DRIVE

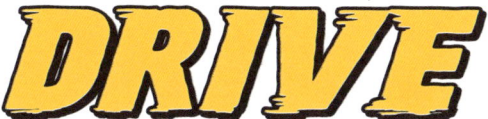

ALSO BY CYNTHIA L. COPELAND

Cub

Really Important Stuff My Dog Has Taught Me

DRIVE

CYNTHIA L. COPELAND
COLORING BY RONDA PATTISON

ALGONQUIN YOUNG READERS
WORKMAN PUBLISHING
New York

This book is a work of historical fiction. In order to give a sense of the times, some names or real people or places have been included in the book. However, the events depicted in this book are imaginary, and the names of nonhistorical persons or events are the product of the author's imagination or are used fictitiously. Any resemblance of such nonhistorical persons or events to actual ones is purely coincidental.

Copyright © 2025 by Cynthia L. Copeland

Hachette Book Group supports the right to free expression and the value of copyright. The purpose of copyright is to encourage writers and artists to produce the creative works that enrich our culture.

The scanning, uploading, and distribution of this book without permission is a theft of the author's intellectual property. If you would like permission to use material from the book (other than for review purposes), please contact permissions@hbgusa.com. Thank you for your support of the author's rights.

Algonquin Young Readers
Workman Publishing
Hachette Book Group, Inc.
1290 Avenue of the Americas
New York, NY 10104
workman.com

Algonquin Young Readers is an imprint of Workman Publishing, a division of Hachette Book Group, Inc. The Workman name and logo are registered trademarks of Hachette Book Group, Inc.

Design by Neil Swaab
Coloring by Ronda Pattison

The publisher is not responsible for websites (or their content) that are not owned by the publisher.

Workman books may be purchased in bulk for business, educational, or promotional use. For information, please contact your local bookseller or the Hachette Book Group Special Markets Department at special.markets@hbgusa.com.

Library of Congress Cataloging-in-Publication Data is available.
ISBNs 978-1-5235-2725-0 (paperback); 978-1-6437-5194-8 (paper over board)
ebook ISBNs 978-1-5235-3230-8, 978-1-5235-3232-2, 978-1-5235-3233-9
First Edition January 2025 APS
Printed in Dongguan, China, on responsibly sourced paper.

10 9 8 7 6 5 4 3 2 1

For Faye

THEN

NOW

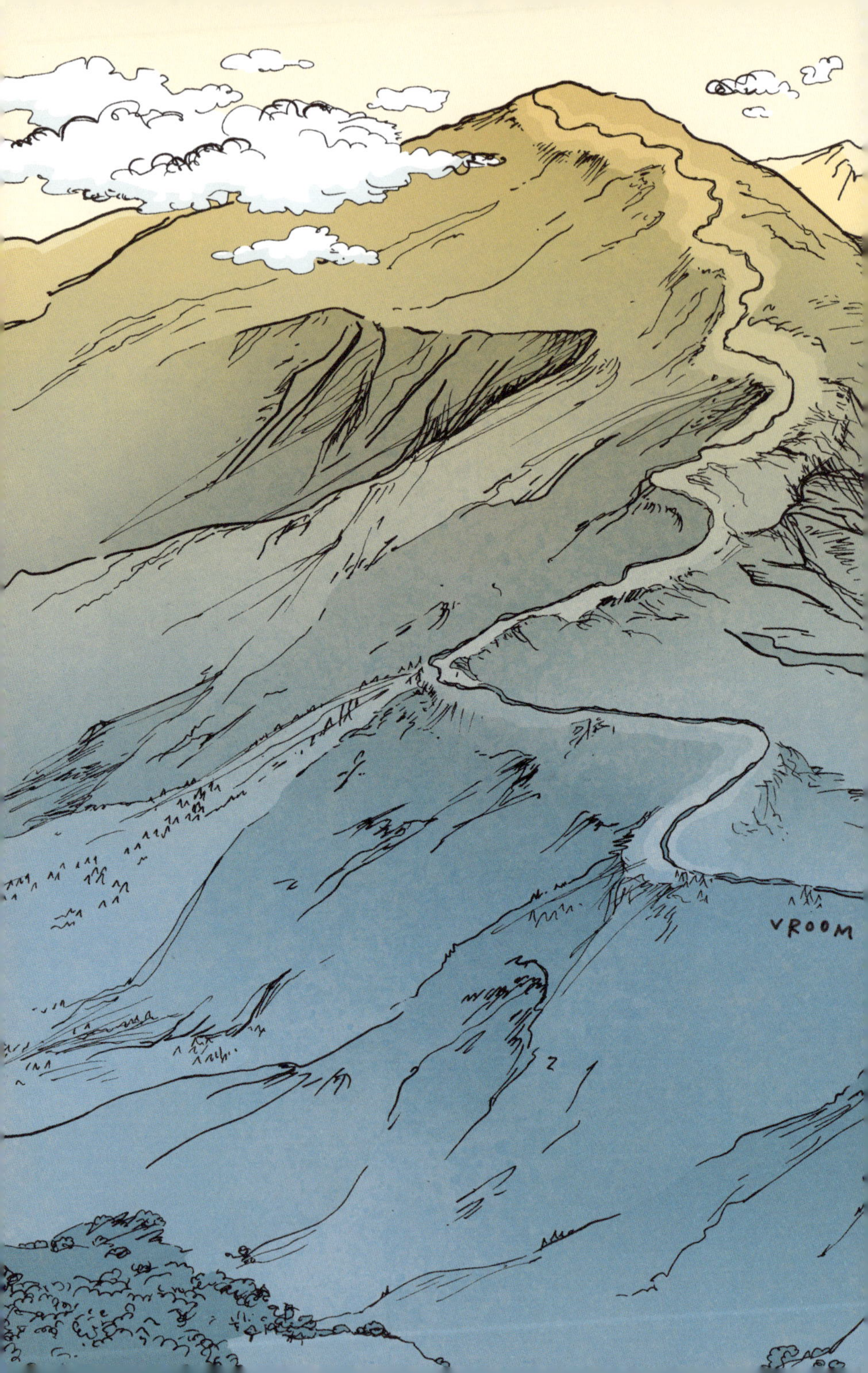
VROOM

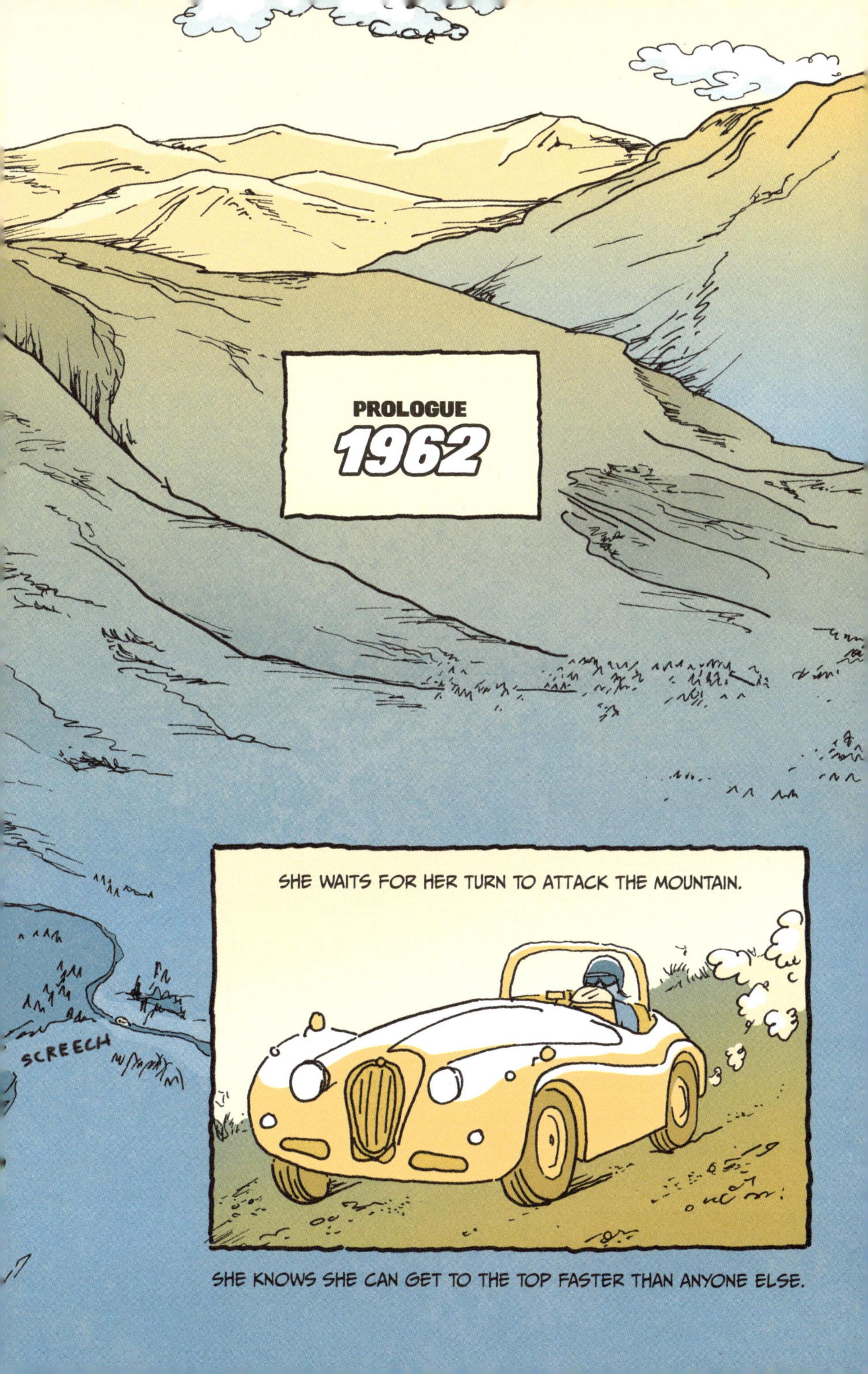

PROLOGUE
1962
SHE WAITS FOR HER TURN TO ATTACK THE MOUNTAIN.
SCREECH
SHE KNOWS SHE CAN GET TO THE TOP FASTER THAN ANYONE ELSE.

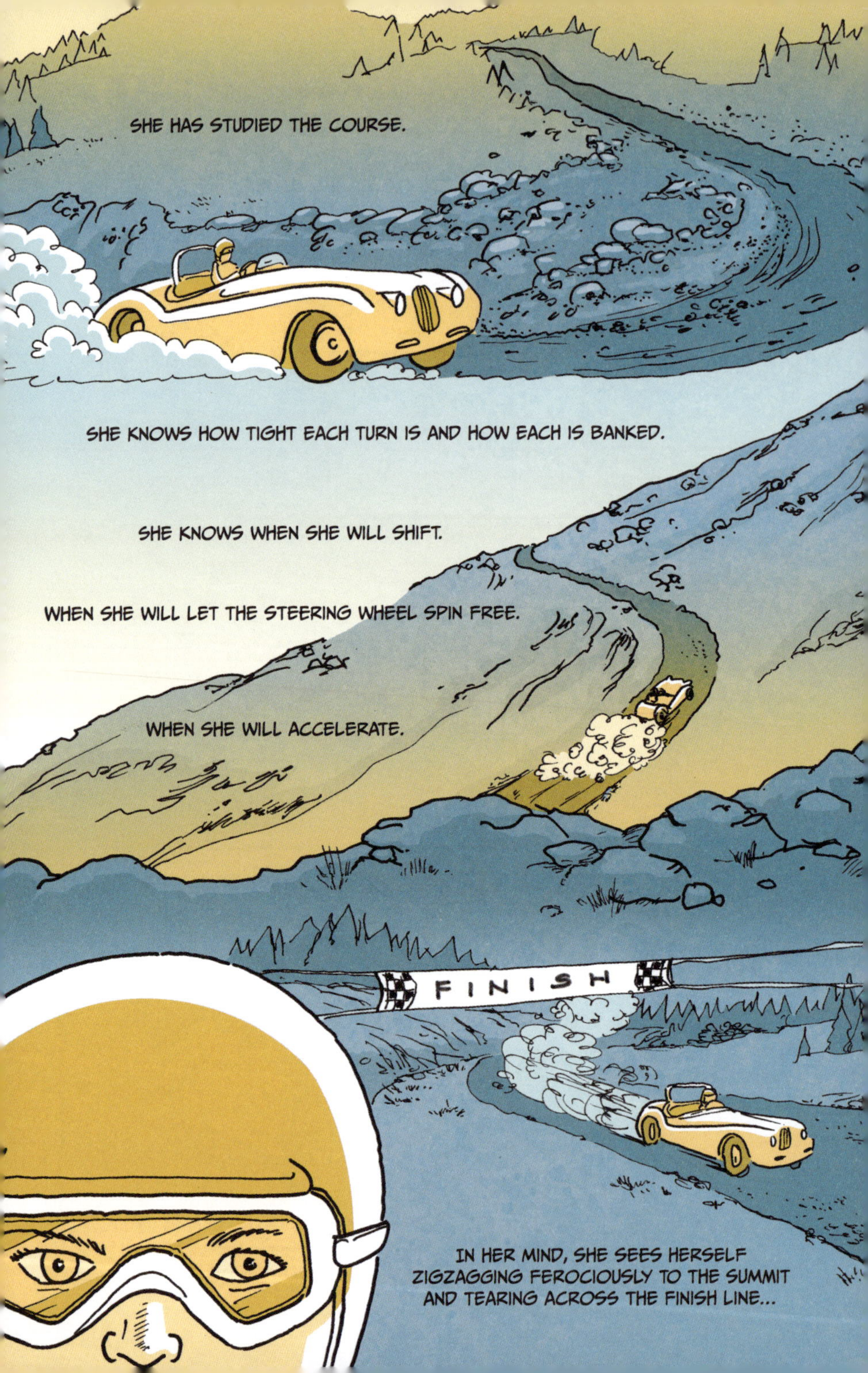
SHE HAS STUDIED THE COURSE.
SHE KNOWS HOW TIGHT EACH TURN IS AND HOW EACH IS BANKED.
SHE KNOWS WHEN SHE WILL SHIFT.
WHEN SHE WILL LET THE STEERING WHEEL SPIN FREE.
WHEN SHE WILL ACCELERATE.
FINISH
IN HER MIND, SHE SEES HERSELF ZIGZAGGING FEROCIOUSLY TO THE SUMMIT AND TEARING ACROSS THE FINISH LINE...

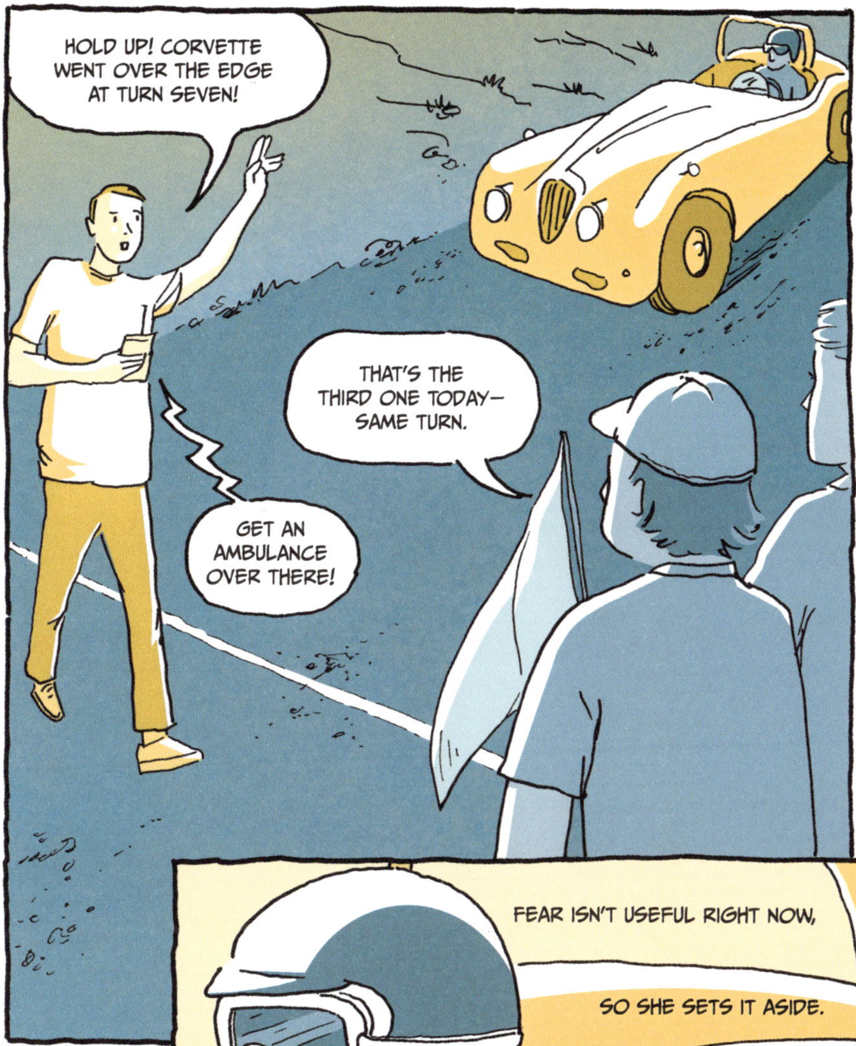
HOLD UP! CORVETTE WENT OVER THE EDGE AT TURN SEVEN!
THAT'S THE THIRD ONE TODAY— SAME TURN.
GET AN AMBULANCE OVER THERE!

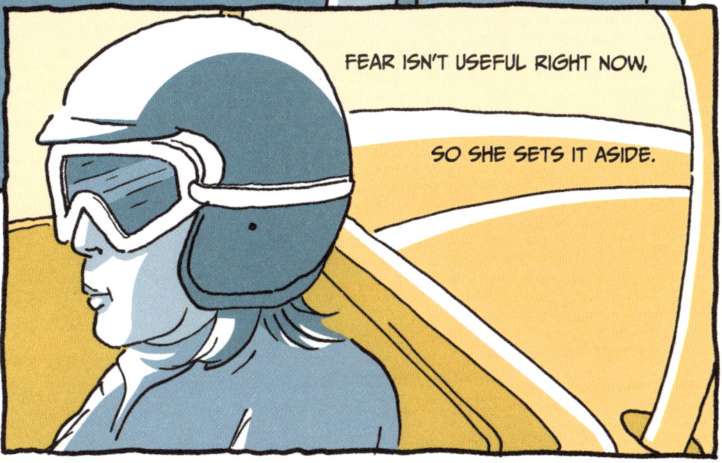
FEAR ISN'T USEFUL RIGHT NOW,
SO SHE SETS IT ASIDE.

BUT SHE MAKES A MENTAL NOTE TO EASE UP SLIGHTLY AT TURN SEVEN.

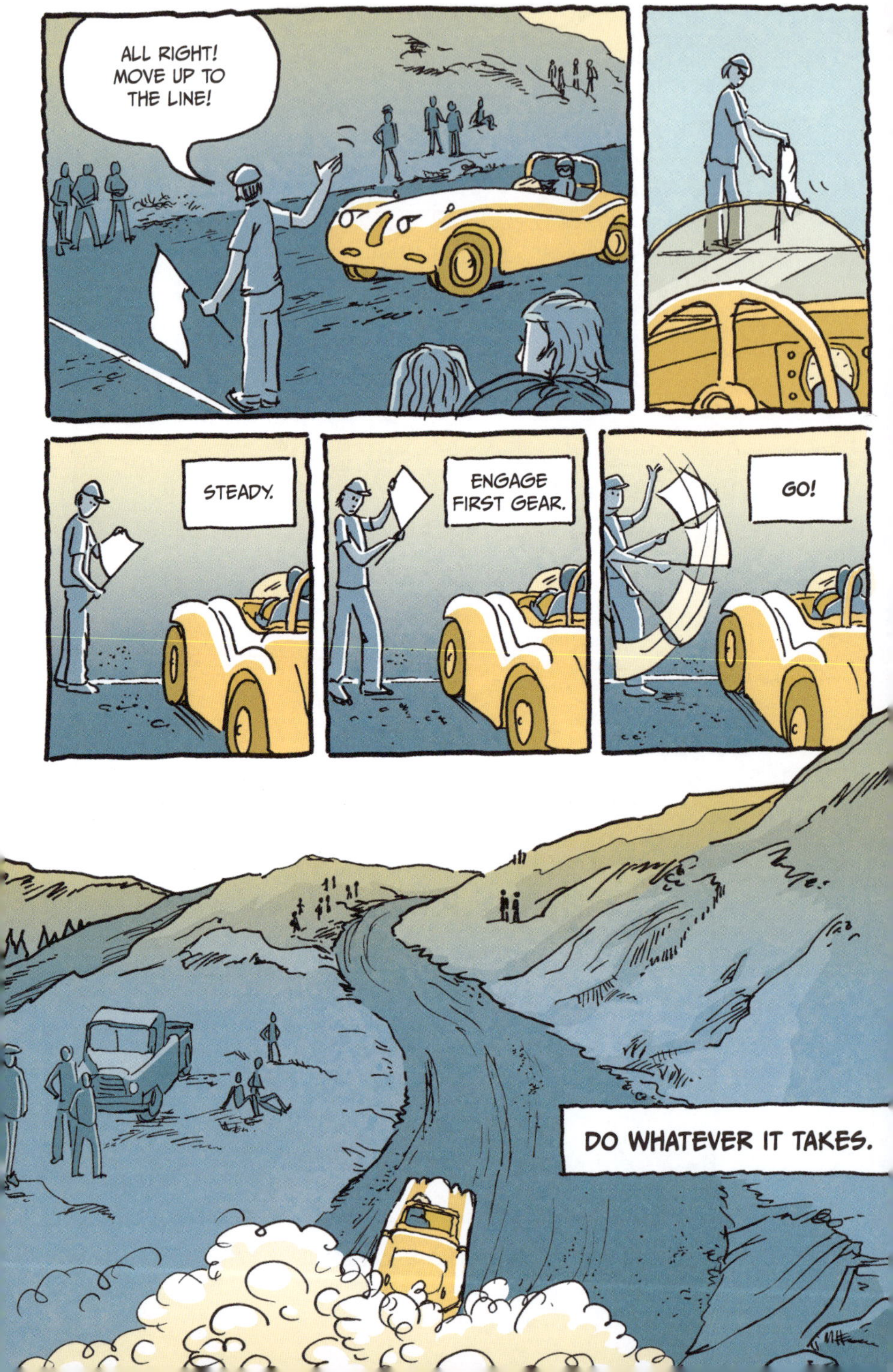
ALL RIGHT! MOVE UP TO THE LINE!
STEADY.
ENGAGE FIRST GEAR.
GO!
DO WHATEVER IT TAKES.

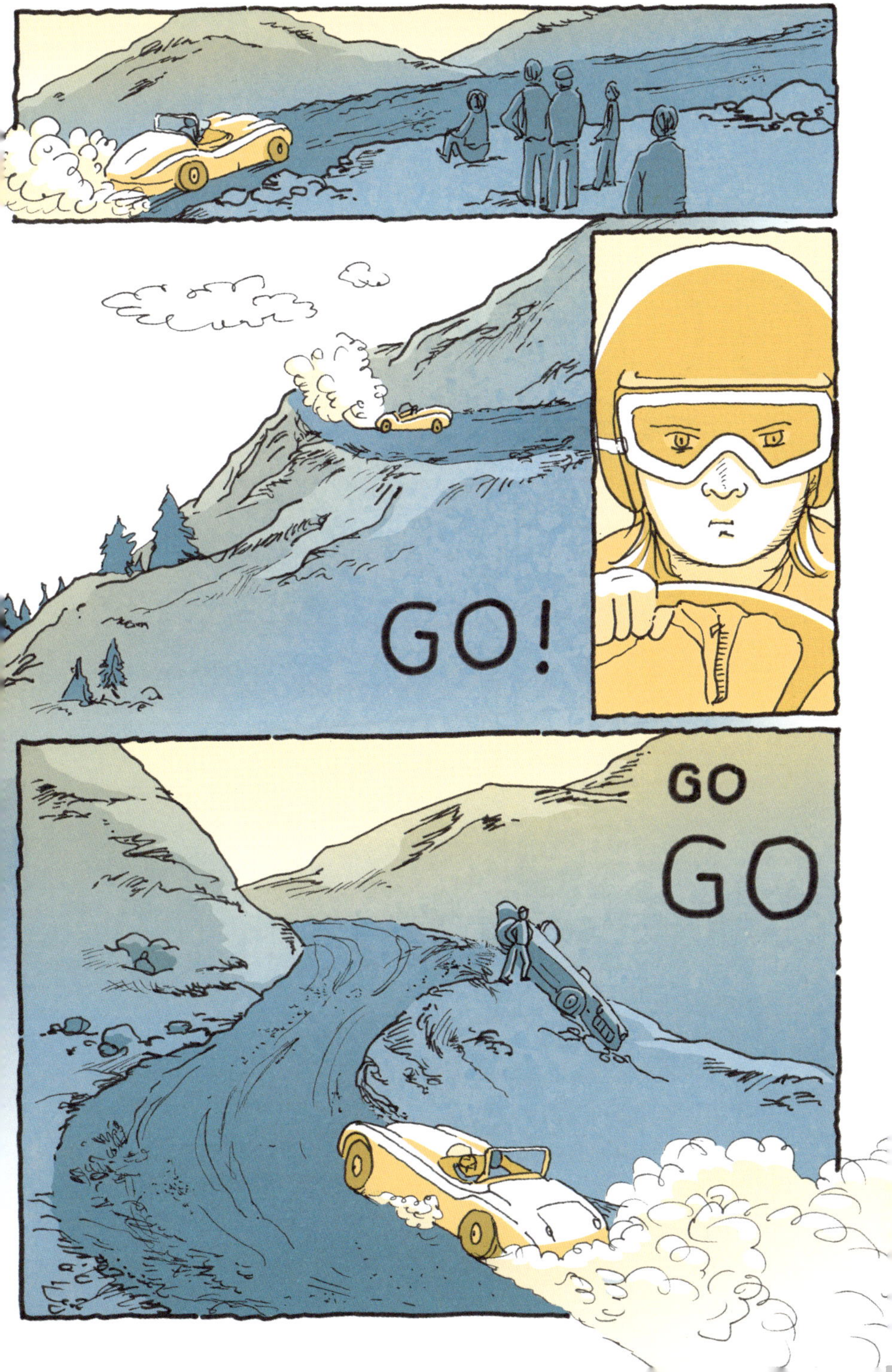
GO!
GO
GO

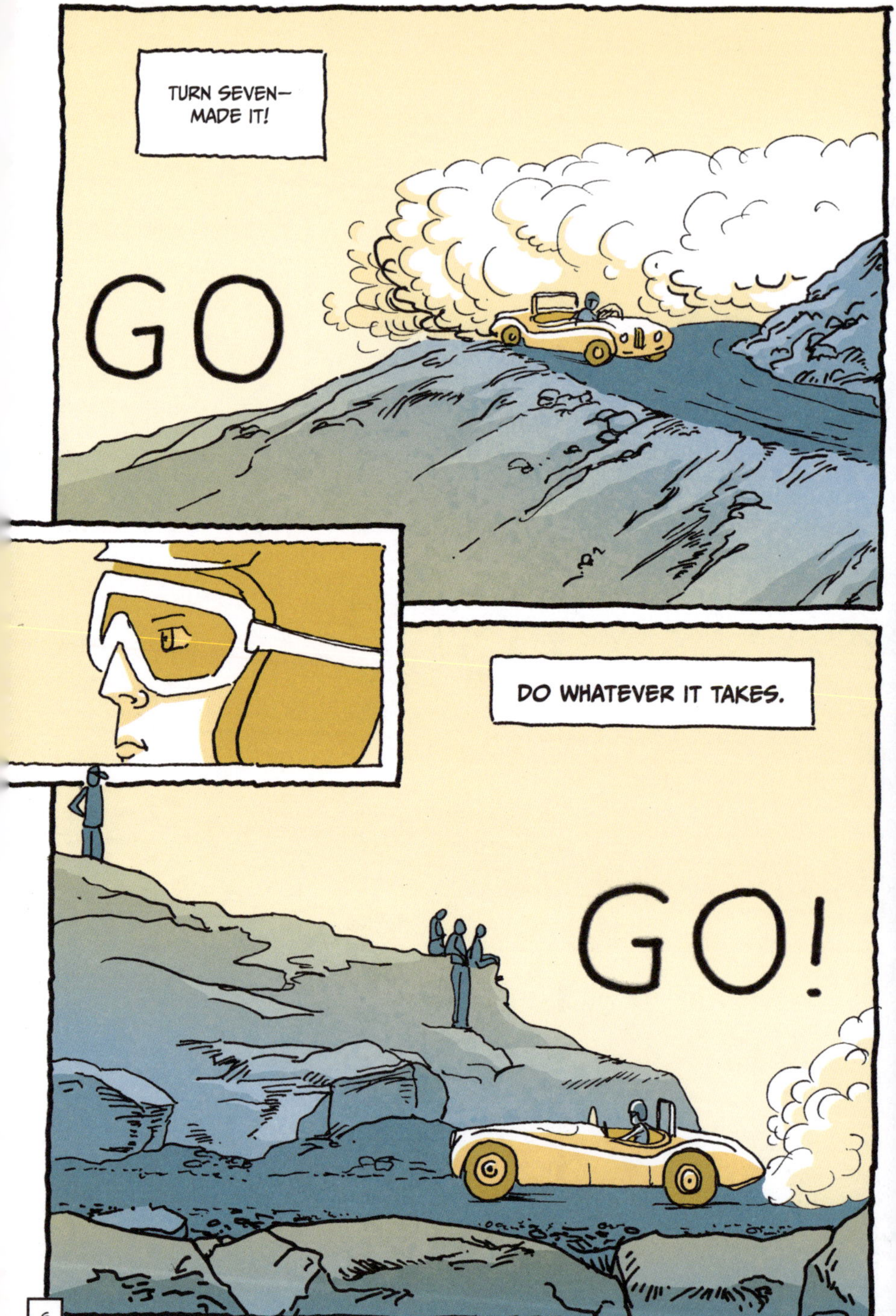
TURN SEVEN—
MADE IT!
GO
DO WHATEVER IT TAKES.
GO!

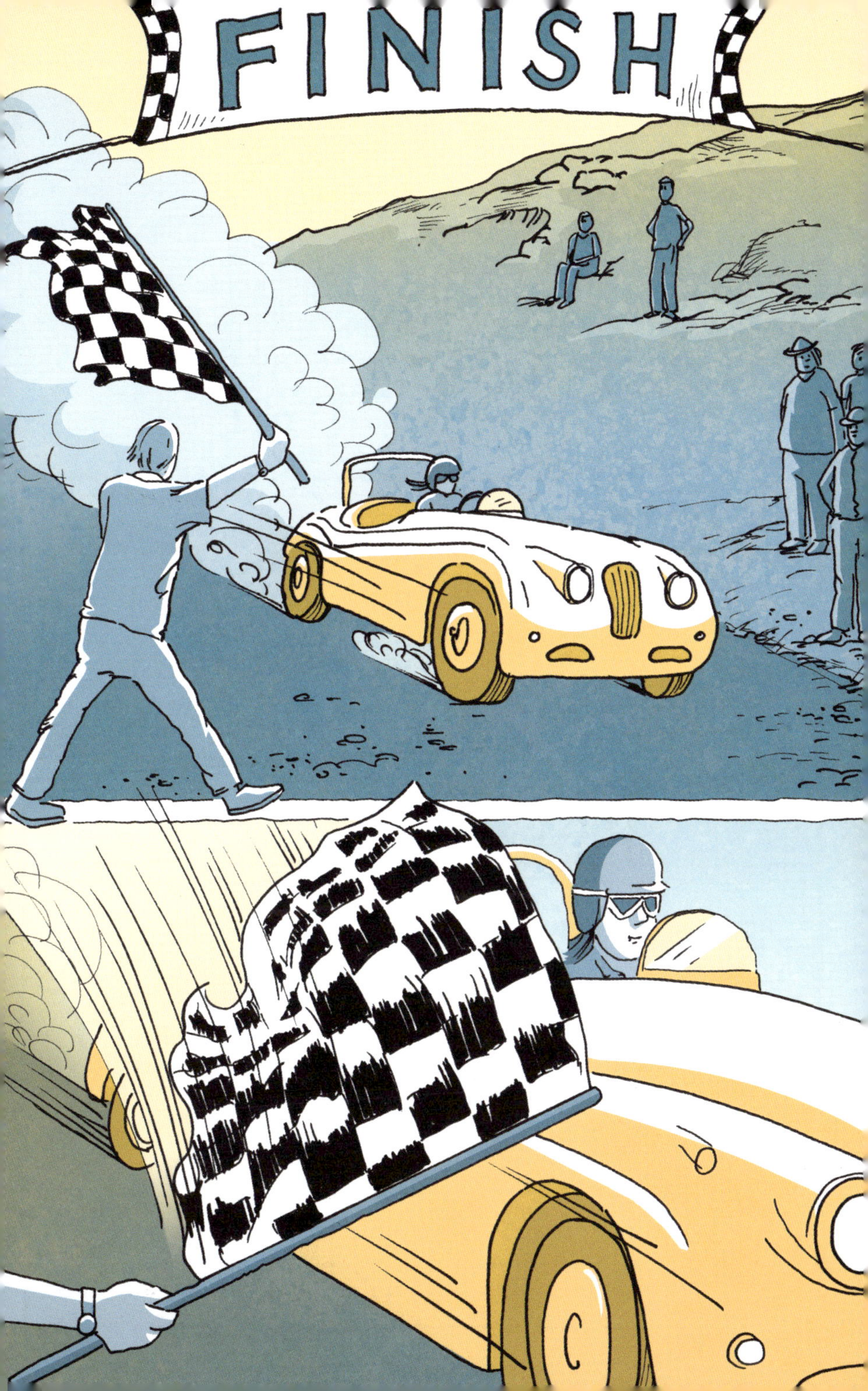
FINISH

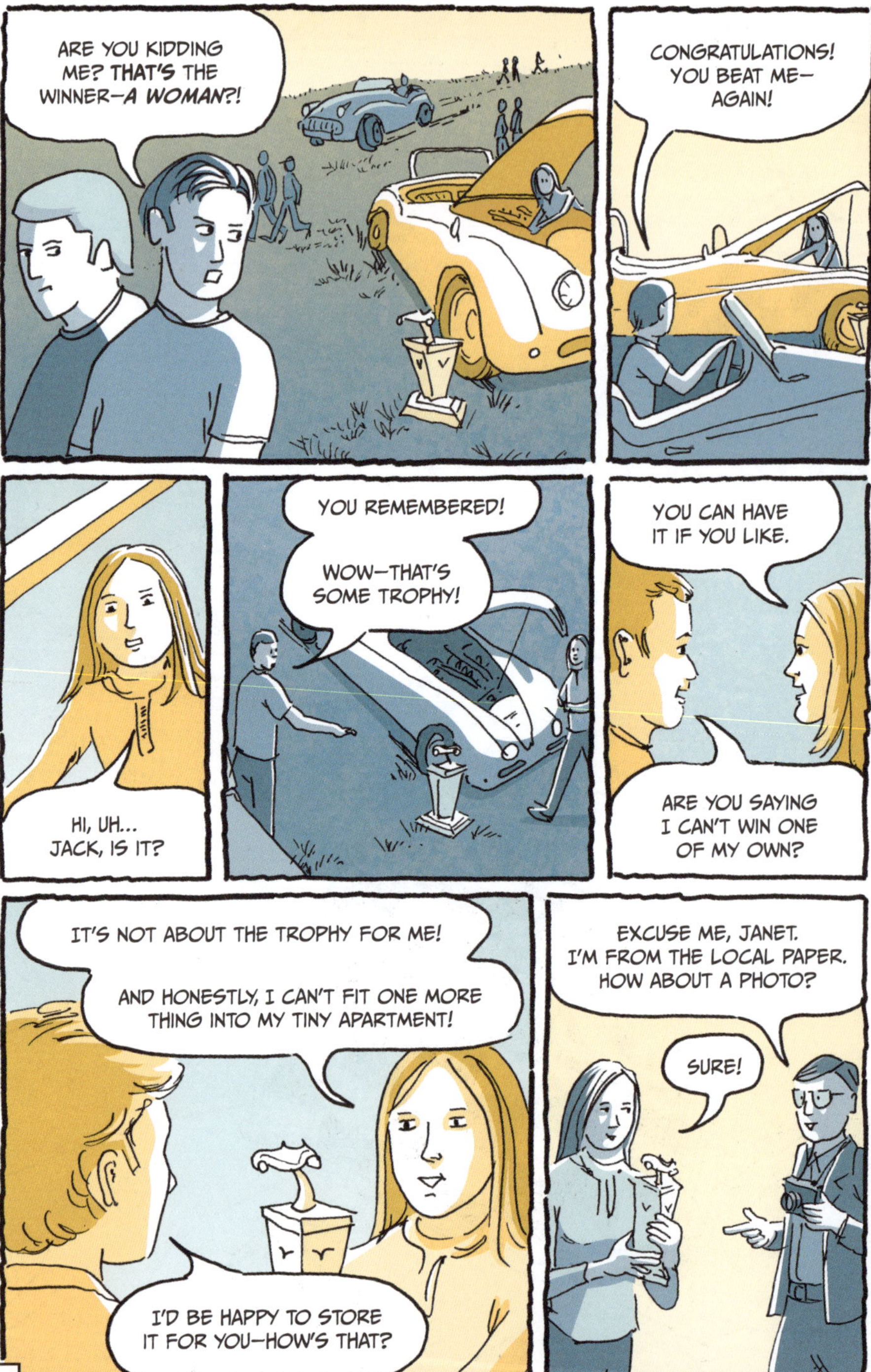
ARE YOU KIDDING ME? **THAT'S** THE WINNER—***A WOMAN***?!
CONGRATULATIONS! YOU BEAT ME— AGAIN!
HI, UH... JACK, IS IT?
YOU REMEMBERED!
WOW—THAT'S SOME TROPHY!
YOU CAN HAVE IT IF YOU LIKE.
ARE YOU SAYING I CAN'T WIN ONE OF MY OWN?
IT'S NOT ABOUT THE TROPHY FOR ME!
AND HONESTLY, I CAN'T FIT ONE MORE THING INTO MY TINY APARTMENT!
I'D BE HAPPY TO STORE IT FOR YOU—HOW'S THAT?
EXCUSE ME, JANET. I'M FROM THE LOCAL PAPER. HOW ABOUT A PHOTO?
SURE!

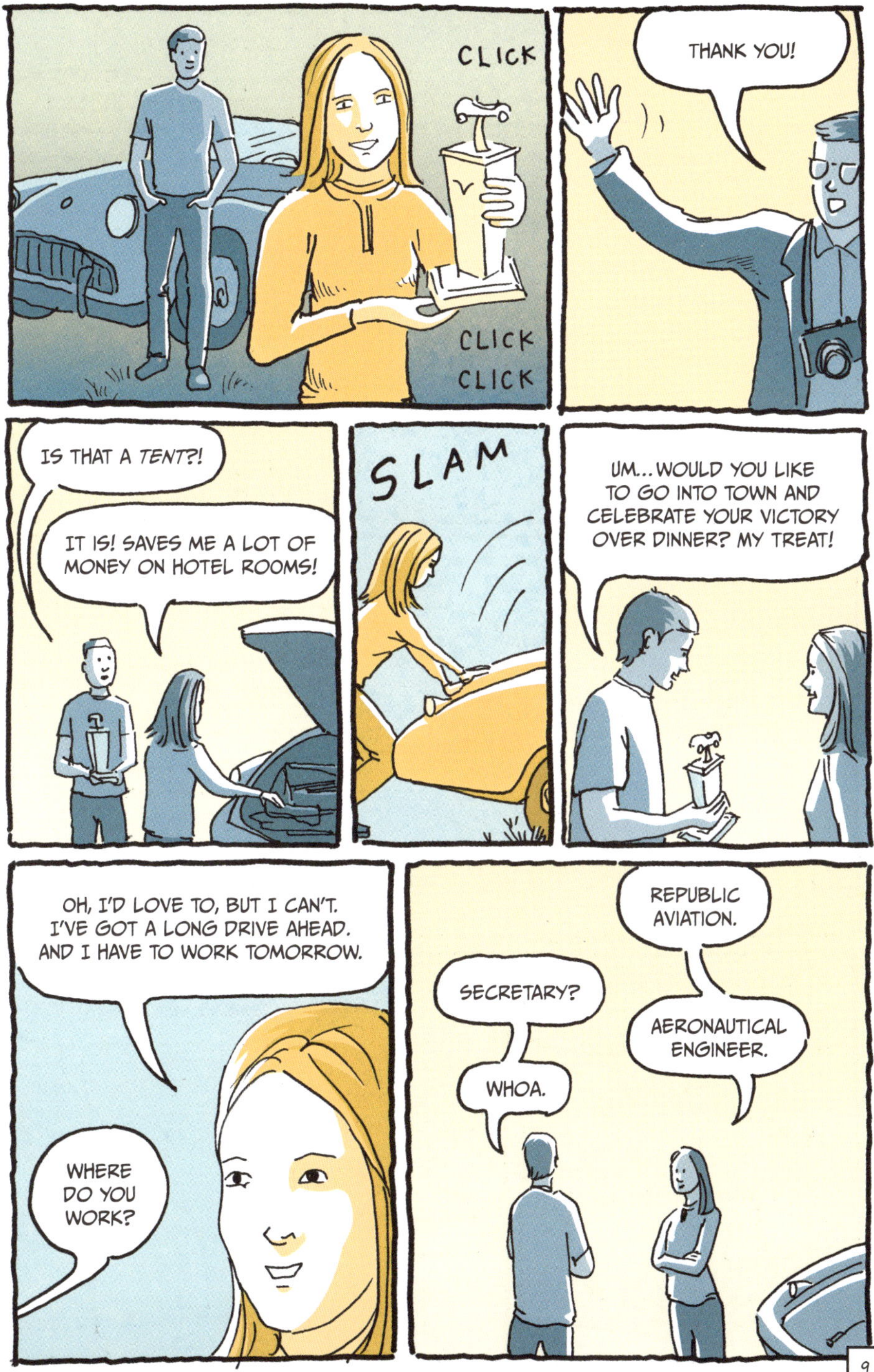
CLICK
CLICK
CLICK
THANK YOU!
IS THAT A *TENT*?!
IT IS! SAVES ME A LOT OF MONEY ON HOTEL ROOMS!
SLAM
UM...WOULD YOU LIKE TO GO INTO TOWN AND CELEBRATE YOUR VICTORY OVER DINNER? MY TREAT!
OH, I'D LOVE TO, BUT I CAN'T. I'VE GOT A LONG DRIVE AHEAD. AND I HAVE TO WORK TOMORROW.
WHERE DO YOU WORK?
REPUBLIC AVIATION.
SECRETARY?
AERONAUTICAL ENGINEER.
WHOA.

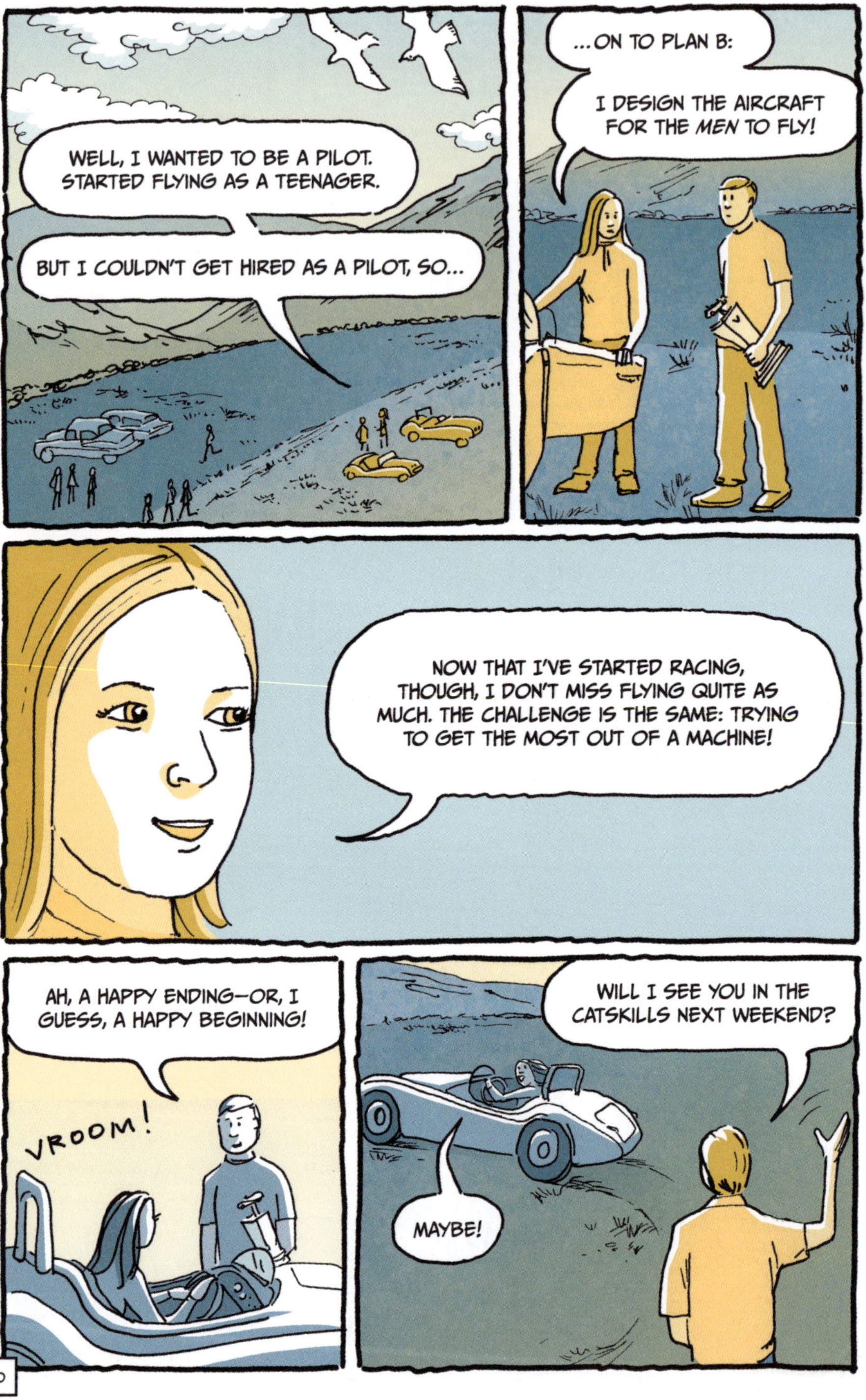
WELL, I WANTED TO BE A PILOT. STARTED FLYING AS A TEENAGER.
BUT I COULDN'T GET HIRED AS A PILOT, SO...
...ON TO PLAN B:
I DESIGN THE AIRCRAFT FOR THE *MEN* TO FLY!
NOW THAT I'VE STARTED RACING, THOUGH, I DON'T MISS FLYING QUITE AS MUCH. THE CHALLENGE IS THE SAME: TRYING TO GET THE MOST OUT OF A MACHINE!
AH, A HAPPY ENDING—OR, I GUESS, A HAPPY BEGINNING!
VROOM!
WILL I SEE YOU IN THE CATSKILLS NEXT WEEKEND?
MAYBE!

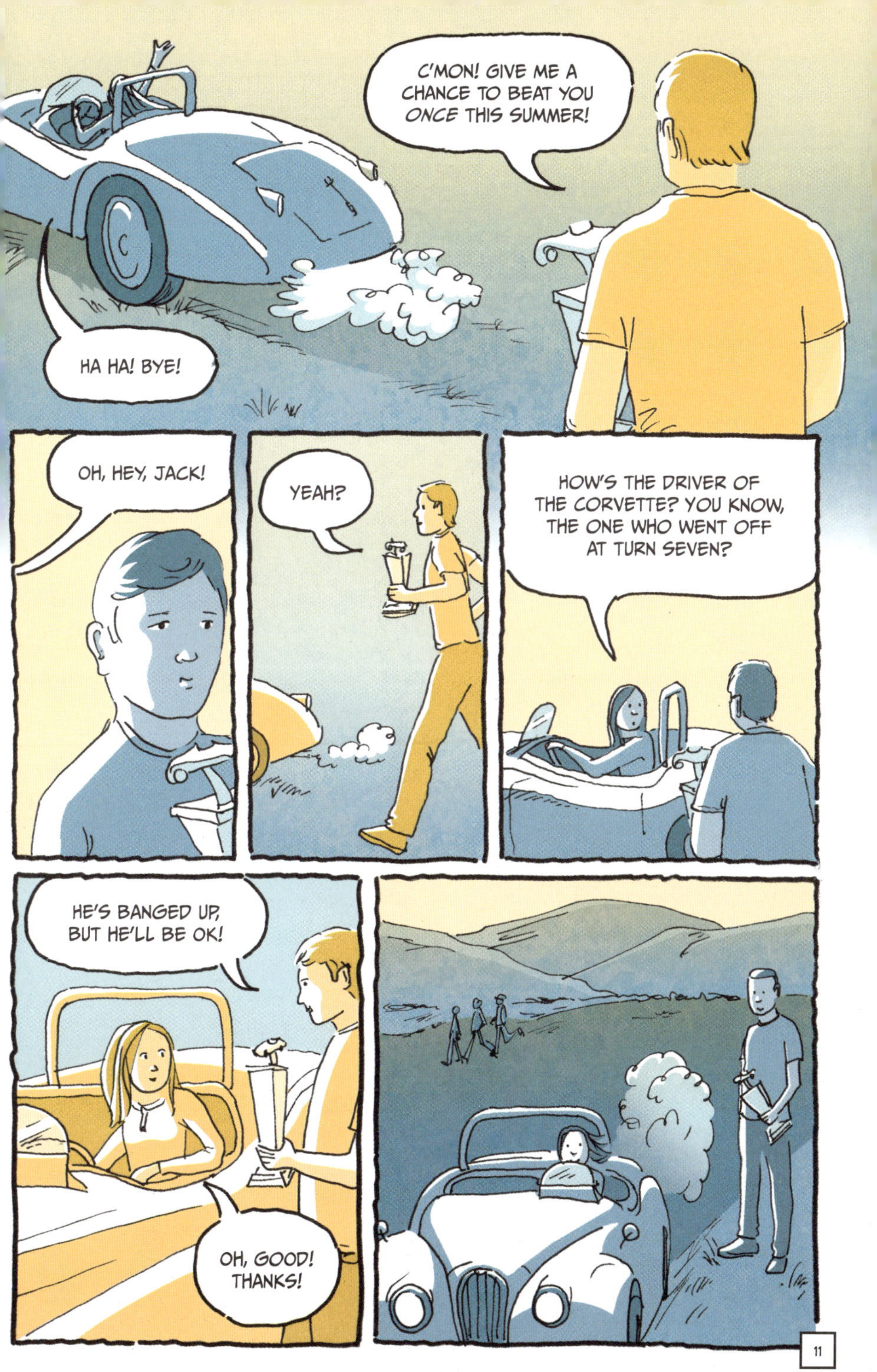
C'MON! GIVE ME A CHANCE TO BEAT YOU ONCE THIS SUMMER!
HA HA! BYE!
OH, HEY, JACK!
YEAH?
HOW'S THE DRIVER OF THE CORVETTE? YOU KNOW, THE ONE WHO WENT OFF AT TURN SEVEN?
HE'S BANGED UP, BUT HE'LL BE OK!
OH, GOOD! THANKS!

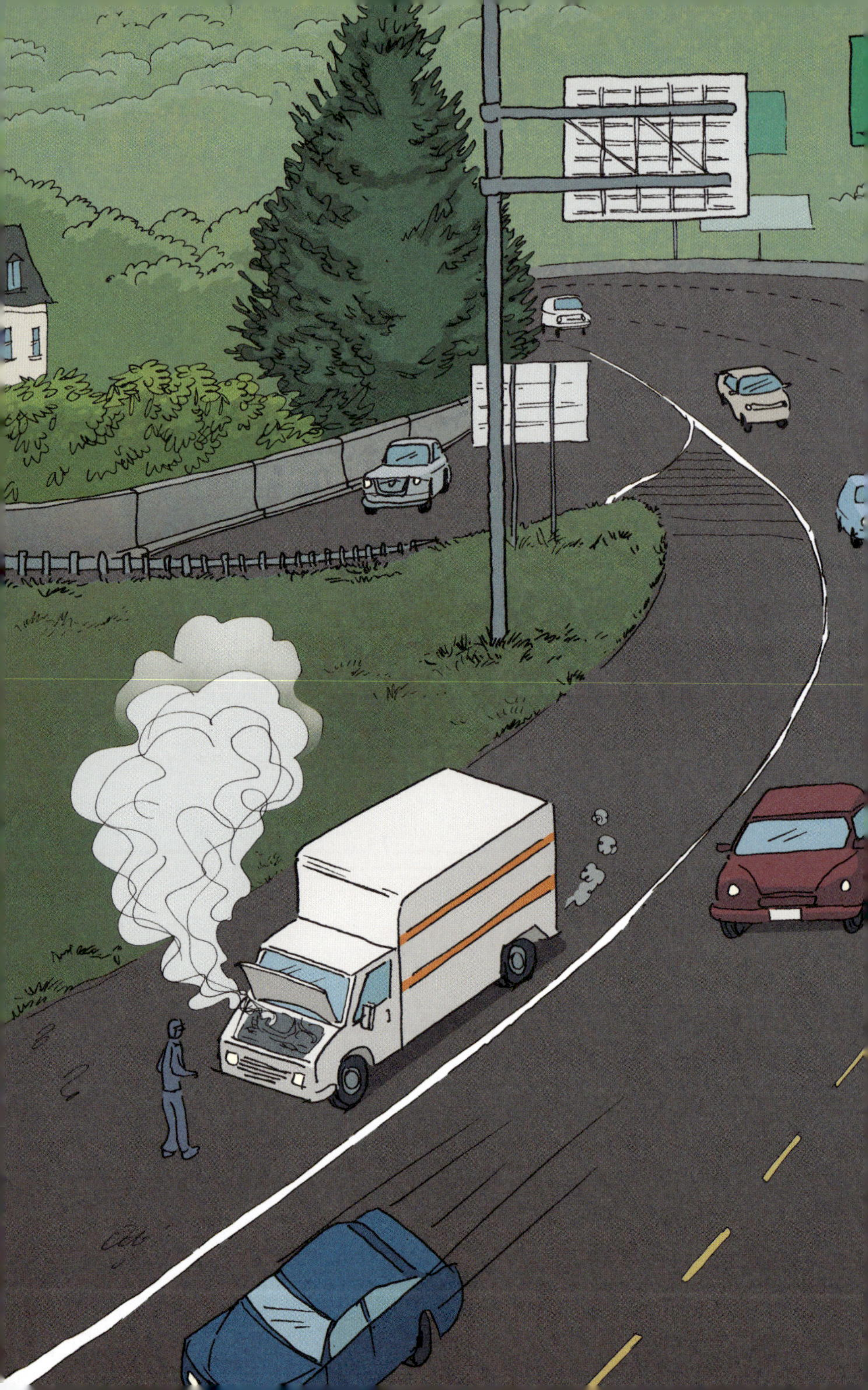

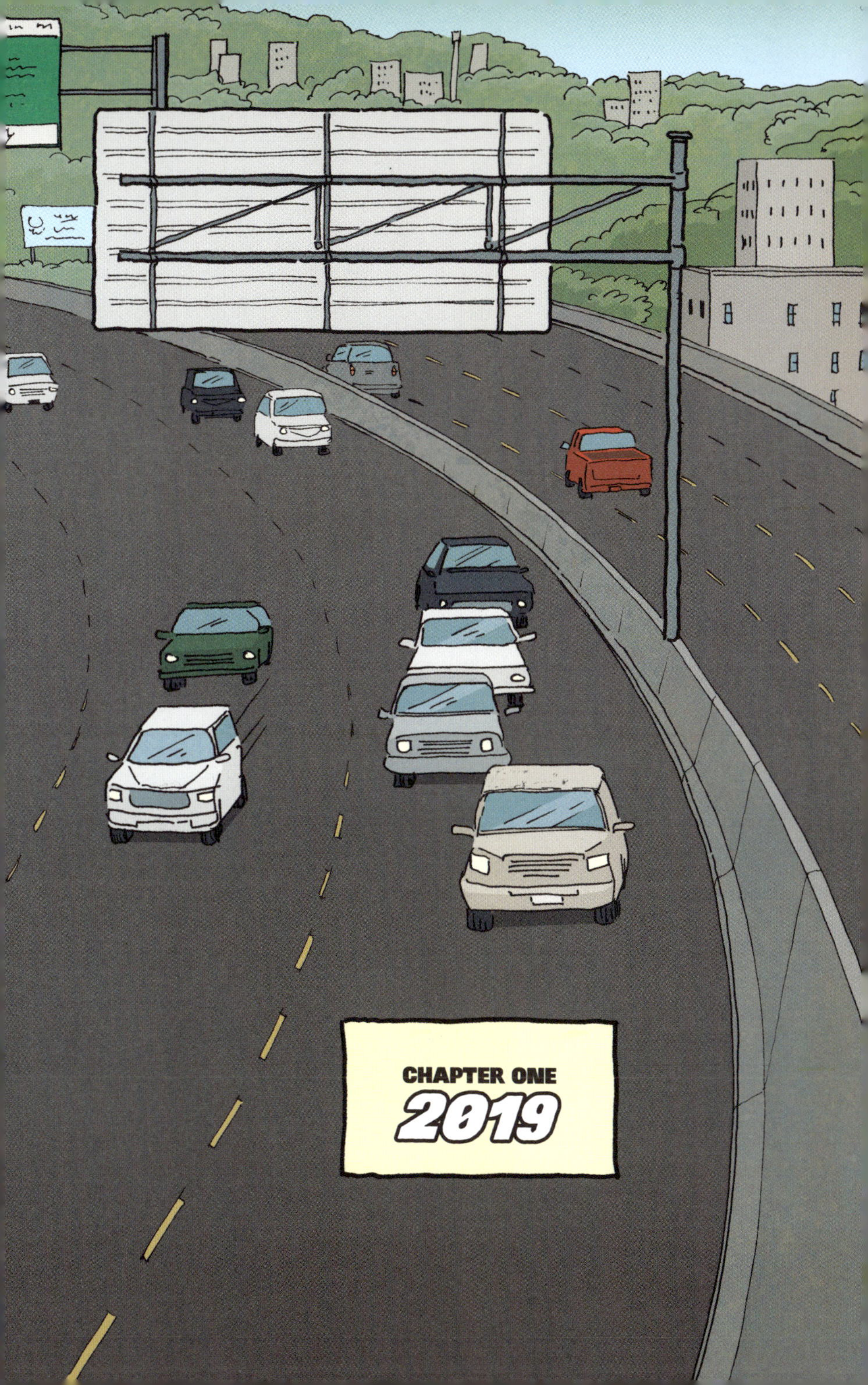
CHAPTER ONE
2019

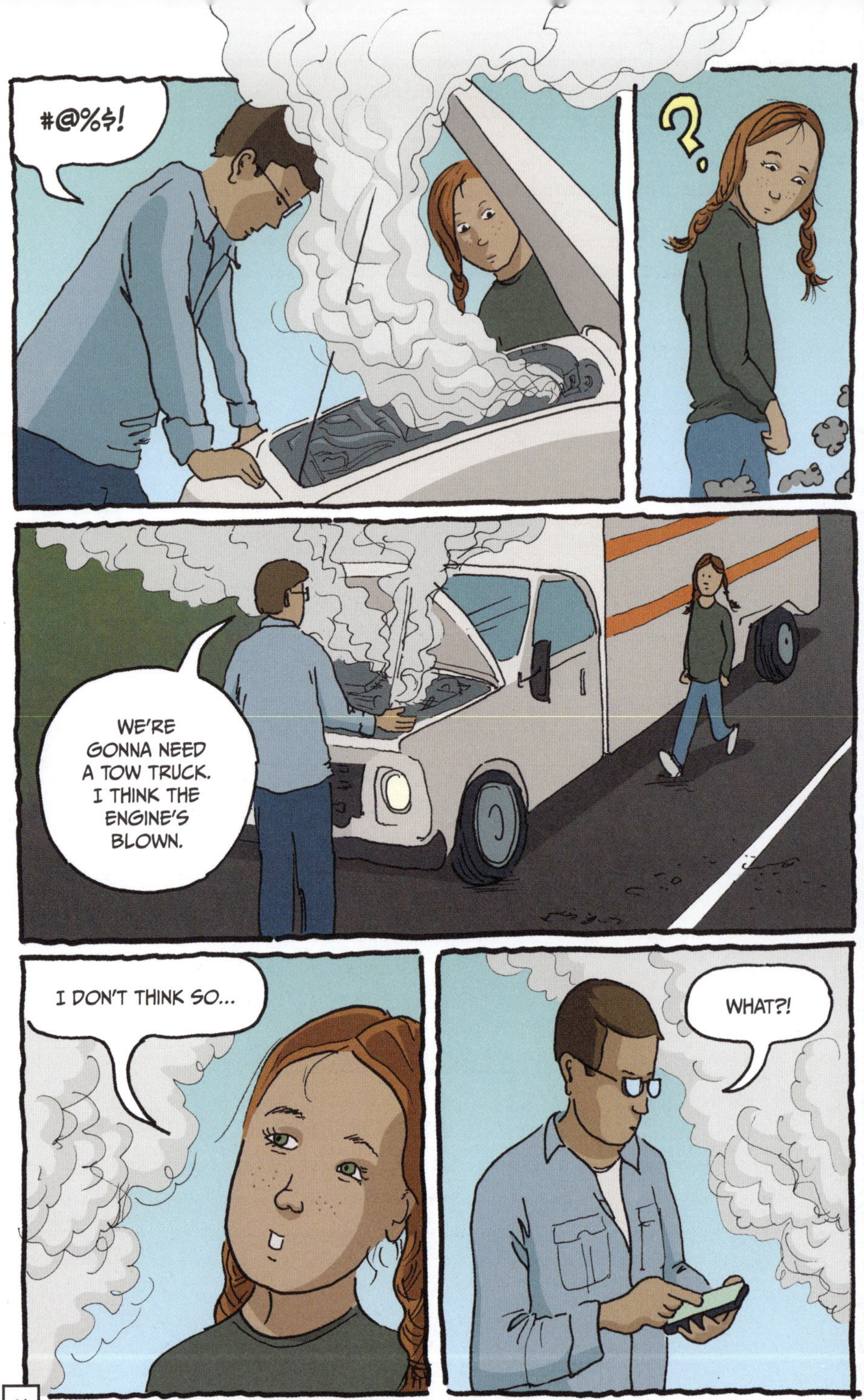
#@%$!
?
WE'RE GONNA NEED A TOW TRUCK. I THINK THE ENGINE'S BLOWN.
I DON'T THINK SO...
WHAT?!

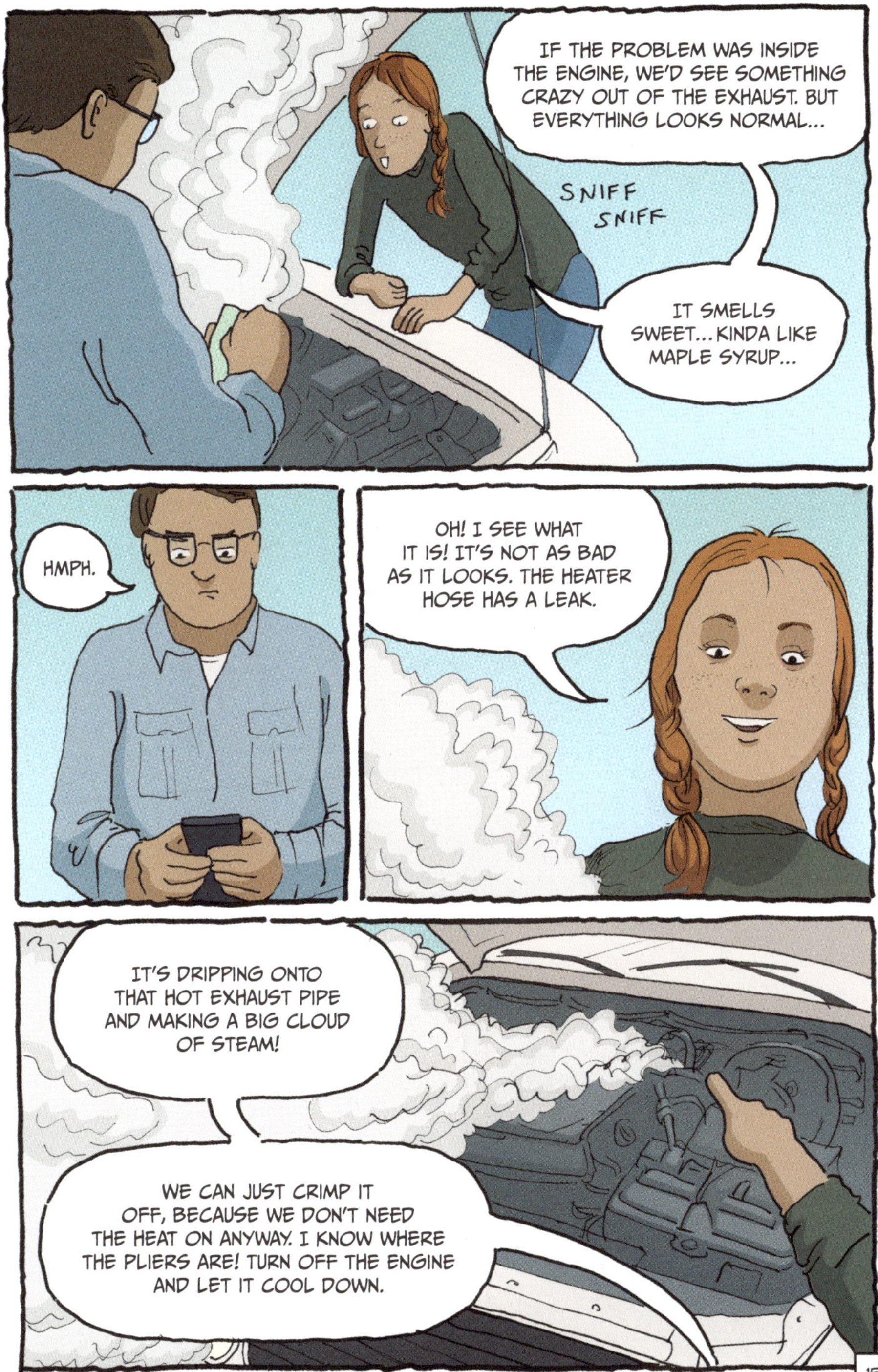
IF THE PROBLEM WAS INSIDE THE ENGINE, WE'D SEE SOMETHING CRAZY OUT OF THE EXHAUST. BUT EVERYTHING LOOKS NORMAL...
SNIFF SNIFF
IT SMELLS SWEET... KINDA LIKE MAPLE SYRUP...
HMPH.
OH! I SEE WHAT IT IS! IT'S NOT AS BAD AS IT LOOKS. THE HEATER HOSE HAS A LEAK.
IT'S DRIPPING ONTO THAT HOT EXHAUST PIPE AND MAKING A BIG CLOUD OF STEAM!
WE CAN JUST CRIMP IT OFF, BECAUSE WE DON'T NEED THE HEAT ON ANYWAY. I KNOW WHERE THE PLIERS ARE! TURN OFF THE ENGINE AND LET IT COOL DOWN.

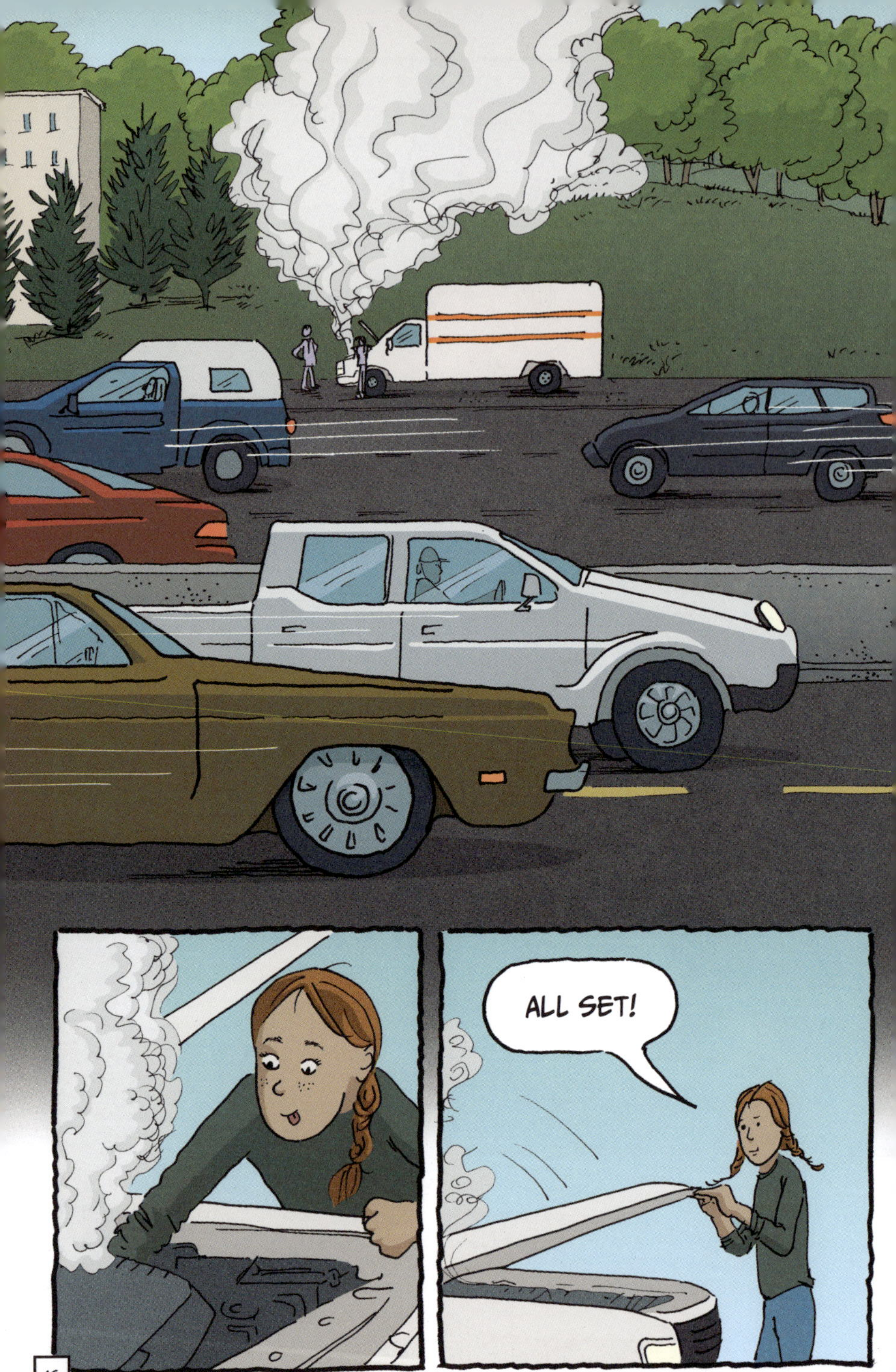
ALL SET!

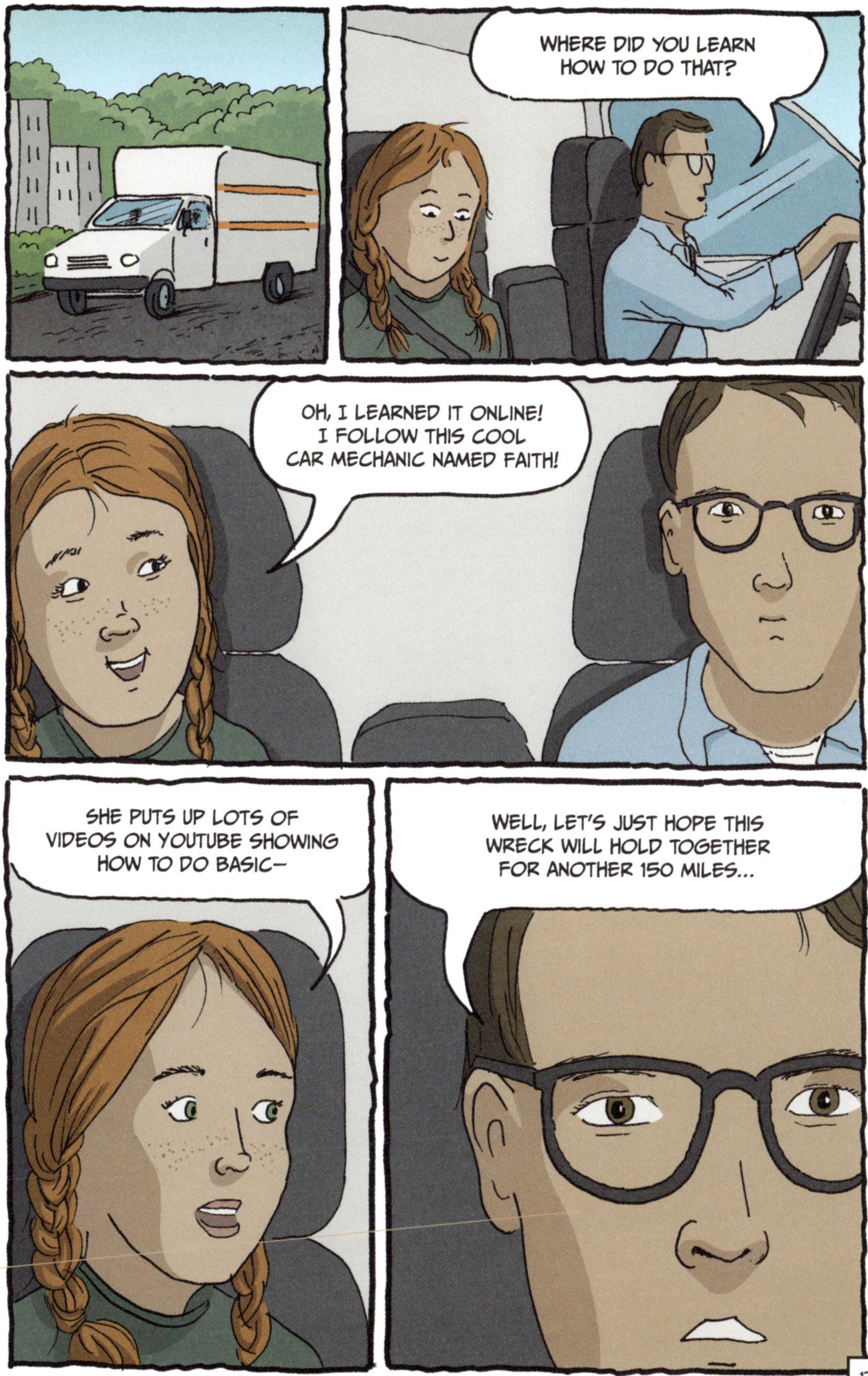
WHERE DID YOU LEARN HOW TO DO THAT?
OH, I LEARNED IT ONLINE! I FOLLOW THIS COOL CAR MECHANIC NAMED FAITH!
SHE PUTS UP LOTS OF VIDEOS ON YOUTUBE SHOWING HOW TO DO BASIC—
WELL, LET'S JUST HOPE THIS WRECK WILL HOLD TOGETHER FOR ANOTHER 150 MILES...

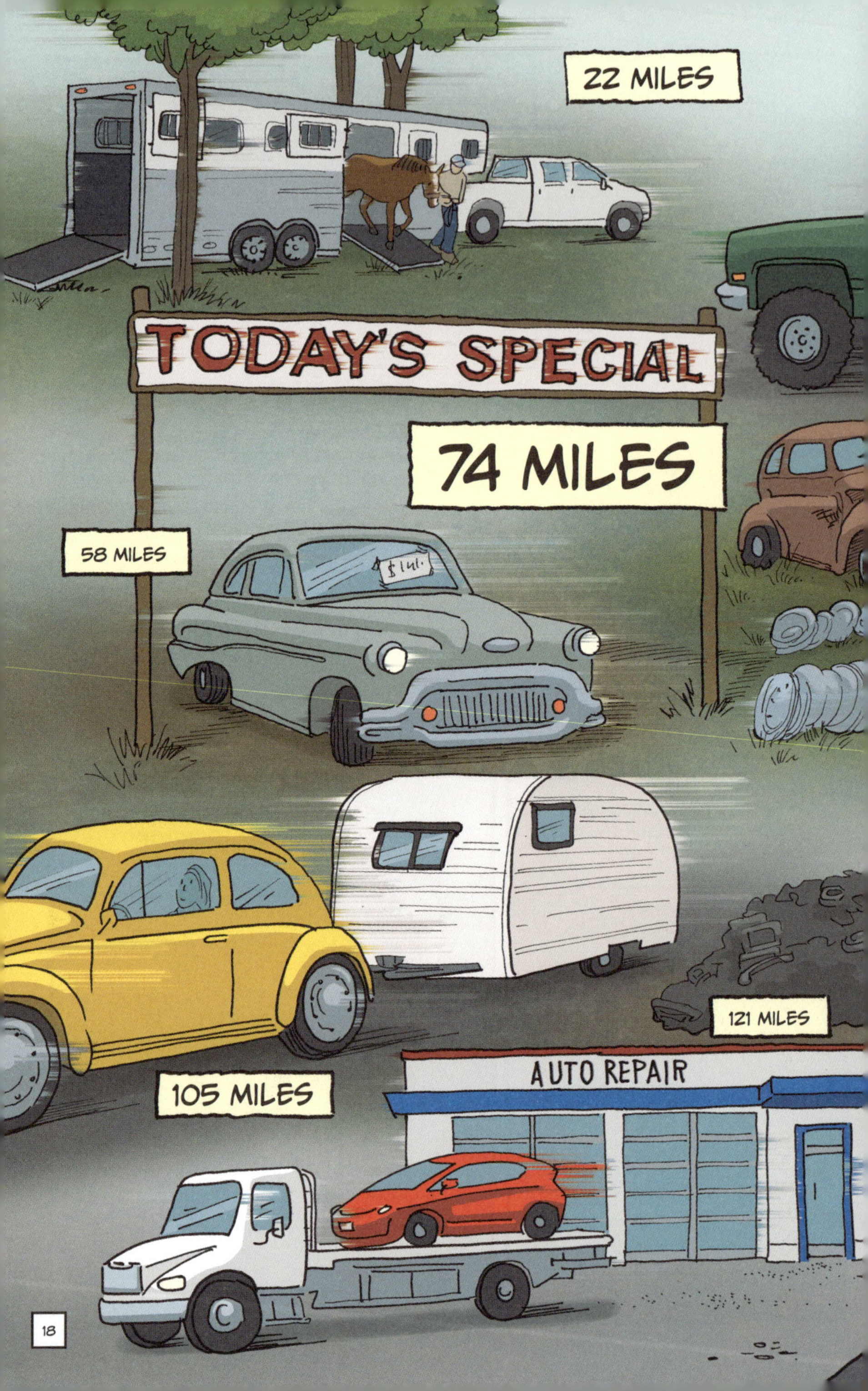
22 MILES
TODAY'S SPECIAL
74 MILES
58 MILES
$141
121 MILES
AUTO REPAIR
105 MILES

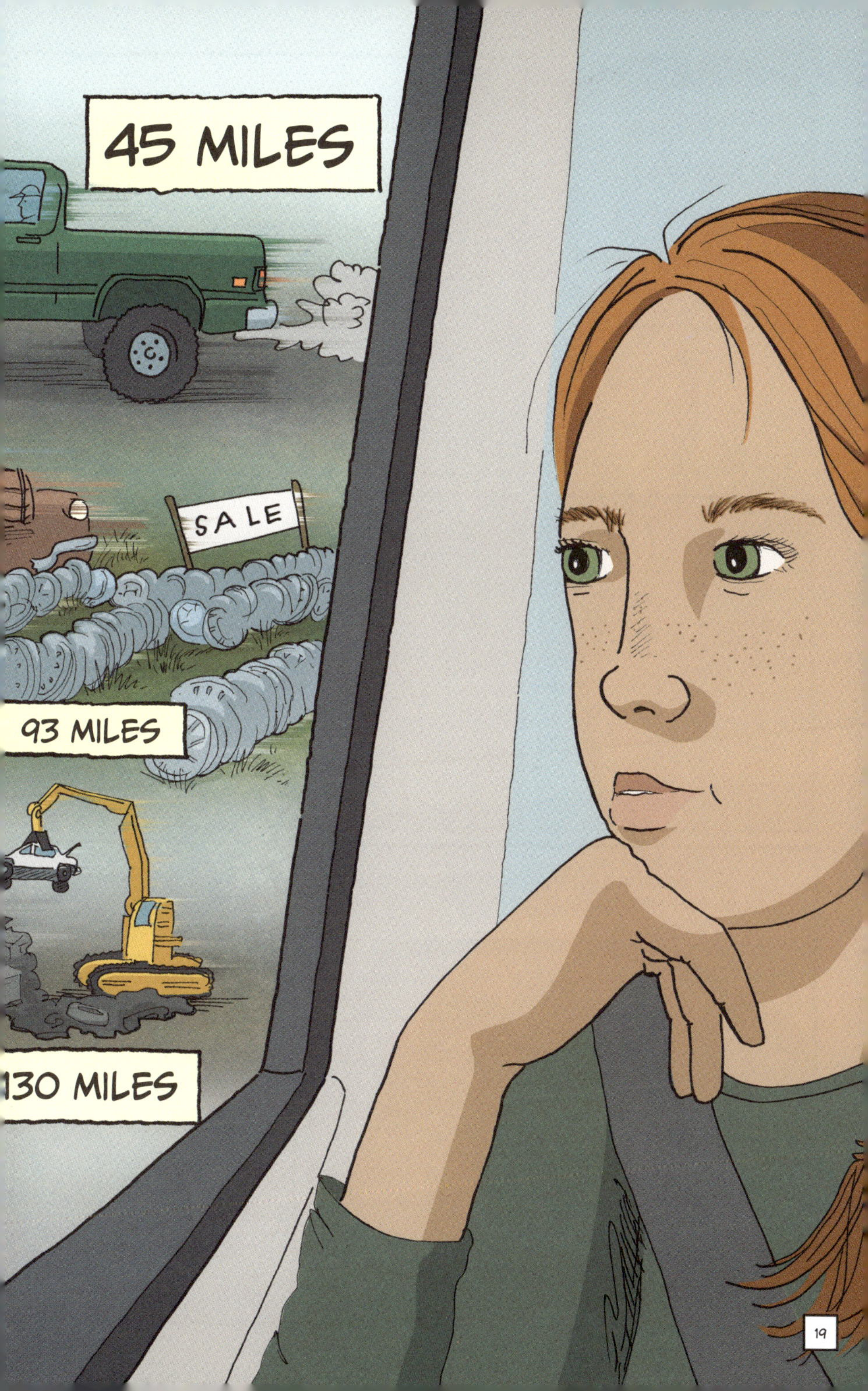
45 MILES
SALE
93 MILES
130 MILES

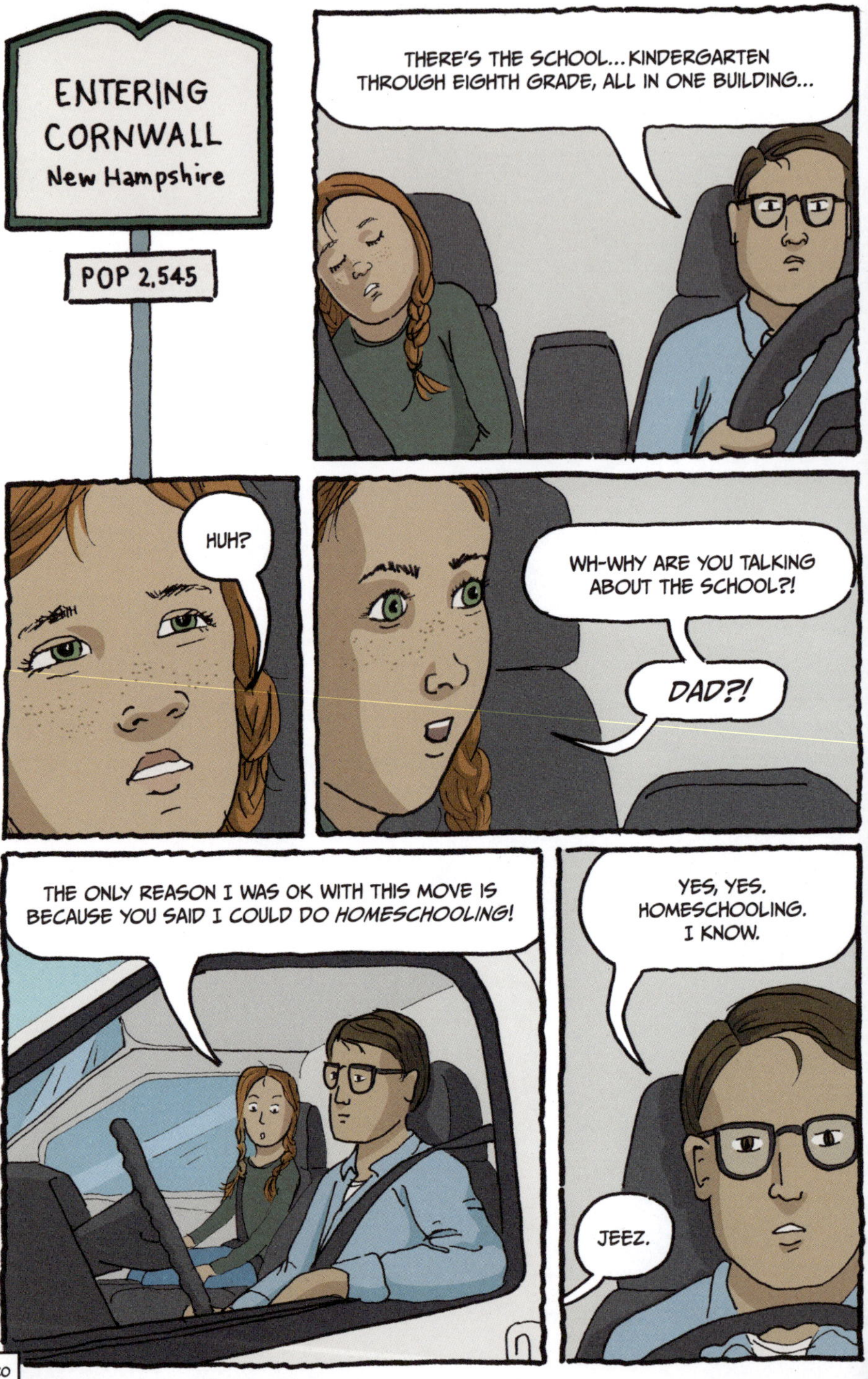
ENTERING
CORNWALL
New Hampshire
POP 2,545
THERE'S THE SCHOOL...KINDERGARTEN THROUGH EIGHTH GRADE, ALL IN ONE BUILDING...
HUH?
WH-WHY ARE YOU TALKING ABOUT THE SCHOOL?!
DAD?!
THE ONLY REASON I WAS OK WITH THIS MOVE IS BECAUSE YOU SAID I COULD DO *HOMESCHOOLING*!
YES, YES. HOMESCHOOLING. I KNOW.
JEEZ.

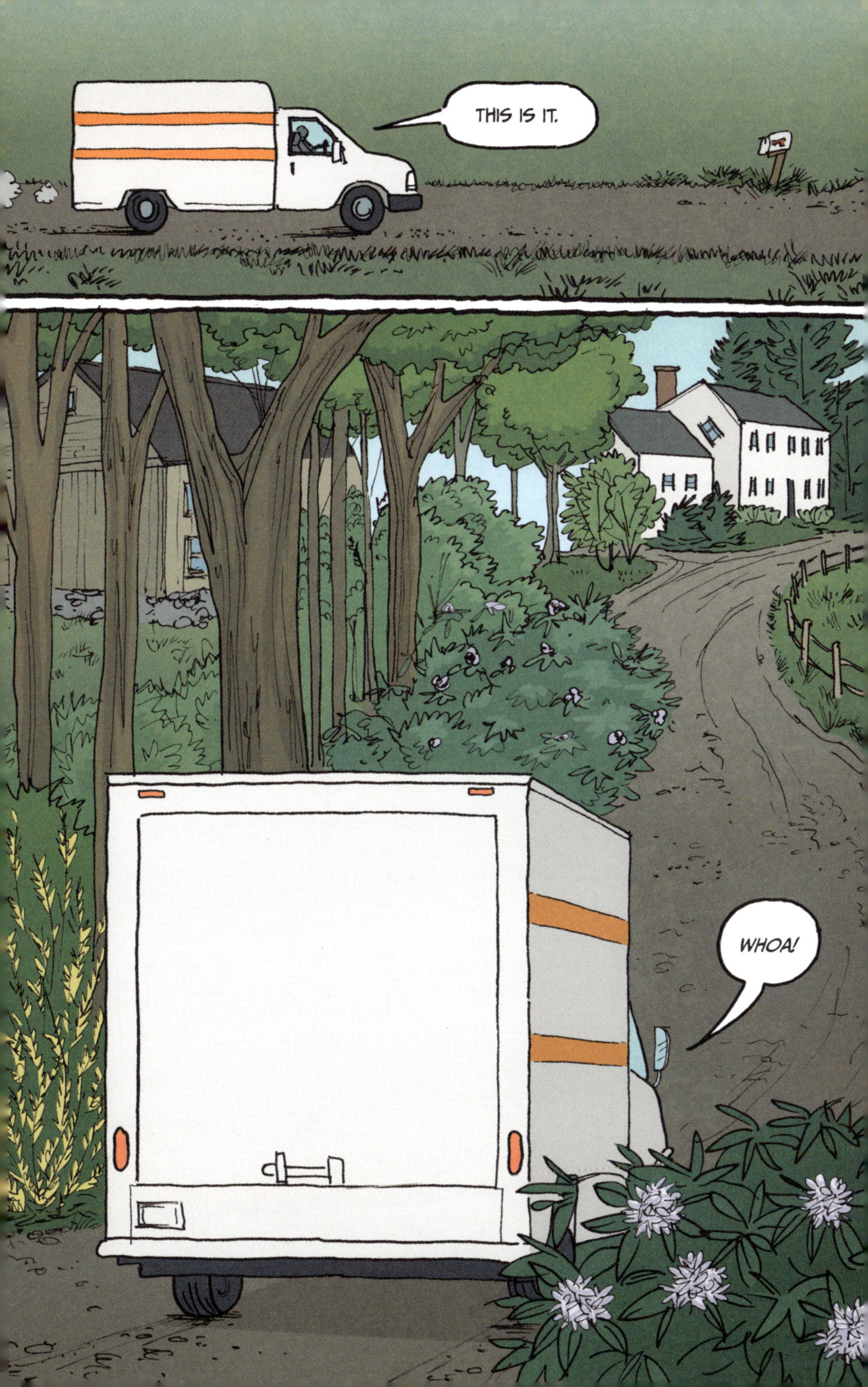
THIS IS IT.
WHOA!

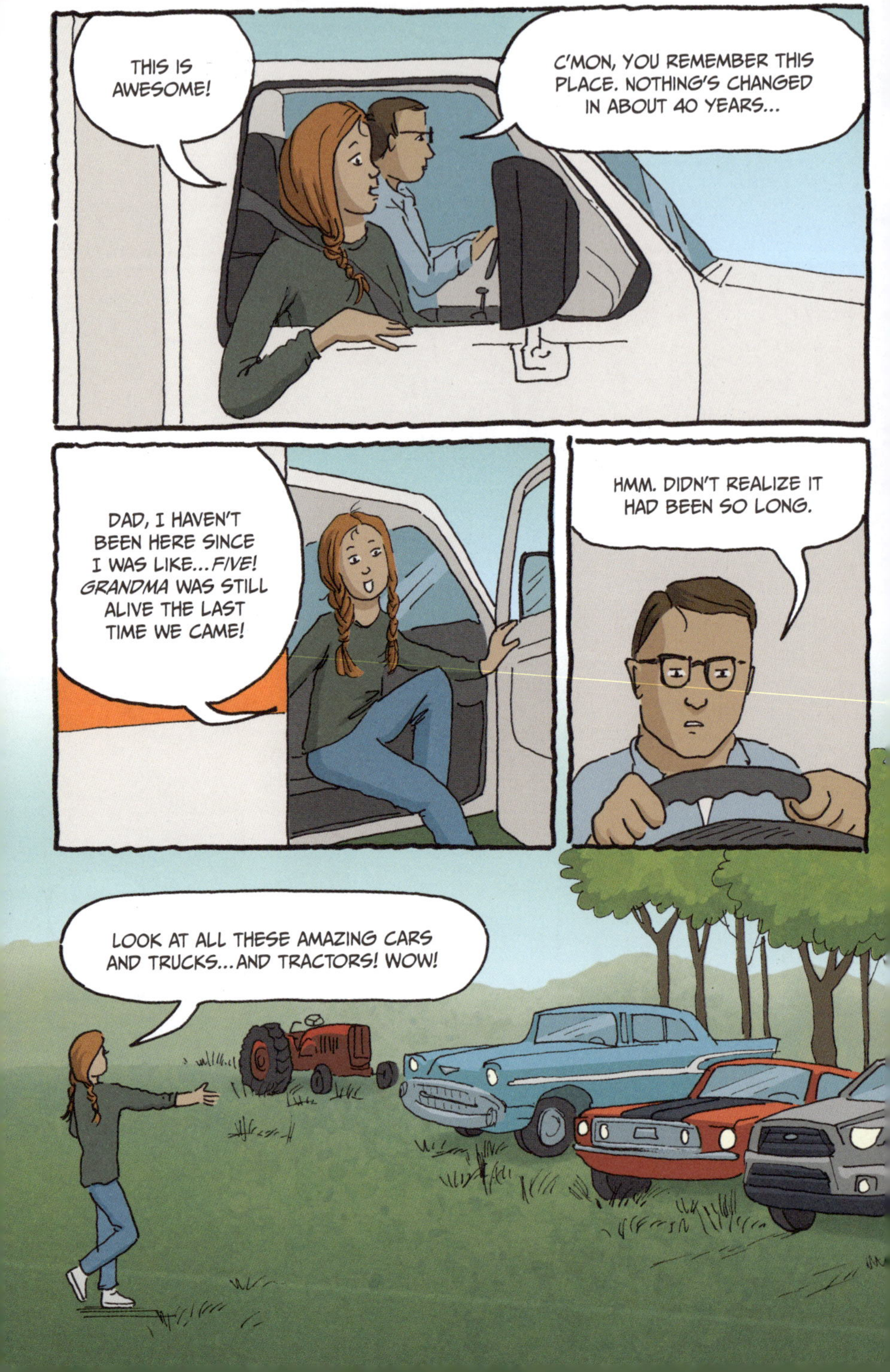
THIS IS AWESOME!
C'MON, YOU REMEMBER THIS PLACE. NOTHING'S CHANGED IN ABOUT 40 YEARS...
DAD, I HAVEN'T BEEN HERE SINCE I WAS LIKE... *FIVE*! *GRANDMA* WAS STILL ALIVE THE LAST TIME WE CAME!
HMM. DIDN'T REALIZE IT HAD BEEN SO LONG.
LOOK AT ALL THESE AMAZING CARS AND TRUCKS... AND TRACTORS! WOW!

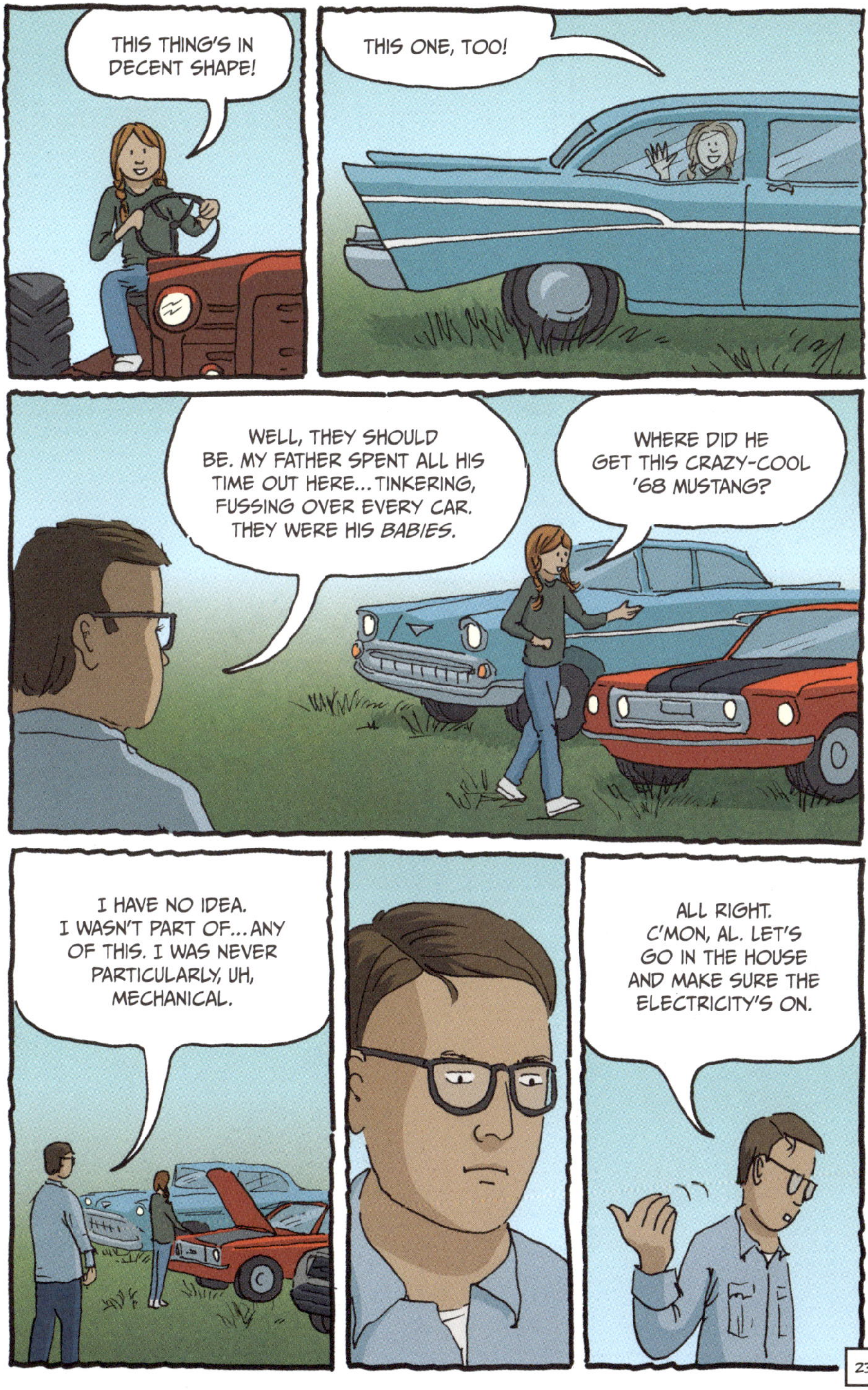
THIS THING'S IN DECENT SHAPE!
THIS ONE, TOO!
WELL, THEY SHOULD BE. MY FATHER SPENT ALL HIS TIME OUT HERE... TINKERING, FUSSING OVER EVERY CAR. THEY WERE HIS *BABIES*.
WHERE DID HE GET THIS CRAZY-COOL '68 MUSTANG?
I HAVE NO IDEA. I WASN'T PART OF... ANY OF THIS. I WAS NEVER PARTICULARLY, UH, MECHANICAL.
ALL RIGHT. C'MON, AL. LET'S GO IN THE HOUSE AND MAKE SURE THE ELECTRICITY'S ON.

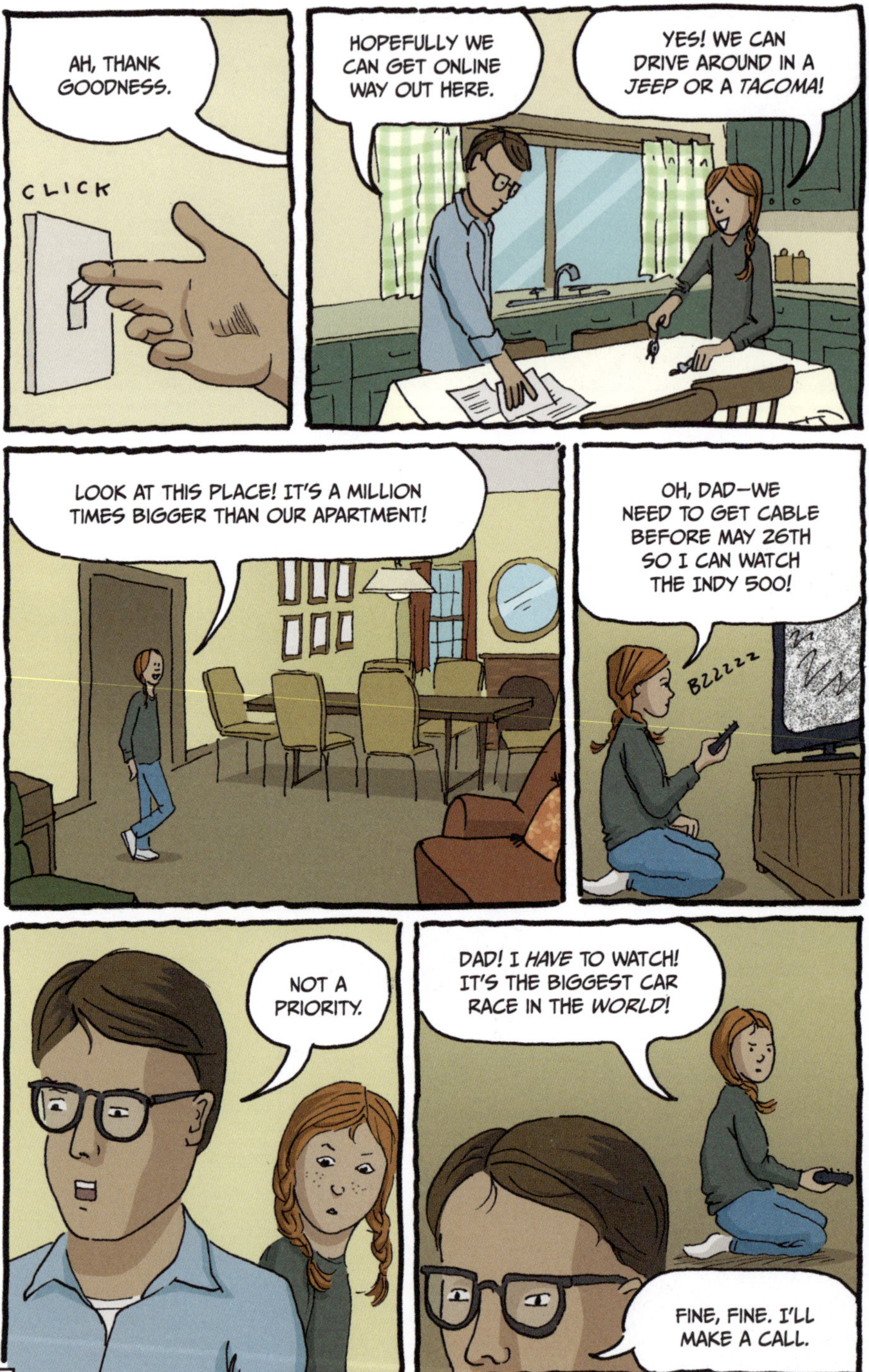
AH, THANK GOODNESS.
CLICK
HOPEFULLY WE CAN GET ONLINE WAY OUT HERE.
YES! WE CAN DRIVE AROUND IN A *JEEP* OR A *TACOMA*!
LOOK AT THIS PLACE! IT'S A MILLION TIMES BIGGER THAN OUR APARTMENT!
OH, DAD—WE NEED TO GET CABLE BEFORE MAY 26TH SO I CAN WATCH THE INDY 500!
BZZZZZ
NOT A PRIORITY.
DAD! I *HAVE* TO WATCH! IT'S THE BIGGEST CAR RACE IN THE *WORLD*!
FINE, FINE. I'LL MAKE A CALL.

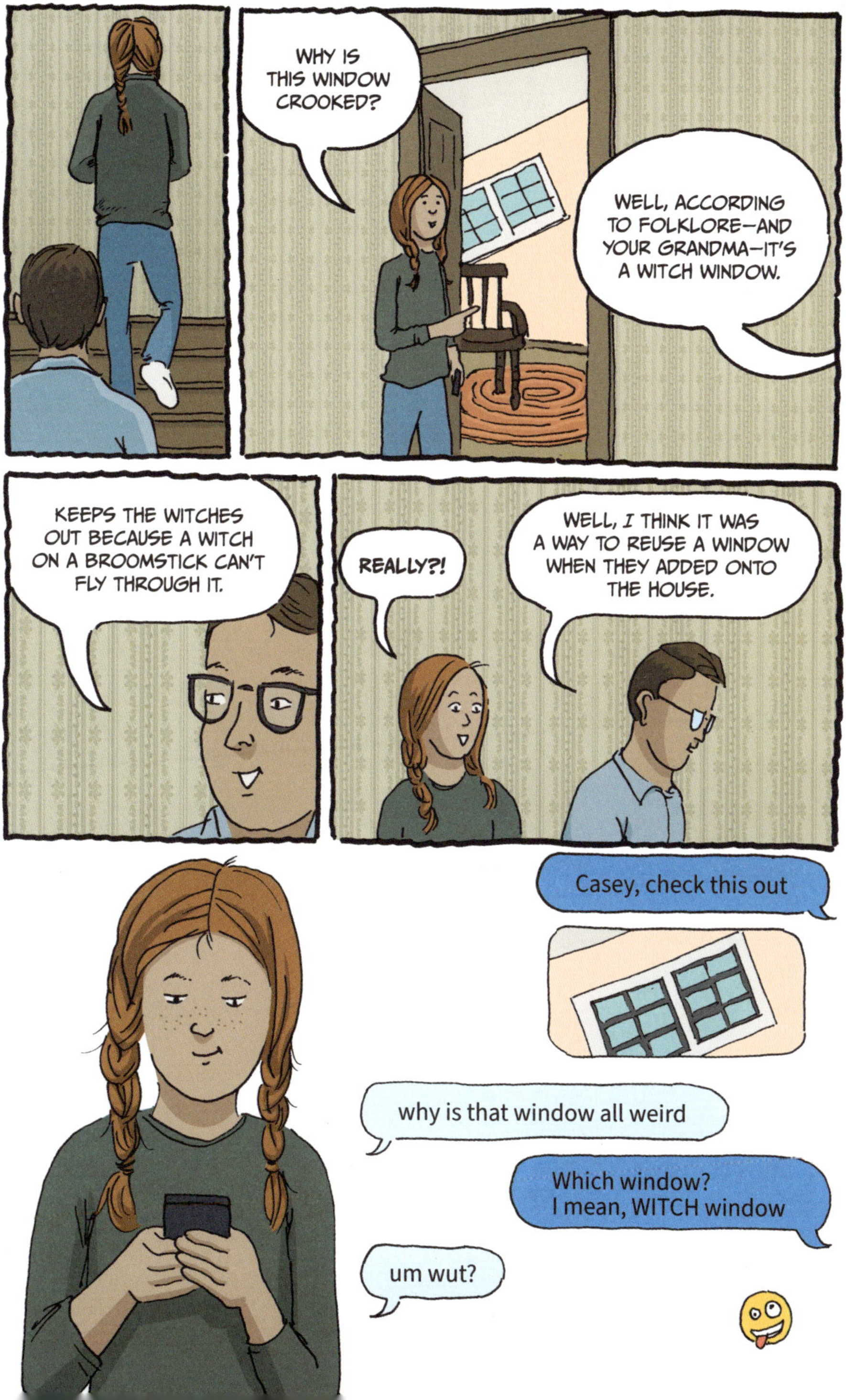
WHY IS THIS WINDOW CROOKED?
WELL, ACCORDING TO FOLKLORE—AND YOUR GRANDMA—IT'S A WITCH WINDOW.
KEEPS THE WITCHES OUT BECAUSE A WITCH ON A BROOMSTICK CAN'T FLY THROUGH IT.
REALLY?!
WELL, I THINK IT WAS A WAY TO REUSE A WINDOW WHEN THEY ADDED ONTO THE HOUSE.
Casey, check this out
why is that window all weird
Which window?
I mean, WITCH window
um wut?

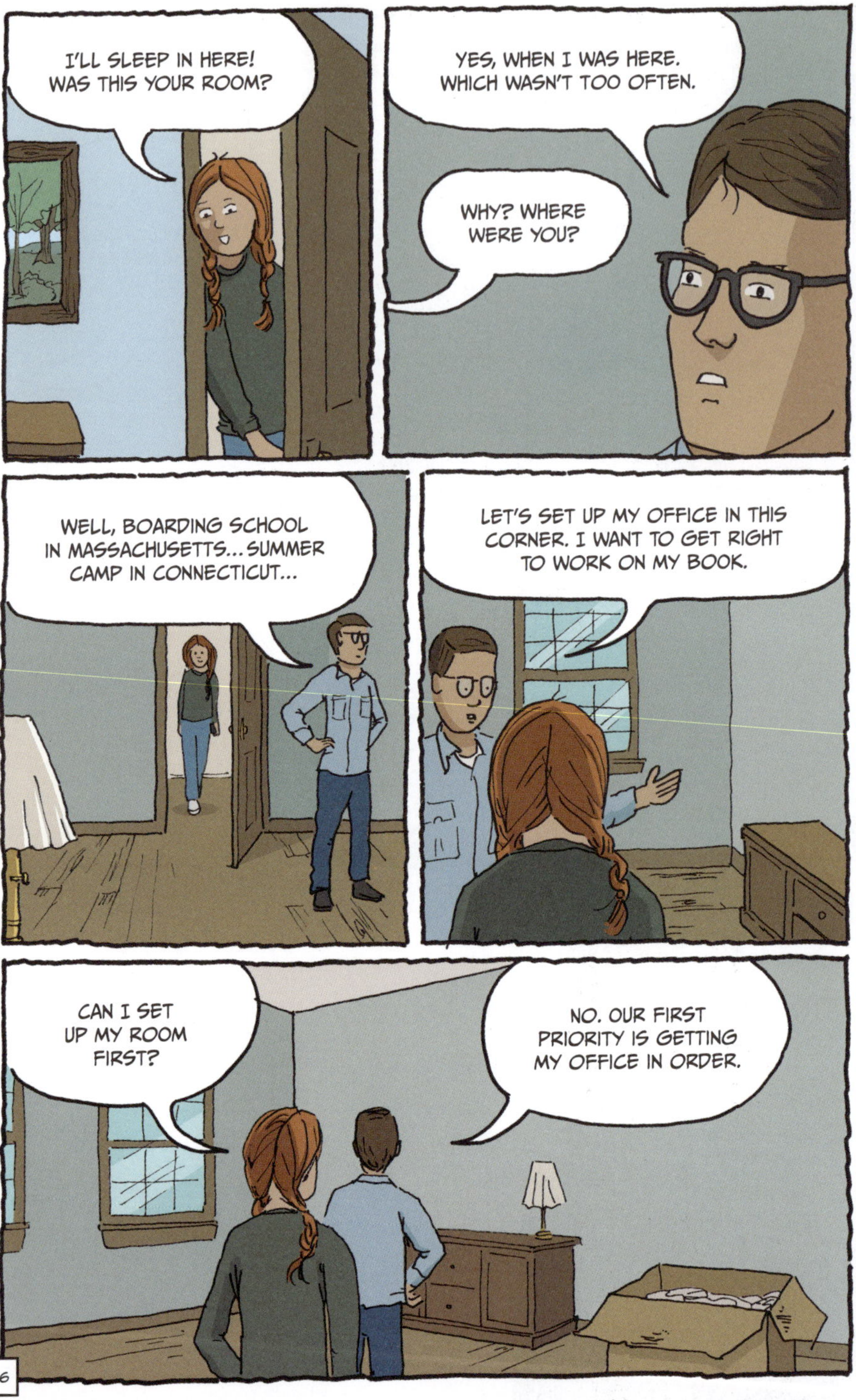
I'LL SLEEP IN HERE! WAS THIS YOUR ROOM?
YES, WHEN I WAS HERE. WHICH WASN'T TOO OFTEN.
WHY? WHERE WERE YOU?
WELL, BOARDING SCHOOL IN MASSACHUSETTS... SUMMER CAMP IN CONNECTICUT...
LET'S SET UP MY OFFICE IN THIS CORNER. I WANT TO GET RIGHT TO WORK ON MY BOOK.
CAN I SET UP MY ROOM FIRST?
NO. OUR FIRST PRIORITY IS GETTING MY OFFICE IN ORDER.

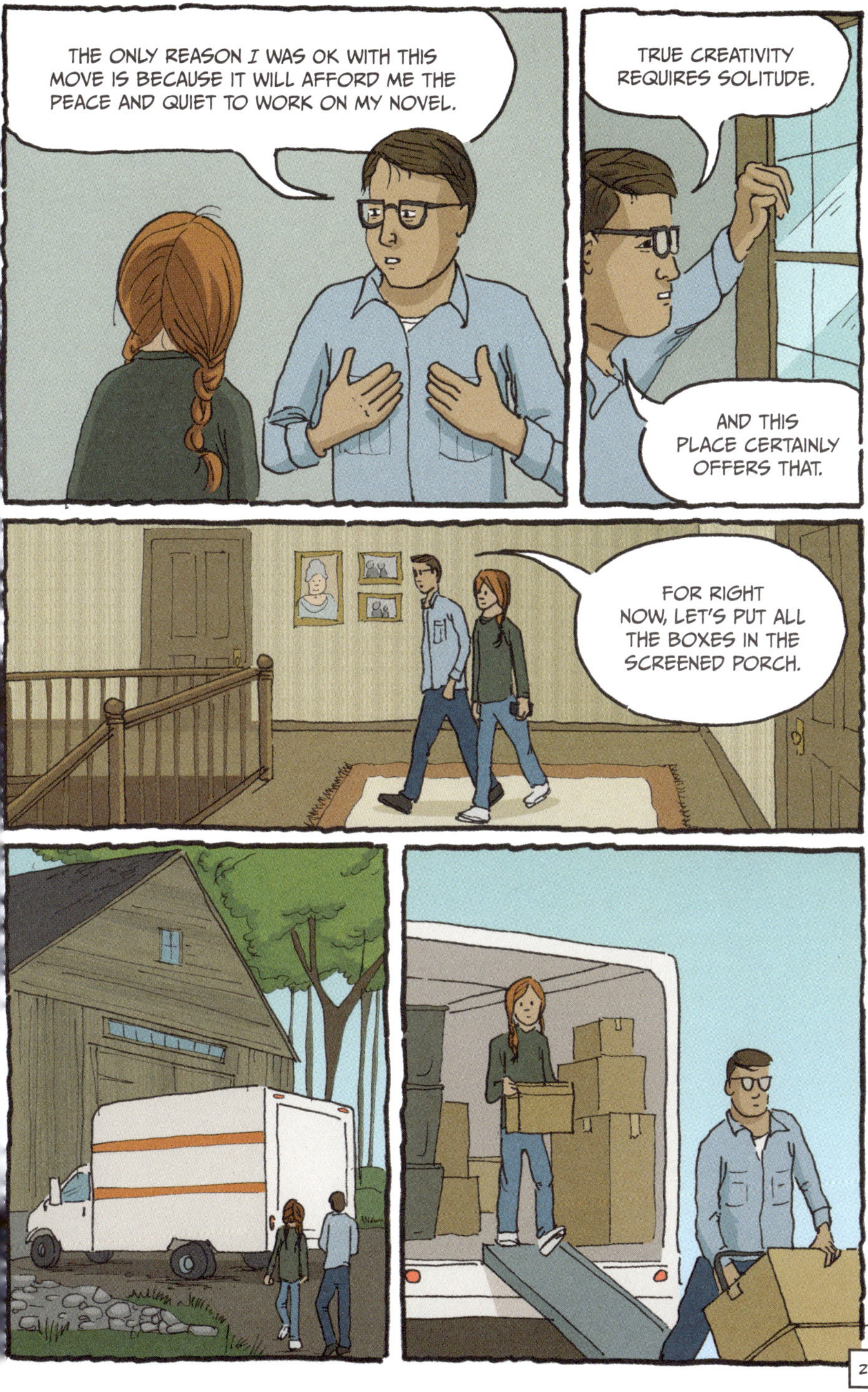
THE ONLY REASON I WAS OK WITH THIS MOVE IS BECAUSE IT WILL AFFORD ME THE PEACE AND QUIET TO WORK ON MY NOVEL.
TRUE CREATIVITY REQUIRES SOLITUDE.
AND THIS PLACE CERTAINLY OFFERS THAT.
FOR RIGHT NOW, LET'S PUT ALL THE BOXES IN THE SCREENED PORCH.

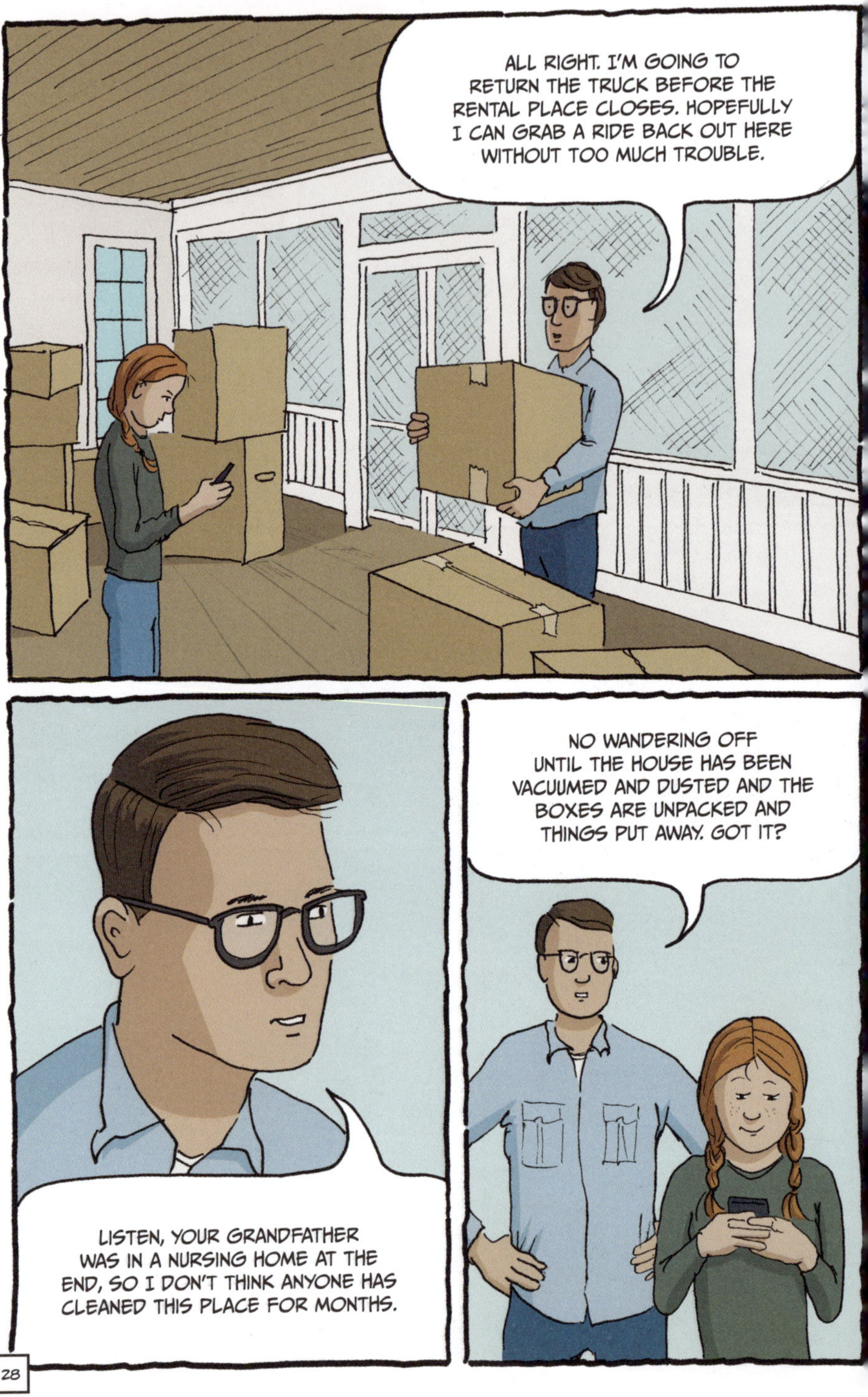
ALL RIGHT. I'M GOING TO RETURN THE TRUCK BEFORE THE RENTAL PLACE CLOSES. HOPEFULLY I CAN GRAB A RIDE BACK OUT HERE WITHOUT TOO MUCH TROUBLE.
LISTEN, YOUR GRANDFATHER WAS IN A NURSING HOME AT THE END, SO I DON'T THINK ANYONE HAS CLEANED THIS PLACE FOR MONTHS.
NO WANDERING OFF UNTIL THE HOUSE HAS BEEN VACUUMED AND DUSTED AND THE BOXES ARE UNPACKED AND THINGS PUT AWAY. GOT IT?

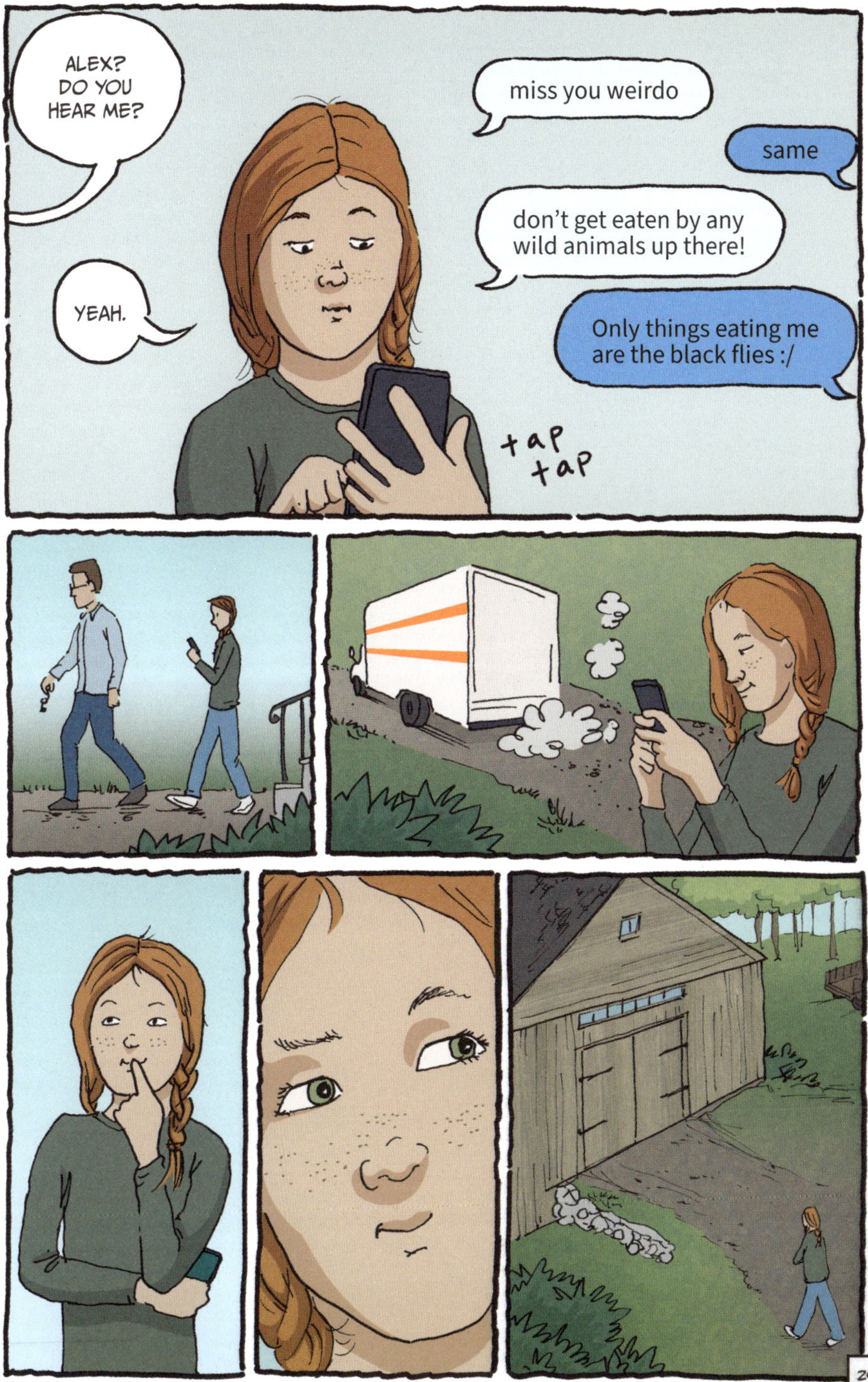
ALEX? DO YOU HEAR ME?
miss you weirdo
same
don't get eaten by any wild animals up there!
YEAH.
Only things eating me are the black flies :/
tap tap

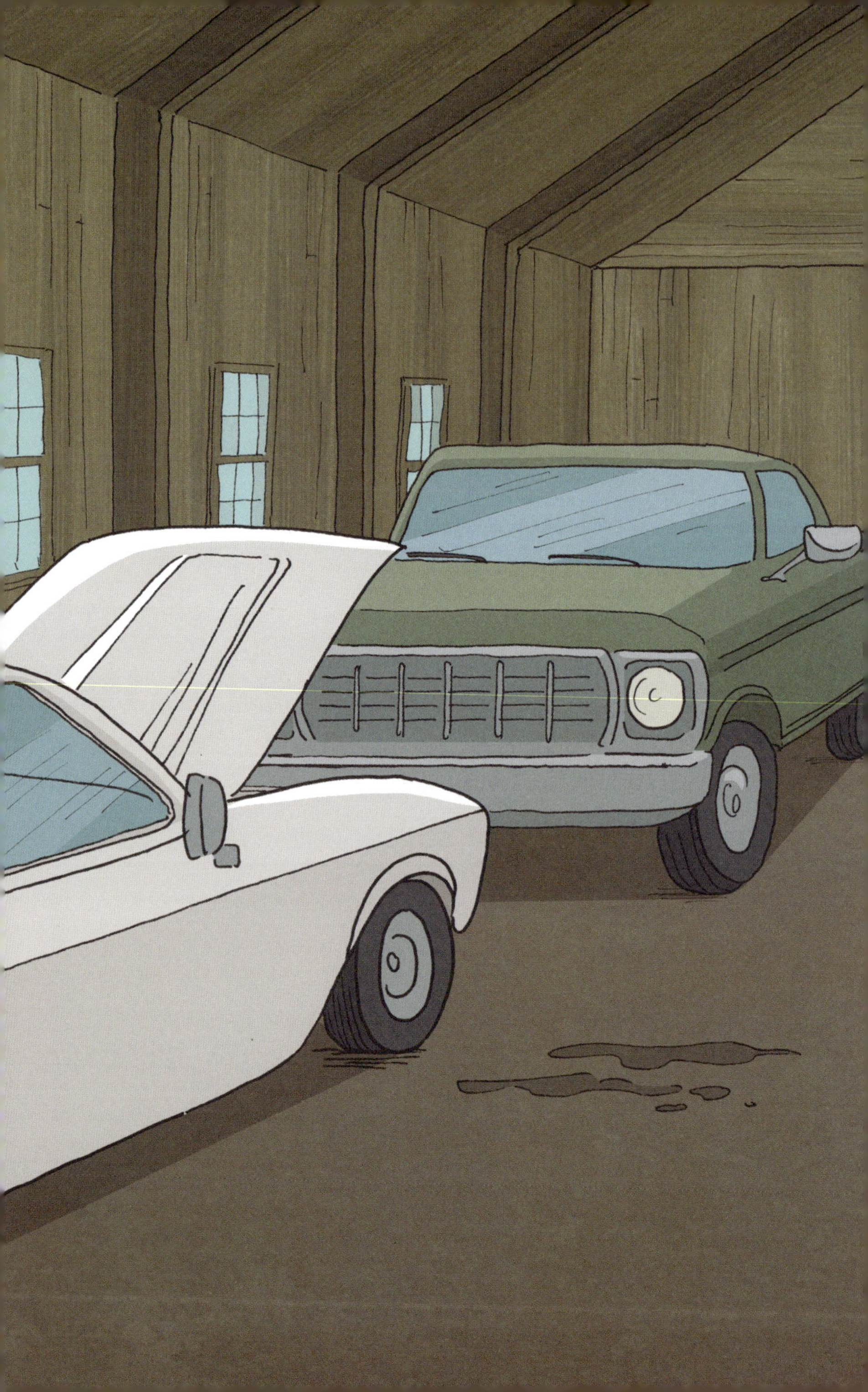

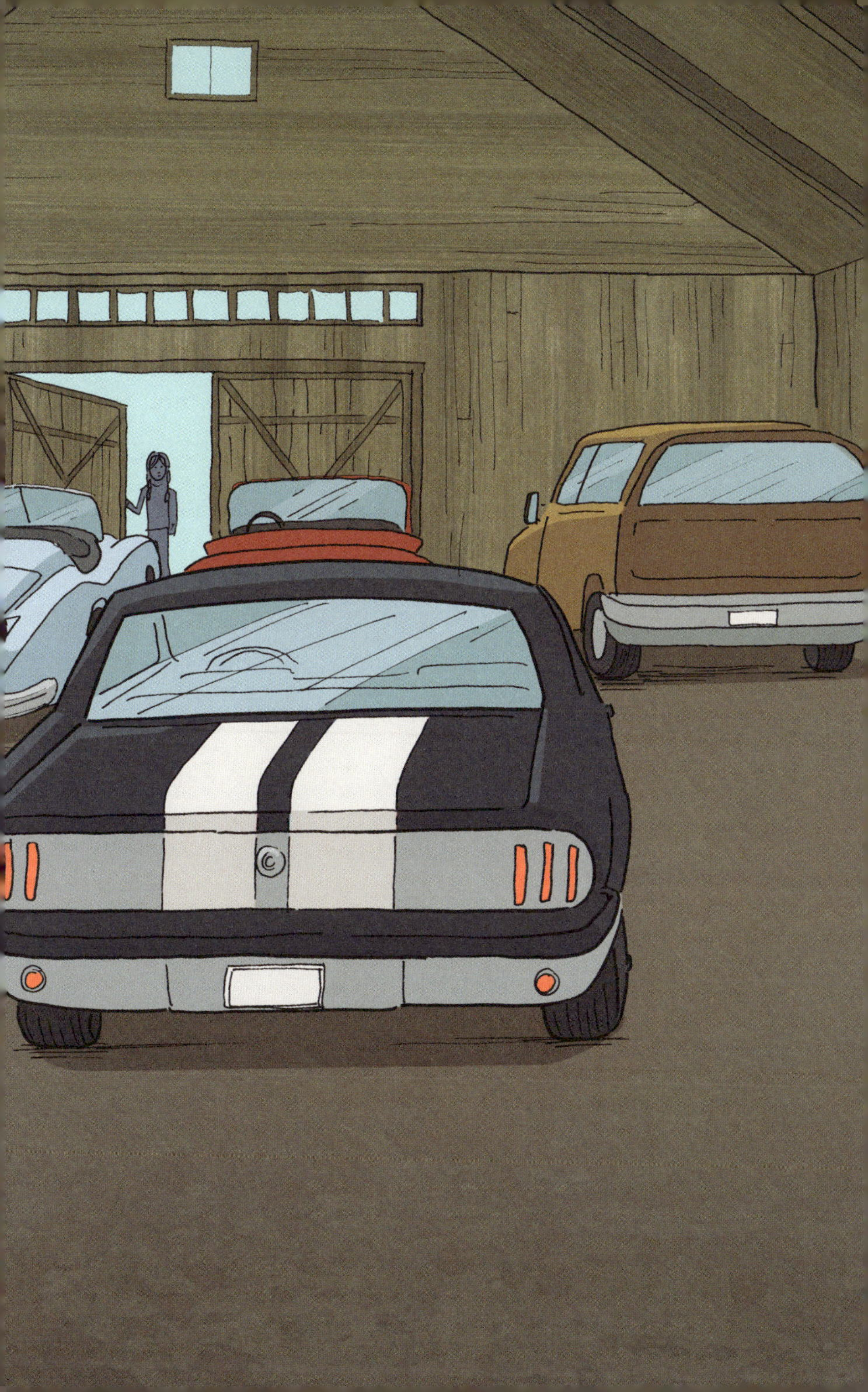

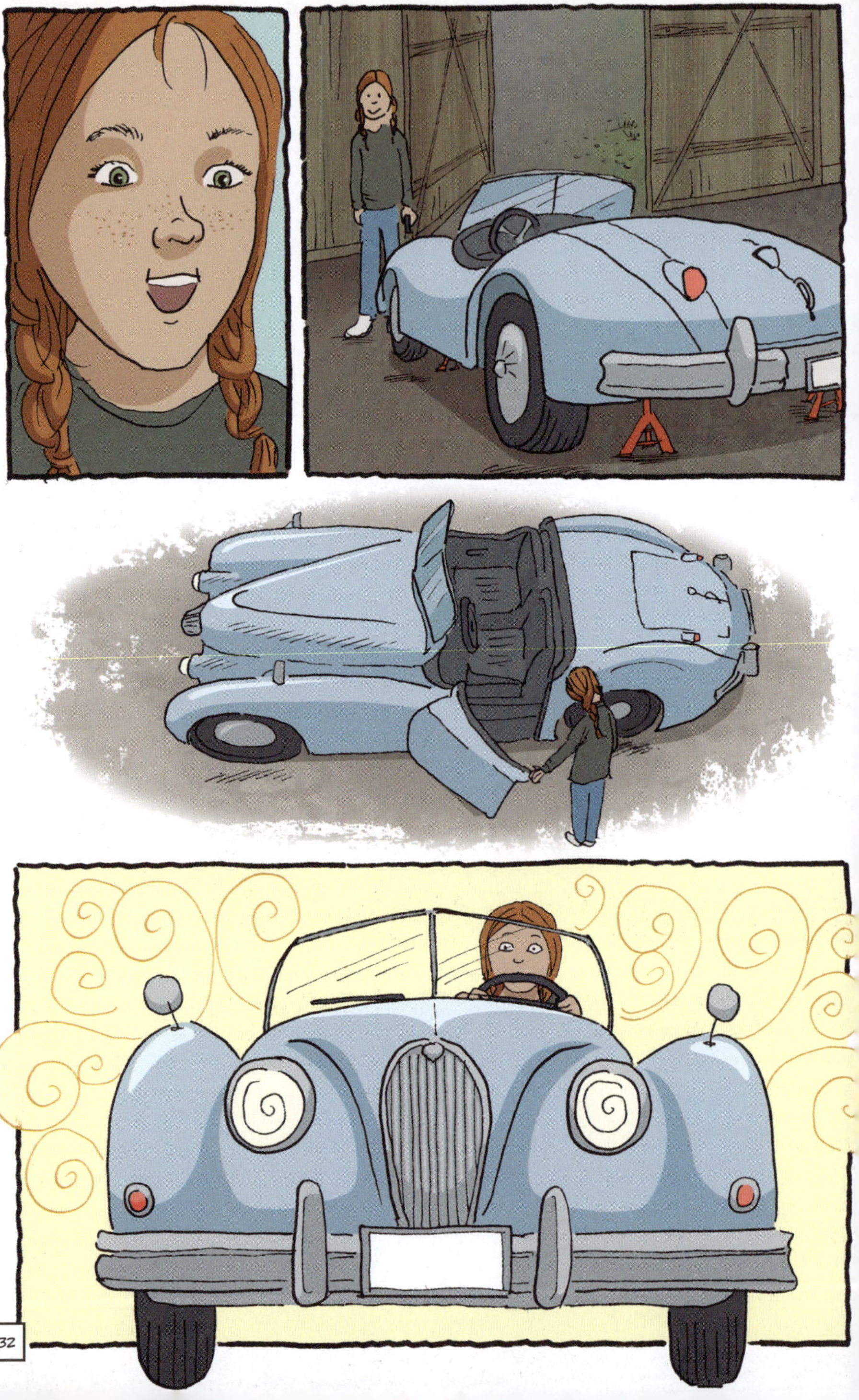

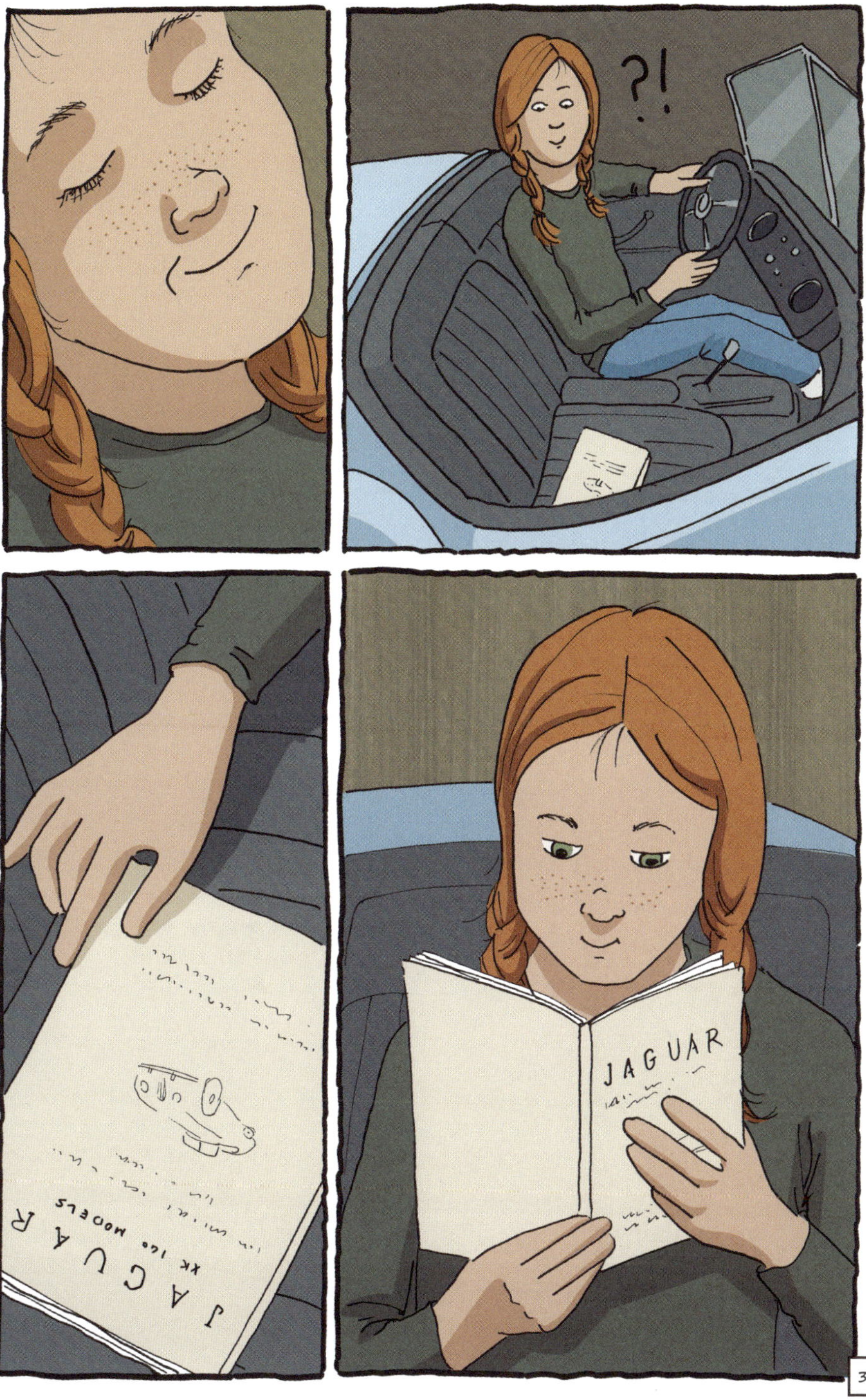
?!
JAGUAR
XK 120 MODELS
JAGUAR

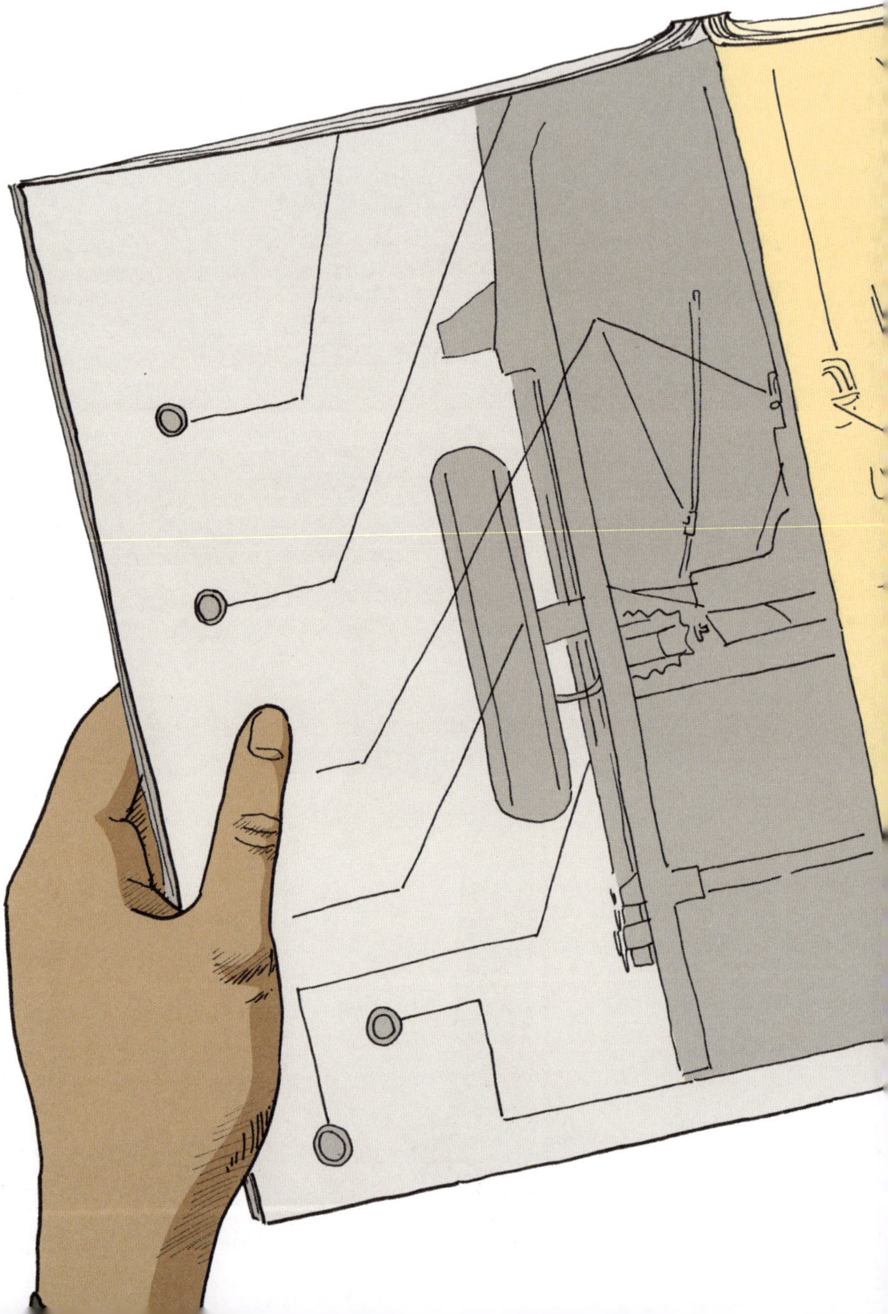

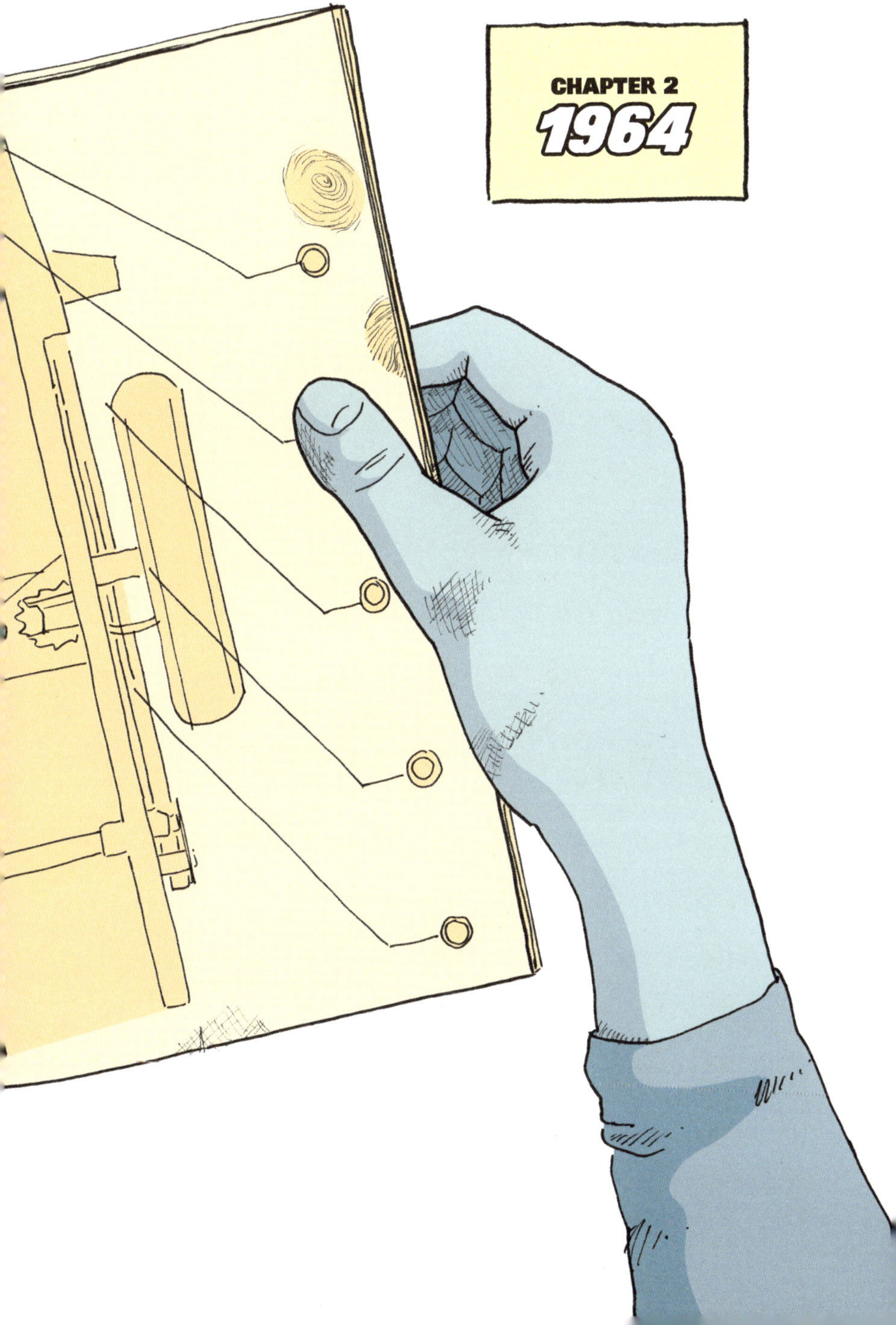
CHAPTER 2
1964

Dear Jack,

Thank you for your recent letter. I'm glad you are well. Congratulations on the purchase of your farm—it sounds lovely!

As you may know, I'm now the graduate of <u>two</u> race car driving schools! My last instructor encouraged me to try sports car racing, so I'm using the winter months to get the Jaguar in tip-top shape.

Because I can't afford to hire a mechanic, I'm teaching myself to be my own mechanic!

After work, I drive my station wagon to an old barn I've rented, where I work on the Jaguar by flashlight because there is no electricity—or heat! Brrr! The rats that scurry around in the barn's dark corners are my only company.

But I don't mind any of it, because it's such a joy to explore every inch of this beautiful car! Using basic hand tools (and the service manual to guide me), I've taken the engine apart down to the last nut and bolt.

After I rebuild it, I plan to putty and sand the fenders and finish the job with a new coat of paint.

My Jaguar and I will be ready to race by summer! I can't wait!

It's almost midnight, so I'll sign off. Good night, dear Jack!

J.

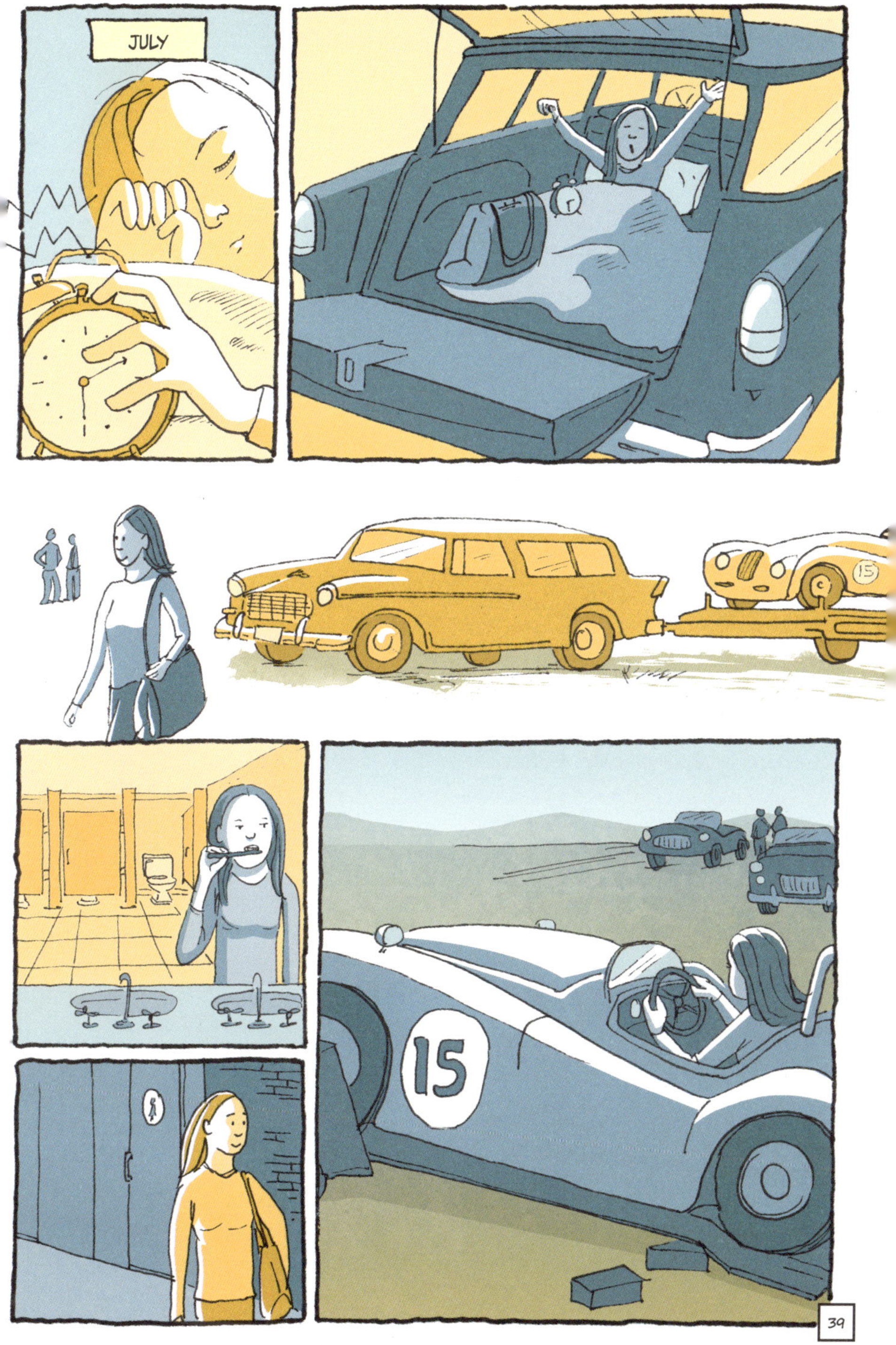

JULY
15
15

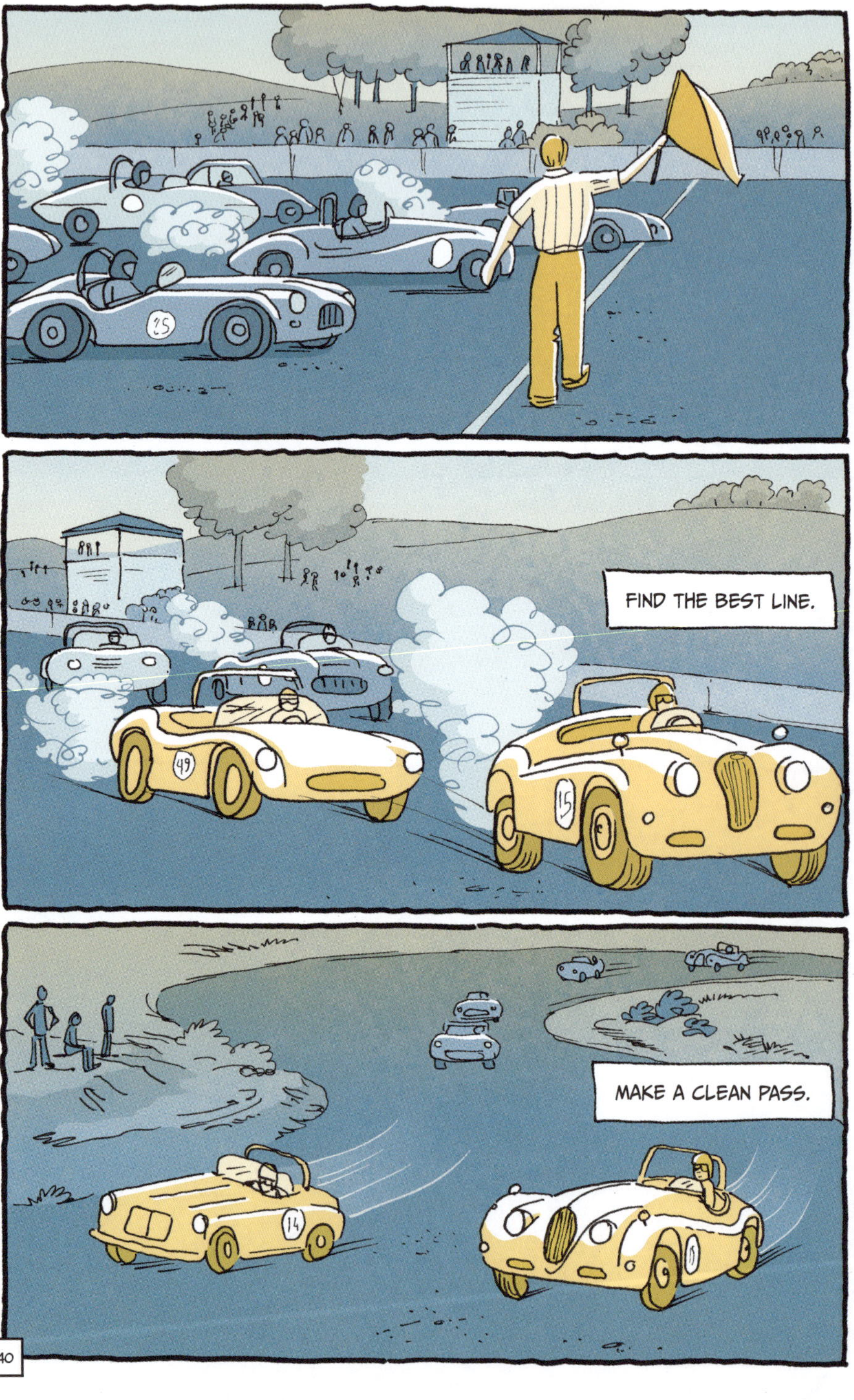
FIND THE BEST LINE.
MAKE A CLEAN PASS.

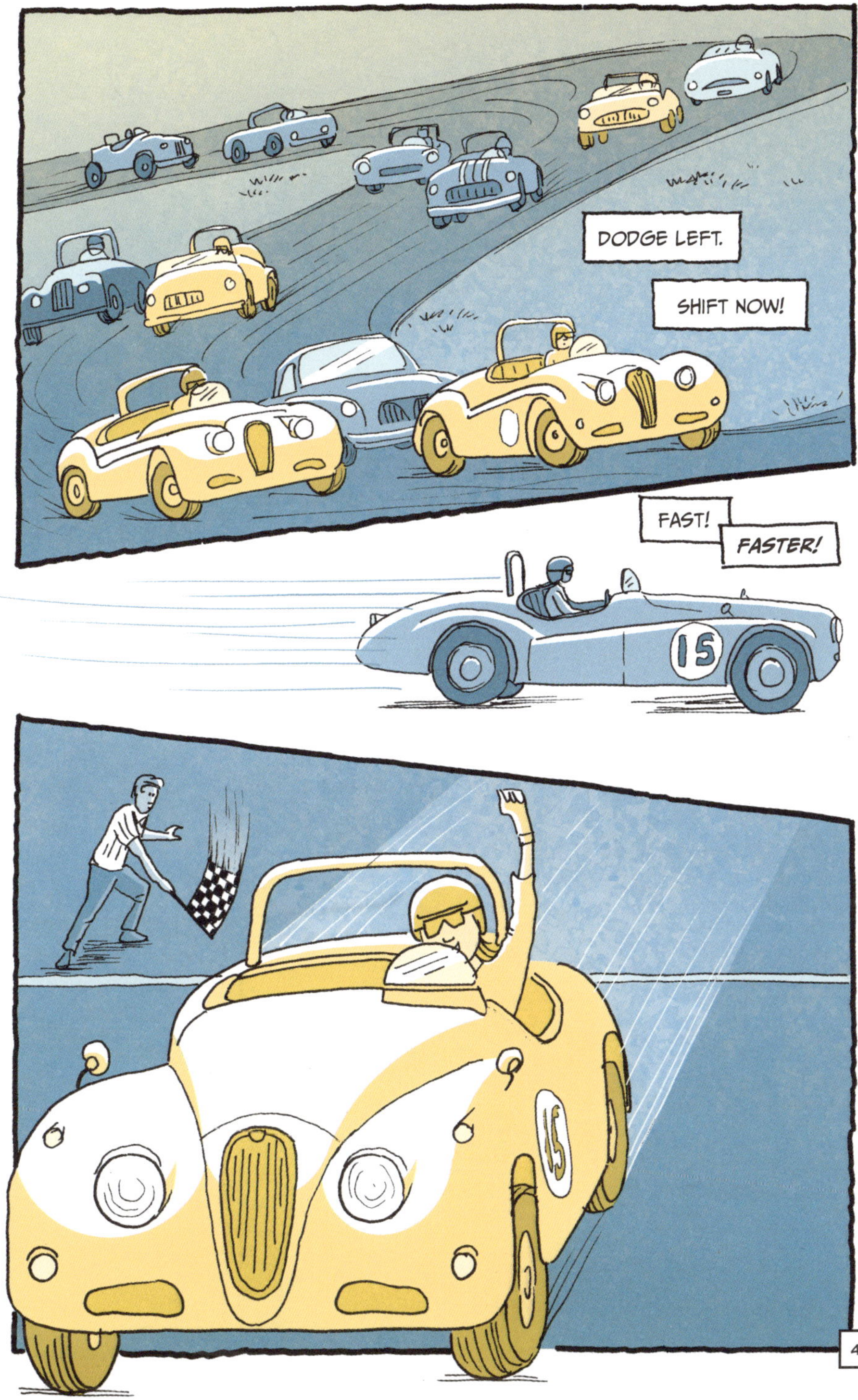
DODGE LEFT.
SHIFT NOW!
FAST!
FASTER!
15
15

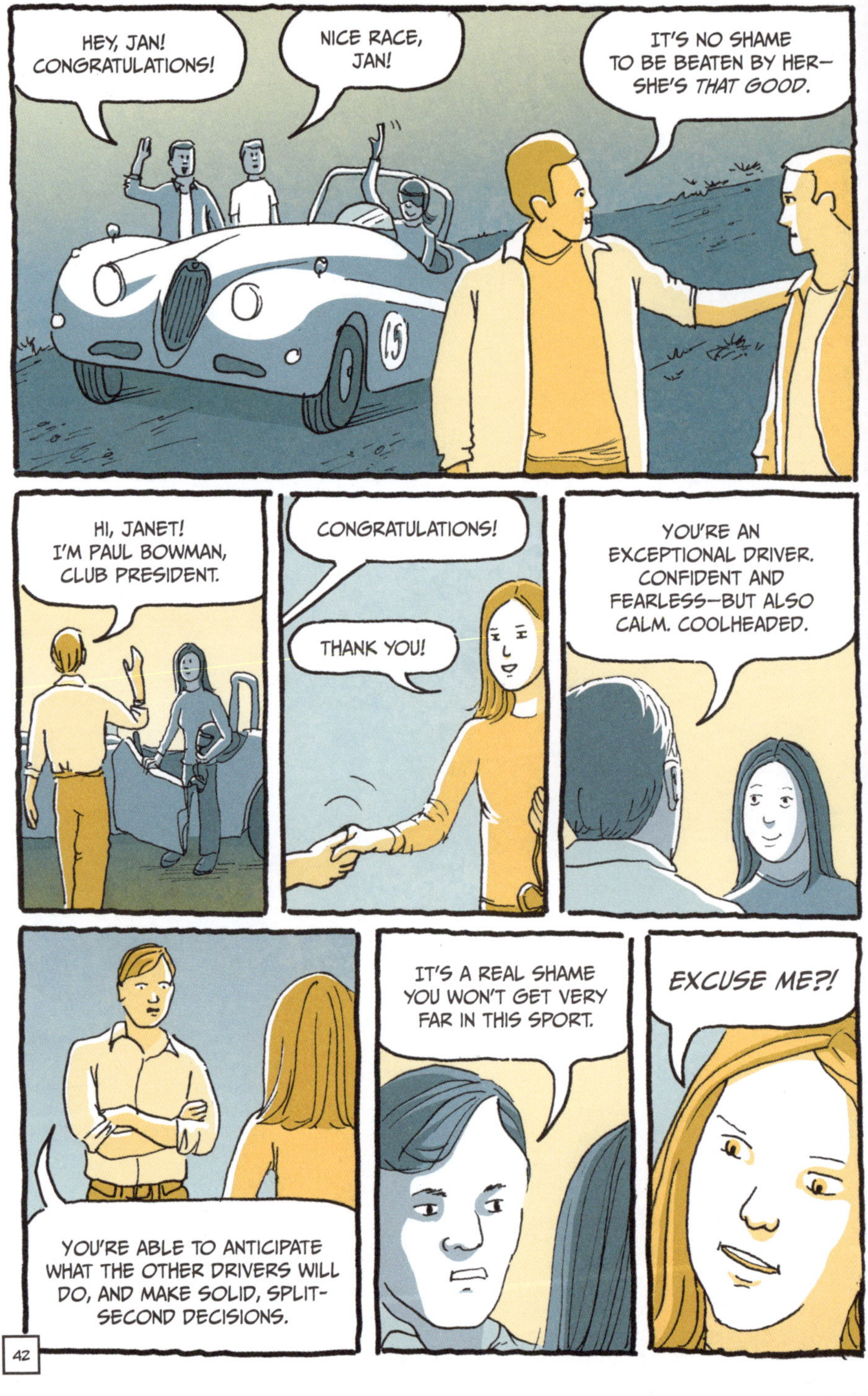
HEY, JAN! CONGRATULATIONS!
NICE RACE, JAN!
IT'S NO SHAME TO BE BEATEN BY HER—SHE'S *THAT GOOD.*
HI, JANET! I'M PAUL BOWMAN, CLUB PRESIDENT.
CONGRATULATIONS!
THANK YOU!
YOU'RE AN EXCEPTIONAL DRIVER. CONFIDENT AND FEARLESS—BUT ALSO CALM. COOLHEADED.
YOU'RE ABLE TO ANTICIPATE WHAT THE OTHER DRIVERS WILL DO, AND MAKE SOLID, SPLIT-SECOND DECISIONS.
IT'S A REAL SHAME YOU WON'T GET VERY FAR IN THIS SPORT.
EXCUSE ME?!

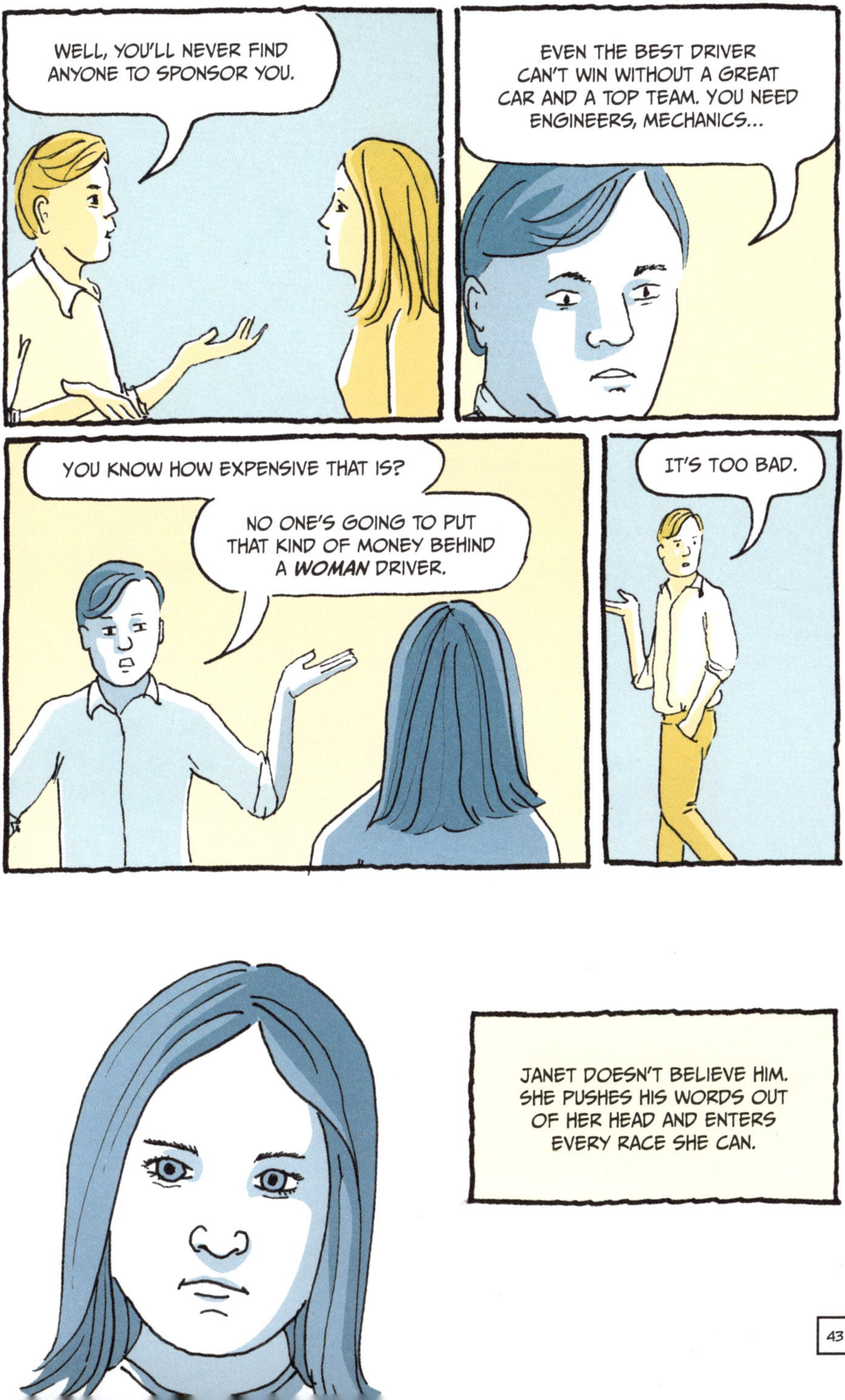
WELL, YOU'LL NEVER FIND ANYONE TO SPONSOR YOU.
EVEN THE BEST DRIVER CAN'T WIN WITHOUT A GREAT CAR AND A TOP TEAM. YOU NEED ENGINEERS, MECHANICS...
YOU KNOW HOW EXPENSIVE THAT IS?
NO ONE'S GOING TO PUT THAT KIND OF MONEY BEHIND A *WOMAN* DRIVER.
IT'S TOO BAD.
JANET DOESN'T BELIEVE HIM. SHE PUSHES HIS WORDS OUT OF HER HEAD AND ENTERS EVERY RACE SHE CAN.

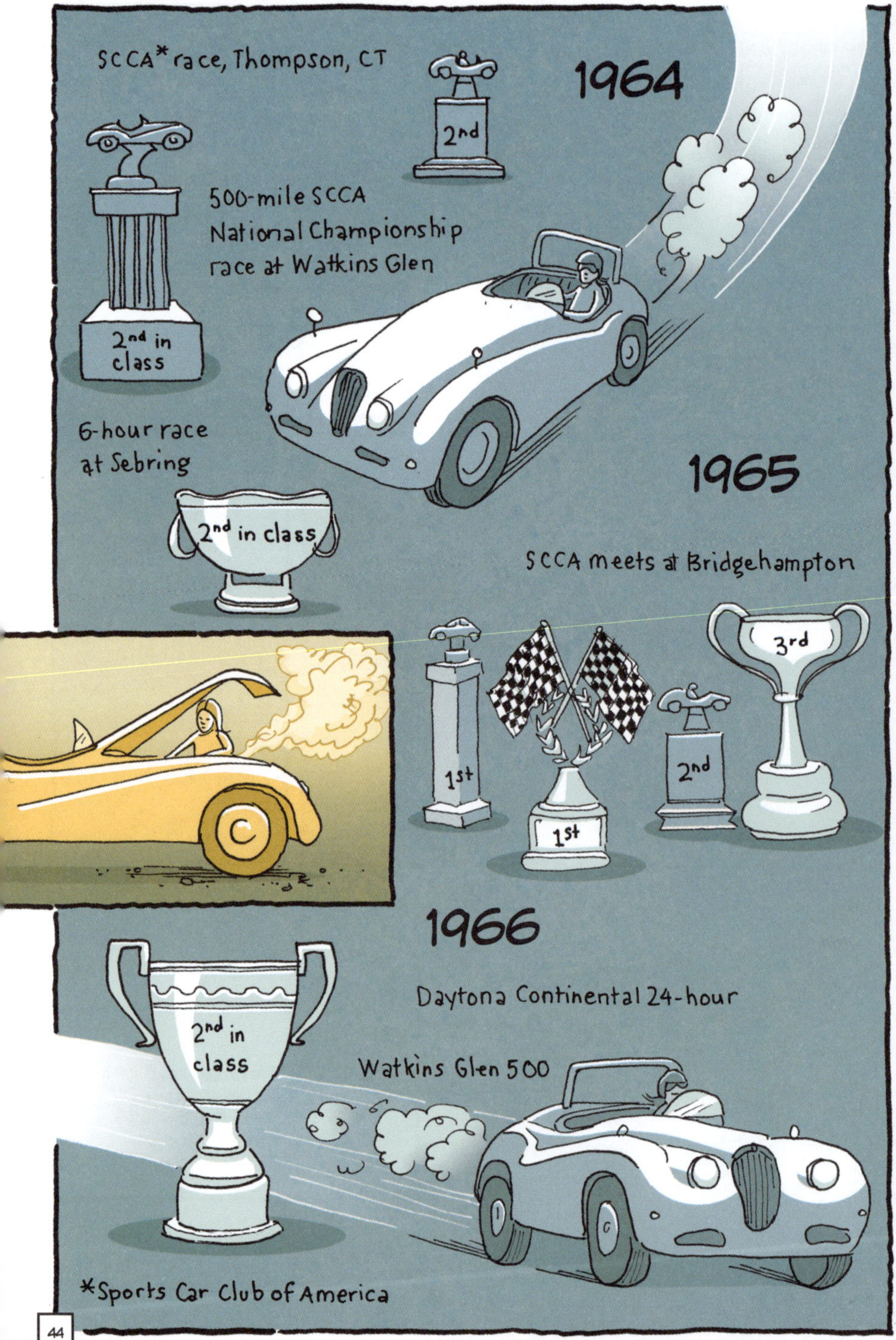
SCCA* race, Thompson, CT
2nd
1964
500-mile SCCA National Championship race at Watkins Glen
2nd in class
6-hour race at Sebring
2nd in class
1965
SCCA meets at Bridgehampton
1st
1st
2nd
3rd
1966
Daytona Continental 24-hour
2nd in class
Watkins Glen 500
*Sports Car Club of America

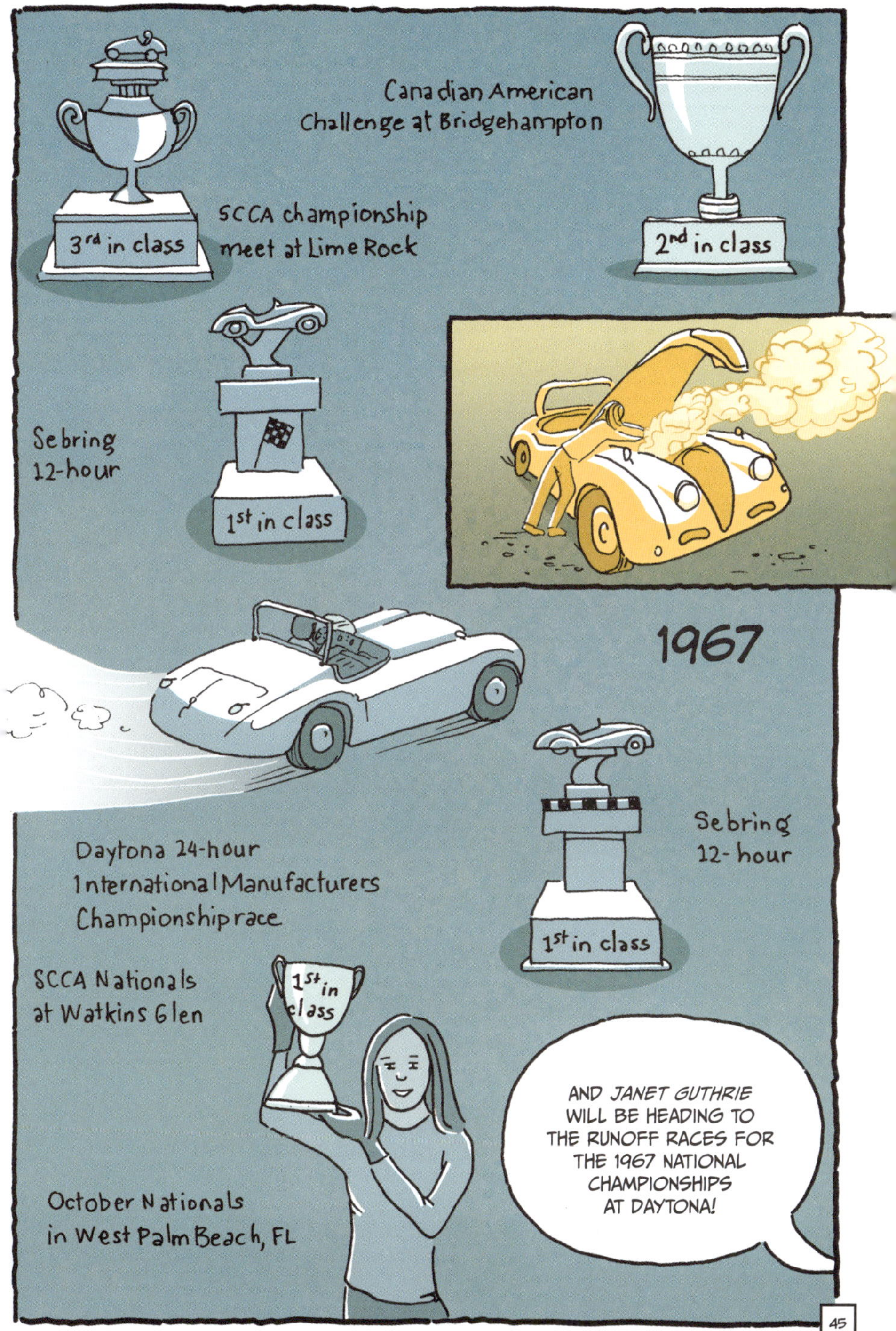

Canadian American Challenge at Bridgehampton
3rd in class
SCCA championship meet at Lime Rock
2nd in class
Sebring 12-hour
1st in class
1967
Daytona 24-hour International Manufacturers Championship race
Sebring 12-hour
1st in class
SCCA Nationals at Watkins Glen
1st in class
October Nationals in West Palm Beach, FL
AND JANET GUTHRIE WILL BE HEADING TO THE RUNOFF RACES FOR THE 1967 NATIONAL CHAMPIONSHIPS AT DAYTONA!

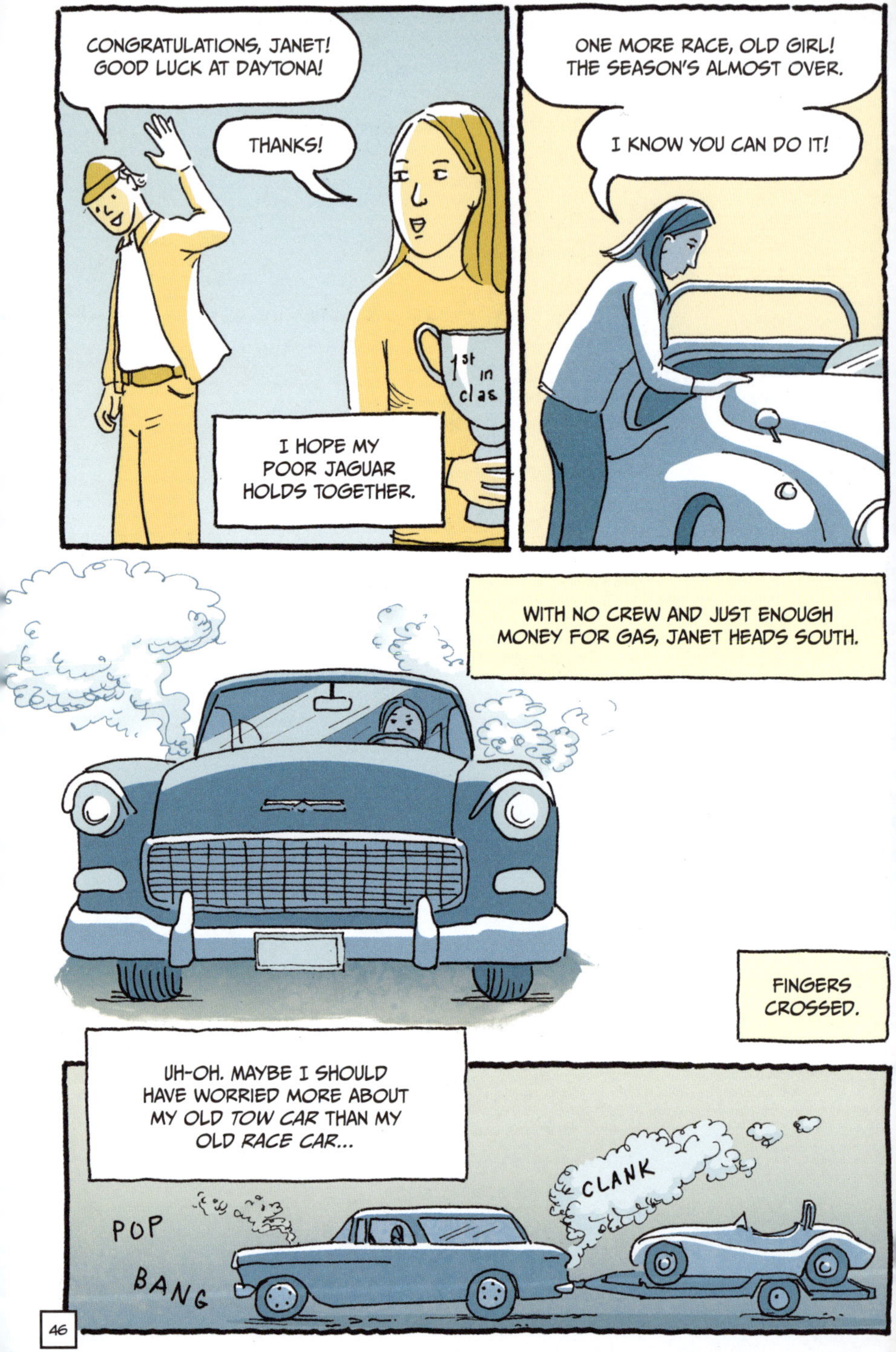
CONGRATULATIONS, JANET! GOOD LUCK AT DAYTONA!
THANKS!
1st in clas
I HOPE MY POOR JAGUAR HOLDS TOGETHER.
ONE MORE RACE, OLD GIRL! THE SEASON'S ALMOST OVER.
I KNOW YOU CAN DO IT!
WITH NO CREW AND JUST ENOUGH MONEY FOR GAS, JANET HEADS SOUTH.
FINGERS CROSSED.
UH-OH. MAYBE I SHOULD HAVE WORRIED MORE ABOUT MY OLD *TOW CAR* THAN MY OLD *RACE CAR*...
CLANK
POP
BANG

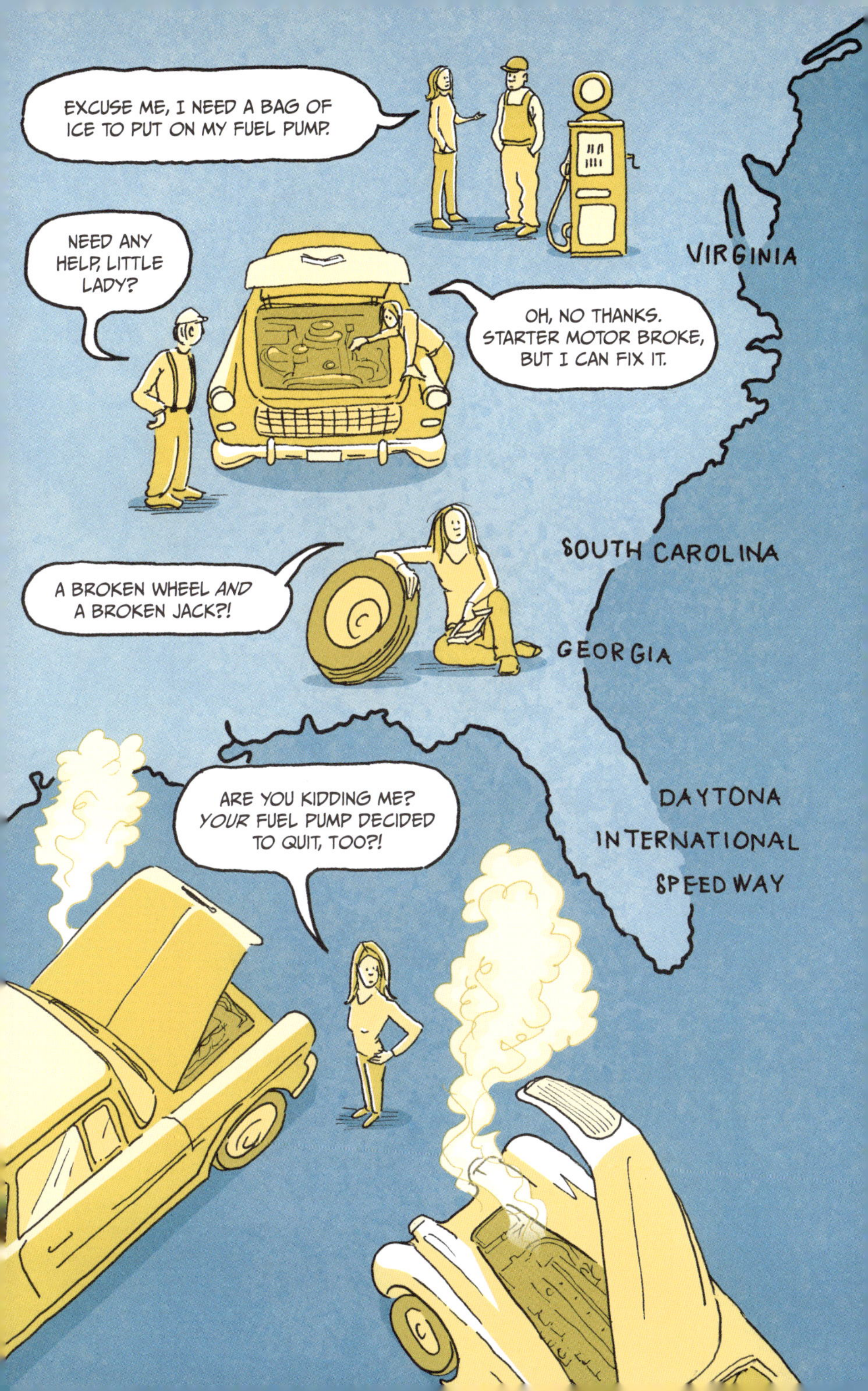
EXCUSE ME, I NEED A BAG OF ICE TO PUT ON MY FUEL PUMP.
NEED ANY HELP, LITTLE LADY?
OH, NO THANKS. STARTER MOTOR BROKE, BUT I CAN FIX IT.
VIRGINIA
SOUTH CAROLINA
A BROKEN WHEEL *AND* A BROKEN JACK?!
GEORGIA
ARE YOU KIDDING ME? *YOUR* FUEL PUMP DECIDED TO QUIT, TOO?!
DAYTONA INTERNATIONAL SPEEDWAY

Dear Jack,

What a wild trip to the Daytona runoffs!

The course was made for the Jaguar, and I was racing <u>so well</u>—until the car threw a rod at 143 miles an hour, becoming a pile of scrap metal in a matter of seconds. I was heartbroken.

On the way home, my tow car gave up in Quantico, Virginia, where I was forced to abandon the entire rig at a Gulf station. The station owner—a racing fan!—promised to keep the cars safe for me and pointed to a bus headed north. I joked with him that if he could find a buyer, I'd happily sell the whole rig! I do know the Jaguar's racing days are over, but it will be nearly impossible to say good-bye. No car will ever mean as much.

Don't worry, though—I will find a way to race. I always do!
Onward!

XO
J.

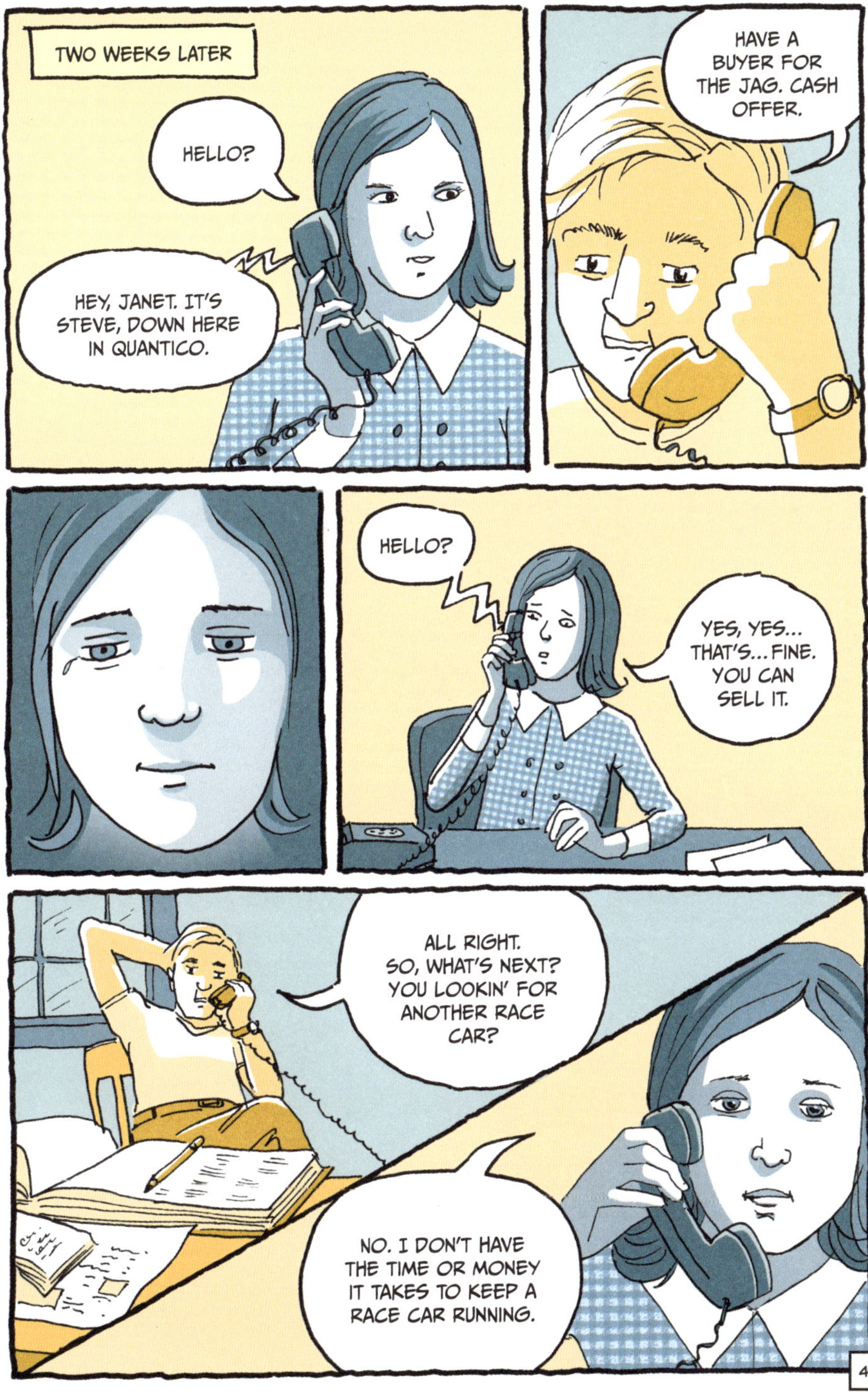
TWO WEEKS LATER
HELLO?
HEY, JANET. IT'S STEVE, DOWN HERE IN QUANTICO.
HAVE A BUYER FOR THE JAG. CASH OFFER.
HELLO?
YES, YES... THAT'S... FINE. YOU CAN SELL IT.
ALL RIGHT. SO, WHAT'S NEXT? YOU LOOKIN' FOR ANOTHER RACE CAR?
NO. I DON'T HAVE THE TIME OR MONEY IT TAKES TO KEEP A RACE CAR RUNNING.

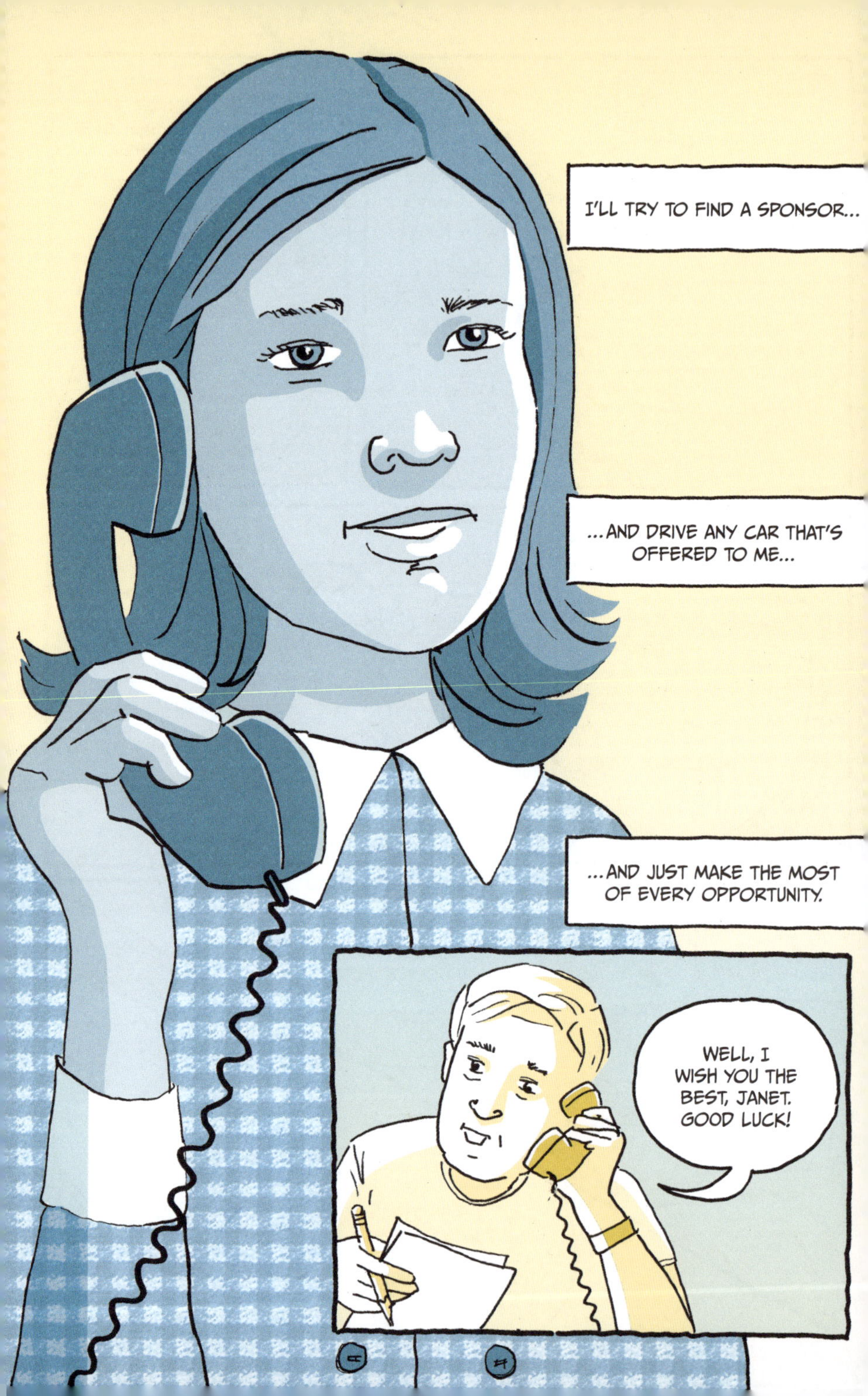
I'LL TRY TO FIND A SPONSOR...
...AND DRIVE ANY CAR THAT'S OFFERED TO ME...
...AND JUST MAKE THE MOST OF EVERY OPPORTUNITY.
WELL, I WISH YOU THE BEST, JANET. GOOD LUCK!

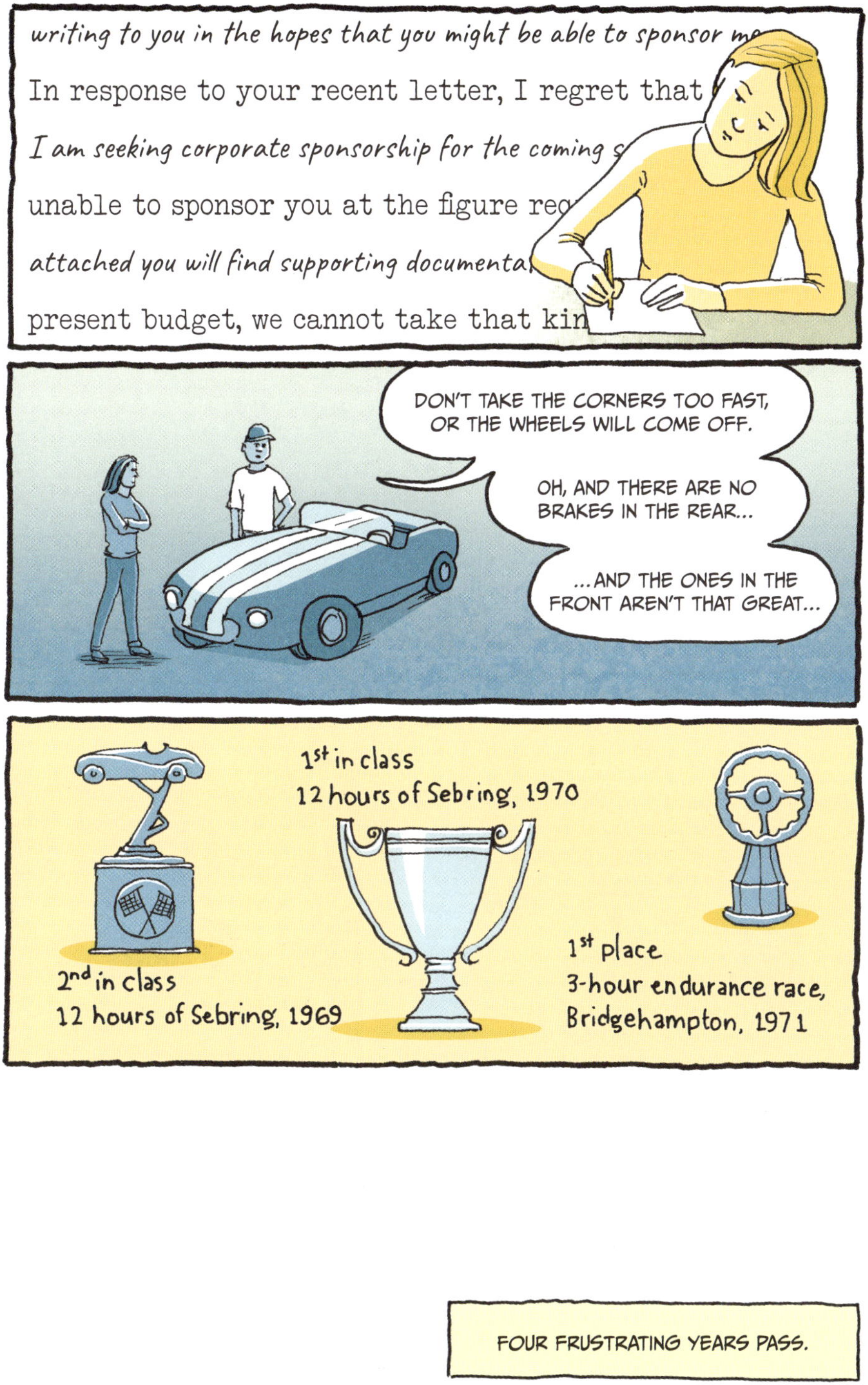
writing to you in the hopes that you might be able to sponsor m
In response to your recent letter, I regret that
I am seeking corporate sponsorship for the coming s
unable to sponsor you at the figure req
attached you will find supporting documenta
present budget, we cannot take that kin
DON'T TAKE THE CORNERS TOO FAST, OR THE WHEELS WILL COME OFF.
OH, AND THERE ARE NO BRAKES IN THE REAR...
...AND THE ONES IN THE FRONT AREN'T THAT GREAT...
2nd in class 12 hours of Sebring, 1969
1st in class 12 hours of Sebring, 1970
1st place 3-hour endurance race, Bridgehampton, 1971
FOUR FRUSTRATING YEARS PASS.

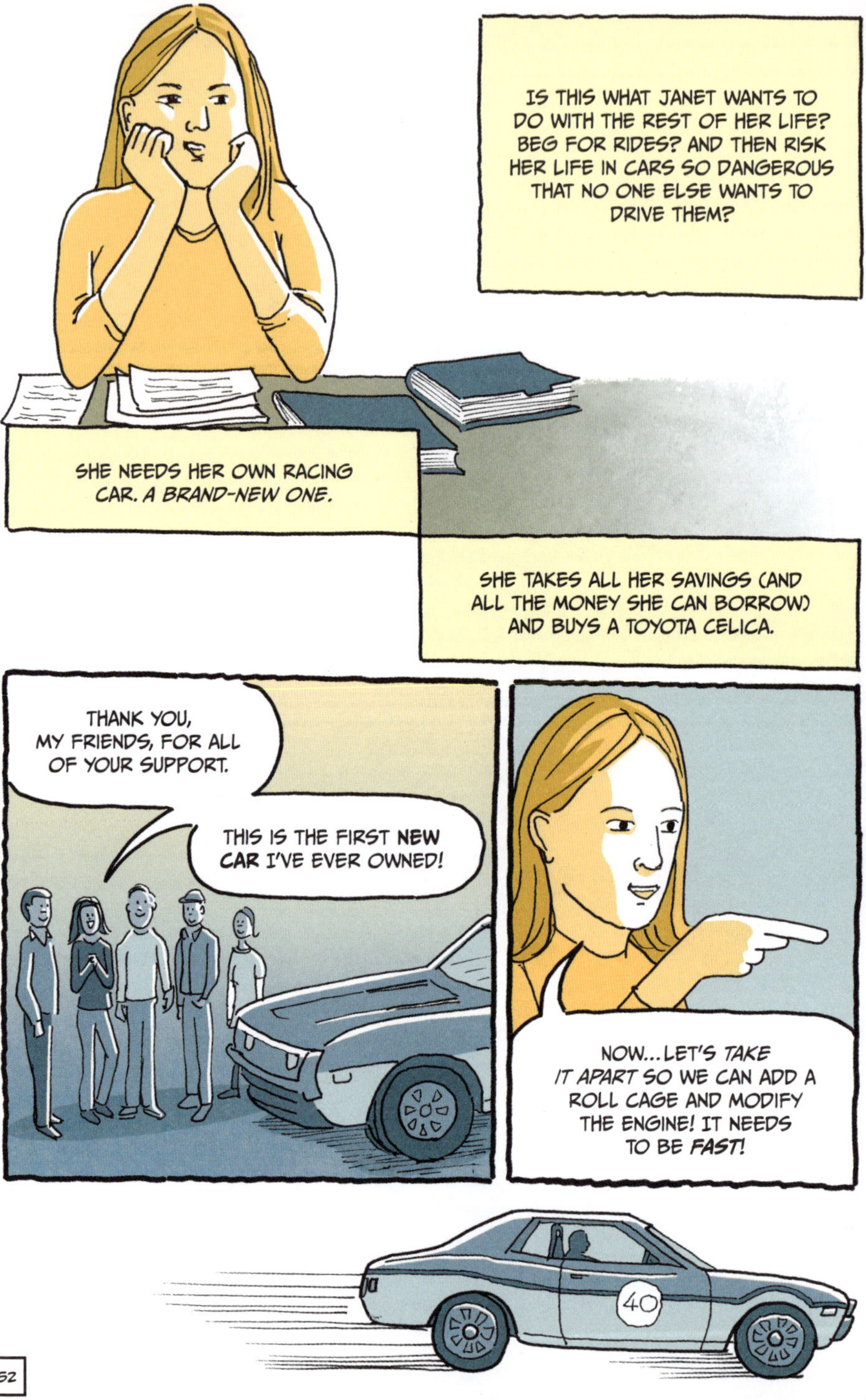
IS THIS WHAT JANET WANTS TO DO WITH THE REST OF HER LIFE? BEG FOR RIDES? AND THEN RISK HER LIFE IN CARS SO DANGEROUS THAT NO ONE ELSE WANTS TO DRIVE THEM?
SHE NEEDS HER OWN RACING CAR. A BRAND-NEW ONE.
SHE TAKES ALL HER SAVINGS (AND ALL THE MONEY SHE CAN BORROW) AND BUYS A TOYOTA CELICA.
THANK YOU, MY FRIENDS, FOR ALL OF YOUR SUPPORT.
THIS IS THE FIRST NEW CAR I'VE EVER OWNED!
NOW...LET'S TAKE IT APART SO WE CAN ADD A ROLL CAGE AND MODIFY THE ENGINE! IT NEEDS TO BE FAST!
40

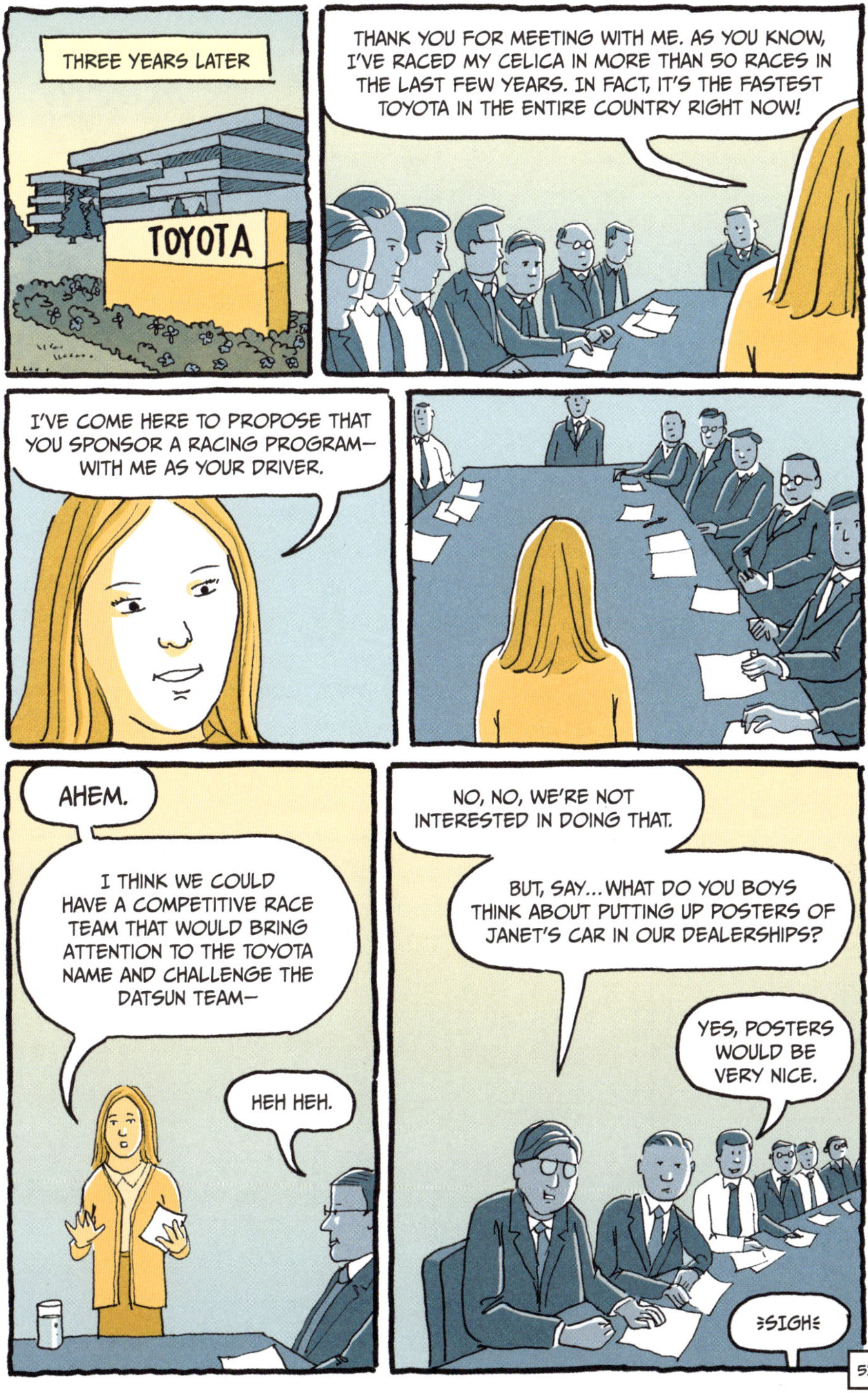
THREE YEARS LATER
TOYOTA
THANK YOU FOR MEETING WITH ME. AS YOU KNOW, I'VE RACED MY CELICA IN MORE THAN 50 RACES IN THE LAST FEW YEARS. IN FACT, IT'S THE FASTEST TOYOTA IN THE ENTIRE COUNTRY RIGHT NOW!
I'VE COME HERE TO PROPOSE THAT YOU SPONSOR A RACING PROGRAM—WITH ME AS YOUR DRIVER.
AHEM.
I THINK WE COULD HAVE A COMPETITIVE RACE TEAM THAT WOULD BRING ATTENTION TO THE TOYOTA NAME AND CHALLENGE THE DATSUN TEAM—
HEH HEH.
NO, NO, WE'RE NOT INTERESTED IN DOING THAT.
BUT, SAY... WHAT DO YOU BOYS THINK ABOUT PUTTING UP POSTERS OF JANET'S CAR IN OUR DEALERSHIPS?
YES, POSTERS WOULD BE VERY NICE.
SIGH

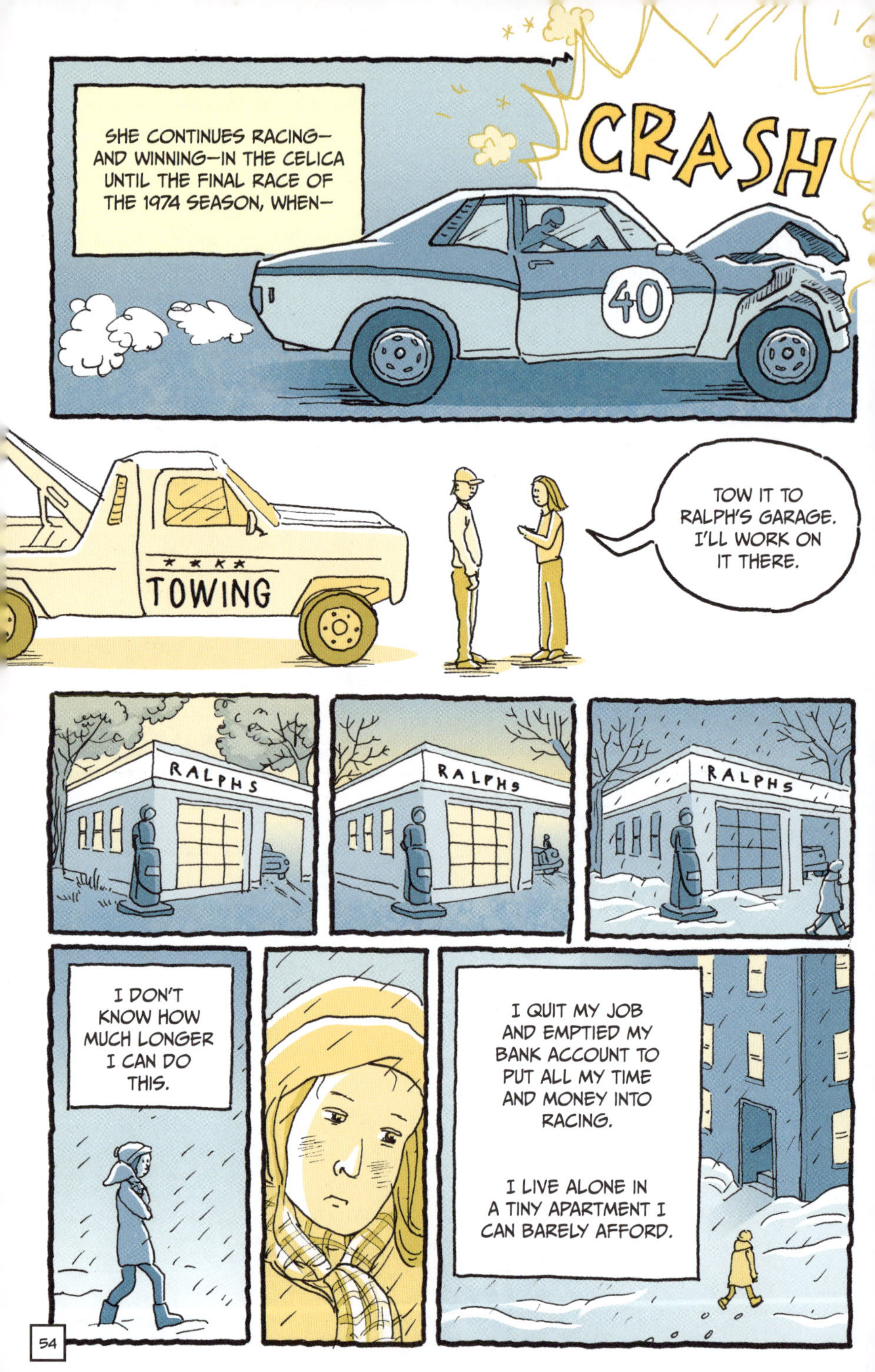
SHE CONTINUES RACING—AND WINNING—IN THE CELICA UNTIL THE FINAL RACE OF THE 1974 SEASON, WHEN—
CRASH
40
TOWING
TOW IT TO RALPH'S GARAGE. I'LL WORK ON IT THERE.
RALPHS
RALPHS
RALPHS
I DON'T KNOW HOW MUCH LONGER I CAN DO THIS.
I QUIT MY JOB AND EMPTIED MY BANK ACCOUNT TO PUT ALL MY TIME AND MONEY INTO RACING.
I LIVE ALONE IN A TINY APARTMENT I CAN BARELY AFFORD.

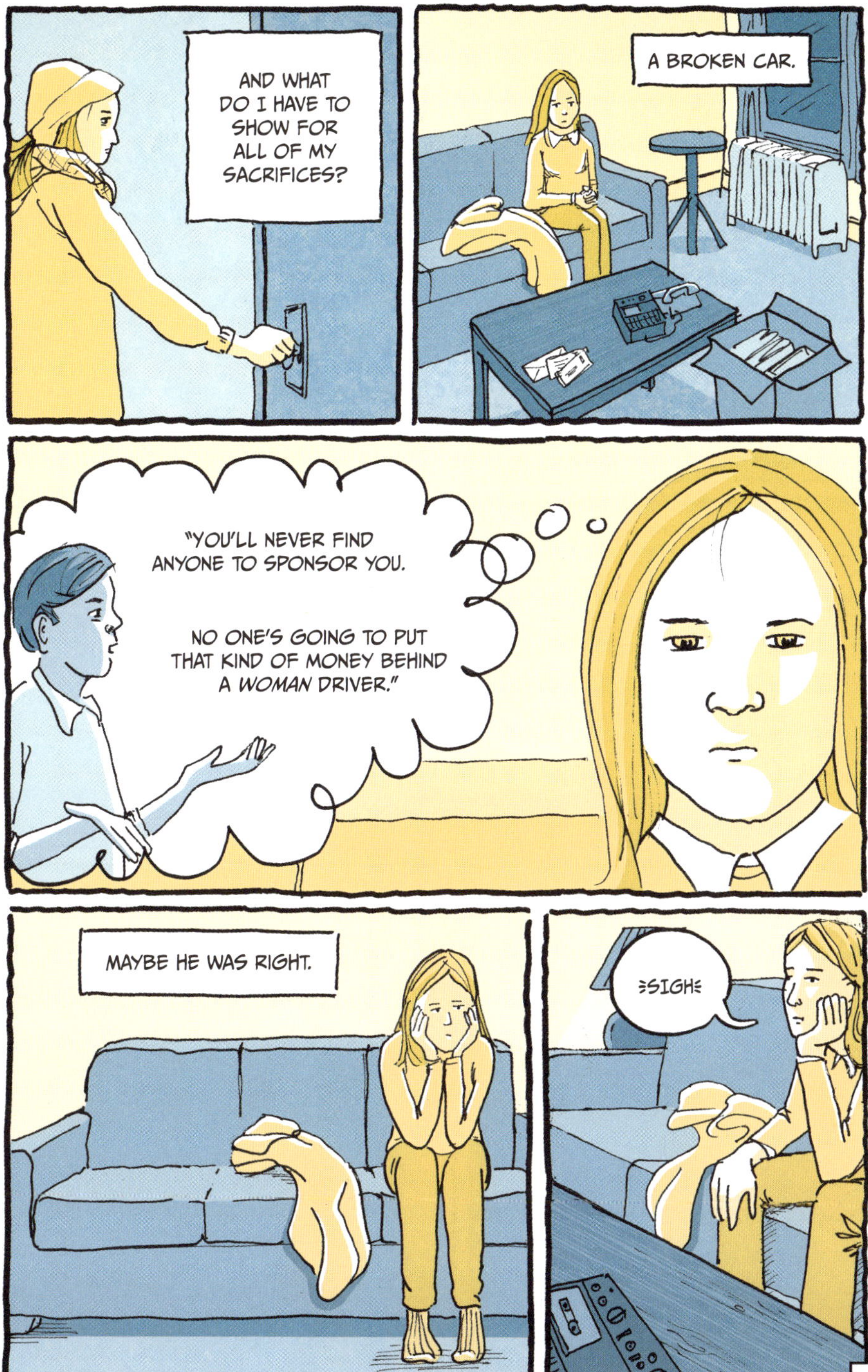
AND WHAT DO I HAVE TO SHOW FOR ALL OF MY SACRIFICES?
A BROKEN CAR.
"YOU'LL NEVER FIND ANYONE TO SPONSOR YOU.
NO ONE'S GOING TO PUT THAT KIND OF MONEY BEHIND A *WOMAN* DRIVER."
MAYBE HE WAS RIGHT.
SIGH

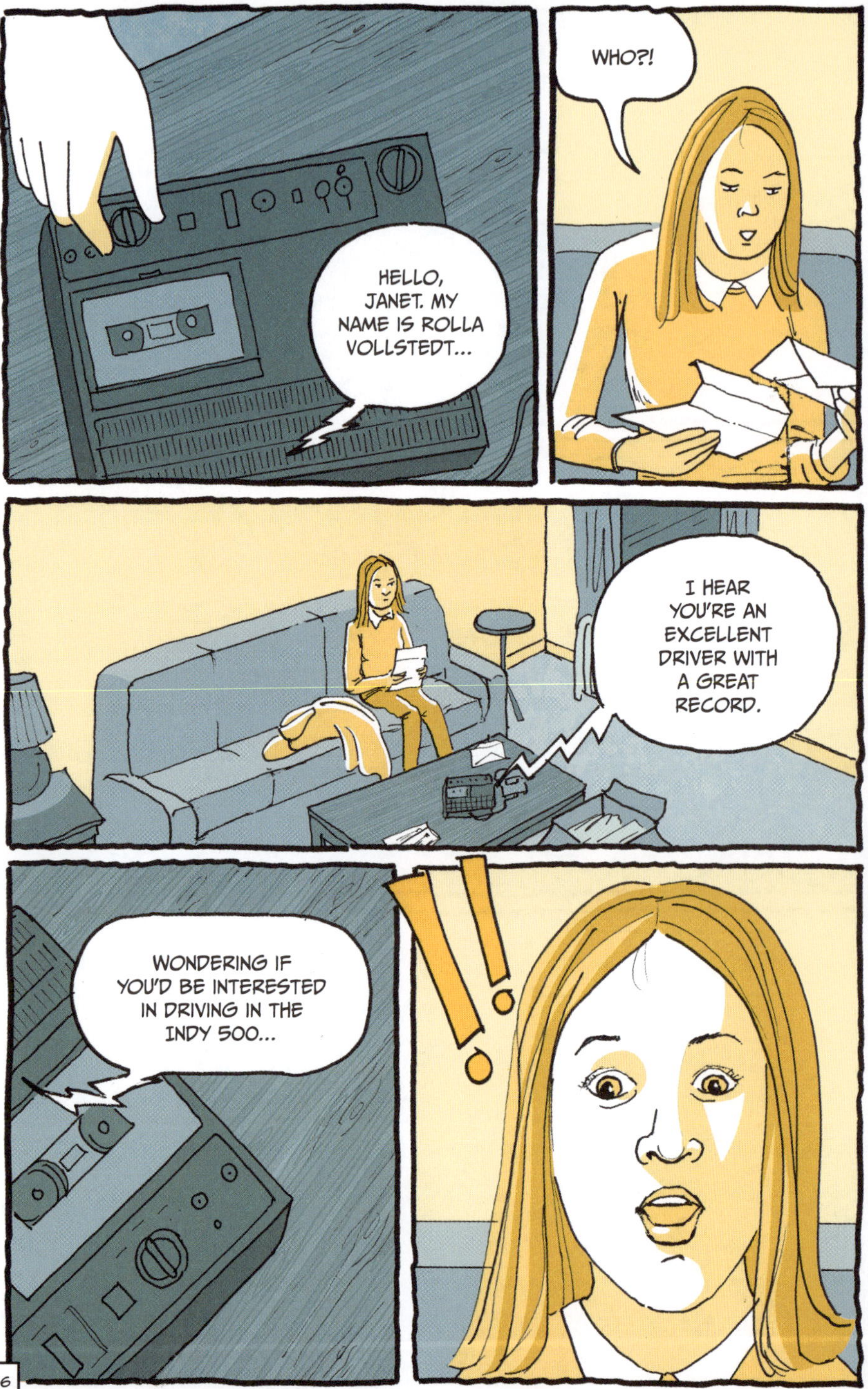
HELLO, JANET. MY NAME IS ROLLA VOLLSTEDT...
WHO?!
I HEAR YOU'RE AN EXCELLENT DRIVER WITH A GREAT RECORD.
WONDERING IF YOU'D BE INTERESTED IN DRIVING IN THE INDY 500...
!!

CHAPTER 3
2019

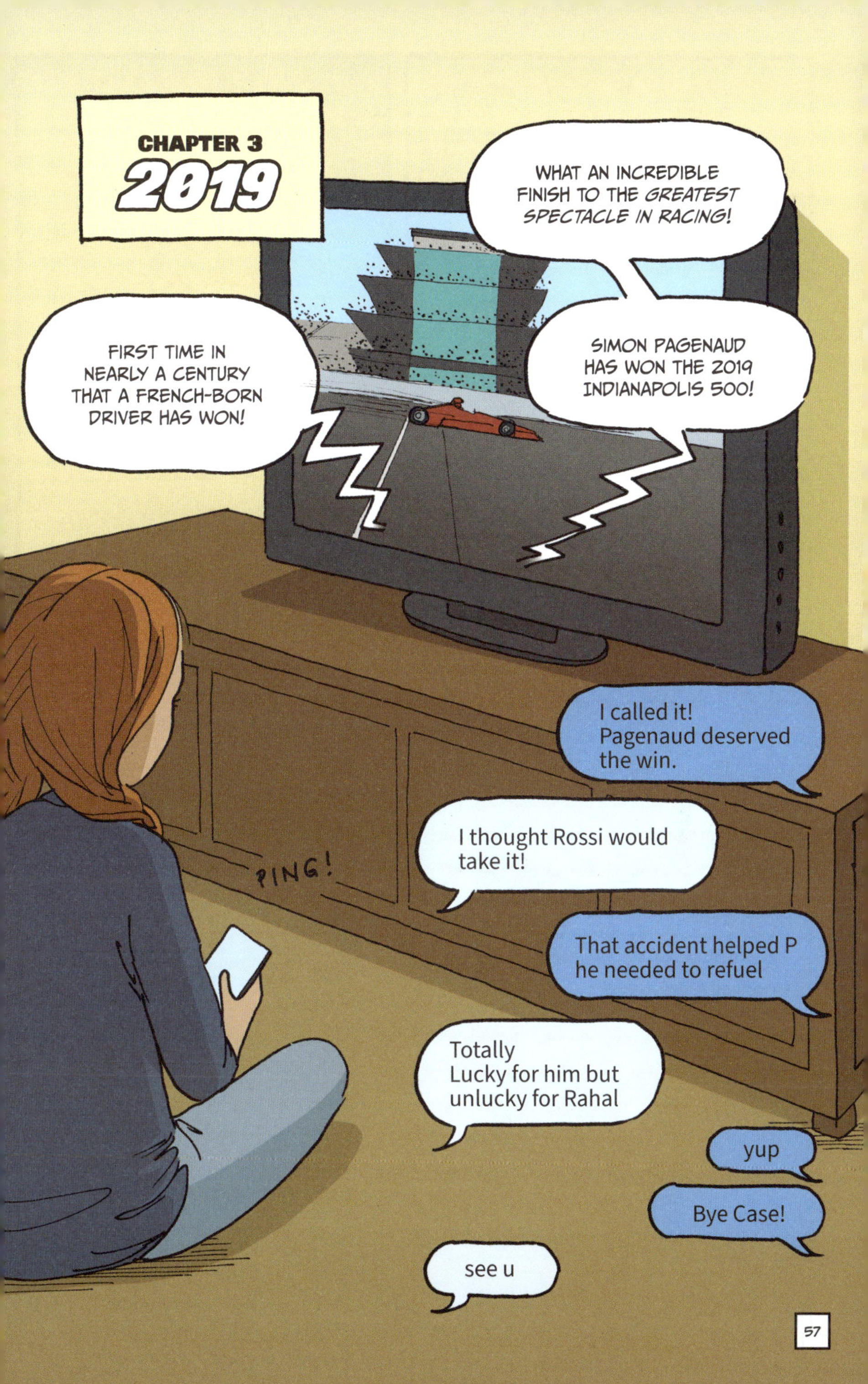

WHAT AN INCREDIBLE FINISH TO THE *GREATEST SPECTACLE IN RACING!*
SIMON PAGENAUD HAS WON THE 2019 INDIANAPOLIS 500!
FIRST TIME IN NEARLY A CENTURY THAT A FRENCH-BORN DRIVER HAS WON!
I called it! Pagenaud deserved the win.
PING!
I thought Rossi would take it!
That accident helped P he needed to refuel
Totally Lucky for him but unlucky for Rahal
yup
Bye Case!
see u

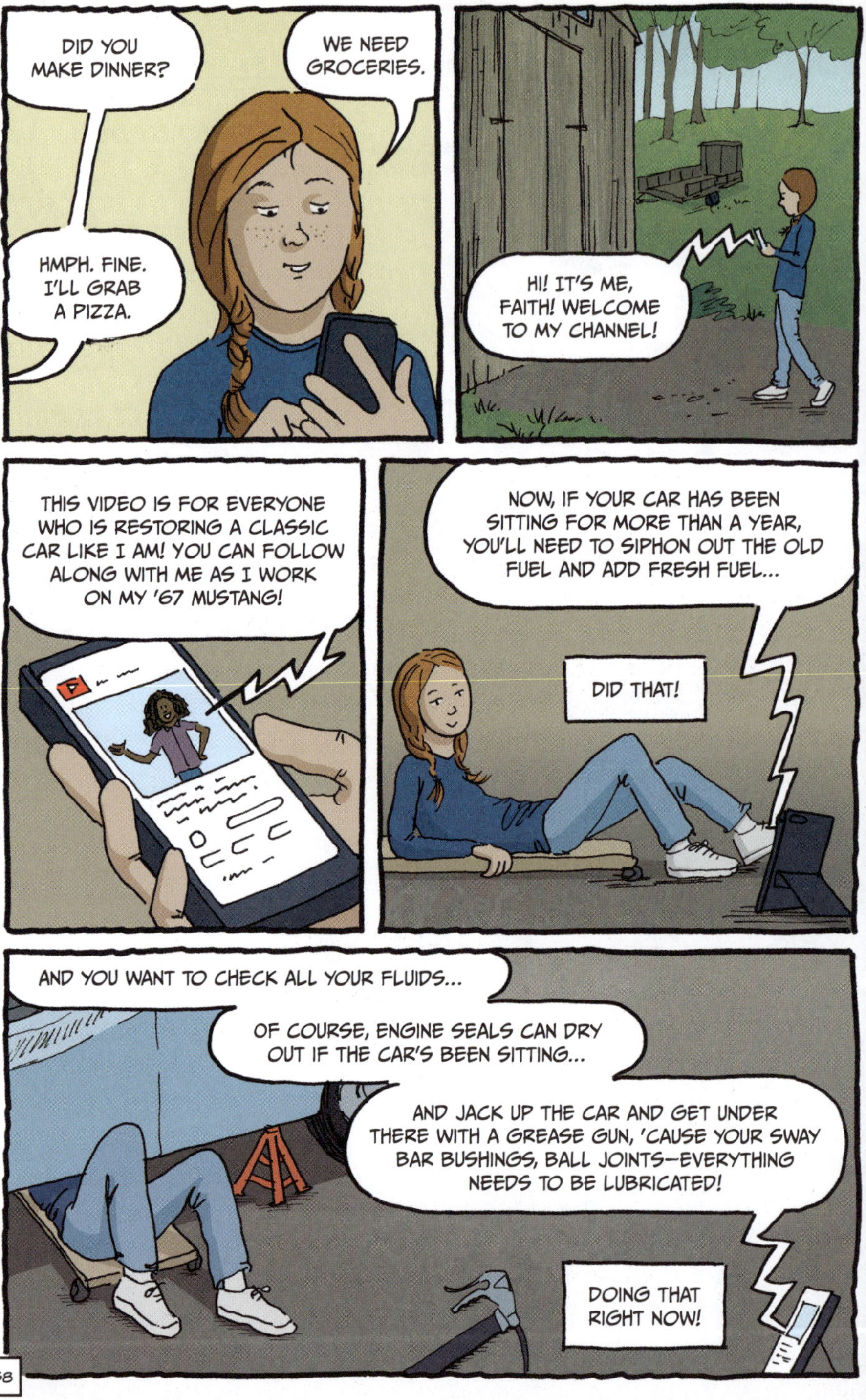
DID YOU MAKE DINNER?
WE NEED GROCERIES.
HMPH. FINE. I'LL GRAB A PIZZA.
HI! IT'S ME, FAITH! WELCOME TO MY CHANNEL!
THIS VIDEO IS FOR EVERYONE WHO IS RESTORING A CLASSIC CAR LIKE I AM! YOU CAN FOLLOW ALONG WITH ME AS I WORK ON MY '67 MUSTANG!
NOW, IF YOUR CAR HAS BEEN SITTING FOR MORE THAN A YEAR, YOU'LL NEED TO SIPHON OUT THE OLD FUEL AND ADD FRESH FUEL...
DID THAT!
AND YOU WANT TO CHECK ALL YOUR FLUIDS...
OF COURSE, ENGINE SEALS CAN DRY OUT IF THE CAR'S BEEN SITTING...
AND JACK UP THE CAR AND GET UNDER THERE WITH A GREASE GUN, 'CAUSE YOUR SWAY BAR BUSHINGS, BALL JOINTS—EVERYTHING NEEDS TO BE LUBRICATED!
DOING THAT RIGHT NOW!

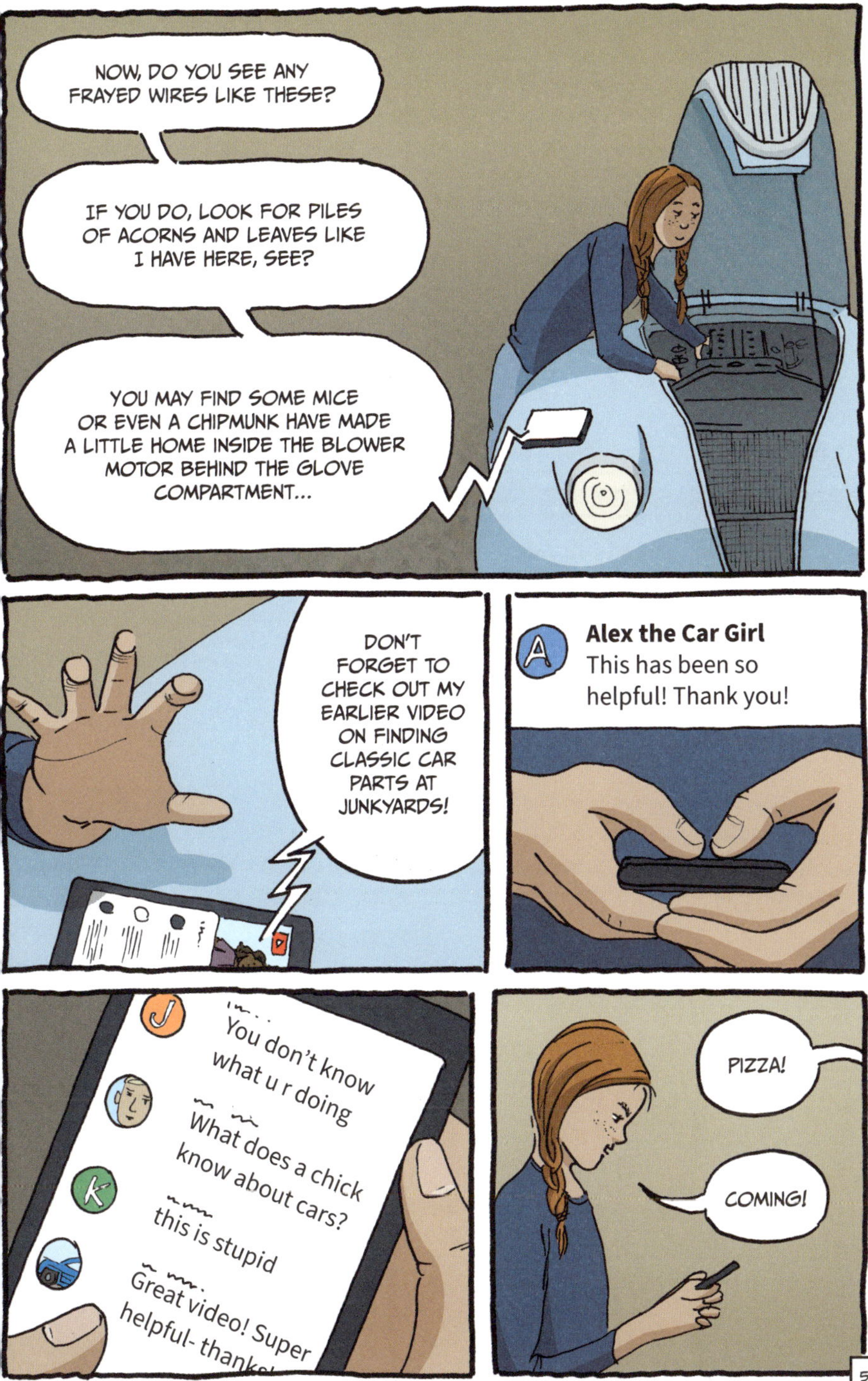
NOW, DO YOU SEE ANY FRAYED WIRES LIKE THESE?
IF YOU DO, LOOK FOR PILES OF ACORNS AND LEAVES LIKE I HAVE HERE, SEE?
YOU MAY FIND SOME MICE OR EVEN A CHIPMUNK HAVE MADE A LITTLE HOME INSIDE THE BLOWER MOTOR BEHIND THE GLOVE COMPARTMENT...
DON'T FORGET TO CHECK OUT MY EARLIER VIDEO ON FINDING CLASSIC CAR PARTS AT JUNKYARDS!
Alex the Car Girl
This has been so helpful! Thank you!
You don't know what u r doing
What does a chick know about cars?
this is stupid
Great video! Super helpful- thanks!
PIZZA!
COMING!

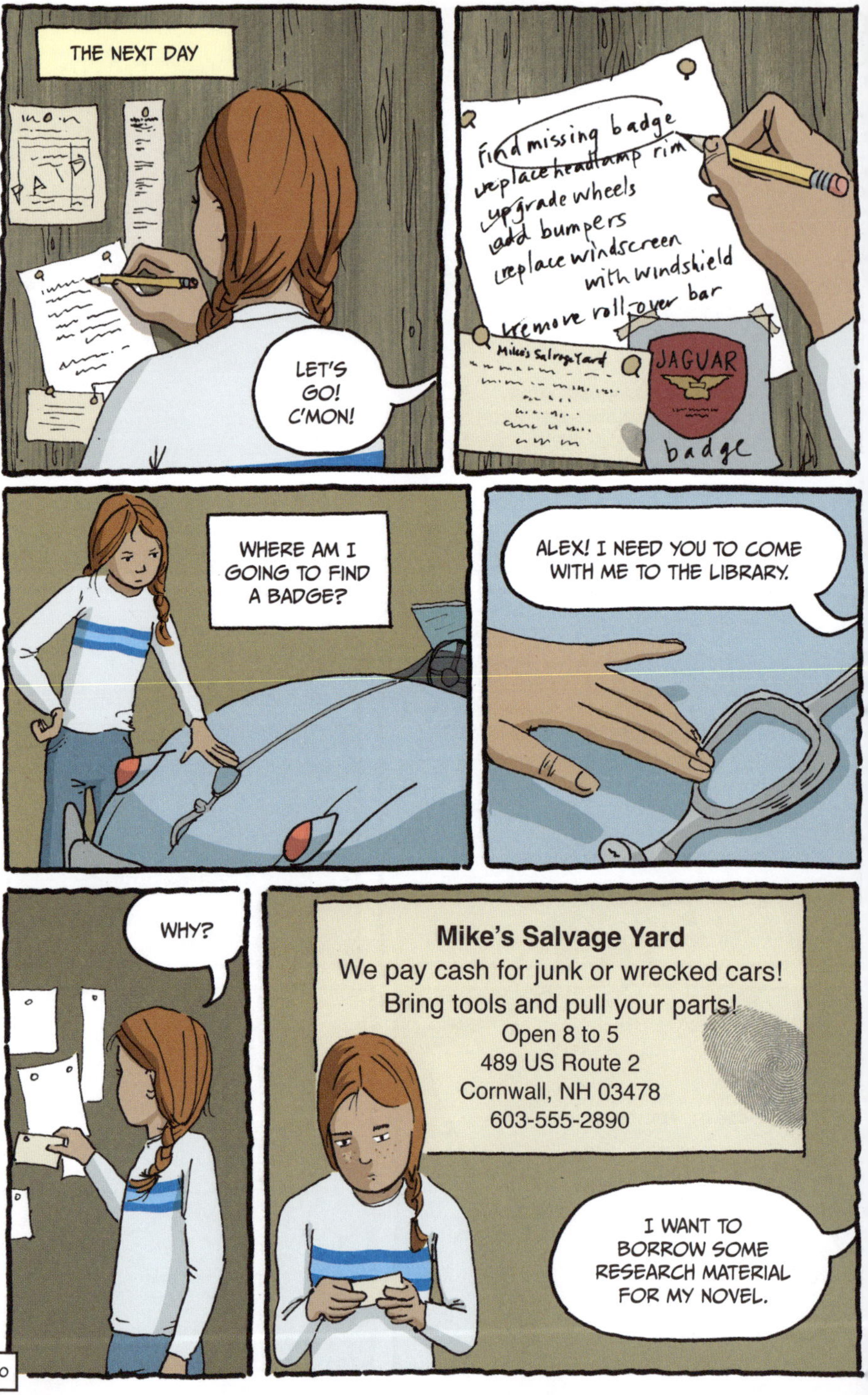
THE NEXT DAY
LET'S GO! C'MON!
find missing badge
replace headlamp rim
upgrade wheels
add bumpers
replace windscreen with windshield
remove roll-over bar
Mike's Salvage Yard
JAGUAR
badge
WHERE AM I GOING TO FIND A BADGE?
ALEX! I NEED YOU TO COME WITH ME TO THE LIBRARY.
WHY?
Mike's Salvage Yard
We pay cash for junk or wrecked cars!
Bring tools and pull your parts!
Open 8 to 5
489 US Route 2
Cornwall, NH 03478
603-555-2890
I WANT TO BORROW SOME RESEARCH MATERIAL FOR MY NOVEL.

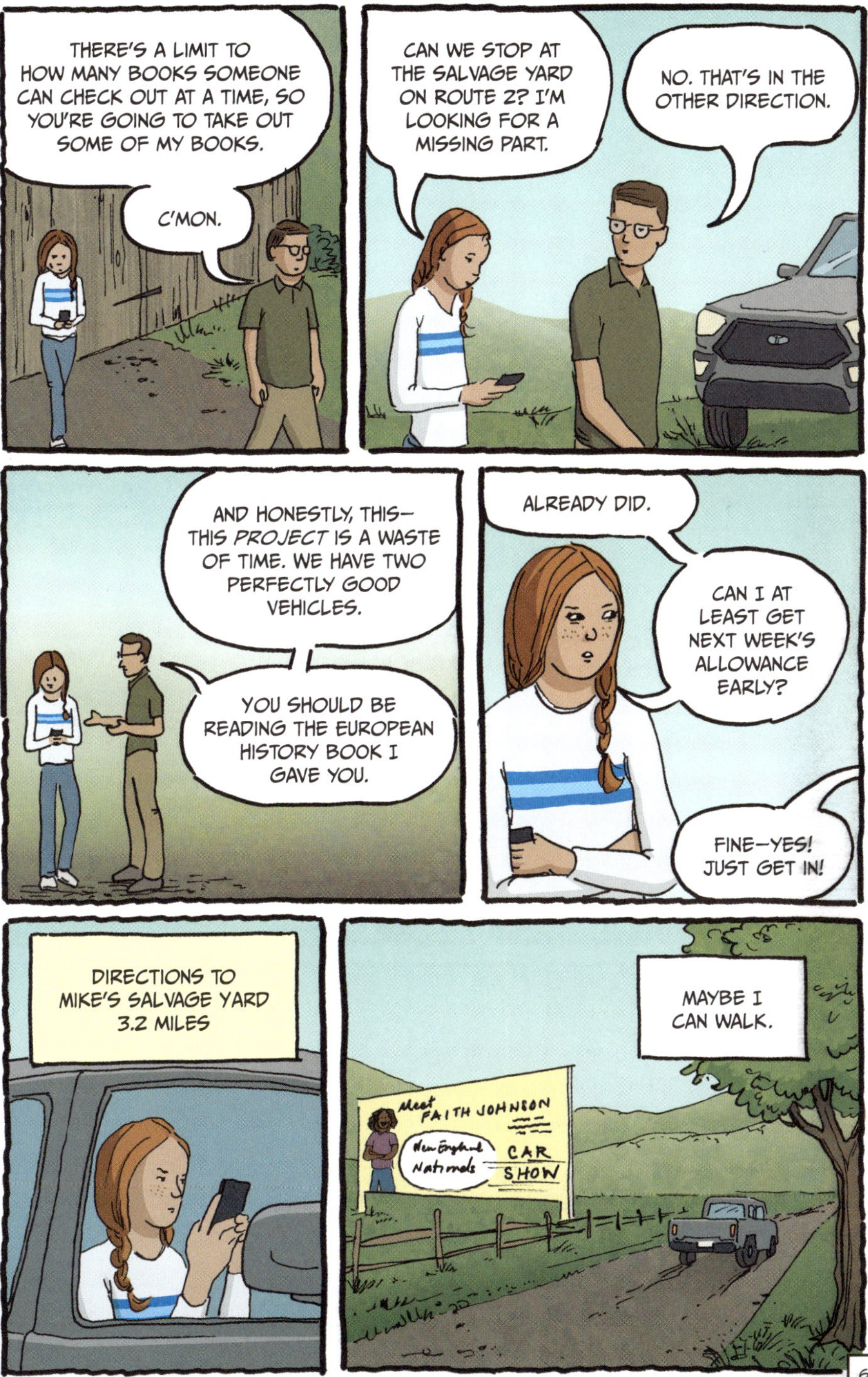
THERE'S A LIMIT TO HOW MANY BOOKS SOMEONE CAN CHECK OUT AT A TIME, SO YOU'RE GOING TO TAKE OUT SOME OF MY BOOKS.
C'MON.
CAN WE STOP AT THE SALVAGE YARD ON ROUTE 2? I'M LOOKING FOR A MISSING PART.
NO. THAT'S IN THE OTHER DIRECTION.
AND HONESTLY, THIS— THIS *PROJECT* IS A WASTE OF TIME. WE HAVE TWO PERFECTLY GOOD VEHICLES.
YOU SHOULD BE READING THE EUROPEAN HISTORY BOOK I GAVE YOU.
ALREADY DID.
CAN I AT LEAST GET NEXT WEEK'S ALLOWANCE EARLY?
FINE—YES! JUST GET IN!
DIRECTIONS TO MIKE'S SALVAGE YARD 3.2 MILES
Meet FAITH JOHNSON
New England Nationals
CAR SHOW
MAYBE I CAN WALK.

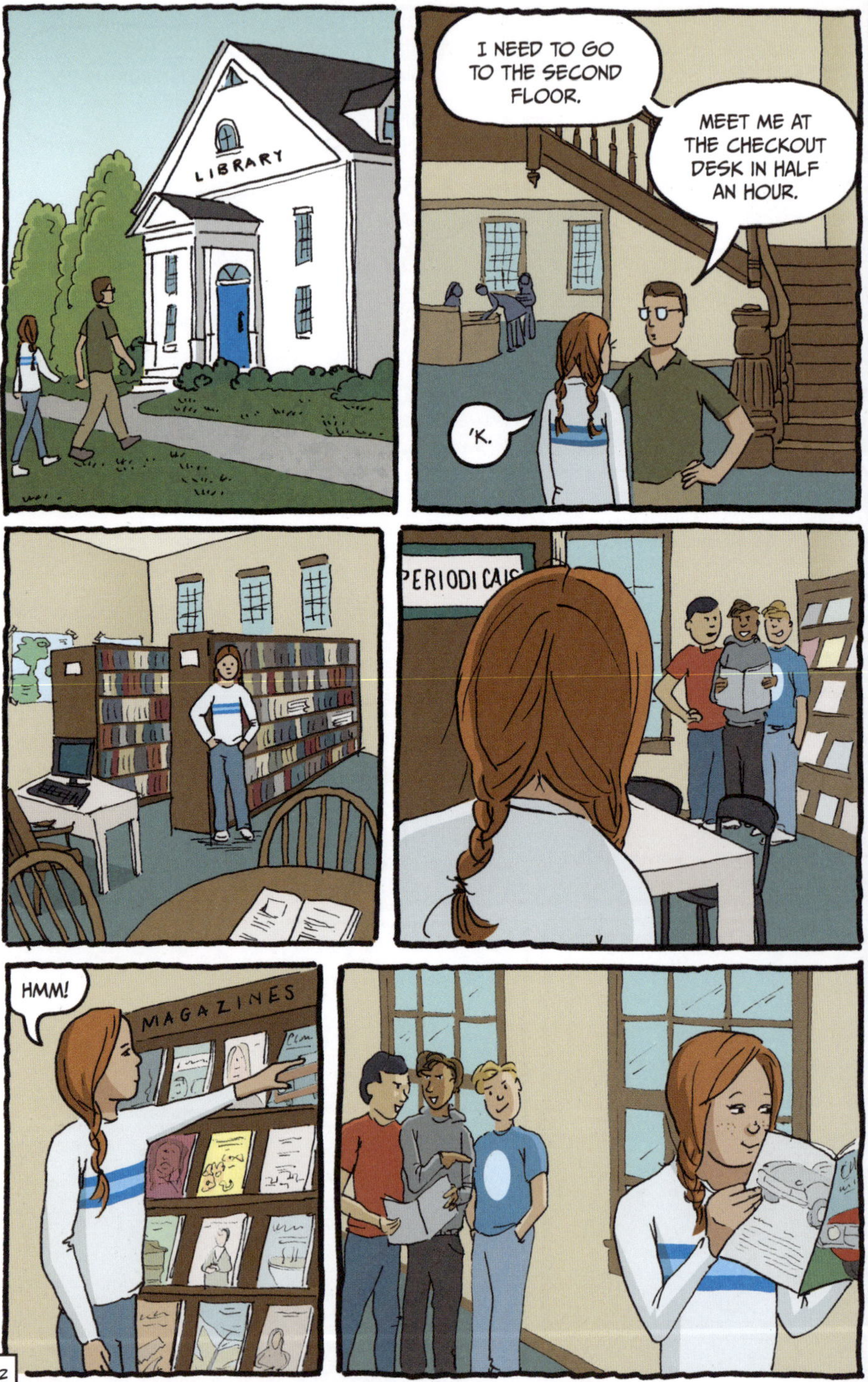
LIBRARY
I NEED TO GO TO THE SECOND FLOOR.
MEET ME AT THE CHECKOUT DESK IN HALF AN HOUR.
'K.
PERIODICALS
HMM!
MAGAZINES

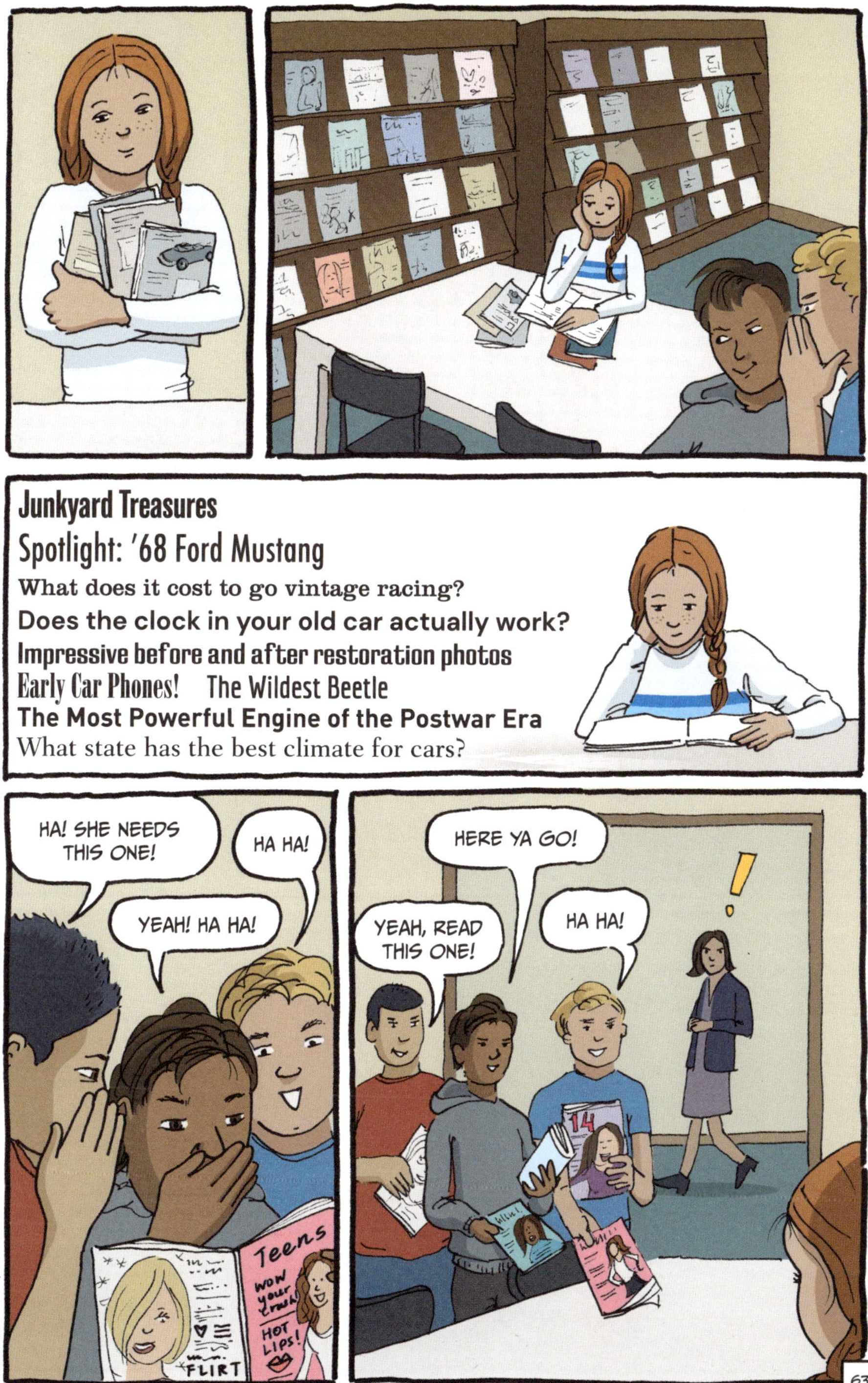
Junkyard Treasures
Spotlight: '68 Ford Mustang
What does it cost to go vintage racing?
Does the clock in your old car actually work?
Impressive before and after restoration photos
Early Car Phones!
The Wildest Beetle
The Most Powerful Engine of the Postwar Era
What state has the best climate for cars?
HA! SHE NEEDS THIS ONE!
HA HA!
YEAH! HA HA!
Teens
WOW your crush!
HOT LIPS!
FLIRT
HERE YA GO!
YEAH, READ THIS ONE!
HA HA!
!
14

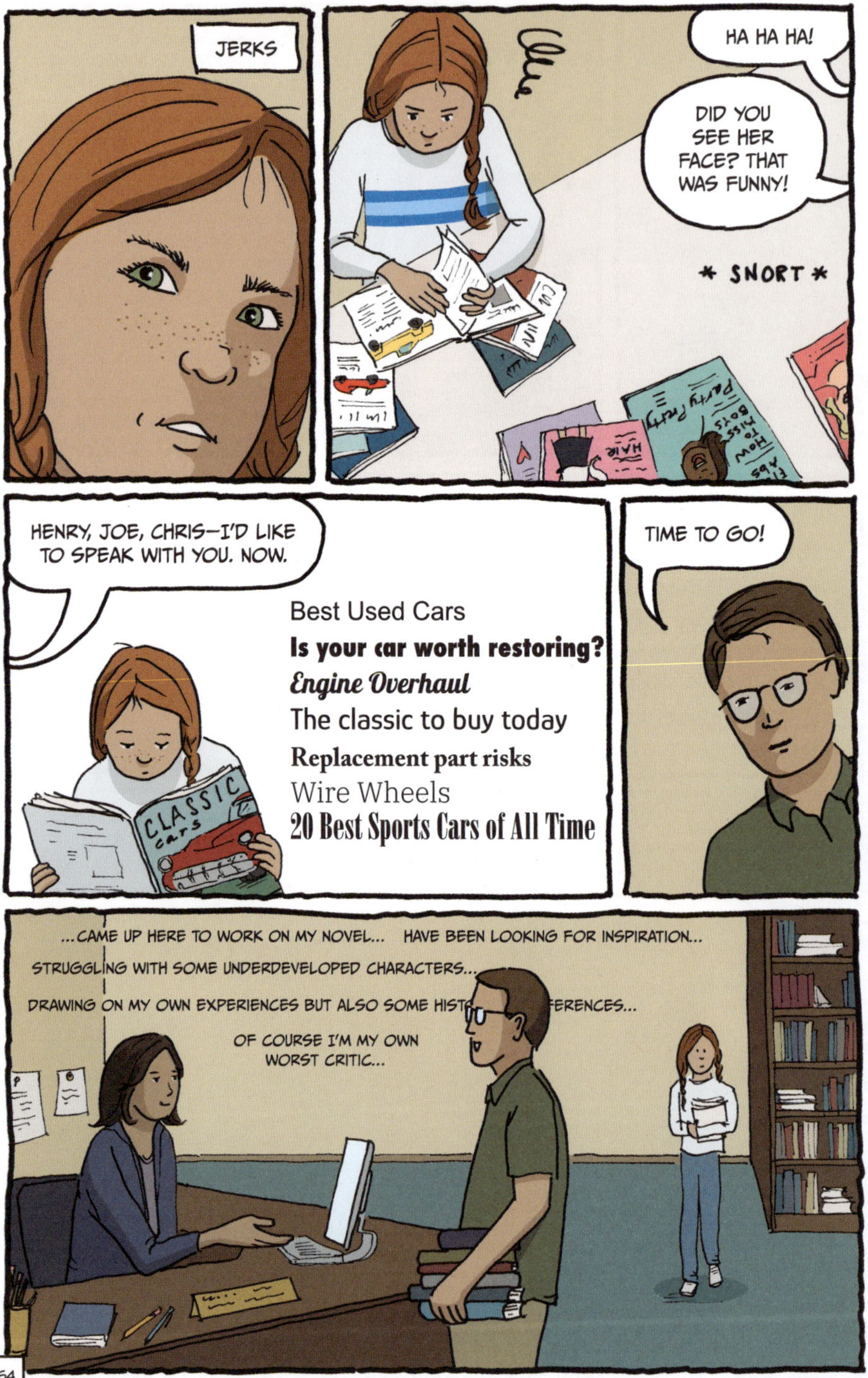
JERKS
HA HA HA!
DID YOU SEE HER FACE? THAT WAS FUNNY!
* SNORT *
HENRY, JOE, CHRIS—I'D LIKE TO SPEAK WITH YOU. NOW.
Best Used Cars
Is your car worth restoring?
Engine Overhaul
The classic to buy today
Replacement part risks
Wire Wheels
20 Best Sports Cars of All Time
CLASSIC CARS
TIME TO GO!
...CAME UP HERE TO WORK ON MY NOVEL... HAVE BEEN LOOKING FOR INSPIRATION...
STRUGGLING WITH SOME UNDERDEVELOPED CHARACTERS...
DRAWING ON MY OWN EXPERIENCES BUT ALSO SOME HIST... ...FERENCES...
OF COURSE I'M MY OWN WORST CRITIC...

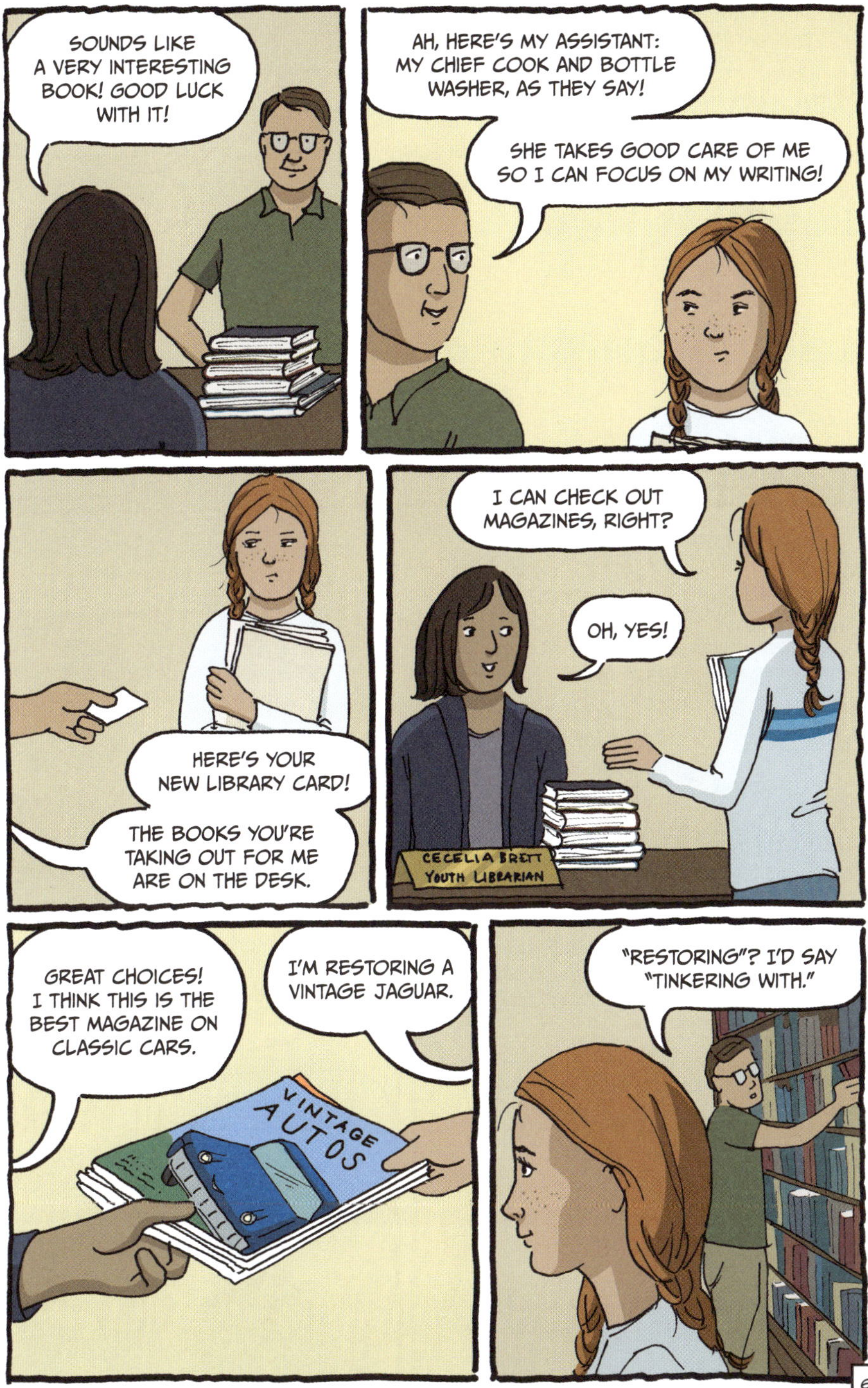
SOUNDS LIKE A VERY INTERESTING BOOK! GOOD LUCK WITH IT!
AH, HERE'S MY ASSISTANT: MY CHIEF COOK AND BOTTLE WASHER, AS THEY SAY!
SHE TAKES GOOD CARE OF ME SO I CAN FOCUS ON MY WRITING!
HERE'S YOUR NEW LIBRARY CARD!
THE BOOKS YOU'RE TAKING OUT FOR ME ARE ON THE DESK.
I CAN CHECK OUT MAGAZINES, RIGHT?
OH, YES!
CECELIA BRETT
YOUTH LIBRARIAN
GREAT CHOICES! I THINK THIS IS THE BEST MAGAZINE ON CLASSIC CARS.
I'M RESTORING A VINTAGE JAGUAR.
VINTAGE AUTOS
"RESTORING"? I'D SAY "TINKERING WITH."

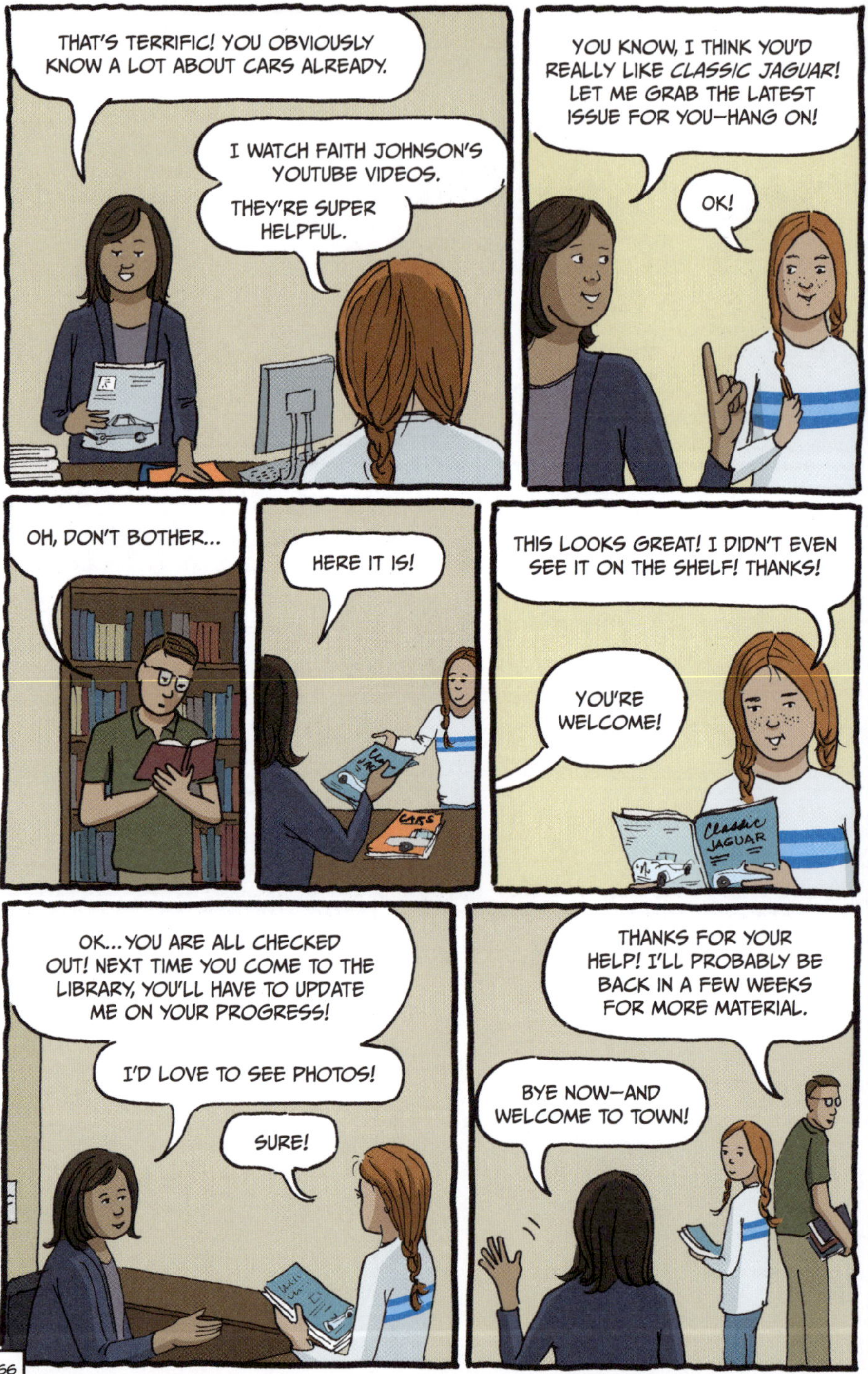
THAT'S TERRIFIC! YOU OBVIOUSLY KNOW A LOT ABOUT CARS ALREADY.
I WATCH FAITH JOHNSON'S YOUTUBE VIDEOS.
THEY'RE SUPER HELPFUL.
YOU KNOW, I THINK YOU'D REALLY LIKE *CLASSIC JAGUAR*! LET ME GRAB THE LATEST ISSUE FOR YOU—HANG ON!
OK!
OH, DON'T BOTHER...
HERE IT IS!
THIS LOOKS GREAT! I DIDN'T EVEN SEE IT ON THE SHELF! THANKS!
YOU'RE WELCOME!
Classic JAGUAR
OK...YOU ARE ALL CHECKED OUT! NEXT TIME YOU COME TO THE LIBRARY, YOU'LL HAVE TO UPDATE ME ON YOUR PROGRESS!
I'D LOVE TO SEE PHOTOS!
SURE!
THANKS FOR YOUR HELP! I'LL PROBABLY BE BACK IN A FEW WEEKS FOR MORE MATERIAL.
BYE NOW—AND WELCOME TO TOWN!

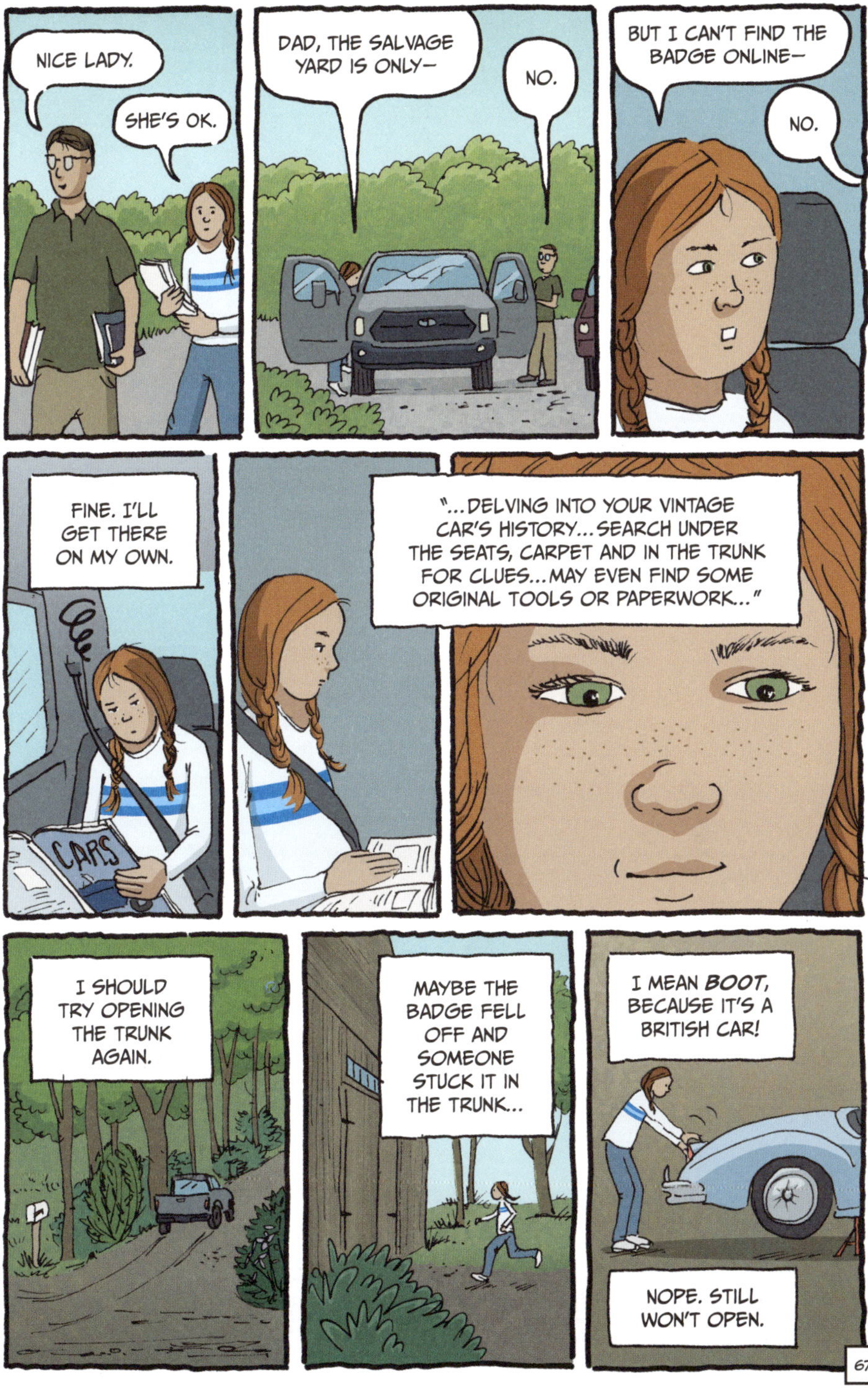
NICE LADY.
SHE'S OK.
DAD, THE SALVAGE YARD IS ONLY–
NO.
BUT I CAN'T FIND THE BADGE ONLINE–
NO.
FINE. I'LL GET THERE ON MY OWN.
CARS
"...DELVING INTO YOUR VINTAGE CAR'S HISTORY...SEARCH UNDER THE SEATS, CARPET AND IN THE TRUNK FOR CLUES...MAY EVEN FIND SOME ORIGINAL TOOLS OR PAPERWORK..."
I SHOULD TRY OPENING THE TRUNK AGAIN.
MAYBE THE BADGE FELL OFF AND SOMEONE STUCK IT IN THE TRUNK...
I MEAN *BOOT*, BECAUSE IT'S A BRITISH CAR!
NOPE. STILL WON'T OPEN.

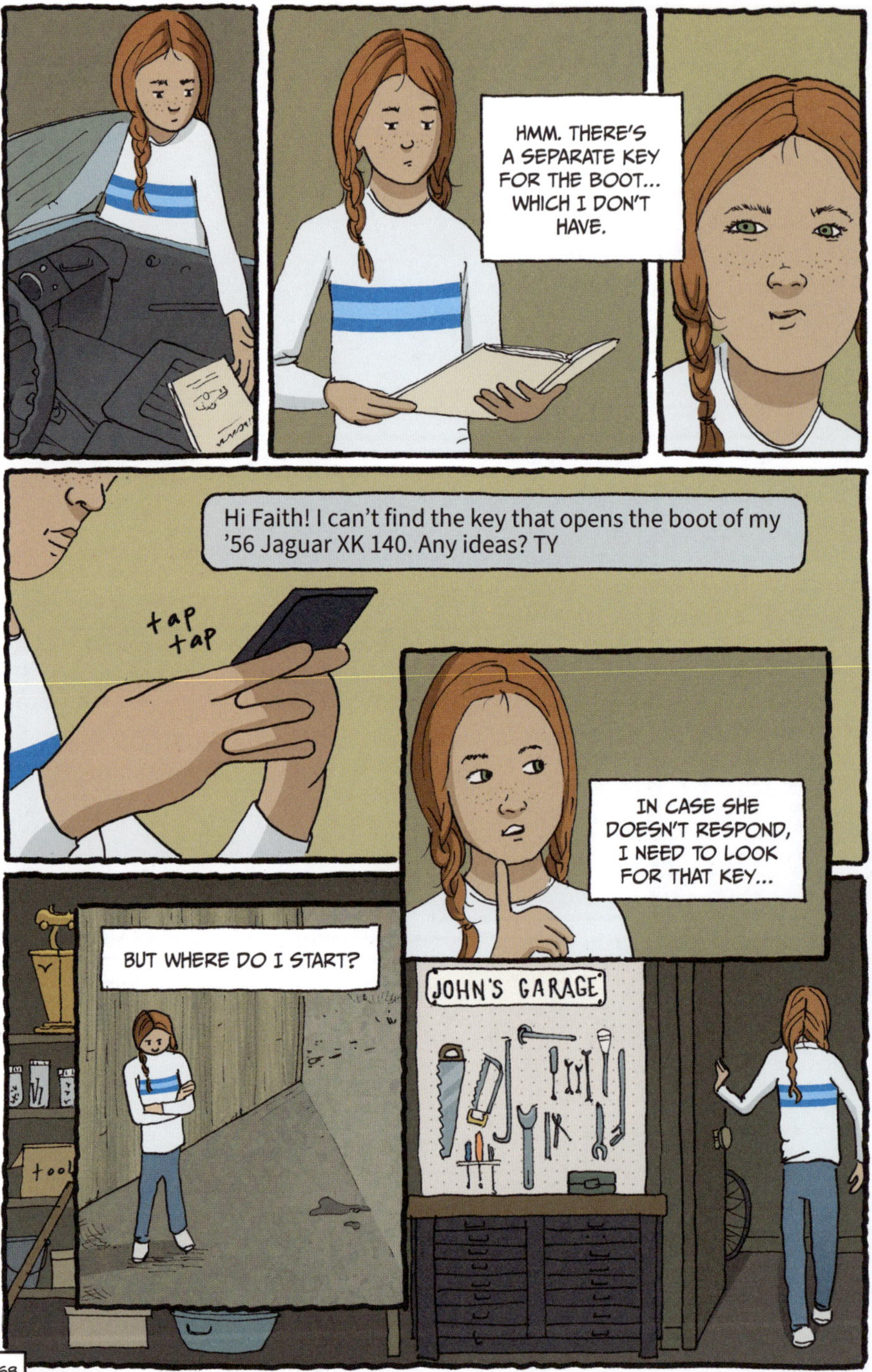

HMM. THERE'S A SEPARATE KEY FOR THE BOOT... WHICH I DON'T HAVE.
Hi Faith! I can't find the key that opens the boot of my '56 Jaguar XK 140. Any ideas? TY
tap tap
IN CASE SHE DOESN'T RESPOND, I NEED TO LOOK FOR THAT KEY...
BUT WHERE DO I START?
JOHN'S GARAGE
tool

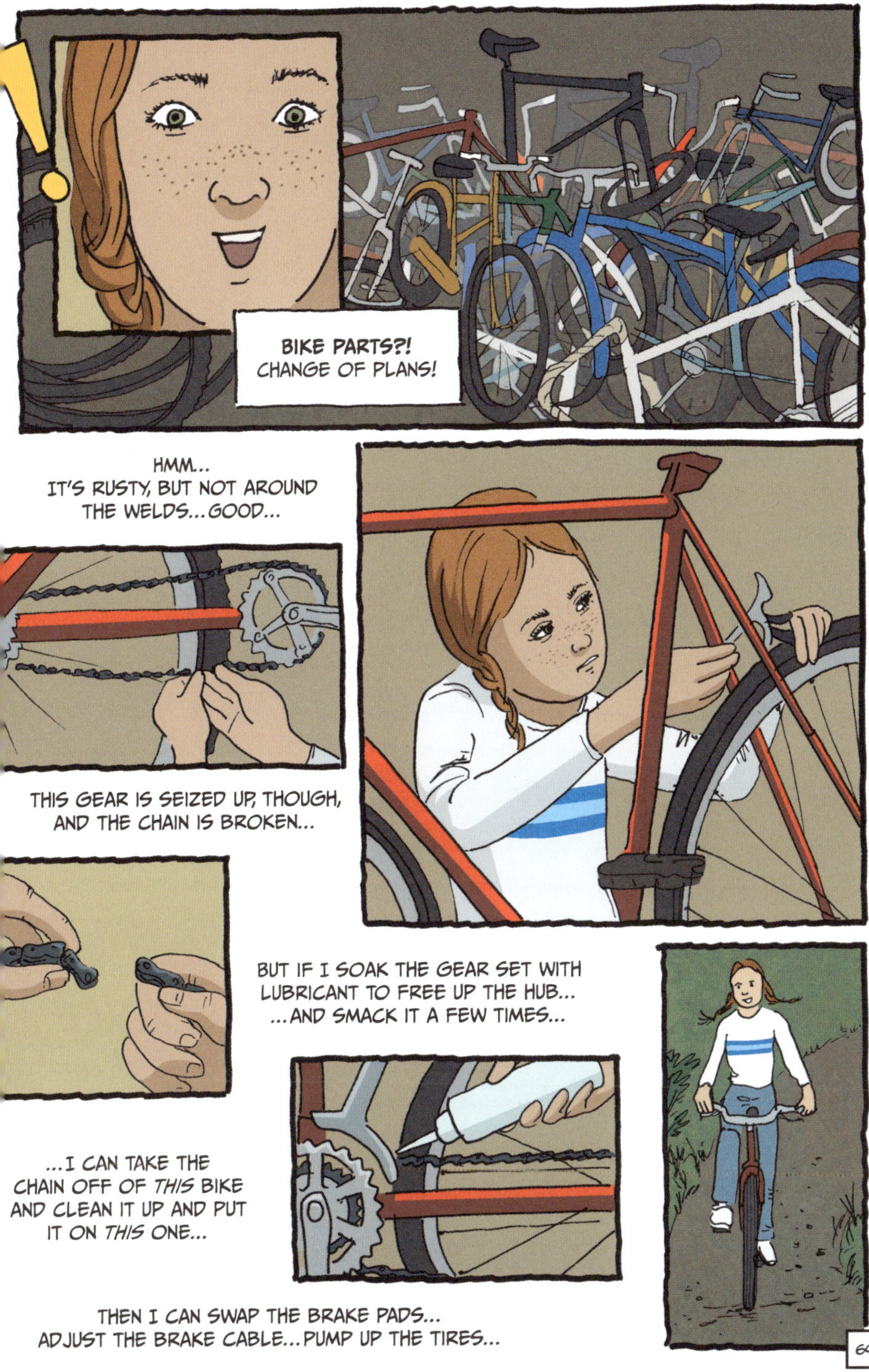
BIKE PARTS?! CHANGE OF PLANS!
HMM... IT'S RUSTY, BUT NOT AROUND THE WELDS... GOOD...
THIS GEAR IS SEIZED UP, THOUGH, AND THE CHAIN IS BROKEN...
BUT IF I SOAK THE GEAR SET WITH LUBRICANT TO FREE UP THE HUB... ...AND SMACK IT A FEW TIMES...
...I CAN TAKE THE CHAIN OFF OF *THIS* BIKE AND CLEAN IT UP AND PUT IT ON *THIS* ONE...
THEN I CAN SWAP THE BRAKE PADS... ADJUST THE BRAKE CABLE... PUMP UP THE TIRES...

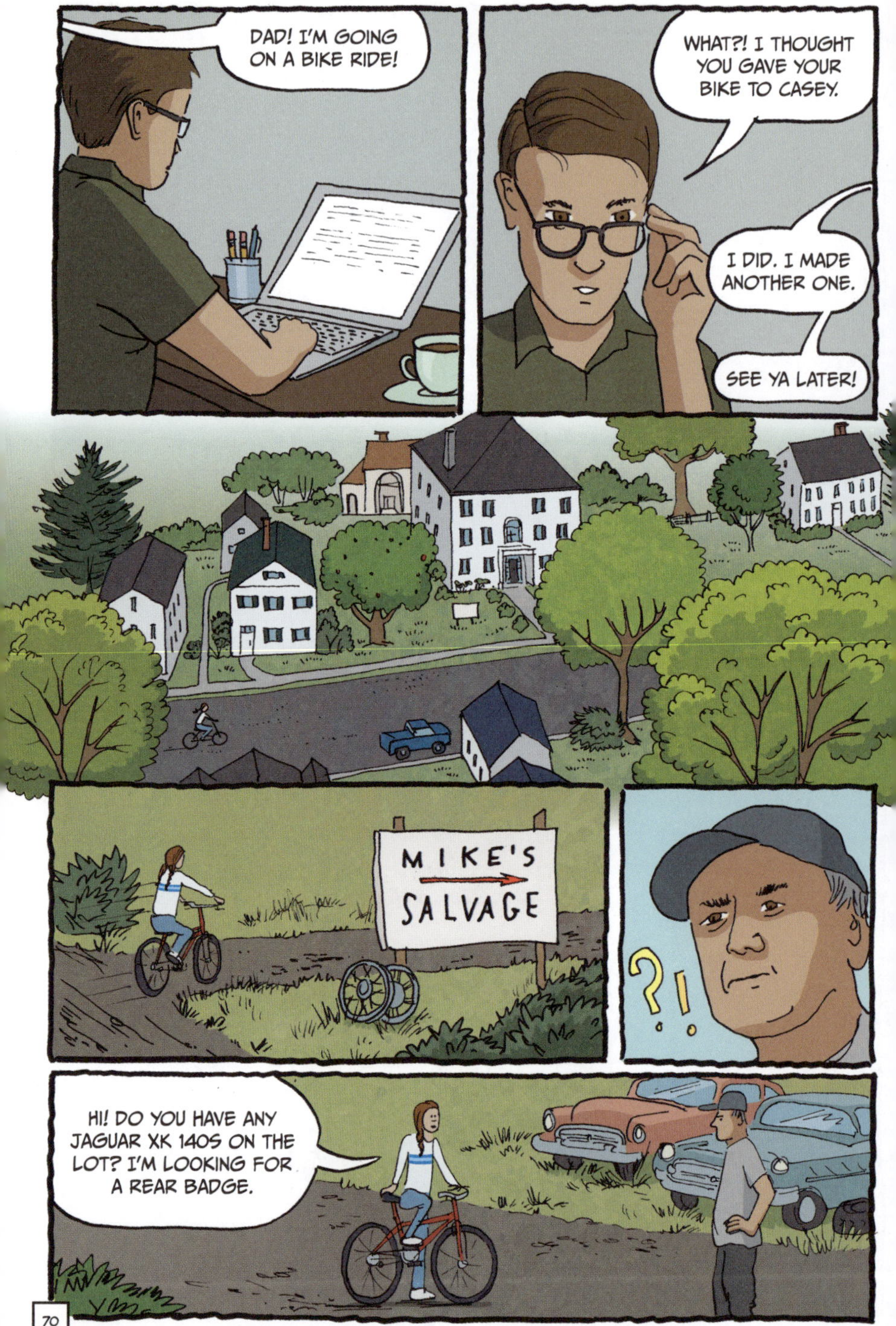
DAD! I'M GOING ON A BIKE RIDE!
WHAT?! I THOUGHT YOU GAVE YOUR BIKE TO CASEY.
I DID. I MADE ANOTHER ONE.
SEE YA LATER!
MIKE'S SALVAGE
?!
HI! DO YOU HAVE ANY JAGUAR XK 140S ON THE LOT? I'M LOOKING FOR A REAR BADGE.

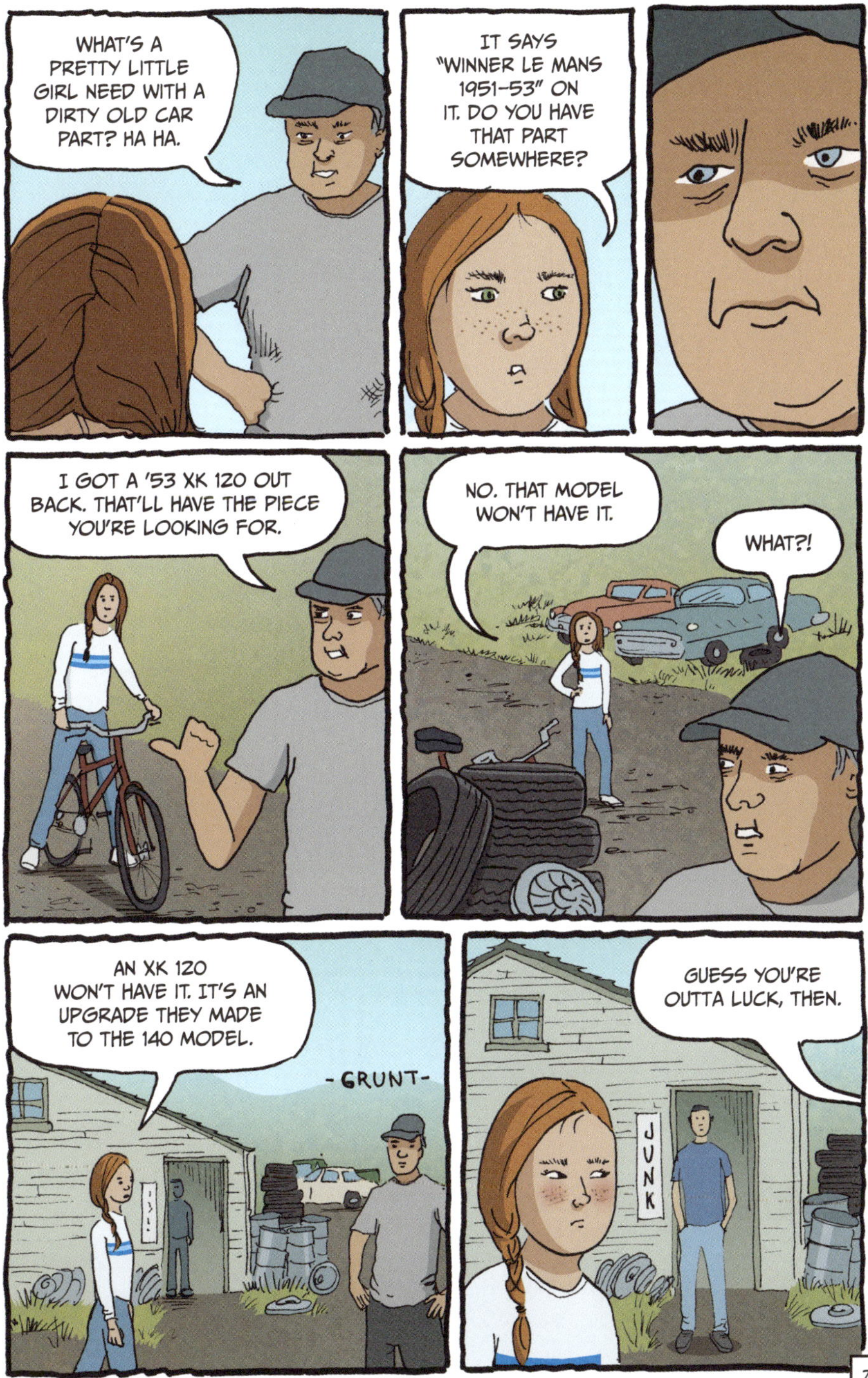
WHAT'S A PRETTY LITTLE GIRL NEED WITH A DIRTY OLD CAR PART? HA HA.
IT SAYS "WINNER LE MANS 1951–53" ON IT. DO YOU HAVE THAT PART SOMEWHERE?
I GOT A '53 XK 120 OUT BACK. THAT'LL HAVE THE PIECE YOU'RE LOOKING FOR.
NO. THAT MODEL WON'T HAVE IT.
WHAT?!
AN XK 120 WON'T HAVE IT. IT'S AN UPGRADE THEY MADE TO THE 140 MODEL.
-GRUNT-
GUESS YOU'RE OUTTA LUCK, THEN.
JUNK

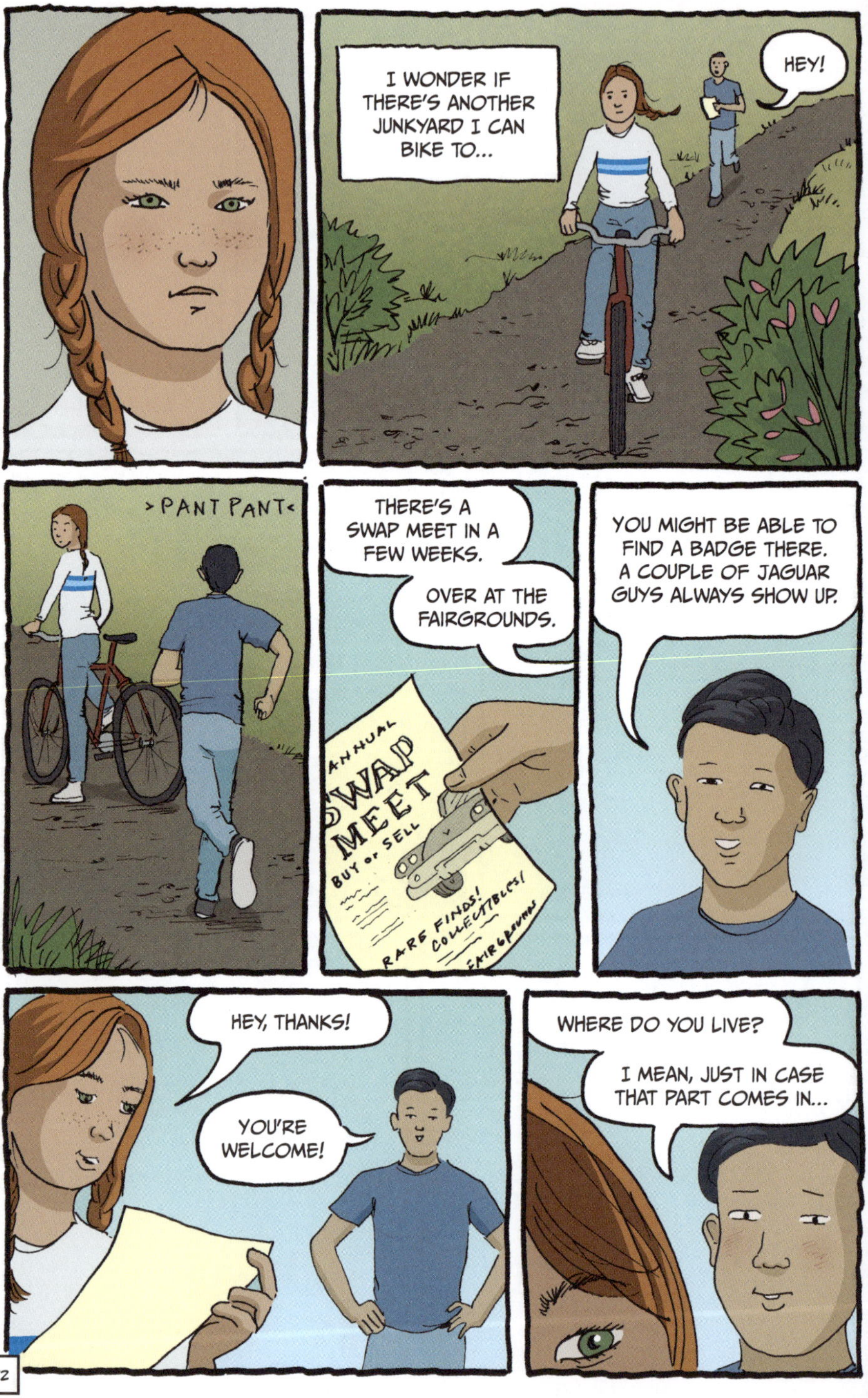
I WONDER IF THERE'S ANOTHER JUNKYARD I CAN BIKE TO...
HEY!
>PANT PANT<
THERE'S A SWAP MEET IN A FEW WEEKS.
OVER AT THE FAIRGROUNDS.
ANNUAL SWAP MEET
BUY or SELL
RARE FINDS!
COLLECTIBLES!
FAIRGROUNDS
YOU MIGHT BE ABLE TO FIND A BADGE THERE. A COUPLE OF JAGUAR GUYS ALWAYS SHOW UP.
HEY, THANKS!
YOU'RE WELCOME!
WHERE DO YOU LIVE?
I MEAN, JUST IN CASE THAT PART COMES IN...

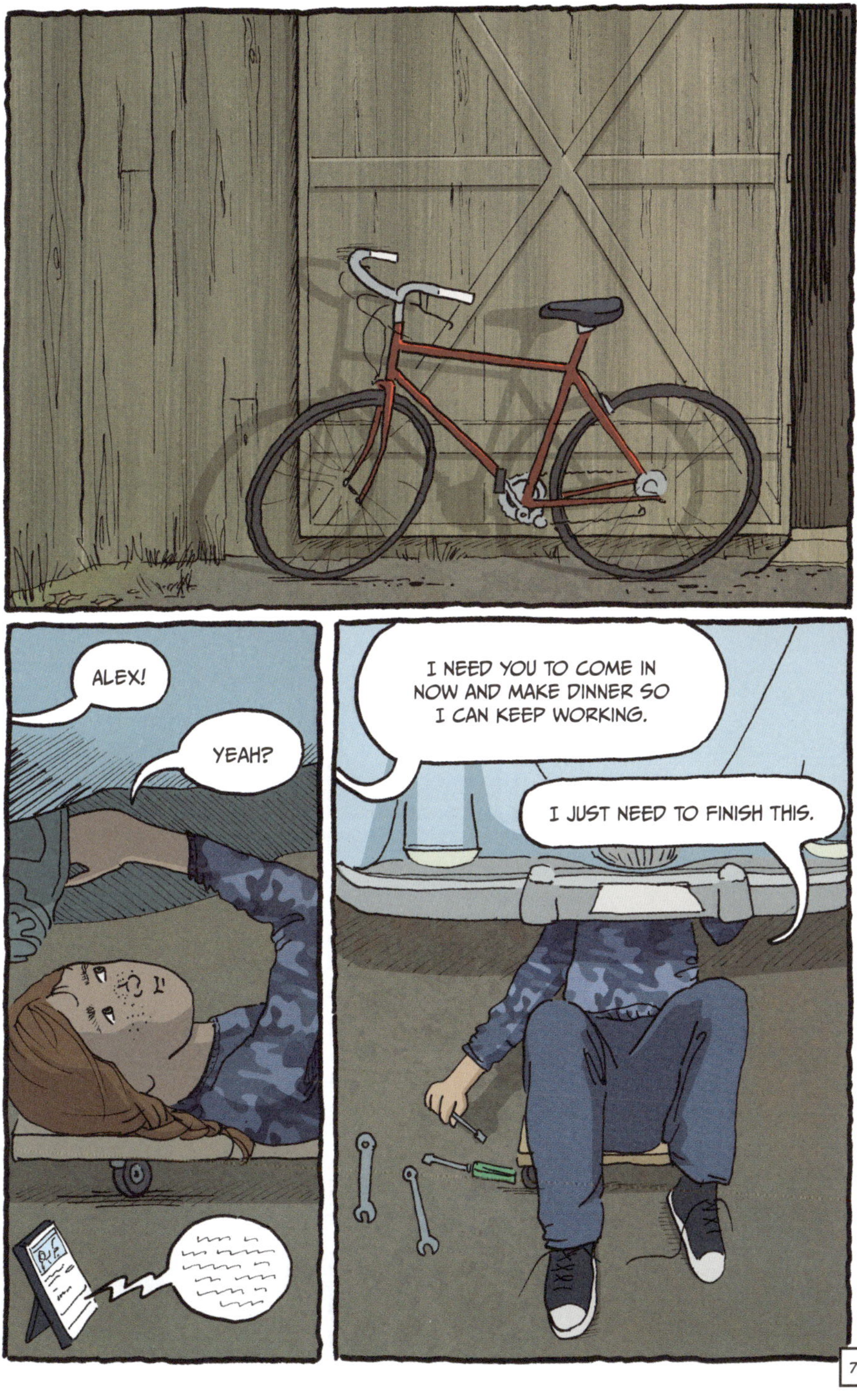
ALEX!
YEAH?
I NEED YOU TO COME IN NOW AND MAKE DINNER SO I CAN KEEP WORKING.
I JUST NEED TO FINISH THIS.

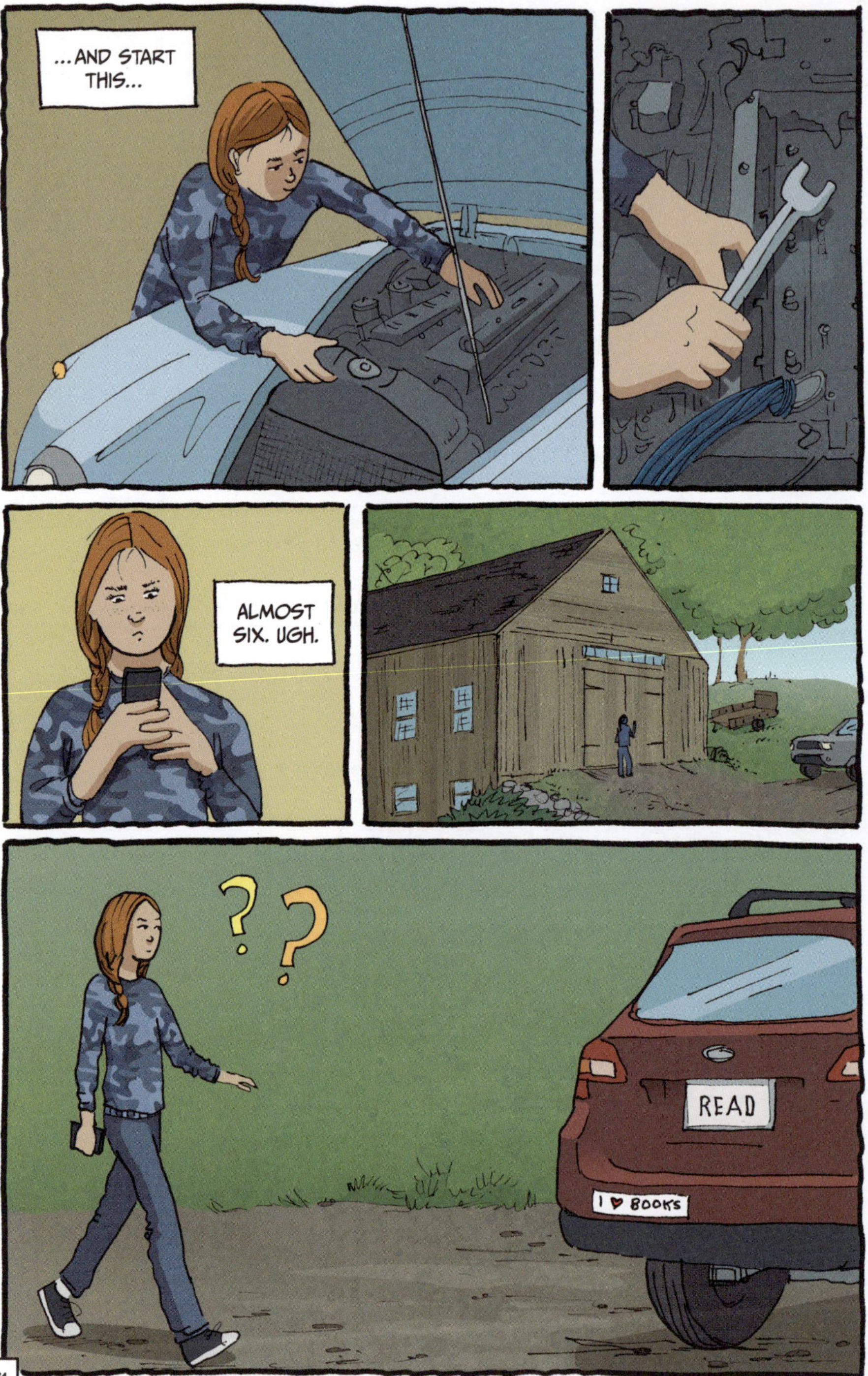
...AND START THIS...
ALMOST SIX. UGH.
READ
I ♥ BOOKS

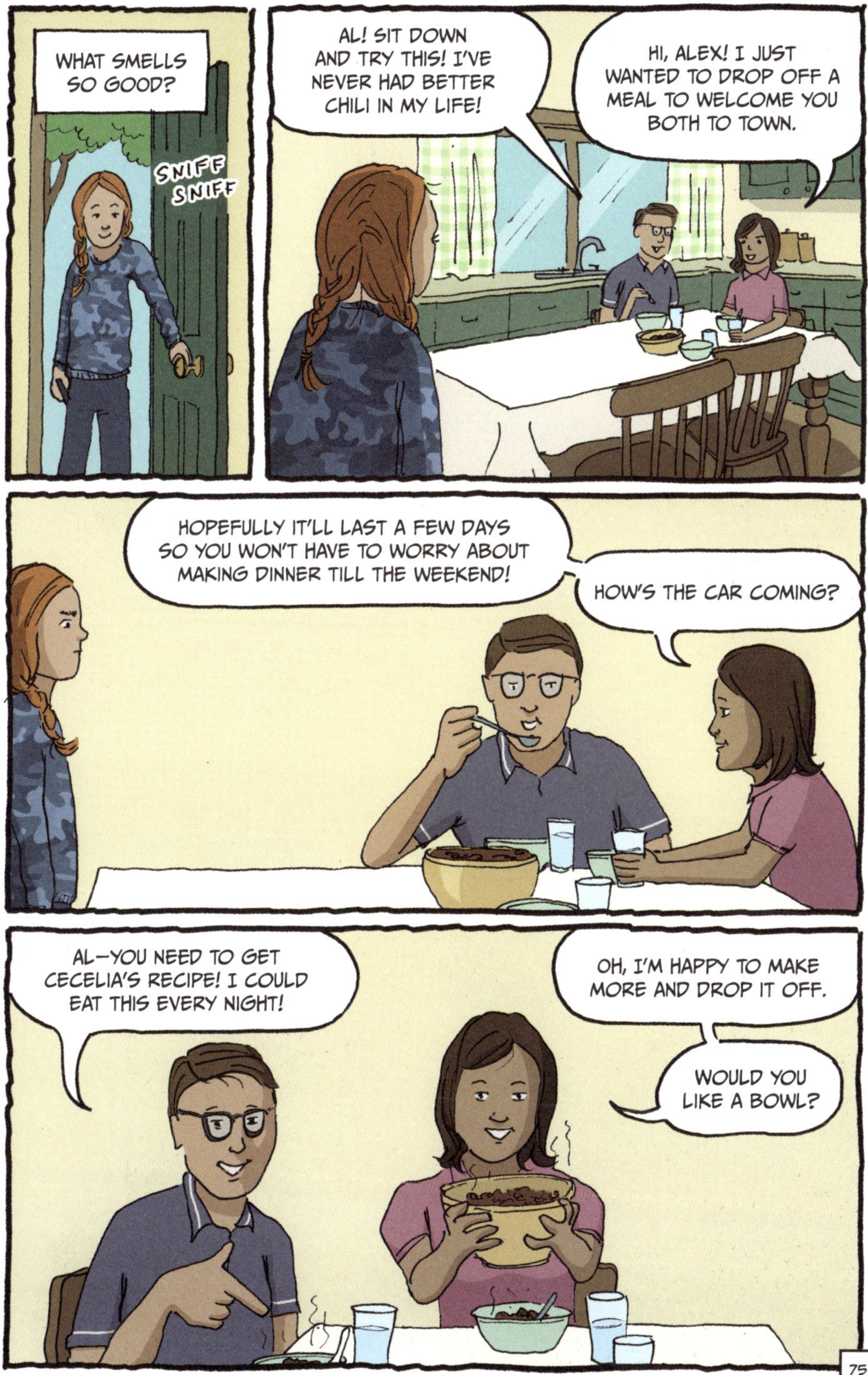
WHAT SMELLS SO GOOD?
SNIFF SNIFF
AL! SIT DOWN AND TRY THIS! I'VE NEVER HAD BETTER CHILI IN MY LIFE!
HI, ALEX! I JUST WANTED TO DROP OFF A MEAL TO WELCOME YOU BOTH TO TOWN.
HOPEFULLY IT'LL LAST A FEW DAYS SO YOU WON'T HAVE TO WORRY ABOUT MAKING DINNER TILL THE WEEKEND!
HOW'S THE CAR COMING?
AL—YOU NEED TO GET CECELIA'S RECIPE! I COULD EAT THIS EVERY NIGHT!
OH, I'M HAPPY TO MAKE MORE AND DROP IT OFF.
WOULD YOU LIKE A BOWL?

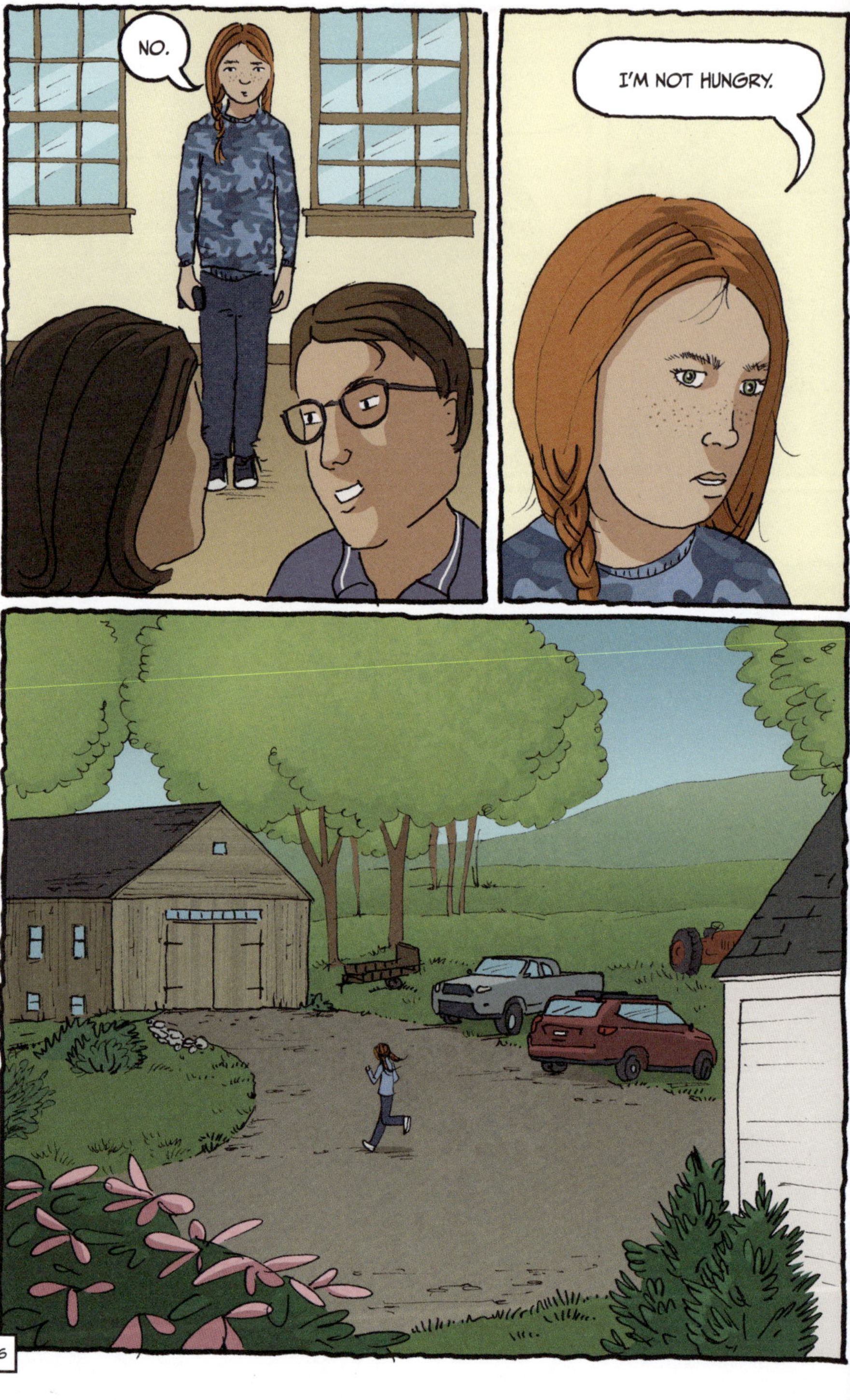
NO.
I'M NOT HUNGRY.

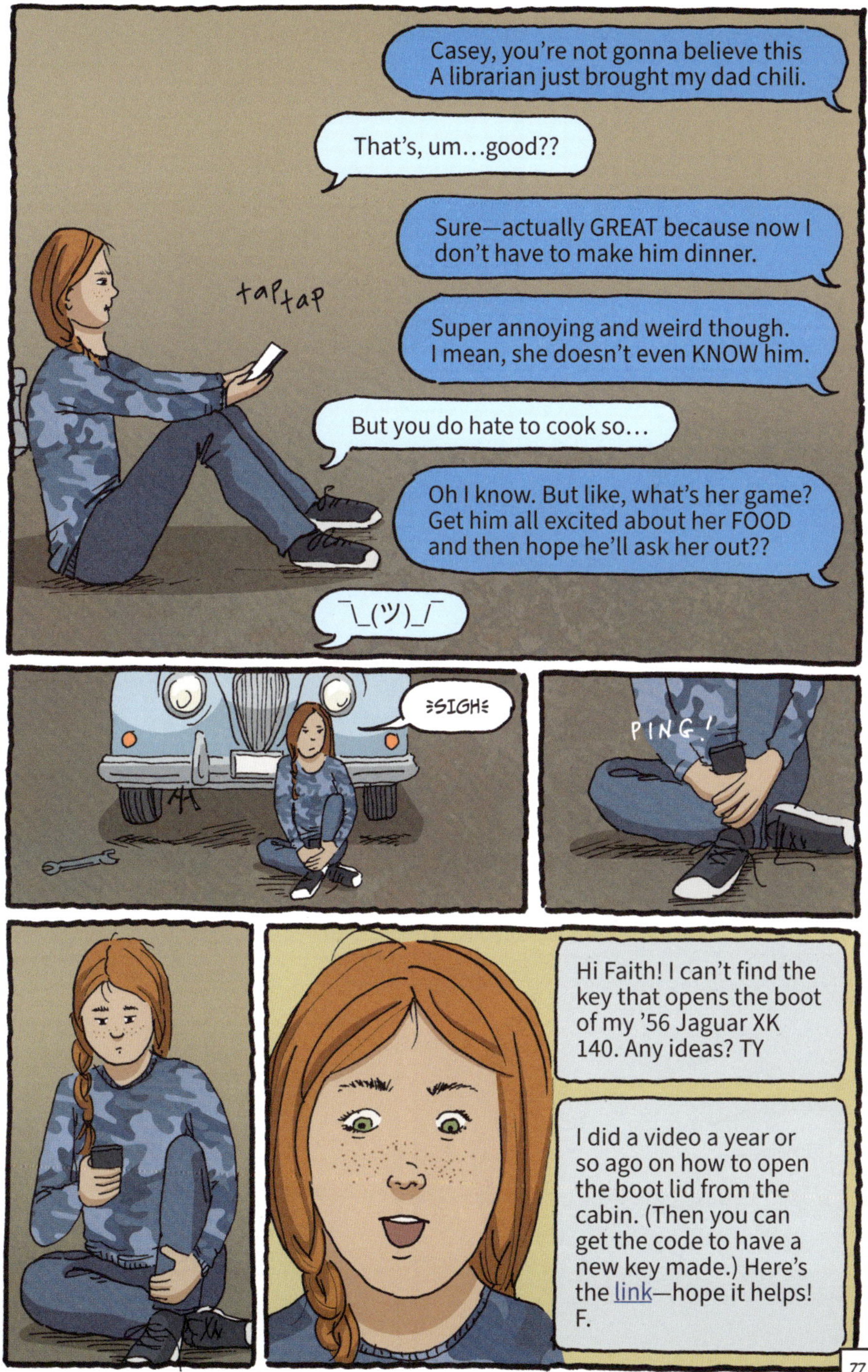
Casey, you're not gonna believe this A librarian just brought my dad chili.
That's, um…good??
Sure—actually GREAT because now I don't have to make him dinner.
tap tap
Super annoying and weird though. I mean, she doesn't even KNOW him.
But you do hate to cook so…
Oh I know. But like, what's her game? Get him all excited about her FOOD and then hope he'll ask her out??
¯_(ツ)_/¯
SIGH
PING!
Hi Faith! I can't find the key that opens the boot of my '56 Jaguar XK 140. Any ideas? TY
I did a video a year or so ago on how to open the boot lid from the cabin. (Then you can get the code to have a new key made.) Here's the link—hope it helps! F.

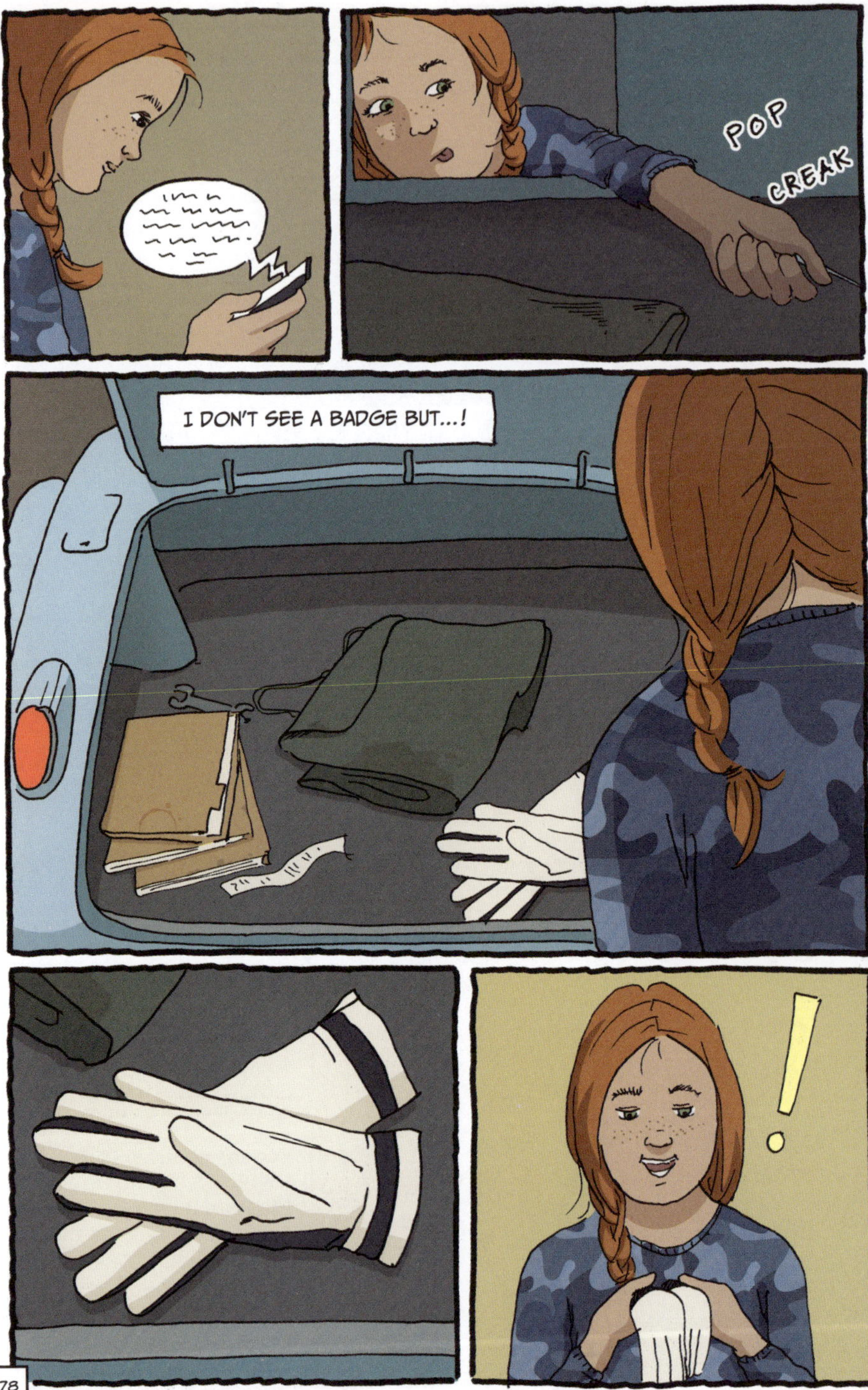
POP
CREAK
I DON'T SEE A BADGE BUT...!
!

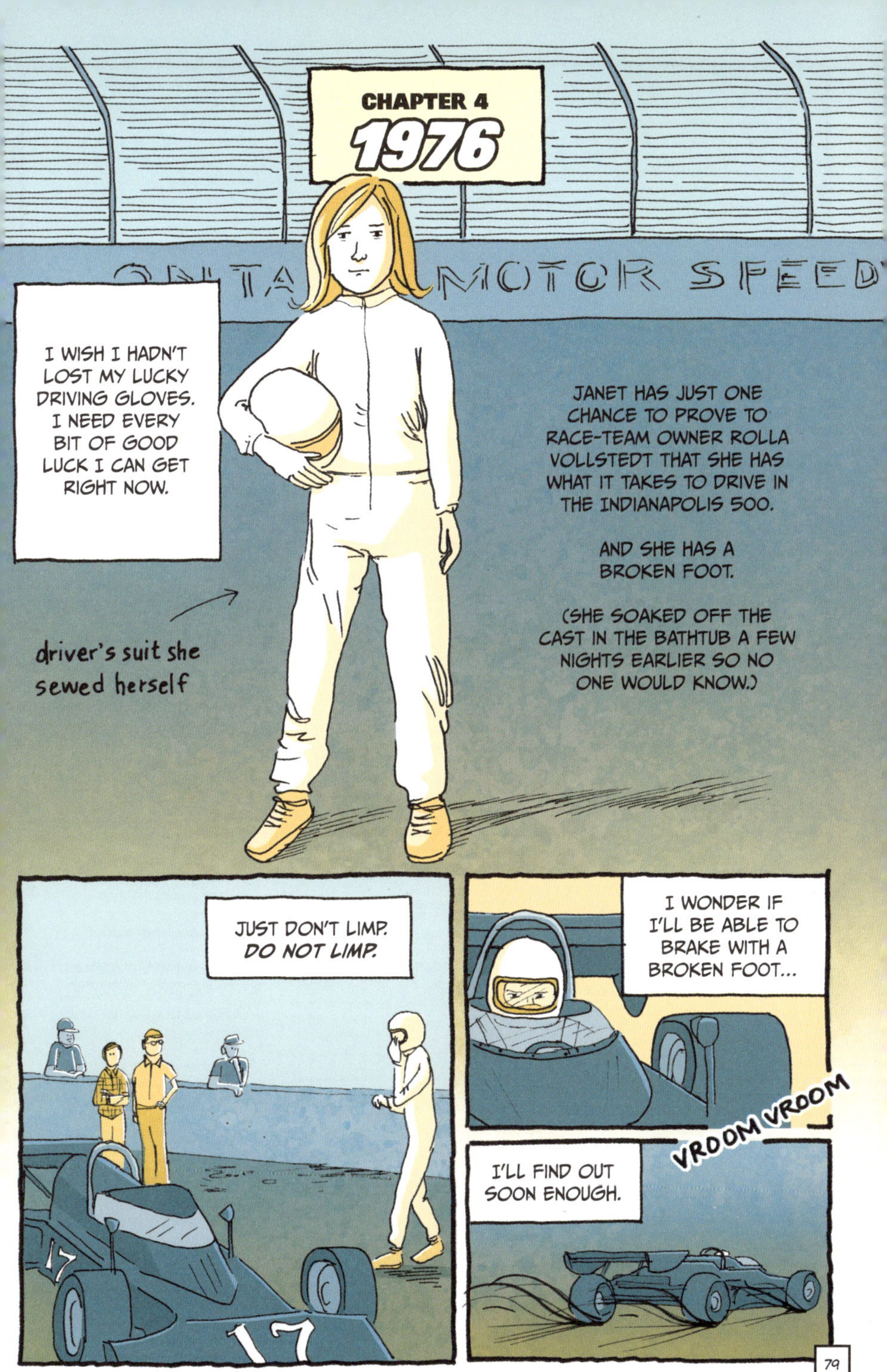
CHAPTER 4
1976
ONTARIO MOTOR SPEEDWAY
I WISH I HADN'T LOST MY LUCKY DRIVING GLOVES. I NEED EVERY BIT OF GOOD LUCK I CAN GET RIGHT NOW.
JANET HAS JUST ONE CHANCE TO PROVE TO RACE-TEAM OWNER ROLLA VOLLSTEDT THAT SHE HAS WHAT IT TAKES TO DRIVE IN THE INDIANAPOLIS 500.
AND SHE HAS A BROKEN FOOT.
(SHE SOAKED OFF THE CAST IN THE BATHTUB A FEW NIGHTS EARLIER SO NO ONE WOULD KNOW.)
driver's suit she sewed herself
JUST DON'T LIMP. *DO NOT LIMP.*
17
17
I WONDER IF I'LL BE ABLE TO BRAKE WITH A BROKEN FOOT...
VROOM VROOM
I'LL FIND OUT SOON ENOUGH.

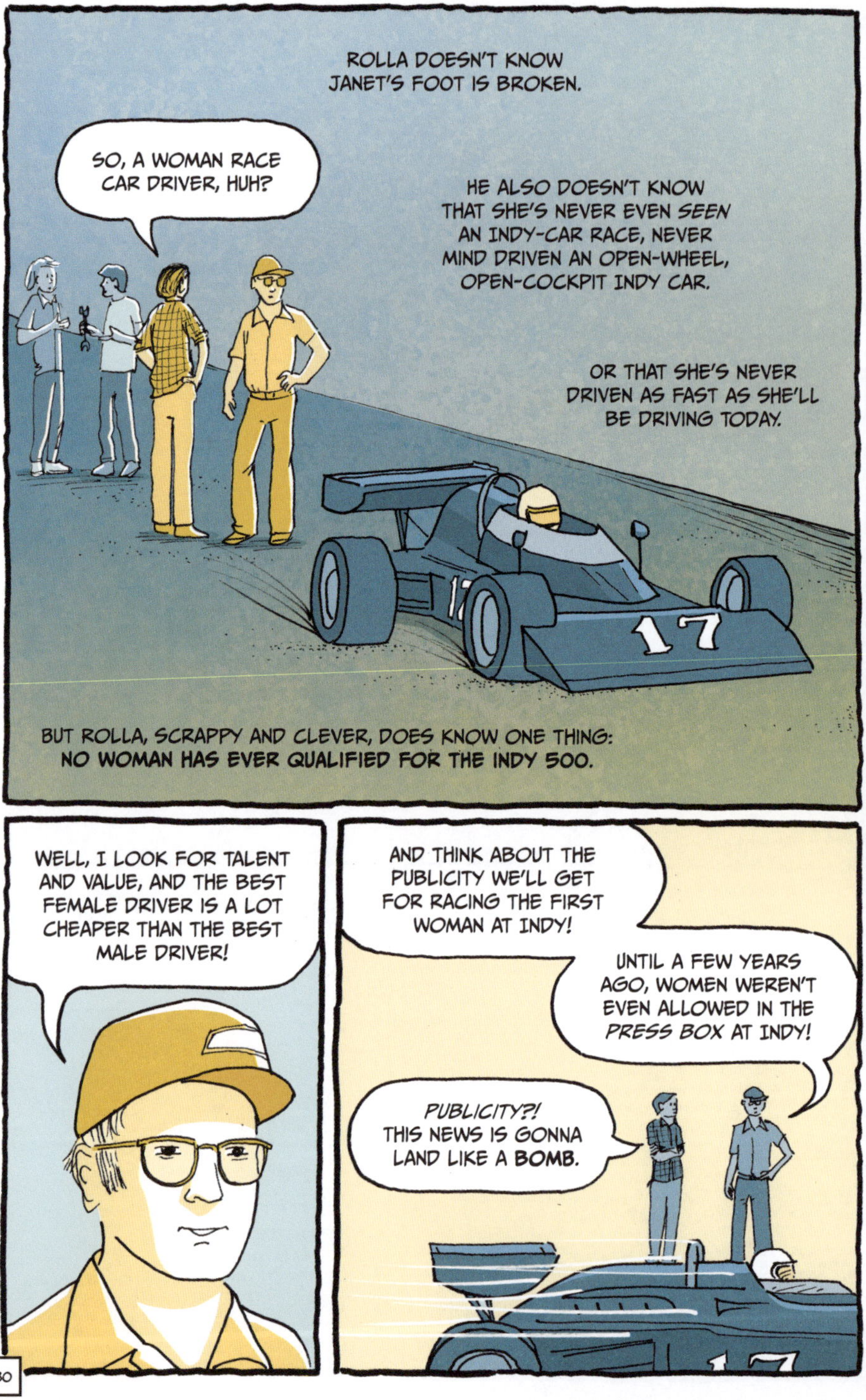
ROLLA DOESN'T KNOW JANET'S FOOT IS BROKEN.
SO, A WOMAN RACE CAR DRIVER, HUH?
HE ALSO DOESN'T KNOW THAT SHE'S NEVER EVEN *SEEN* AN INDY-CAR RACE, NEVER MIND DRIVEN AN OPEN-WHEEL, OPEN-COCKPIT INDY CAR.
OR THAT SHE'S NEVER DRIVEN AS FAST AS SHE'LL BE DRIVING TODAY.
17
BUT ROLLA, SCRAPPY AND CLEVER, DOES KNOW ONE THING:
NO WOMAN HAS EVER QUALIFIED FOR THE INDY 500.
WELL, I LOOK FOR TALENT AND VALUE, AND THE BEST FEMALE DRIVER IS A LOT CHEAPER THAN THE BEST MALE DRIVER!
AND THINK ABOUT THE PUBLICITY WE'LL GET FOR RACING THE FIRST WOMAN AT INDY!
UNTIL A FEW YEARS AGO, WOMEN WEREN'T EVEN ALLOWED IN THE *PRESS BOX* AT INDY!
PUBLICITY?! THIS NEWS IS GONNA LAND LIKE A **BOMB.**

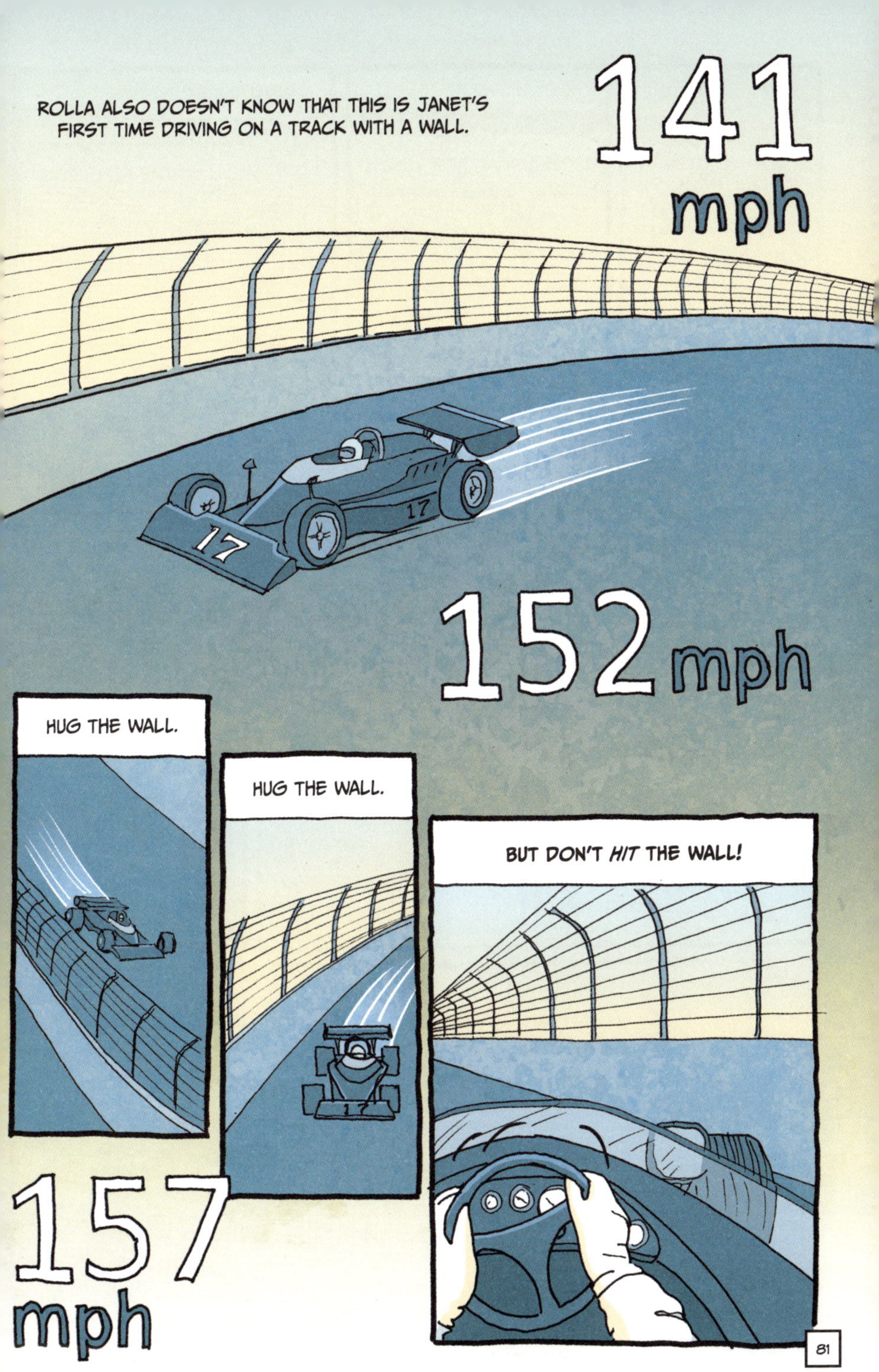
ROLLA ALSO DOESN'T KNOW THAT THIS IS JANET'S FIRST TIME DRIVING ON A TRACK WITH A WALL.
141 mph
17
17
152 mph
HUG THE WALL.
HUG THE WALL.
BUT DON'T *HIT* THE WALL!
157 mph

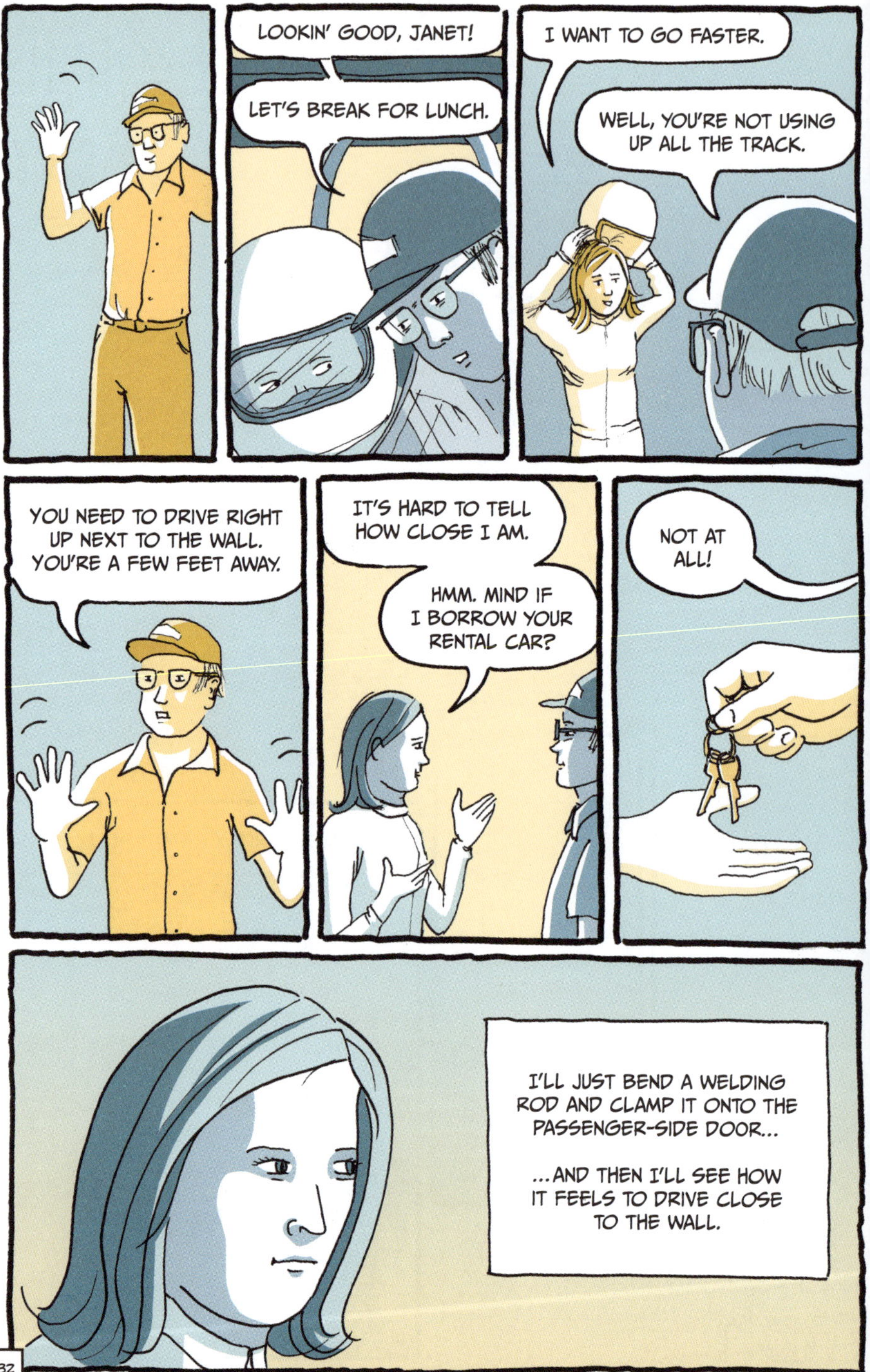
LOOKIN' GOOD, JANET!
LET'S BREAK FOR LUNCH.
I WANT TO GO FASTER.
WELL, YOU'RE NOT USING UP ALL THE TRACK.
YOU NEED TO DRIVE RIGHT UP NEXT TO THE WALL. YOU'RE A FEW FEET AWAY.
IT'S HARD TO TELL HOW CLOSE I AM.
HMM. MIND IF I BORROW YOUR RENTAL CAR?
NOT AT ALL!
I'LL JUST BEND A WELDING ROD AND CLAMP IT ONTO THE PASSENGER-SIDE DOOR...
...AND THEN I'LL SEE HOW IT FEELS TO DRIVE CLOSE TO THE WALL.

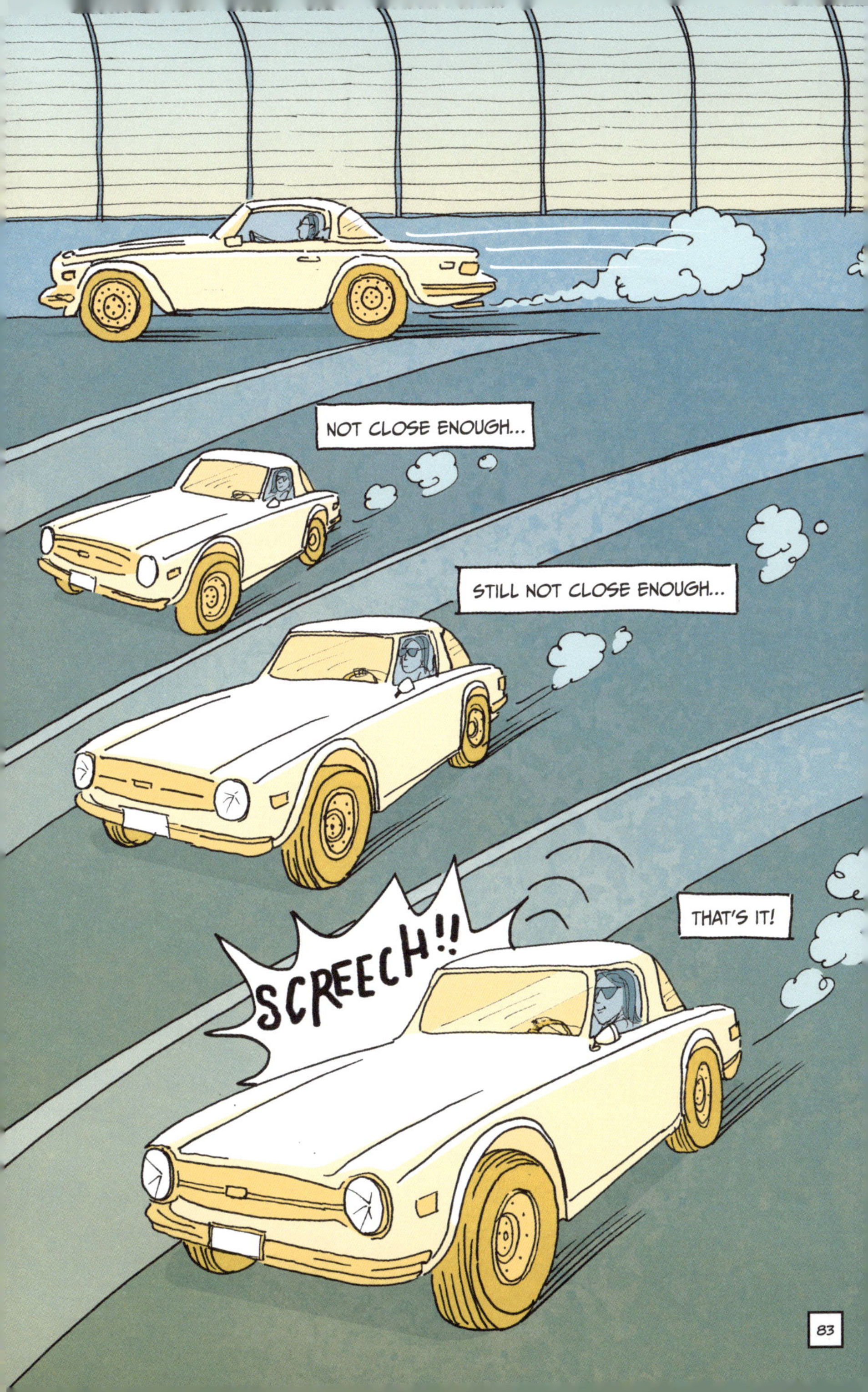
NOT CLOSE ENOUGH...
STILL NOT CLOSE ENOUGH...
THAT'S IT!
SCREECH!!

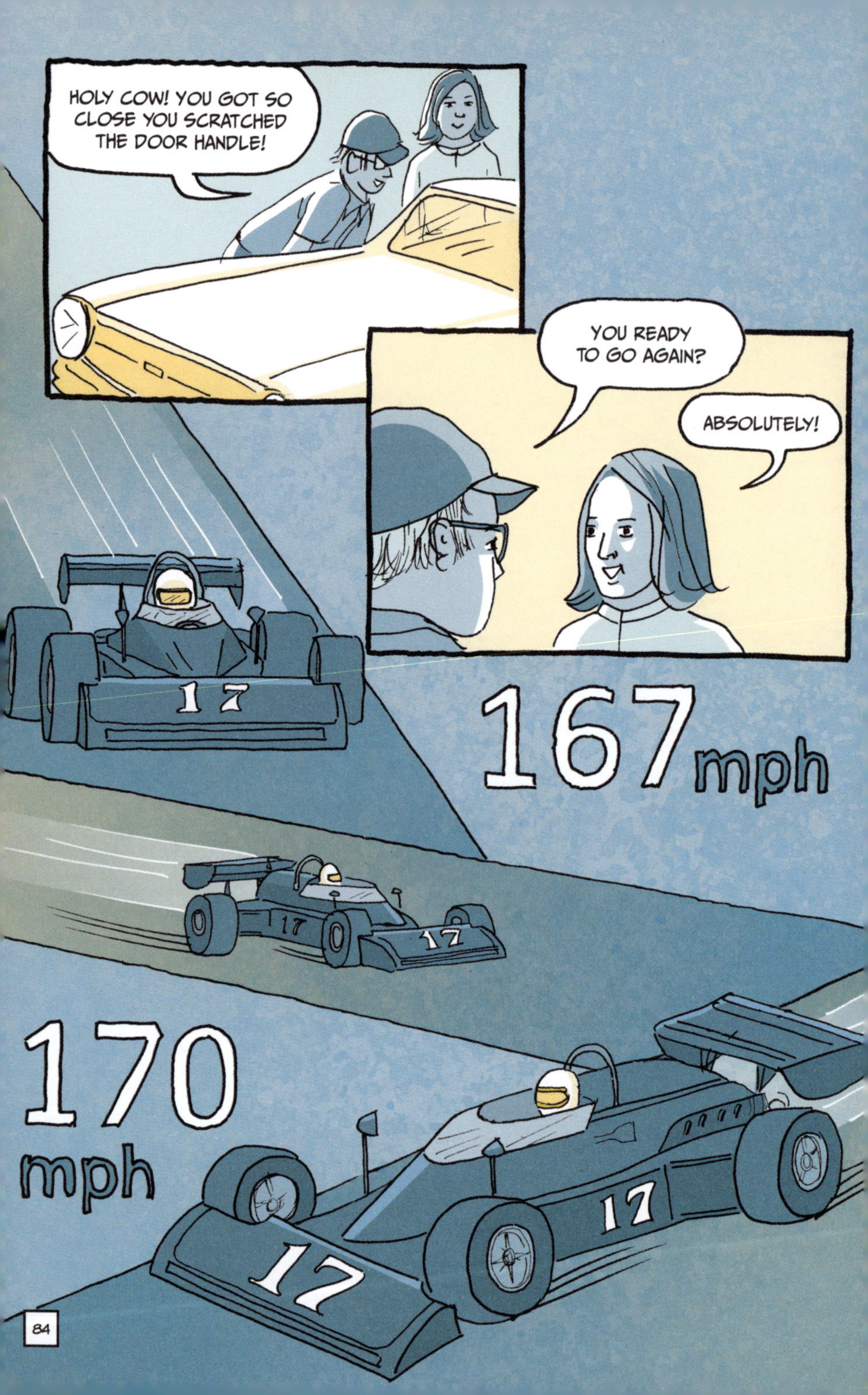
HOLY COW! YOU GOT SO CLOSE YOU SCRATCHED THE DOOR HANDLE!
YOU READY TO GO AGAIN?
ABSOLUTELY!
167mph
170 mph

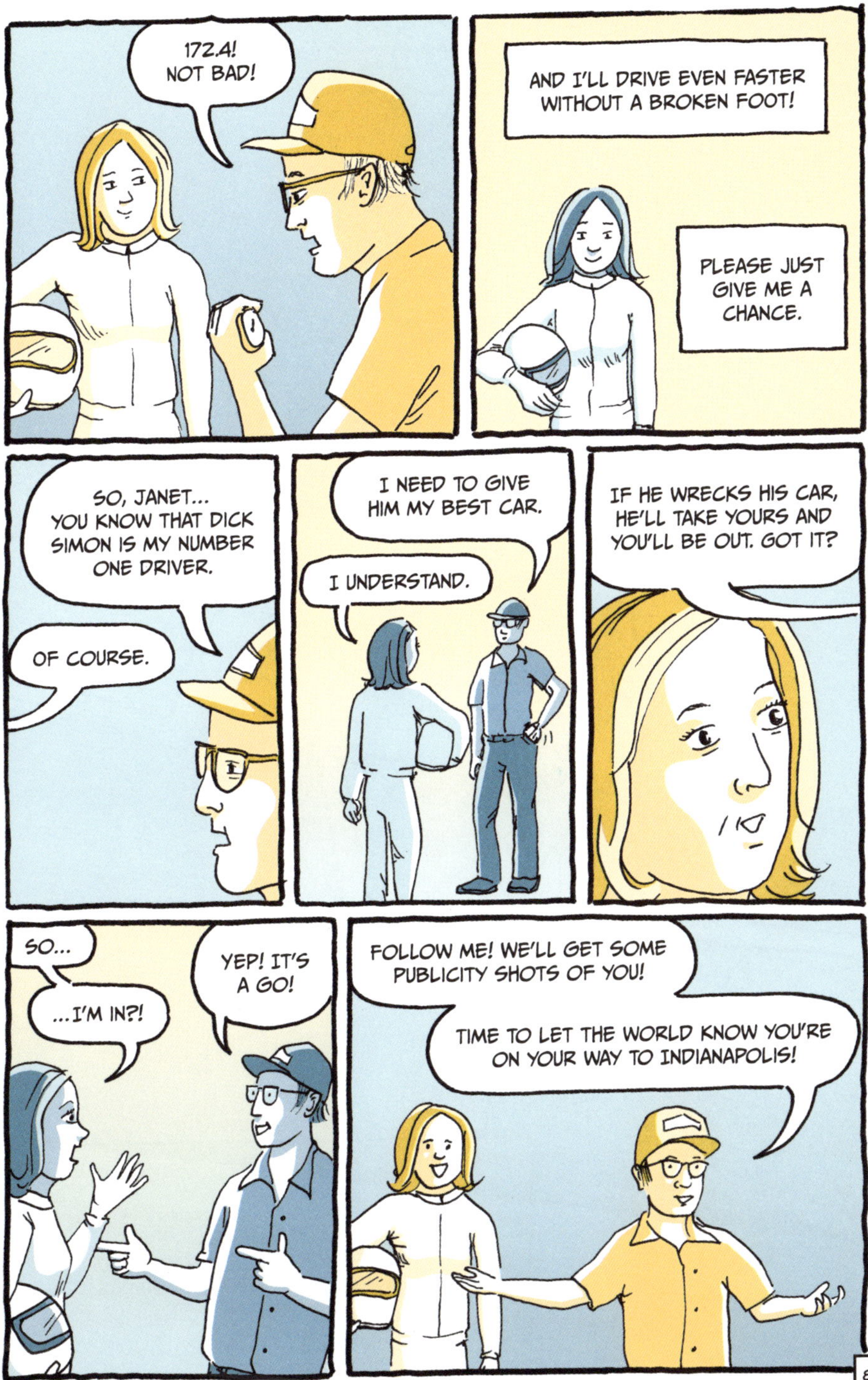

172.4! NOT BAD!
AND I'LL DRIVE EVEN FASTER WITHOUT A BROKEN FOOT!
PLEASE JUST GIVE ME A CHANCE.
SO, JANET... YOU KNOW THAT DICK SIMON IS MY NUMBER ONE DRIVER.
OF COURSE.
I NEED TO GIVE HIM MY BEST CAR.
I UNDERSTAND.
IF HE WRECKS HIS CAR, HE'LL TAKE YOURS AND YOU'LL BE OUT. GOT IT?
SO...
...I'M IN?!
YEP! IT'S A GO!
FOLLOW ME! WE'LL GET SOME PUBLICITY SHOTS OF YOU!
TIME TO LET THE WORLD KNOW YOU'RE ON YOUR WAY TO INDIANAPOLIS!

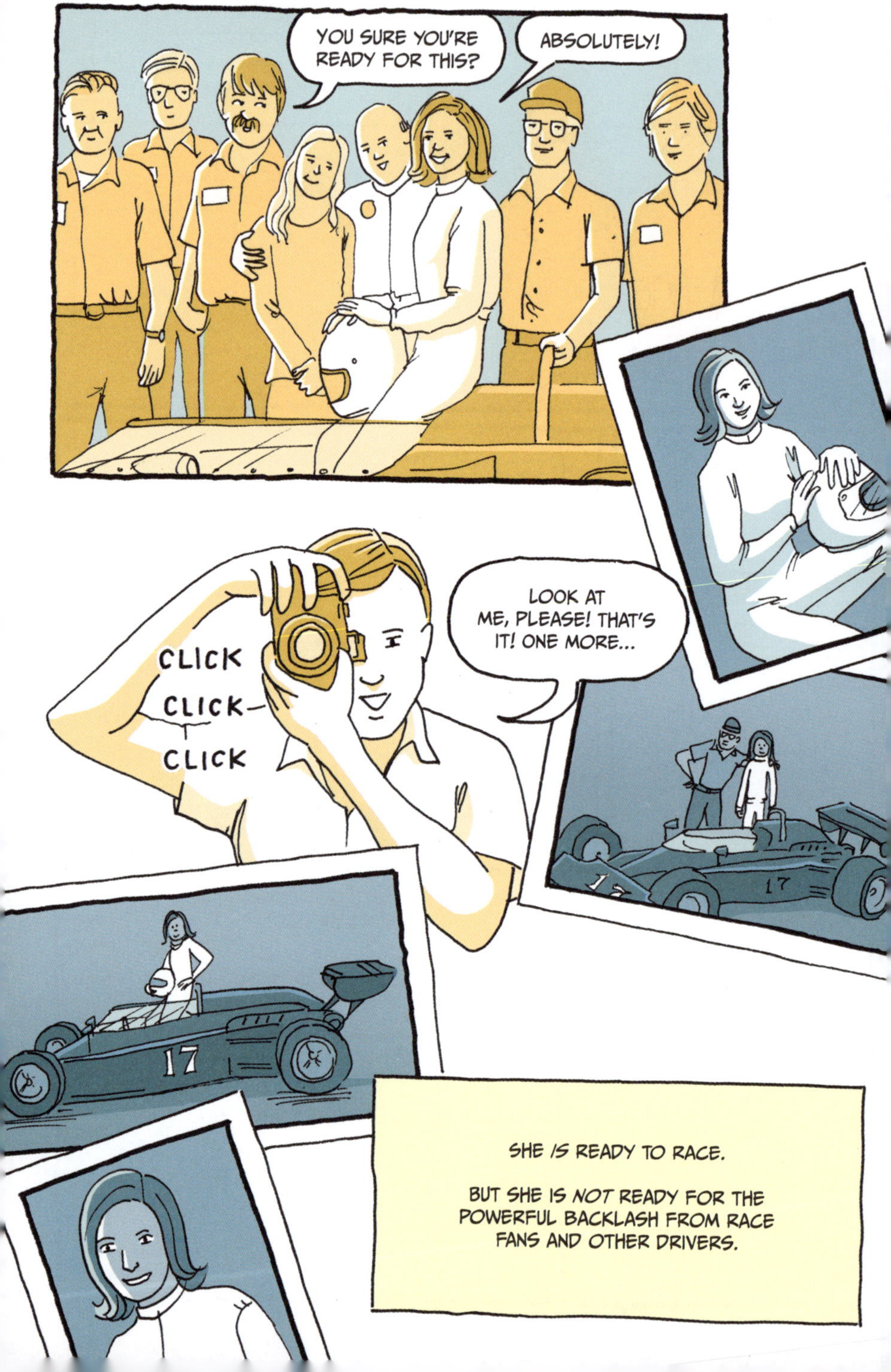
YOU SURE YOU'RE READY FOR THIS?
ABSOLUTELY!
CLICK
CLICK
CLICK
LOOK AT ME, PLEASE! THAT'S IT! ONE MORE...
17
17
17
SHE *IS* READY TO RACE.
BUT SHE IS *NOT* READY FOR THE POWERFUL BACKLASH FROM RACE FANS AND OTHER DRIVERS.

"SHE IS ONLY RACING BECAUSE SHE'S A WOMAN AND VOLLSTEDT WANTS ALL THE MEDIA ATTENTION."

A WOMAN DRIVER AT INDY? "It's idiotic!"

GUTHRIE HAS RACERS FUMING

Guthrie Hopes to Be First Woman to Qualify for Indy 500... but How Will Fans React?

"WHERE DID THIS WOMAN COME FROM, ANYWAY?"

RACERS REBEL AGAINST NOTION OF WOMEN ON TRACK
Hint at Boycott

"SHE'S A PROBLEM."

Women Invading Indianapolis?!
Women Lack Physical Strength to Win

Indy Race Officials Inundated with Hate Mail after Guthrie Announces Plan to Race

A SHE at Indy? No Comment!

Indy Stunt
Unqualified!

Women Racers a "Joke"

Will she faint the pressure of race? Ladies s... stay at...

dangero...
...unqualified and inco...
should be at home wh...
...is the world comin...
...overtake a...
lady c...
...would you

Women are not capa... or calm enough to sta... up under the pressure ...racing cars. Half of th... won't even be...
and...

Women are too emotional and likely to overreact... another racer gets... to them...

To the Indianapolis Race Committee:
I am outraged that you are allowing a FEMALE DRIVER to try to qualify for t... Someone is going to get killed and you ...insist that no wome...

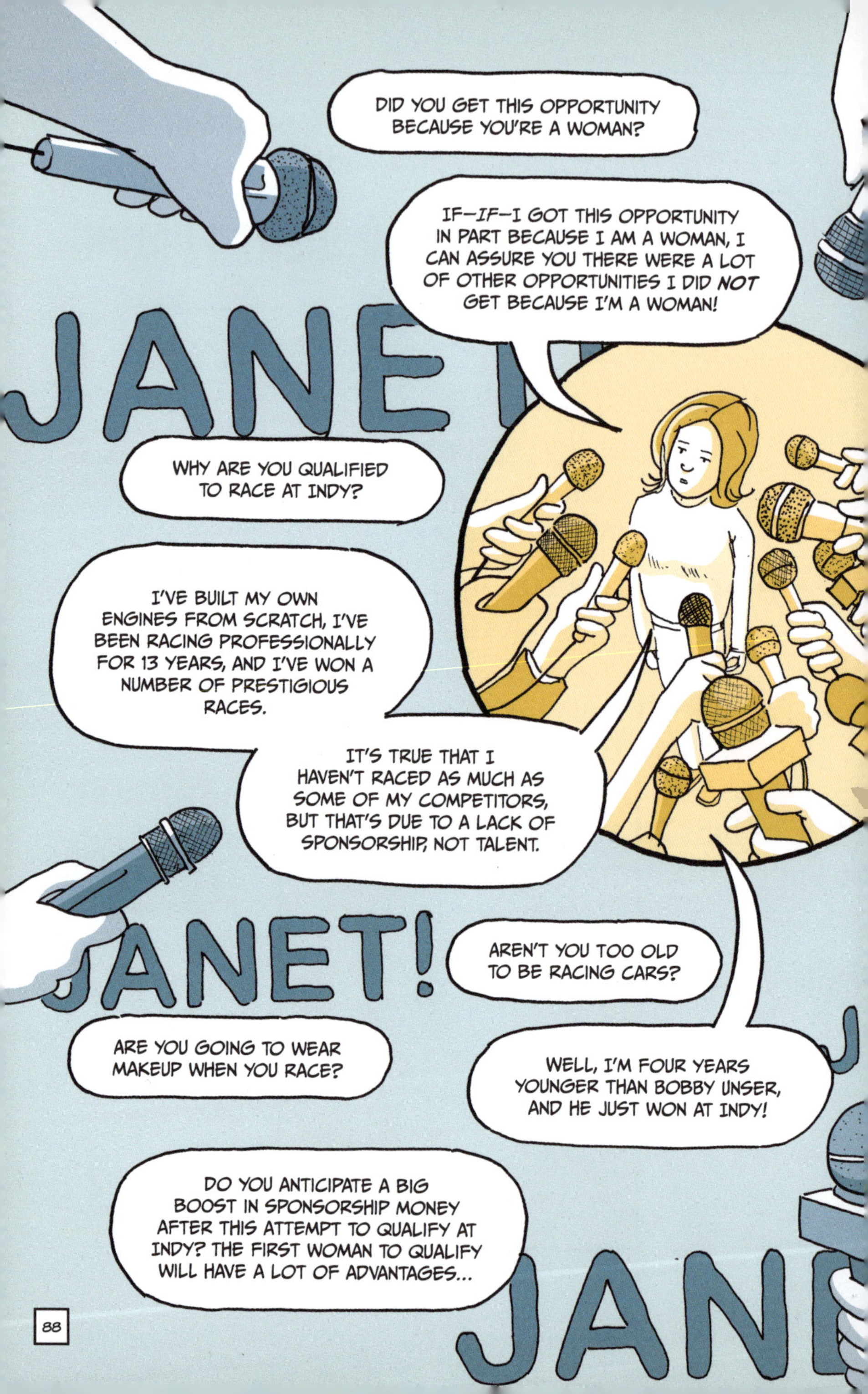
DID YOU GET THIS OPPORTUNITY BECAUSE YOU'RE A WOMAN?
IF—*IF*—I GOT THIS OPPORTUNITY IN PART BECAUSE I AM A WOMAN, I CAN ASSURE YOU THERE WERE A LOT OF OTHER OPPORTUNITIES I DID ***NOT*** GET BECAUSE I'M A WOMAN!
JANET
WHY ARE YOU QUALIFIED TO RACE AT INDY?
I'VE BUILT MY OWN ENGINES FROM SCRATCH, I'VE BEEN RACING PROFESSIONALLY FOR 13 YEARS, AND I'VE WON A NUMBER OF PRESTIGIOUS RACES.
IT'S TRUE THAT I HAVEN'T RACED AS MUCH AS SOME OF MY COMPETITORS, BUT THAT'S DUE TO A LACK OF SPONSORSHIP, NOT TALENT.
JANET!
AREN'T YOU TOO OLD TO BE RACING CARS?
ARE YOU GOING TO WEAR MAKEUP WHEN YOU RACE?
WELL, I'M FOUR YEARS YOUNGER THAN BOBBY UNSER, AND HE JUST WON AT INDY!
DO YOU ANTICIPATE A BIG BOOST IN SPONSORSHIP MONEY AFTER THIS ATTEMPT TO QUALIFY AT INDY? THE FIRST WOMAN TO QUALIFY WILL HAVE A LOT OF ADVANTAGES...
JAN

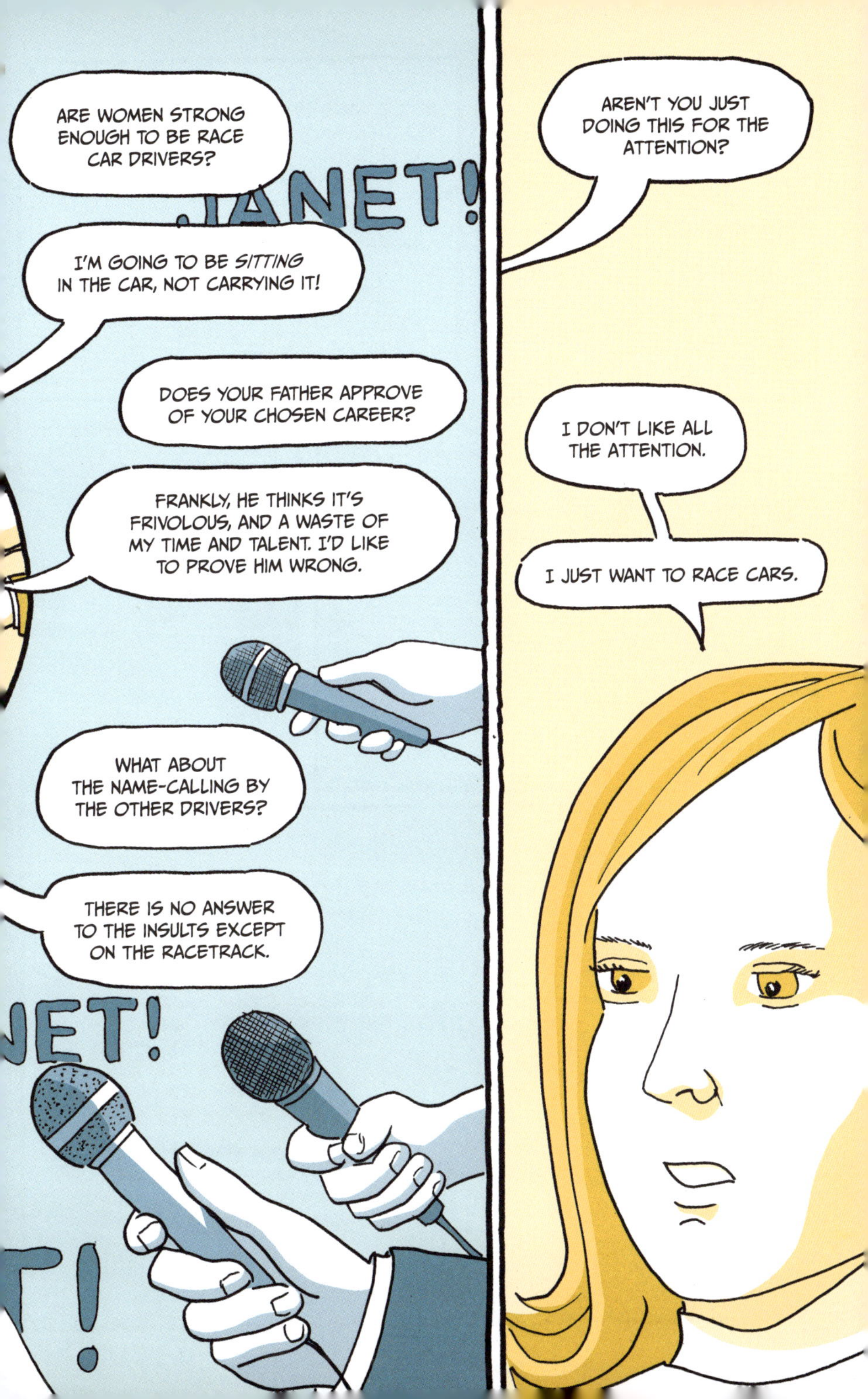
ARE WOMEN STRONG ENOUGH TO BE RACE CAR DRIVERS?
JANET!
I'M GOING TO BE *SITTING* IN THE CAR, NOT CARRYING IT!
DOES YOUR FATHER APPROVE OF YOUR CHOSEN CAREER?
FRANKLY, HE THINKS IT'S FRIVOLOUS, AND A WASTE OF MY TIME AND TALENT. I'D LIKE TO PROVE HIM WRONG.
WHAT ABOUT THE NAME-CALLING BY THE OTHER DRIVERS?
THERE IS NO ANSWER TO THE INSULTS EXCEPT ON THE RACETRACK.
ET!
T!
AREN'T YOU JUST DOING THIS FOR THE ATTENTION?
I DON'T LIKE ALL THE ATTENTION.
I JUST WANT TO RACE CARS.

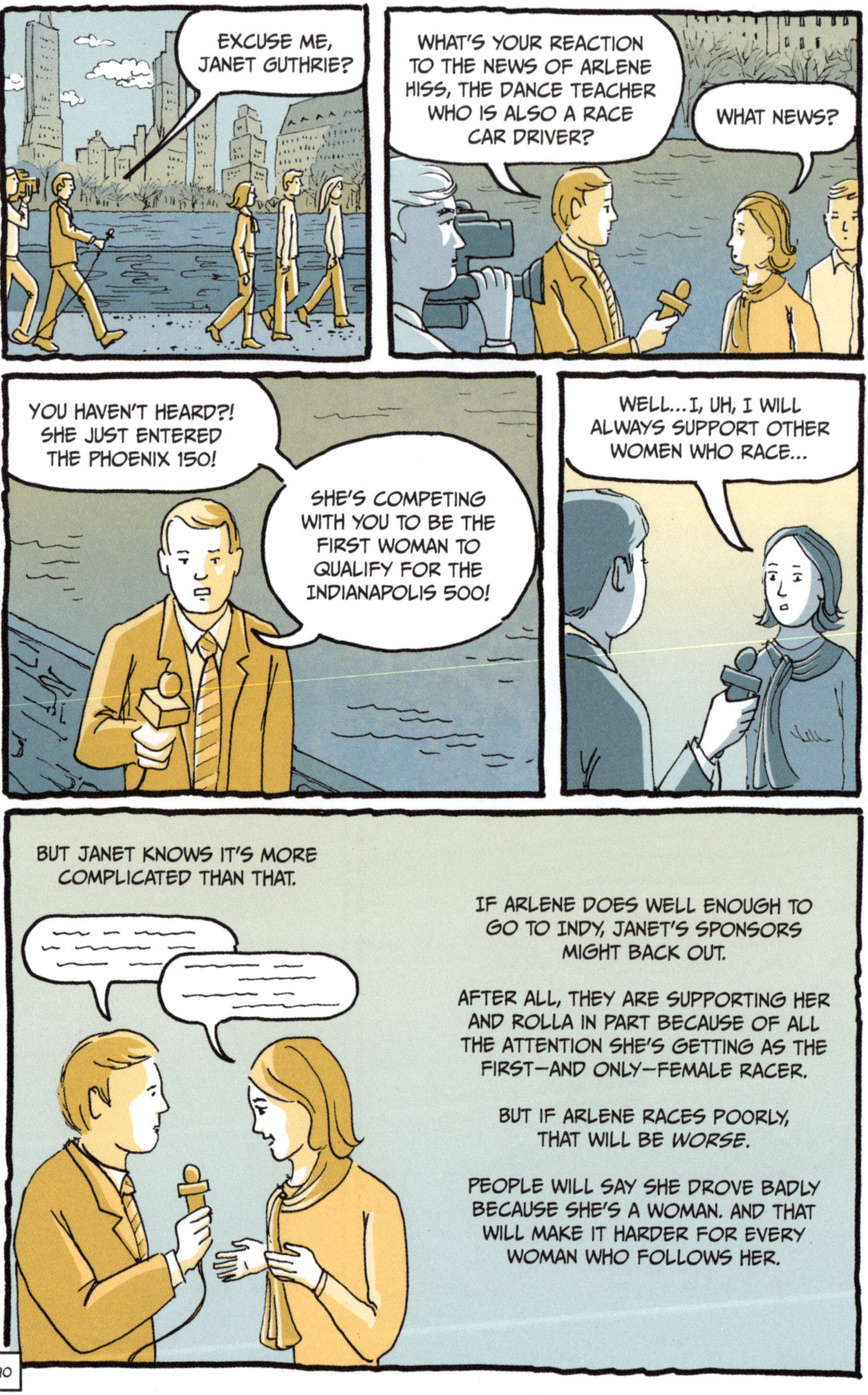
EXCUSE ME, JANET GUTHRIE?
WHAT'S YOUR REACTION TO THE NEWS OF ARLENE HISS, THE DANCE TEACHER WHO IS ALSO A RACE CAR DRIVER?
WHAT NEWS?
YOU HAVEN'T HEARD?! SHE JUST ENTERED THE PHOENIX 150!
SHE'S COMPETING WITH YOU TO BE THE FIRST WOMAN TO QUALIFY FOR THE INDIANAPOLIS 500!
WELL...I, UH, I WILL ALWAYS SUPPORT OTHER WOMEN WHO RACE...
BUT JANET KNOWS IT'S MORE COMPLICATED THAN THAT.
IF ARLENE DOES WELL ENOUGH TO GO TO INDY, JANET'S SPONSORS MIGHT BACK OUT.
AFTER ALL, THEY ARE SUPPORTING HER AND ROLLA IN PART BECAUSE OF ALL THE ATTENTION SHE'S GETTING AS THE FIRST—AND ONLY—FEMALE RACER.
BUT IF ARLENE RACES POORLY, THAT WILL BE *WORSE*.
PEOPLE WILL SAY SHE DROVE BADLY BECAUSE SHE'S A WOMAN. AND THAT WILL MAKE IT HARDER FOR EVERY WOMAN WHO FOLLOWS HER.

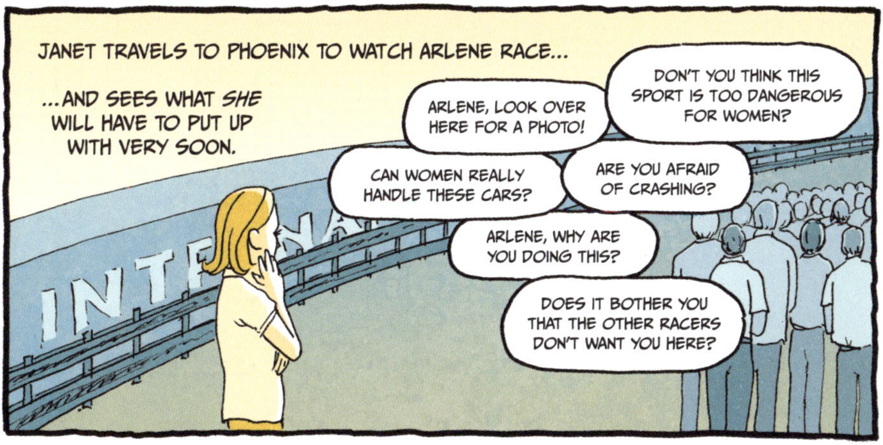
JANET TRAVELS TO PHOENIX TO WATCH ARLENE RACE...
...AND SEES WHAT *SHE* WILL HAVE TO PUT UP WITH VERY SOON.
ARLENE, LOOK OVER HERE FOR A PHOTO!
DON'T YOU THINK THIS SPORT IS TOO DANGEROUS FOR WOMEN?
CAN WOMEN REALLY HANDLE THESE CARS?
ARE YOU AFRAID OF CRASHING?
ARLENE, WHY ARE YOU DOING THIS?
DOES IT BOTHER YOU THAT THE OTHER RACERS DON'T WANT YOU HERE?

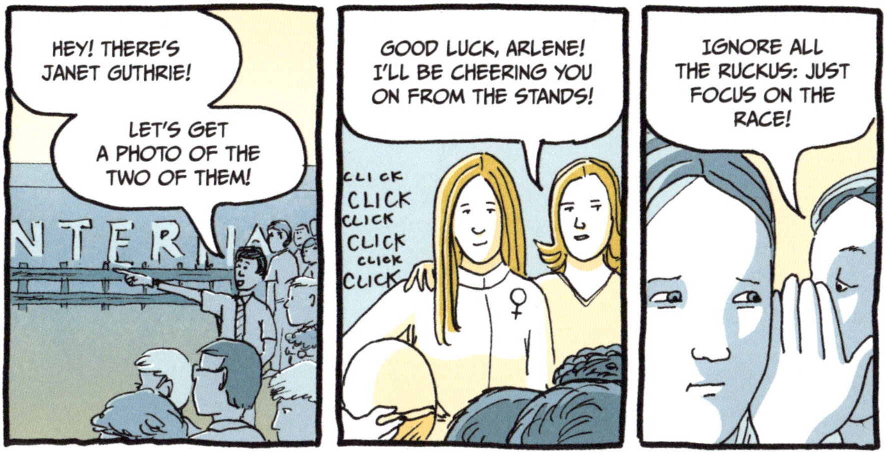
HEY! THERE'S JANET GUTHRIE!
LET'S GET A PHOTO OF THE TWO OF THEM!
GOOD LUCK, ARLENE! I'LL BE CHEERING YOU ON FROM THE STANDS!
CLICK
CLICK
CLICK
CLICK
CLICK
CLICK
IGNORE ALL THE RUCKUS: JUST FOCUS ON THE RACE!

BUT ARLENE ISN'T ABLE TO DO THAT.

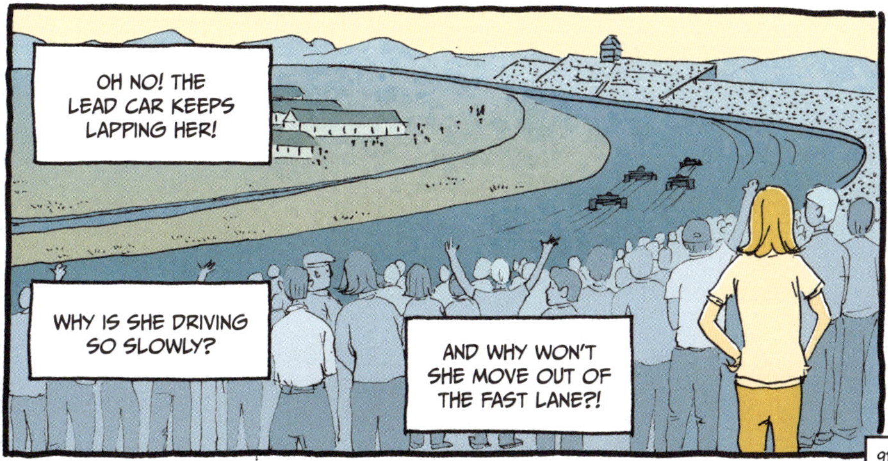
OH NO! THE LEAD CAR KEEPS LAPPING HER!
WHY IS SHE DRIVING SO SLOWLY?
AND WHY WON'T SHE MOVE OUT OF THE FAST LANE?!

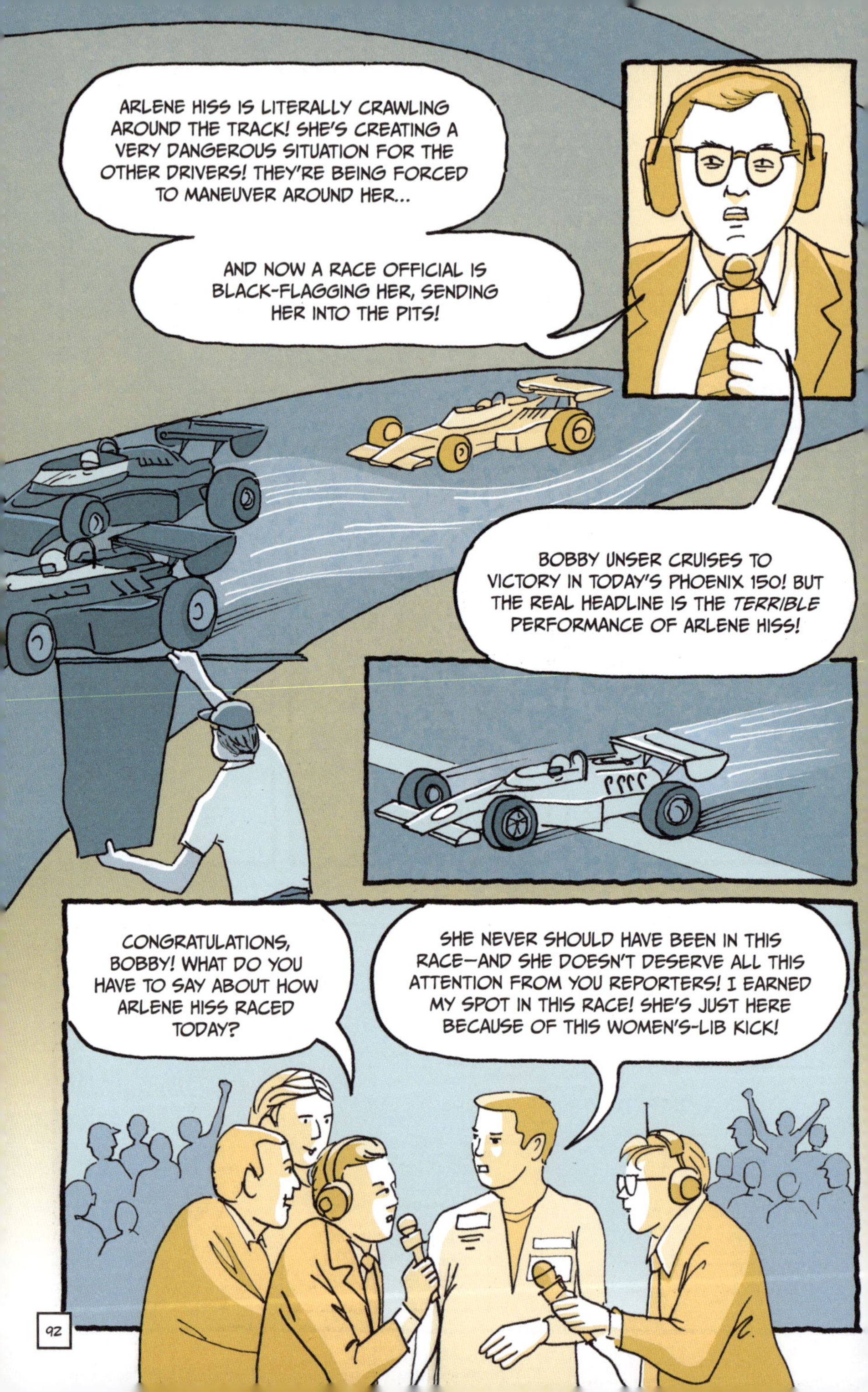
ARLENE HISS IS LITERALLY CRAWLING AROUND THE TRACK! SHE'S CREATING A VERY DANGEROUS SITUATION FOR THE OTHER DRIVERS! THEY'RE BEING FORCED TO MANEUVER AROUND HER...
AND NOW A RACE OFFICIAL IS BLACK-FLAGGING HER, SENDING HER INTO THE PITS!
BOBBY UNSER CRUISES TO VICTORY IN TODAY'S PHOENIX 150! BUT THE REAL HEADLINE IS THE *TERRIBLE* PERFORMANCE OF ARLENE HISS!
CONGRATULATIONS, BOBBY! WHAT DO YOU HAVE TO SAY ABOUT HOW ARLENE HISS RACED TODAY?
SHE NEVER SHOULD HAVE BEEN IN THIS RACE—AND SHE DOESN'T DESERVE ALL THIS ATTENTION FROM YOU REPORTERS! I EARNED MY SPOT IN THIS RACE! SHE'S JUST HERE BECAUSE OF THIS WOMEN'S-LIB KICK!

ARLENE HISS WILL NEVER COMPETE IN ANOTHER INDY-CAR EVENT. SHE RETURNS TO HER LIFE AS A DANCE INSTRUCTOR.

BUT SHE LEAVES ANGER AND TURMOIL IN HER WAKE.

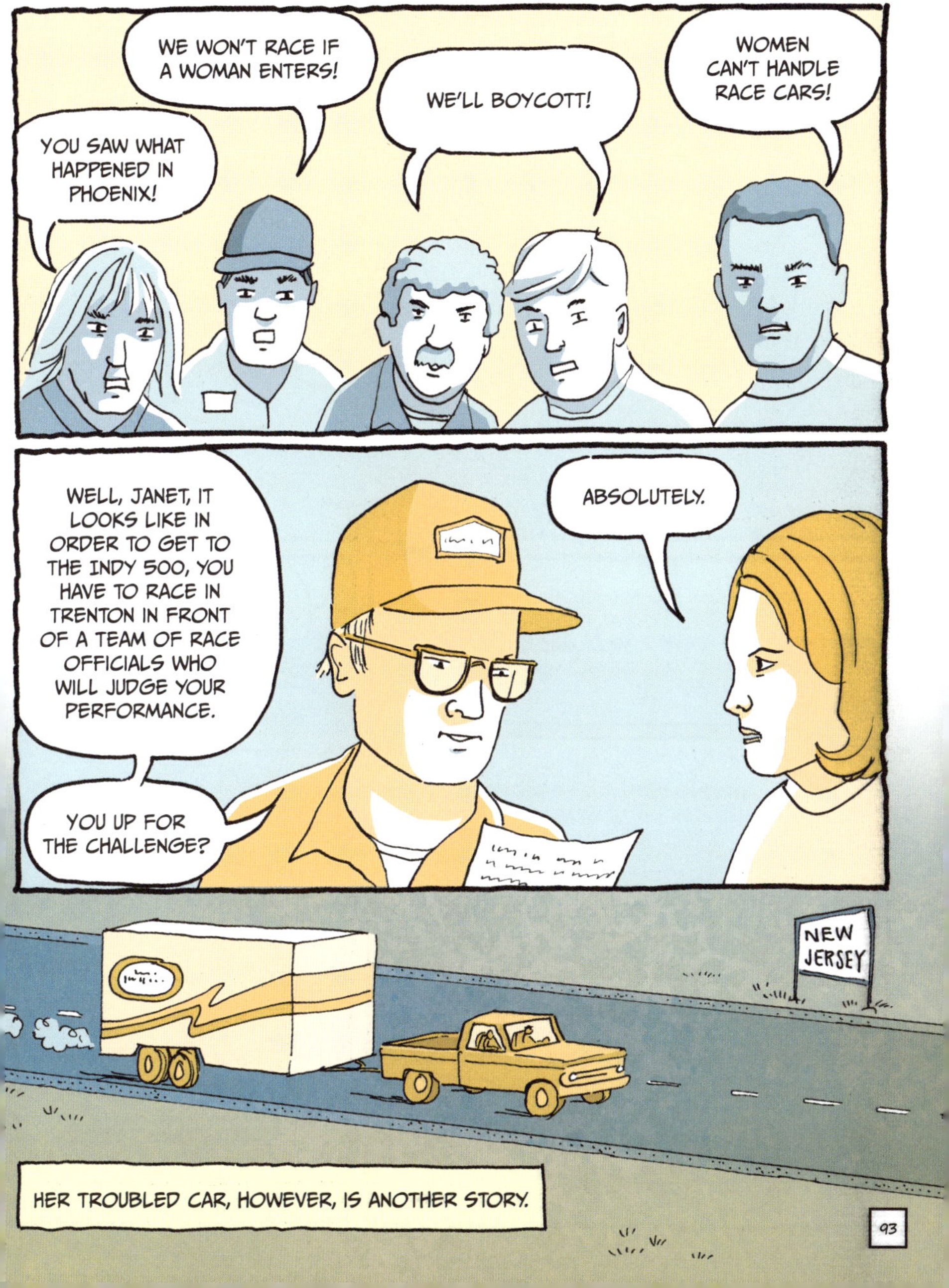
YOU SAW WHAT HAPPENED IN PHOENIX!
WE WON'T RACE IF A WOMAN ENTERS!
WE'LL BOYCOTT!
WOMEN CAN'T HANDLE RACE CARS!
WELL, JANET, IT LOOKS LIKE IN ORDER TO GET TO THE INDY 500, YOU HAVE TO RACE IN TRENTON IN FRONT OF A TEAM OF RACE OFFICIALS WHO WILL JUDGE YOUR PERFORMANCE.
YOU UP FOR THE CHALLENGE?
ABSOLUTELY.
NEW JERSEY
HER TROUBLED CAR, HOWEVER, IS ANOTHER STORY.

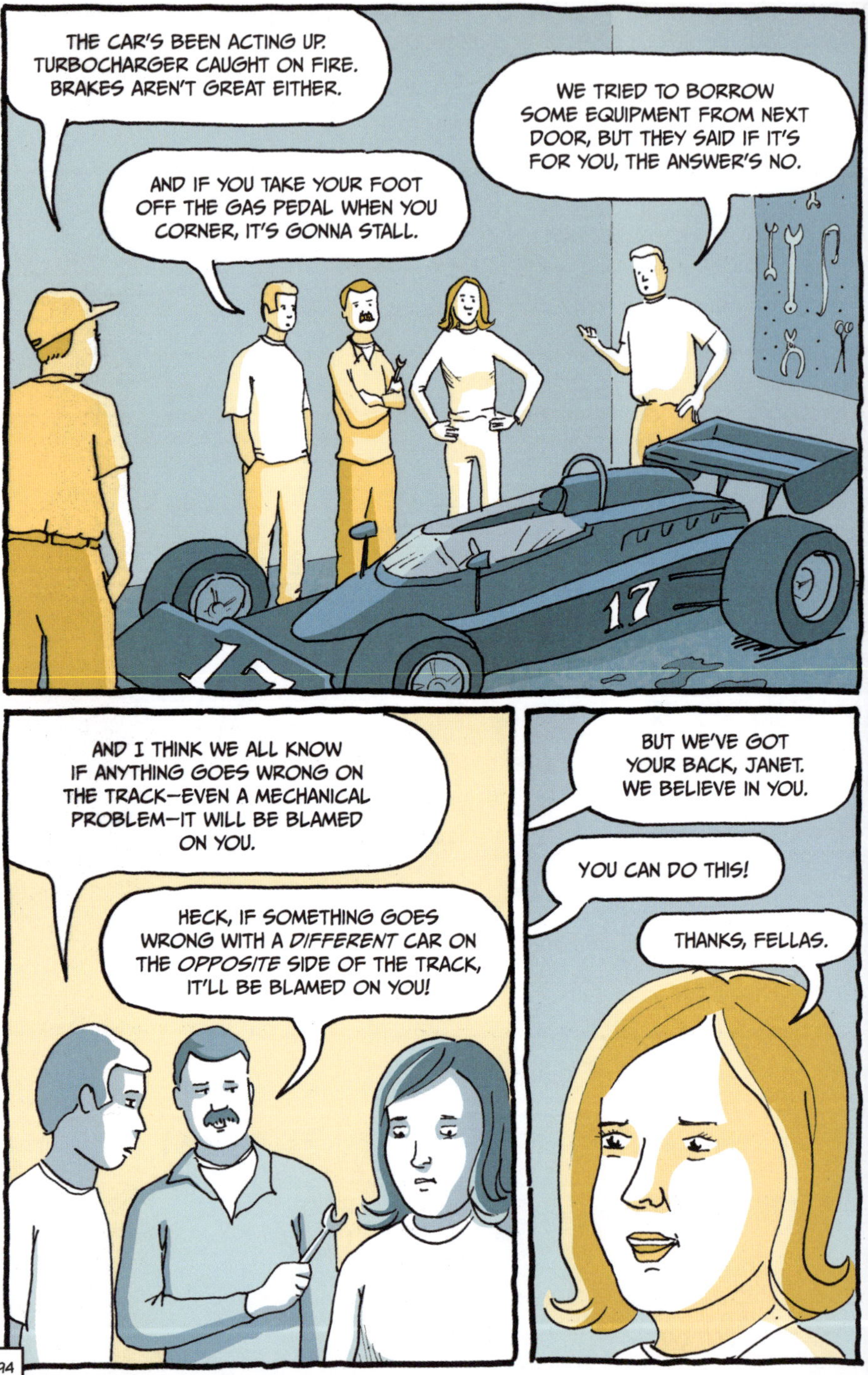
THE CAR'S BEEN ACTING UP. TURBOCHARGER CAUGHT ON FIRE. BRAKES AREN'T GREAT EITHER.
AND IF YOU TAKE YOUR FOOT OFF THE GAS PEDAL WHEN YOU CORNER, IT'S GONNA STALL.
WE TRIED TO BORROW SOME EQUIPMENT FROM NEXT DOOR, BUT THEY SAID IF IT'S FOR YOU, THE ANSWER'S NO.
17
AND I THINK WE ALL KNOW IF ANYTHING GOES WRONG ON THE TRACK—EVEN A MECHANICAL PROBLEM—IT WILL BE BLAMED ON YOU.
HECK, IF SOMETHING GOES WRONG WITH A *DIFFERENT* CAR ON THE *OPPOSITE* SIDE OF THE TRACK, IT'LL BE BLAMED ON YOU!
BUT WE'VE GOT YOUR BACK, JANET. WE BELIEVE IN YOU.
YOU CAN DO THIS!
THANKS, FELLAS.

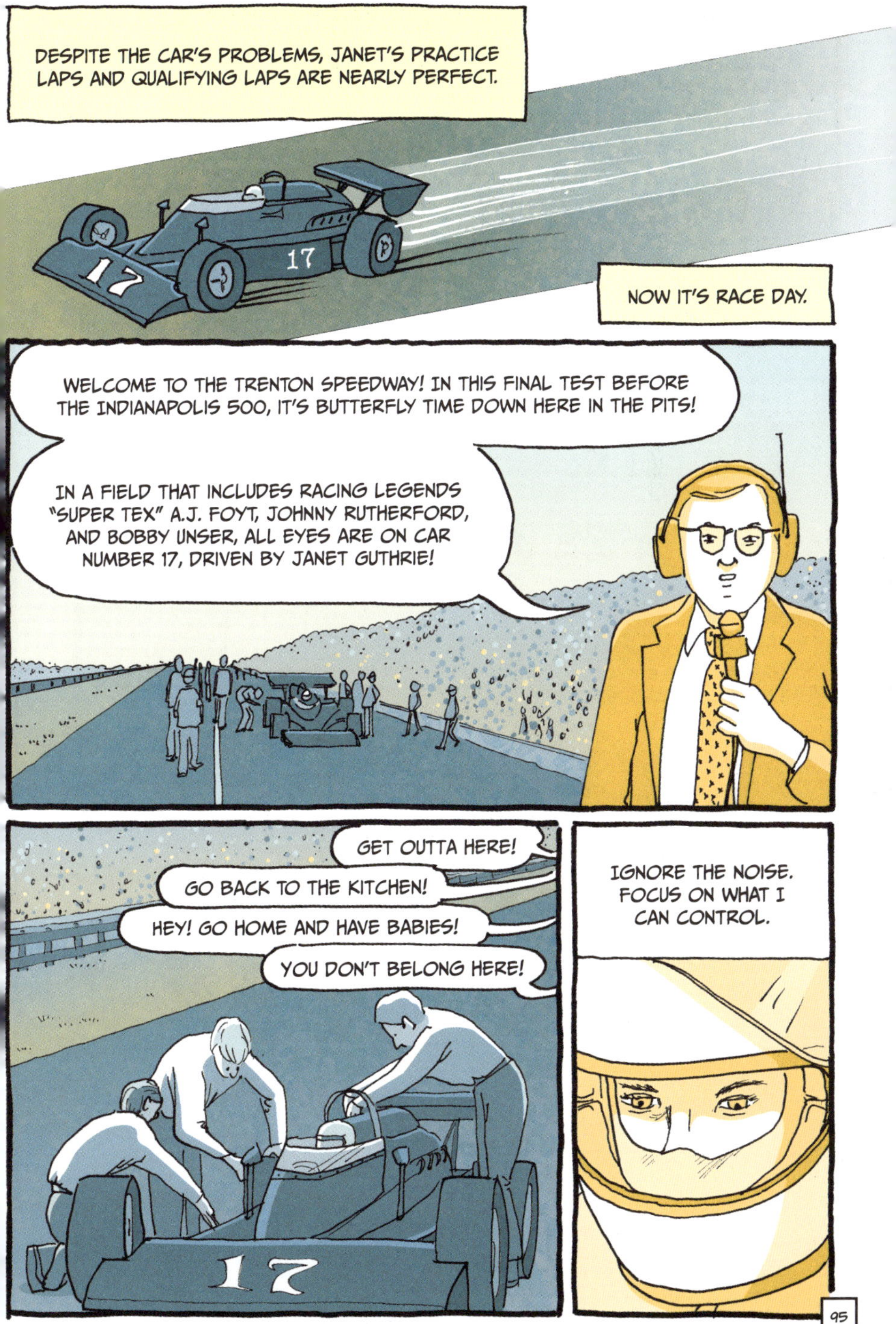
DESPITE THE CAR'S PROBLEMS, JANET'S PRACTICE LAPS AND QUALIFYING LAPS ARE NEARLY PERFECT.
17
17
NOW IT'S RACE DAY.
WELCOME TO THE TRENTON SPEEDWAY! IN THIS FINAL TEST BEFORE THE INDIANAPOLIS 500, IT'S BUTTERFLY TIME DOWN HERE IN THE PITS!
IN A FIELD THAT INCLUDES RACING LEGENDS "SUPER TEX" A.J. FOYT, JOHNNY RUTHERFORD, AND BOBBY UNSER, ALL EYES ARE ON CAR NUMBER 17, DRIVEN BY JANET GUTHRIE!
GET OUTTA HERE!
GO BACK TO THE KITCHEN!
HEY! GO HOME AND HAVE BABIES!
YOU DON'T BELONG HERE!
17
IGNORE THE NOISE. FOCUS ON WHAT I CAN CONTROL.

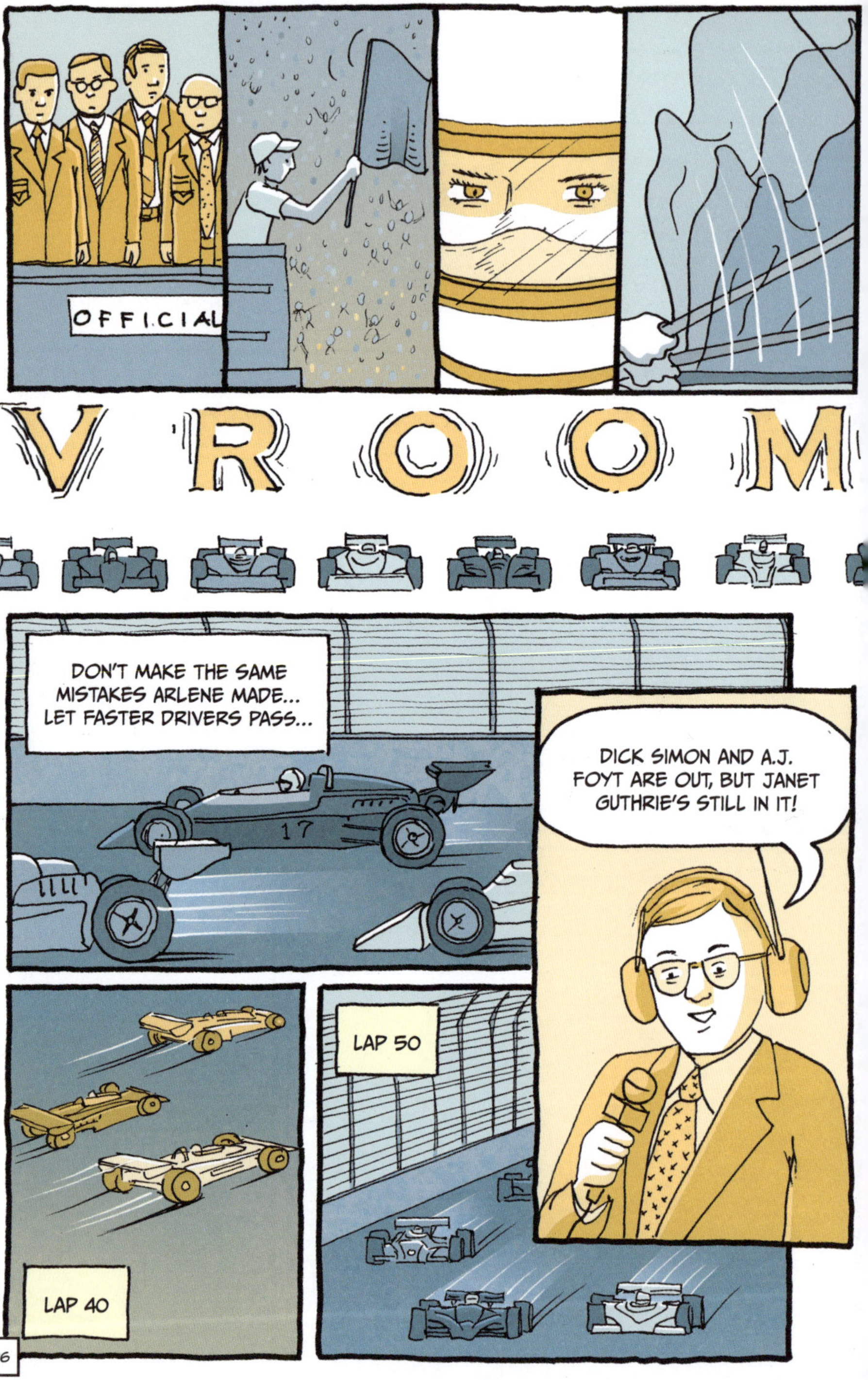
OFFICIAL
VROOM
DON'T MAKE THE SAME MISTAKES ARLENE MADE... LET FASTER DRIVERS PASS...
17
DICK SIMON AND A.J. FOYT ARE OUT, BUT JANET GUTHRIE'S STILL IN IT!
LAP 40
LAP 50

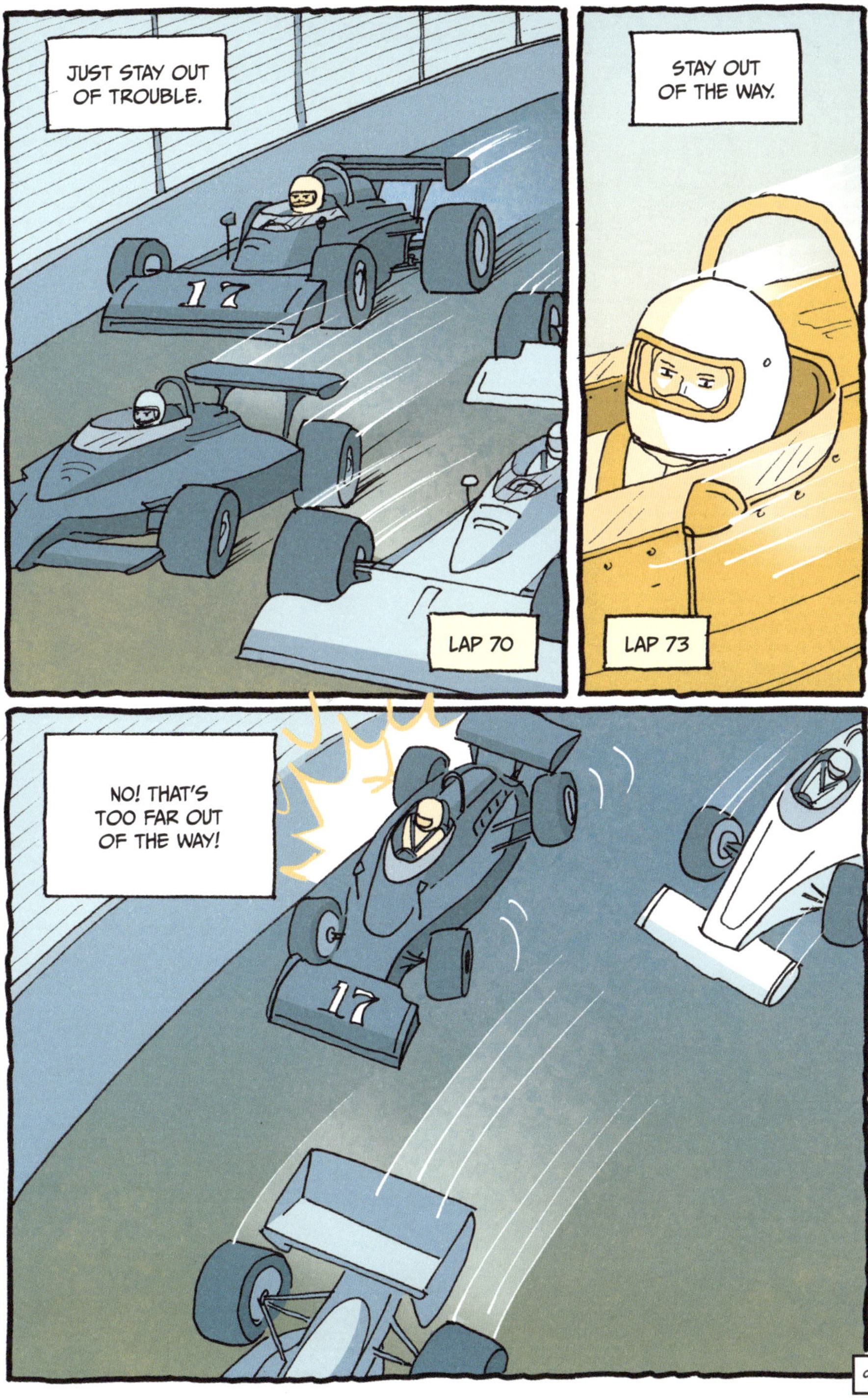
JUST STAY OUT OF TROUBLE.
LAP 70
STAY OUT OF THE WAY.
LAP 73
NO! THAT'S TOO FAR OUT OF THE WAY!
17

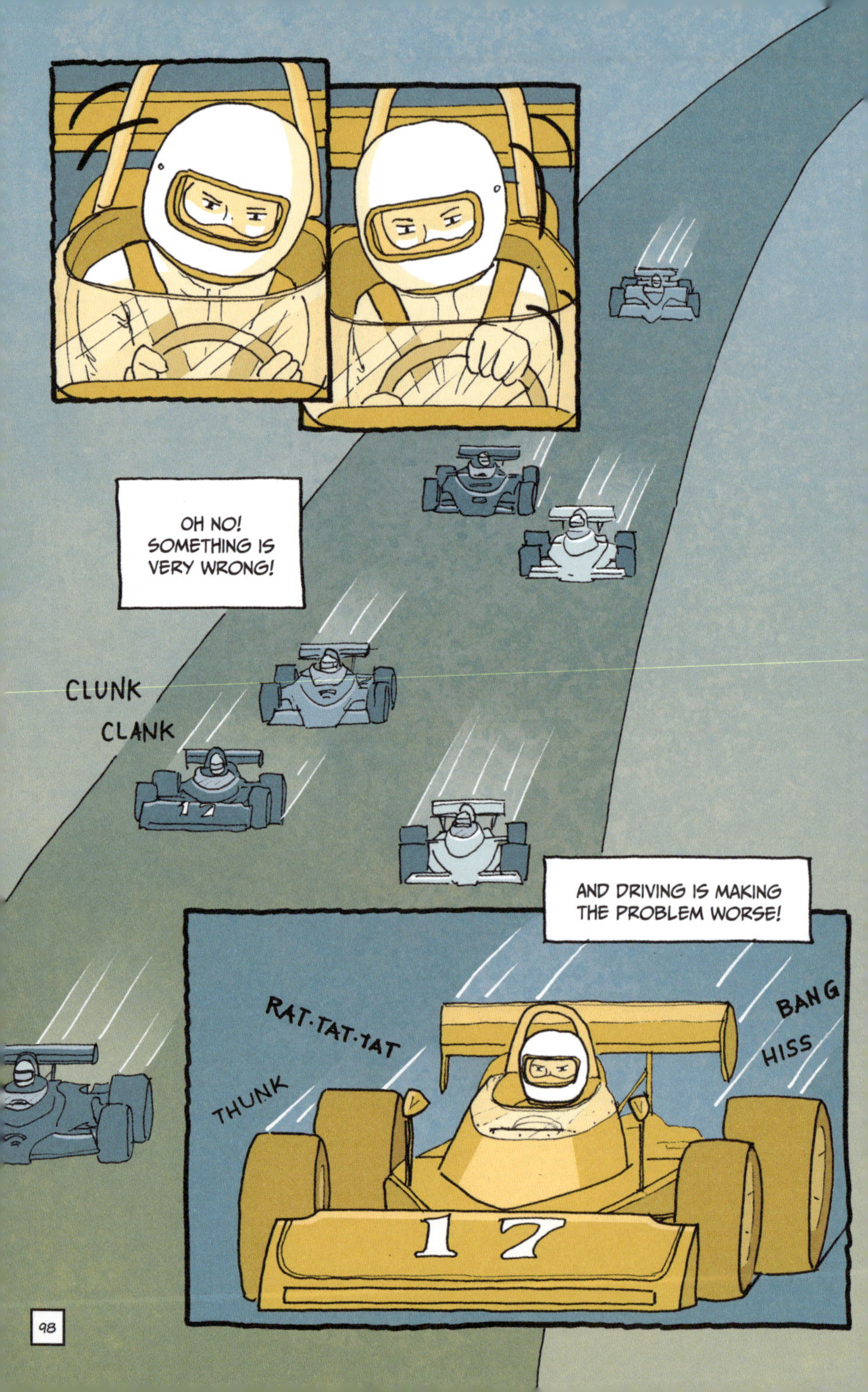
OH NO! SOMETHING IS VERY WRONG!
CLUNK
CLANK
AND DRIVING IS MAKING THE PROBLEM WORSE!
RAT-TAT-TAT
THUNK
BANG
HISS
17

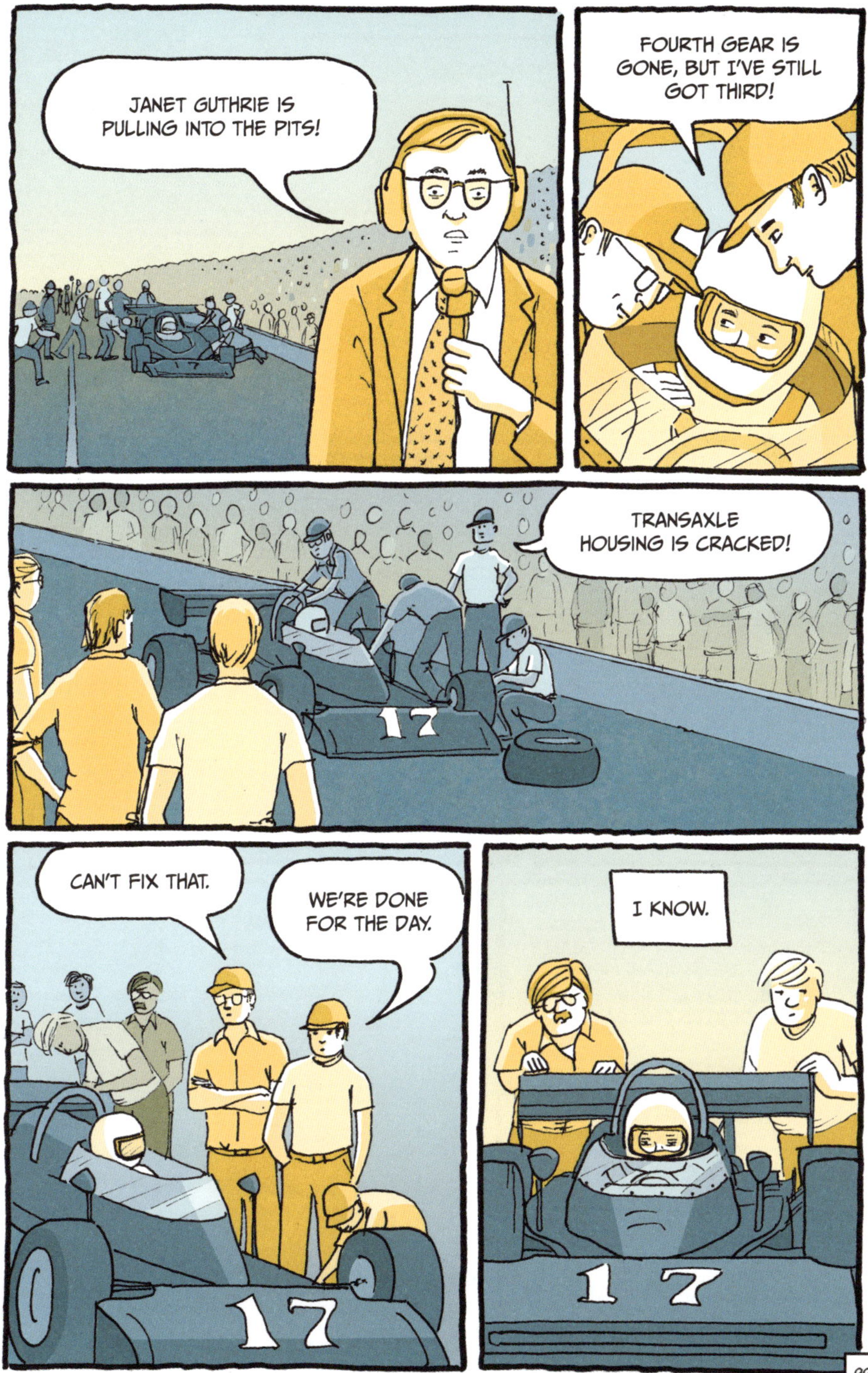
JANET GUTHRIE IS PULLING INTO THE PITS!
FOURTH GEAR IS GONE, BUT I'VE STILL GOT THIRD!
TRANSAXLE HOUSING IS CRACKED!
17
CAN'T FIX THAT.
WE'RE DONE FOR THE DAY.
17
I KNOW.
17

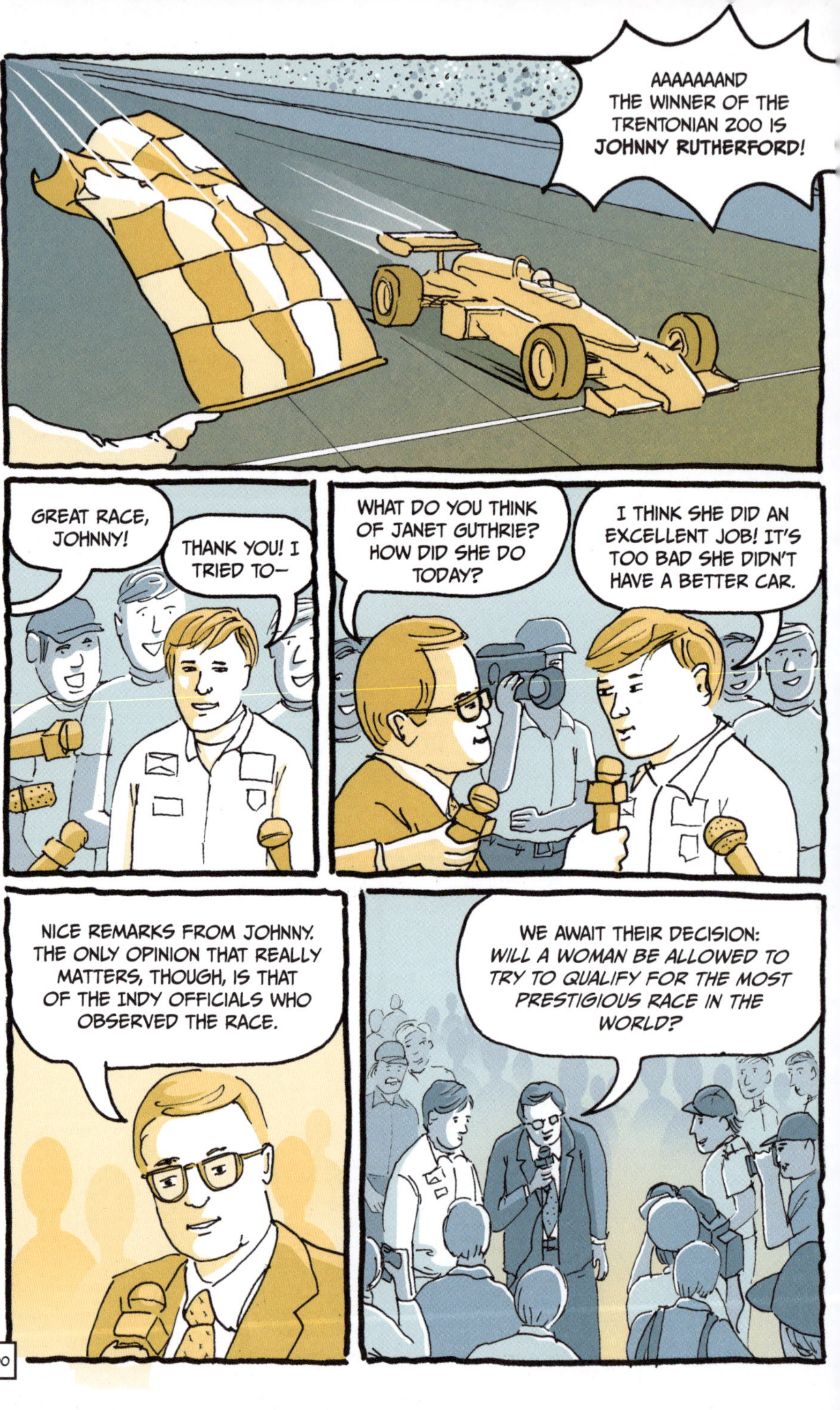
AAAAAAAND THE WINNER OF THE TRENTONIAN 200 IS **JOHNNY RUTHERFORD!**
GREAT RACE, JOHNNY!
THANK YOU! I TRIED TO—
WHAT DO YOU THINK OF JANET GUTHRIE? HOW DID SHE DO TODAY?
I THINK SHE DID AN EXCELLENT JOB! IT'S TOO BAD SHE DIDN'T HAVE A BETTER CAR.
NICE REMARKS FROM JOHNNY. THE ONLY OPINION THAT REALLY MATTERS, THOUGH, IS THAT OF THE INDY OFFICIALS WHO OBSERVED THE RACE.
WE AWAIT THEIR DECISION: *WILL A WOMAN BE ALLOWED TO TRY TO QUALIFY FOR THE MOST PRESTIGIOUS RACE IN THE WORLD?*

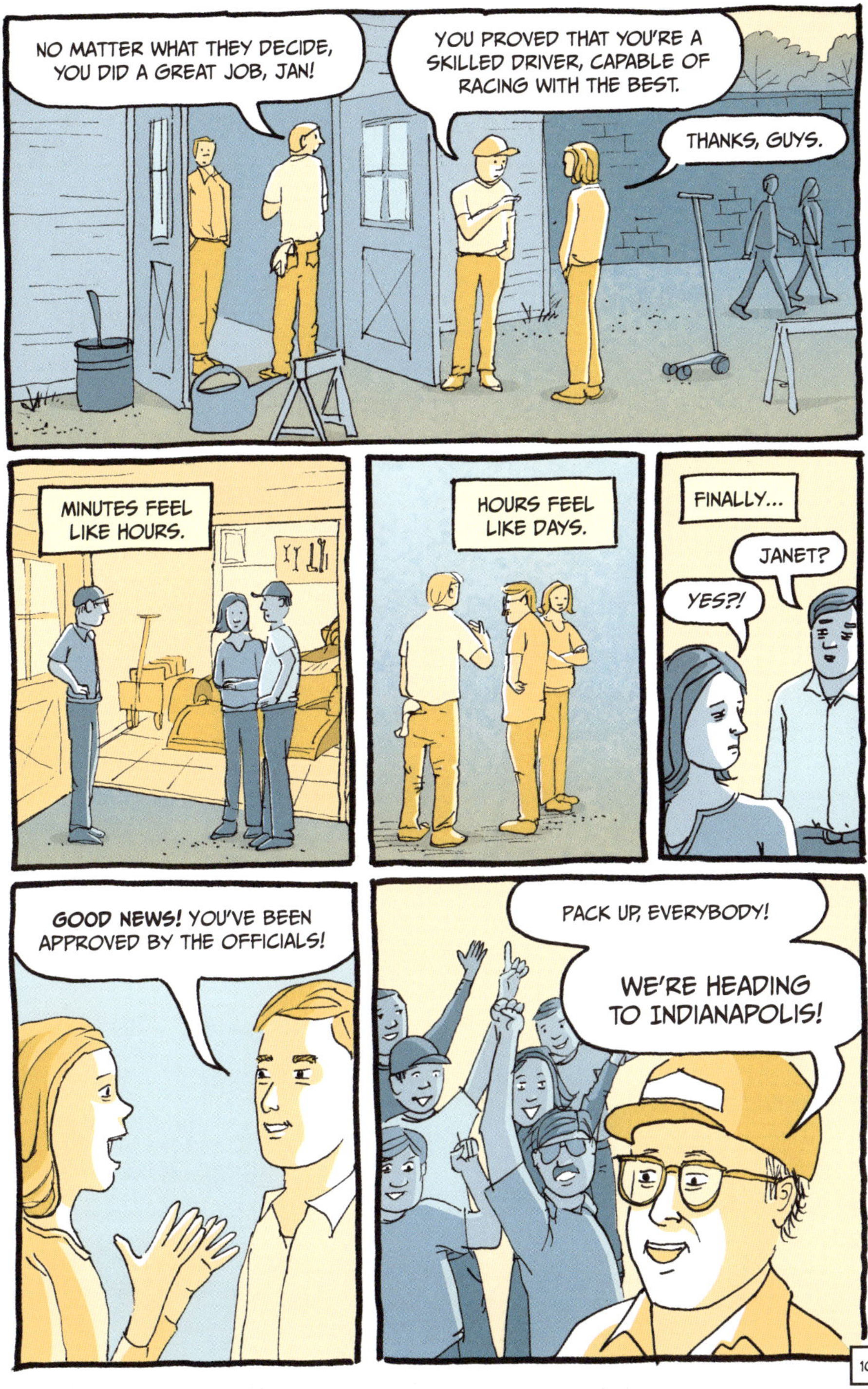
NO MATTER WHAT THEY DECIDE, YOU DID A GREAT JOB, JAN!
YOU PROVED THAT YOU'RE A SKILLED DRIVER, CAPABLE OF RACING WITH THE BEST.
THANKS, GUYS.
MINUTES FEEL LIKE HOURS.
HOURS FEEL LIKE DAYS.
FINALLY...
JANET?
YES?!
GOOD NEWS! YOU'VE BEEN APPROVED BY THE OFFICIALS!
PACK UP, EVERYBODY!
WE'RE HEADING TO INDIANAPOLIS!

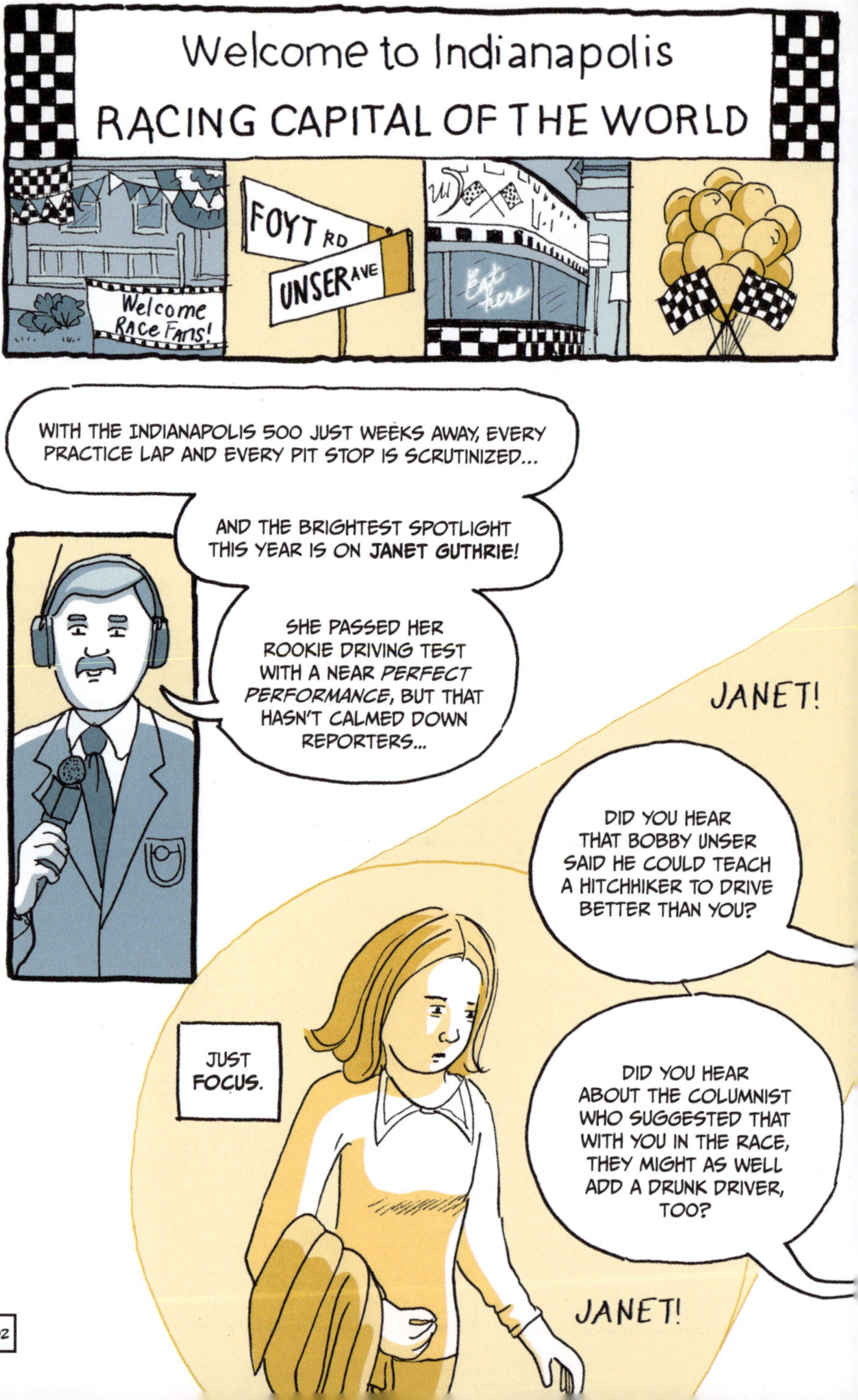

Welcome to Indianapolis
RACING CAPITAL OF THE WORLD
Welcome Race Fans!
FOYT RD
UNSER AVE
Eat here
WITH THE INDIANAPOLIS 500 JUST WEEKS AWAY, EVERY PRACTICE LAP AND EVERY PIT STOP IS SCRUTINIZED...
AND THE BRIGHTEST SPOTLIGHT THIS YEAR IS ON JANET GUTHRIE!
SHE PASSED HER ROOKIE DRIVING TEST WITH A NEAR *PERFECT PERFORMANCE*, BUT THAT HASN'T CALMED DOWN REPORTERS...
JANET!
DID YOU HEAR THAT BOBBY UNSER SAID HE COULD TEACH A HITCHHIKER TO DRIVE BETTER THAN YOU?
JUST FOCUS.
DID YOU HEAR ABOUT THE COLUMNIST WHO SUGGESTED THAT WITH YOU IN THE RACE, THEY MIGHT AS WELL ADD A DRUNK DRIVER, TOO?
JANET!

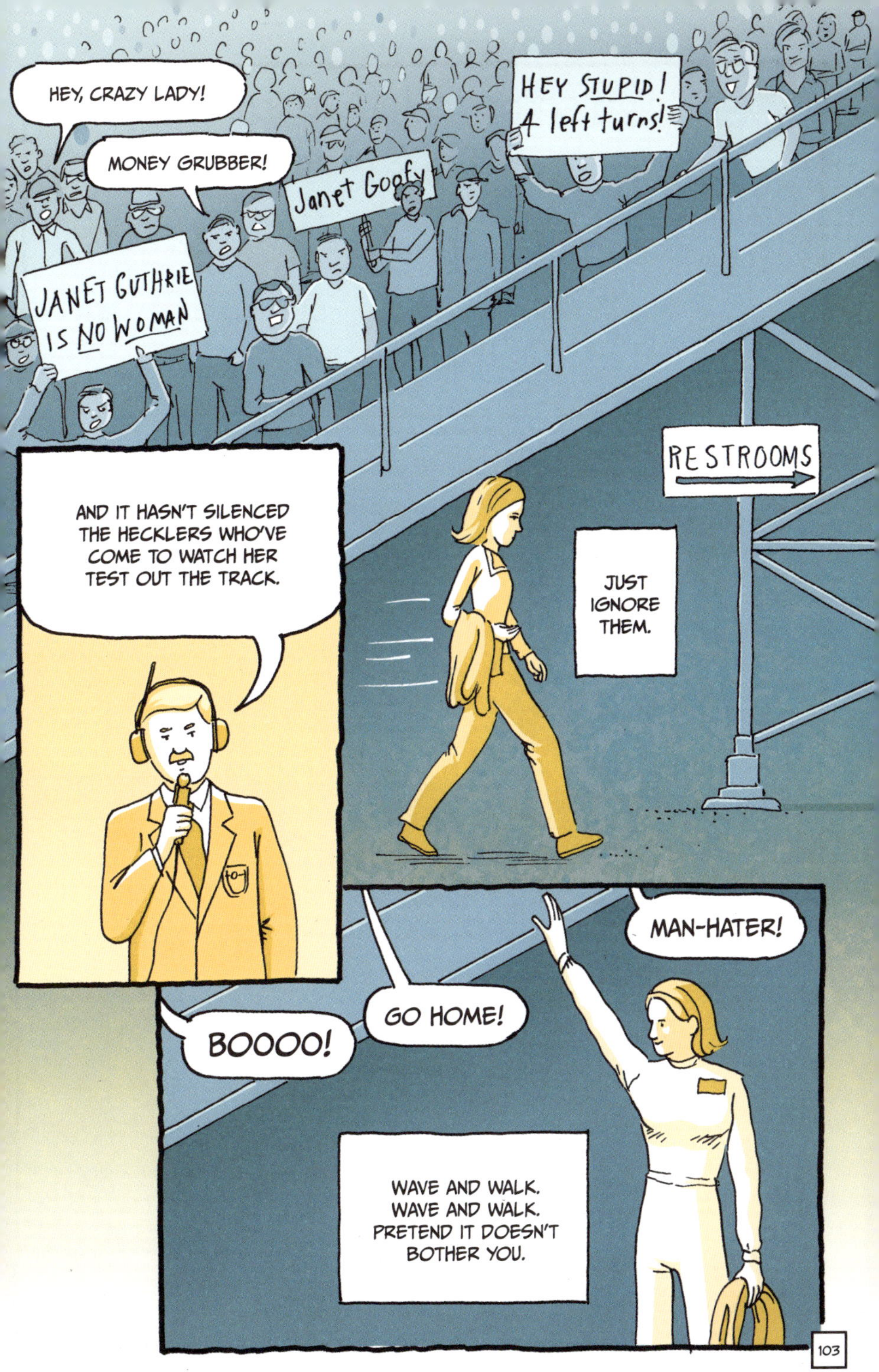
HEY, CRAZY LADY!
MONEY GRUBBER!
Janet Goofy
HEY STUPID! 4 left turns!
JANET GUTHRIE IS NO WOMAN
AND IT HASN'T SILENCED THE HECKLERS WHO'VE COME TO WATCH HER TEST OUT THE TRACK.
RESTROOMS
JUST IGNORE THEM.
MAN-HATER!
GO HOME!
BOOOO!
WAVE AND WALK. WAVE AND WALK. PRETEND IT DOESN'T BOTHER YOU.

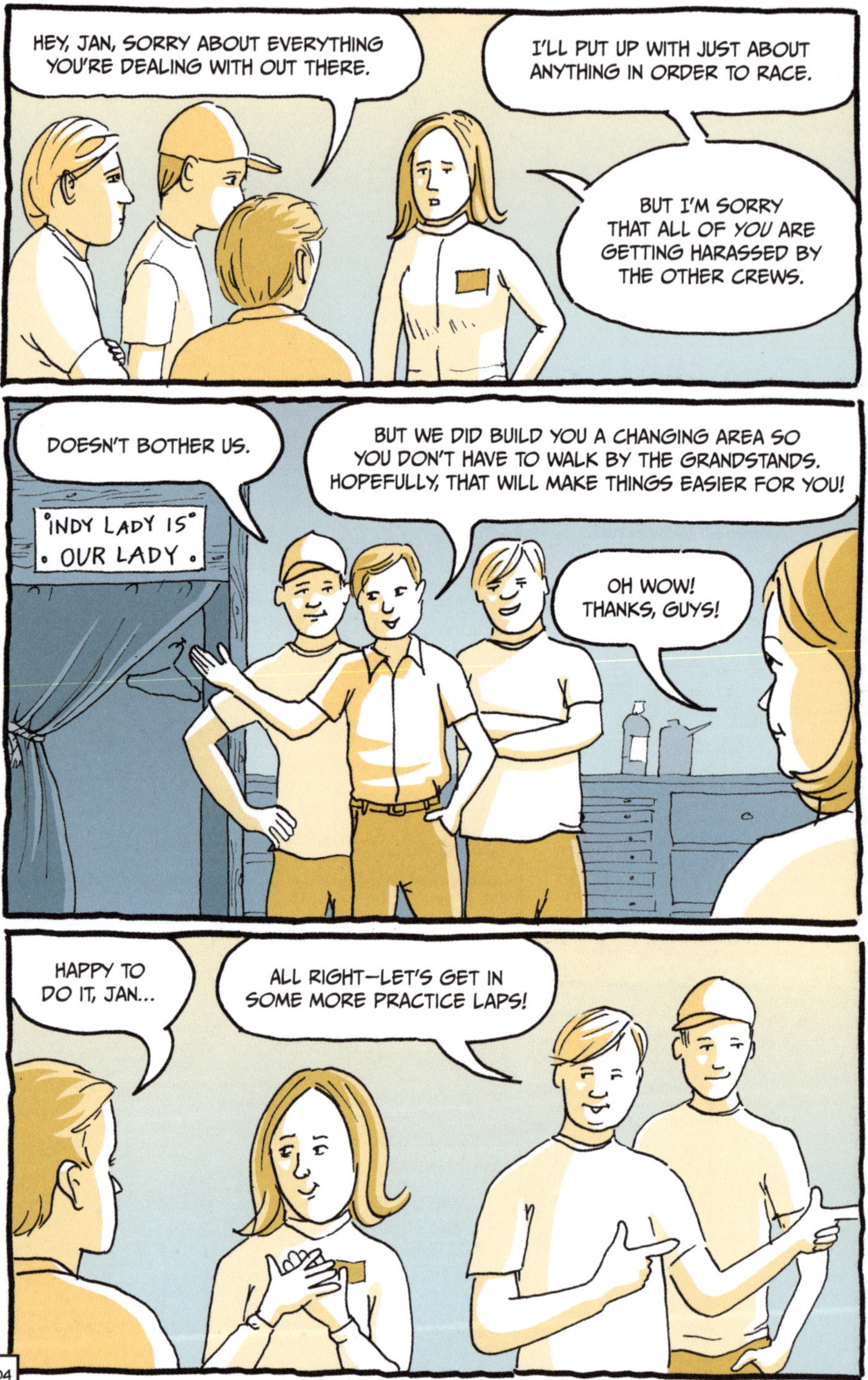
HEY, JAN, SORRY ABOUT EVERYTHING YOU'RE DEALING WITH OUT THERE.
I'LL PUT UP WITH JUST ABOUT ANYTHING IN ORDER TO RACE.
BUT I'M SORRY THAT ALL OF *YOU* ARE GETTING HARASSED BY THE OTHER CREWS.
DOESN'T BOTHER US.
BUT WE DID BUILD YOU A CHANGING AREA SO YOU DON'T HAVE TO WALK BY THE GRANDSTANDS. HOPEFULLY, THAT WILL MAKE THINGS EASIER FOR YOU!
INDY LADY IS OUR LADY
OH WOW! THANKS, GUYS!
HAPPY TO DO IT, JAN...
ALL RIGHT—LET'S GET IN SOME MORE PRACTICE LAPS!

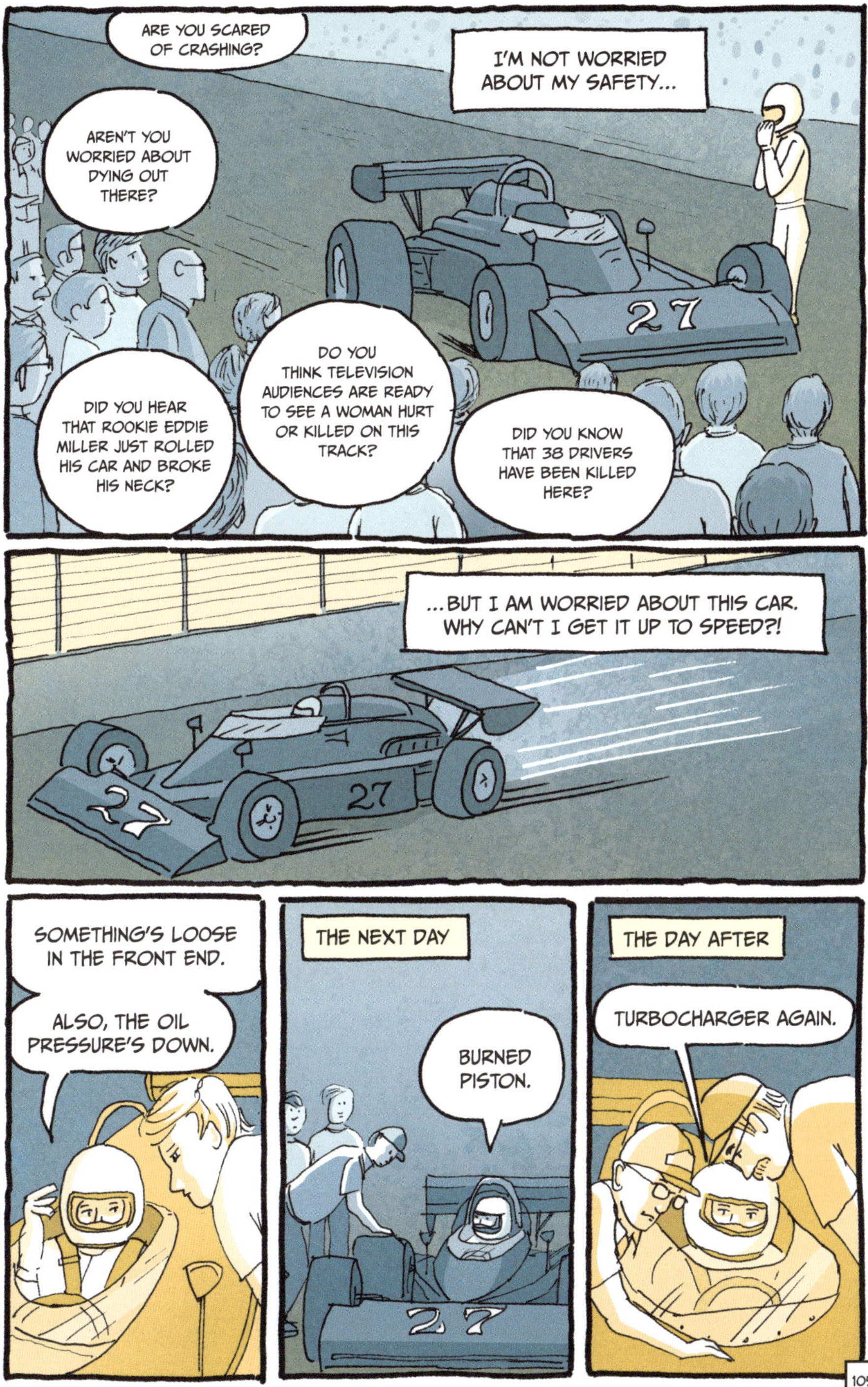
ARE YOU SCARED OF CRASHING?
I'M NOT WORRIED ABOUT MY SAFETY...
AREN'T YOU WORRIED ABOUT DYING OUT THERE?
DID YOU HEAR THAT ROOKIE EDDIE MILLER JUST ROLLED HIS CAR AND BROKE HIS NECK?
DO YOU THINK TELEVISION AUDIENCES ARE READY TO SEE A WOMAN HURT OR KILLED ON THIS TRACK?
DID YOU KNOW THAT 38 DRIVERS HAVE BEEN KILLED HERE?
27
...BUT I AM WORRIED ABOUT THIS CAR. WHY CAN'T I GET IT UP TO SPEED?!
27
27
SOMETHING'S LOOSE IN THE FRONT END.
ALSO, THE OIL PRESSURE'S DOWN.
THE NEXT DAY
BURNED PISTON.
27
THE DAY AFTER
TURBOCHARGER AGAIN.

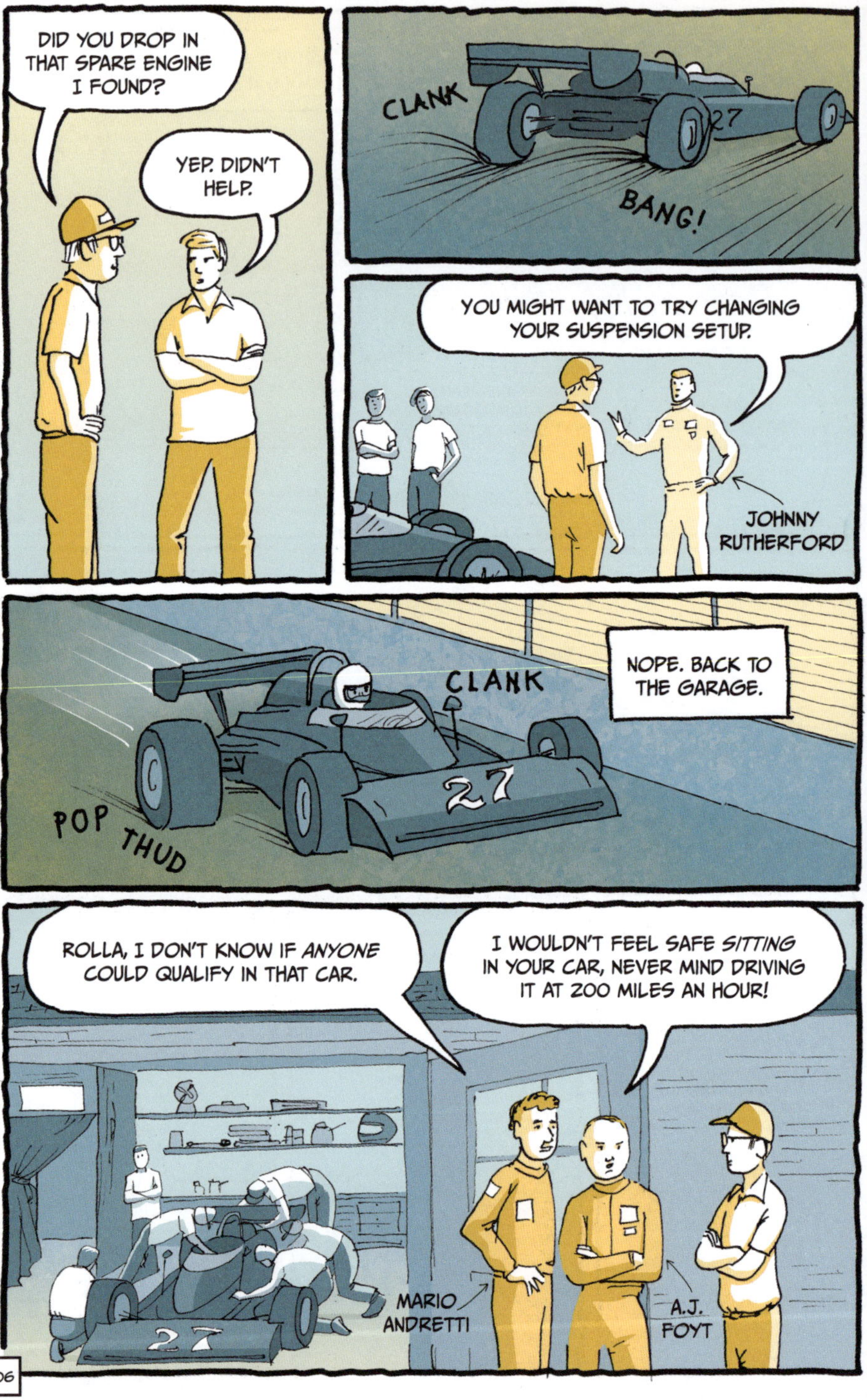
DID YOU DROP IN THAT SPARE ENGINE I FOUND?
YEP. DIDN'T HELP.
CLANK
BANG!
YOU MIGHT WANT TO TRY CHANGING YOUR SUSPENSION SETUP.
JOHNNY RUTHERFORD
CLANK
NOPE. BACK TO THE GARAGE.
POP
THUD
ROLLA, I DON'T KNOW IF *ANYONE* COULD QUALIFY IN THAT CAR.
I WOULDN'T FEEL SAFE *SITTING* IN YOUR CAR, NEVER MIND DRIVING IT AT 200 MILES AN HOUR!
MARIO ANDRETTI
A.J. FOYT

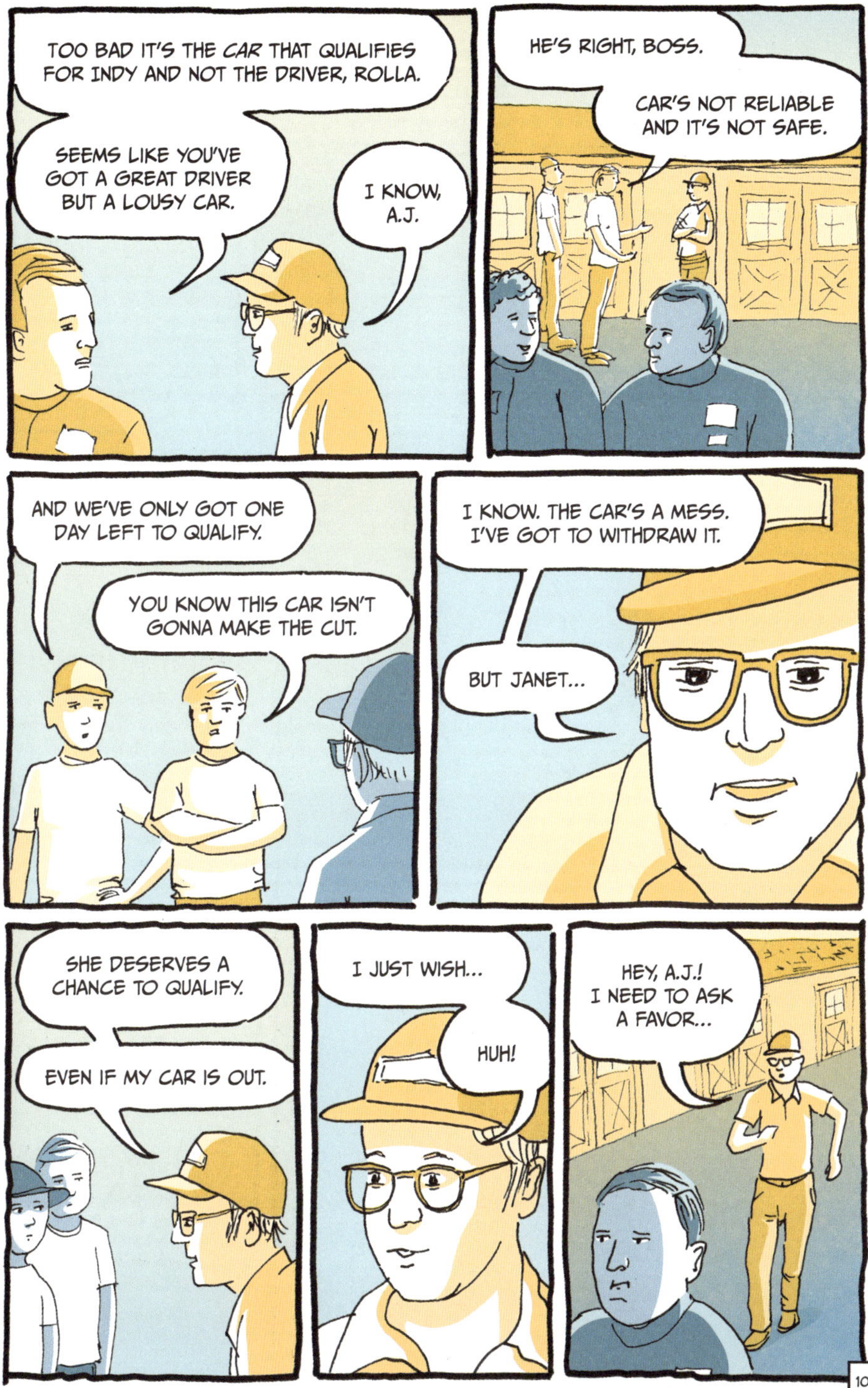
TOO BAD IT'S THE *CAR* THAT QUALIFIES FOR INDY AND NOT THE DRIVER, ROLLA.
SEEMS LIKE YOU'VE GOT A GREAT DRIVER BUT A LOUSY CAR.
I KNOW, A.J.
HE'S RIGHT, BOSS.
CAR'S NOT RELIABLE AND IT'S NOT SAFE.
AND WE'VE ONLY GOT ONE DAY LEFT TO QUALIFY.
YOU KNOW THIS CAR ISN'T GONNA MAKE THE CUT.
I KNOW. THE CAR'S A MESS. I'VE GOT TO WITHDRAW IT.
BUT JANET...
SHE DESERVES A CHANCE TO QUALIFY.
EVEN IF MY CAR IS OUT.
I JUST WISH...
HUH!
HEY, A.J.! I NEED TO ASK A FAVOR...

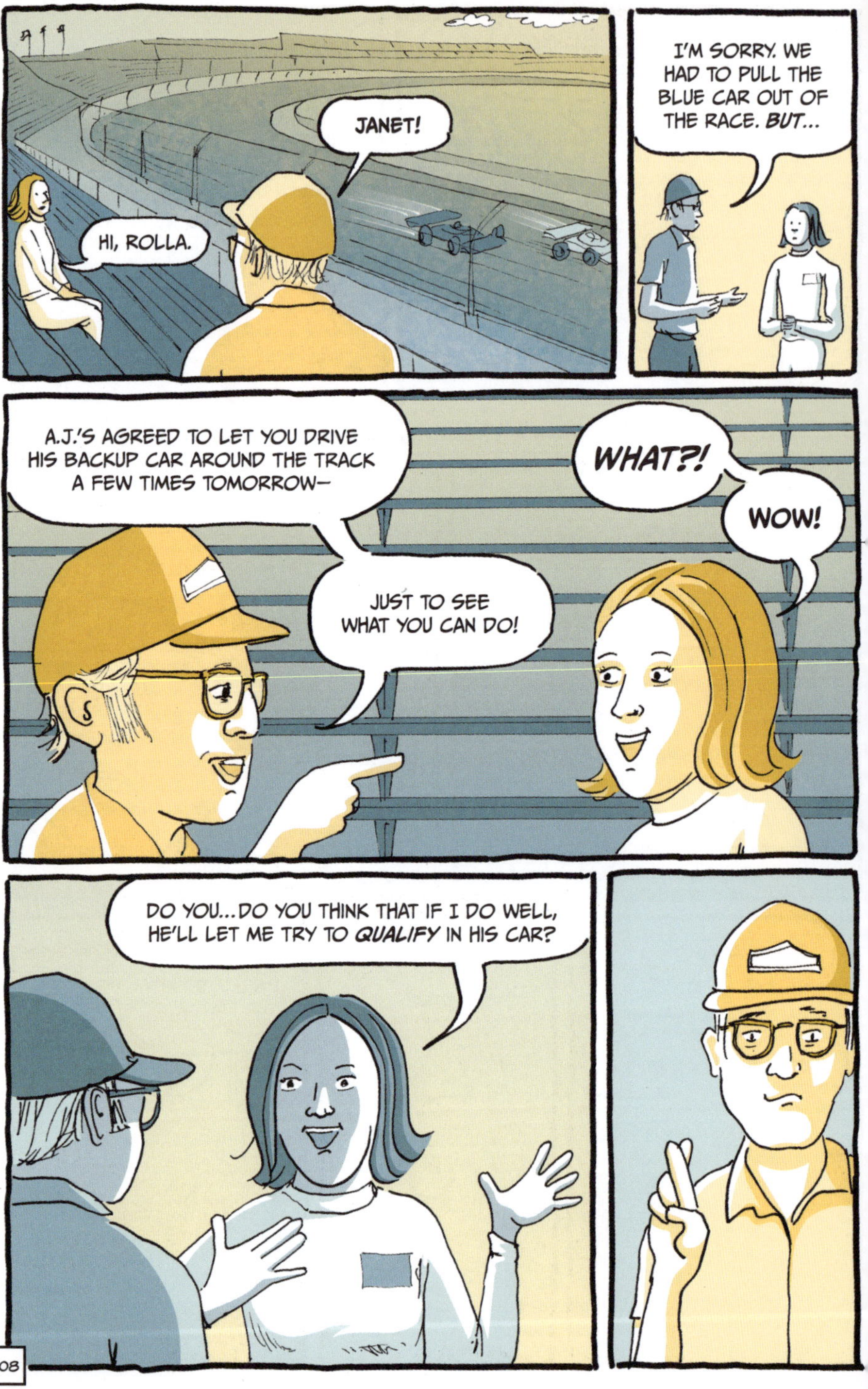
JANET!
HI, ROLLA.
I'M SORRY. WE HAD TO PULL THE BLUE CAR OUT OF THE RACE. *BUT*...
A.J.'S AGREED TO LET YOU DRIVE HIS BACKUP CAR AROUND THE TRACK A FEW TIMES TOMORROW–
JUST TO SEE WHAT YOU CAN DO!
WHAT?!
WOW!
DO YOU...DO YOU THINK THAT IF I DO WELL, HE'LL LET ME TRY TO *QUALIFY* IN HIS CAR?

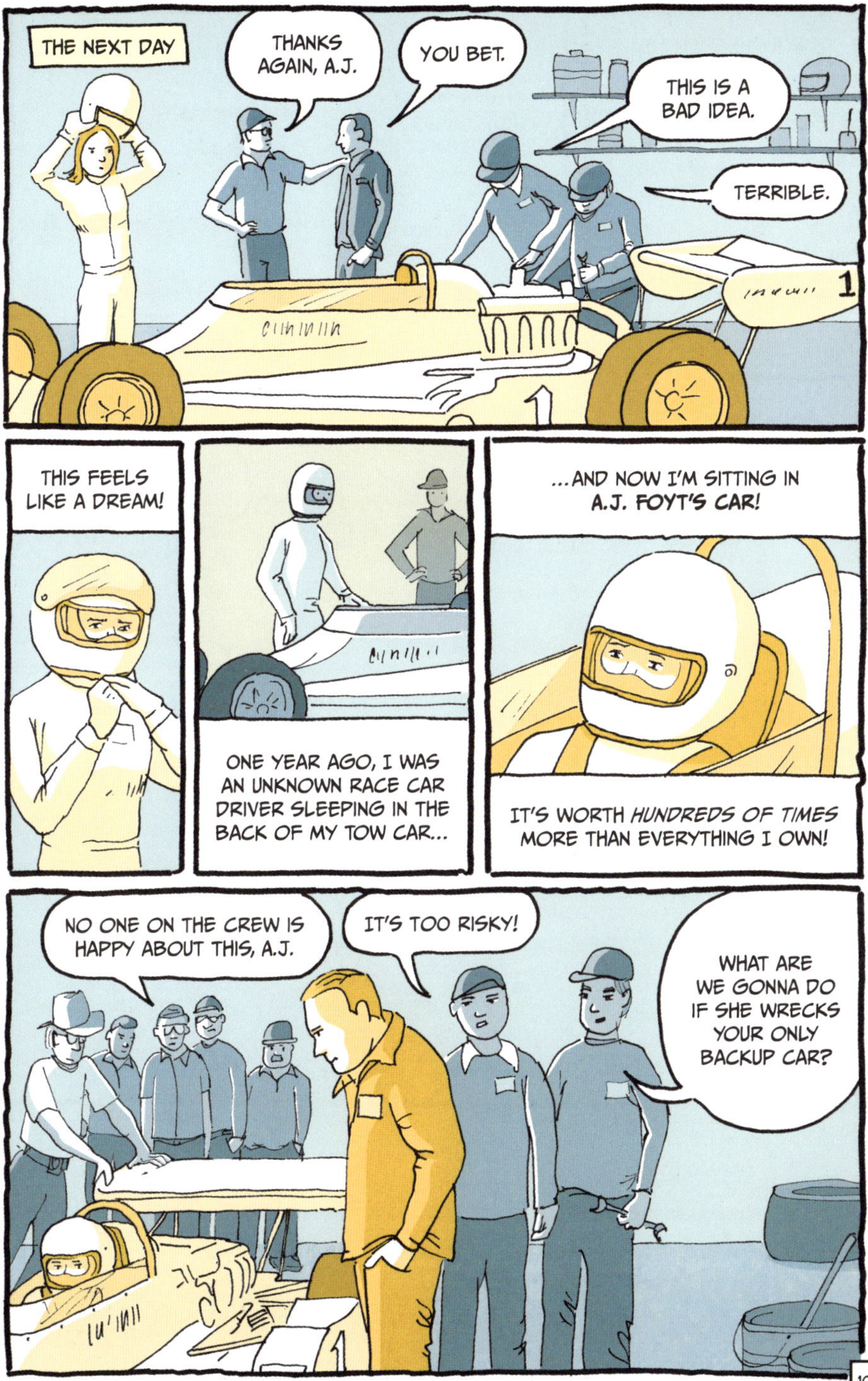
THE NEXT DAY
THANKS AGAIN, A.J.
YOU BET.
THIS IS A BAD IDEA.
TERRIBLE.
THIS FEELS LIKE A DREAM!
ONE YEAR AGO, I WAS AN UNKNOWN RACE CAR DRIVER SLEEPING IN THE BACK OF MY TOW CAR...
...AND NOW I'M SITTING IN A.J. FOYT'S CAR!
IT'S WORTH *HUNDREDS OF TIMES* MORE THAN EVERYTHING I OWN!
NO ONE ON THE CREW IS HAPPY ABOUT THIS, A.J.
IT'S TOO RISKY!
WHAT ARE WE GONNA DO IF SHE WRECKS YOUR ONLY BACKUP CAR?

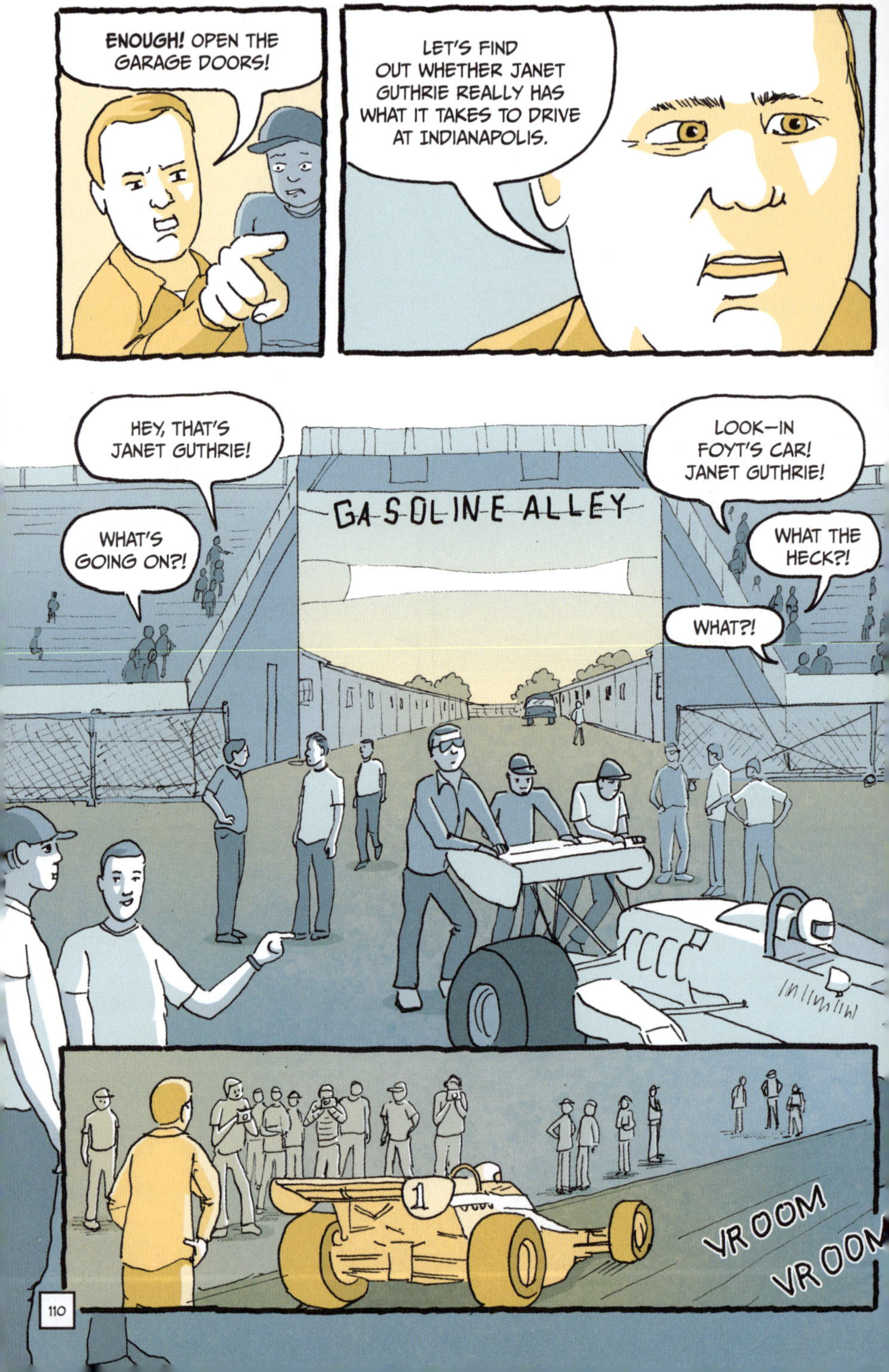
ENOUGH! OPEN THE GARAGE DOORS!
LET'S FIND OUT WHETHER JANET GUTHRIE REALLY HAS WHAT IT TAKES TO DRIVE AT INDIANAPOLIS.
HEY, THAT'S JANET GUTHRIE!
WHAT'S GOING ON?!
GASOLINE ALLEY
LOOK—IN FOYT'S CAR! JANET GUTHRIE!
WHAT THE HECK?!
WHAT?!
VROOM
VROOM

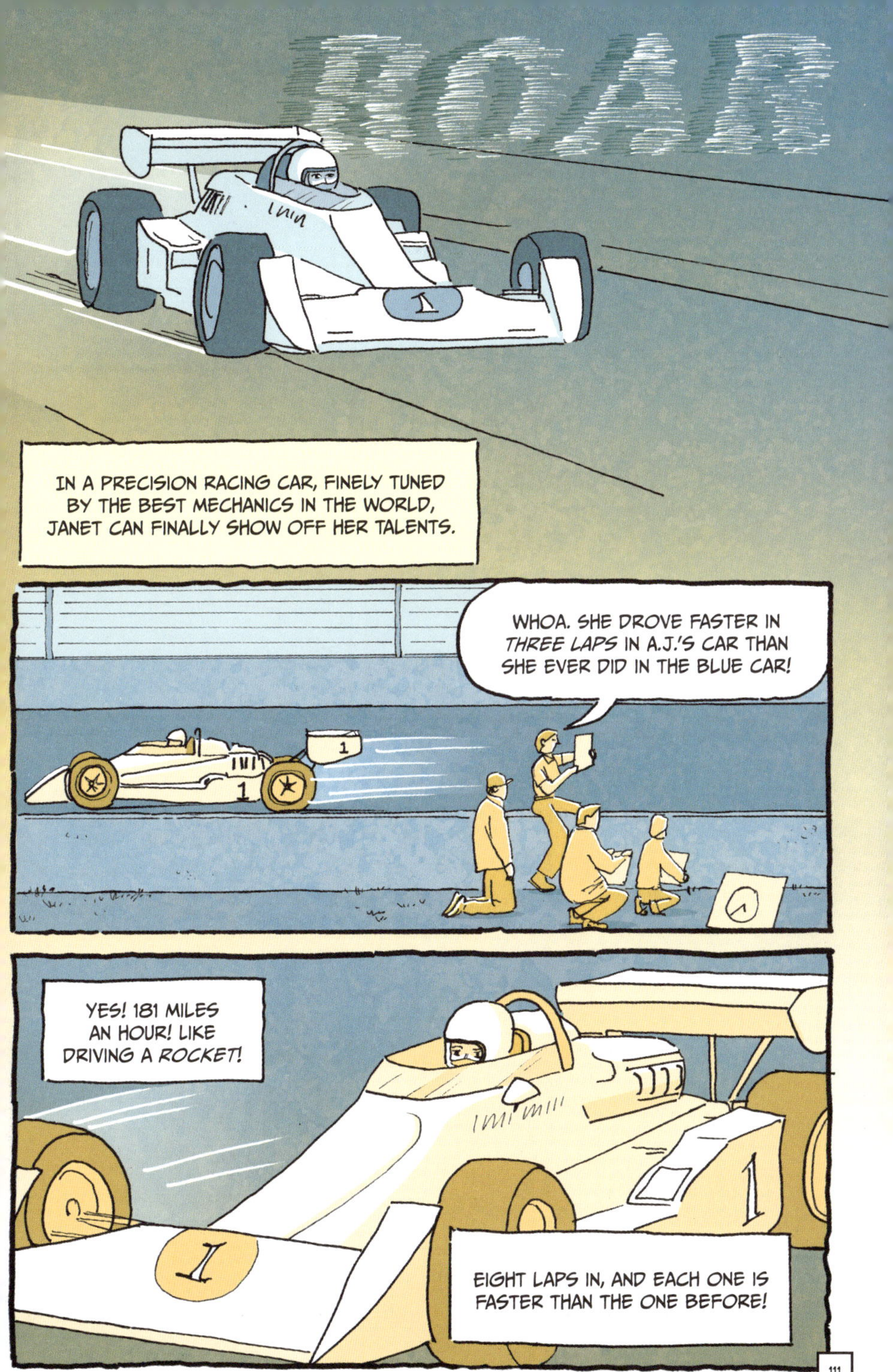
ROAR
IN A PRECISION RACING CAR, FINELY TUNED BY THE BEST MECHANICS IN THE WORLD, JANET CAN FINALLY SHOW OFF HER TALENTS.
WHOA. SHE DROVE FASTER IN *THREE LAPS* IN A.J.'S CAR THAN SHE EVER DID IN THE BLUE CAR!
YES! 181 MILES AN HOUR! LIKE DRIVING A *ROCKET*!
EIGHT LAPS IN, AND EACH ONE IS FASTER THAN THE ONE BEFORE!

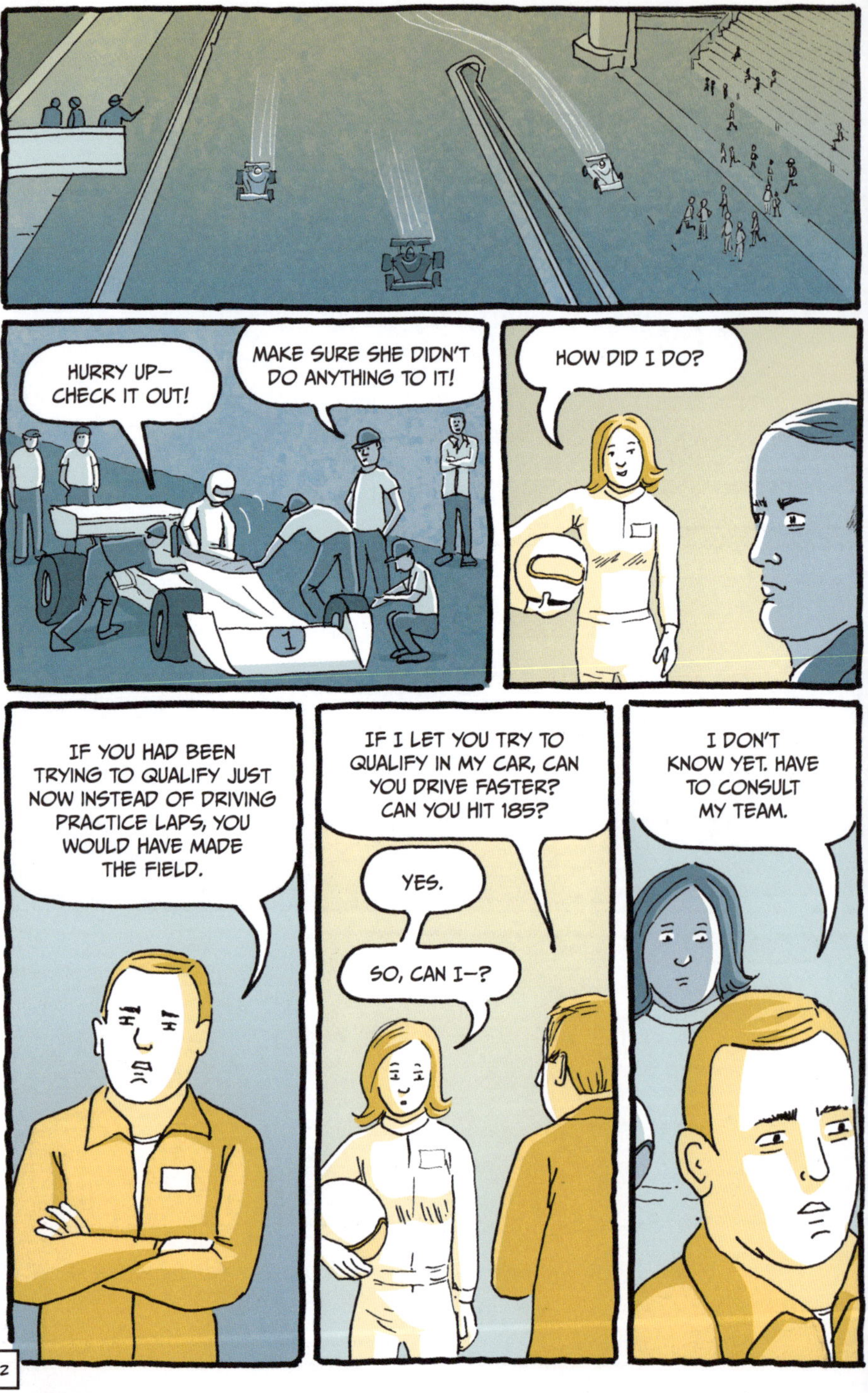
HURRY UP—
CHECK IT OUT!
MAKE SURE SHE DIDN'T DO ANYTHING TO IT!
HOW DID I DO?
IF YOU HAD BEEN TRYING TO QUALIFY JUST NOW INSTEAD OF DRIVING PRACTICE LAPS, YOU WOULD HAVE MADE THE FIELD.
IF I LET YOU TRY TO QUALIFY IN MY CAR, CAN YOU DRIVE FASTER? CAN YOU HIT 185?
YES.
SO, CAN I—?
I DON'T KNOW YET. HAVE TO CONSULT MY TEAM.

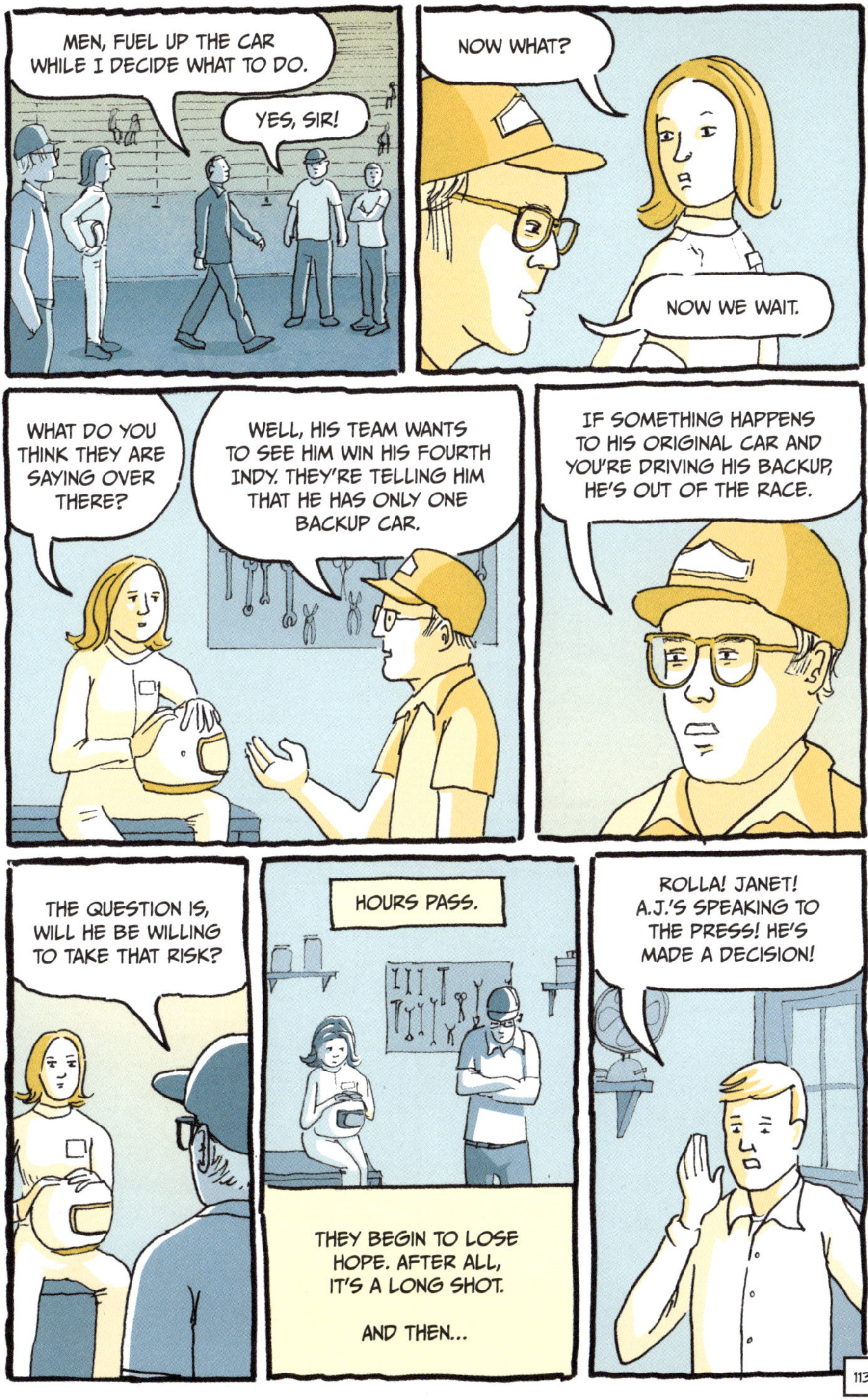
MEN, FUEL UP THE CAR WHILE I DECIDE WHAT TO DO.
YES, SIR!
NOW WHAT?
NOW WE WAIT.
WHAT DO YOU THINK THEY ARE SAYING OVER THERE?
WELL, HIS TEAM WANTS TO SEE HIM WIN HIS FOURTH INDY. THEY'RE TELLING HIM THAT HE HAS ONLY ONE BACKUP CAR.
IF SOMETHING HAPPENS TO HIS ORIGINAL CAR AND YOU'RE DRIVING HIS BACKUP, HE'S OUT OF THE RACE.
THE QUESTION IS, WILL HE BE WILLING TO TAKE THAT RISK?
HOURS PASS.
THEY BEGIN TO LOSE HOPE. AFTER ALL, IT'S A LONG SHOT.
AND THEN...
ROLLA! JANET! A.J.'S SPEAKING TO THE PRESS! HE'S MADE A DECISION!

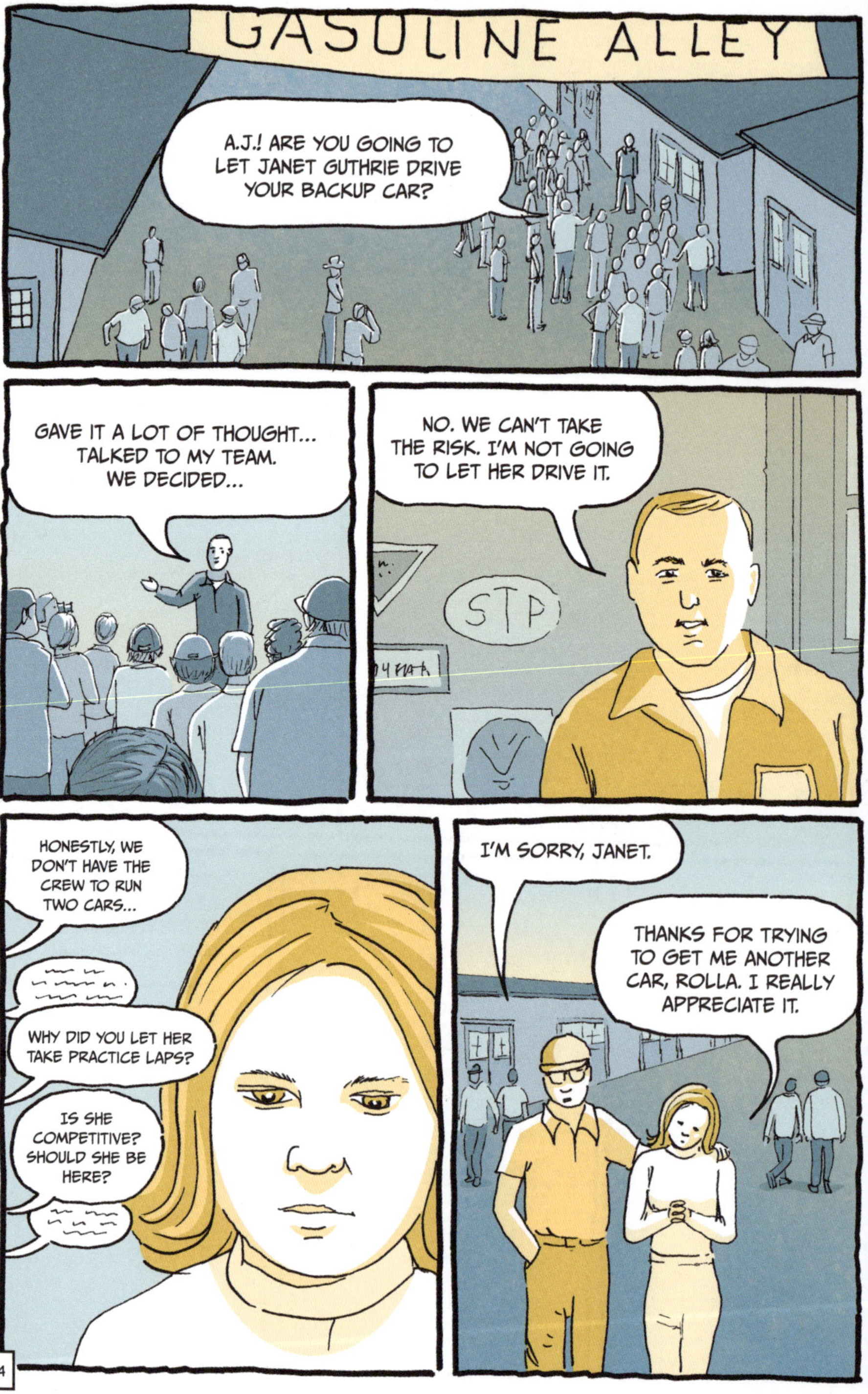

GASOLINE ALLEY
A.J.! ARE YOU GOING TO LET JANET GUTHRIE DRIVE YOUR BACKUP CAR?
GAVE IT A LOT OF THOUGHT... TALKED TO MY TEAM. WE DECIDED...
NO. WE CAN'T TAKE THE RISK. I'M NOT GOING TO LET HER DRIVE IT.
STP
HONESTLY, WE DON'T HAVE THE CREW TO RUN TWO CARS...
WHY DID YOU LET HER TAKE PRACTICE LAPS?
IS SHE COMPETITIVE? SHOULD SHE BE HERE?
I'M SORRY, JANET.
THANKS FOR TRYING TO GET ME ANOTHER CAR, ROLLA. I REALLY APPRECIATE IT.

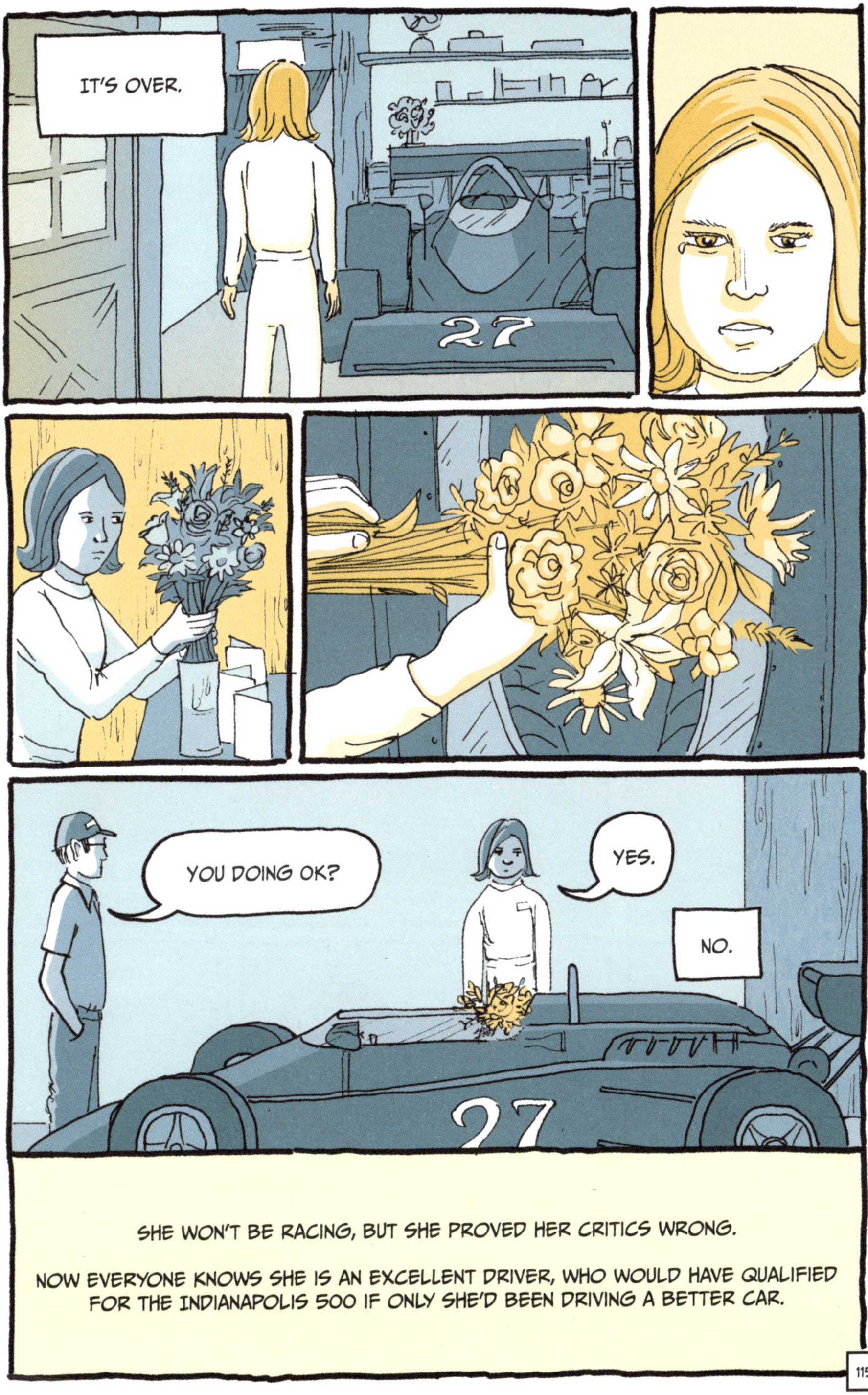
IT'S OVER.
YOU DOING OK?
YES.
NO.
SHE WON'T BE RACING, BUT SHE PROVED HER CRITICS WRONG.
NOW EVERYONE KNOWS SHE IS AN EXCELLENT DRIVER, WHO WOULD HAVE QUALIFIED FOR THE INDIANAPOLIS 500 IF ONLY SHE'D BEEN DRIVING A BETTER CAR.

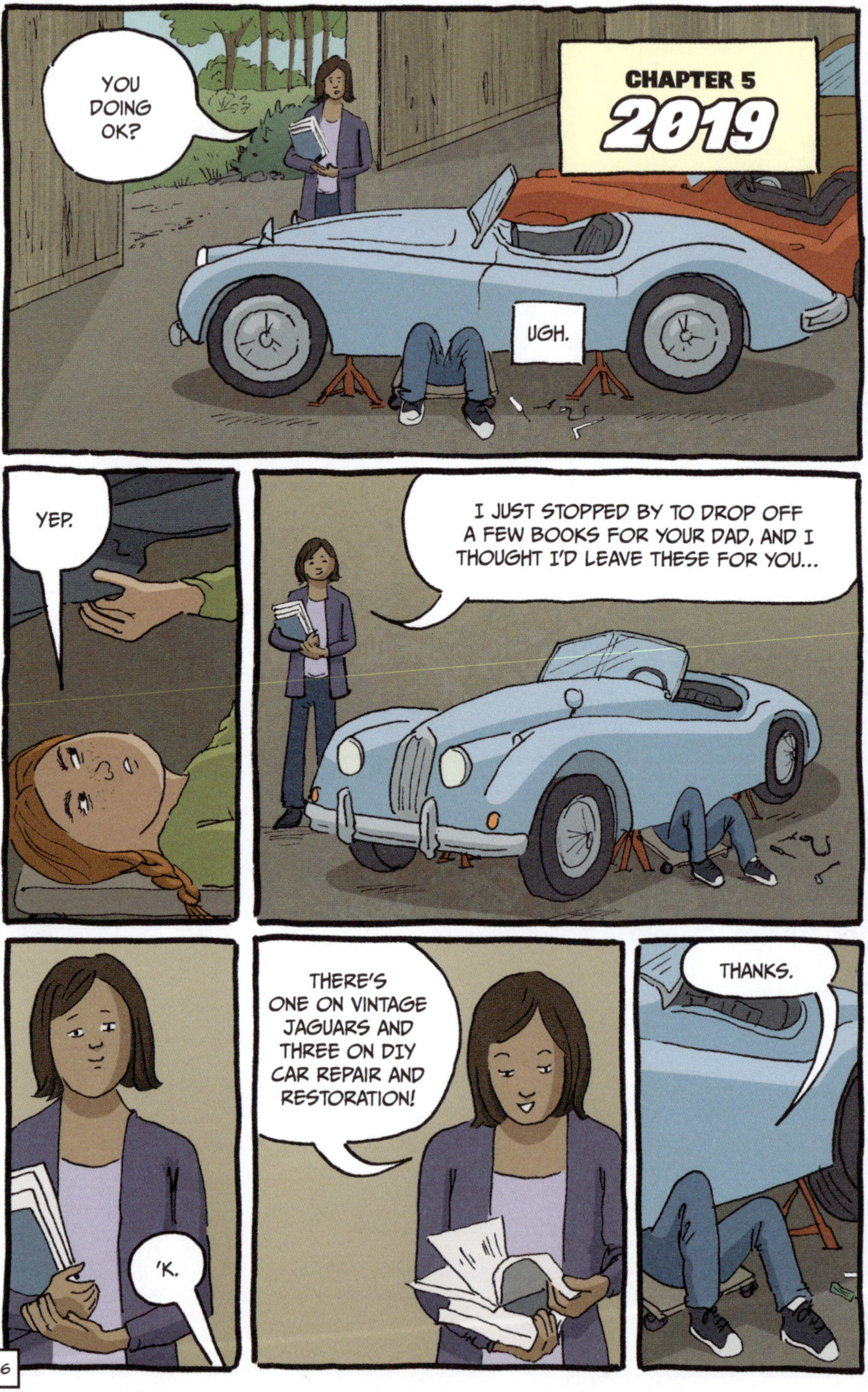
CHAPTER 5
2019
YOU DOING OK?
UGH.
YEP.
I JUST STOPPED BY TO DROP OFF A FEW BOOKS FOR YOUR DAD, AND I THOUGHT I'D LEAVE THESE FOR YOU...
'K.
THERE'S ONE ON VINTAGE JAGUARS AND THREE ON DIY CAR REPAIR AND RESTORATION!
THANKS.

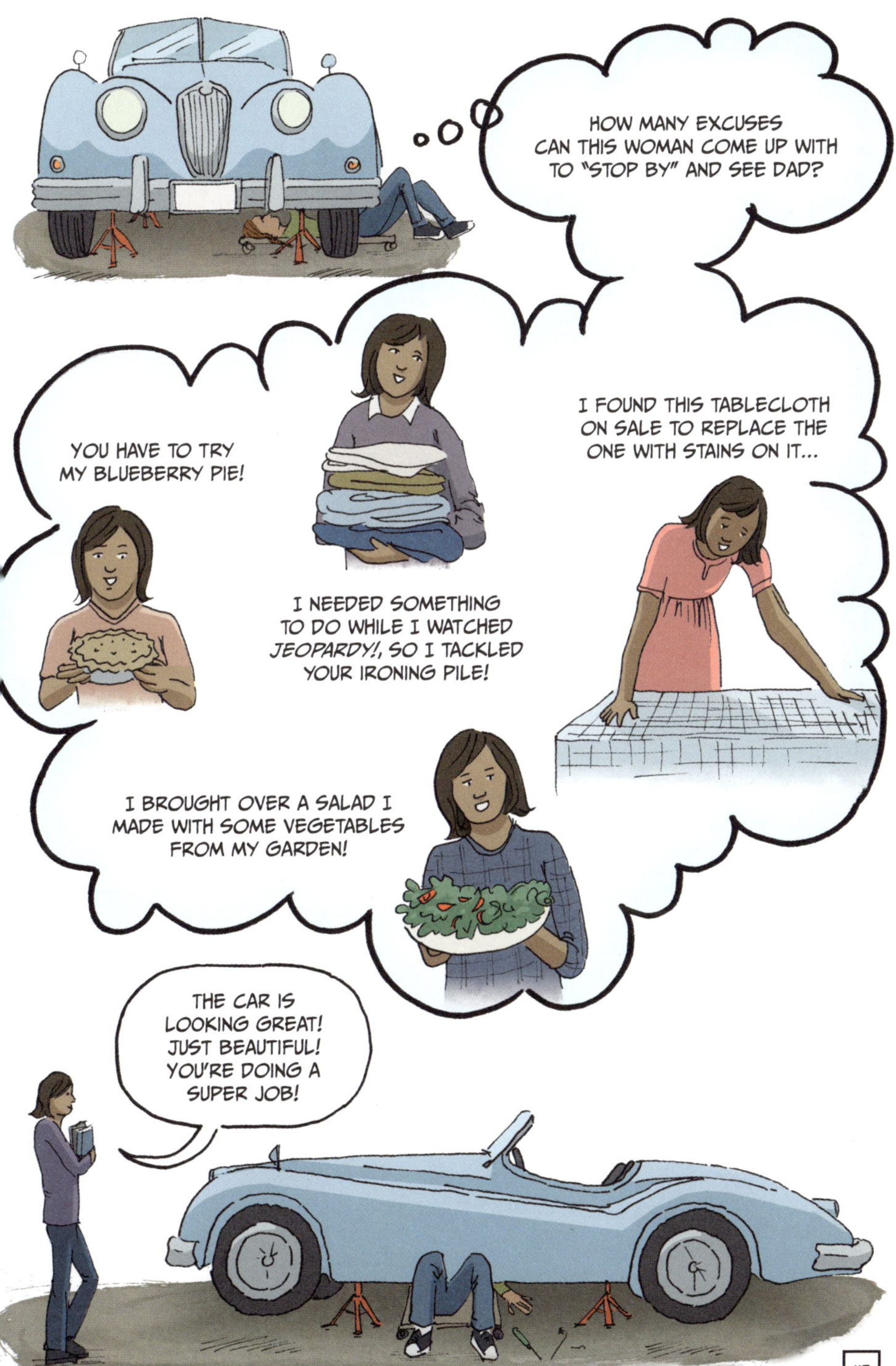
HOW MANY EXCUSES CAN THIS WOMAN COME UP WITH TO "STOP BY" AND SEE DAD?
YOU HAVE TO TRY MY BLUEBERRY PIE!
I FOUND THIS TABLECLOTH ON SALE TO REPLACE THE ONE WITH STAINS ON IT...
I NEEDED SOMETHING TO DO WHILE I WATCHED *JEOPARDY!*, SO I TACKLED YOUR IRONING PILE!
I BROUGHT OVER A SALAD I MADE WITH SOME VEGETABLES FROM MY GARDEN!
THE CAR IS LOOKING GREAT! JUST BEAUTIFUL! YOU'RE DOING A SUPER JOB!

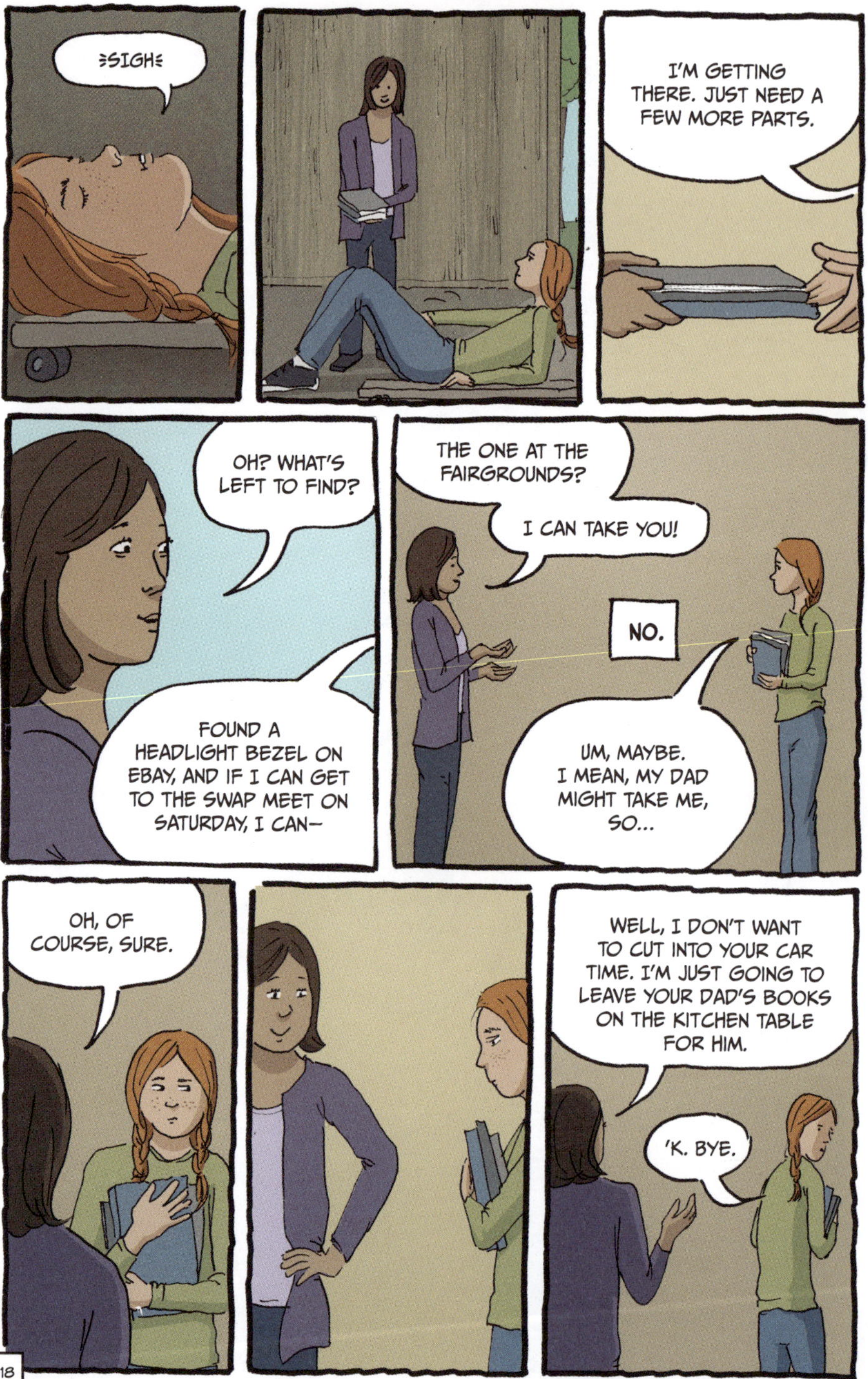
SIGH
I'M GETTING THERE. JUST NEED A FEW MORE PARTS.
OH? WHAT'S LEFT TO FIND?
FOUND A HEADLIGHT BEZEL ON EBAY, AND IF I CAN GET TO THE SWAP MEET ON SATURDAY, I CAN–
THE ONE AT THE FAIRGROUNDS?
I CAN TAKE YOU!
NO.
UM, MAYBE. I MEAN, MY DAD MIGHT TAKE ME, SO...
OH, OF COURSE, SURE.
WELL, I DON'T WANT TO CUT INTO YOUR CAR TIME. I'M JUST GOING TO LEAVE YOUR DAD'S BOOKS ON THE KITCHEN TABLE FOR HIM.
'K. BYE.

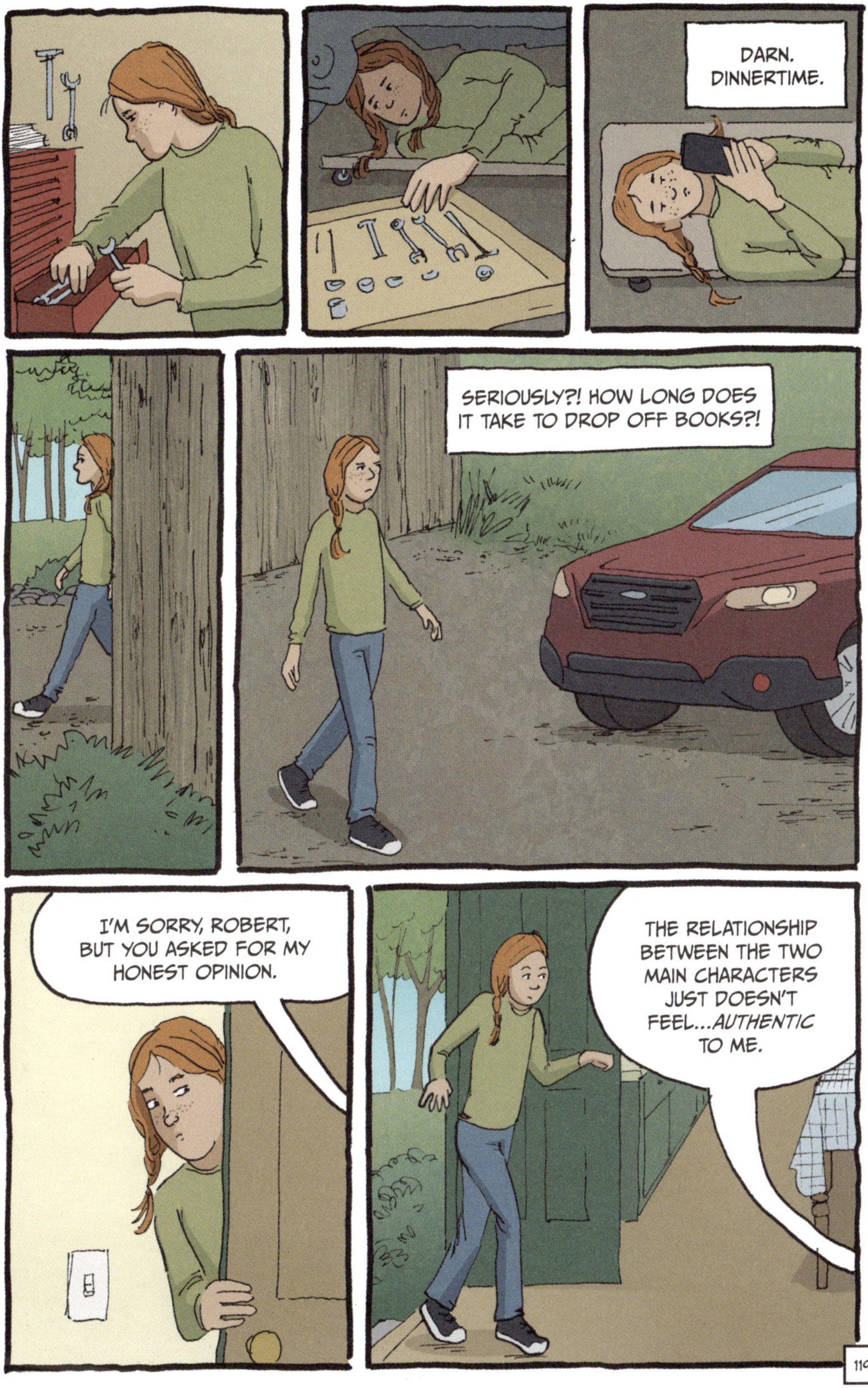
DARN. DINNERTIME.
SERIOUSLY?! HOW LONG DOES IT TAKE TO DROP OFF BOOKS?!
I'M SORRY, ROBERT, BUT YOU ASKED FOR MY HONEST OPINION.
THE RELATIONSHIP BETWEEN THE TWO MAIN CHARACTERS JUST DOESN'T FEEL...*AUTHENTIC* TO ME.

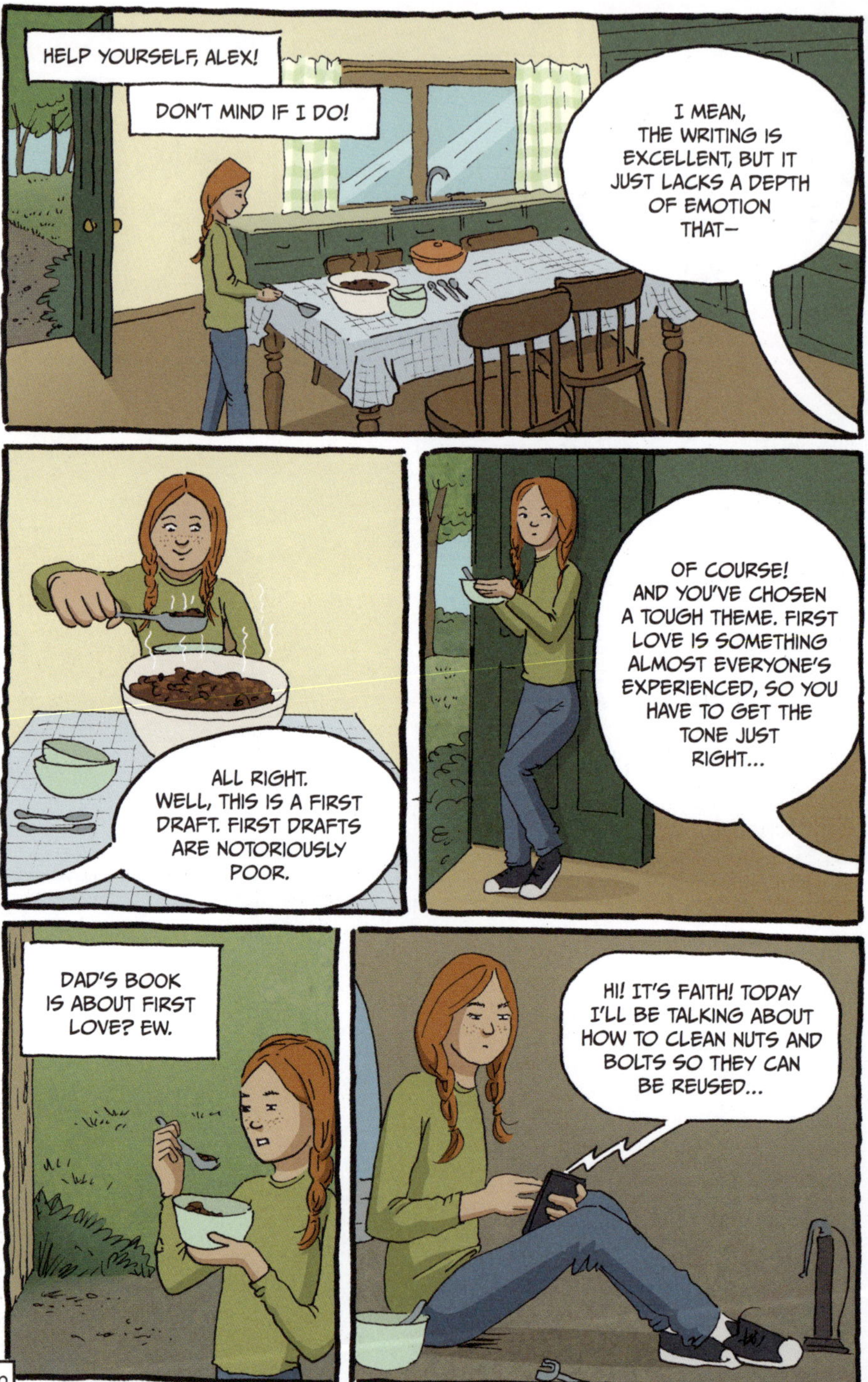
HELP YOURSELF, ALEX!
DON'T MIND IF I DO!
I MEAN, THE WRITING IS EXCELLENT, BUT IT JUST LACKS A DEPTH OF EMOTION THAT—
ALL RIGHT. WELL, THIS IS A FIRST DRAFT. FIRST DRAFTS ARE NOTORIOUSLY POOR.
OF COURSE! AND YOU'VE CHOSEN A TOUGH THEME. FIRST LOVE IS SOMETHING ALMOST EVERYONE'S EXPERIENCED, SO YOU HAVE TO GET THE TONE JUST RIGHT...
DAD'S BOOK IS ABOUT FIRST LOVE? EW.
HI! IT'S FAITH! TODAY I'LL BE TALKING ABOUT HOW TO CLEAN NUTS AND BOLTS SO THEY CAN BE REUSED...

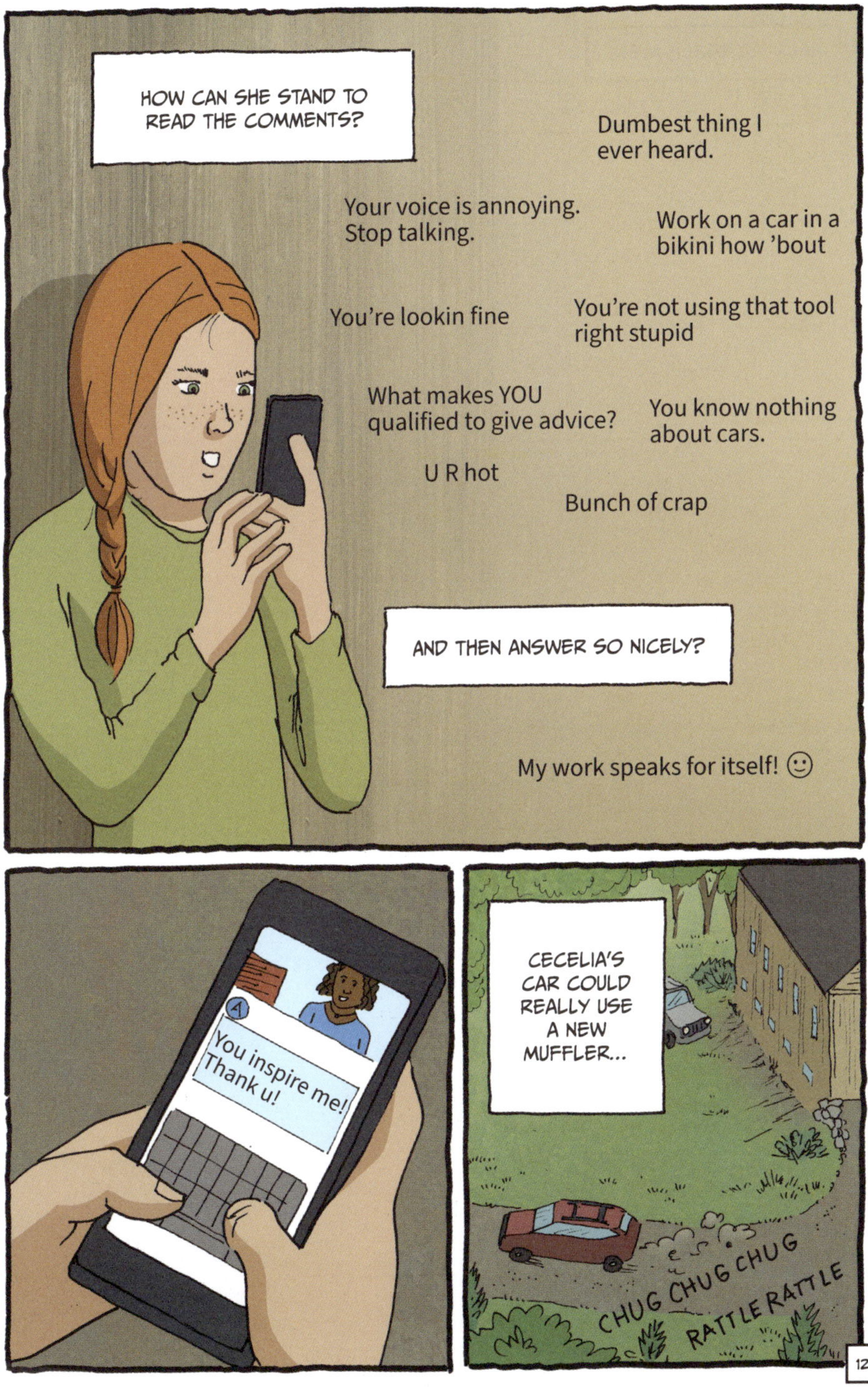
HOW CAN SHE STAND TO READ THE COMMENTS?
Dumbest thing I ever heard.
Your voice is annoying. Stop talking.
Work on a car in a bikini how 'bout
You're lookin fine
You're not using that tool right stupid
What makes YOU qualified to give advice?
You know nothing about cars.
U R hot
Bunch of crap
AND THEN ANSWER SO NICELY?
My work speaks for itself! ☺
You inspire me!
Thank u!
CECELIA'S CAR COULD REALLY USE A NEW MUFFLER...
CHUG CHUG CHUG
RATTLE RATTLE

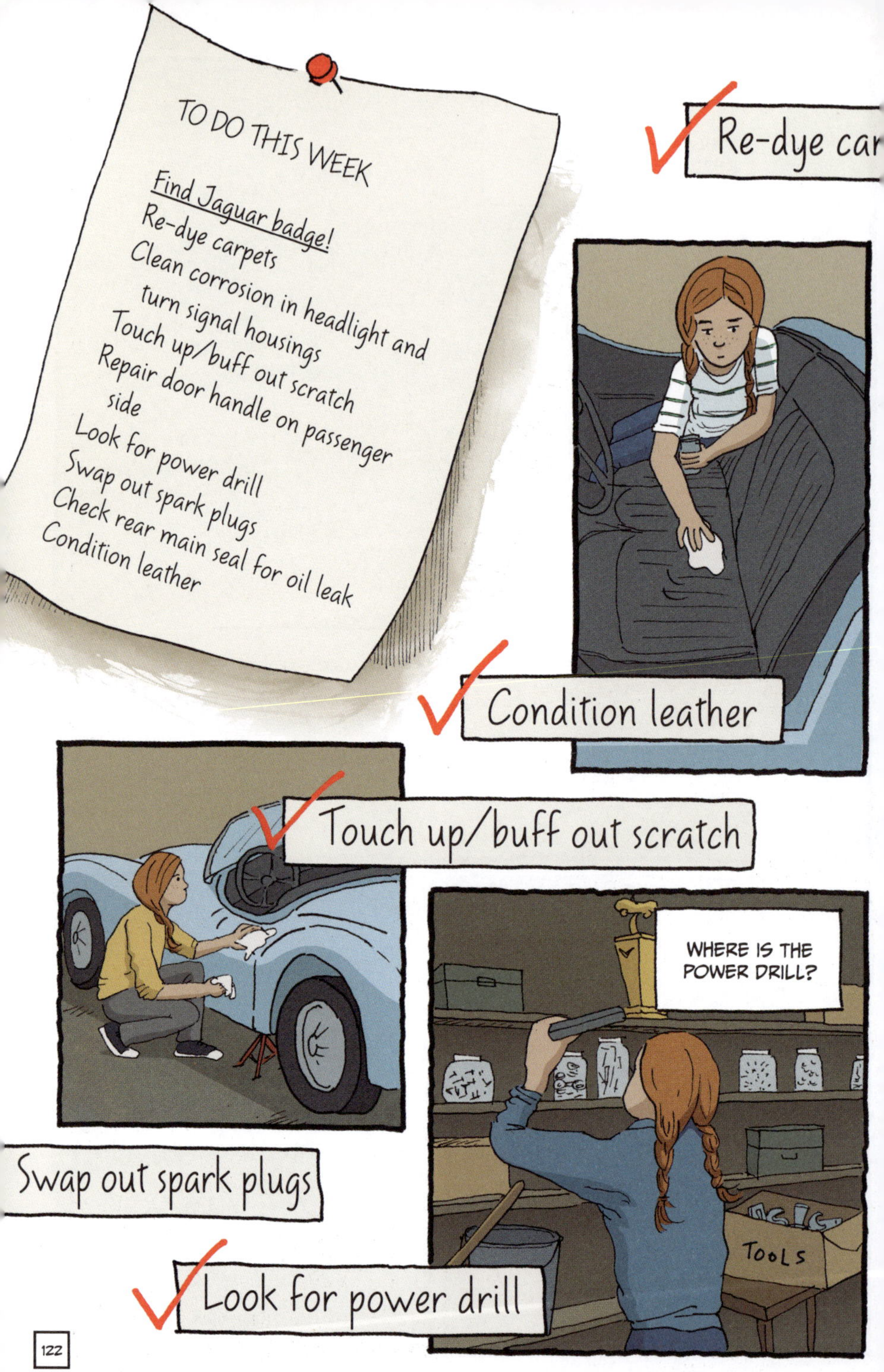
TO DO THIS WEEK
Find Jaguar badge!
Re-dye carpets
Clean corrosion in headlight and turn signal housings
Touch up/buff out scratch
Repair door handle on passenger side
Look for power drill
Swap out spark plugs
Check rear main seal for oil leak
Condition leather
Re-dye car
Condition leather
Touch up/buff out scratch
WHERE IS THE POWER DRILL?
TOOLS
Swap out spark plugs
Look for power drill

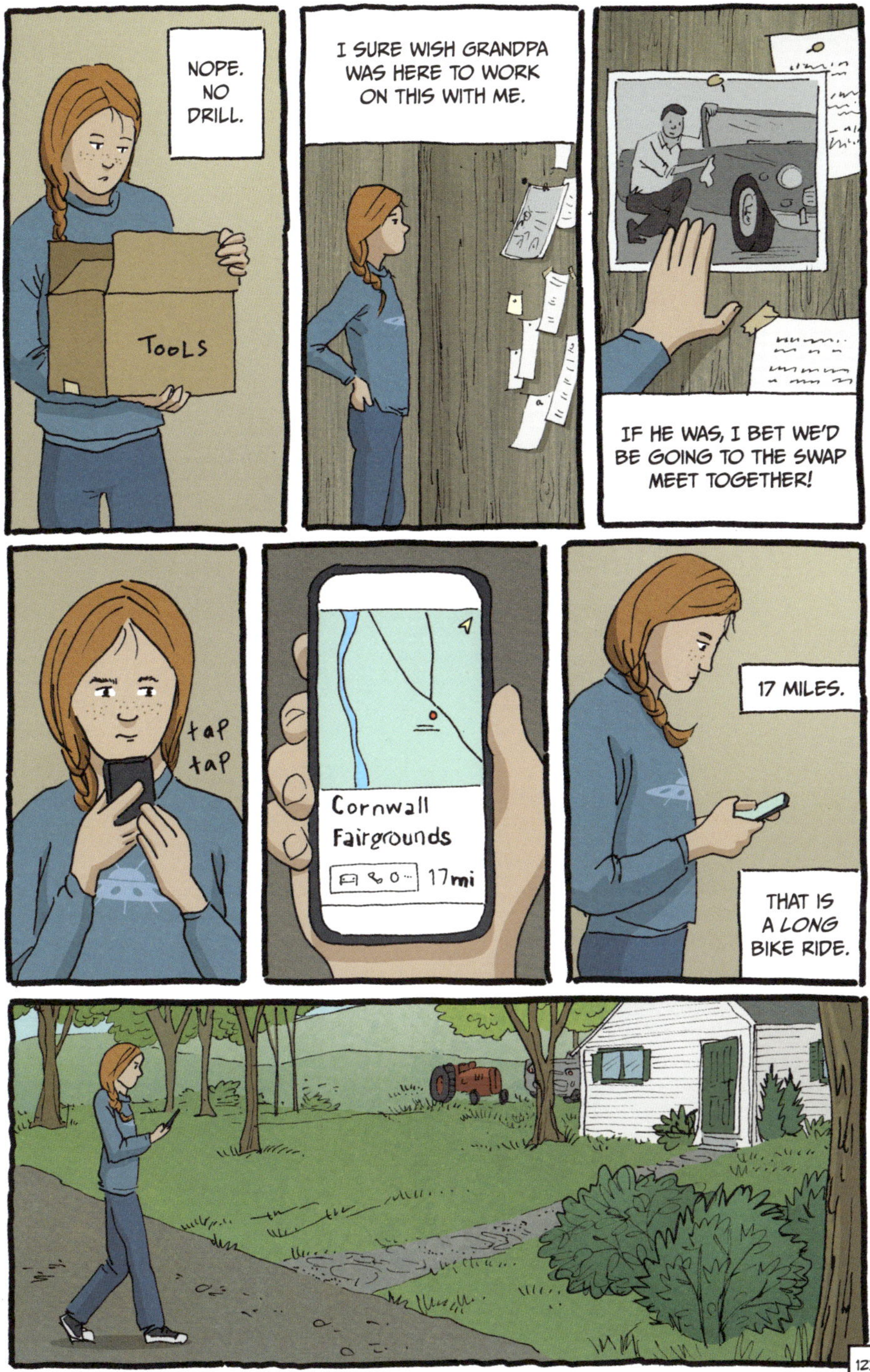
NOPE. NO DRILL.
TOOLS
I SURE WISH GRANDPA WAS HERE TO WORK ON THIS WITH ME.
IF HE WAS, I BET WE'D BE GOING TO THE SWAP MEET TOGETHER!
tap tap
Cornwall Fairgrounds
17mi
17 MILES.
THAT IS A *LONG* BIKE RIDE.

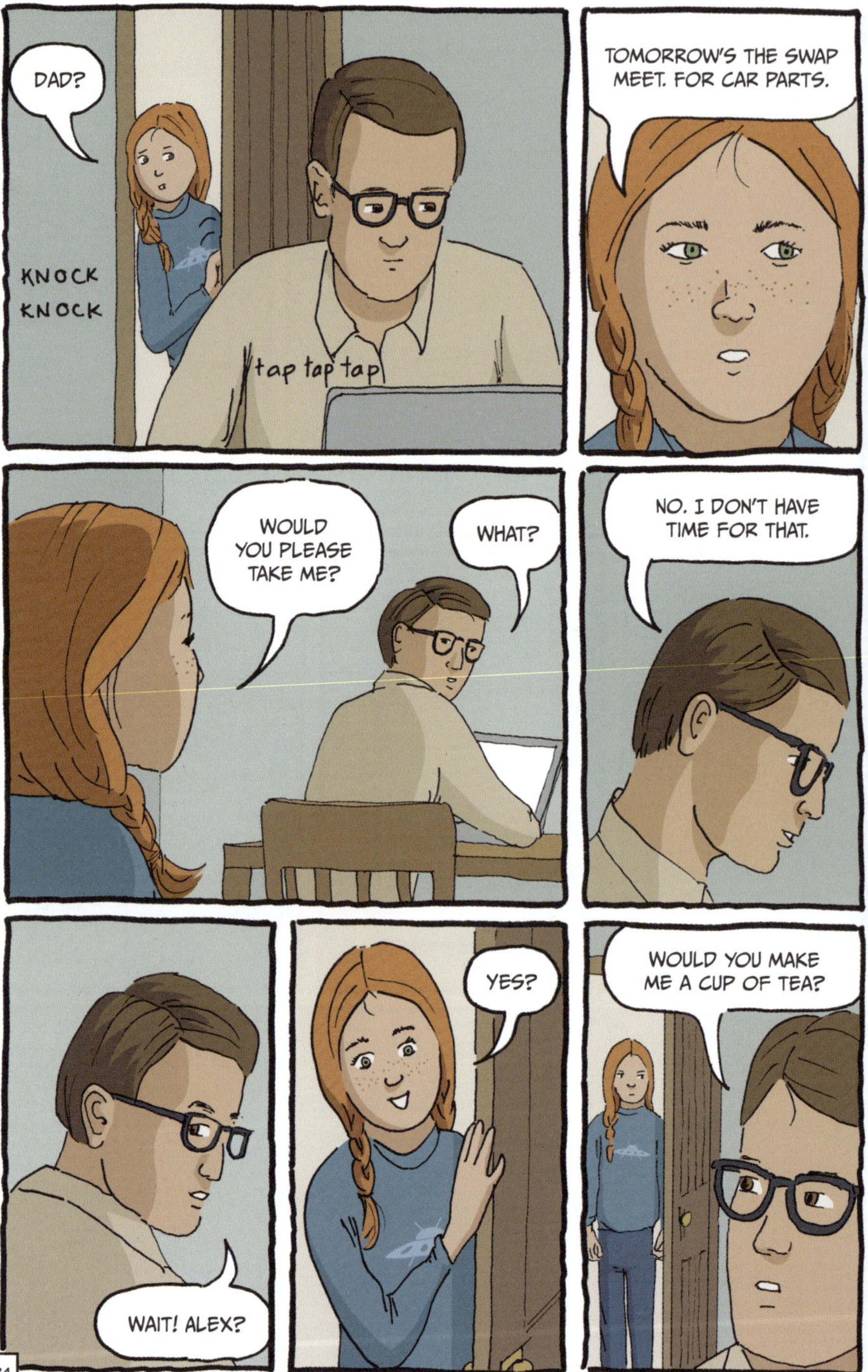
DAD?
KNOCK KNOCK
tap tap tap
TOMORROW'S THE SWAP MEET. FOR CAR PARTS.
WOULD YOU PLEASE TAKE ME?
WHAT?
NO. I DON'T HAVE TIME FOR THAT.
WAIT! ALEX?
YES?
WOULD YOU MAKE ME A CUP OF TEA?

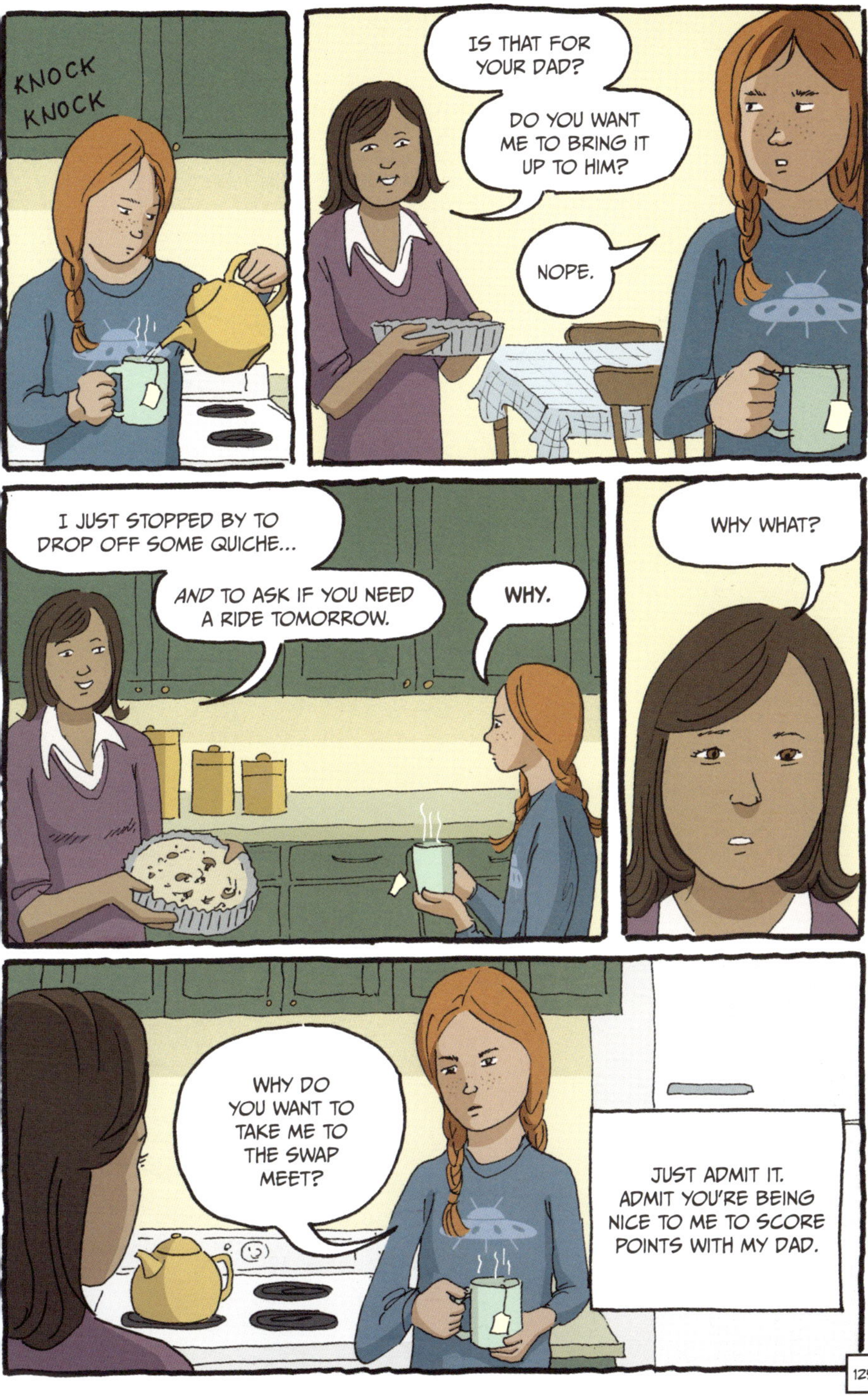
KNOCK KNOCK
IS THAT FOR YOUR DAD?
DO YOU WANT ME TO BRING IT UP TO HIM?
NOPE.
I JUST STOPPED BY TO DROP OFF SOME QUICHE...
AND TO ASK IF YOU NEED A RIDE TOMORROW.
WHY.
WHY WHAT?
WHY DO YOU WANT TO TAKE ME TO THE SWAP MEET?
JUST ADMIT IT. ADMIT YOU'RE BEING NICE TO ME TO SCORE POINTS WITH MY DAD.

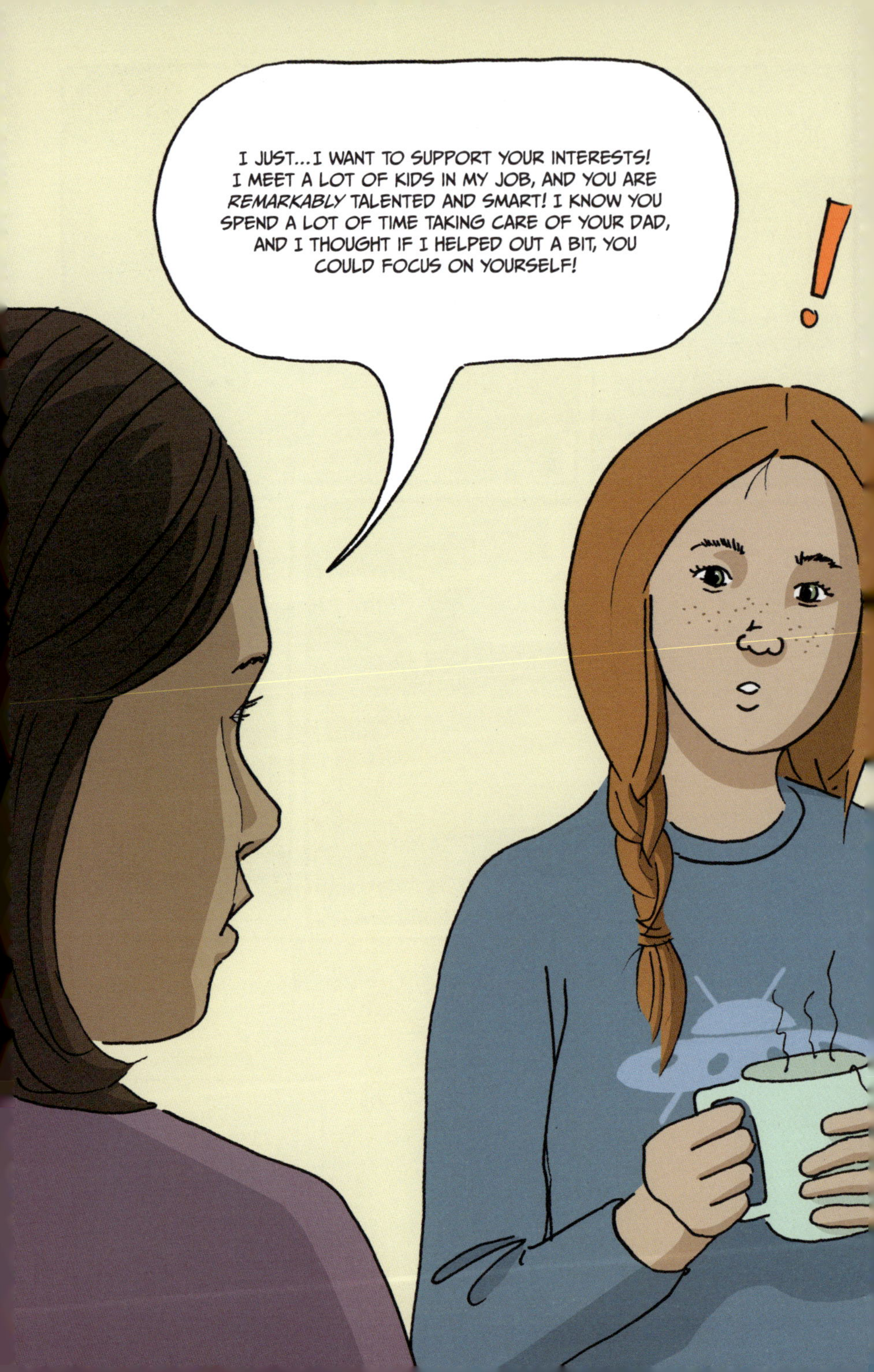
I JUST...I WANT TO SUPPORT YOUR INTERESTS! I MEET A LOT OF KIDS IN MY JOB, AND YOU ARE *REMARKABLY* TALENTED AND SMART! I KNOW YOU SPEND A LOT OF TIME TAKING CARE OF YOUR DAD, AND I THOUGHT IF I HELPED OUT A BIT, YOU COULD FOCUS ON YOURSELF!
!

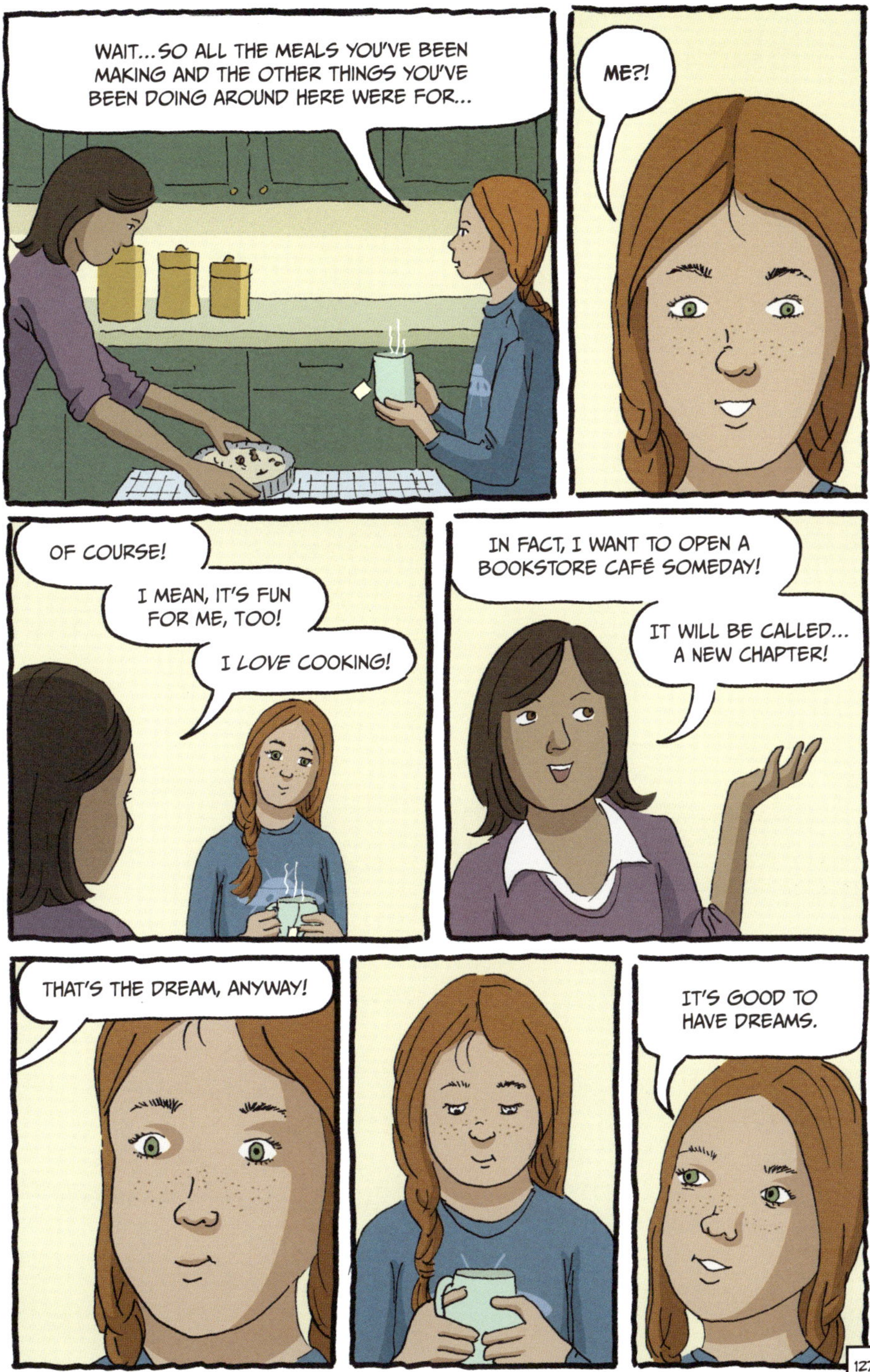
WAIT...SO ALL THE MEALS YOU'VE BEEN MAKING AND THE OTHER THINGS YOU'VE BEEN DOING AROUND HERE WERE FOR...
ME?!
OF COURSE!
I MEAN, IT'S FUN FOR ME, TOO!
I *LOVE* COOKING!
IN FACT, I WANT TO OPEN A BOOKSTORE CAFÉ SOMEDAY!
IT WILL BE CALLED... A NEW CHAPTER!
THAT'S THE DREAM, ANYWAY!
IT'S GOOD TO HAVE DREAMS.

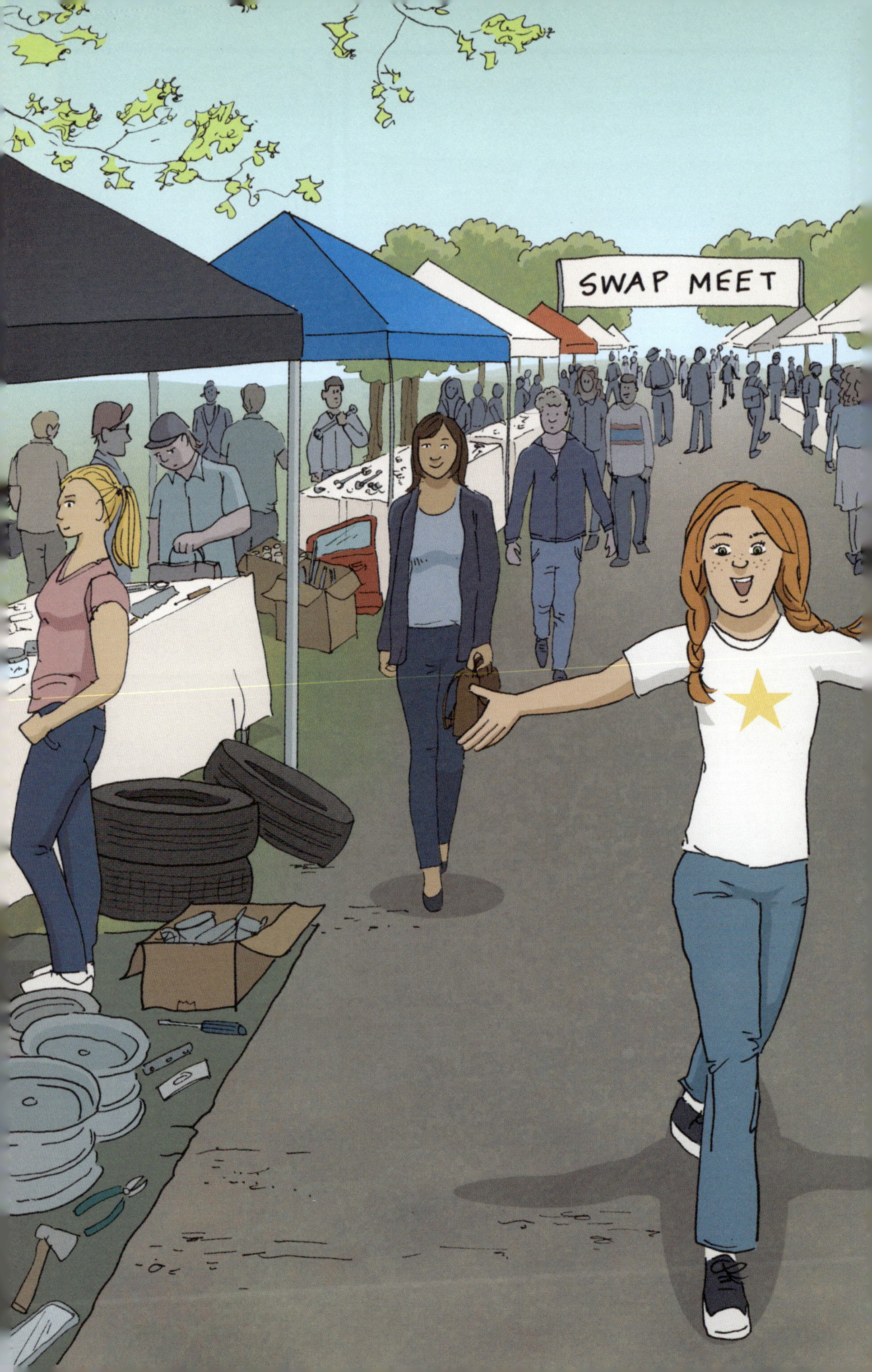
SWAP MEET

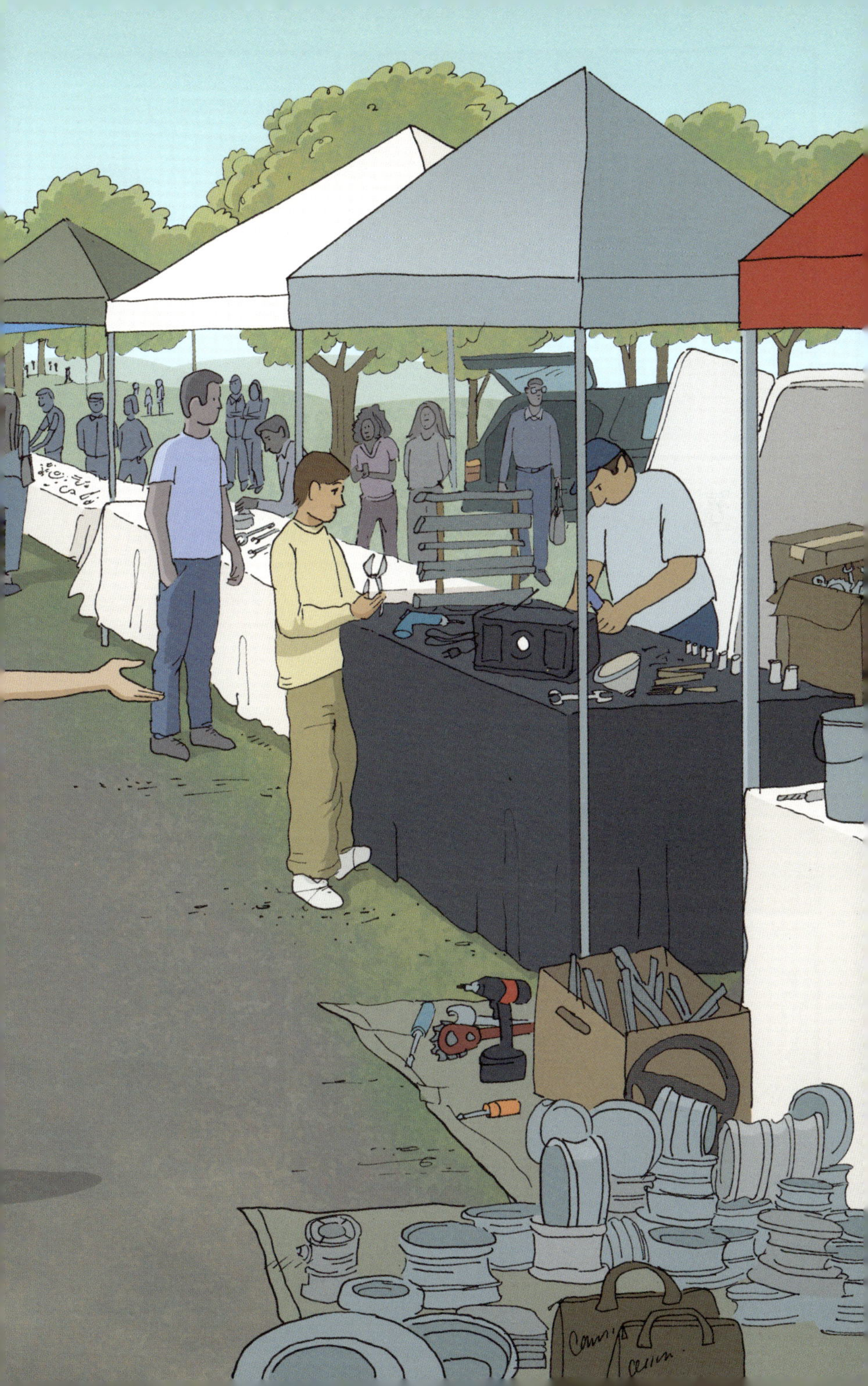

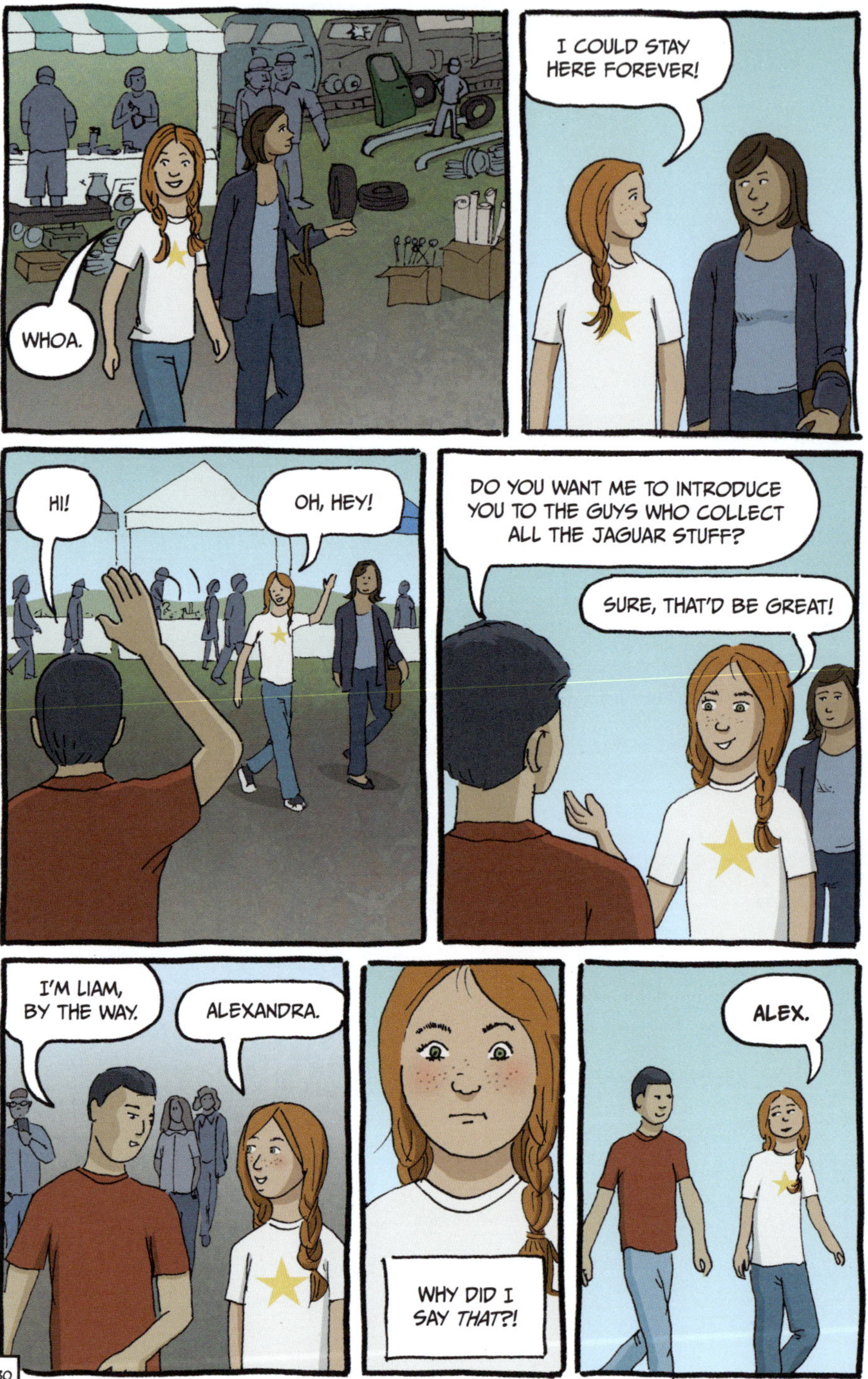
WHOA.
I COULD STAY HERE FOREVER!
HI!
OH, HEY!
DO YOU WANT ME TO INTRODUCE YOU TO THE GUYS WHO COLLECT ALL THE JAGUAR STUFF?
SURE, THAT'D BE GREAT!
I'M LIAM, BY THE WAY.
ALEXANDRA.
WHY DID I SAY *THAT*?!
ALEX.

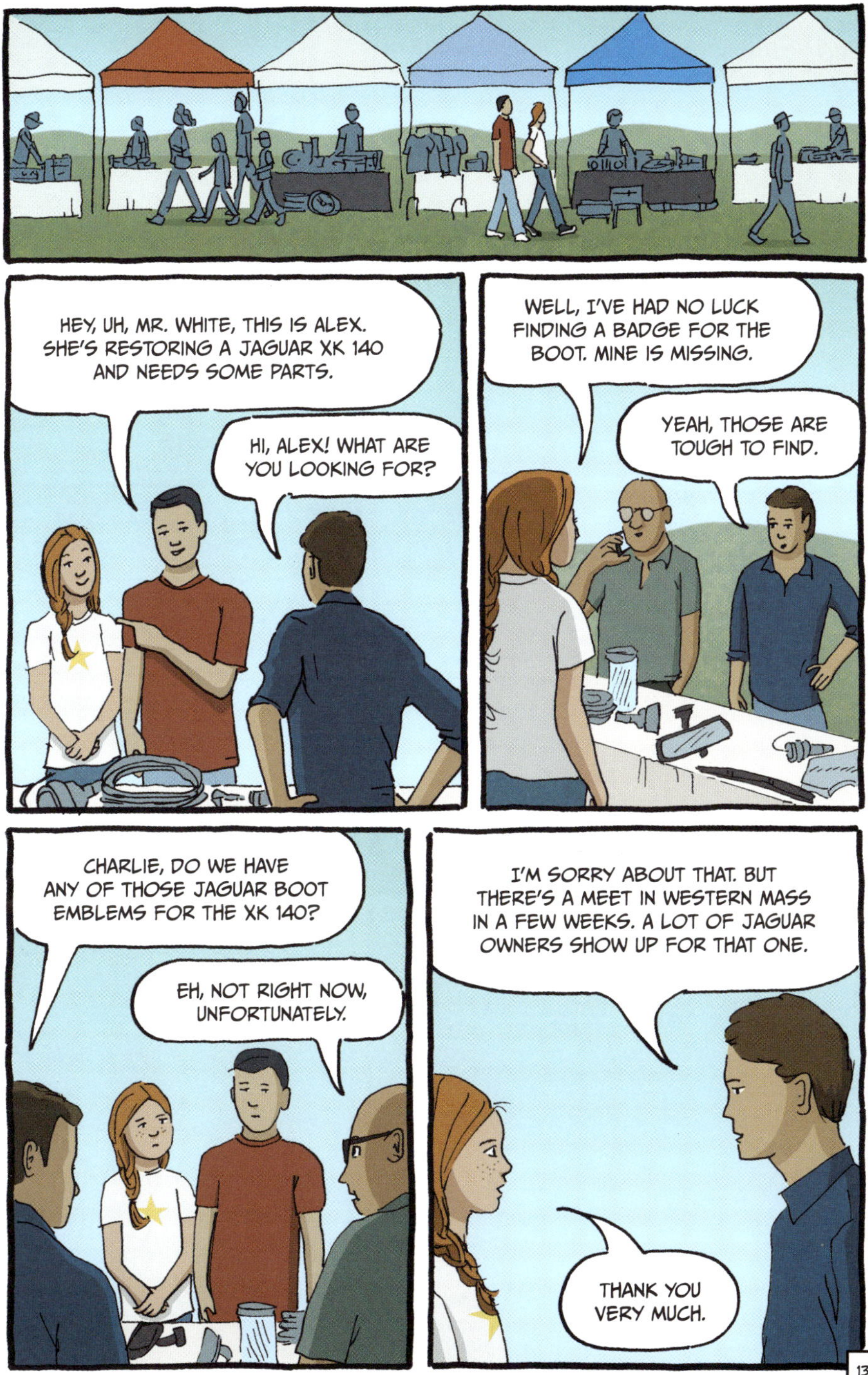
HEY, UH, MR. WHITE, THIS IS ALEX. SHE'S RESTORING A JAGUAR XK 140 AND NEEDS SOME PARTS.
HI, ALEX! WHAT ARE YOU LOOKING FOR?
WELL, I'VE HAD NO LUCK FINDING A BADGE FOR THE BOOT. MINE IS MISSING.
YEAH, THOSE ARE TOUGH TO FIND.
CHARLIE, DO WE HAVE ANY OF THOSE JAGUAR BOOT EMBLEMS FOR THE XK 140?
EH, NOT RIGHT NOW, UNFORTUNATELY.
I'M SORRY ABOUT THAT. BUT THERE'S A MEET IN WESTERN MASS IN A FEW WEEKS. A LOT OF JAGUAR OWNERS SHOW UP FOR THAT ONE.
THANK YOU VERY MUCH.

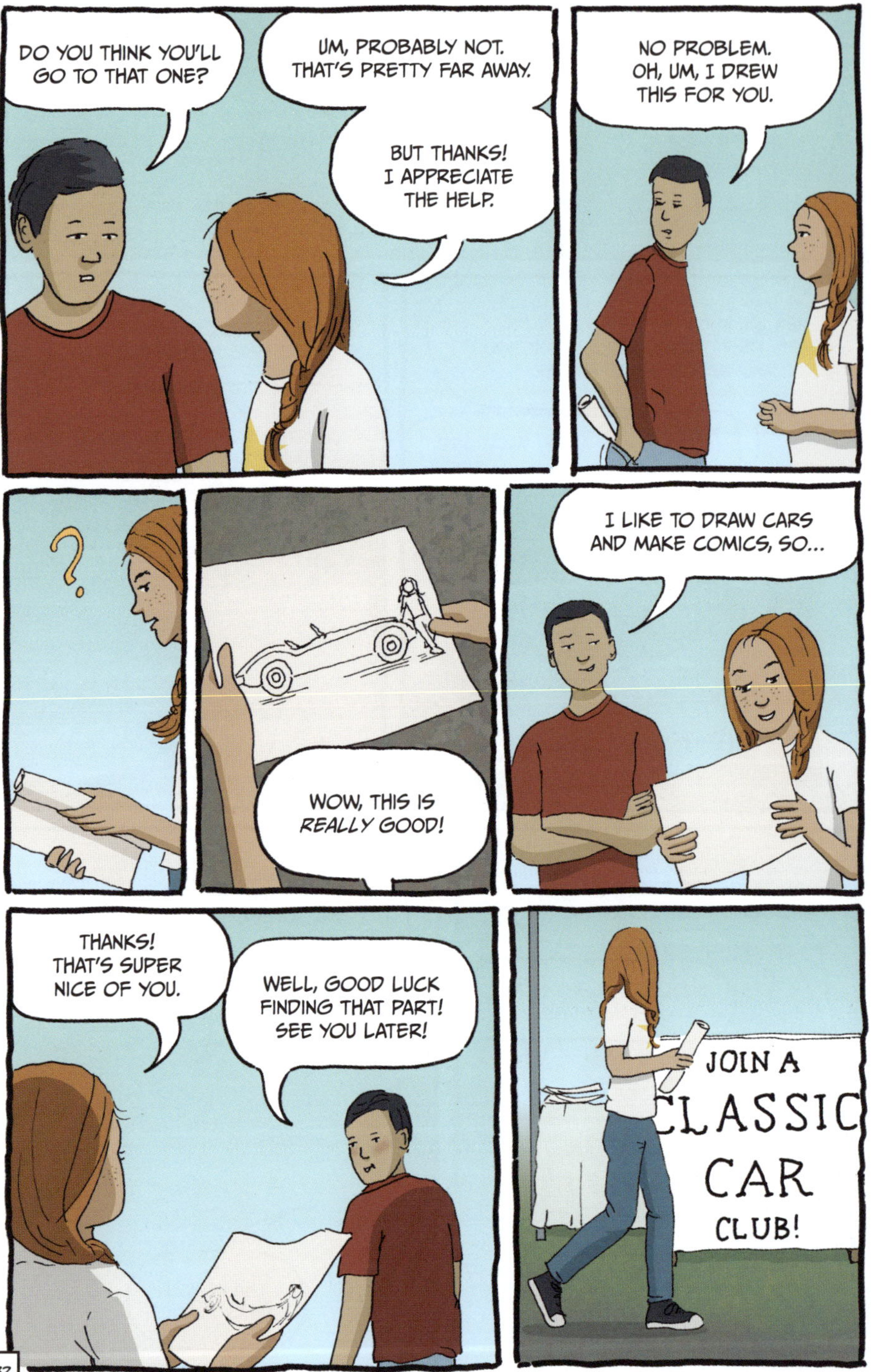
DO YOU THINK YOU'LL GO TO THAT ONE?
UM, PROBABLY NOT. THAT'S PRETTY FAR AWAY.
BUT THANKS! I APPRECIATE THE HELP.
NO PROBLEM. OH, UM, I DREW THIS FOR YOU.
?
WOW, THIS IS *REALLY* GOOD!
I LIKE TO DRAW CARS AND MAKE COMICS, SO...
THANKS! THAT'S SUPER NICE OF YOU.
WELL, GOOD LUCK FINDING THAT PART! SEE YOU LATER!
JOIN A CLASSIC CAR CLUB!

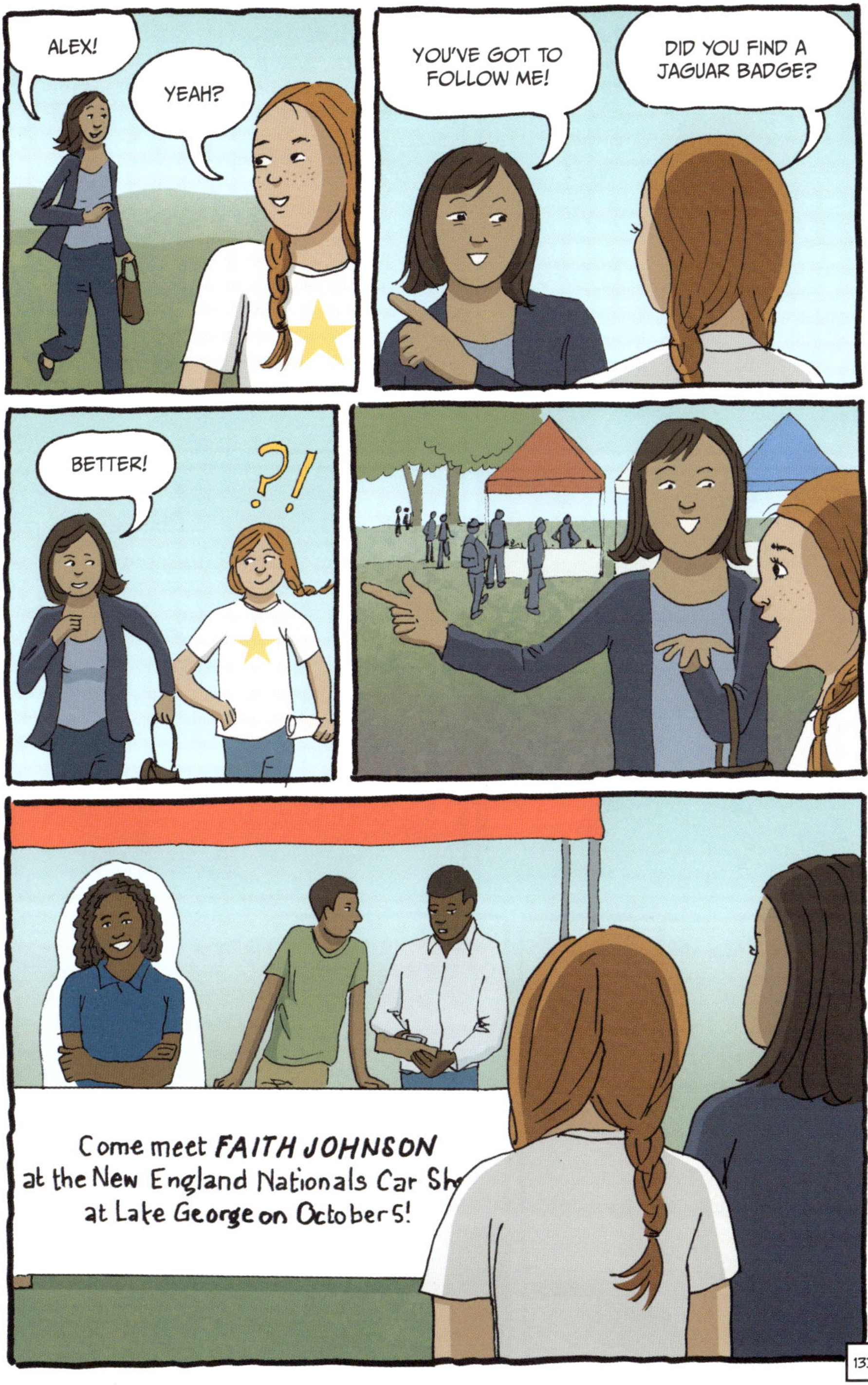
ALEX!
YEAH?
YOU'VE GOT TO FOLLOW ME!
DID YOU FIND A JAGUAR BADGE?
BETTER!
?!
Come meet FAITH JOHNSON
at the New England Nationals Car Sh
at Lake George on October 5!

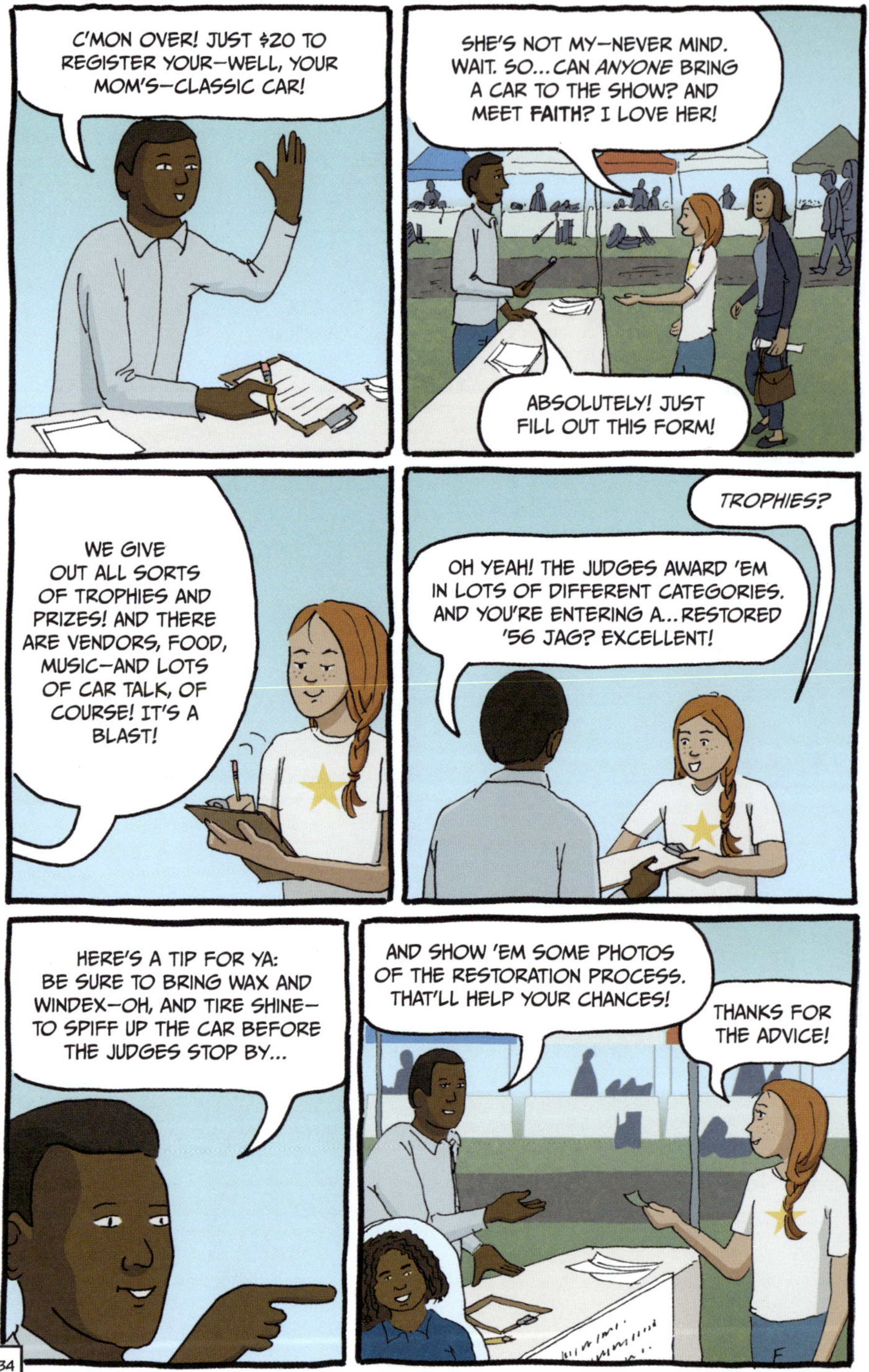

C'MON OVER! JUST $20 TO REGISTER YOUR—WELL, YOUR MOM'S—CLASSIC CAR!
SHE'S NOT MY—NEVER MIND. WAIT. SO...CAN ANYONE BRING A CAR TO THE SHOW? AND MEET FAITH? I LOVE HER!
ABSOLUTELY! JUST FILL OUT THIS FORM!
WE GIVE OUT ALL SORTS OF TROPHIES AND PRIZES! AND THERE ARE VENDORS, FOOD, MUSIC—AND LOTS OF CAR TALK, OF COURSE! IT'S A BLAST!
TROPHIES?
OH YEAH! THE JUDGES AWARD 'EM IN LOTS OF DIFFERENT CATEGORIES. AND YOU'RE ENTERING A...RESTORED '56 JAG? EXCELLENT!
HERE'S A TIP FOR YA: BE SURE TO BRING WAX AND WINDEX—OH, AND TIRE SHINE—TO SPIFF UP THE CAR BEFORE THE JUDGES STOP BY...
AND SHOW 'EM SOME PHOTOS OF THE RESTORATION PROCESS. THAT'LL HELP YOUR CHANCES!
THANKS FOR THE ADVICE!

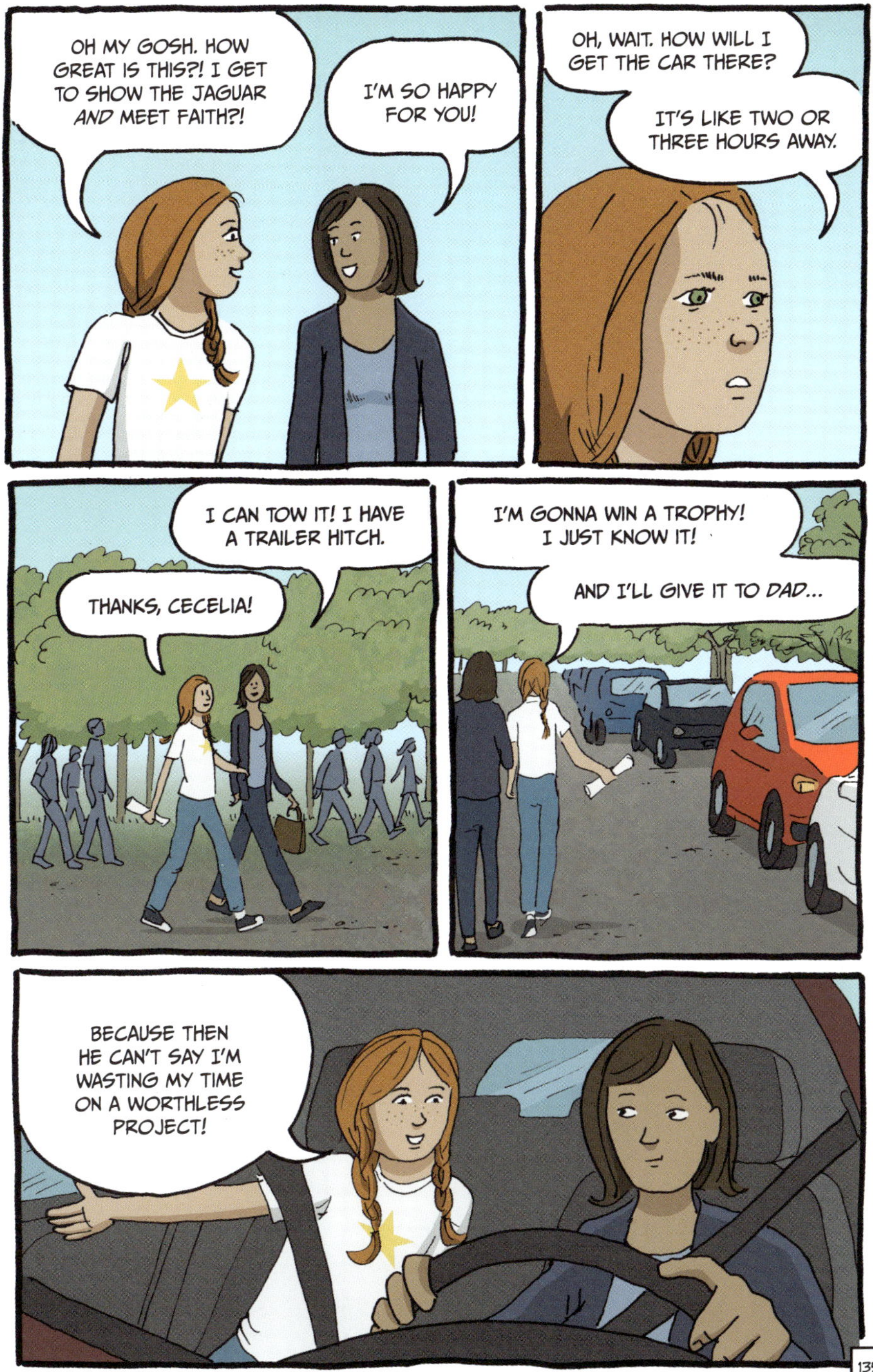
OH MY GOSH. HOW GREAT IS THIS?! I GET TO SHOW THE JAGUAR *AND* MEET FAITH?!
I'M SO HAPPY FOR YOU!
OH, WAIT. HOW WILL I GET THE CAR THERE?
IT'S LIKE TWO OR THREE HOURS AWAY.
I CAN TOW IT! I HAVE A TRAILER HITCH.
THANKS, CECELIA!
I'M GONNA WIN A TROPHY! I JUST KNOW IT!
AND I'LL GIVE IT TO *DAD*...
BECAUSE THEN HE CAN'T SAY I'M WASTING MY TIME ON A WORTHLESS PROJECT!

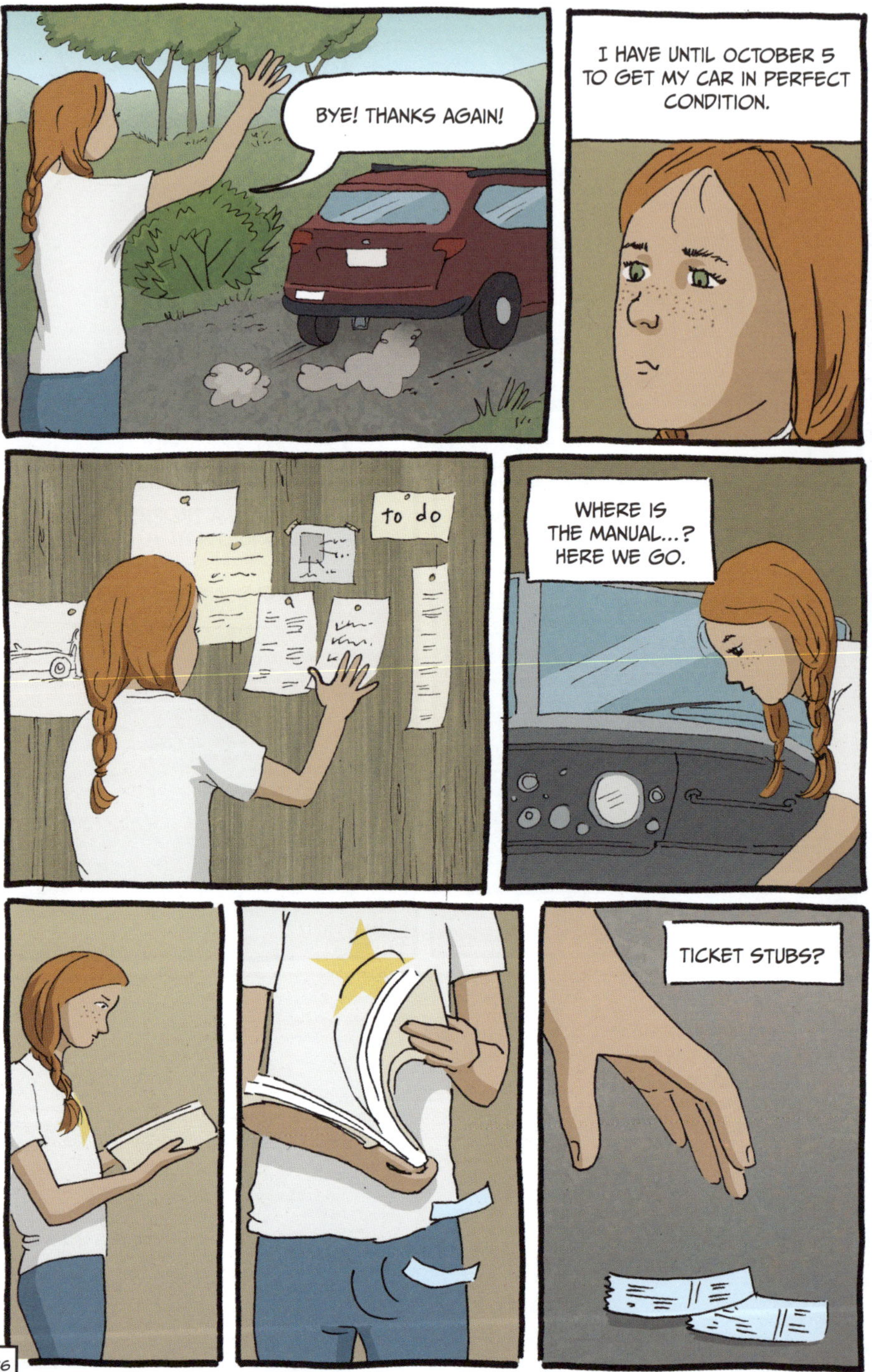
BYE! THANKS AGAIN!
I HAVE UNTIL OCTOBER 5 TO GET MY CAR IN PERFECT CONDITION.
to do
WHERE IS THE MANUAL...? HERE WE GO.
TICKET STUBS?

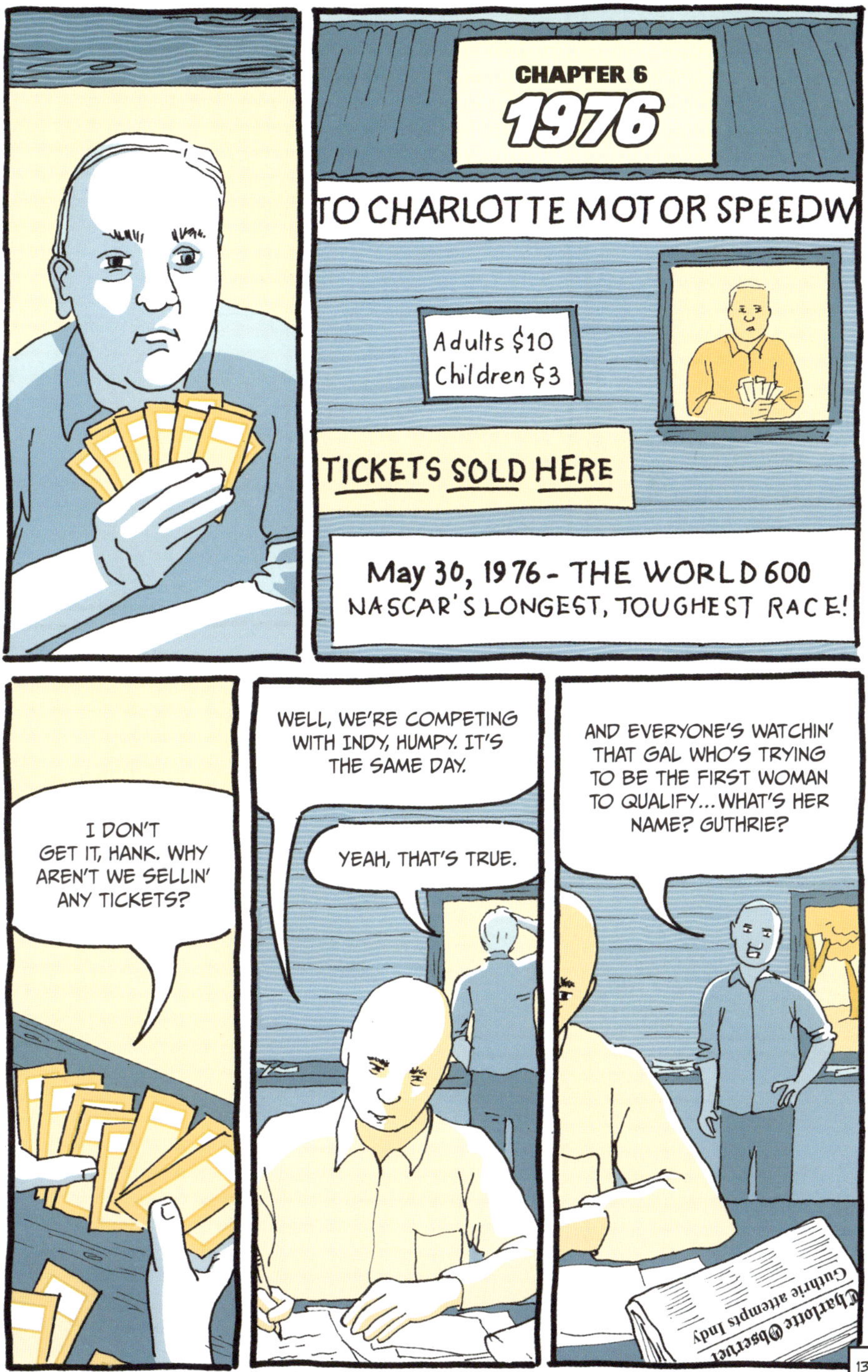
CHAPTER 6
1976
TO CHARLOTTE MOTOR SPEEDW
Adults $10
Children $3
TICKETS SOLD HERE
May 30, 1976 - THE WORLD 600
NASCAR'S LONGEST, TOUGHEST RACE!
I DON'T GET IT, HANK. WHY AREN'T WE SELLIN' ANY TICKETS?
WELL, WE'RE COMPETING WITH INDY, HUMPY. IT'S THE SAME DAY.
YEAH, THAT'S TRUE.
AND EVERYONE'S WATCHIN' THAT GAL WHO'S TRYING TO BE THE FIRST WOMAN TO QUALIFY... WHAT'S HER NAME? GUTHRIE?
Charlotte Observer
Guthrie attempts Indy

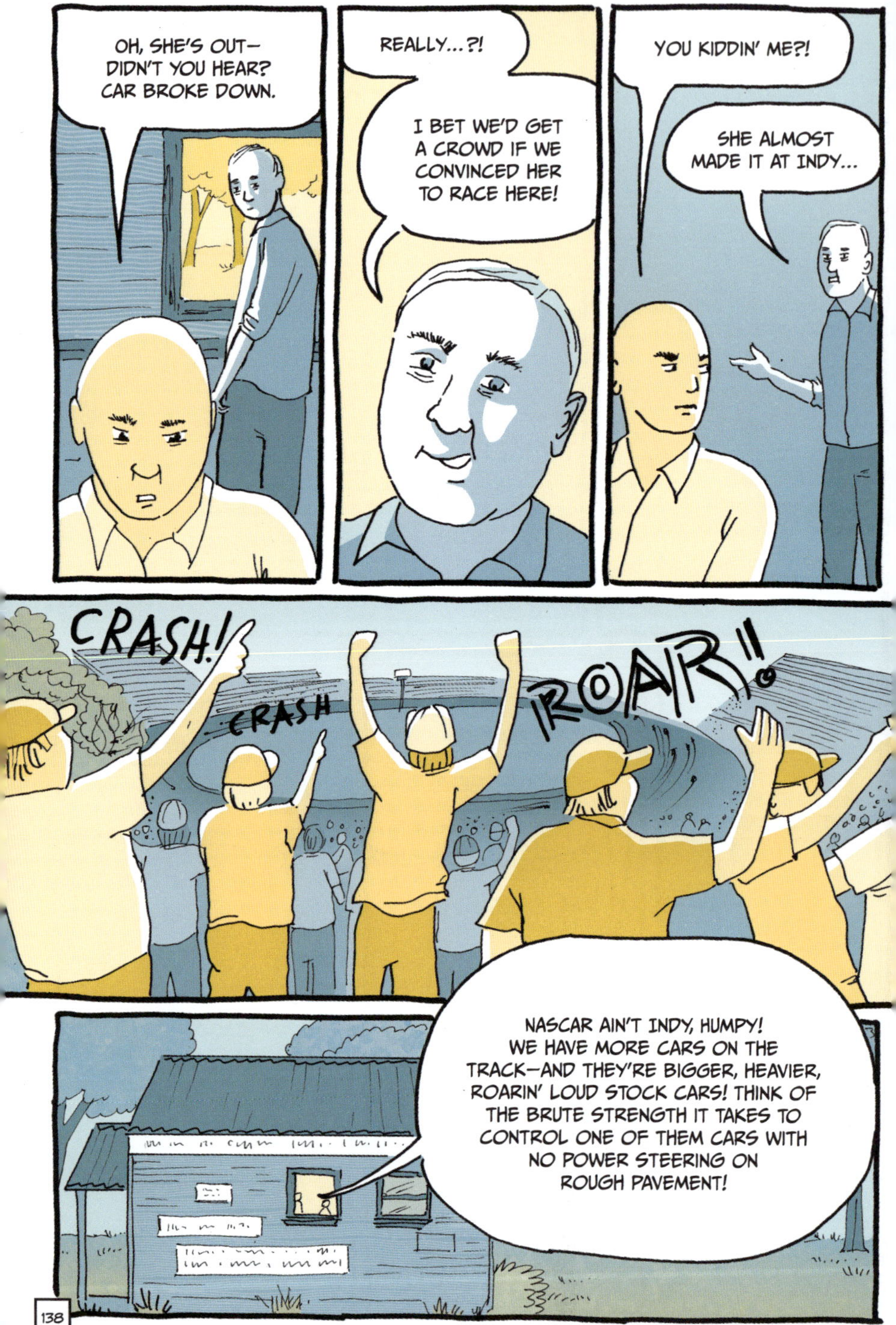
OH, SHE'S OUT— DIDN'T YOU HEAR? CAR BROKE DOWN.
REALLY...?!
I BET WE'D GET A CROWD IF WE CONVINCED HER TO RACE HERE!
YOU KIDDIN' ME?!
SHE ALMOST MADE IT AT INDY...
CRASH!
CRASH
ROAR!!
NASCAR AIN'T INDY, HUMPY! WE HAVE MORE CARS ON THE TRACK—AND THEY'RE BIGGER, HEAVIER, ROARIN' LOUD STOCK CARS! THINK OF THE BRUTE STRENGTH IT TAKES TO CONTROL ONE OF THEM CARS WITH NO POWER STEERING ON ROUGH PAVEMENT!

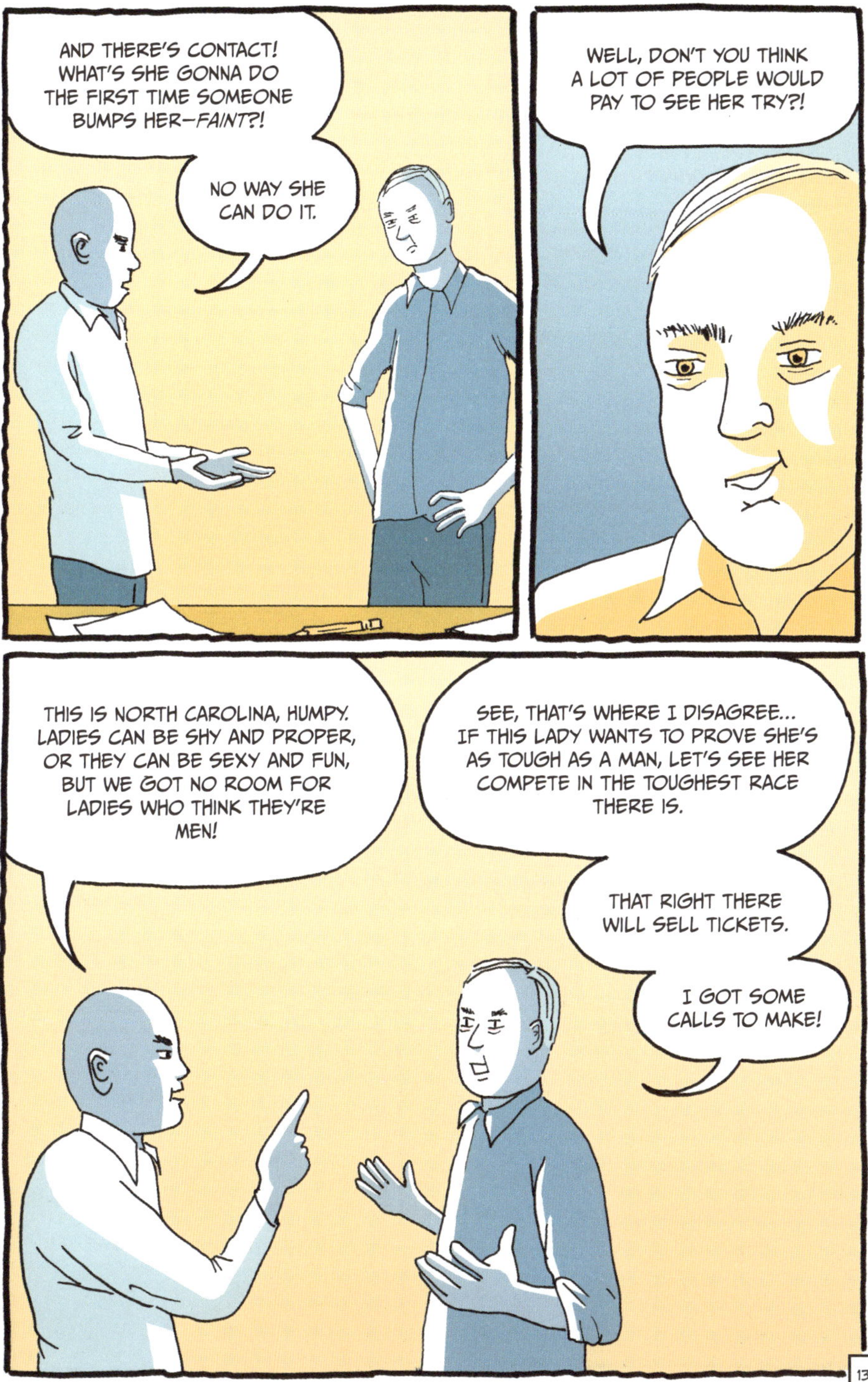
AND THERE'S CONTACT! WHAT'S SHE GONNA DO THE FIRST TIME SOMEONE BUMPS HER—*FAINT*?!
NO WAY SHE CAN DO IT.
WELL, DON'T YOU THINK A LOT OF PEOPLE WOULD PAY TO SEE HER TRY?!
THIS IS NORTH CAROLINA, HUMPY. LADIES CAN BE SHY AND PROPER, OR THEY CAN BE SEXY AND FUN, BUT WE GOT NO ROOM FOR LADIES WHO THINK THEY'RE MEN!
SEE, THAT'S WHERE I DISAGREE... IF THIS LADY WANTS TO PROVE SHE'S AS TOUGH AS A MAN, LET'S SEE HER COMPETE IN THE TOUGHEST RACE THERE IS.
THAT RIGHT THERE WILL SELL TICKETS.
I GOT SOME CALLS TO MAKE!

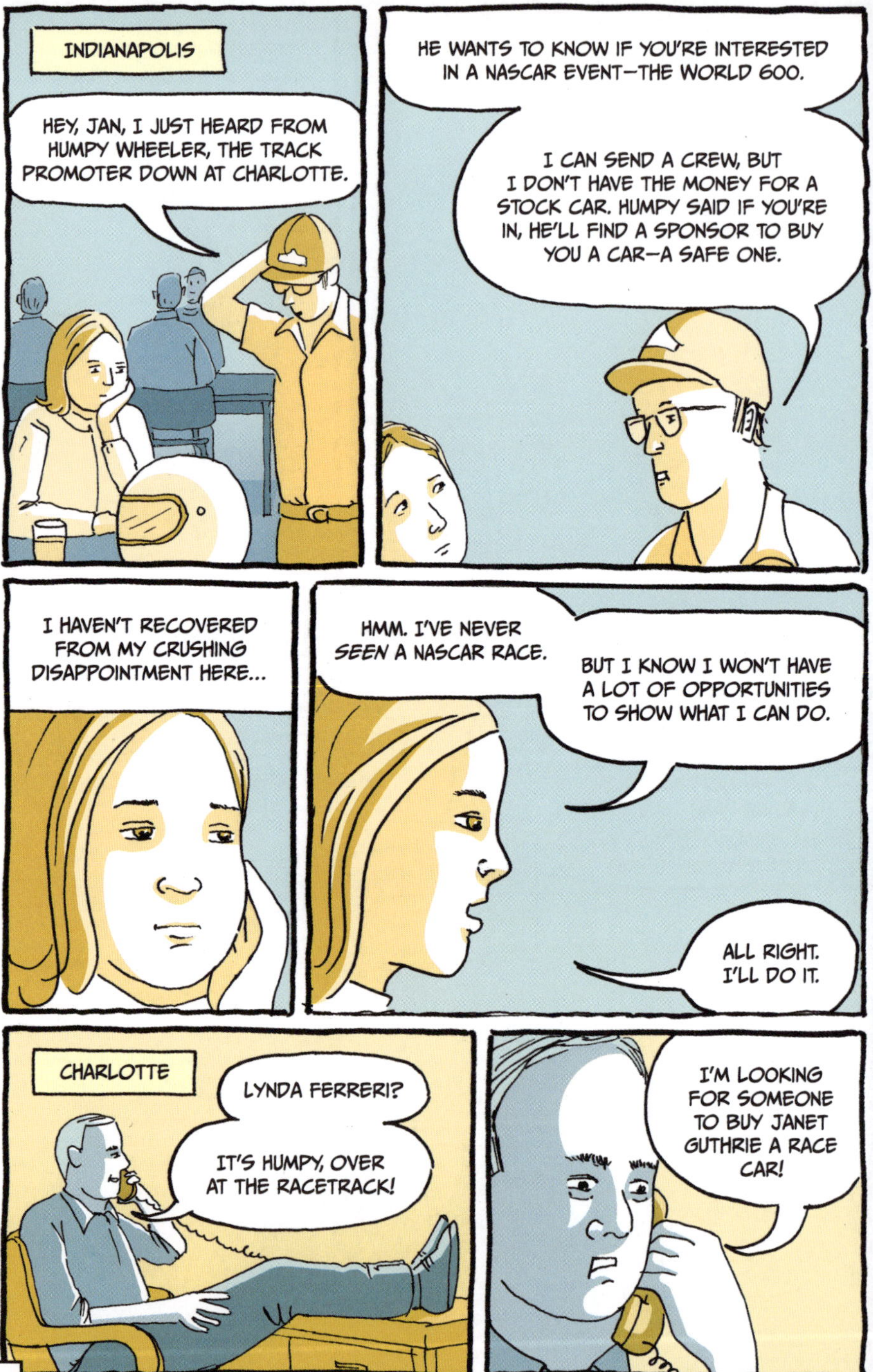
INDIANAPOLIS
HEY, JAN, I JUST HEARD FROM HUMPY WHEELER, THE TRACK PROMOTER DOWN AT CHARLOTTE.
HE WANTS TO KNOW IF YOU'RE INTERESTED IN A NASCAR EVENT—THE WORLD 600.
I CAN SEND A CREW, BUT I DON'T HAVE THE MONEY FOR A STOCK CAR. HUMPY SAID IF YOU'RE IN, HE'LL FIND A SPONSOR TO BUY YOU A CAR—A SAFE ONE.
I HAVEN'T RECOVERED FROM MY CRUSHING DISAPPOINTMENT HERE...
HMM. I'VE NEVER *SEEN* A NASCAR RACE.
BUT I KNOW I WON'T HAVE A LOT OF OPPORTUNITIES TO SHOW WHAT I CAN DO.
ALL RIGHT. I'LL DO IT.
CHARLOTTE
LYNDA FERRERI?
IT'S HUMPY, OVER AT THE RACETRACK!
I'M LOOKING FOR SOMEONE TO BUY JANET GUTHRIE A RACE CAR!

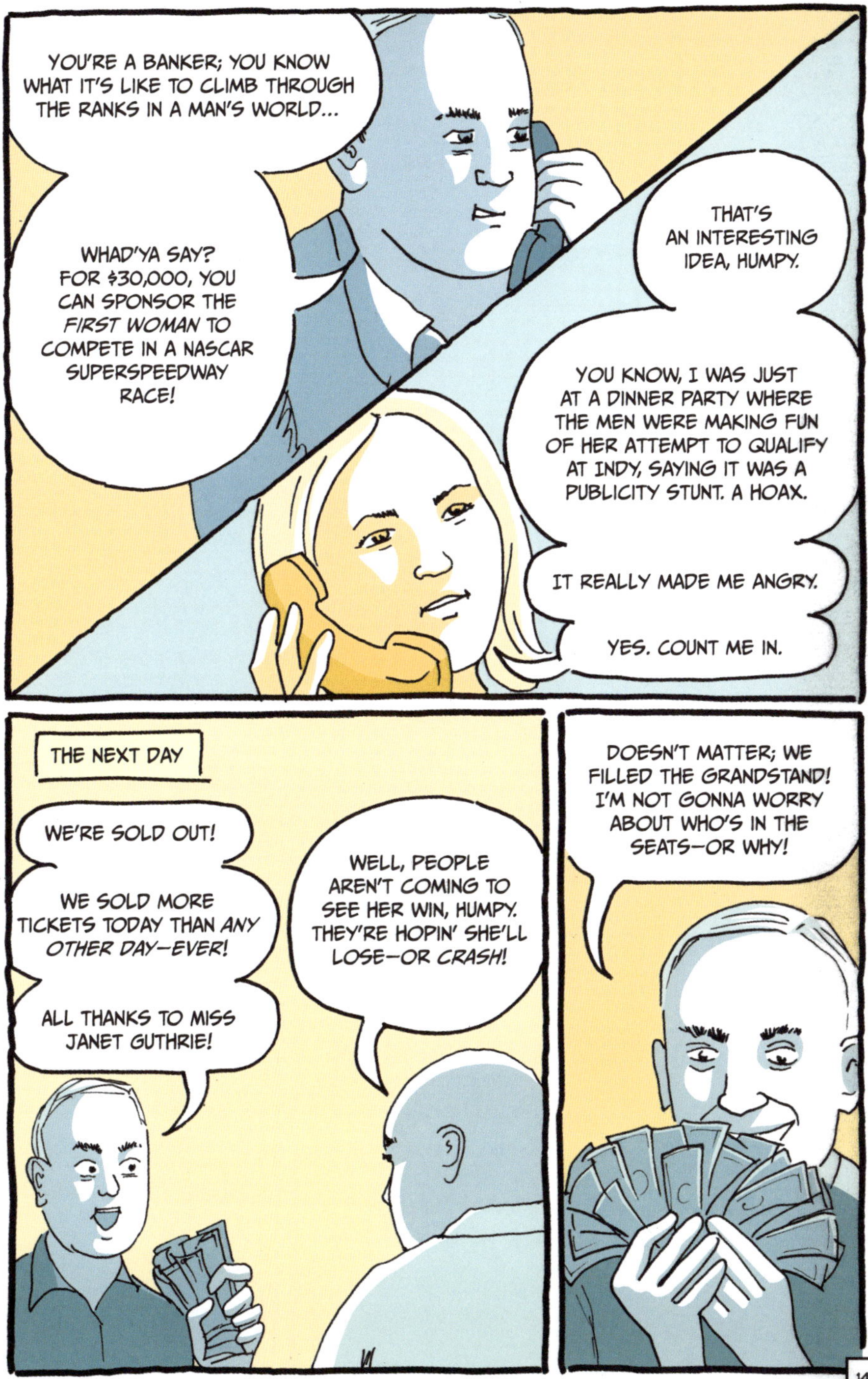
YOU'RE A BANKER; YOU KNOW WHAT IT'S LIKE TO CLIMB THROUGH THE RANKS IN A MAN'S WORLD...
WHAD'YA SAY? FOR $30,000, YOU CAN SPONSOR THE *FIRST WOMAN* TO COMPETE IN A NASCAR SUPERSPEEDWAY RACE!
THAT'S AN INTERESTING IDEA, HUMPY.
YOU KNOW, I WAS JUST AT A DINNER PARTY WHERE THE MEN WERE MAKING FUN OF HER ATTEMPT TO QUALIFY AT INDY, SAYING IT WAS A PUBLICITY STUNT. A HOAX.
IT REALLY MADE ME ANGRY.
YES. COUNT ME IN.
THE NEXT DAY
WE'RE SOLD OUT!
WE SOLD MORE TICKETS TODAY THAN *ANY OTHER DAY—EVER!*
ALL THANKS TO MISS JANET GUTHRIE!
WELL, PEOPLE AREN'T COMING TO SEE HER WIN, HUMPY. THEY'RE HOPIN' SHE'LL LOSE—OR *CRASH!*
DOESN'T MATTER; WE FILLED THE GRANDSTAND! I'M NOT GONNA WORRY ABOUT WHO'S IN THE SEATS—OR WHY!

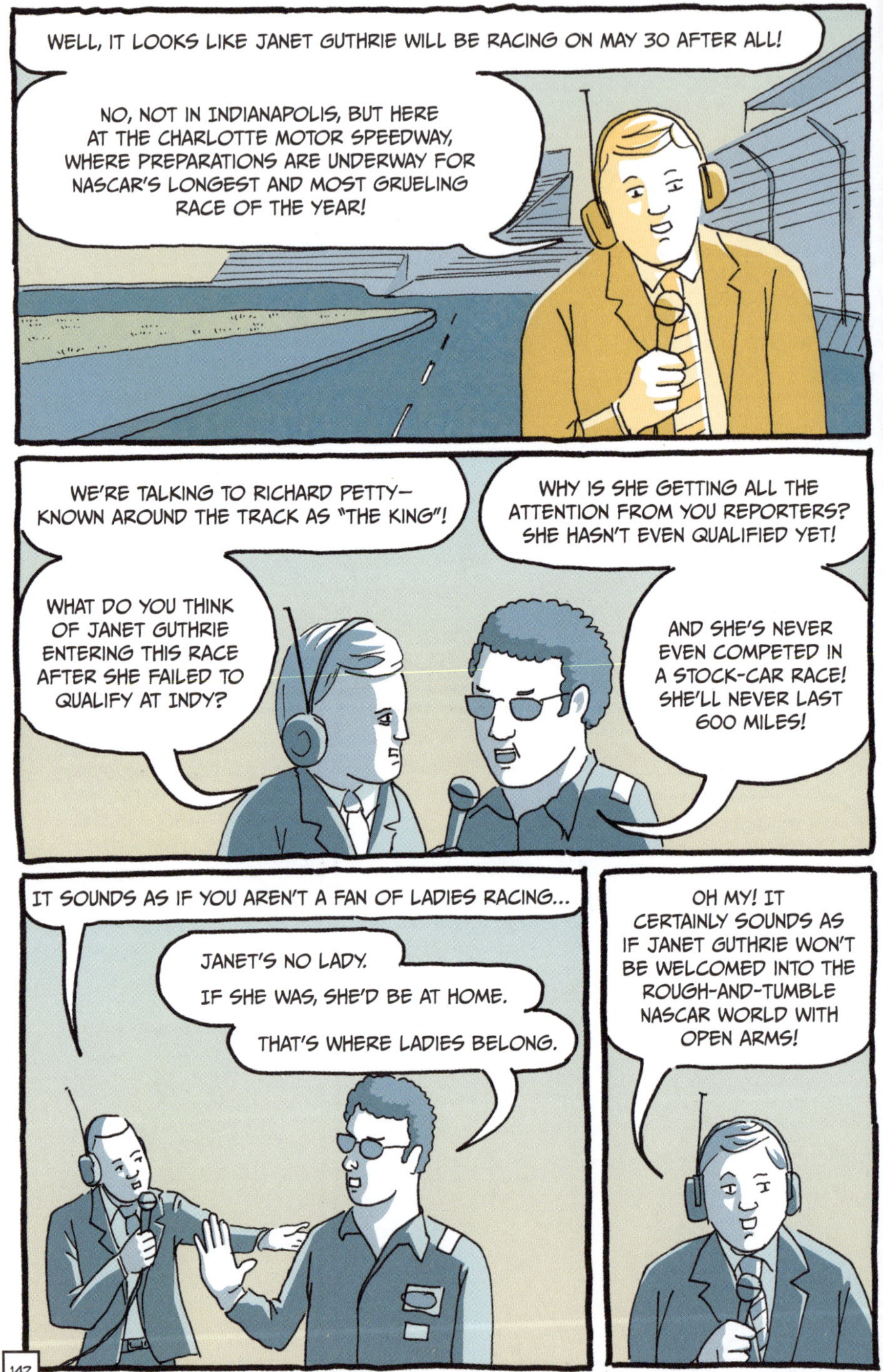
WELL, IT LOOKS LIKE JANET GUTHRIE WILL BE RACING ON MAY 30 AFTER ALL!
NO, NOT IN INDIANAPOLIS, BUT HERE AT THE CHARLOTTE MOTOR SPEEDWAY, WHERE PREPARATIONS ARE UNDERWAY FOR NASCAR'S LONGEST AND MOST GRUELING RACE OF THE YEAR!
WE'RE TALKING TO RICHARD PETTY— KNOWN AROUND THE TRACK AS "THE KING"!
WHAT DO YOU THINK OF JANET GUTHRIE ENTERING THIS RACE AFTER SHE FAILED TO QUALIFY AT INDY?
WHY IS SHE GETTING ALL THE ATTENTION FROM YOU REPORTERS? SHE HASN'T EVEN QUALIFIED YET!
AND SHE'S NEVER EVEN COMPETED IN A STOCK-CAR RACE! SHE'LL NEVER LAST 600 MILES!
IT SOUNDS AS IF YOU AREN'T A FAN OF LADIES RACING...
JANET'S NO LADY.
IF SHE WAS, SHE'D BE AT HOME.
THAT'S WHERE LADIES BELONG.
OH MY! IT CERTAINLY SOUNDS AS IF JANET GUTHRIE WON'T BE WELCOMED INTO THE ROUGH-AND-TUMBLE NASCAR WORLD WITH OPEN ARMS!

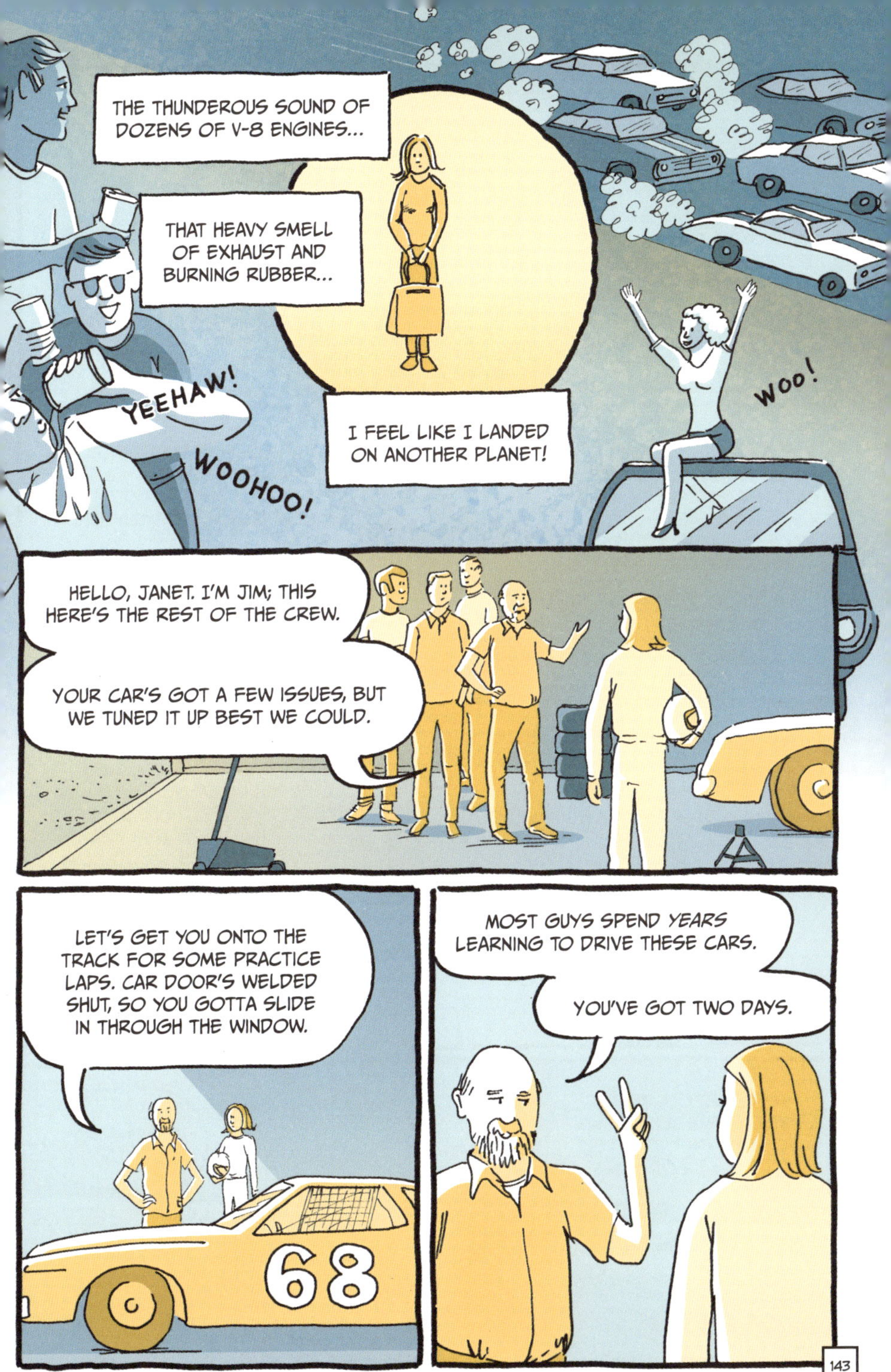

THE THUNDEROUS SOUND OF DOZENS OF V-8 ENGINES...
THAT HEAVY SMELL OF EXHAUST AND BURNING RUBBER...
YEEHAW!
WOOHOO!
I FEEL LIKE I LANDED ON ANOTHER PLANET!
WOO!
HELLO, JANET. I'M JIM; THIS HERE'S THE REST OF THE CREW.
YOUR CAR'S GOT A FEW ISSUES, BUT WE TUNED IT UP BEST WE COULD.
LET'S GET YOU ONTO THE TRACK FOR SOME PRACTICE LAPS. CAR DOOR'S WELDED SHUT, SO YOU GOTTA SLIDE IN THROUGH THE WINDOW.
68
MOST GUYS SPEND *YEARS* LEARNING TO DRIVE THESE CARS.
YOU'VE GOT TWO DAYS.

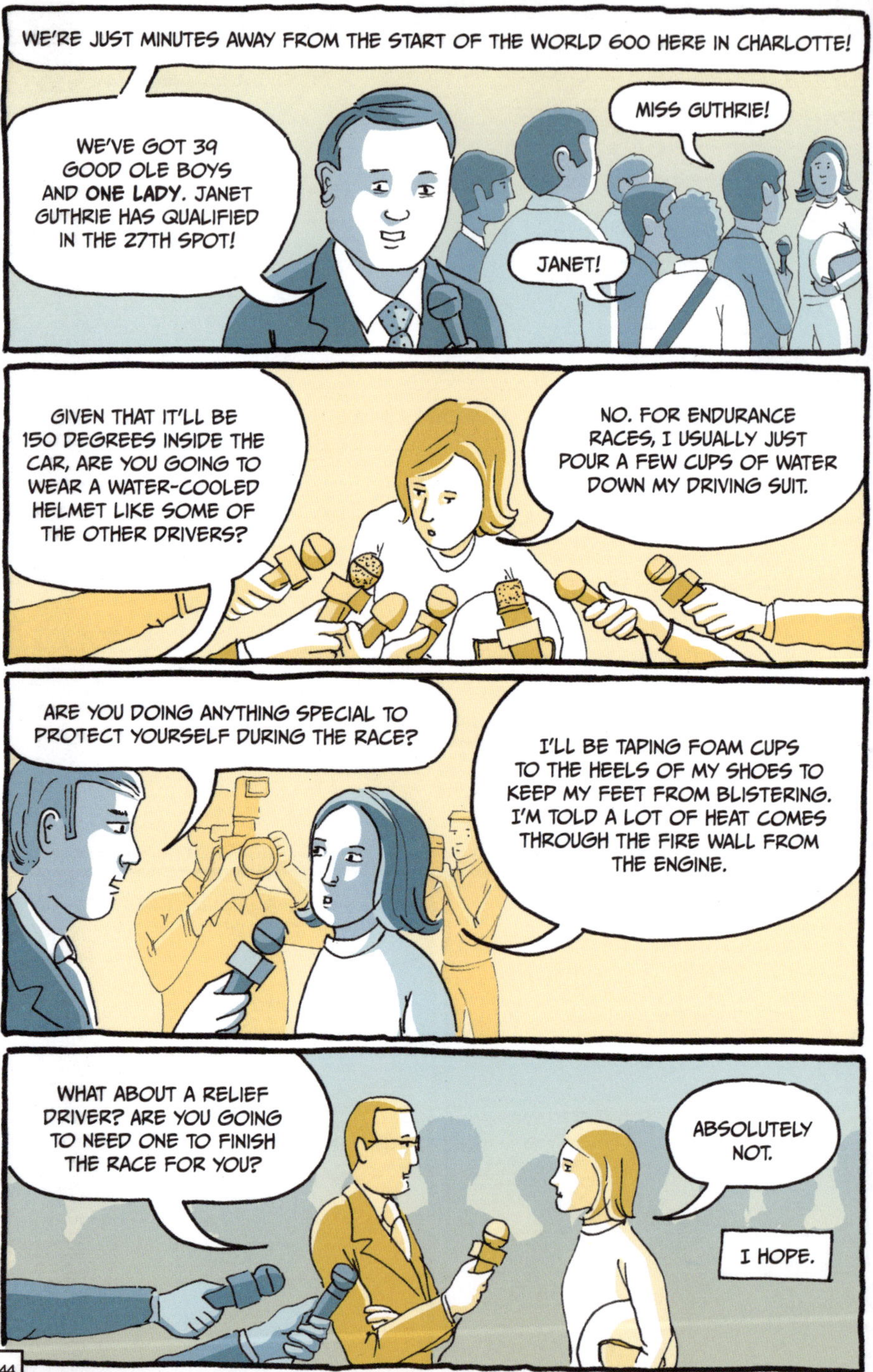
WE'RE JUST MINUTES AWAY FROM THE START OF THE WORLD 600 HERE IN CHARLOTTE!
WE'VE GOT 39 GOOD OLE BOYS AND **ONE LADY**. JANET GUTHRIE HAS QUALIFIED IN THE 27TH SPOT!
MISS GUTHRIE!
JANET!
GIVEN THAT IT'LL BE 150 DEGREES INSIDE THE CAR, ARE YOU GOING TO WEAR A WATER-COOLED HELMET LIKE SOME OF THE OTHER DRIVERS?
NO. FOR ENDURANCE RACES, I USUALLY JUST POUR A FEW CUPS OF WATER DOWN MY DRIVING SUIT.
ARE YOU DOING ANYTHING SPECIAL TO PROTECT YOURSELF DURING THE RACE?
I'LL BE TAPING FOAM CUPS TO THE HEELS OF MY SHOES TO KEEP MY FEET FROM BLISTERING. I'M TOLD A LOT OF HEAT COMES THROUGH THE FIRE WALL FROM THE ENGINE.
WHAT ABOUT A RELIEF DRIVER? ARE YOU GOING TO NEED ONE TO FINISH THE RACE FOR YOU?
ABSOLUTELY NOT.
I HOPE.

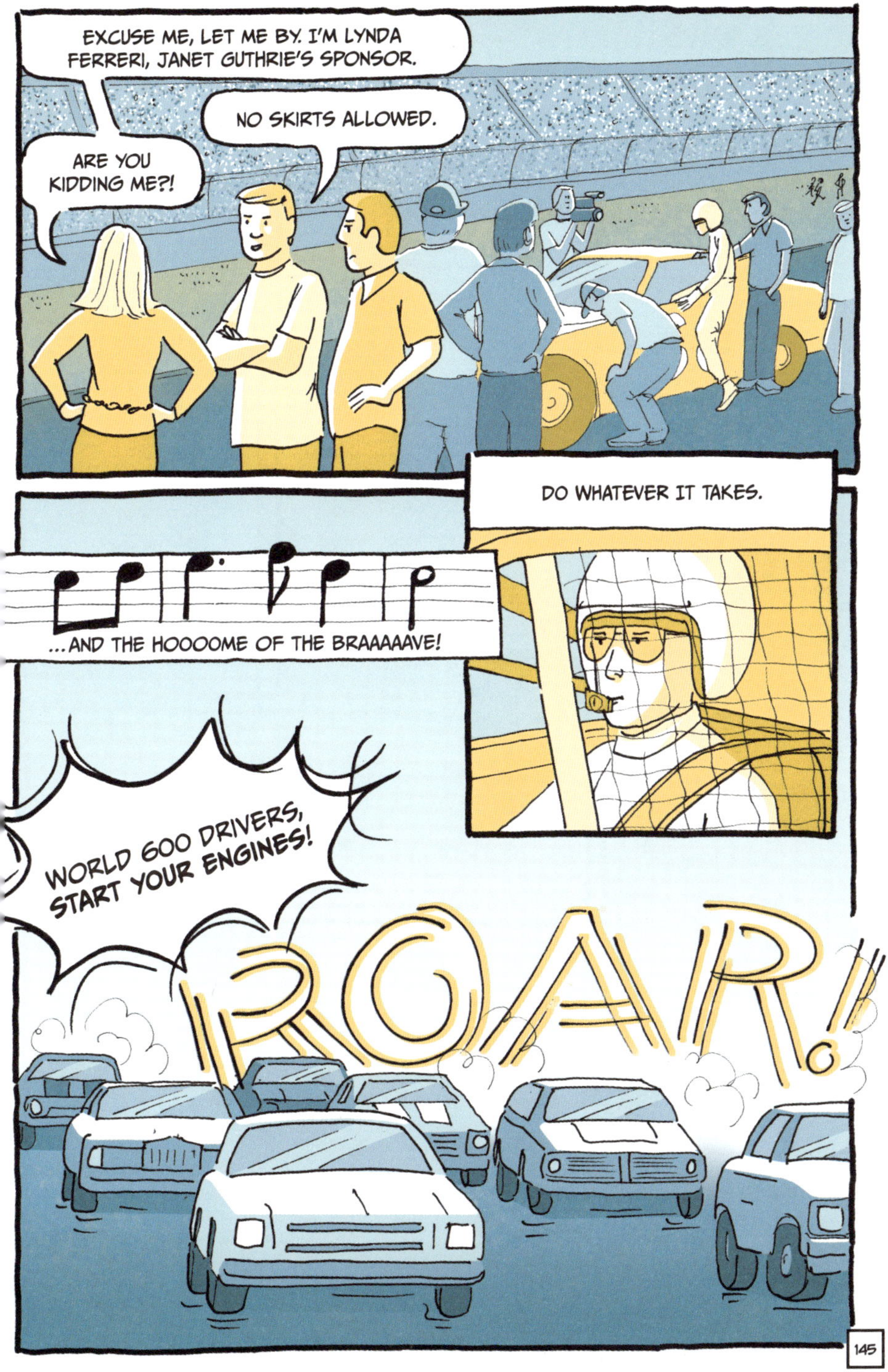
EXCUSE ME, LET ME BY. I'M LYNDA FERRERI, JANET GUTHRIE'S SPONSOR.
NO SKIRTS ALLOWED.
ARE YOU KIDDING ME?!
DO WHATEVER IT TAKES.
...AND THE HOOOOME OF THE BRAAAAAVE!
WORLD 600 DRIVERS, START YOUR ENGINES!
ROAR!

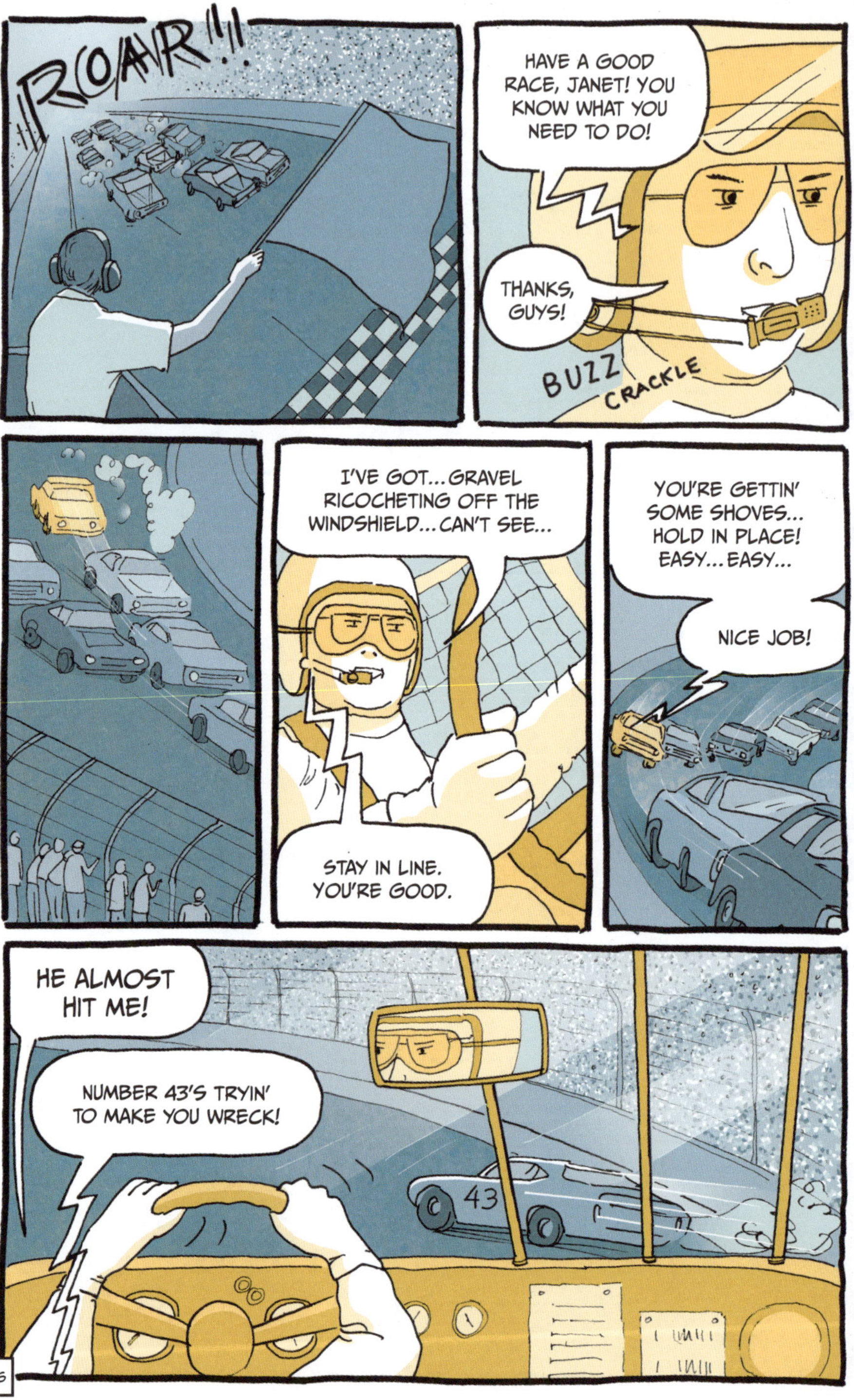
ROAR!!!
HAVE A GOOD RACE, JANET! YOU KNOW WHAT YOU NEED TO DO!
THANKS, GUYS!
BUZZ
CRACKLE
I'VE GOT...GRAVEL RICOCHETING OFF THE WINDSHIELD...CAN'T SEE...
STAY IN LINE. YOU'RE GOOD.
YOU'RE GETTIN' SOME SHOVES... HOLD IN PLACE! EASY...EASY...
NICE JOB!
HE ALMOST HIT ME!
NUMBER 43'S TRYIN' TO MAKE YOU WRECK!
43

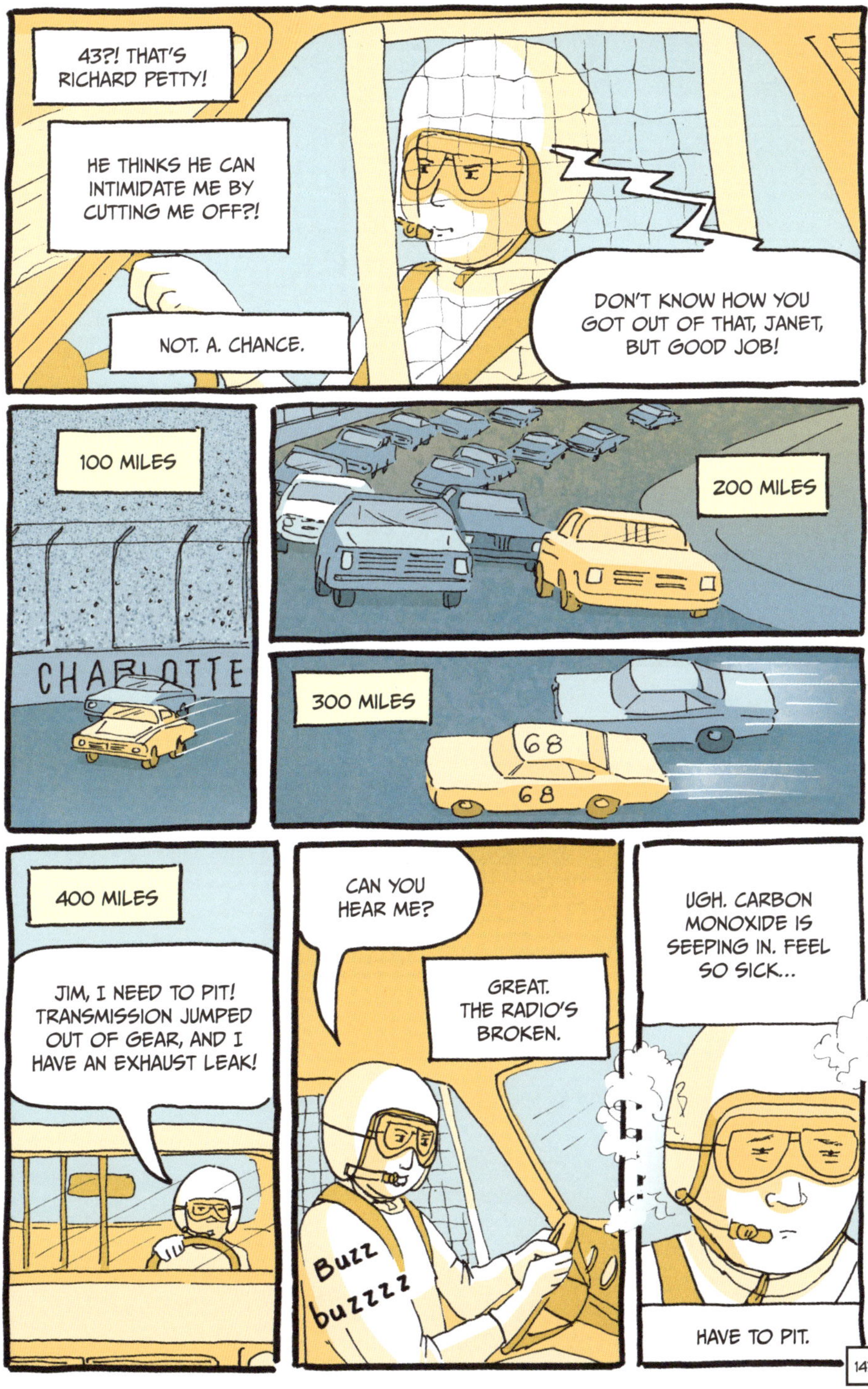
43?! THAT'S RICHARD PETTY!
HE THINKS HE CAN INTIMIDATE ME BY CUTTING ME OFF?!
NOT. A. CHANCE.
DON'T KNOW HOW YOU GOT OUT OF THAT, JANET, BUT GOOD JOB!
100 MILES
CHARLOTTE
200 MILES
300 MILES
68
68
400 MILES
JIM, I NEED TO PIT! TRANSMISSION JUMPED OUT OF GEAR, AND I HAVE AN EXHAUST LEAK!
CAN YOU HEAR ME?
GREAT. THE RADIO'S BROKEN.
Buzz buzzzzz
UGH. CARBON MONOXIDE IS SEEPING IN. FEEL SO SICK...
HAVE TO PIT.

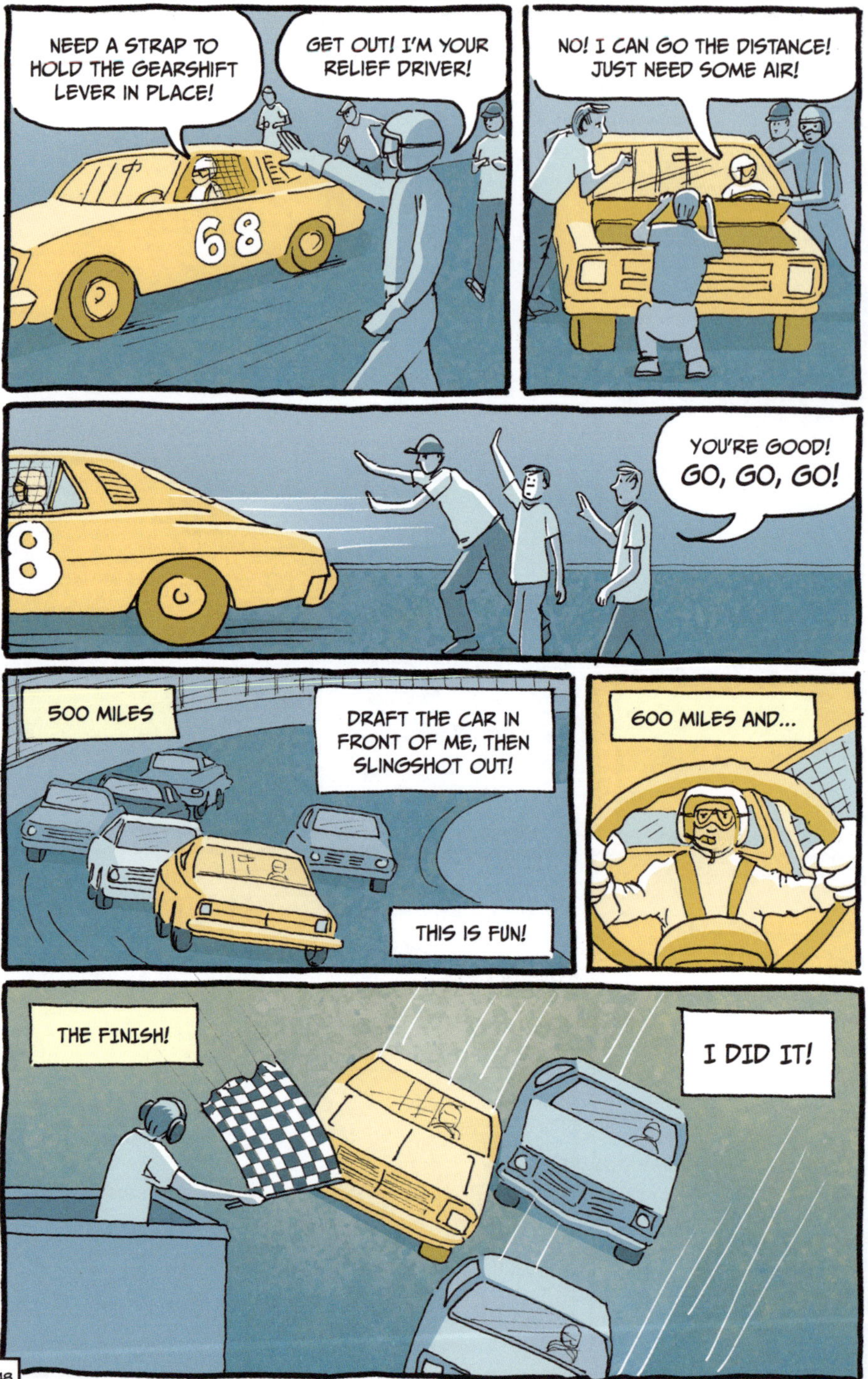
NEED A STRAP TO HOLD THE GEARSHIFT LEVER IN PLACE!
GET OUT! I'M YOUR RELIEF DRIVER!
68
NO! I CAN GO THE DISTANCE! JUST NEED SOME AIR!
YOU'RE GOOD! GO, GO, GO!
500 MILES
DRAFT THE CAR IN FRONT OF ME, THEN SLINGSHOT OUT!
THIS IS FUN!
600 MILES AND...
THE FINISH!
I DID IT!

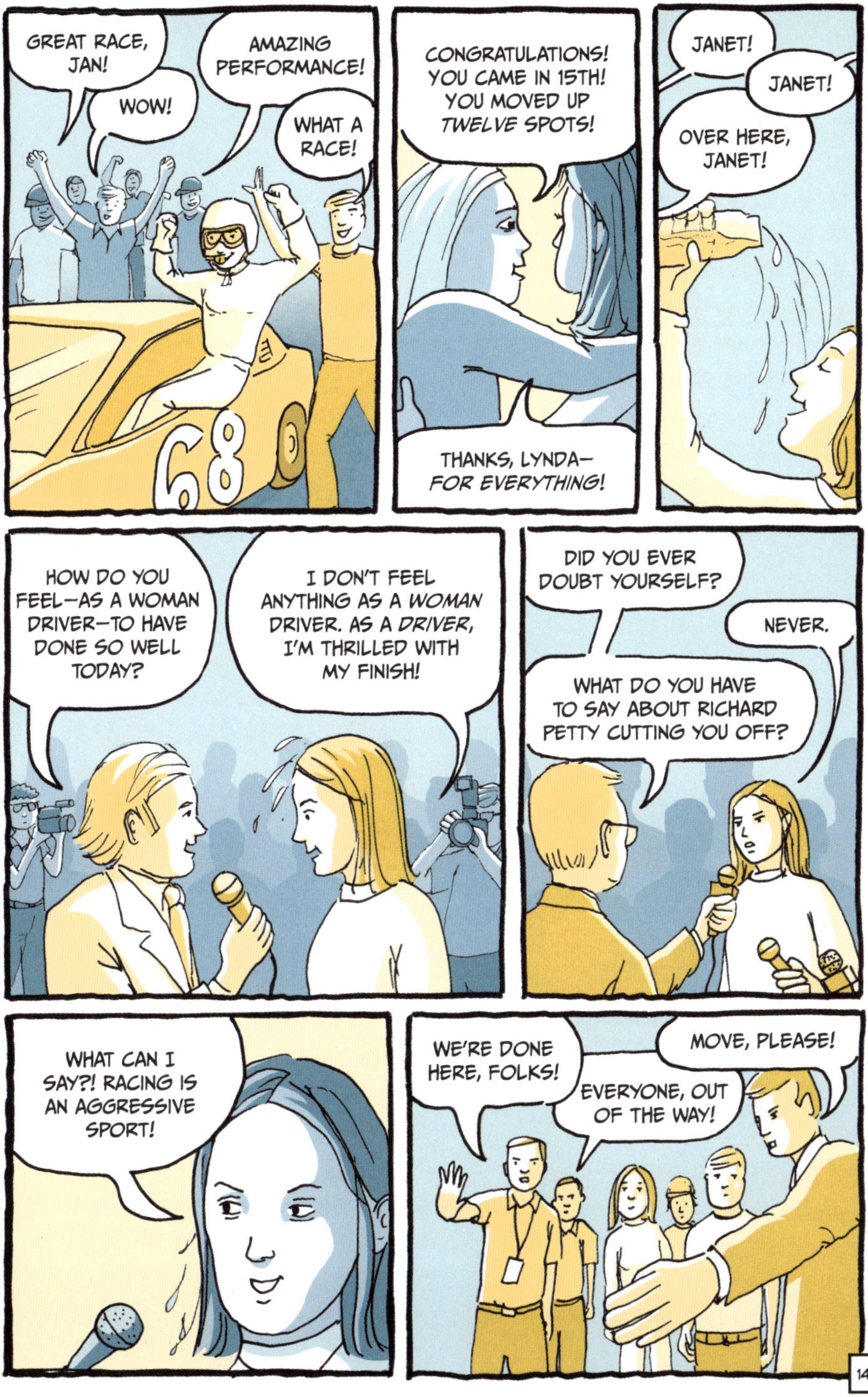
GREAT RACE, JAN!
WOW!
AMAZING PERFORMANCE!
WHAT A RACE!
CONGRATULATIONS! YOU CAME IN 15TH! YOU MOVED UP *TWELVE* SPOTS!
THANKS, LYNDA— *FOR EVERYTHING!*
JANET!
JANET!
OVER HERE, JANET!
HOW DO YOU FEEL—AS A WOMAN DRIVER—TO HAVE DONE SO WELL TODAY?
I DON'T FEEL ANYTHING AS A *WOMAN* DRIVER. AS A *DRIVER,* I'M THRILLED WITH MY FINISH!
DID YOU EVER DOUBT YOURSELF?
NEVER.
WHAT DO YOU HAVE TO SAY ABOUT RICHARD PETTY CUTTING YOU OFF?
WHAT CAN I SAY?! RACING IS AN AGGRESSIVE SPORT!
WE'RE DONE HERE, FOLKS!
EVERYONE, OUT OF THE WAY!
MOVE, PLEASE!

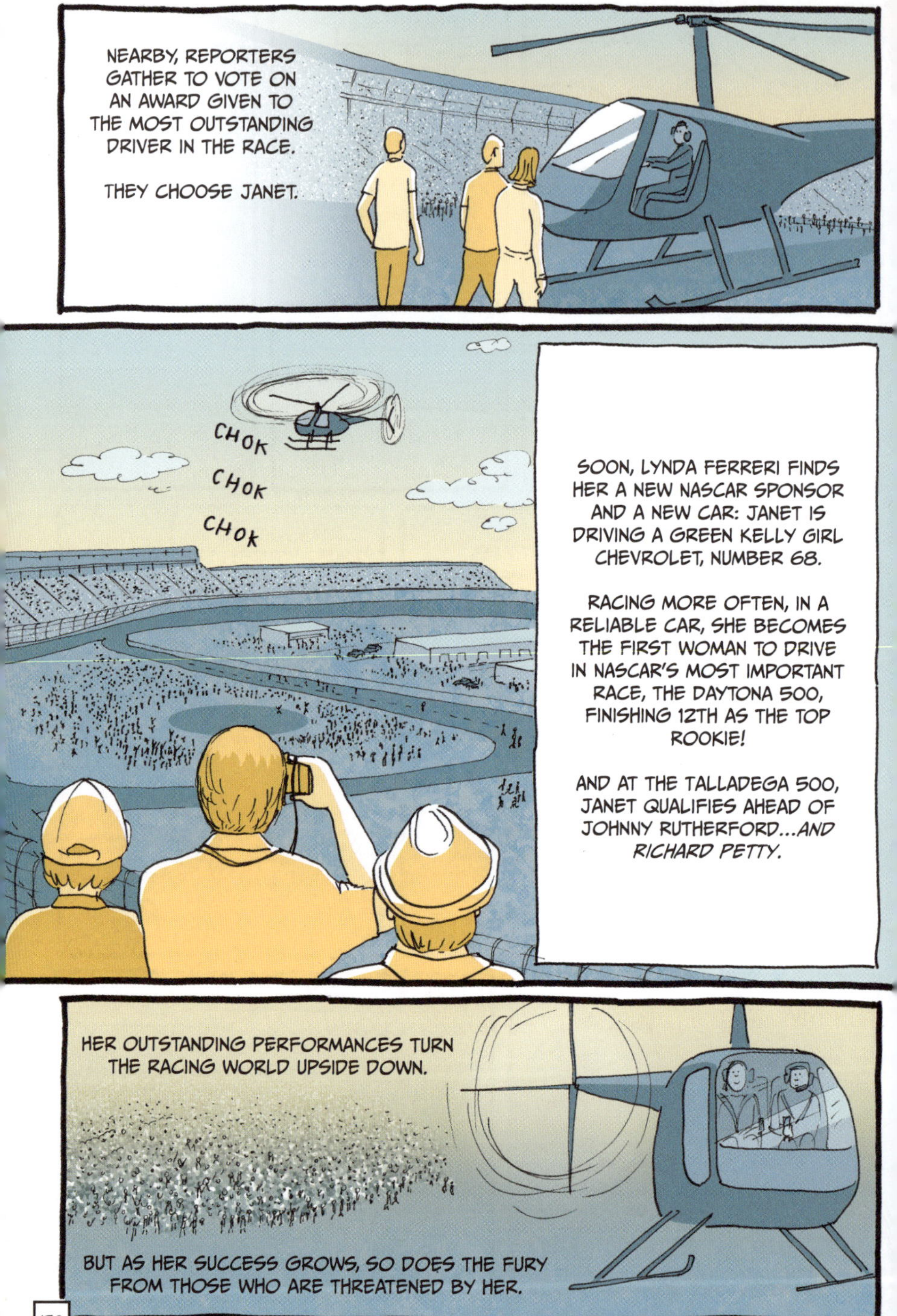
NEARBY, REPORTERS GATHER TO VOTE ON AN AWARD GIVEN TO THE MOST OUTSTANDING DRIVER IN THE RACE.
THEY CHOOSE JANET.
CHOK
CHOK
CHOK
SOON, LYNDA FERRERI FINDS HER A NEW NASCAR SPONSOR AND A NEW CAR: JANET IS DRIVING A GREEN KELLY GIRL CHEVROLET, NUMBER 68.
RACING MORE OFTEN, IN A RELIABLE CAR, SHE BECOMES THE FIRST WOMAN TO DRIVE IN NASCAR'S MOST IMPORTANT RACE, THE DAYTONA 500, FINISHING 12TH AS THE TOP ROOKIE!
AND AT THE TALLADEGA 500, JANET QUALIFIES AHEAD OF JOHNNY RUTHERFORD...*AND RICHARD PETTY.*
HER OUTSTANDING PERFORMANCES TURN THE RACING WORLD UPSIDE DOWN.
BUT AS HER SUCCESS GROWS, SO DOES THE FURY FROM THOSE WHO ARE THREATENED BY HER.

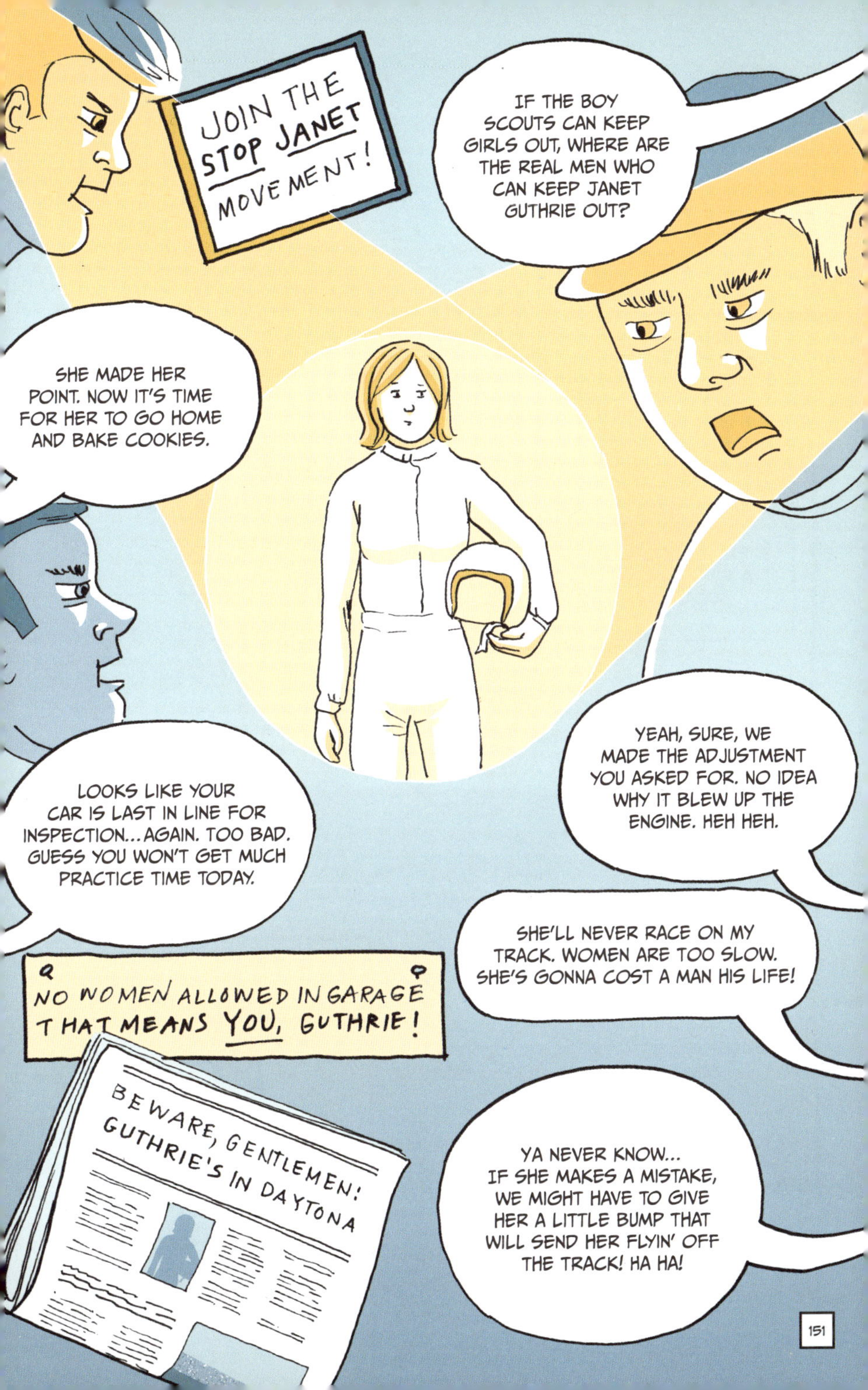
JOIN THE STOP JANET MOVEMENT!
IF THE BOY SCOUTS CAN KEEP GIRLS OUT, WHERE ARE THE REAL MEN WHO CAN KEEP JANET GUTHRIE OUT?
SHE MADE HER POINT. NOW IT'S TIME FOR HER TO GO HOME AND BAKE COOKIES.
YEAH, SURE, WE MADE THE ADJUSTMENT YOU ASKED FOR. NO IDEA WHY IT BLEW UP THE ENGINE. HEH HEH.
LOOKS LIKE YOUR CAR IS LAST IN LINE FOR INSPECTION... AGAIN. TOO BAD. GUESS YOU WON'T GET MUCH PRACTICE TIME TODAY.
SHE'LL NEVER RACE ON MY TRACK. WOMEN ARE TOO SLOW. SHE'S GONNA COST A MAN HIS LIFE!
NO WOMEN ALLOWED IN GARAGE THAT MEANS YOU, GUTHRIE!
BEWARE, GENTLEMEN! GUTHRIE'S IN DAYTONA
YA NEVER KNOW... IF SHE MAKES A MISTAKE, WE MIGHT HAVE TO GIVE HER A LITTLE BUMP THAT WILL SEND HER FLYIN' OFF THE TRACK! HA HA!

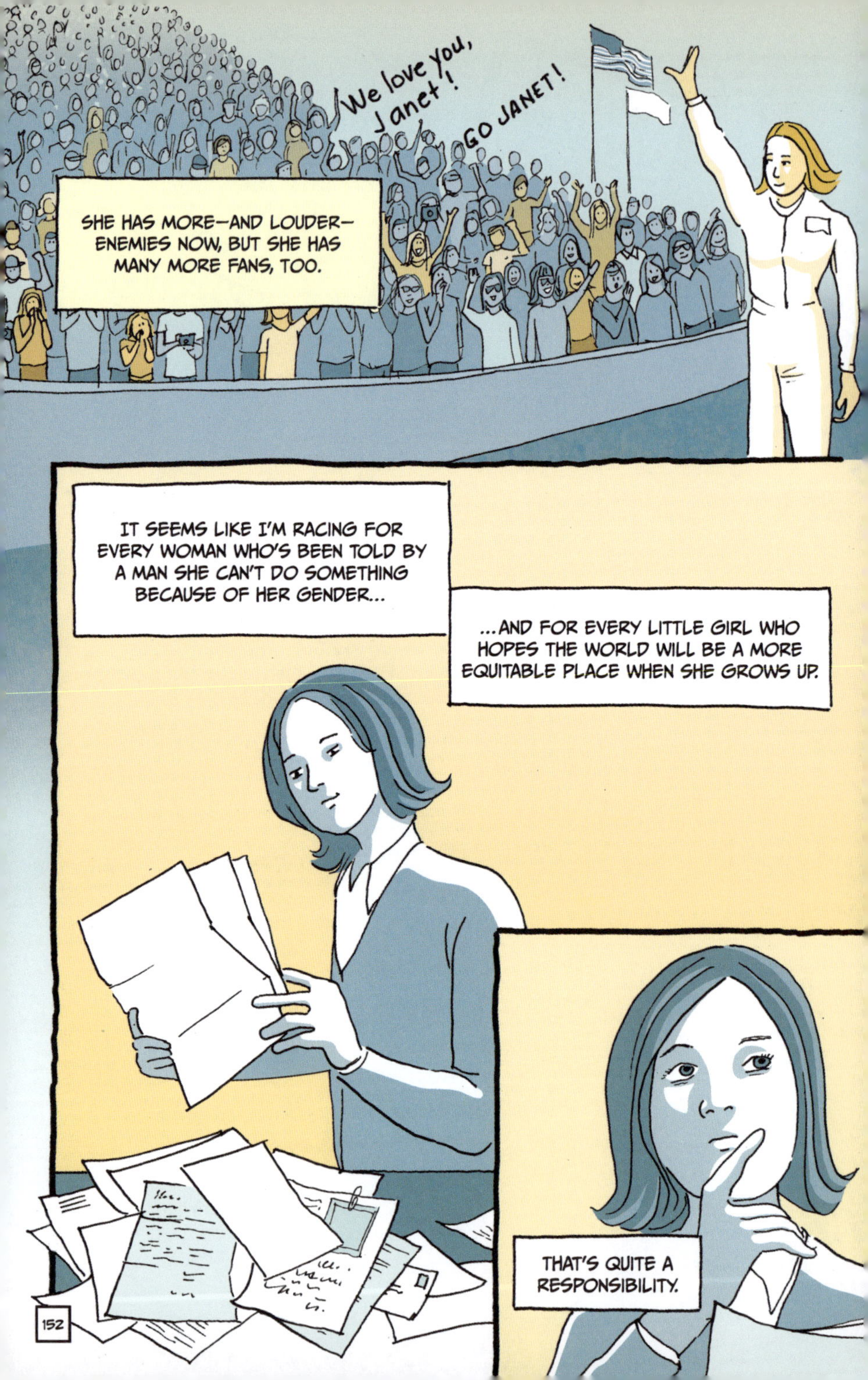
We love you, Janet!
GO JANET!
SHE HAS MORE—AND LOUDER—ENEMIES NOW, BUT SHE HAS MANY MORE FANS, TOO.
IT SEEMS LIKE I'M RACING FOR EVERY WOMAN WHO'S BEEN TOLD BY A MAN SHE CAN'T DO SOMETHING BECAUSE OF HER GENDER...
...AND FOR EVERY LITTLE GIRL WHO HOPES THE WORLD WILL BE A MORE EQUITABLE PLACE WHEN SHE GROWS UP.
THAT'S QUITE A RESPONSIBILITY.

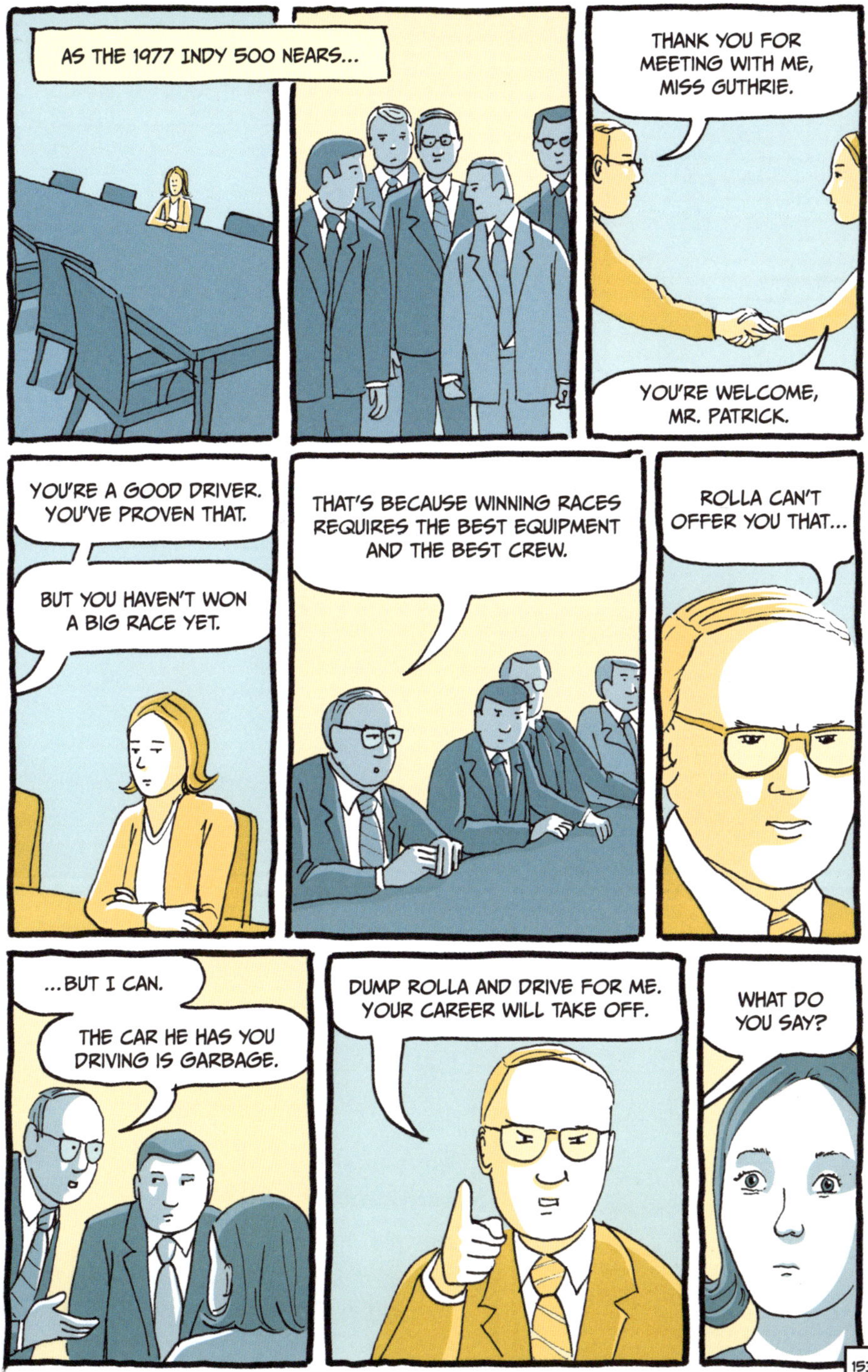
AS THE 1977 INDY 500 NEARS...
THANK YOU FOR MEETING WITH ME, MISS GUTHRIE.
YOU'RE WELCOME, MR. PATRICK.
YOU'RE A GOOD DRIVER. YOU'VE PROVEN THAT.
BUT YOU HAVEN'T WON A BIG RACE YET.
THAT'S BECAUSE WINNING RACES REQUIRES THE BEST EQUIPMENT AND THE BEST CREW.
ROLLA CAN'T OFFER YOU THAT...
...BUT I CAN.
THE CAR HE HAS YOU DRIVING IS GARBAGE.
DUMP ROLLA AND DRIVE FOR ME. YOUR CAREER WILL TAKE OFF.
WHAT DO YOU SAY?

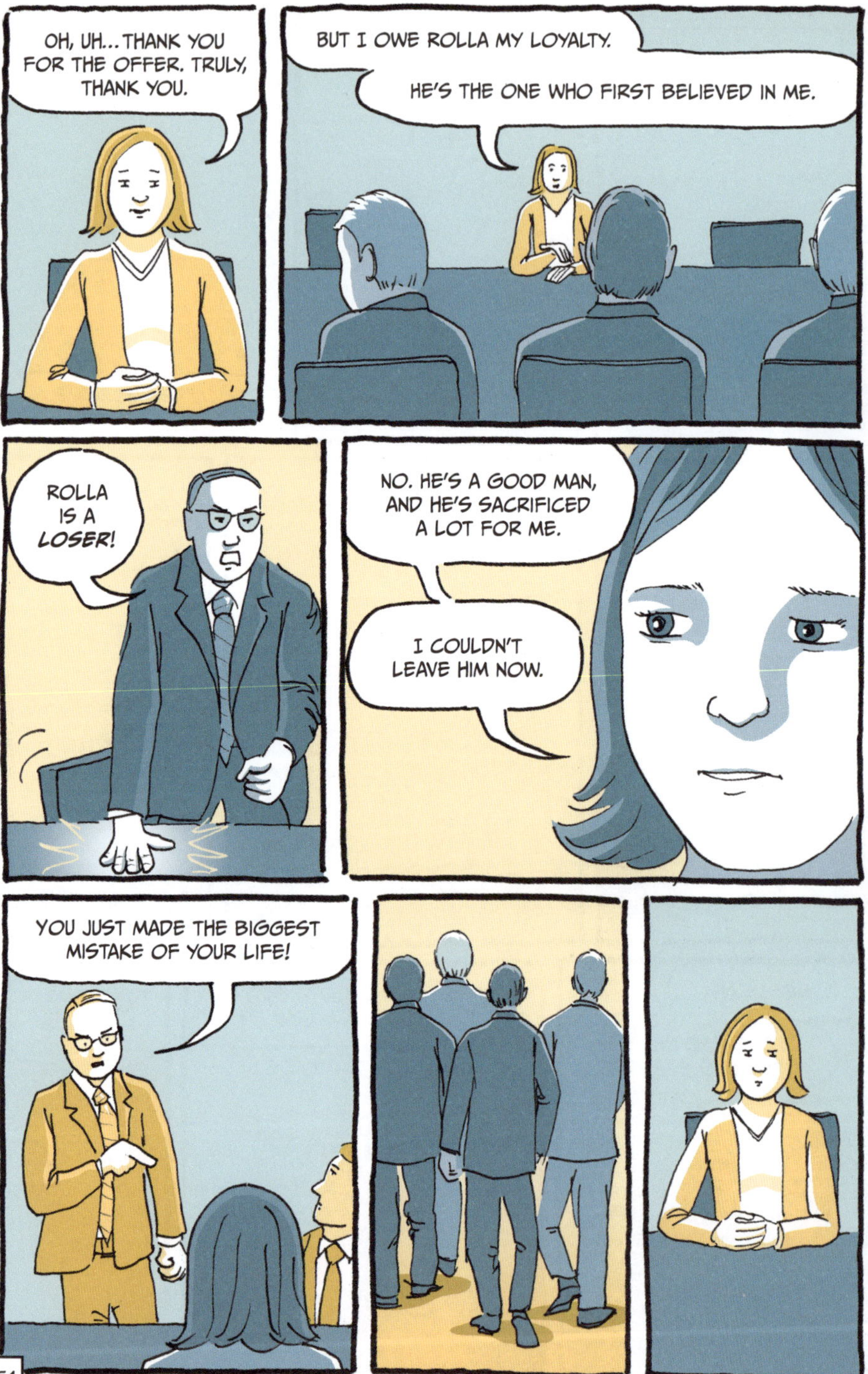

OH, UH...THANK YOU FOR THE OFFER. TRULY, THANK YOU.
BUT I OWE ROLLA MY LOYALTY.
HE'S THE ONE WHO FIRST BELIEVED IN ME.
ROLLA IS A *LOSER!*
NO. HE'S A GOOD MAN, AND HE'S SACRIFICED A LOT FOR ME.
I COULDN'T LEAVE HIM NOW.
YOU JUST MADE THE BIGGEST MISTAKE OF YOUR LIFE!

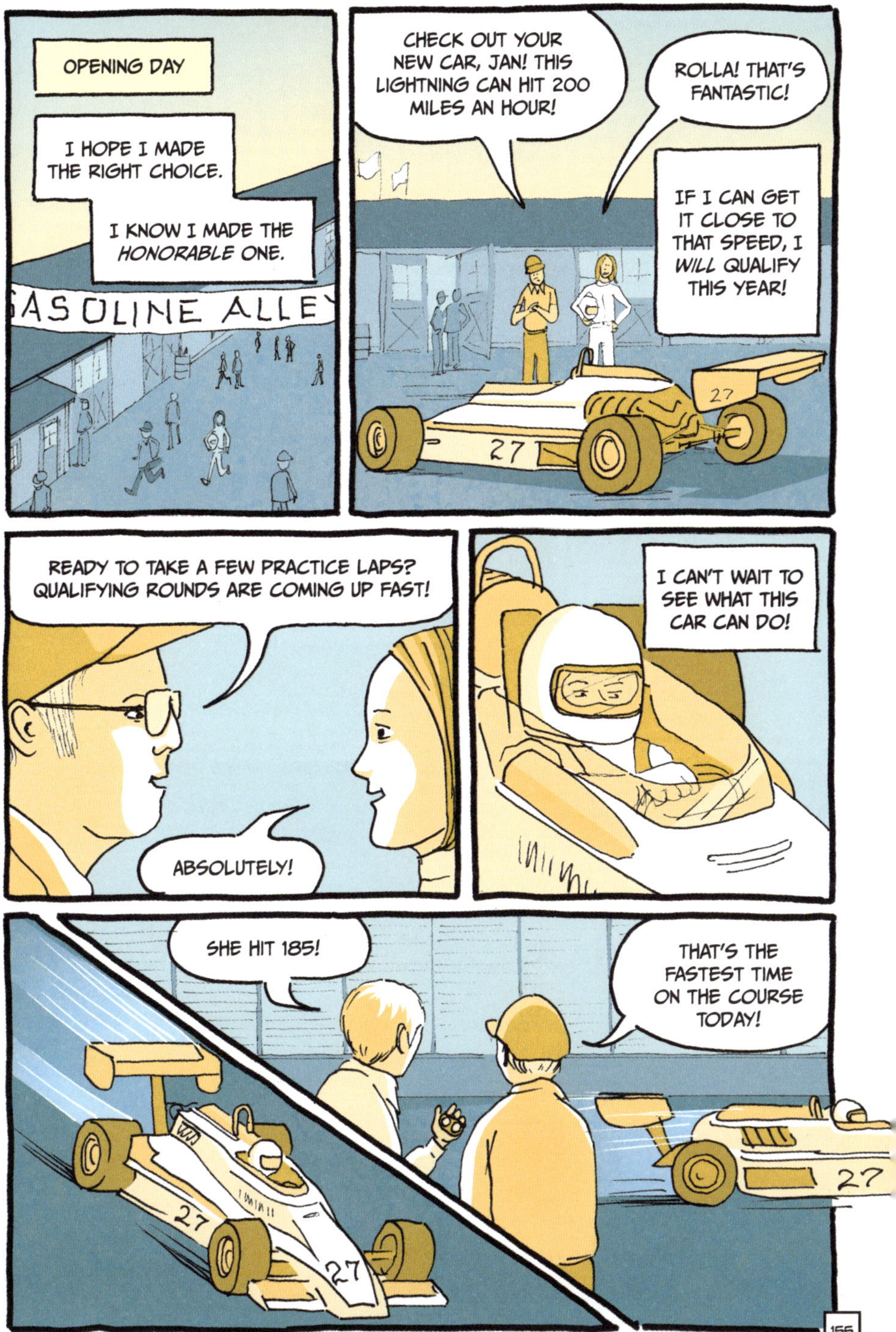
OPENING DAY
I HOPE I MADE THE RIGHT CHOICE.
I KNOW I MADE THE *HONORABLE* ONE.
GASOLINE ALLEY
CHECK OUT YOUR NEW CAR, JAN! THIS LIGHTNING CAN HIT 200 MILES AN HOUR!
ROLLA! THAT'S FANTASTIC!
IF I CAN GET IT CLOSE TO THAT SPEED, I *WILL* QUALIFY THIS YEAR!
27
READY TO TAKE A FEW PRACTICE LAPS? QUALIFYING ROUNDS ARE COMING UP FAST!
ABSOLUTELY!
I CAN'T WAIT TO SEE WHAT THIS CAR CAN DO!
SHE HIT 185!
THAT'S THE FASTEST TIME ON THE COURSE TODAY!
27

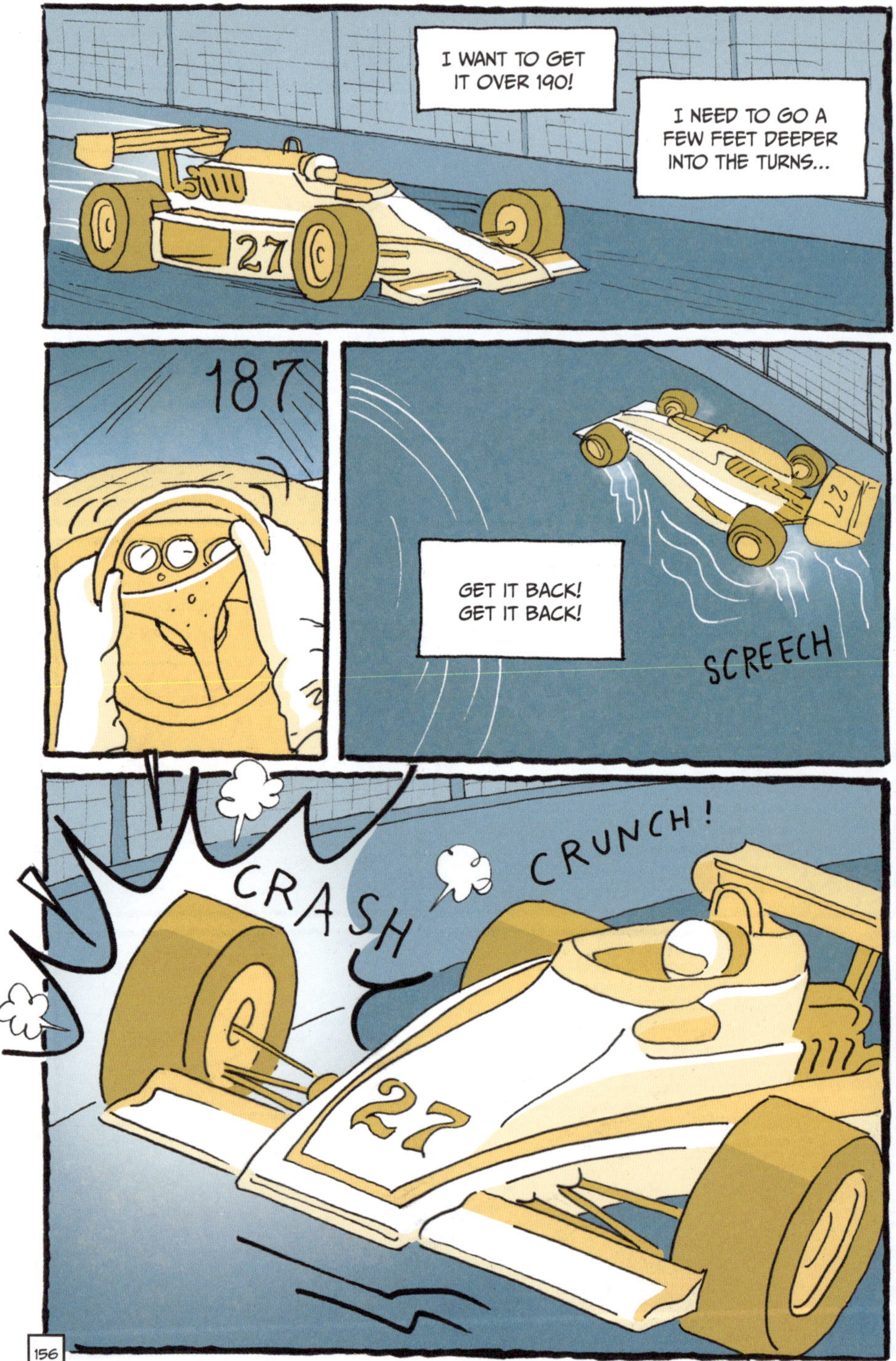
I WANT TO GET IT OVER 190!
I NEED TO GO A FEW FEET DEEPER INTO THE TURNS...
187
GET IT BACK! GET IT BACK!
SCREECH
CRASH
CRUNCH!

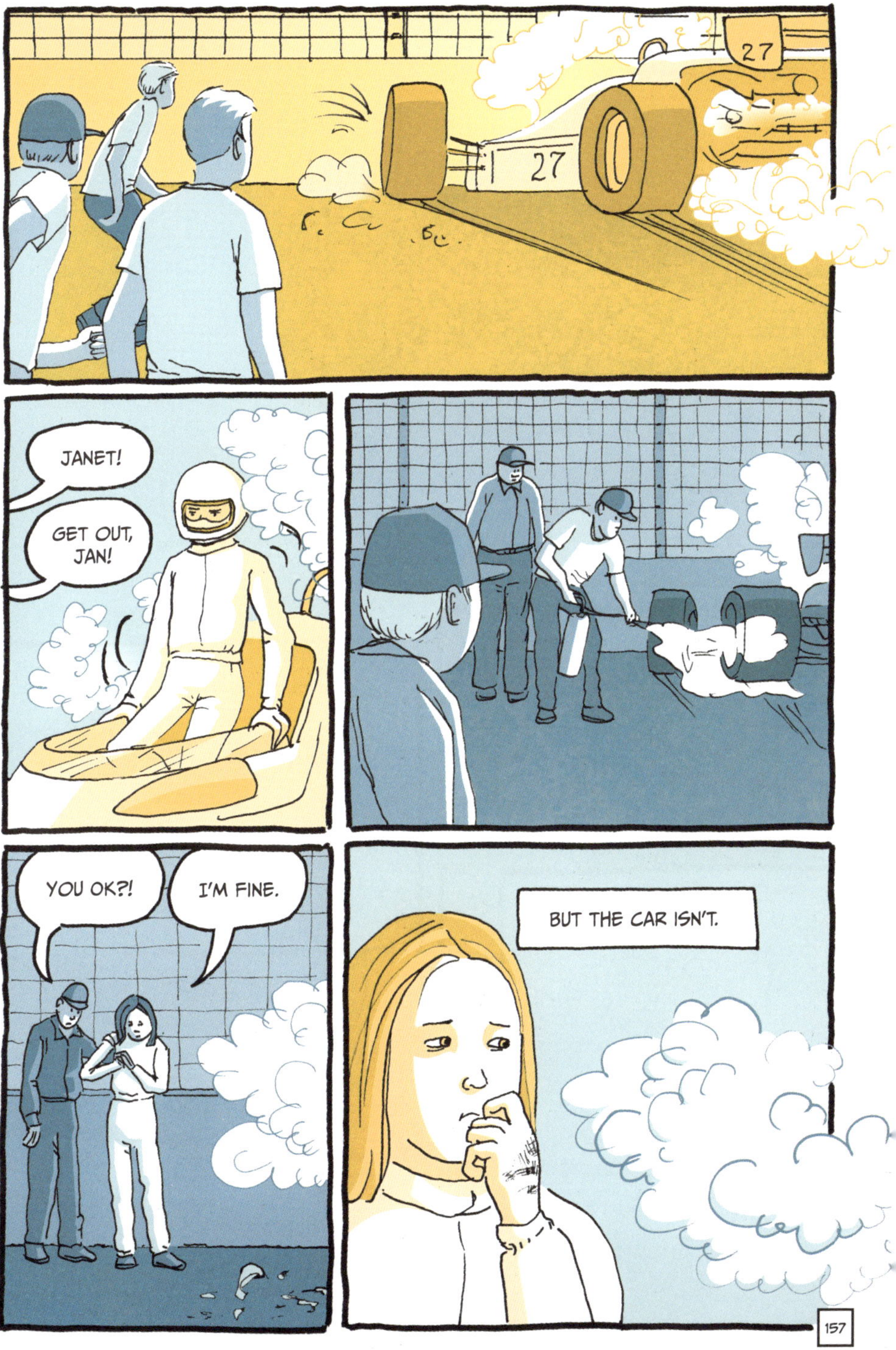
JANET!
GET OUT, JAN!
YOU OK?!
I'M FINE.
BUT THE CAR ISN'T.

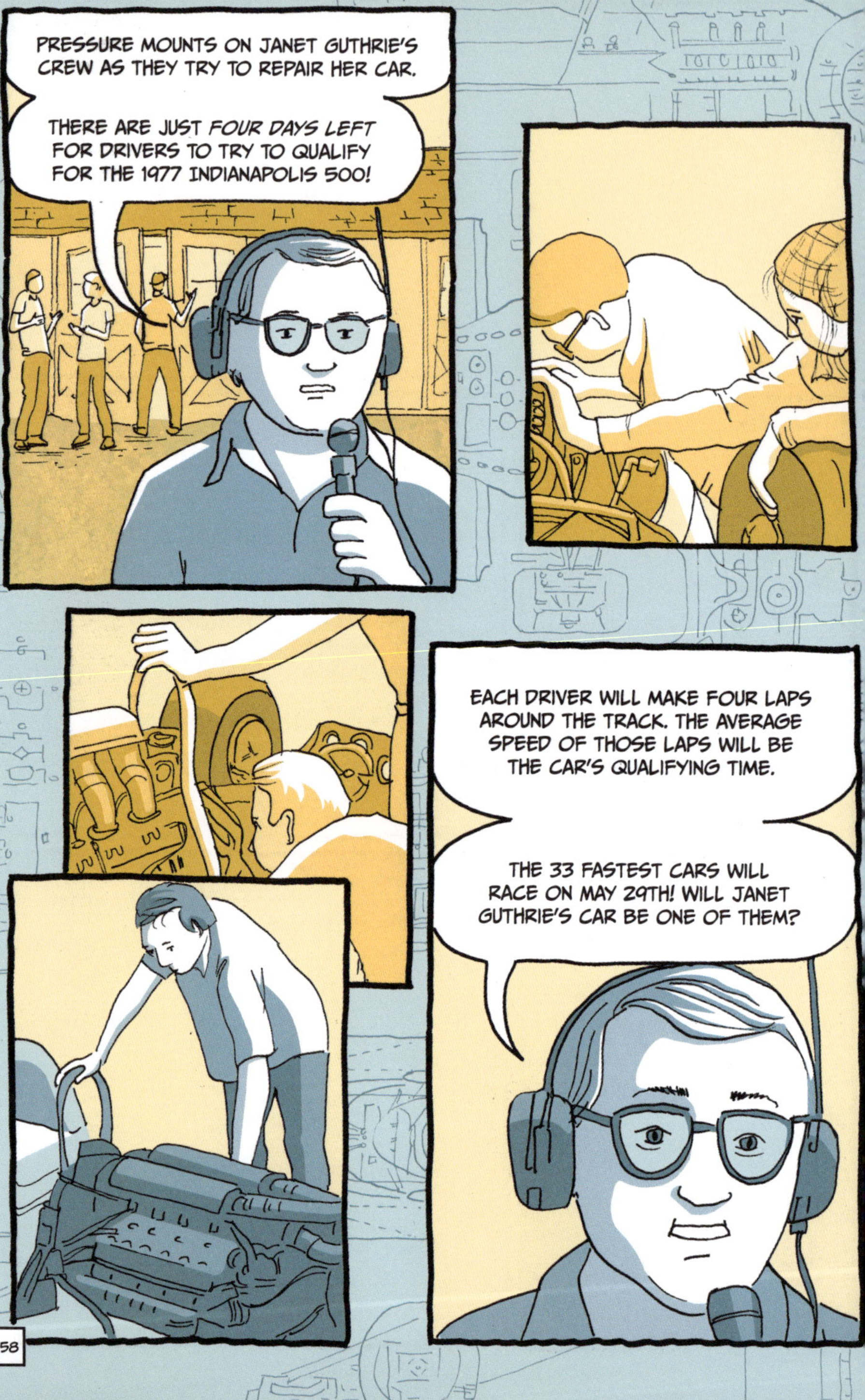
PRESSURE MOUNTS ON JANET GUTHRIE'S CREW AS THEY TRY TO REPAIR HER CAR.
THERE ARE JUST *FOUR DAYS LEFT* FOR DRIVERS TO TRY TO QUALIFY FOR THE 1977 INDIANAPOLIS 500!
EACH DRIVER WILL MAKE FOUR LAPS AROUND THE TRACK. THE AVERAGE SPEED OF THOSE LAPS WILL BE THE CAR'S QUALIFYING TIME.
THE 33 FASTEST CARS WILL RACE ON MAY 29TH! WILL JANET GUTHRIE'S CAR BE ONE OF THEM?

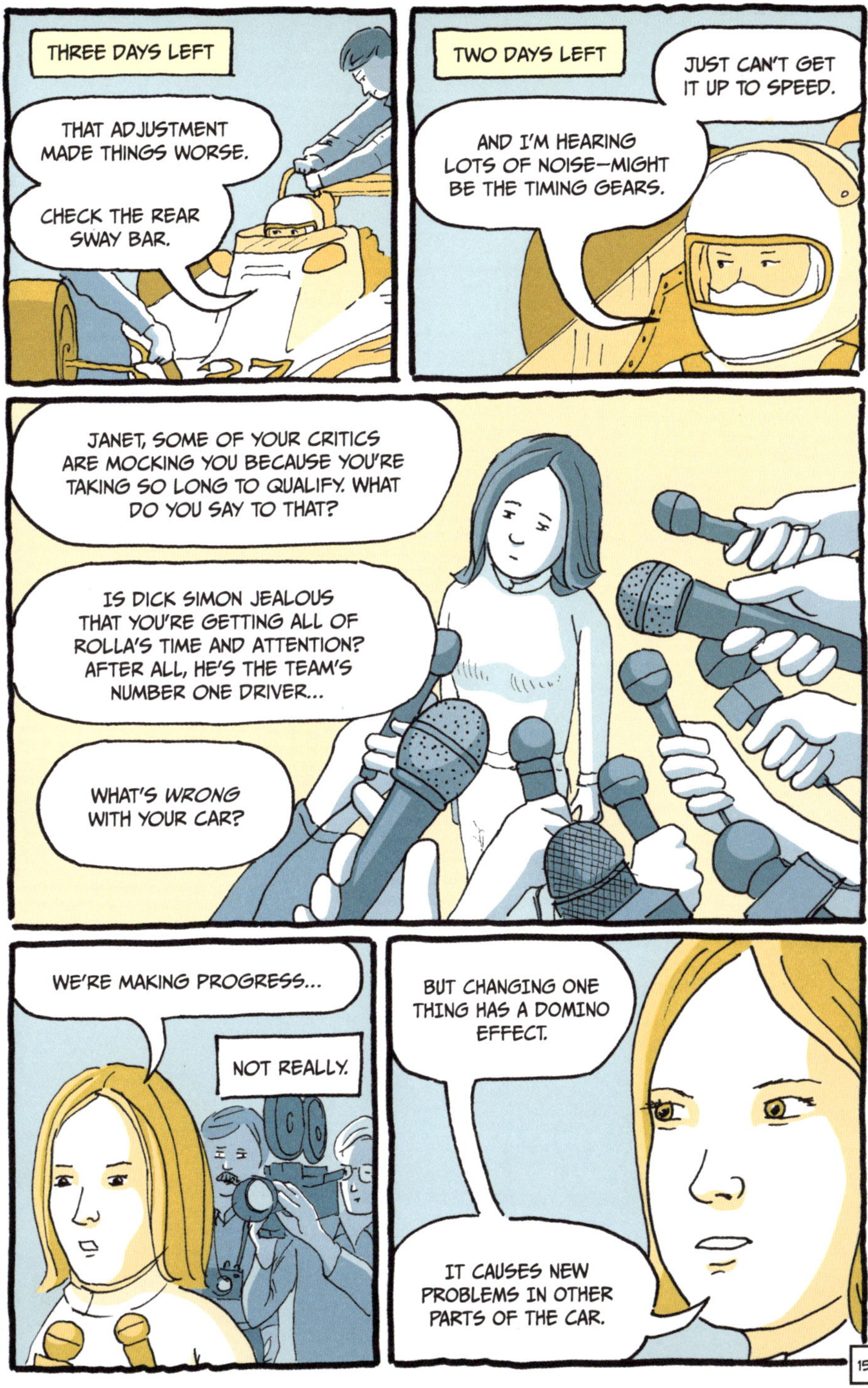
THREE DAYS LEFT
THAT ADJUSTMENT MADE THINGS WORSE.
CHECK THE REAR SWAY BAR.
TWO DAYS LEFT
JUST CAN'T GET IT UP TO SPEED.
AND I'M HEARING LOTS OF NOISE—MIGHT BE THE TIMING GEARS.
JANET, SOME OF YOUR CRITICS ARE MOCKING YOU BECAUSE YOU'RE TAKING SO LONG TO QUALIFY. WHAT DO YOU SAY TO THAT?
IS DICK SIMON JEALOUS THAT YOU'RE GETTING ALL OF ROLLA'S TIME AND ATTENTION? AFTER ALL, HE'S THE TEAM'S NUMBER ONE DRIVER...
WHAT'S *WRONG* WITH YOUR CAR?
WE'RE MAKING PROGRESS...
NOT REALLY.
BUT CHANGING ONE THING HAS A DOMINO EFFECT.
IT CAUSES NEW PROBLEMS IN OTHER PARTS OF THE CAR.

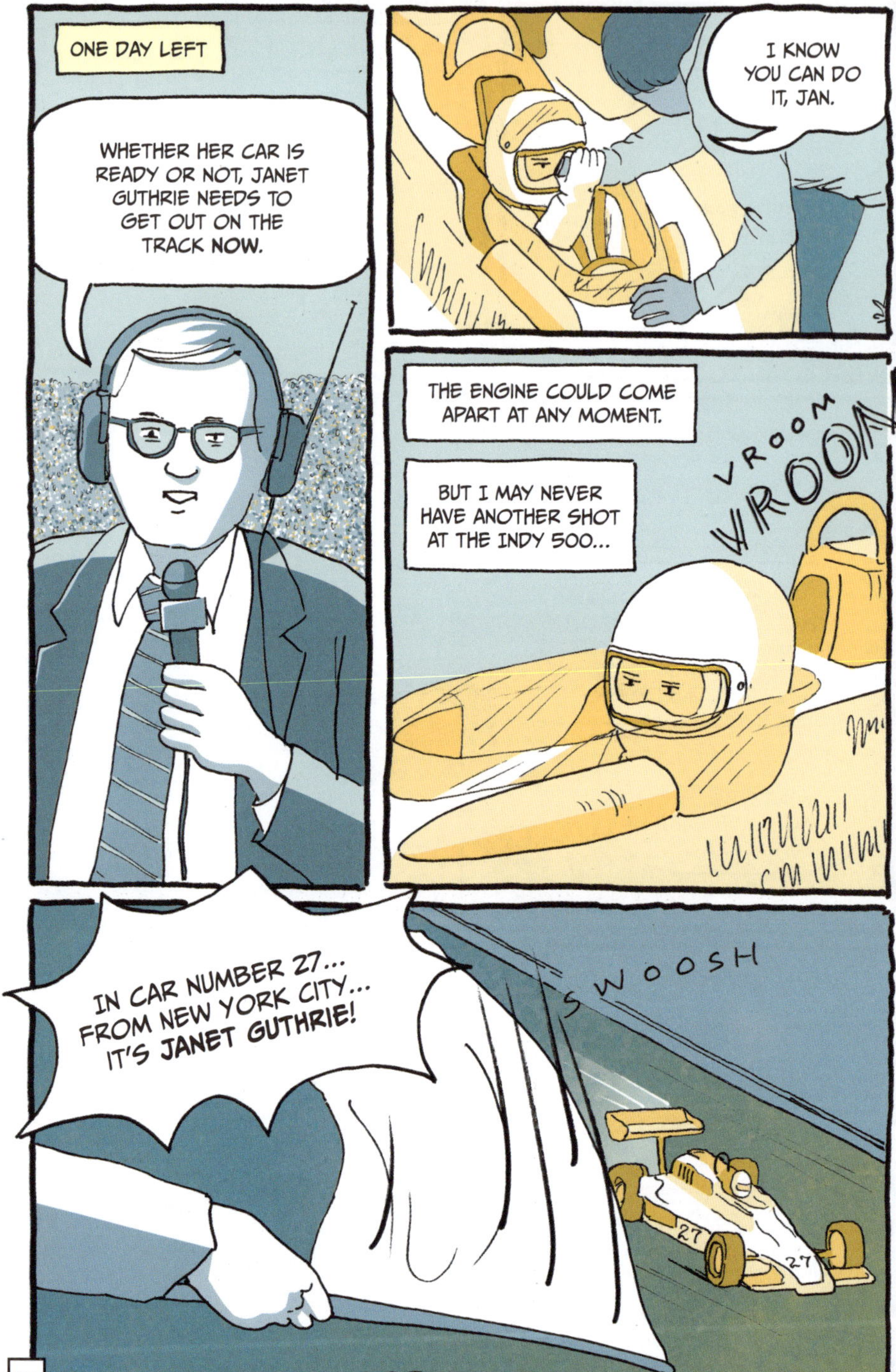
ONE DAY LEFT
WHETHER HER CAR IS READY OR NOT, JANET GUTHRIE NEEDS TO GET OUT ON THE TRACK **NOW**.
I KNOW YOU CAN DO IT, JAN.
THE ENGINE COULD COME APART AT ANY MOMENT.
BUT I MAY NEVER HAVE ANOTHER SHOT AT THE INDY 500...
VROOM
VROOM
IN CAR NUMBER 27... FROM NEW YORK CITY... IT'S **JANET GUTHRIE**!
SWOOSH
27

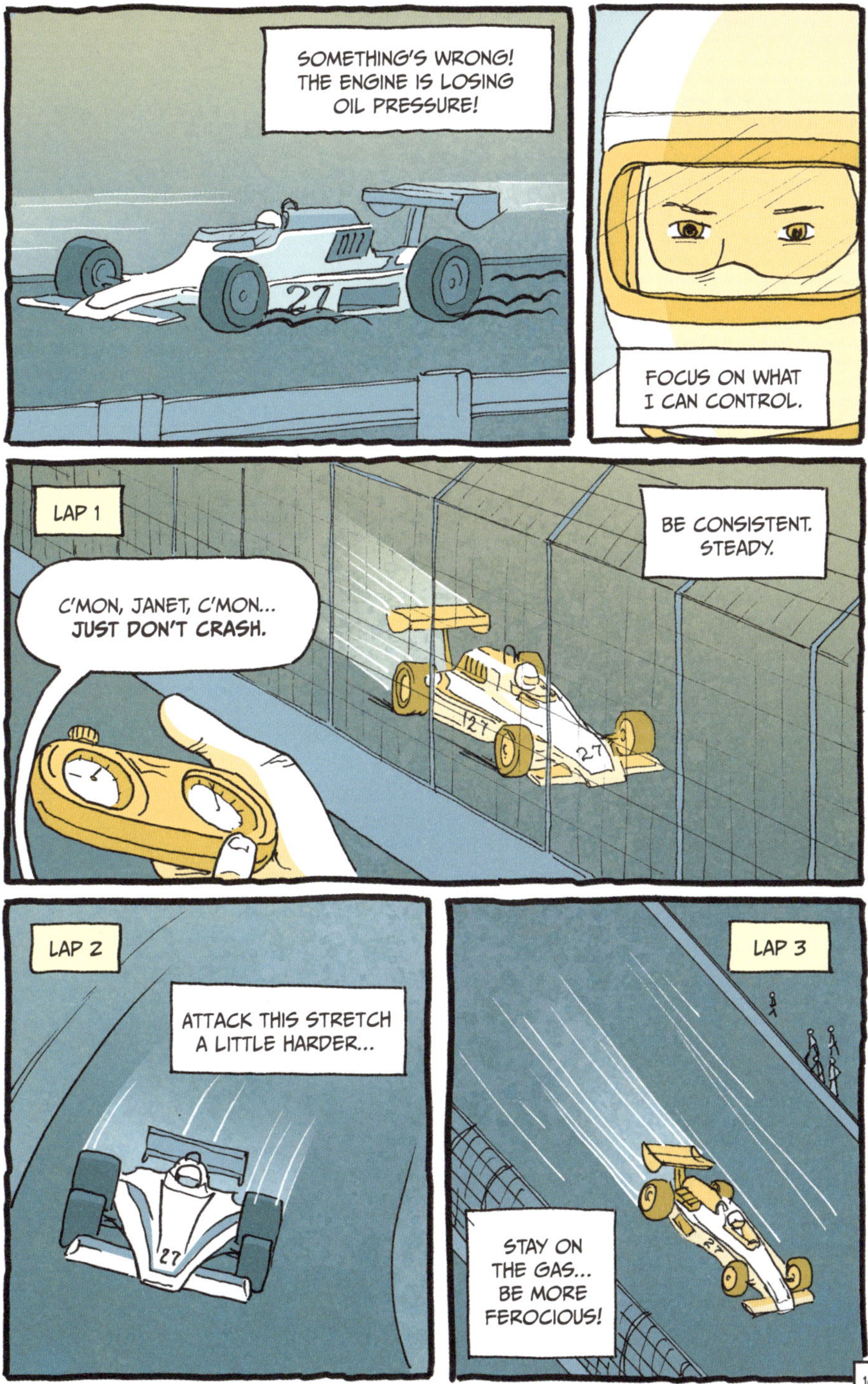
SOMETHING'S WRONG! THE ENGINE IS LOSING OIL PRESSURE!
FOCUS ON WHAT I CAN CONTROL.
LAP 1
BE CONSISTENT. STEADY.
C'MON, JANET, C'MON... **JUST DON'T CRASH.**
LAP 2
ATTACK THIS STRETCH A LITTLE HARDER...
LAP 3
STAY ON THE GAS... BE MORE FEROCIOUS!

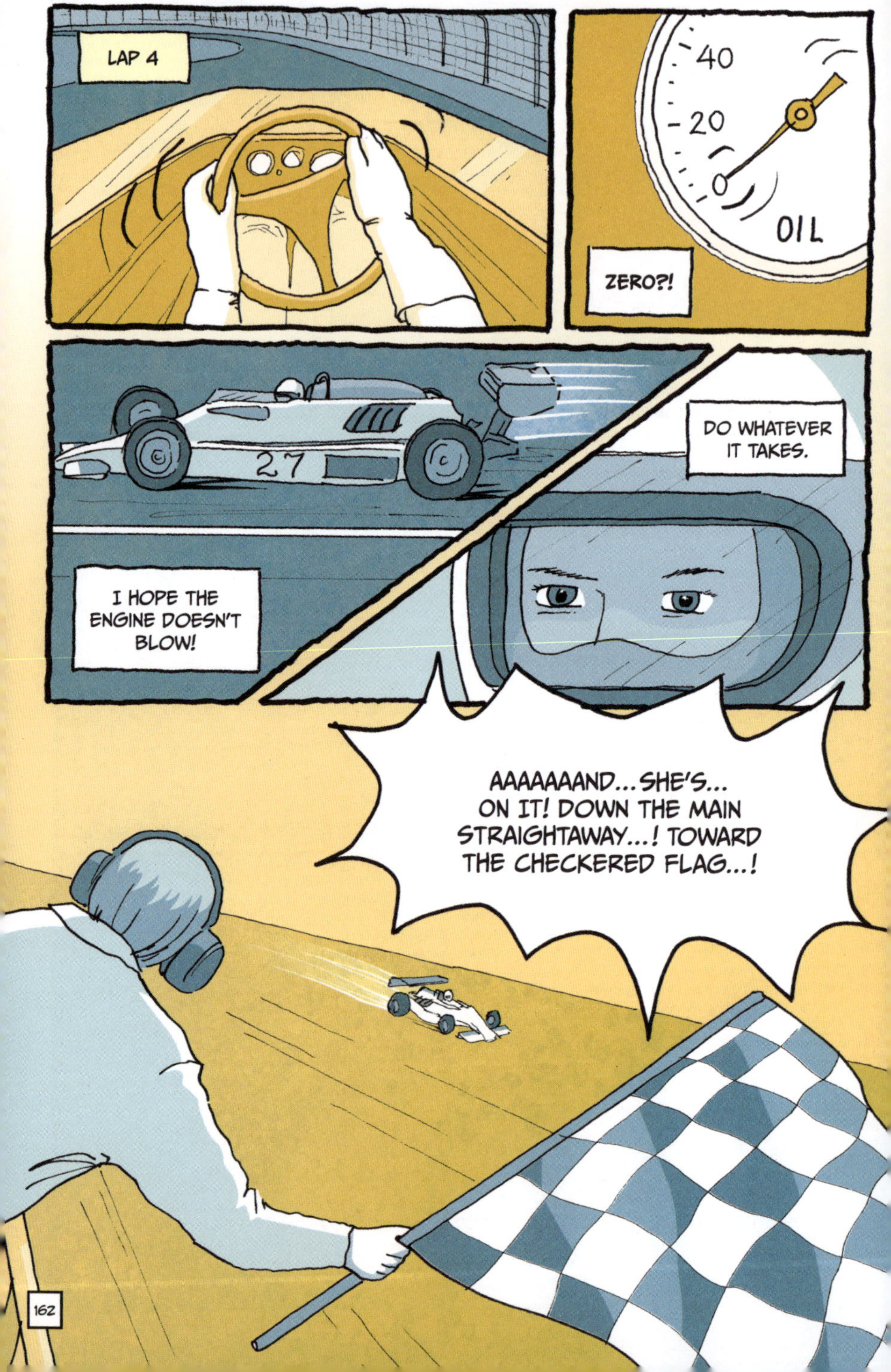
LAP 4
40
20
0
OIL
ZERO?!
27
DO WHATEVER IT TAKES.
I HOPE THE ENGINE DOESN'T BLOW!
AAAAAAAND... SHE'S... ON IT! DOWN THE MAIN STRAIGHTAWAY...! TOWARD THE CHECKERED FLAG...!

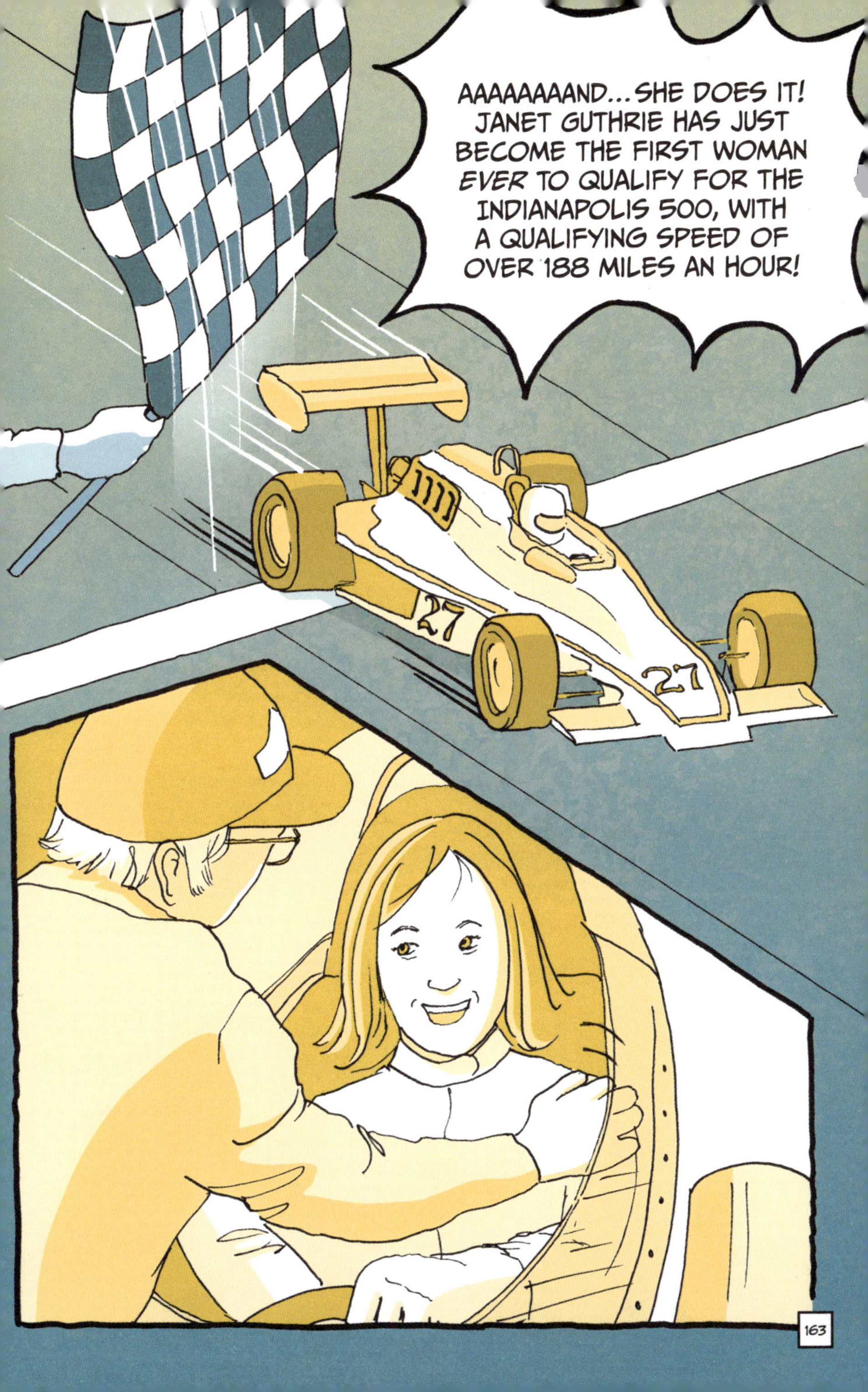
AAAAAAAAND...SHE DOES IT! JANET GUTHRIE HAS JUST BECOME THE FIRST WOMAN *EVER* TO QUALIFY FOR THE INDIANAPOLIS 500, WITH A QUALIFYING SPEED OF OVER 188 MILES AN HOUR!
27
27

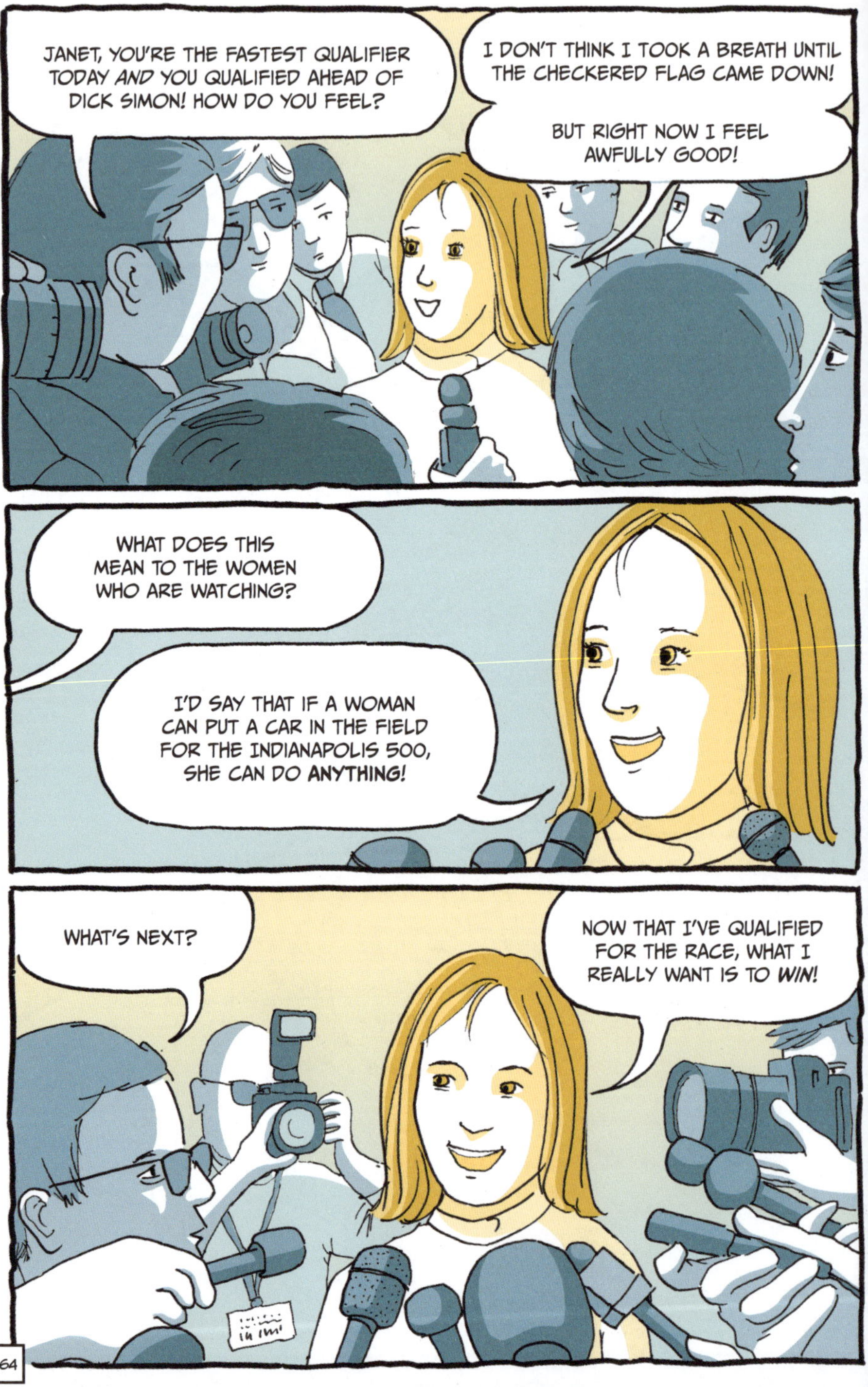
JANET, YOU'RE THE FASTEST QUALIFIER TODAY *AND* YOU QUALIFIED AHEAD OF DICK SIMON! HOW DO YOU FEEL?
I DON'T THINK I TOOK A BREATH UNTIL THE CHECKERED FLAG CAME DOWN!
BUT RIGHT NOW I FEEL AWFULLY GOOD!
WHAT DOES THIS MEAN TO THE WOMEN WHO ARE WATCHING?
I'D SAY THAT IF A WOMAN CAN PUT A CAR IN THE FIELD FOR THE INDIANAPOLIS 500, SHE CAN DO **ANYTHING!**
WHAT'S NEXT?
NOW THAT I'VE QUALIFIED FOR THE RACE, WHAT I REALLY WANT IS TO *WIN!*

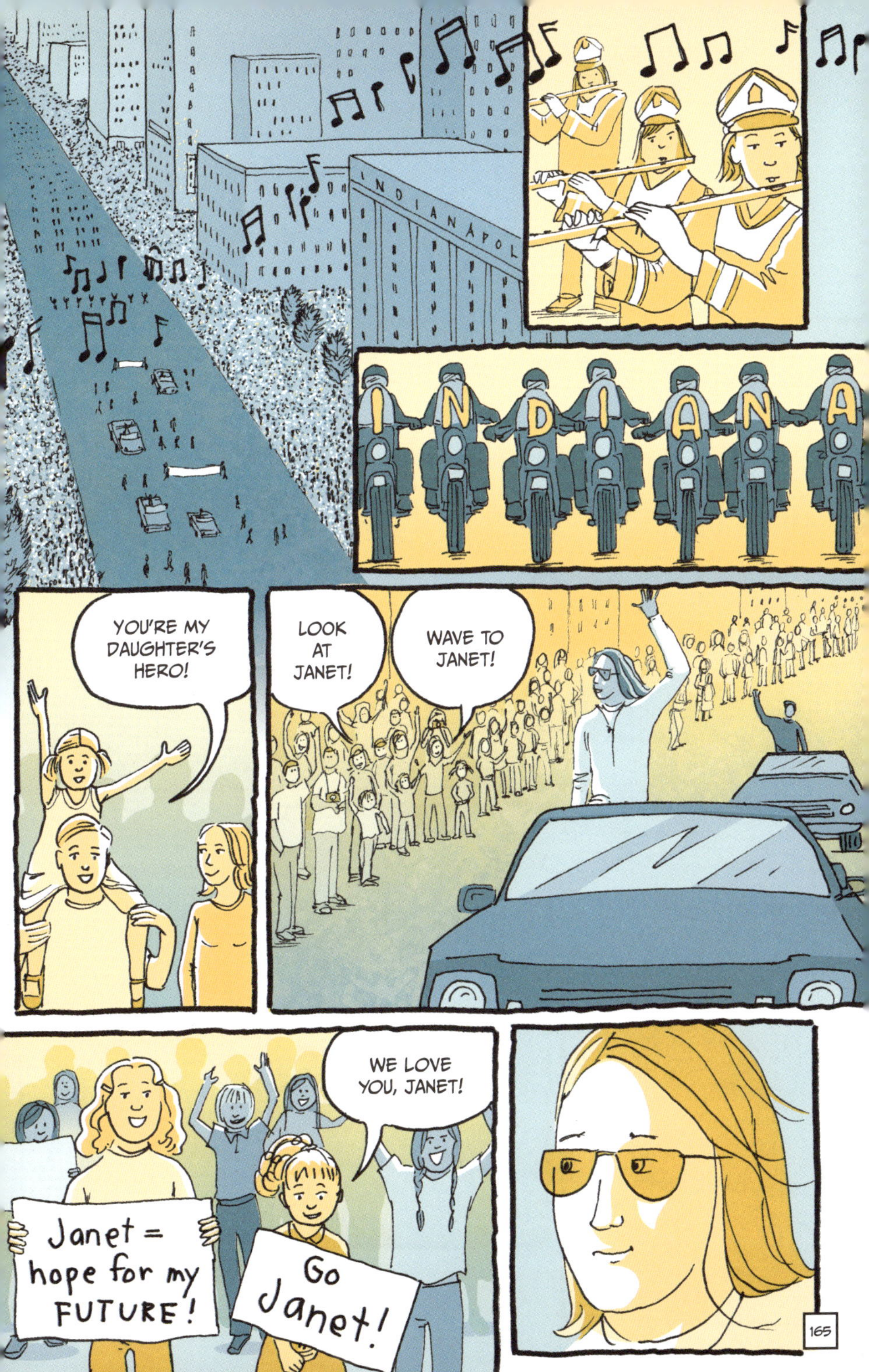
INDIANAPOL
INDIANA
YOU'RE MY DAUGHTER'S HERO!
LOOK AT JANET!
WAVE TO JANET!
WE LOVE YOU, JANET!
Janet = hope for my FUTURE!
Go Janet!

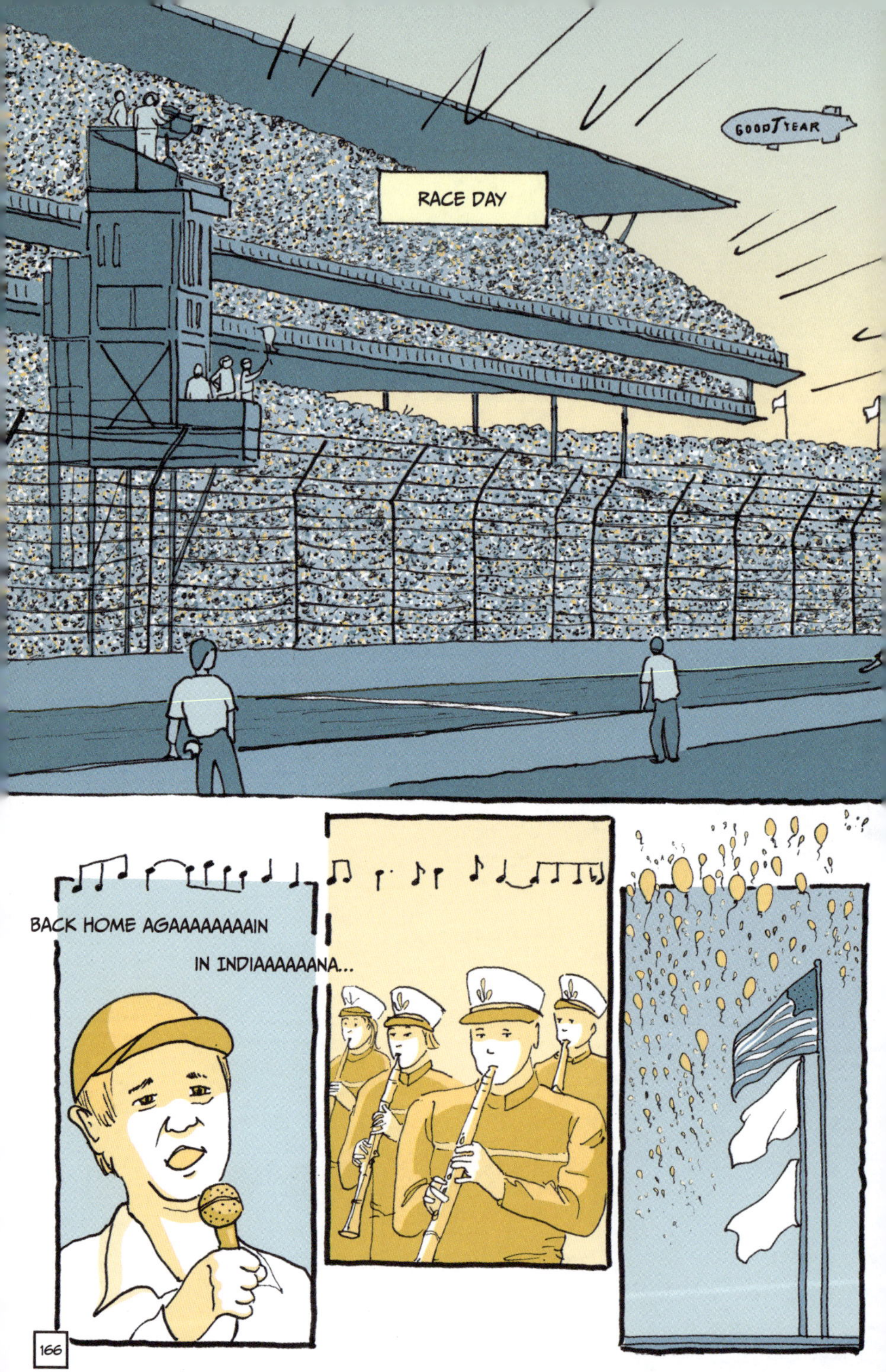
GOODYEAR
RACE DAY
BACK HOME AGAAAAAAAAIN
IN INDIAAAAAANA...

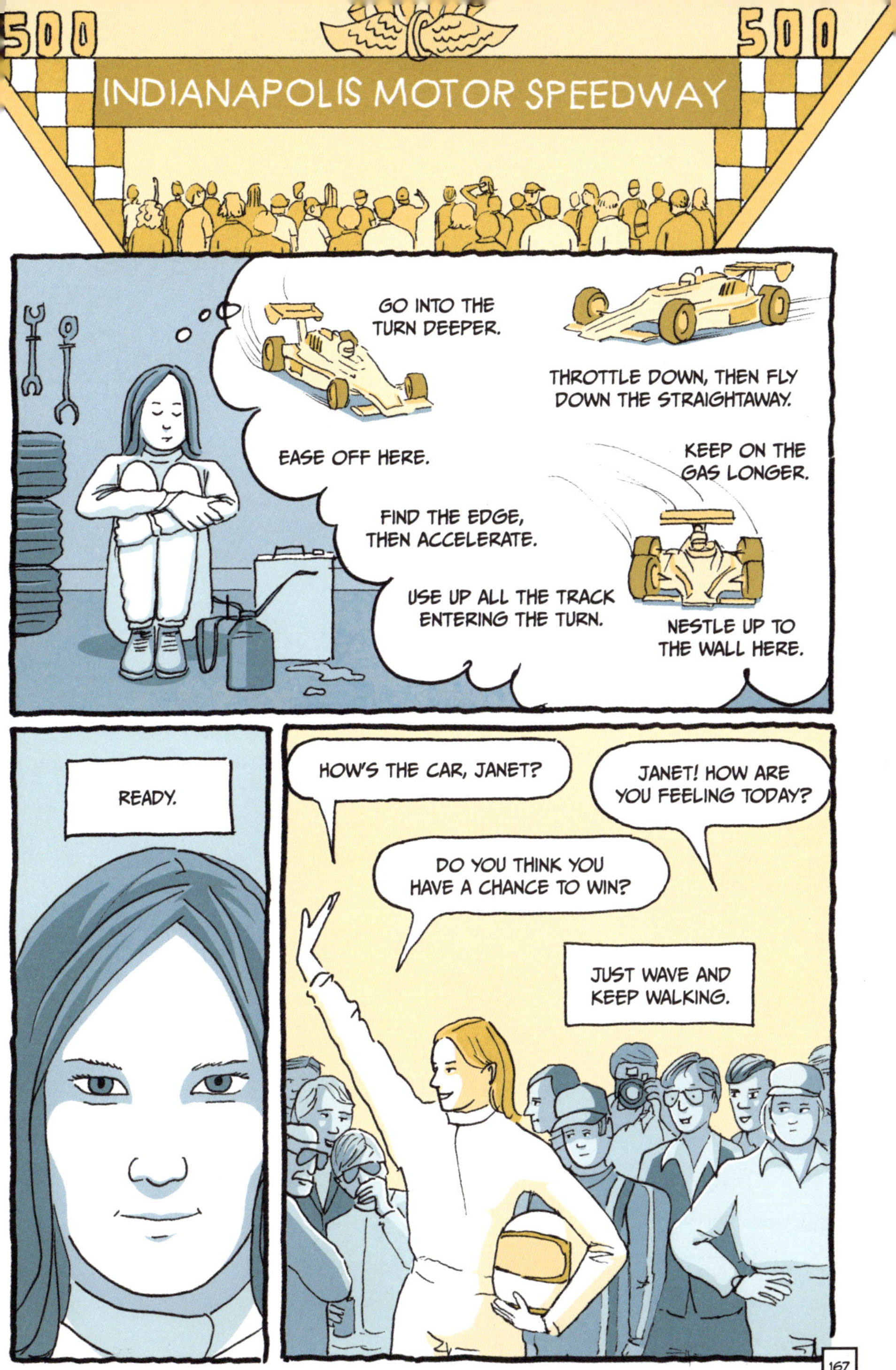
500
500
INDIANAPOLIS MOTOR SPEEDWAY
GO INTO THE TURN DEEPER.
THROTTLE DOWN, THEN FLY DOWN THE STRAIGHTAWAY.
EASE OFF HERE.
KEEP ON THE GAS LONGER.
FIND THE EDGE, THEN ACCELERATE.
USE UP ALL THE TRACK ENTERING THE TURN.
NESTLE UP TO THE WALL HERE.
READY.
HOW'S THE CAR, JANET?
JANET! HOW ARE YOU FEELING TODAY?
DO YOU THINK YOU HAVE A CHANCE TO WIN?
JUST WAVE AND KEEP WALKING.

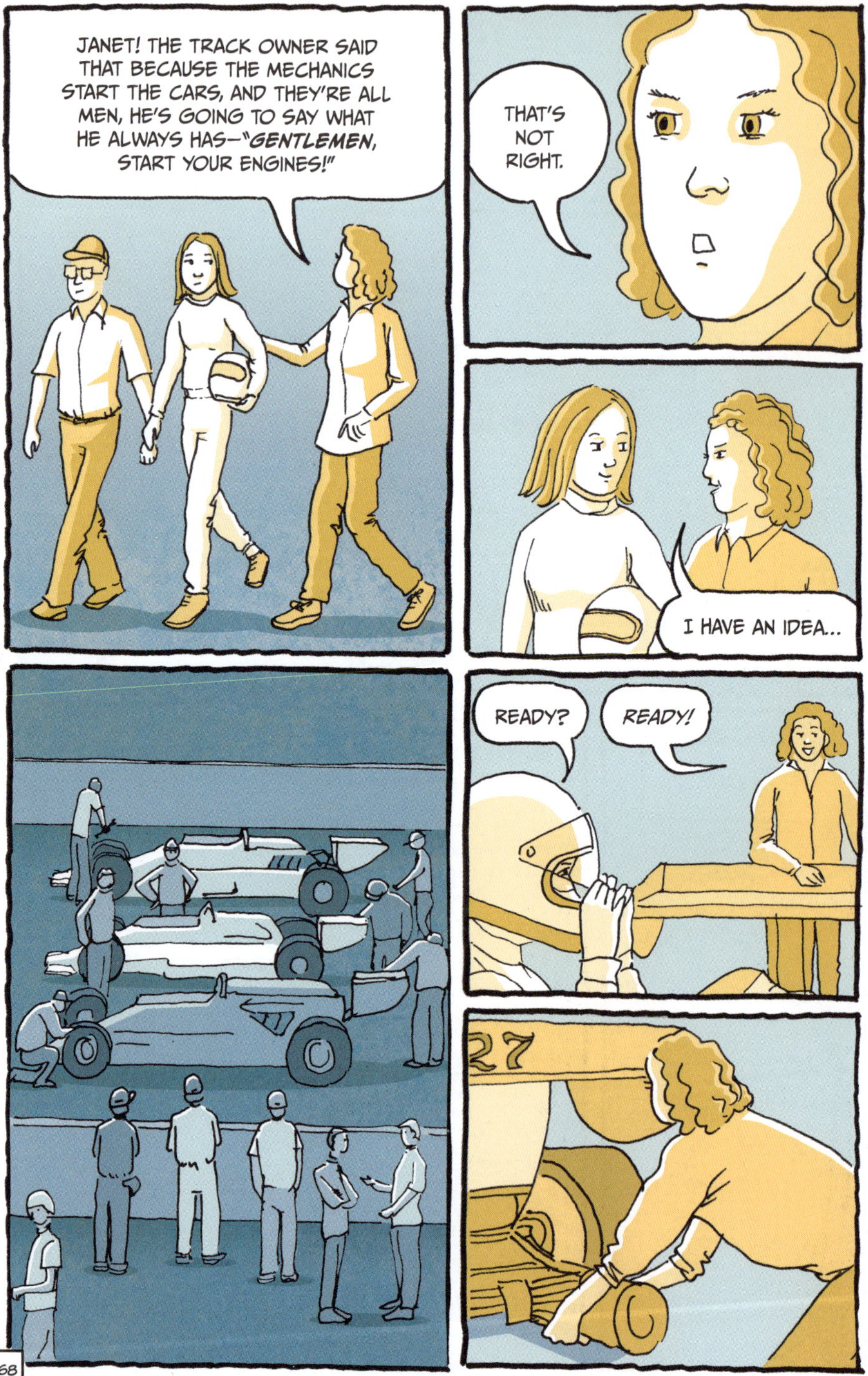
JANET! THE TRACK OWNER SAID THAT BECAUSE THE MECHANICS START THE CARS, AND THEY'RE ALL MEN, HE'S GOING TO SAY WHAT HE ALWAYS HAS—"*GENTLEMEN*, START YOUR ENGINES!"
THAT'S NOT RIGHT.
I HAVE AN IDEA...
READY?
READY!
27

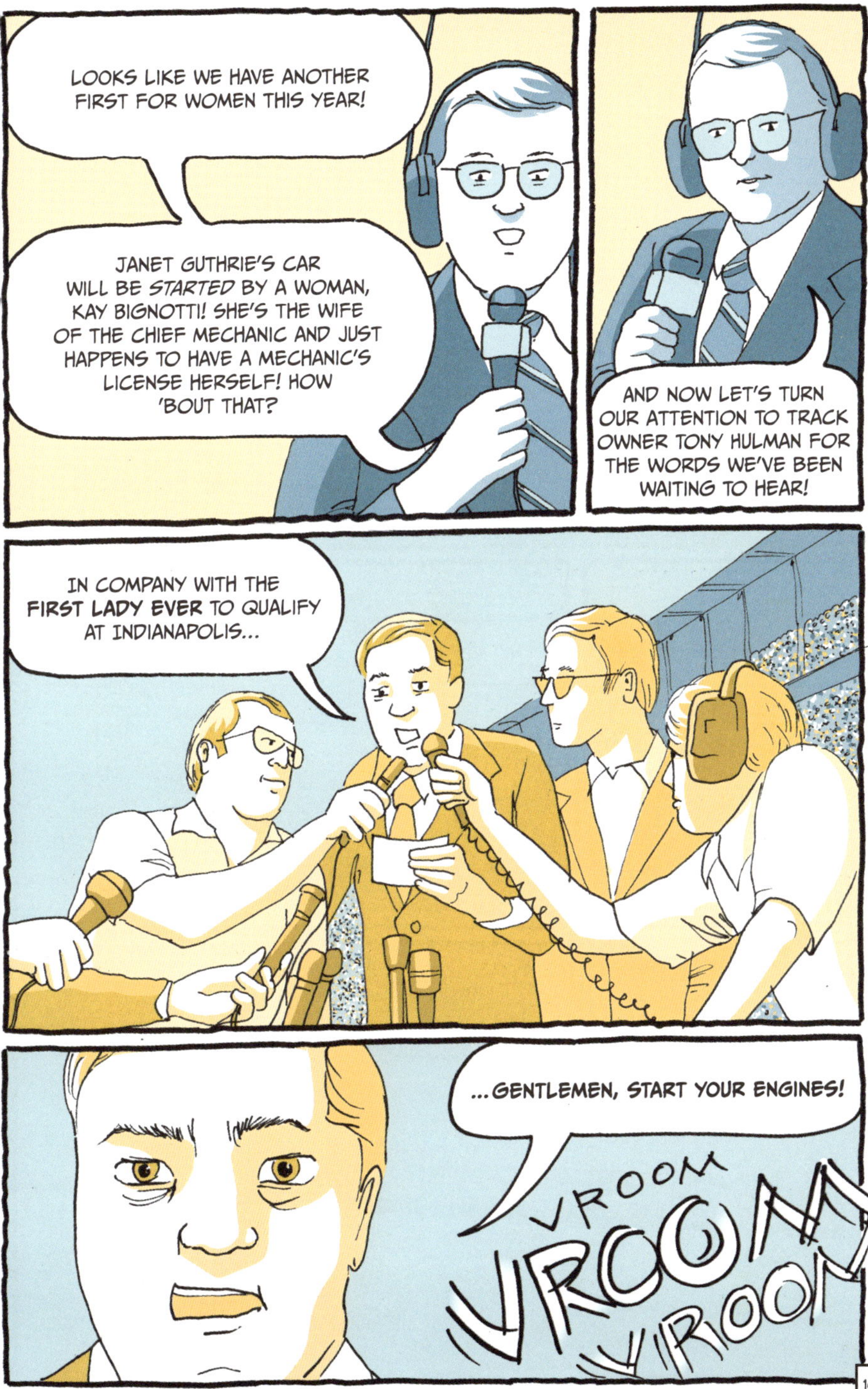
LOOKS LIKE WE HAVE ANOTHER FIRST FOR WOMEN THIS YEAR!
JANET GUTHRIE'S CAR WILL BE *STARTED* BY A WOMAN, KAY BIGNOTTI! SHE'S THE WIFE OF THE CHIEF MECHANIC AND JUST HAPPENS TO HAVE A MECHANIC'S LICENSE HERSELF! HOW 'BOUT THAT?
AND NOW LET'S TURN OUR ATTENTION TO TRACK OWNER TONY HULMAN FOR THE WORDS WE'VE BEEN WAITING TO HEAR!
IN COMPANY WITH THE **FIRST LADY EVER** TO QUALIFY AT INDIANAPOLIS...
...GENTLEMEN, START YOUR ENGINES!
VROOM
VROOM
VROOM

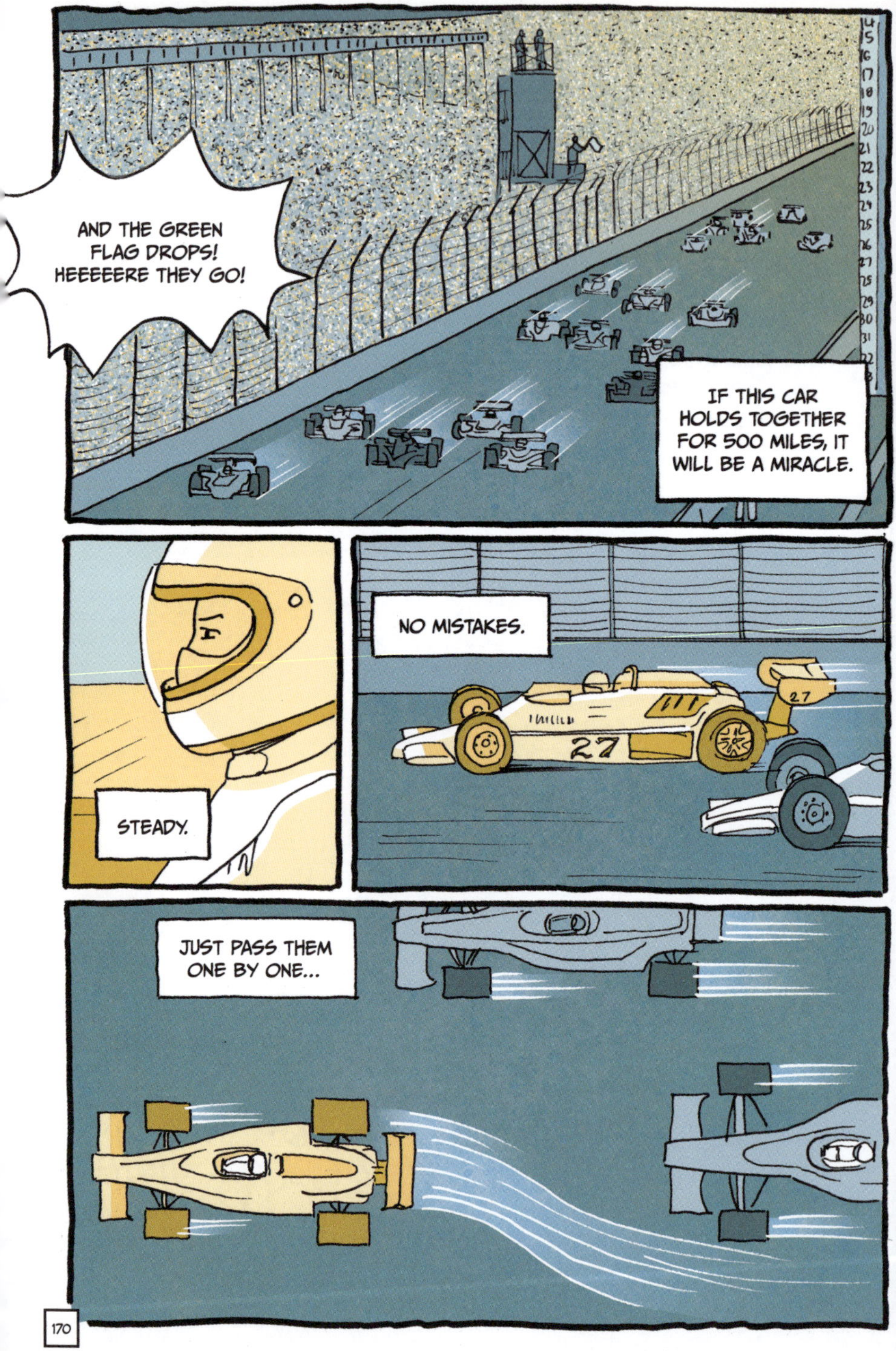
AND THE GREEN FLAG DROPS! HEEEEERE THEY GO!
IF THIS CAR HOLDS TOGETHER FOR 500 MILES, IT WILL BE A MIRACLE.
STEADY.
NO MISTAKES.
27
27
JUST PASS THEM ONE BY ONE...

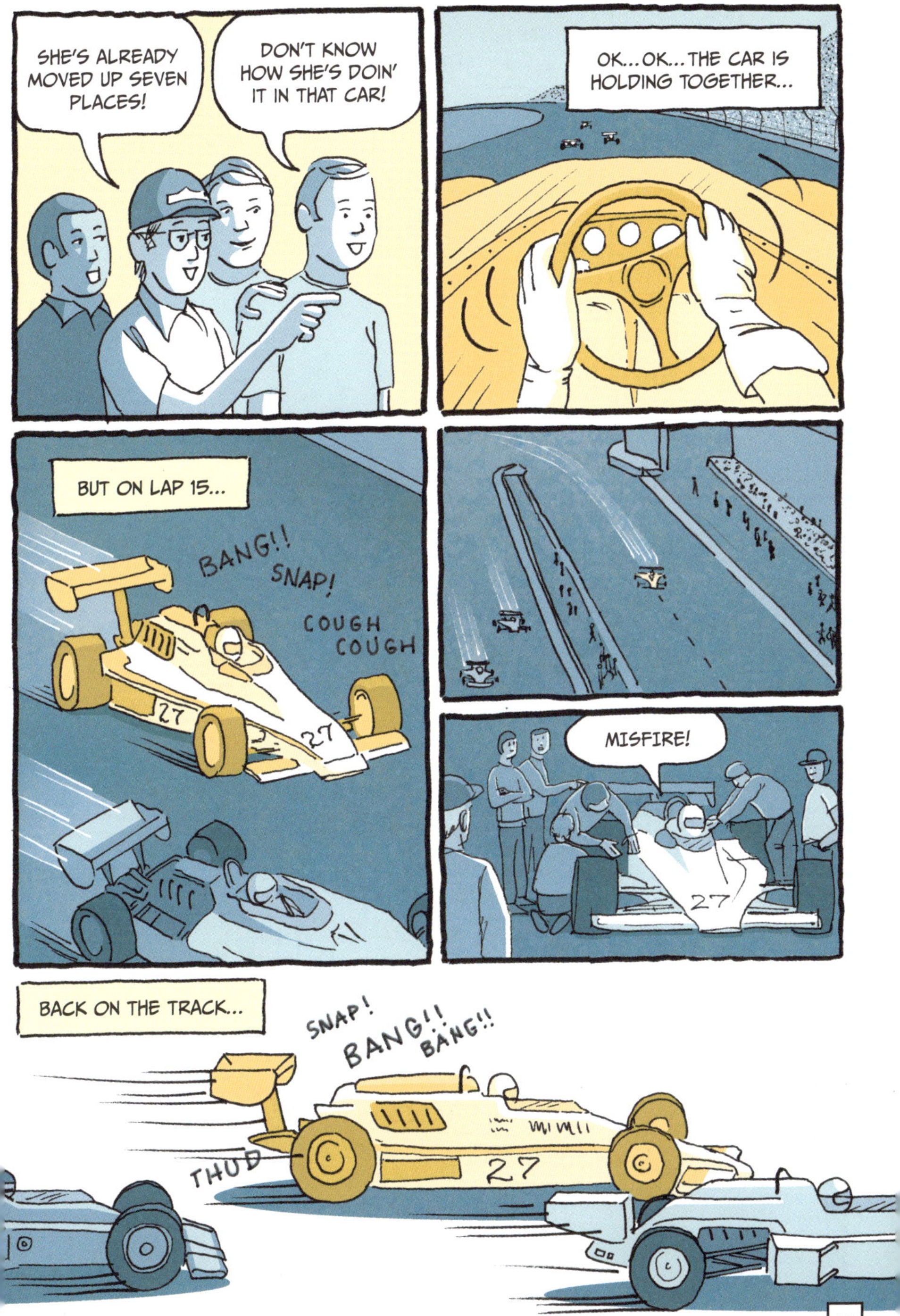
SHE'S ALREADY MOVED UP SEVEN PLACES!
DON'T KNOW HOW SHE'S DOIN' IT IN THAT CAR!
OK...OK...THE CAR IS HOLDING TOGETHER...
BUT ON LAP 15...
BANG!!
SNAP!
COUGH COUGH
27
MISFIRE!
27
BACK ON THE TRACK...
SNAP!
BANG!!
BANG!!
THUD
27

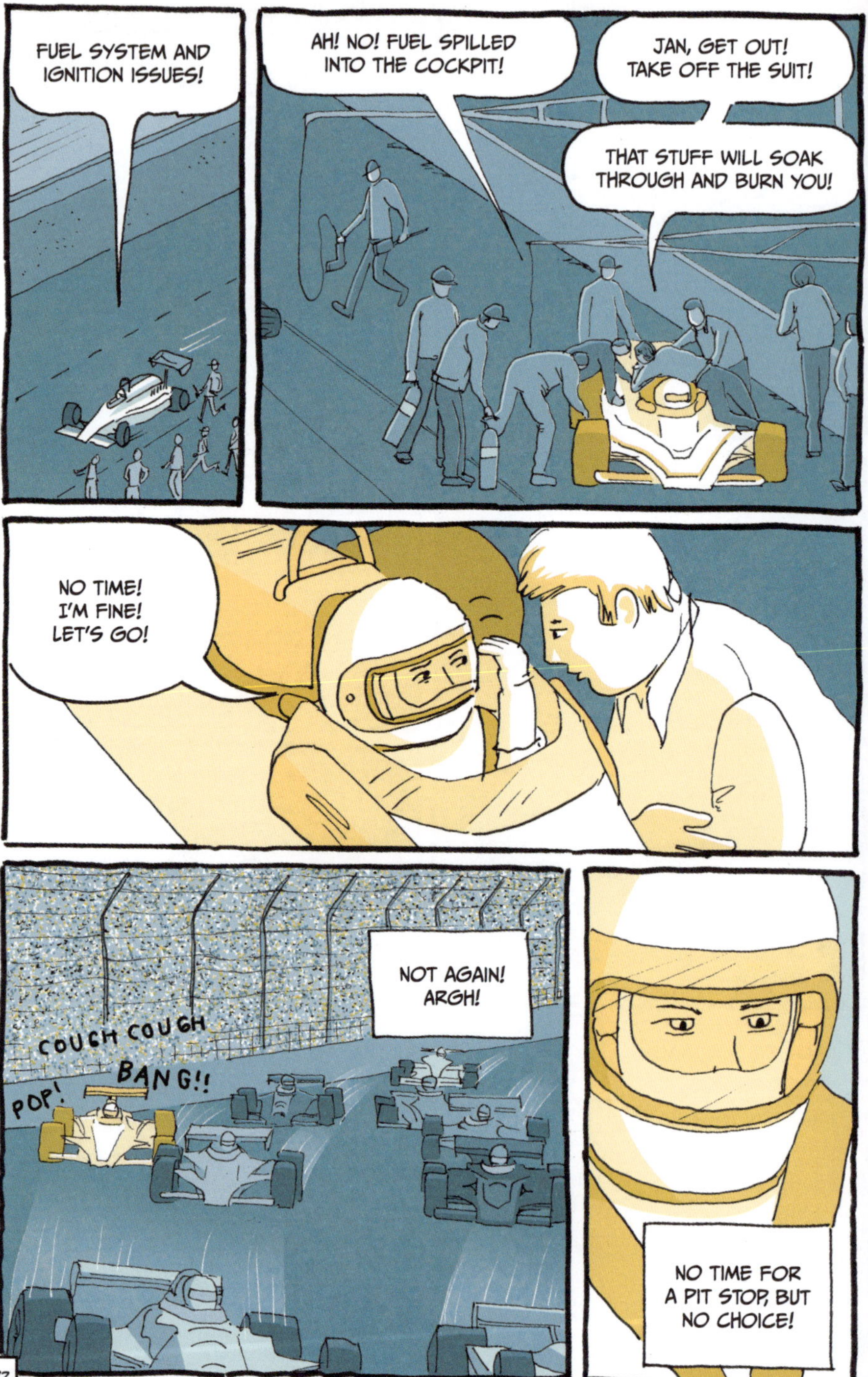
FUEL SYSTEM AND IGNITION ISSUES!
AH! NO! FUEL SPILLED INTO THE COCKPIT!
JAN, GET OUT! TAKE OFF THE SUIT!
THAT STUFF WILL SOAK THROUGH AND BURN YOU!
NO TIME! I'M FINE! LET'S GO!
NOT AGAIN! ARGH!
COUGH COUGH
BANG!!
POP!
NO TIME FOR A PIT STOP, BUT NO CHOICE!

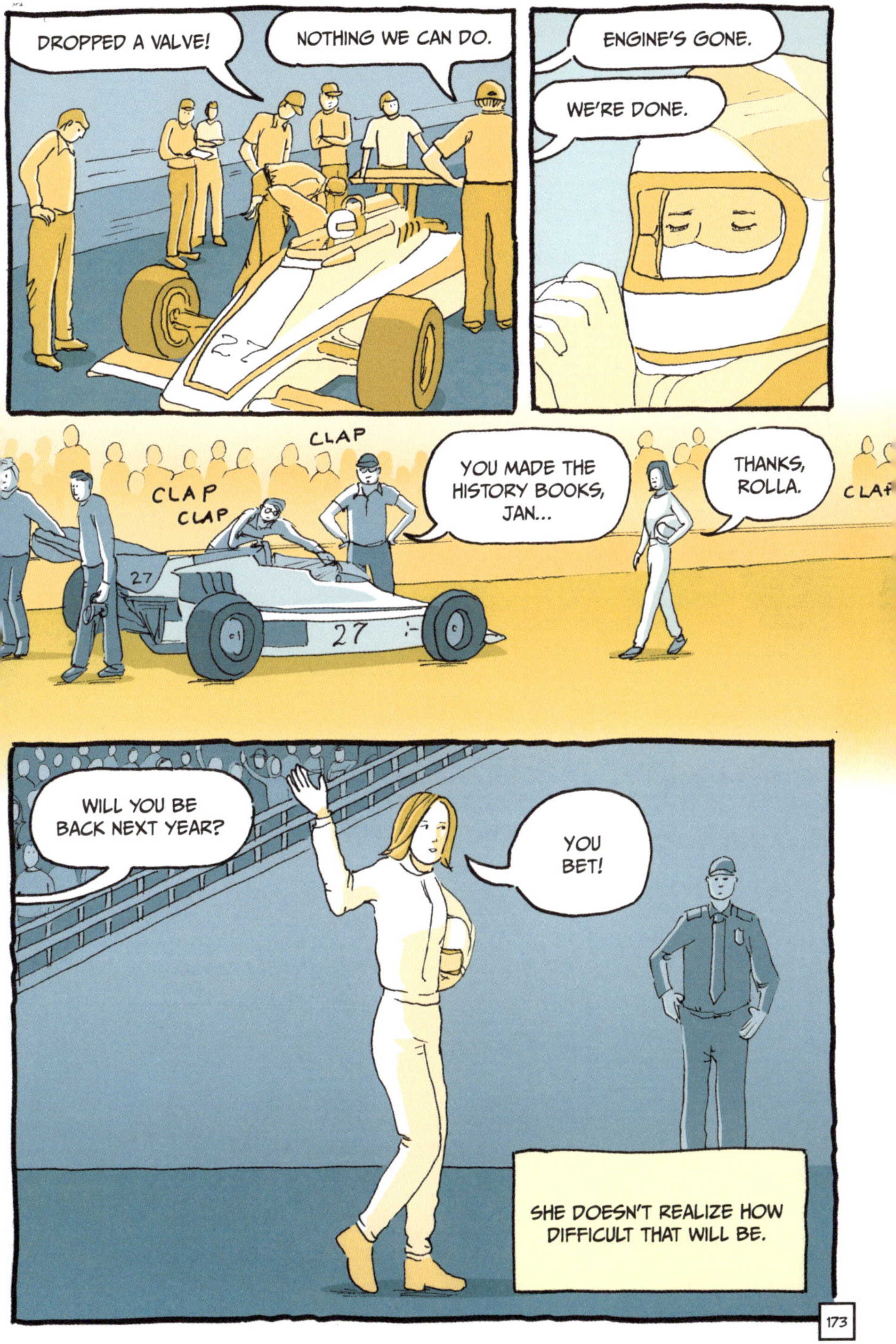
DROPPED A VALVE!
NOTHING WE CAN DO.
ENGINE'S GONE.
WE'RE DONE.
CLAP
CLAP
CLAP
YOU MADE THE HISTORY BOOKS, JAN...
THANKS, ROLLA.
CLAP
WILL YOU BE BACK NEXT YEAR?
YOU BET!
SHE DOESN'T REALIZE HOW DIFFICULT THAT WILL BE.

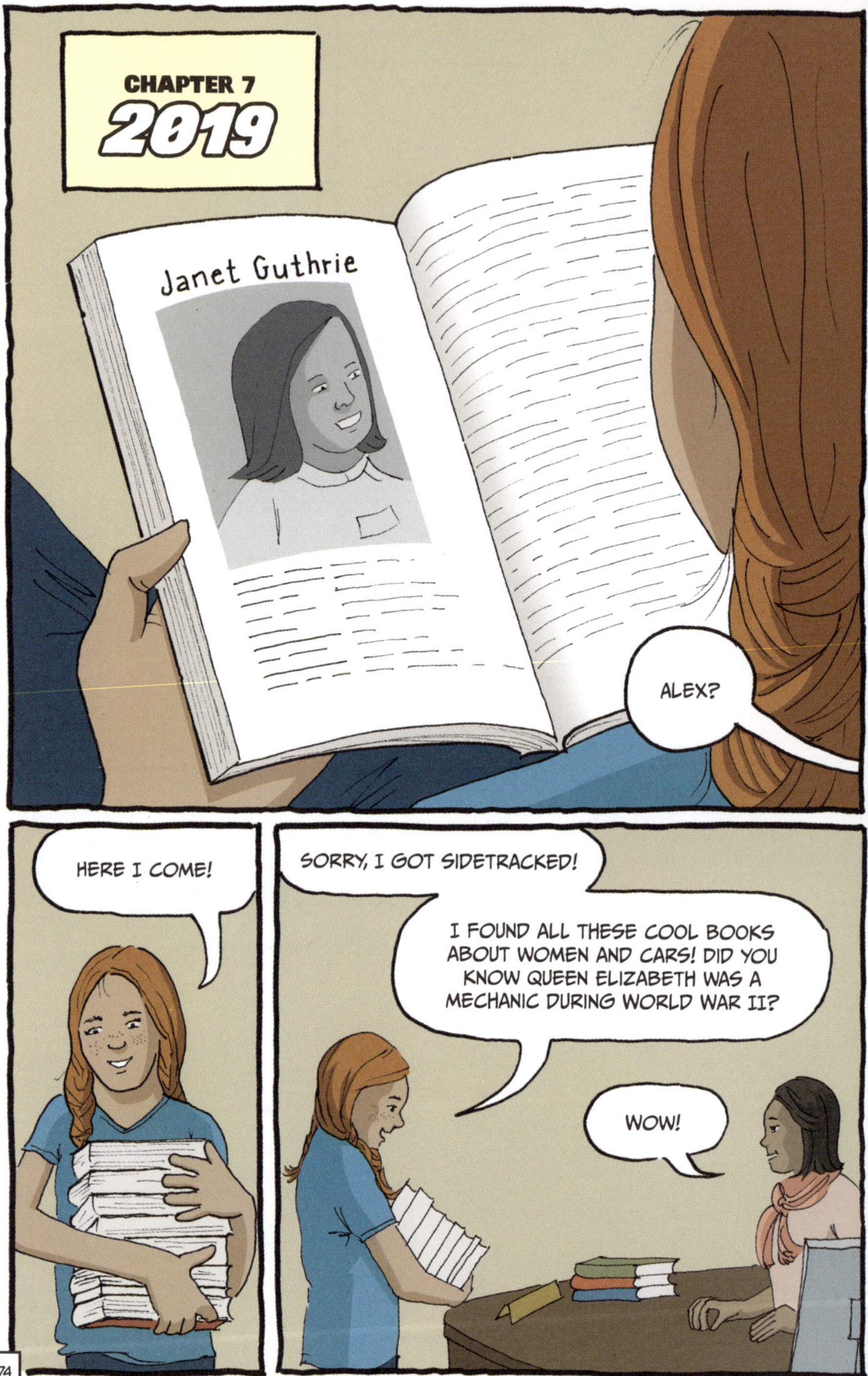
CHAPTER 7
2019
Janet Guthrie
ALEX?
HERE I COME!
SORRY, I GOT SIDETRACKED!
I FOUND ALL THESE COOL BOOKS ABOUT WOMEN AND CARS! DID YOU KNOW QUEEN ELIZABETH WAS A MECHANIC DURING WORLD WAR II?
WOW!

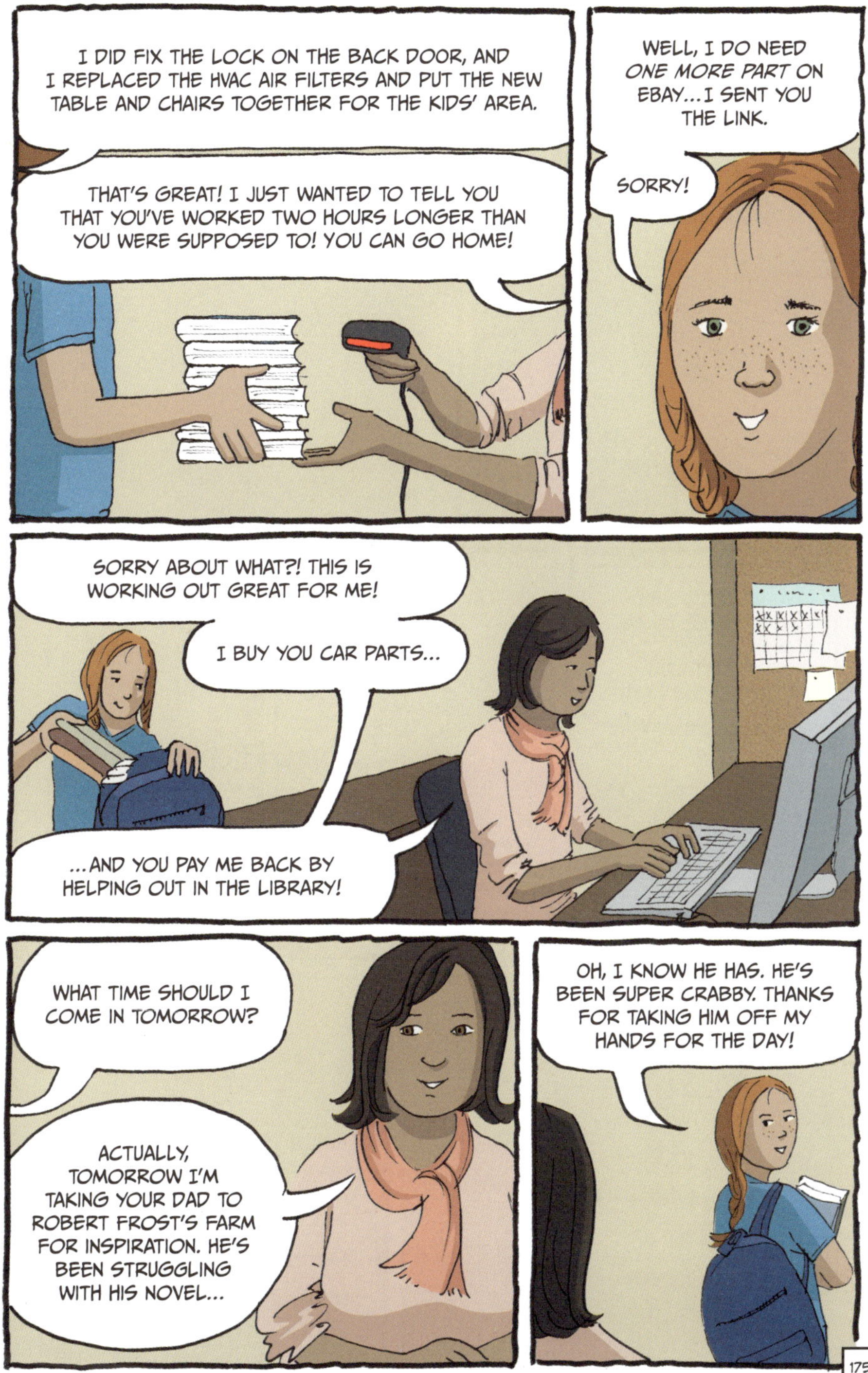
I DID FIX THE LOCK ON THE BACK DOOR, AND I REPLACED THE HVAC AIR FILTERS AND PUT THE NEW TABLE AND CHAIRS TOGETHER FOR THE KIDS' AREA.
THAT'S GREAT! I JUST WANTED TO TELL YOU THAT YOU'VE WORKED TWO HOURS LONGER THAN YOU WERE SUPPOSED TO! YOU CAN GO HOME!
WELL, I DO NEED *ONE MORE PART* ON EBAY...I SENT YOU THE LINK.
SORRY!
SORRY ABOUT WHAT?! THIS IS WORKING OUT GREAT FOR ME!
I BUY YOU CAR PARTS...
...AND YOU PAY ME BACK BY HELPING OUT IN THE LIBRARY!
WHAT TIME SHOULD I COME IN TOMORROW?
ACTUALLY, TOMORROW I'M TAKING YOUR DAD TO ROBERT FROST'S FARM FOR INSPIRATION. HE'S BEEN STRUGGLING WITH HIS NOVEL...
OH, I KNOW HE HAS. HE'S BEEN SUPER CRABBY. THANKS FOR TAKING HIM OFF MY HANDS FOR THE DAY!

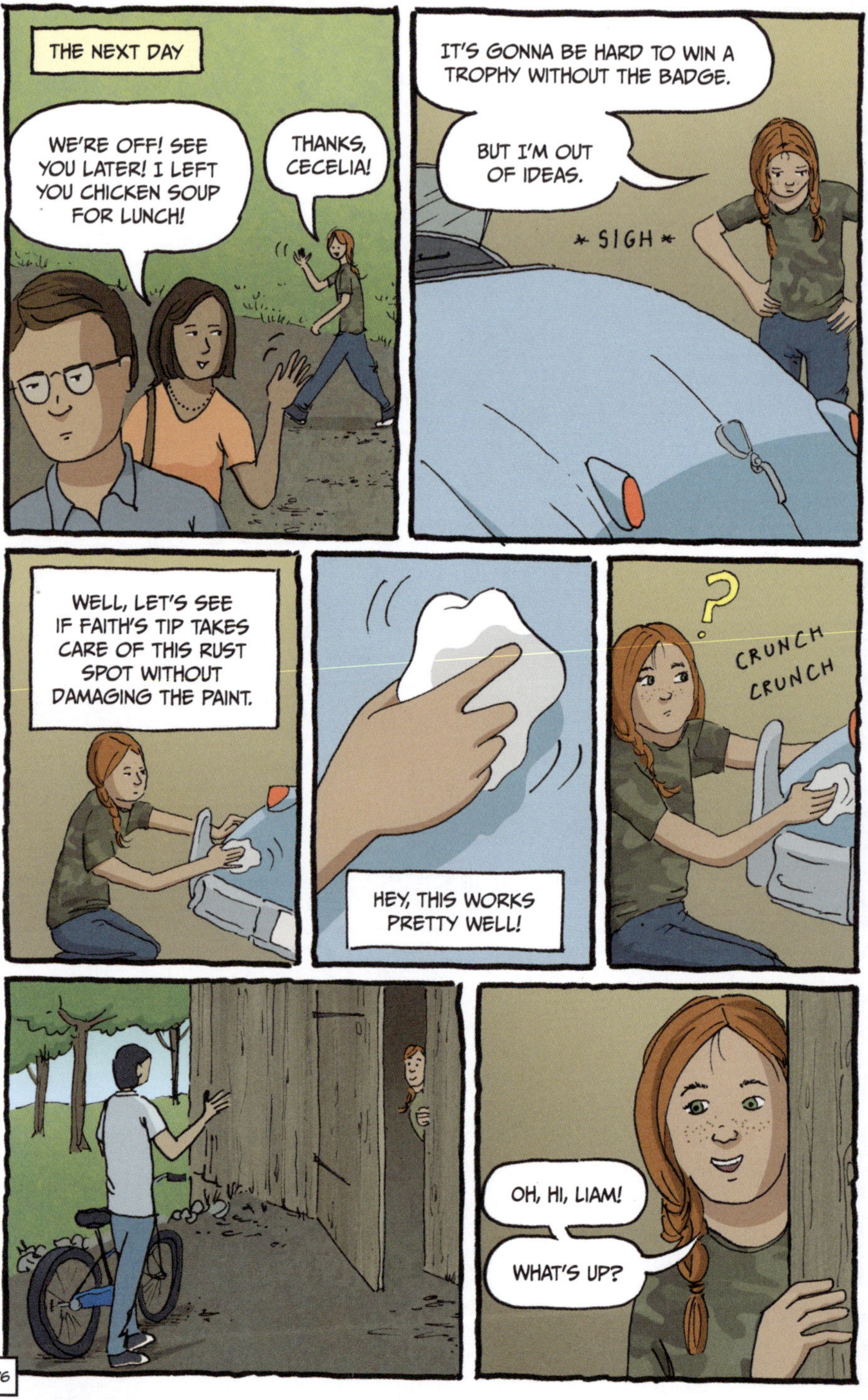

THE NEXT DAY
WE'RE OFF! SEE YOU LATER! I LEFT YOU CHICKEN SOUP FOR LUNCH!
THANKS, CECELIA!
IT'S GONNA BE HARD TO WIN A TROPHY WITHOUT THE BADGE.
BUT I'M OUT OF IDEAS.
SIGH
WELL, LET'S SEE IF FAITH'S TIP TAKES CARE OF THIS RUST SPOT WITHOUT DAMAGING THE PAINT.
HEY, THIS WORKS PRETTY WELL!
?
CRUNCH
CRUNCH
OH, HI, LIAM!
WHAT'S UP?

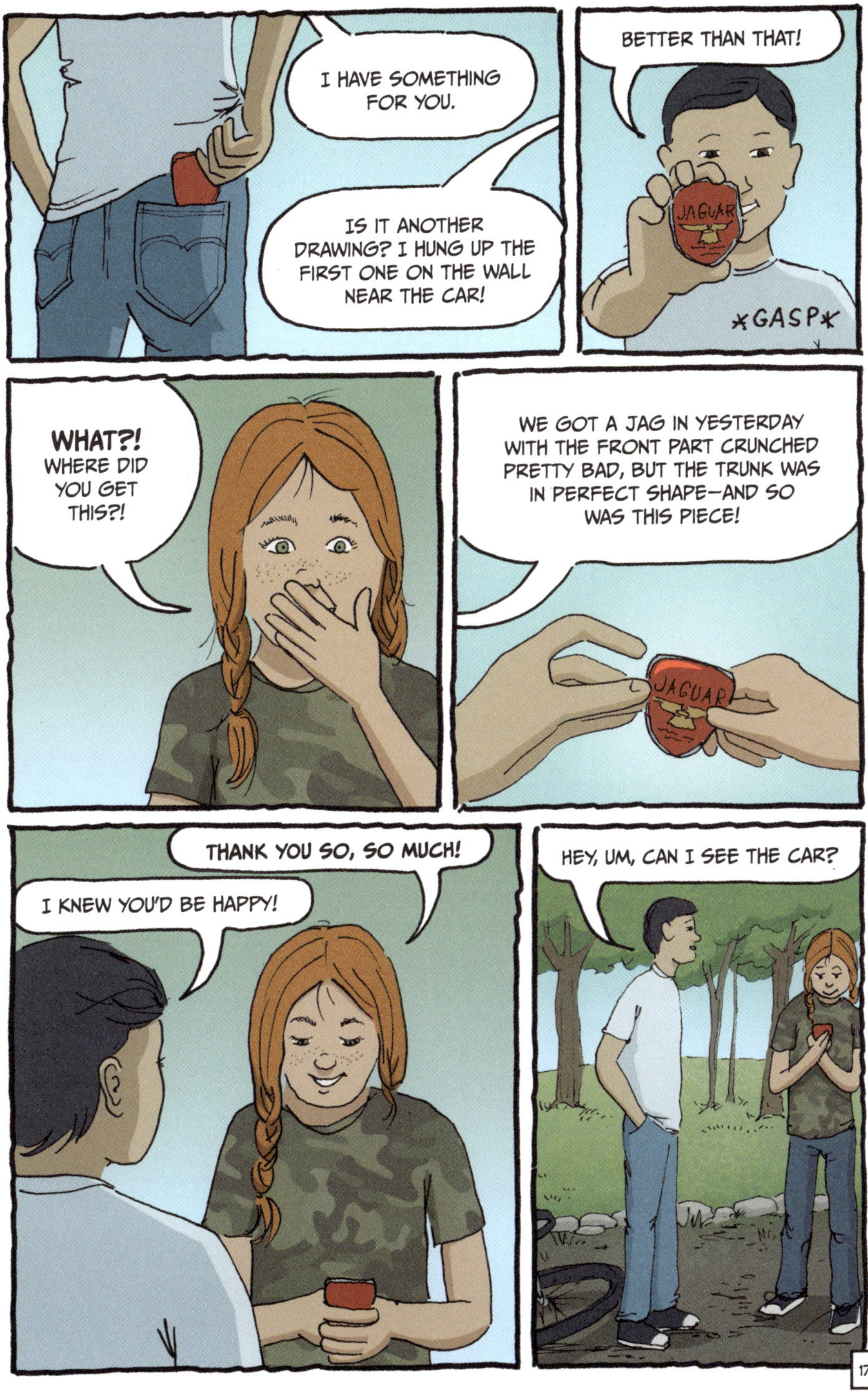
I HAVE SOMETHING FOR YOU.
IS IT ANOTHER DRAWING? I HUNG UP THE FIRST ONE ON THE WALL NEAR THE CAR!
BETTER THAN THAT!
JAGUAR
GASP
WHAT?! WHERE DID YOU GET THIS?!
WE GOT A JAG IN YESTERDAY WITH THE FRONT PART CRUNCHED PRETTY BAD, BUT THE TRUNK WAS IN PERFECT SHAPE—AND SO WAS THIS PIECE!
JAGUAR
THANK YOU SO, SO MUCH!
I KNEW YOU'D BE HAPPY!
HEY, UM, CAN I SEE THE CAR?

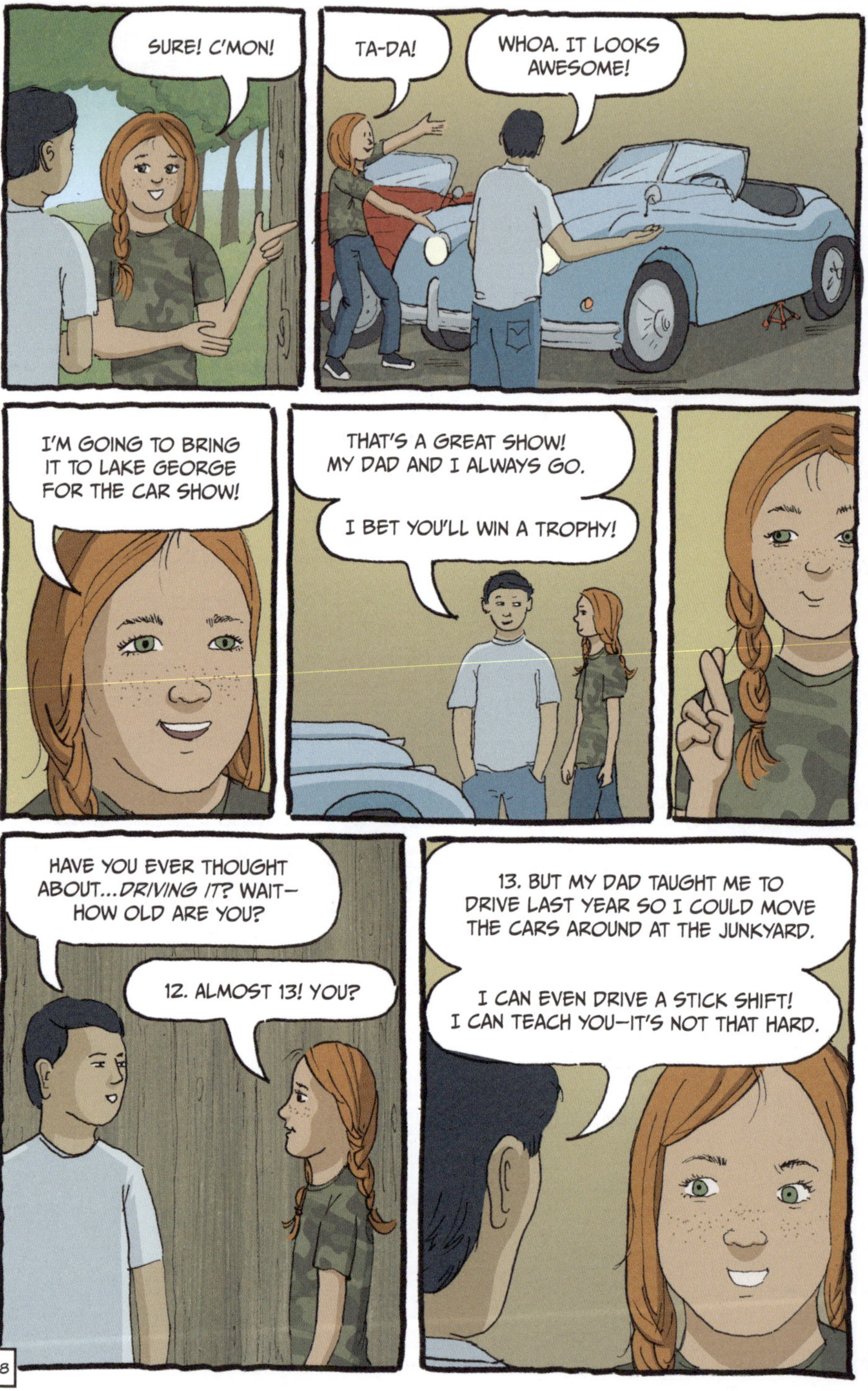
SURE! C'MON!
TA-DA!
WHOA. IT LOOKS AWESOME!
I'M GOING TO BRING IT TO LAKE GEORGE FOR THE CAR SHOW!
THAT'S A GREAT SHOW! MY DAD AND I ALWAYS GO.
I BET YOU'LL WIN A TROPHY!
HAVE YOU EVER THOUGHT ABOUT...*DRIVING IT*? WAIT—HOW OLD ARE YOU?
12. ALMOST 13! YOU?
13. BUT MY DAD TAUGHT ME TO DRIVE LAST YEAR SO I COULD MOVE THE CARS AROUND AT THE JUNKYARD.
I CAN EVEN DRIVE A STICK SHIFT! I CAN TEACH YOU—IT'S NOT THAT HARD.

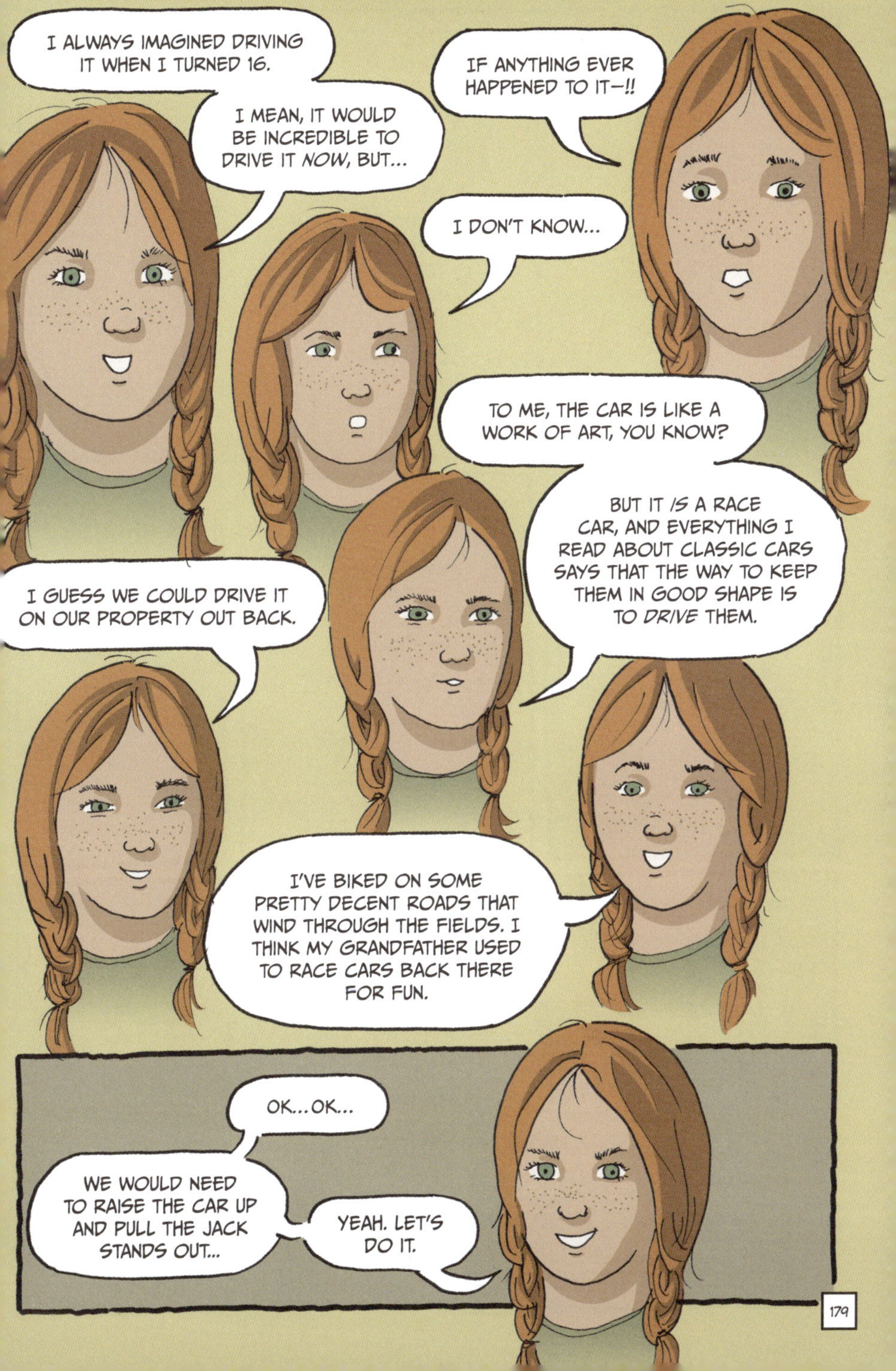
I ALWAYS IMAGINED DRIVING IT WHEN I TURNED 16.
I MEAN, IT WOULD BE INCREDIBLE TO DRIVE IT *NOW*, BUT...
I DON'T KNOW...
IF ANYTHING EVER HAPPENED TO IT—!!
TO ME, THE CAR IS LIKE A WORK OF ART, YOU KNOW?
BUT IT *IS* A RACE CAR, AND EVERYTHING I READ ABOUT CLASSIC CARS SAYS THAT THE WAY TO KEEP THEM IN GOOD SHAPE IS TO *DRIVE* THEM.
I GUESS WE COULD DRIVE IT ON OUR PROPERTY OUT BACK.
I'VE BIKED ON SOME PRETTY DECENT ROADS THAT WIND THROUGH THE FIELDS. I THINK MY GRANDFATHER USED TO RACE CARS BACK THERE FOR FUN.
OK...OK...
WE WOULD NEED TO RAISE THE CAR UP AND PULL THE JACK STANDS OUT...
YEAH. LET'S DO IT.

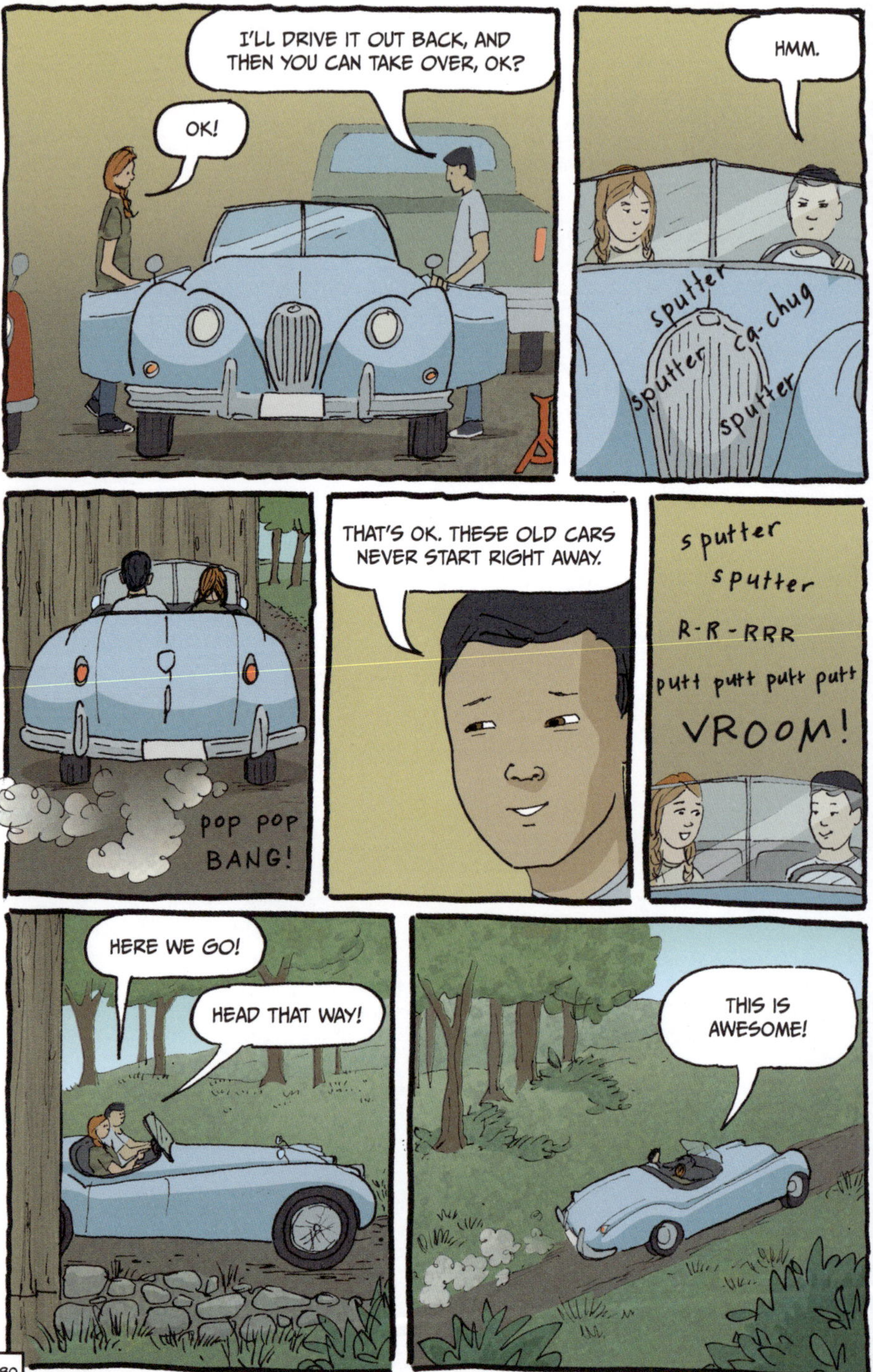

OK!
I'LL DRIVE IT OUT BACK, AND THEN YOU CAN TAKE OVER, OK?
HMM.
sputter
ca-chug
sputter
sputter
pop pop
BANG!
THAT'S OK. THESE OLD CARS NEVER START RIGHT AWAY.
sputter
sputter
R-R-RRR
putt putt putt putt
VROOM!
HERE WE GO!
HEAD THAT WAY!
THIS IS AWESOME!

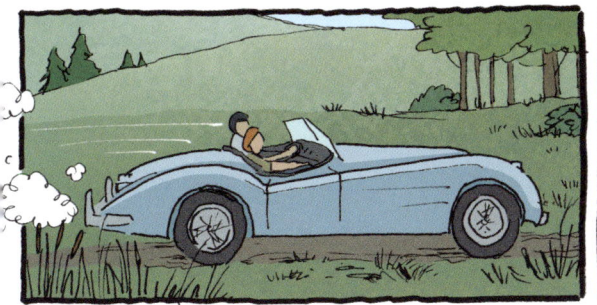

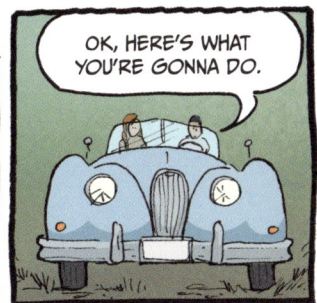

OK, HERE'S WHAT YOU'RE GONNA DO.
WITH YOUR RIGHT FOOT ON THE BRAKE, PRESS THE CLUTCH ALL THE WAY TO THE FLOOR WITH YOUR LEFT FOOT.
SHIFT INTO FIRST, AND TAKE YOUR FOOT OFF THE BRAKE, WHILE SLOWLY STARTING TO RELEASE THE CLUTCH.
AS YOU LET UP ON THE CLUTCH, START GIVING THE CAR A LITTLE GAS.
PRETTY SOON YOU'VE RELEASED THE CLUTCH, AND YOU'RE JUST ACCELERATING!
FOR SECOND GEAR, YOU NEED TO STEP ON THE CLUTCH AGAIN, MOVE INTO SECOND LIKE THIS, AND RELEASE THE CLUTCH AS YOU PRESS DOWN ON THE GAS. GOT IT?
GOT IT!

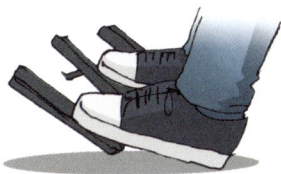

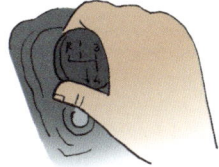

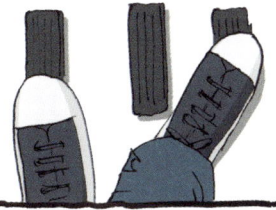

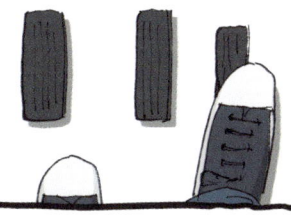

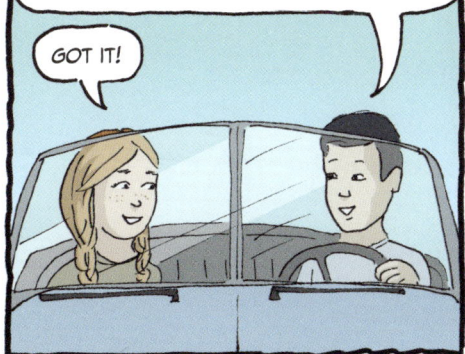

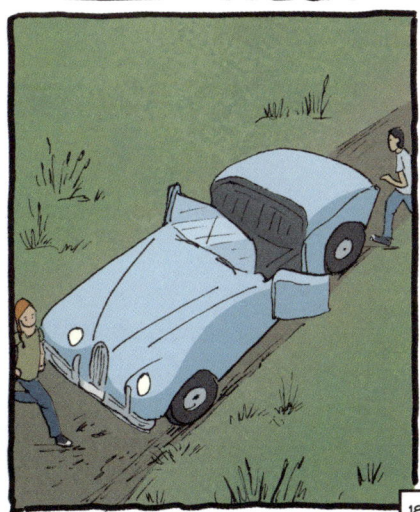

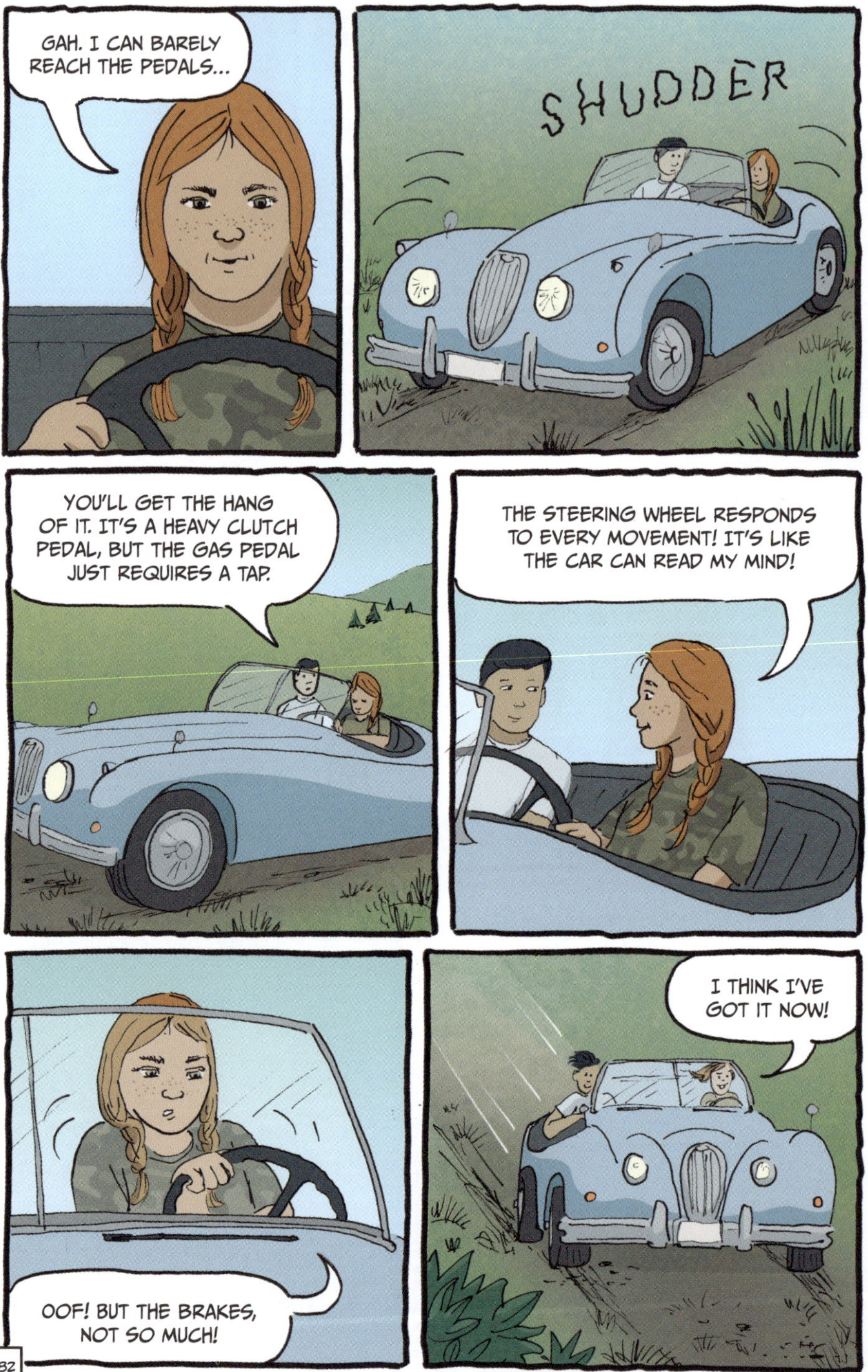
GAH. I CAN BARELY REACH THE PEDALS...
SHUDDER
YOU'LL GET THE HANG OF IT. IT'S A HEAVY CLUTCH PEDAL, BUT THE GAS PEDAL JUST REQUIRES A TAP.
THE STEERING WHEEL RESPONDS TO EVERY MOVEMENT! IT'S LIKE THE CAR CAN READ MY MIND!
OOF! BUT THE BRAKES, NOT SO MUCH!
I THINK I'VE GOT IT NOW!

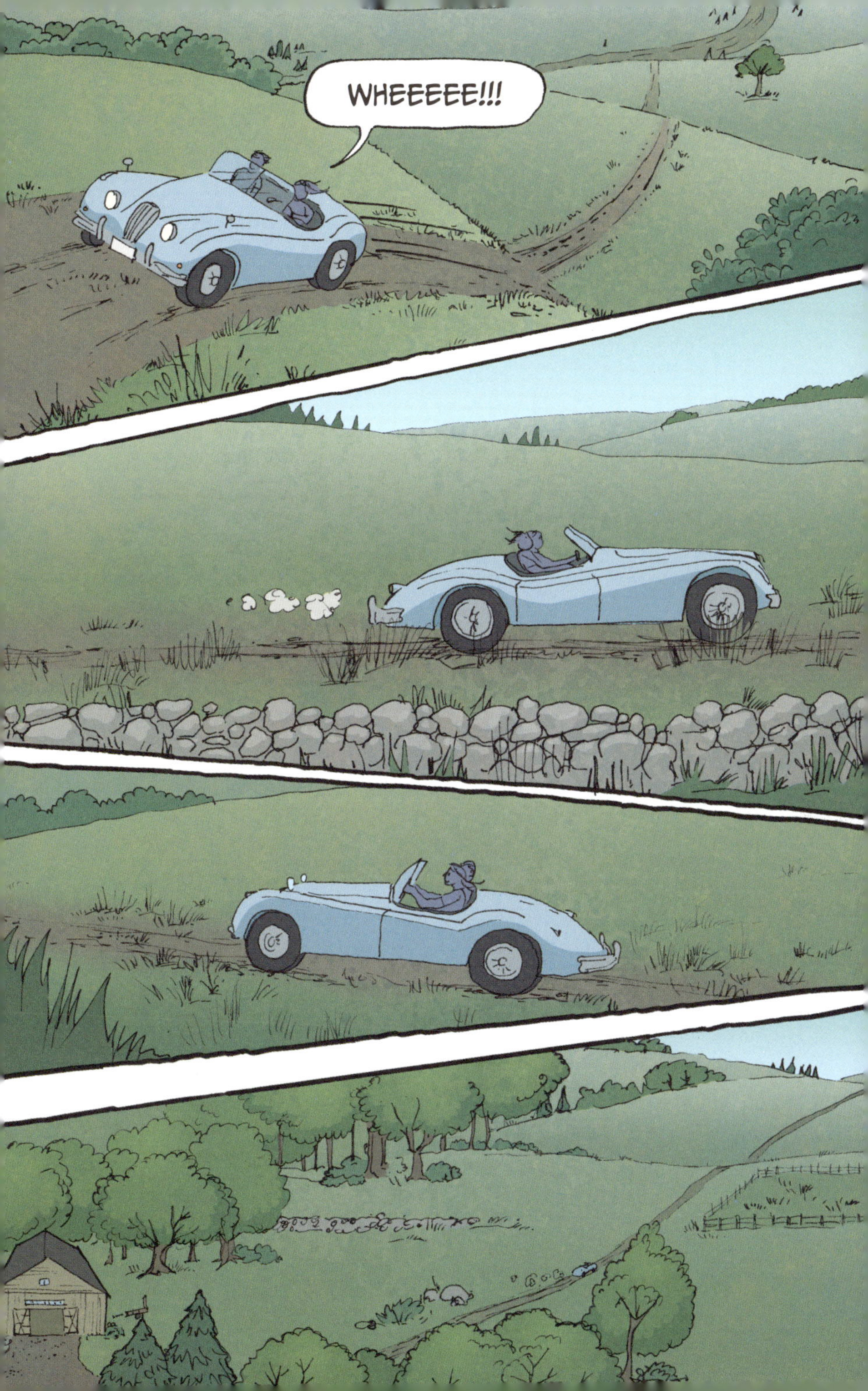
WHEEEEEE!!!

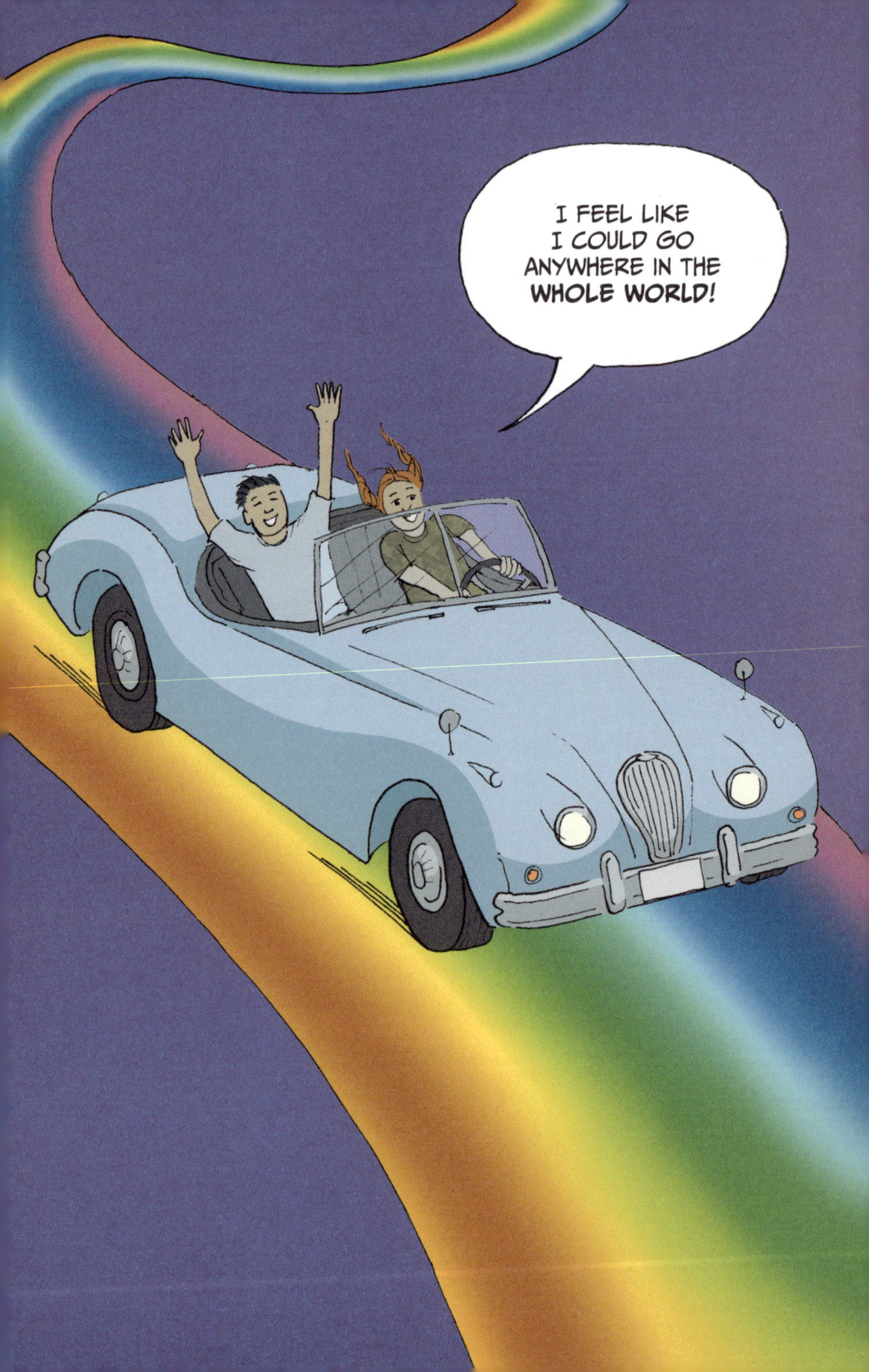
I FEEL LIKE I COULD GO ANYWHERE IN THE WHOLE WORLD!

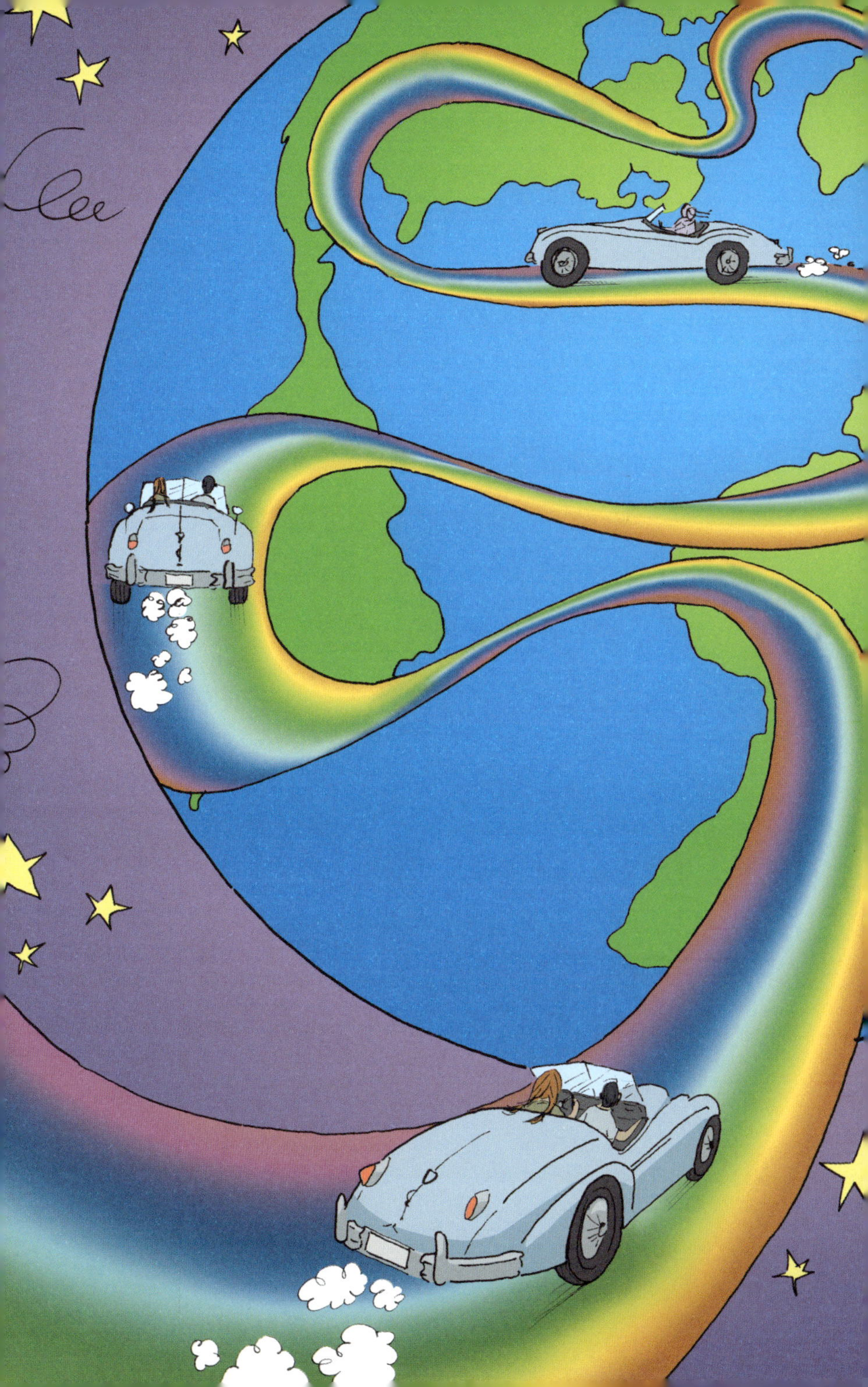

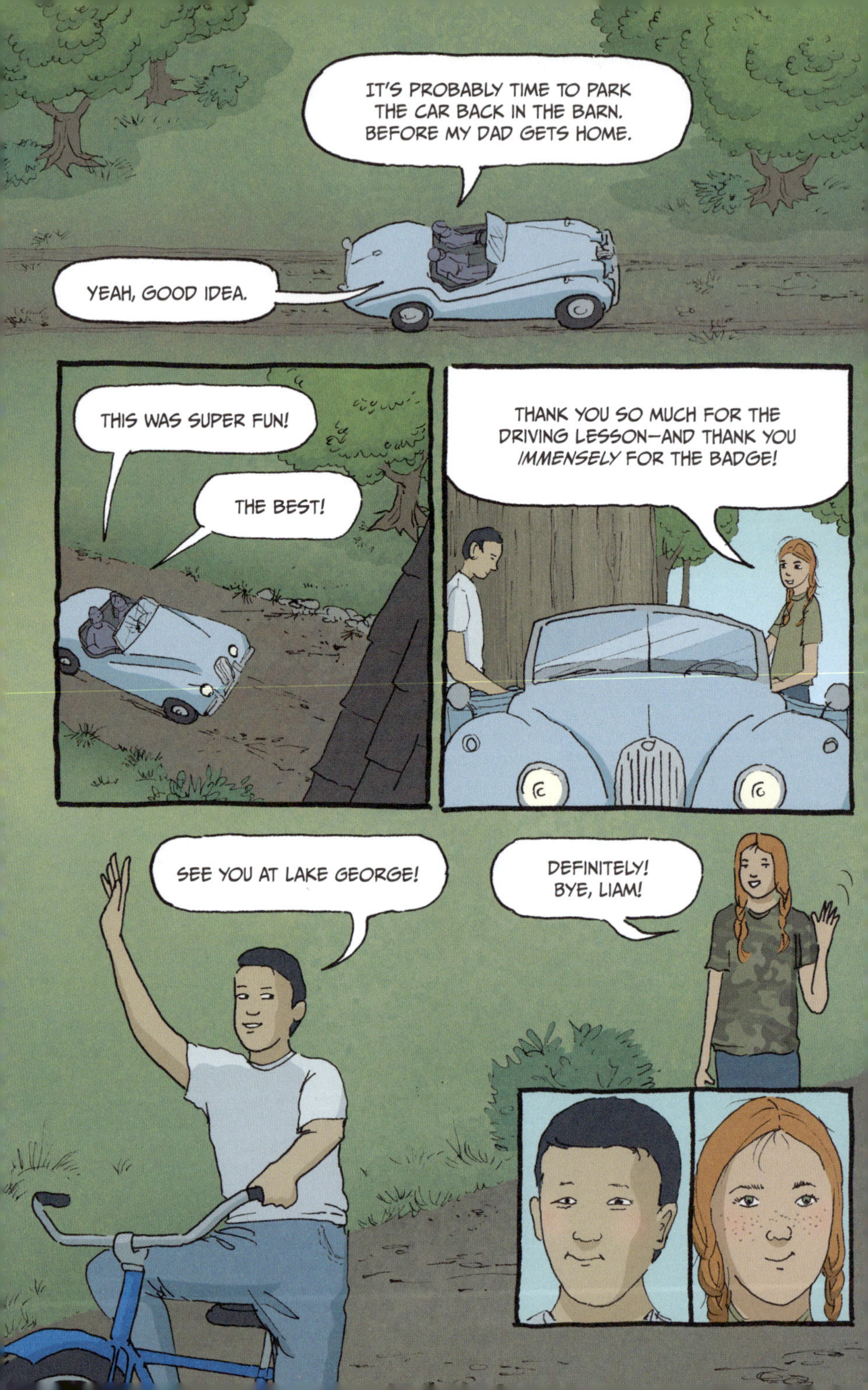
IT'S PROBABLY TIME TO PARK THE CAR BACK IN THE BARN. BEFORE MY DAD GETS HOME.
YEAH, GOOD IDEA.
THIS WAS SUPER FUN!
THE BEST!
THANK YOU SO MUCH FOR THE DRIVING LESSON—AND THANK YOU *IMMENSELY* FOR THE BADGE!
SEE YOU AT LAKE GEORGE!
DEFINITELY! BYE, LIAM!

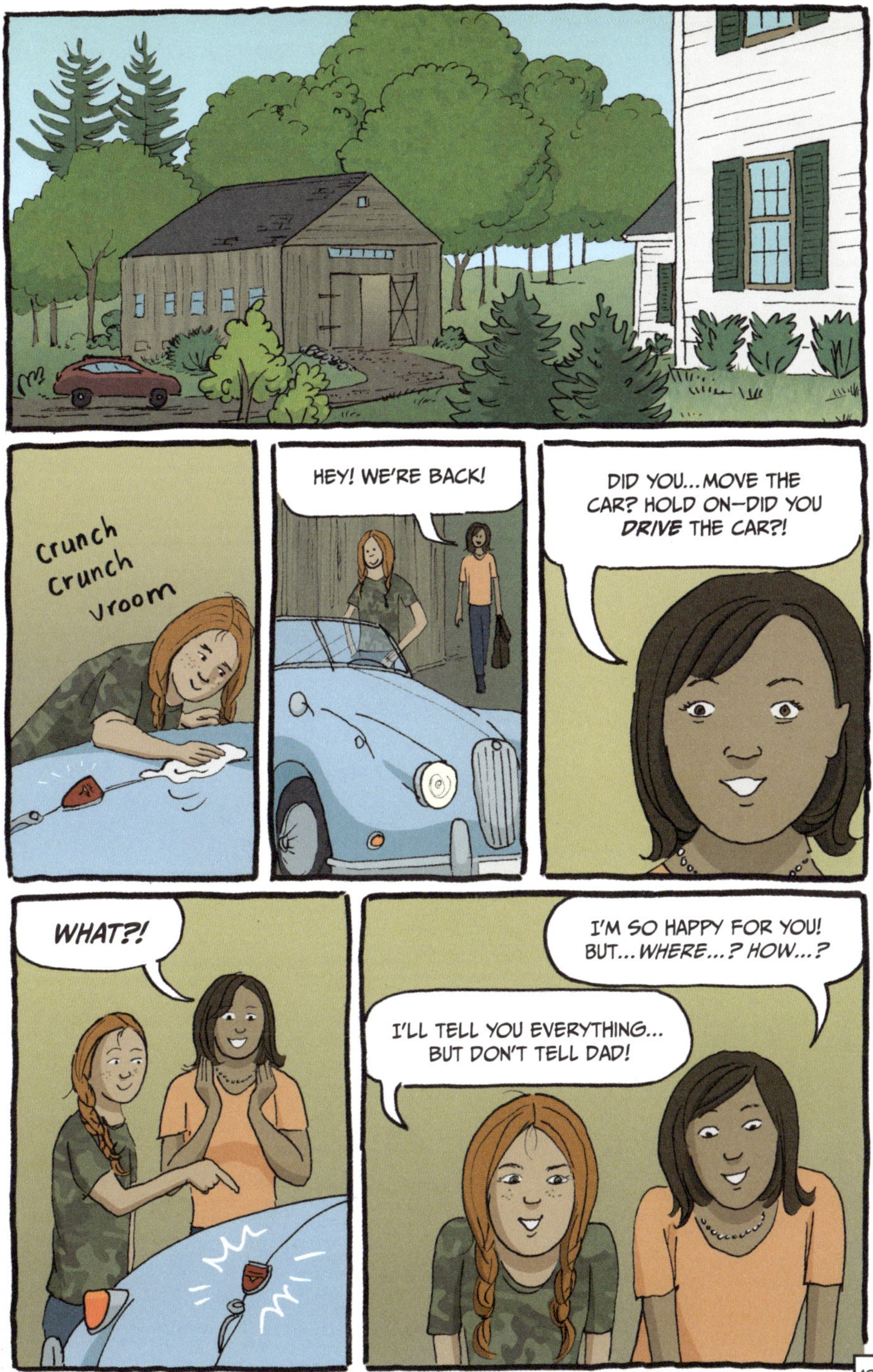
crunch
crunch
vroom
HEY! WE'RE BACK!
DID YOU...MOVE THE CAR? HOLD ON—DID YOU *DRIVE* THE CAR?!
WHAT?!
I'M SO HAPPY FOR YOU! BUT...*WHERE...? HOW...?*
I'LL TELL YOU EVERYTHING... BUT DON'T TELL DAD!

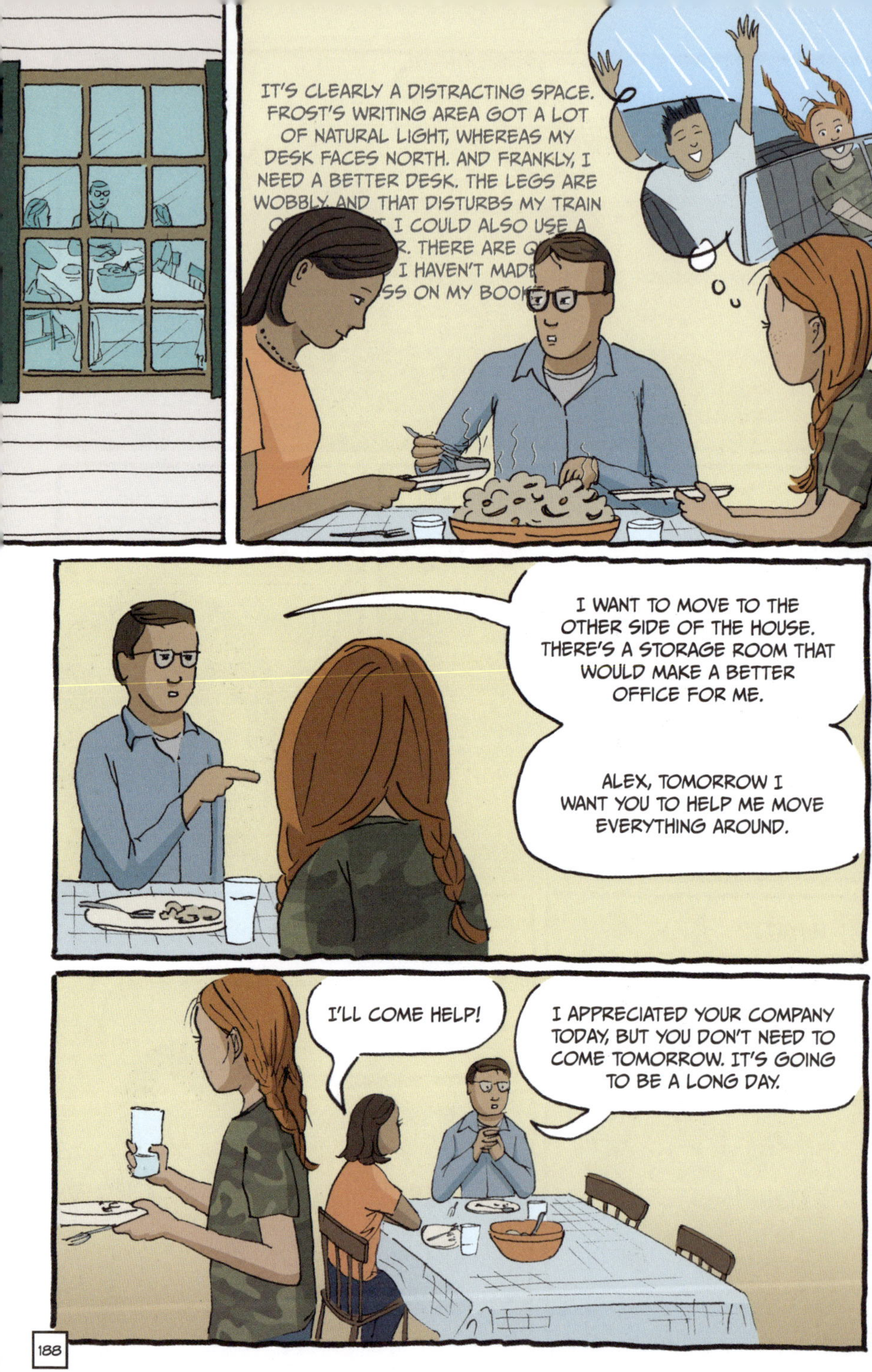

IT'S CLEARLY A DISTRACTING SPACE. FROST'S WRITING AREA GOT A LOT OF NATURAL LIGHT, WHEREAS MY DESK FACES NORTH. AND FRANKLY, I NEED A BETTER DESK. THE LEGS ARE WOBBLY, AND THAT DISTURBS MY TRAIN
I COULD ALSO USE A
R. THERE ARE
I HAVEN'T MADE
SS ON MY BOOK
I WANT TO MOVE TO THE OTHER SIDE OF THE HOUSE. THERE'S A STORAGE ROOM THAT WOULD MAKE A BETTER OFFICE FOR ME.
ALEX, TOMORROW I WANT YOU TO HELP ME MOVE EVERYTHING AROUND.
I'LL COME HELP!
I APPRECIATED YOUR COMPANY TODAY, BUT YOU DON'T NEED TO COME TOMORROW. IT'S GOING TO BE A LONG DAY.

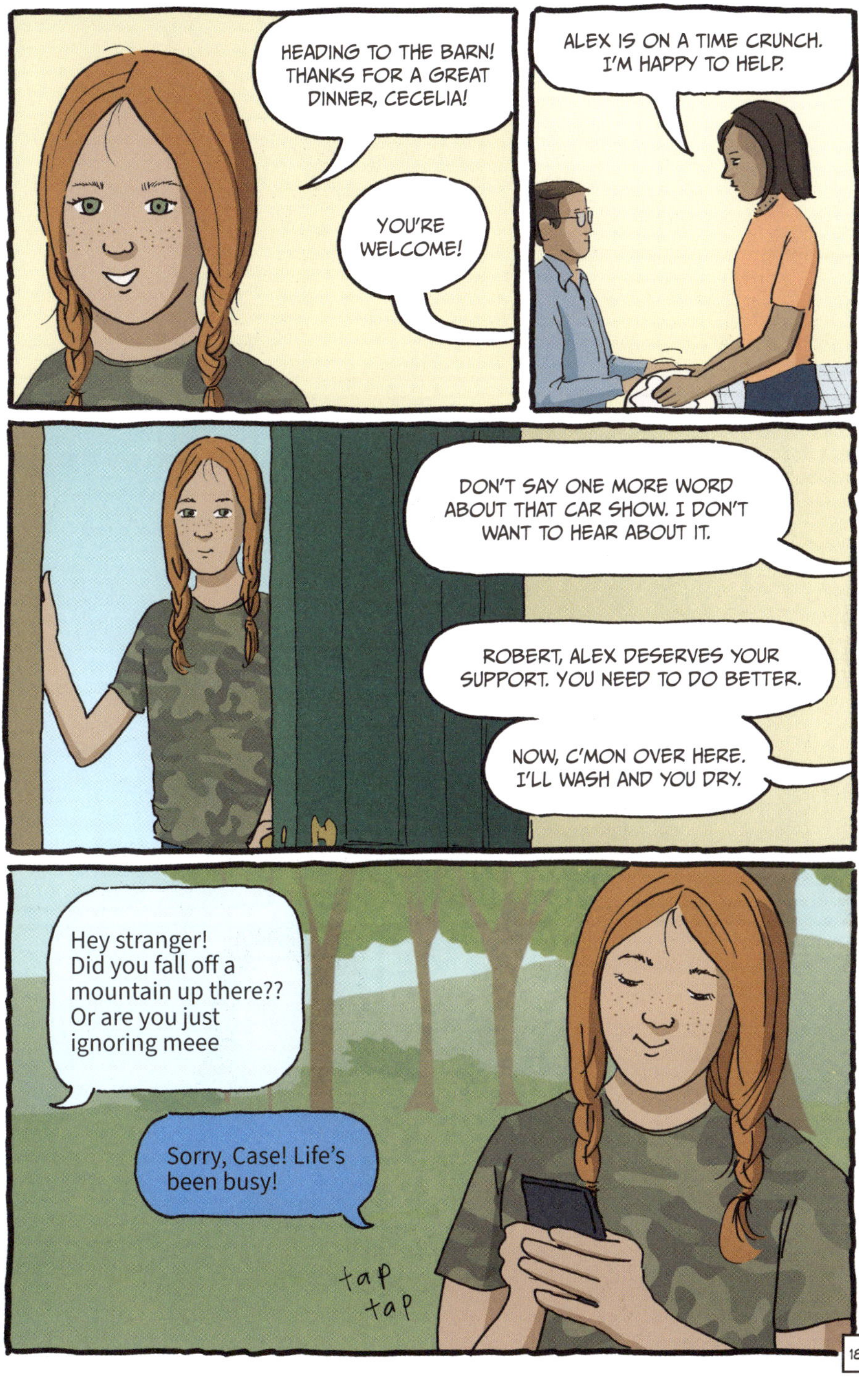

HEADING TO THE BARN! THANKS FOR A GREAT DINNER, CECELIA!
YOU'RE WELCOME!
ALEX IS ON A TIME CRUNCH. I'M HAPPY TO HELP.
DON'T SAY ONE MORE WORD ABOUT THAT CAR SHOW. I DON'T WANT TO HEAR ABOUT IT.
ROBERT, ALEX DESERVES YOUR SUPPORT. YOU NEED TO DO BETTER.
NOW, C'MON OVER HERE. I'LL WASH AND YOU DRY.
Hey stranger! Did you fall off a mountain up there?? Or are you just ignoring meee
Sorry, Case! Life's been busy!
tap tap

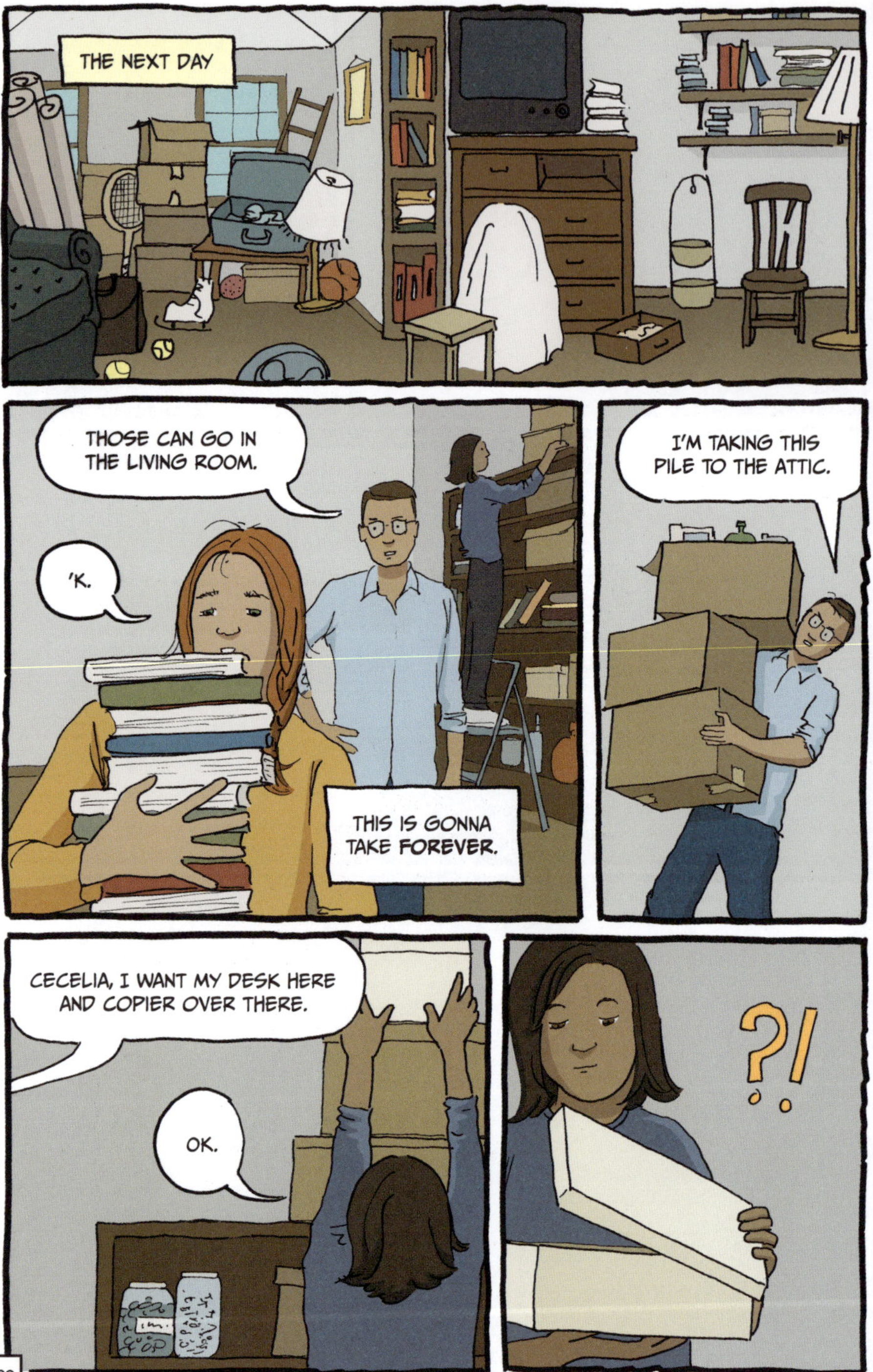
THE NEXT DAY
THOSE CAN GO IN THE LIVING ROOM.
'K.
THIS IS GONNA TAKE FOREVER.
I'M TAKING THIS PILE TO THE ATTIC.
CECELIA, I WANT MY DESK HERE AND COPIER OVER THERE.
OK.
?!

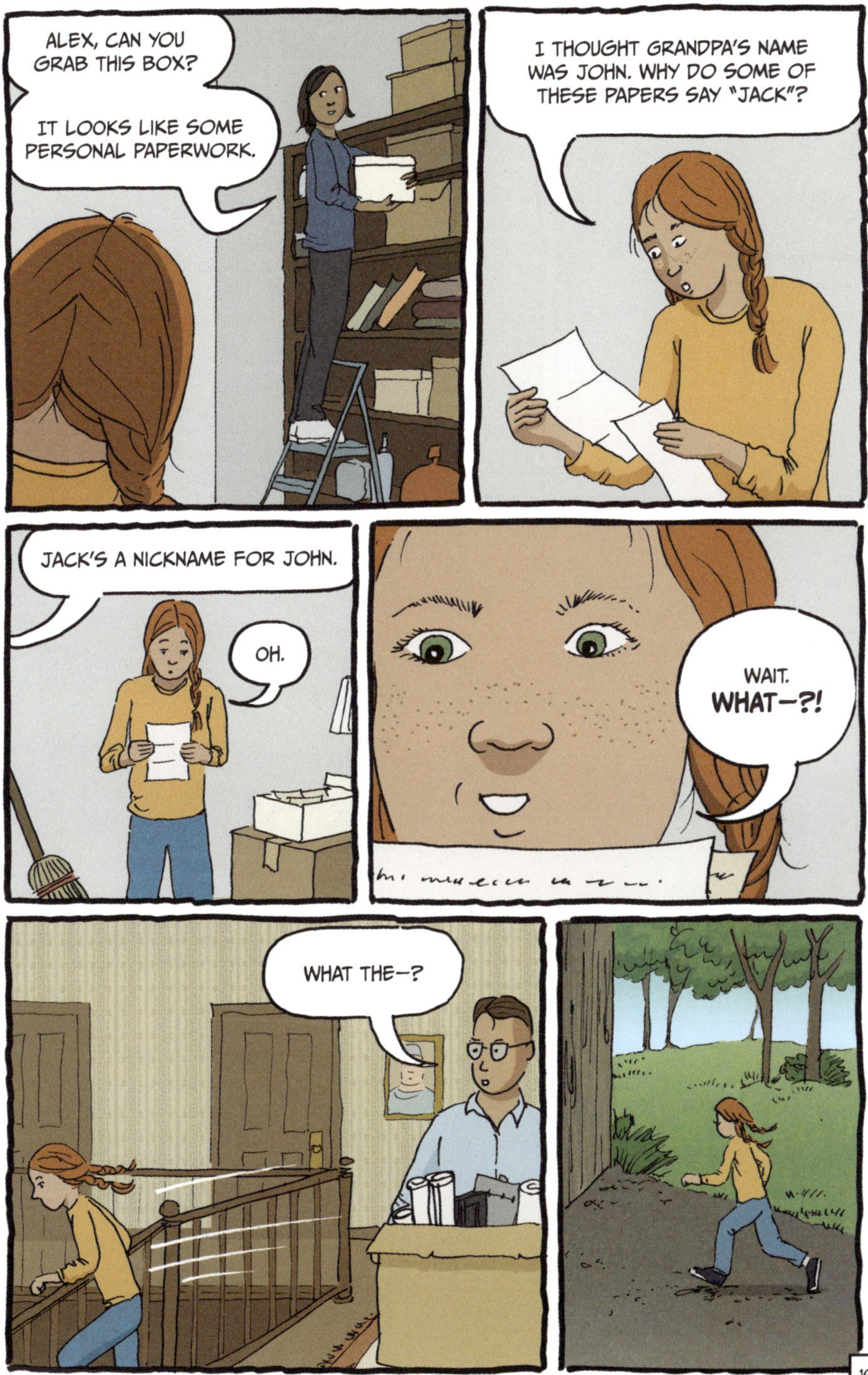
ALEX, CAN YOU GRAB THIS BOX?
IT LOOKS LIKE SOME PERSONAL PAPERWORK.
I THOUGHT GRANDPA'S NAME WAS JOHN. WHY DO SOME OF THESE PAPERS SAY "JACK"?
JACK'S A NICKNAME FOR JOHN.
OH.
WAIT. **WHAT—?!**
WHAT THE—?

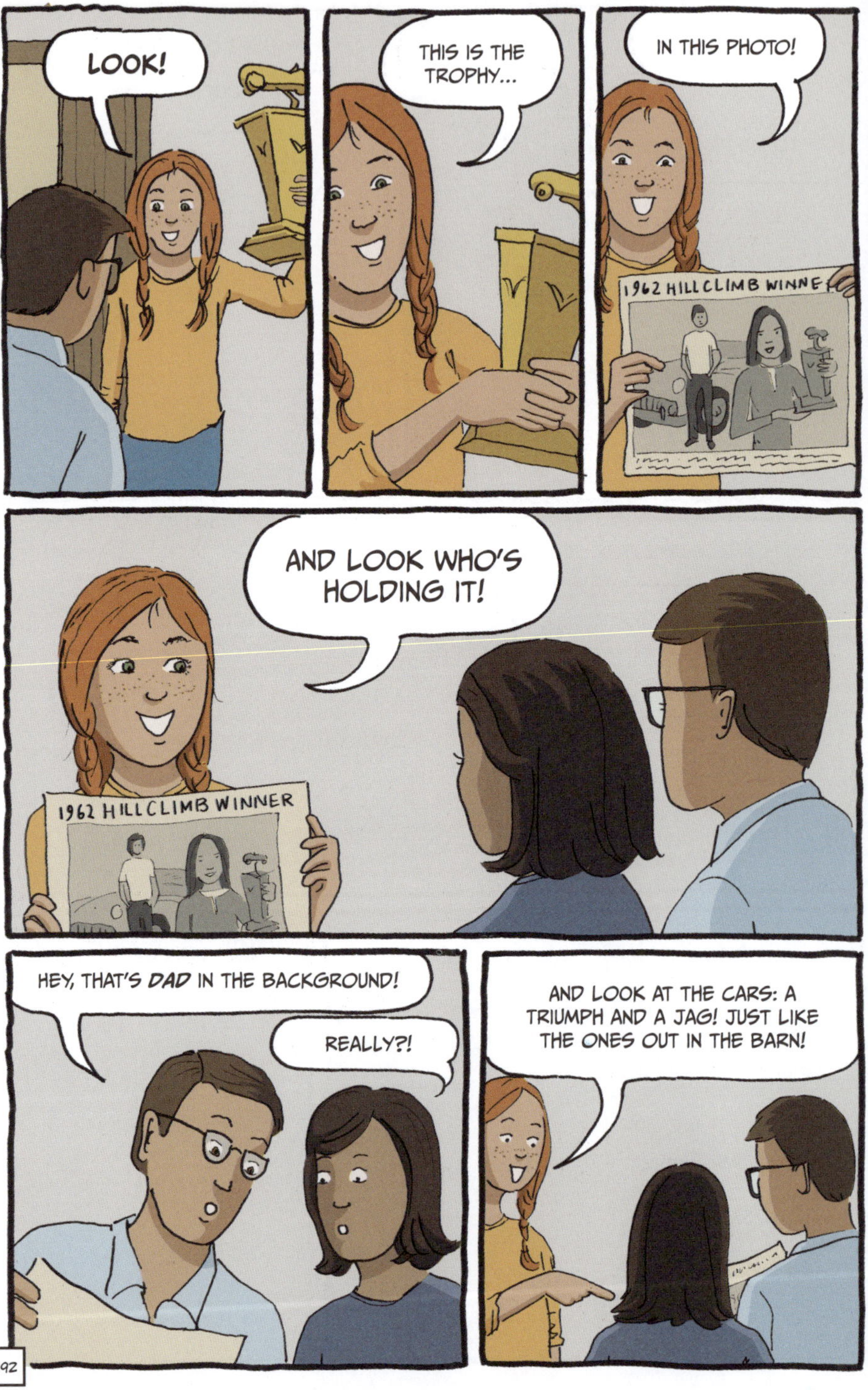
LOOK!
THIS IS THE TROPHY...
IN THIS PHOTO!
1962 HILLCLIMB WINNE
AND LOOK WHO'S HOLDING IT!
1962 HILLCLIMB WINNER
HEY, THAT'S *DAD* IN THE BACKGROUND!
REALLY?!
AND LOOK AT THE CARS: A TRIUMPH AND A JAG! JUST LIKE THE ONES OUT IN THE BARN!

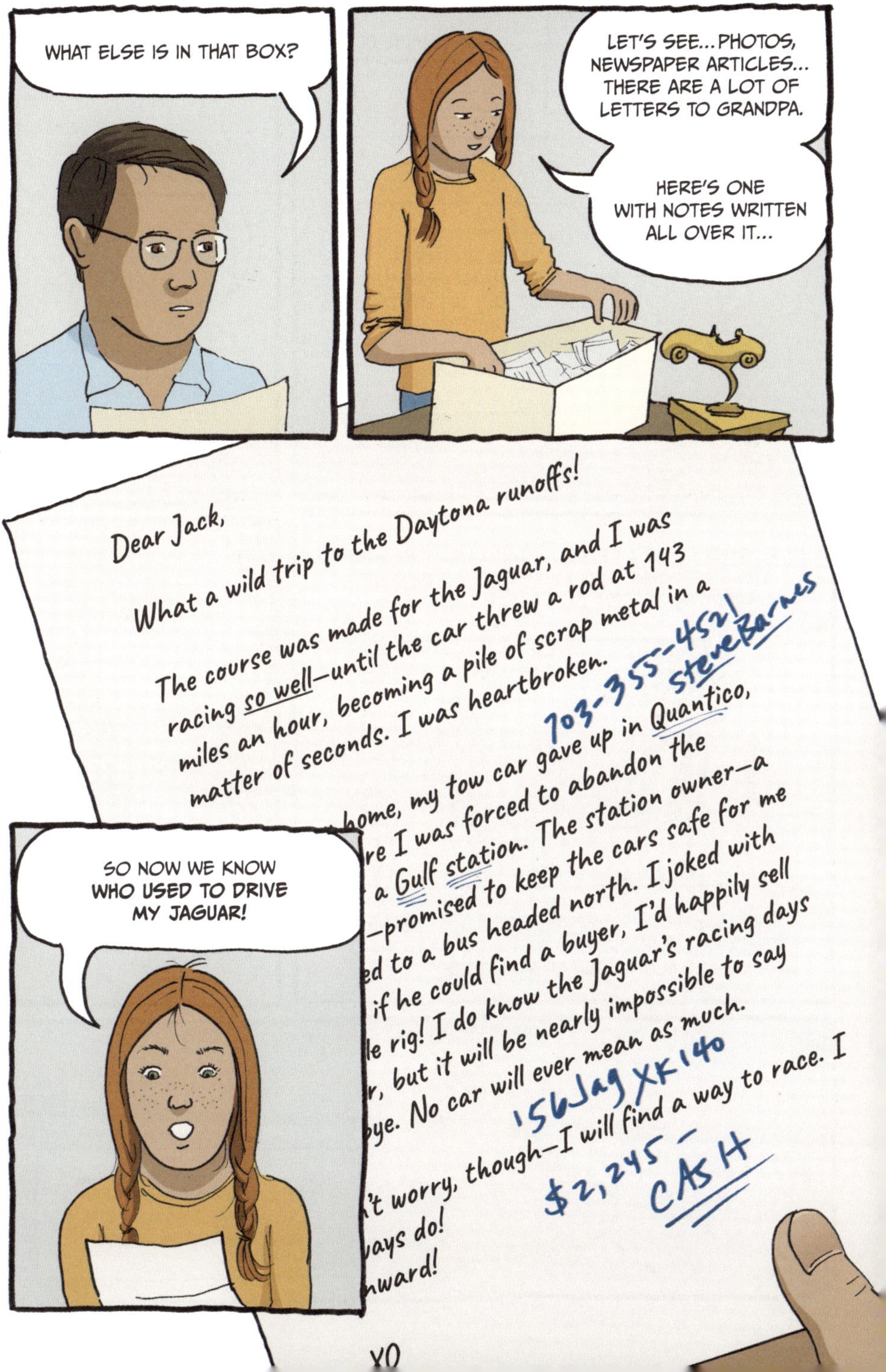

WHAT ELSE IS IN THAT BOX?
LET'S SEE... PHOTOS, NEWSPAPER ARTICLES... THERE ARE A LOT OF LETTERS TO GRANDPA.
HERE'S ONE WITH NOTES WRITTEN ALL OVER IT...
Dear Jack,
What a wild trip to the Daytona runoffs!
The course was made for the Jaguar, and I was racing so well—until the car threw a rod at 143 miles an hour, becoming a pile of scrap metal in a matter of seconds. I was heartbroken.
703-355-4521
Steve Barnes
home, my tow car gave up in Quantico,
re I was forced to abandon the
a Gulf station. The station owner—a
—promised to keep the cars safe for me
ed to a bus headed north. I joked with
if he could find a buyer, I'd happily sell
le rig! I do know the Jaguar's racing days
r, but it will be nearly impossible to say
bye. No car will ever mean as much.
'56 Jag XK140
't worry, though—I will find a way to race. I
ays do!
nward!
$2,245—
CASH
XO
SO NOW WE KNOW WHO USED TO DRIVE MY JAGUAR!

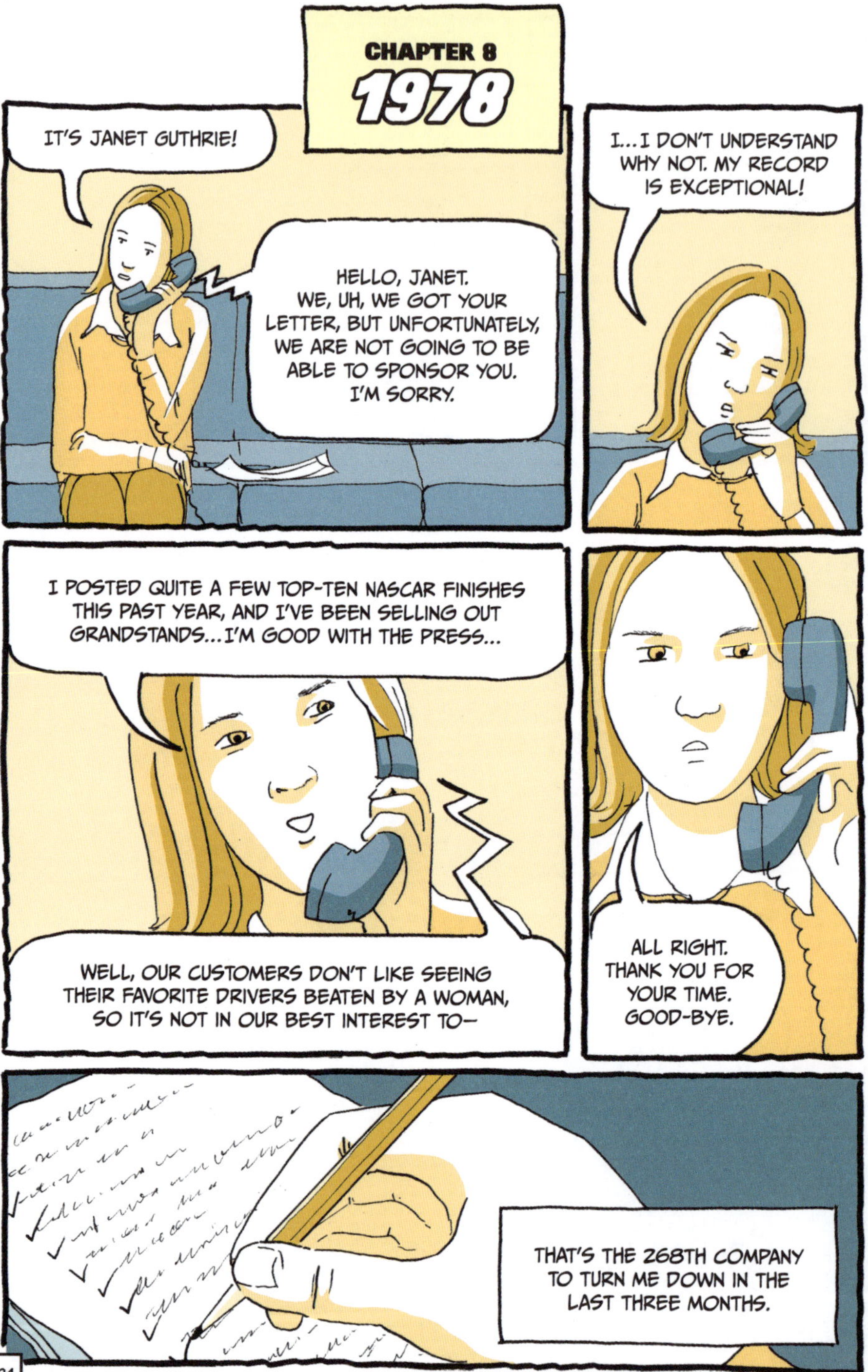
CHAPTER 8
1978
IT'S JANET GUTHRIE!
HELLO, JANET. WE, UH, WE GOT YOUR LETTER, BUT UNFORTUNATELY, WE ARE NOT GOING TO BE ABLE TO SPONSOR YOU. I'M SORRY.
I...I DON'T UNDERSTAND WHY NOT. MY RECORD IS EXCEPTIONAL!
I POSTED QUITE A FEW TOP-TEN NASCAR FINISHES THIS PAST YEAR, AND I'VE BEEN SELLING OUT GRANDSTANDS...I'M GOOD WITH THE PRESS...
WELL, OUR CUSTOMERS DON'T LIKE SEEING THEIR FAVORITE DRIVERS BEATEN BY A WOMAN, SO IT'S NOT IN OUR BEST INTEREST TO—
ALL RIGHT. THANK YOU FOR YOUR TIME. GOOD-BYE.
THAT'S THE 268TH COMPANY TO TURN ME DOWN IN THE LAST THREE MONTHS.

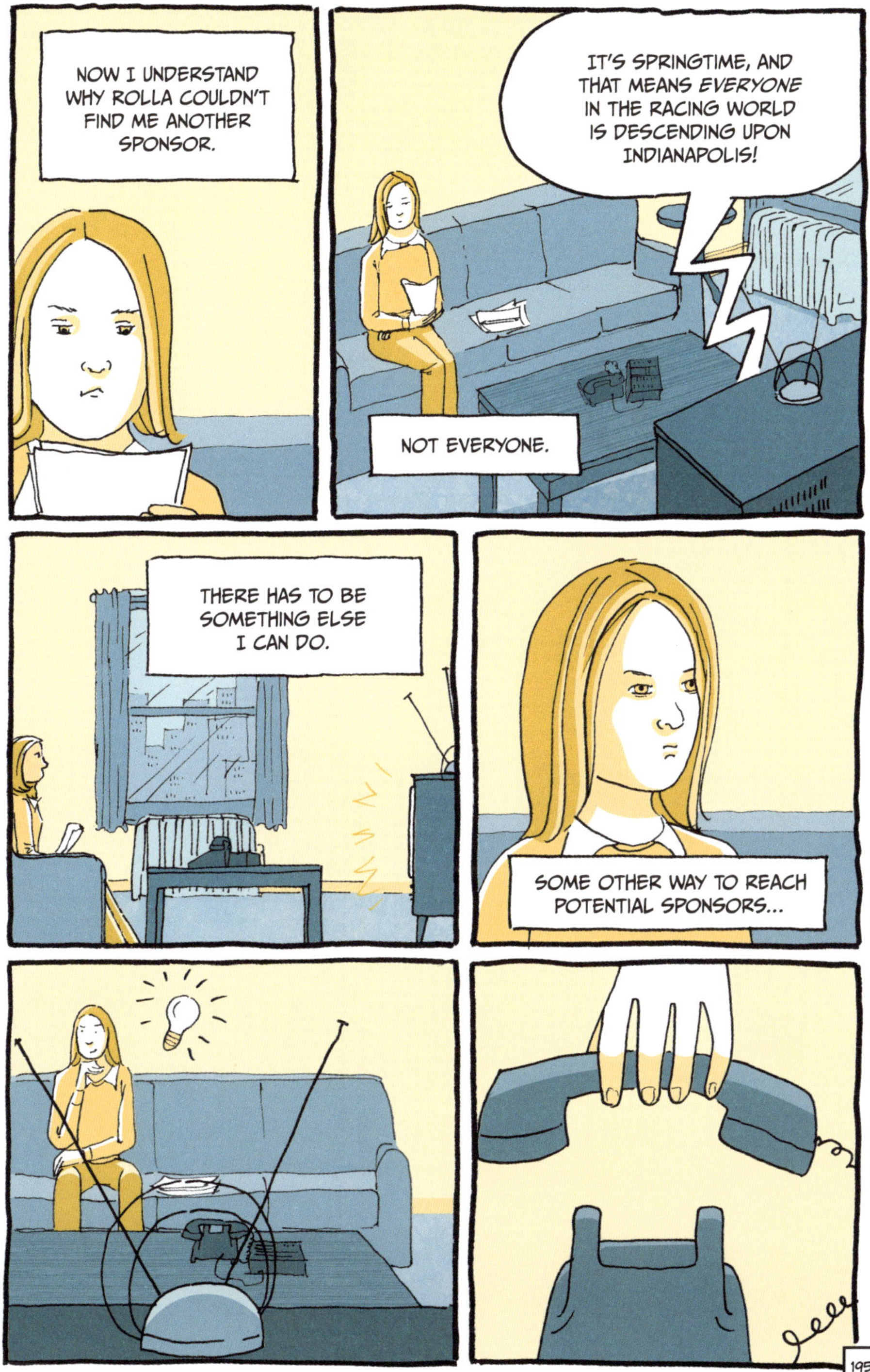
NOW I UNDERSTAND WHY ROLLA COULDN'T FIND ME ANOTHER SPONSOR.
IT'S SPRINGTIME, AND THAT MEANS *EVERYONE* IN THE RACING WORLD IS DESCENDING UPON INDIANAPOLIS!
NOT EVERYONE.
THERE HAS TO BE SOMETHING ELSE I CAN DO.
SOME OTHER WAY TO REACH POTENTIAL SPONSORS...

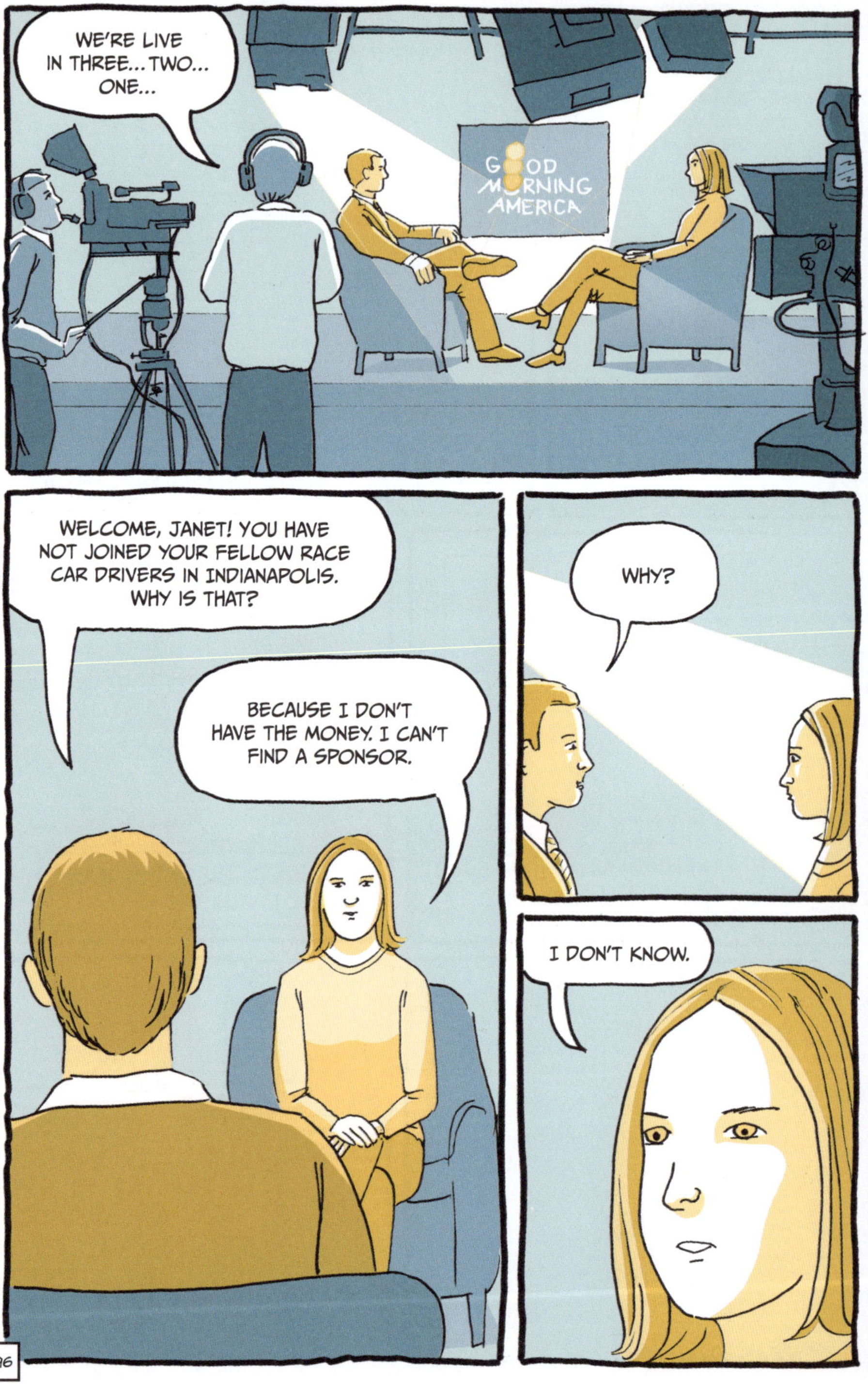
WE'RE LIVE IN THREE... TWO... ONE...
GOOD MORNING AMERICA
WELCOME, JANET! YOU HAVE NOT JOINED YOUR FELLOW RACE CAR DRIVERS IN INDIANAPOLIS. WHY IS THAT?
BECAUSE I DON'T HAVE THE MONEY. I CAN'T FIND A SPONSOR.
WHY?
I DON'T KNOW.

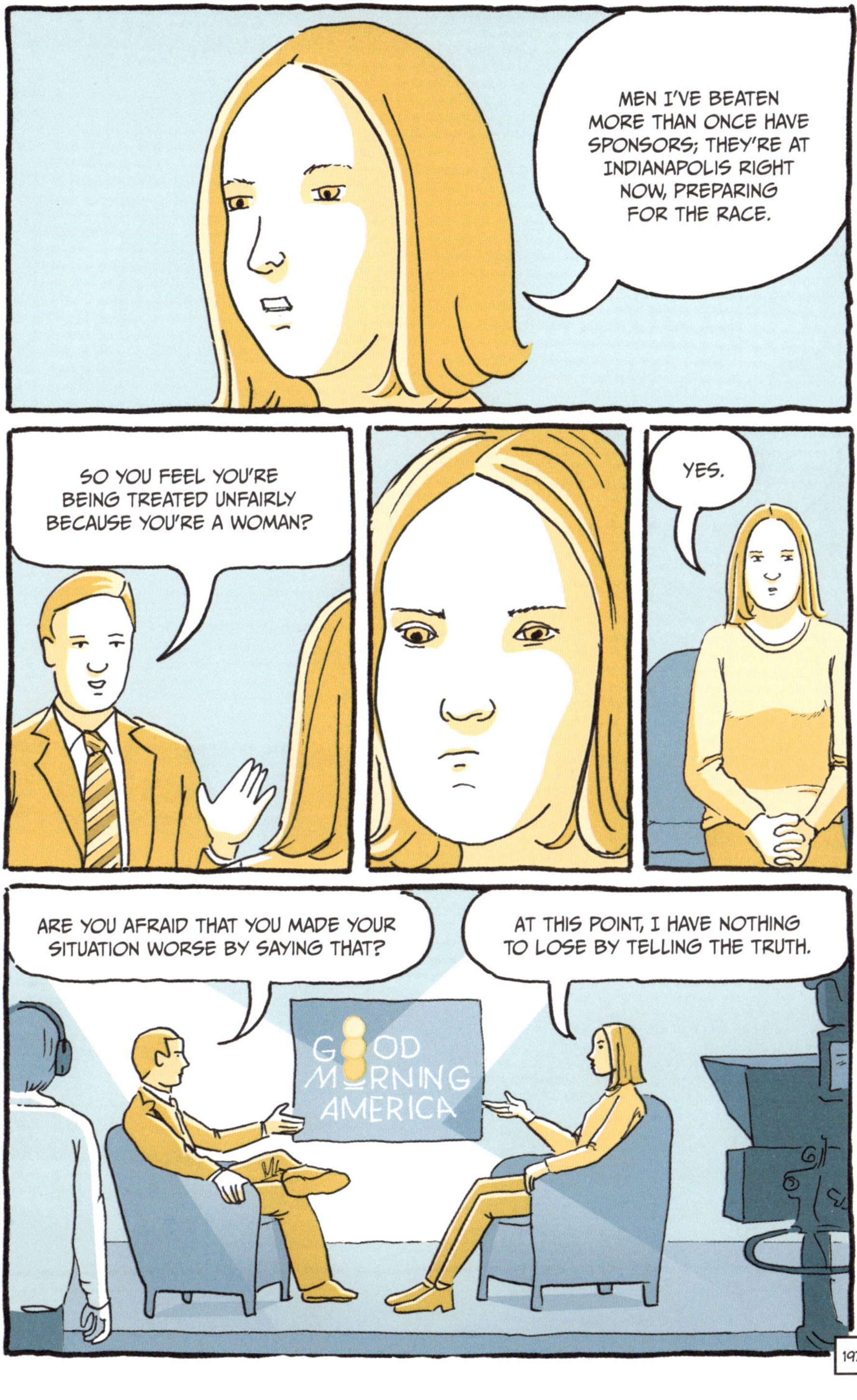
MEN I'VE BEATEN MORE THAN ONCE HAVE SPONSORS; THEY'RE AT INDIANAPOLIS RIGHT NOW, PREPARING FOR THE RACE.
SO YOU FEEL YOU'RE BEING TREATED UNFAIRLY BECAUSE YOU'RE A WOMAN?
YES.
ARE YOU AFRAID THAT YOU MADE YOUR SITUATION WORSE BY SAYING THAT?
AT THIS POINT, I HAVE NOTHING TO LOSE BY TELLING THE TRUTH.
GOOD MORNING AMERICA

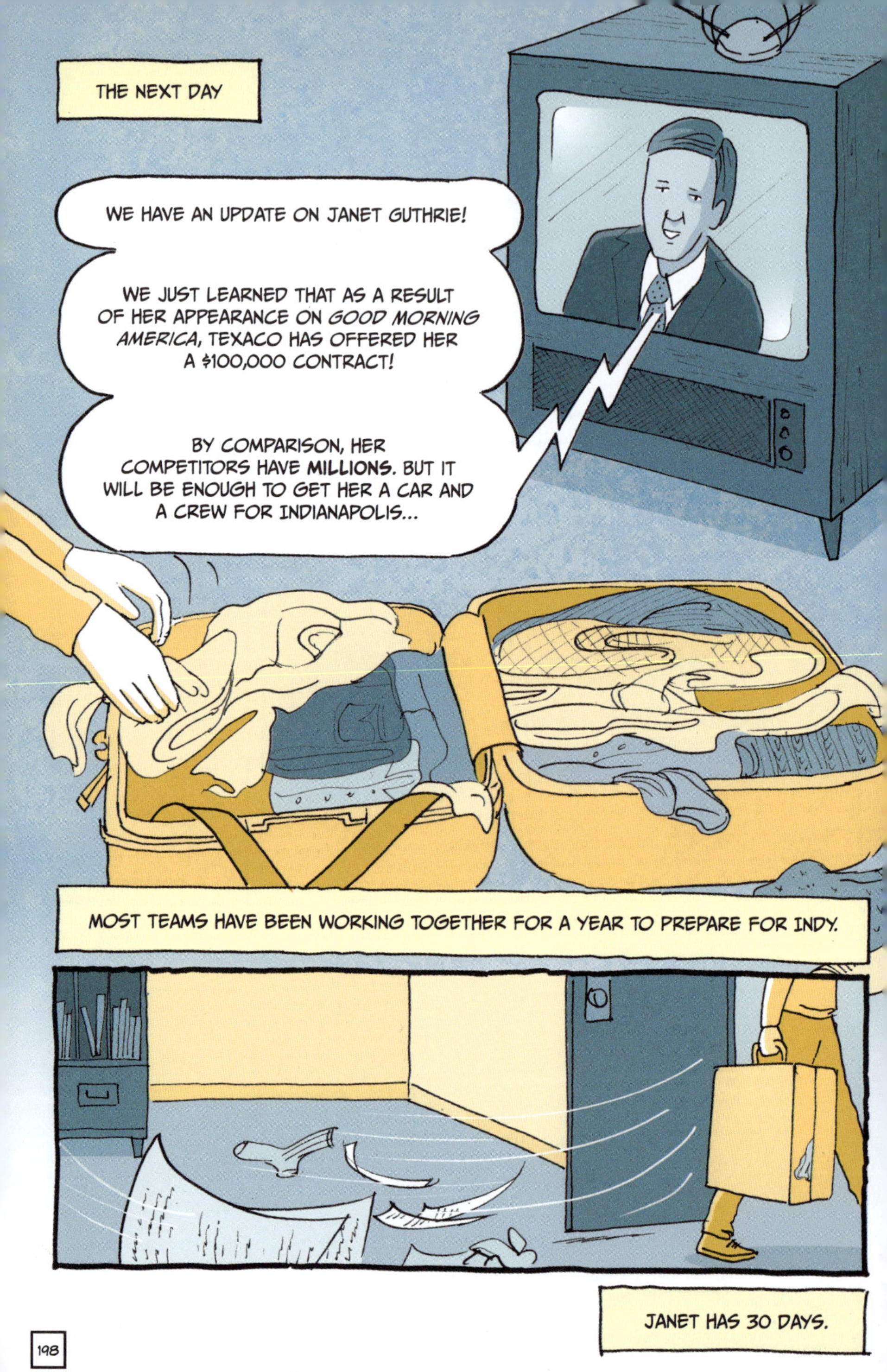
THE NEXT DAY
WE HAVE AN UPDATE ON JANET GUTHRIE!
WE JUST LEARNED THAT AS A RESULT OF HER APPEARANCE ON *GOOD MORNING AMERICA*, TEXACO HAS OFFERED HER A $100,000 CONTRACT!
BY COMPARISON, HER COMPETITORS HAVE **MILLIONS**. BUT IT WILL BE ENOUGH TO GET HER A CAR AND A CREW FOR INDIANAPOLIS...
MOST TEAMS HAVE BEEN WORKING TOGETHER FOR A YEAR TO PREPARE FOR INDY.
JANET HAS 30 DAYS.

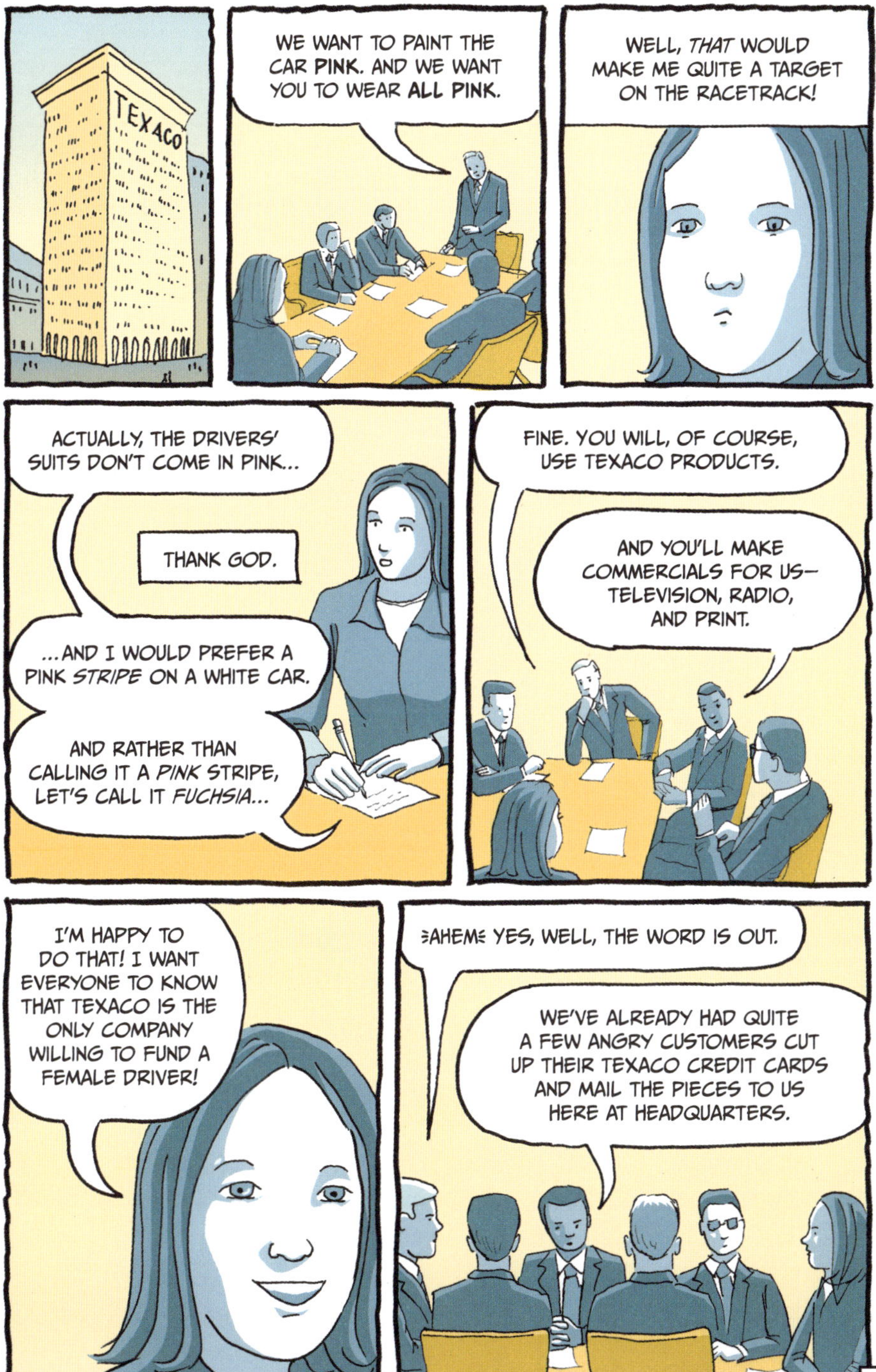
TEXACO
WE WANT TO PAINT THE CAR **PINK**. AND WE WANT YOU TO WEAR **ALL PINK**.
WELL, *THAT* WOULD MAKE ME QUITE A TARGET ON THE RACETRACK!
ACTUALLY, THE DRIVERS' SUITS DON'T COME IN PINK...
THANK GOD.
...AND I WOULD PREFER A PINK *STRIPE* ON A WHITE CAR.
AND RATHER THAN CALLING IT A *PINK* STRIPE, LET'S CALL IT *FUCHSIA*...
FINE. YOU WILL, OF COURSE, USE TEXACO PRODUCTS.
AND YOU'LL MAKE COMMERCIALS FOR US— TELEVISION, RADIO, AND PRINT.
I'M HAPPY TO DO THAT! I WANT EVERYONE TO KNOW THAT TEXACO IS THE ONLY COMPANY WILLING TO FUND A FEMALE DRIVER!
AHEM YES, WELL, THE WORD IS OUT.
WE'VE ALREADY HAD QUITE A FEW ANGRY CUSTOMERS CUT UP THEIR TEXACO CREDIT CARDS AND MAIL THE PIECES TO US HERE AT HEADQUARTERS.

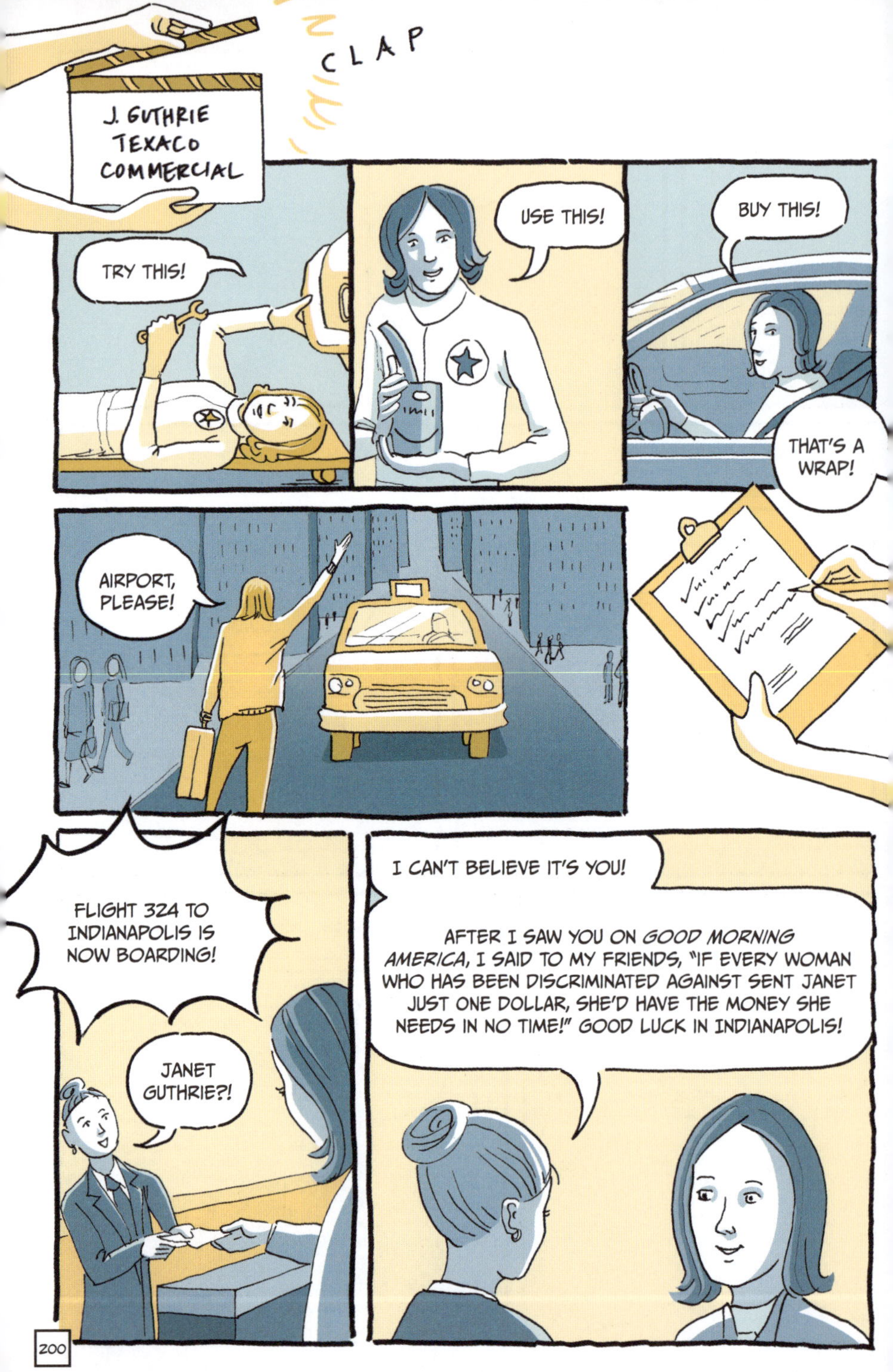

CLAP
J. GUTHRIE TEXACO COMMERCIAL
TRY THIS!
USE THIS!
BUY THIS!
THAT'S A WRAP!
AIRPORT, PLEASE!
FLIGHT 324 TO INDIANAPOLIS IS NOW BOARDING!
JANET GUTHRIE?!
I CAN'T BELIEVE IT'S YOU!
AFTER I SAW YOU ON *GOOD MORNING AMERICA*, I SAID TO MY FRIENDS, "IF EVERY WOMAN WHO HAS BEEN DISCRIMINATED AGAINST SENT JANET JUST ONE DOLLAR, SHE'D HAVE THE MONEY SHE NEEDS IN NO TIME!" GOOD LUCK IN INDIANAPOLIS!

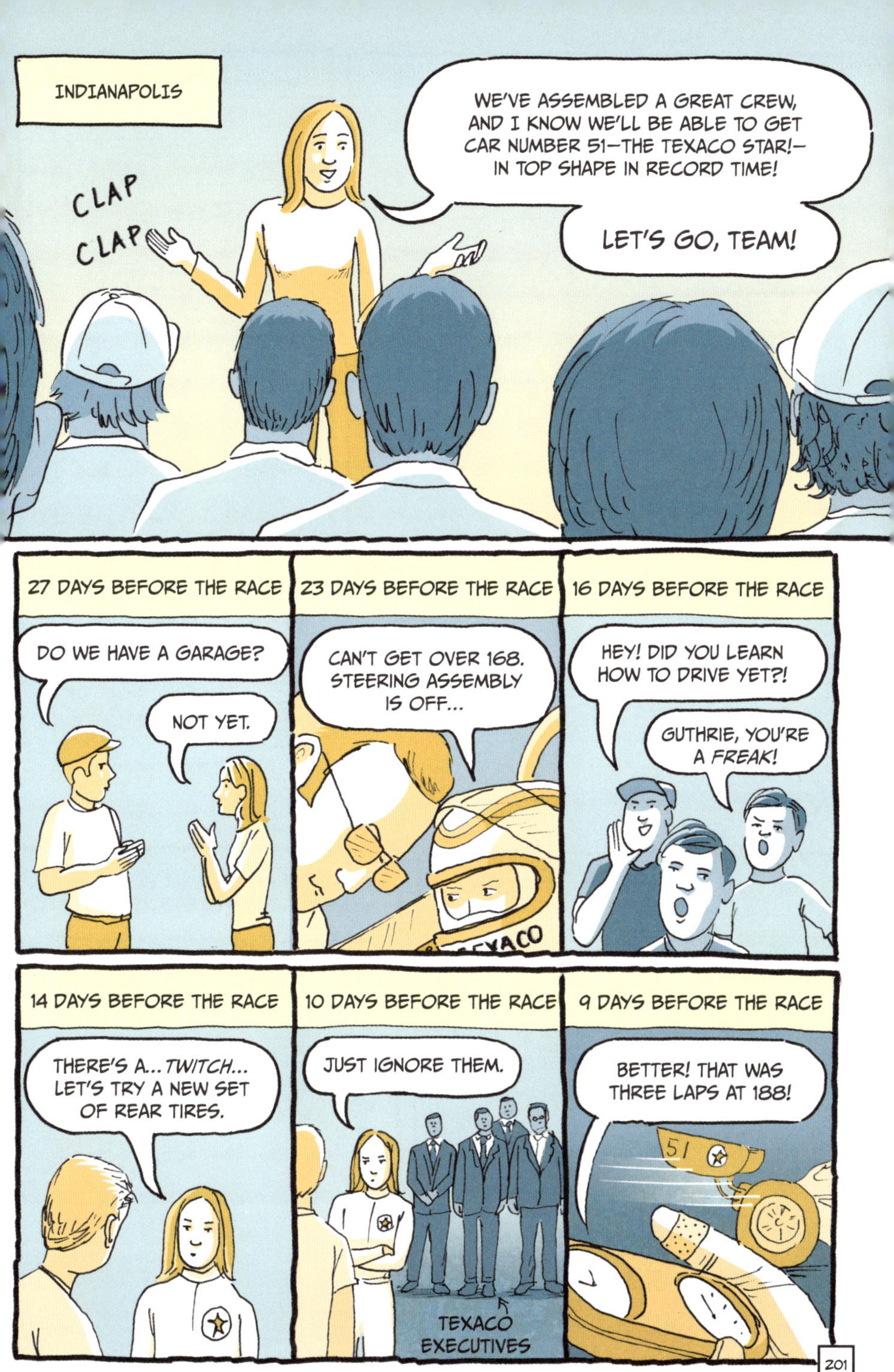
INDIANAPOLIS
WE'VE ASSEMBLED A GREAT CREW, AND I KNOW WE'LL BE ABLE TO GET CAR NUMBER 51—THE TEXACO STAR!—IN TOP SHAPE IN RECORD TIME!
LET'S GO, TEAM!
CLAP
CLAP
27 DAYS BEFORE THE RACE
DO WE HAVE A GARAGE?
NOT YET.
23 DAYS BEFORE THE RACE
CAN'T GET OVER 168. STEERING ASSEMBLY IS OFF...
16 DAYS BEFORE THE RACE
HEY! DID YOU LEARN HOW TO DRIVE YET?!
GUTHRIE, YOU'RE A *FREAK!*
14 DAYS BEFORE THE RACE
THERE'S A... *TWITCH*... LET'S TRY A NEW SET OF REAR TIRES.
10 DAYS BEFORE THE RACE
JUST IGNORE THEM.
TEXACO EXECUTIVES
9 DAYS BEFORE THE RACE
BETTER! THAT WAS THREE LAPS AT 188!

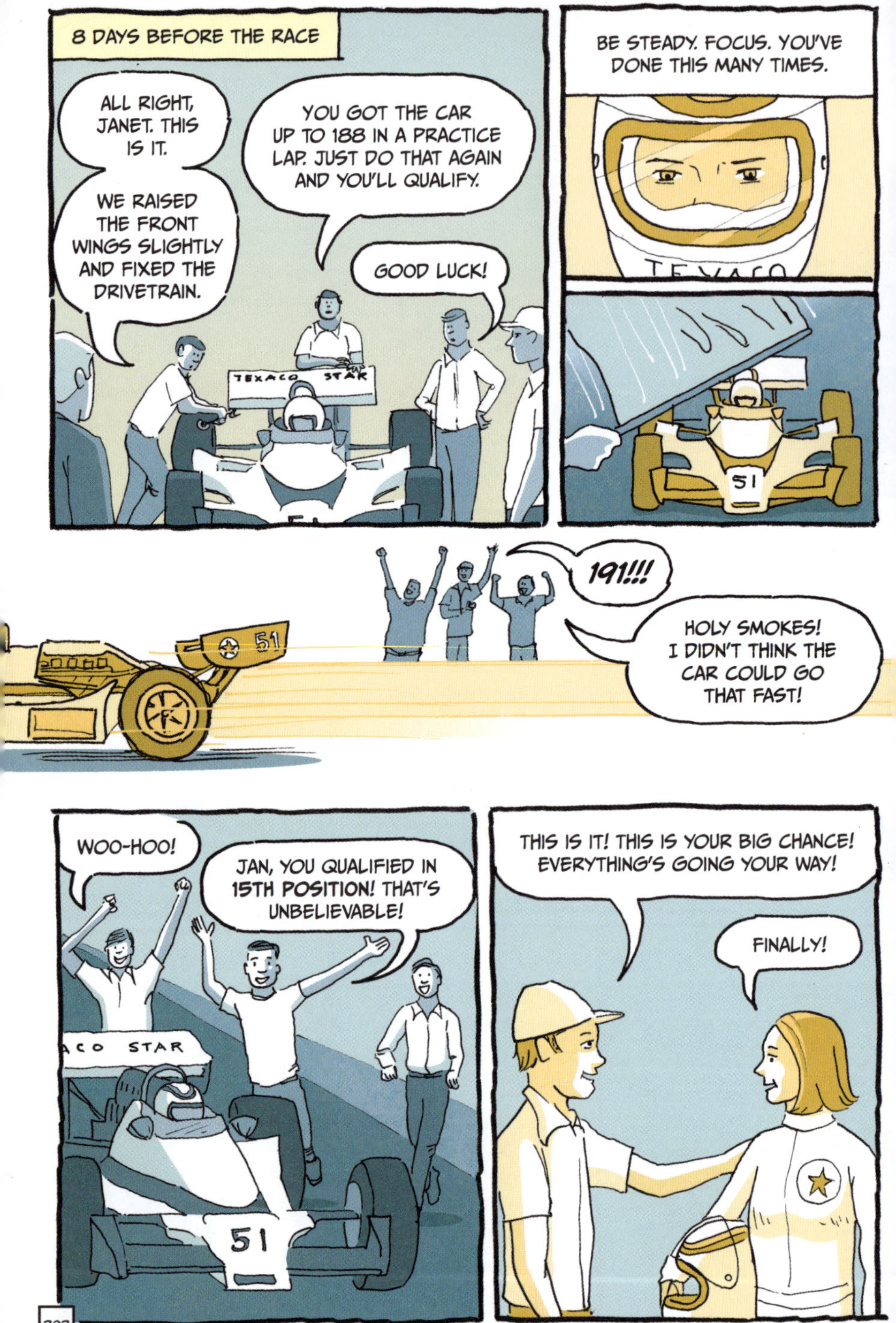
8 DAYS BEFORE THE RACE
ALL RIGHT, JANET. THIS IS IT.
WE RAISED THE FRONT WINGS SLIGHTLY AND FIXED THE DRIVETRAIN.
YOU GOT THE CAR UP TO 188 IN A PRACTICE LAP. JUST DO THAT AGAIN AND YOU'LL QUALIFY.
GOOD LUCK!
TEXACO STAR
BE STEADY. FOCUS. YOU'VE DONE THIS MANY TIMES.
51
191!!!
HOLY SMOKES! I DIDN'T THINK THE CAR COULD GO THAT FAST!
WOO-HOO!
JAN, YOU QUALIFIED IN **15TH POSITION!** THAT'S UNBELIEVABLE!
THIS IS IT! THIS IS YOUR BIG CHANCE! EVERYTHING'S GOING YOUR WAY!
FINALLY!

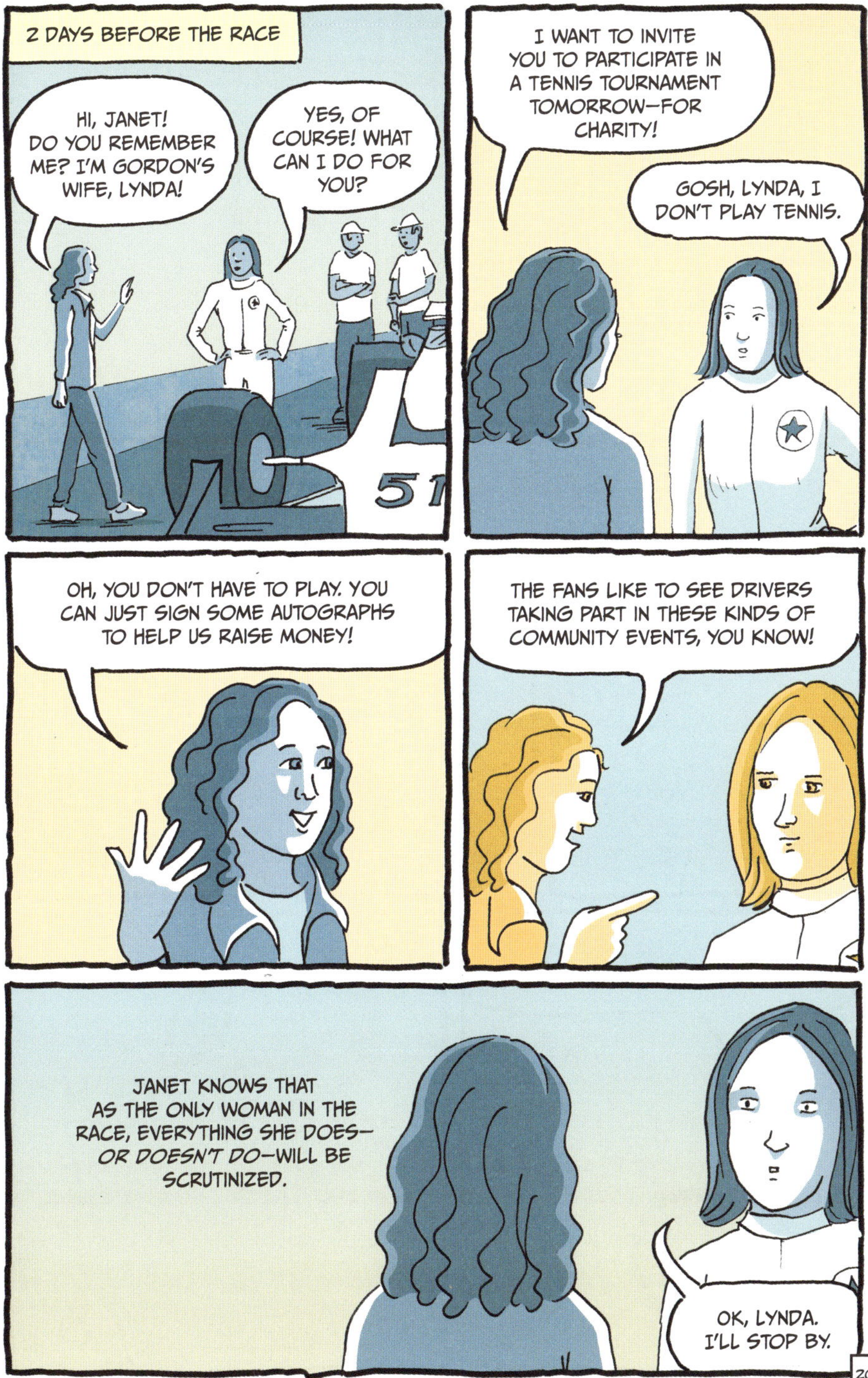
2 DAYS BEFORE THE RACE
HI, JANET! DO YOU REMEMBER ME? I'M GORDON'S WIFE, LYNDA!
YES, OF COURSE! WHAT CAN I DO FOR YOU?
51
I WANT TO INVITE YOU TO PARTICIPATE IN A TENNIS TOURNAMENT TOMORROW—FOR CHARITY!
GOSH, LYNDA, I DON'T PLAY TENNIS.
OH, YOU DON'T HAVE TO PLAY. YOU CAN JUST SIGN SOME AUTOGRAPHS TO HELP US RAISE MONEY!
THE FANS LIKE TO SEE DRIVERS TAKING PART IN THESE KINDS OF COMMUNITY EVENTS, YOU KNOW!
JANET KNOWS THAT AS THE ONLY WOMAN IN THE RACE, EVERYTHING SHE DOES—*OR DOESN'T DO*—WILL BE SCRUTINIZED.
OK, LYNDA. I'LL STOP BY.

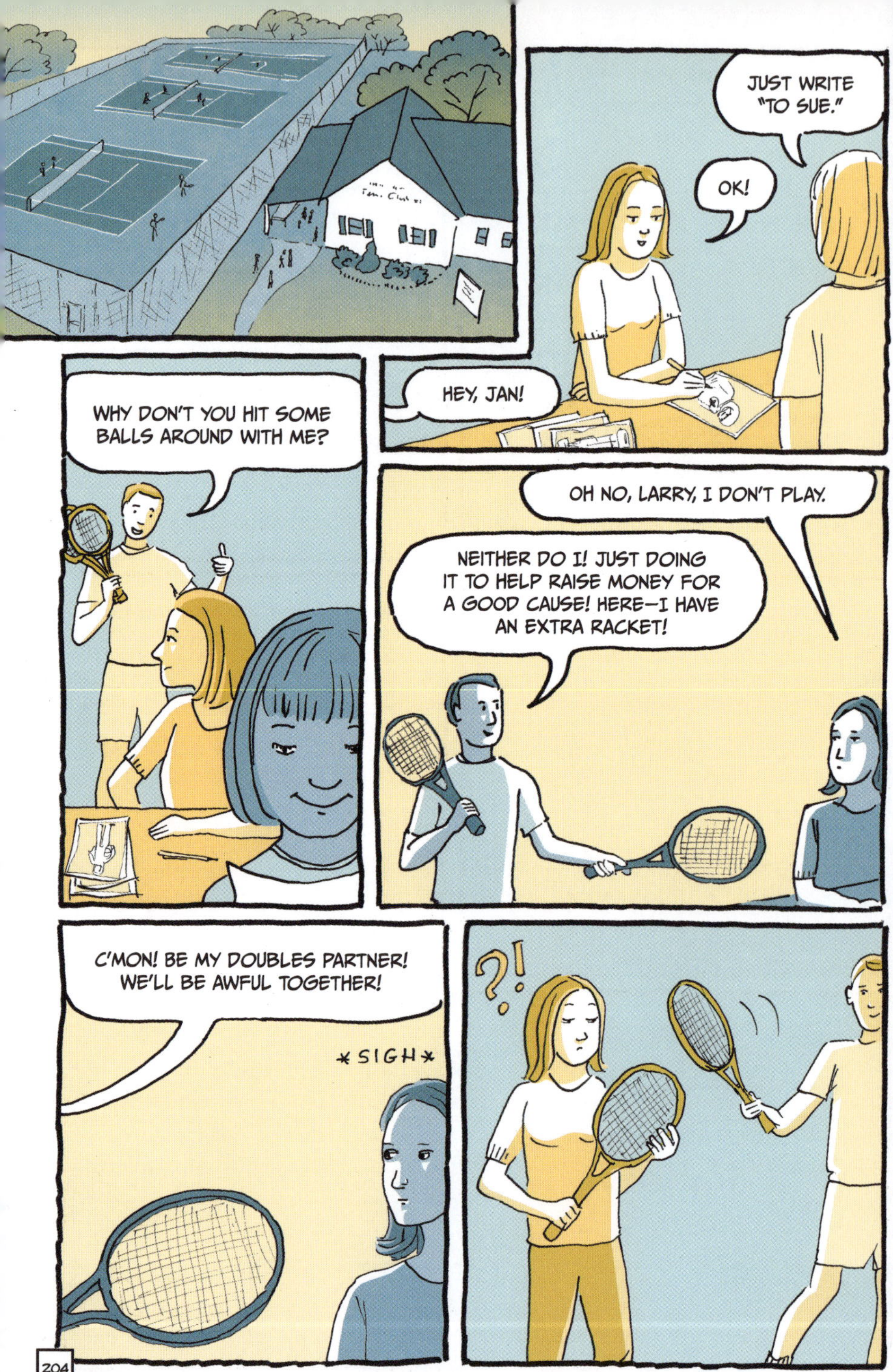

JUST WRITE "TO SUE."
OK!
HEY, JAN!
WHY DON'T YOU HIT SOME BALLS AROUND WITH ME?
OH NO, LARRY, I DON'T PLAY.
NEITHER DO I! JUST DOING IT TO HELP RAISE MONEY FOR A GOOD CAUSE! HERE—I HAVE AN EXTRA RACKET!
C'MON! BE MY DOUBLES PARTNER! WE'LL BE AWFUL TOGETHER!
SIGH
?!

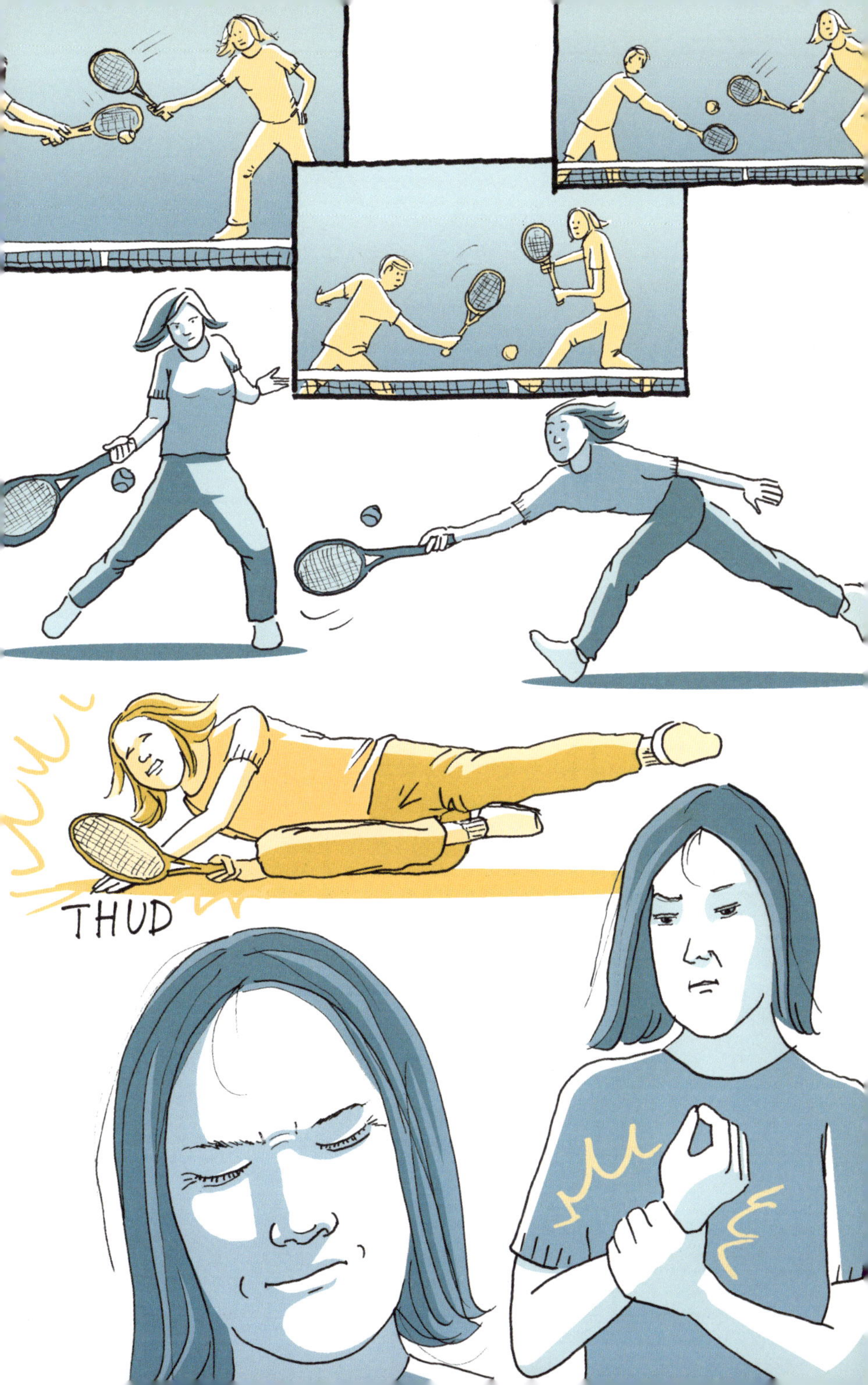
THUD

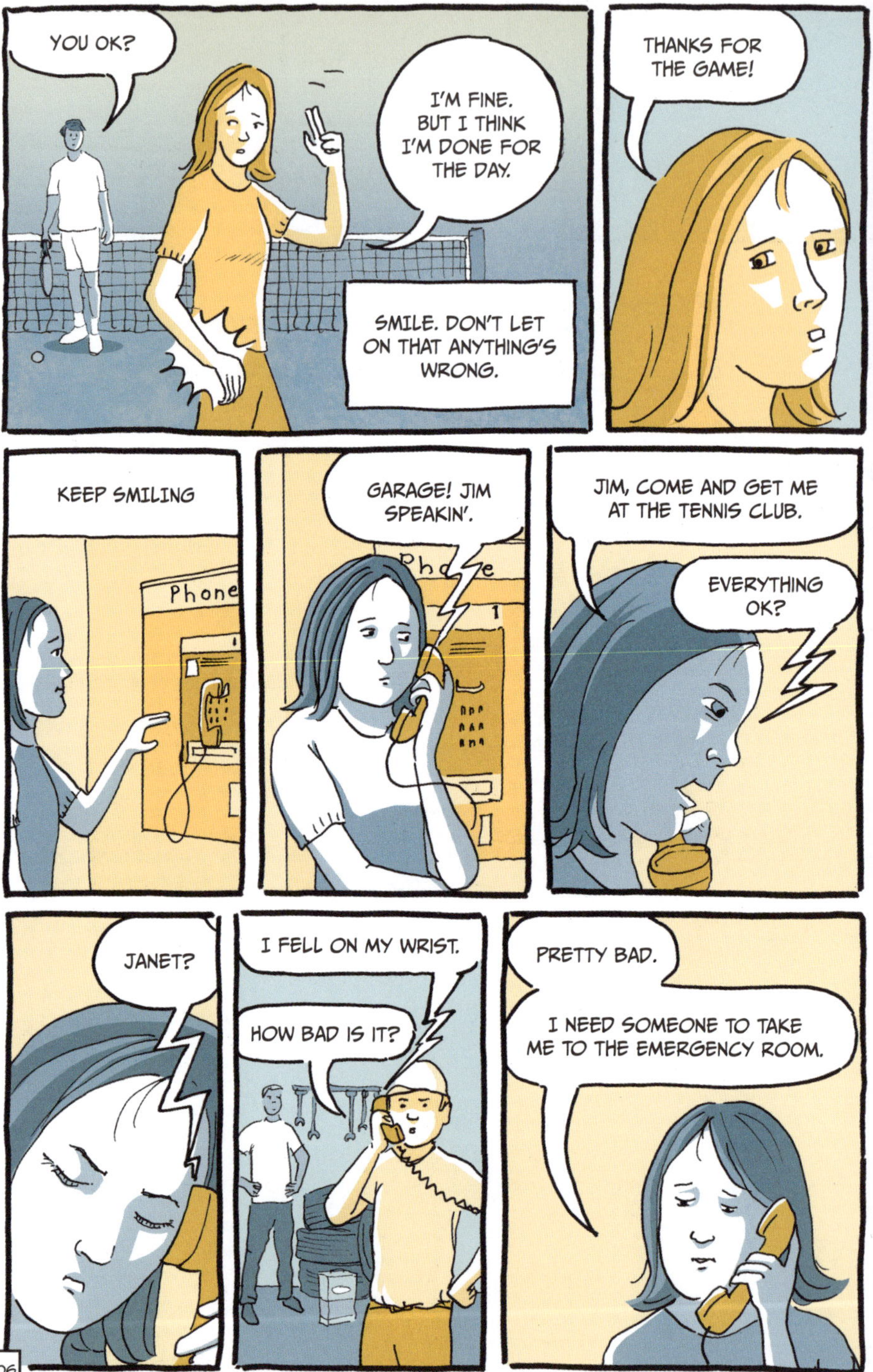
YOU OK?
I'M FINE. BUT I THINK I'M DONE FOR THE DAY.
SMILE. DON'T LET ON THAT ANYTHING'S WRONG.
THANKS FOR THE GAME!
KEEP SMILING
Phone
GARAGE! JIM SPEAKIN'.
JIM, COME AND GET ME AT THE TENNIS CLUB.
EVERYTHING OK?
JANET?
I FELL ON MY WRIST.
HOW BAD IS IT?
PRETTY BAD.
I NEED SOMEONE TO TAKE ME TO THE EMERGENCY ROOM.

EMERGENCY
HMM...
SO, ACCORDING TO THE X-RAY, YOUR WRIST IS BROKEN.
BROKEN?!
PLEASE DON'T TELL ANYONE. THEY'LL NEVER LET ME RACE.
I DON'T KNOW HOW YOU'RE GOING TO DRIVE. YOU CAN'T SHIFT WITH A BROKEN WRIST.
I CAN DO IT.
PLEASE.
SIGH
I'LL MAKE A SPLINT FOR IT.
BUT YOU'RE GOING TO BE IN A LOT OF PAIN.

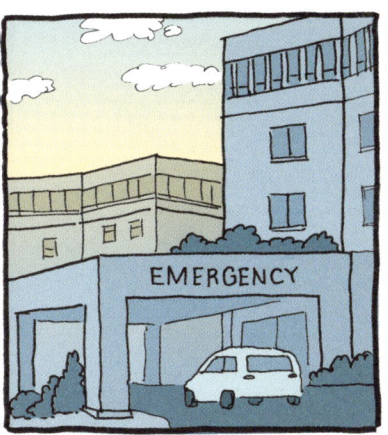

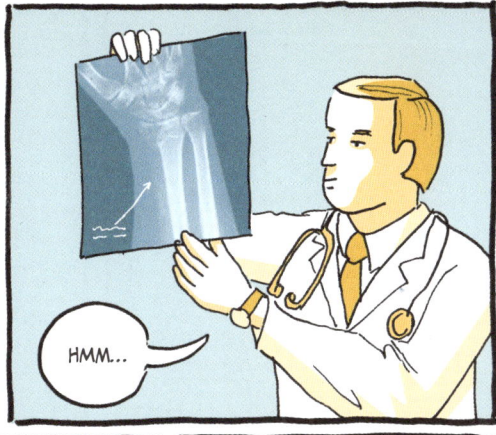

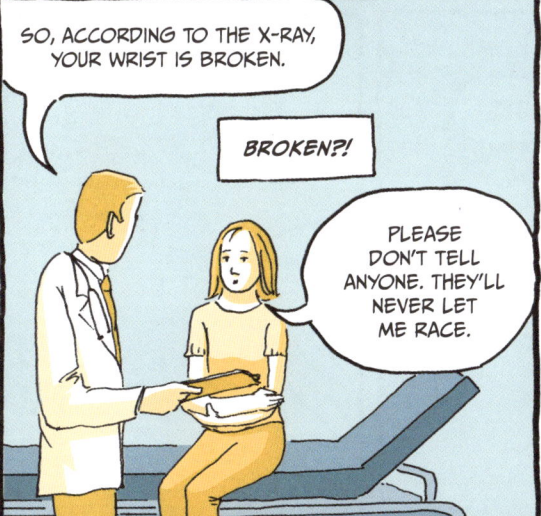

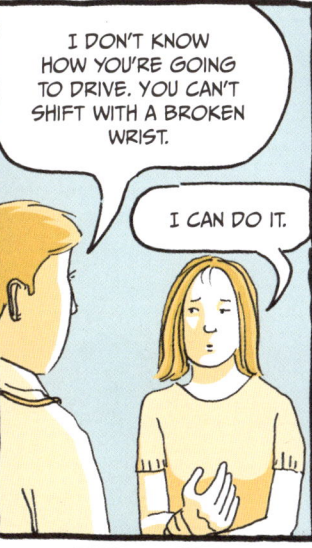

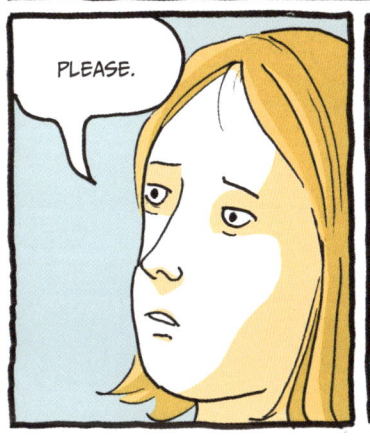

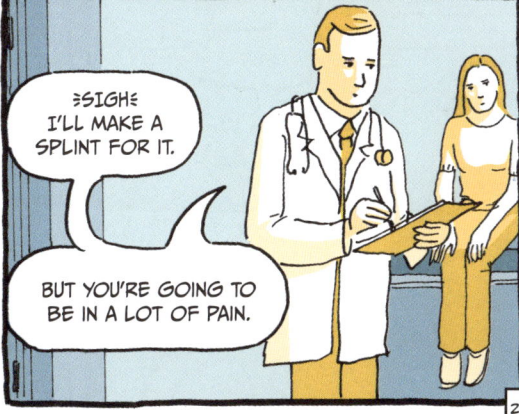

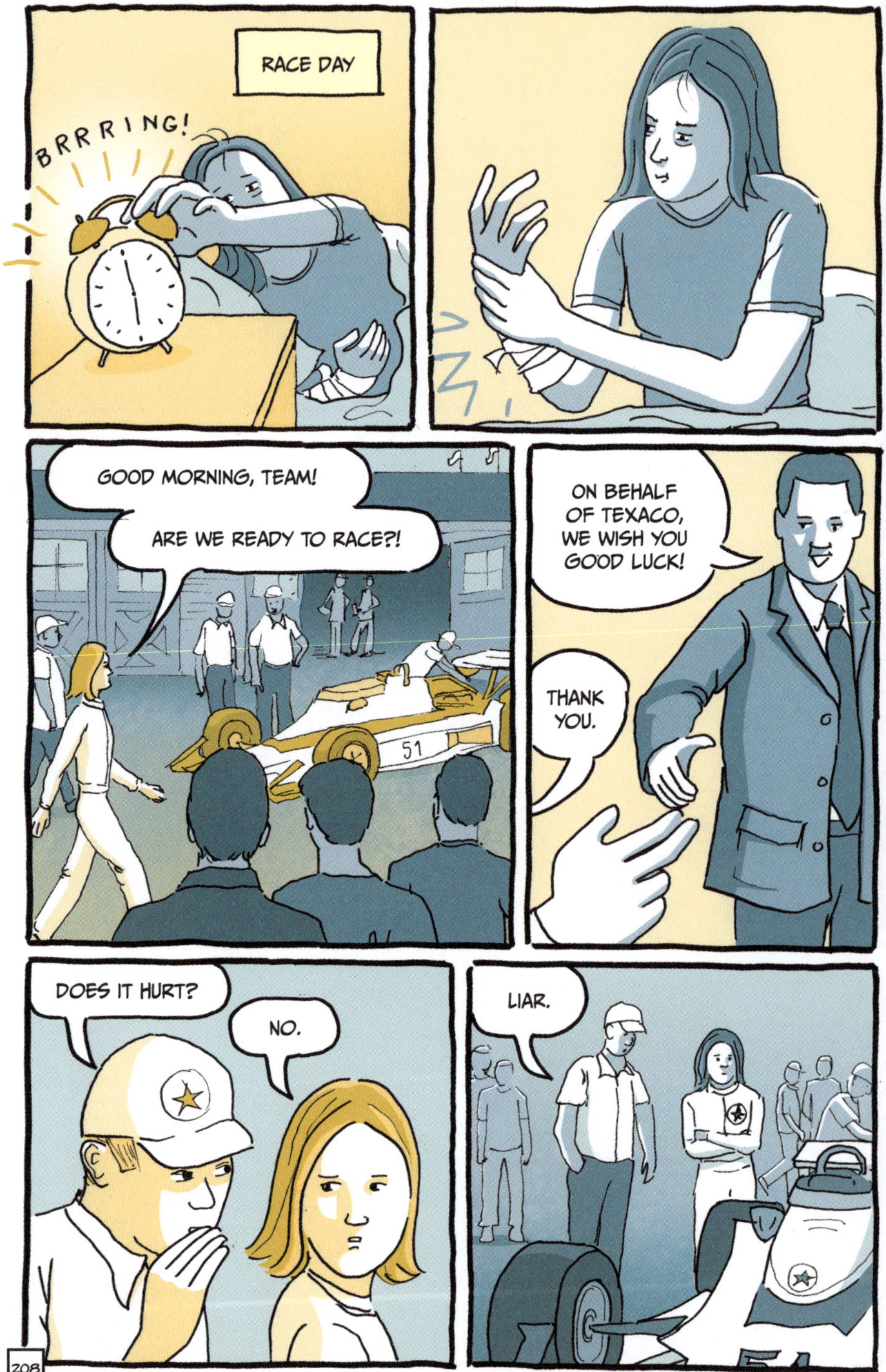
RACE DAY
BRRRING!
GOOD MORNING, TEAM!
ARE WE READY TO RACE?!
ON BEHALF OF TEXACO, WE WISH YOU GOOD LUCK!
THANK YOU.
51
DOES IT HURT?
NO.
LIAR.

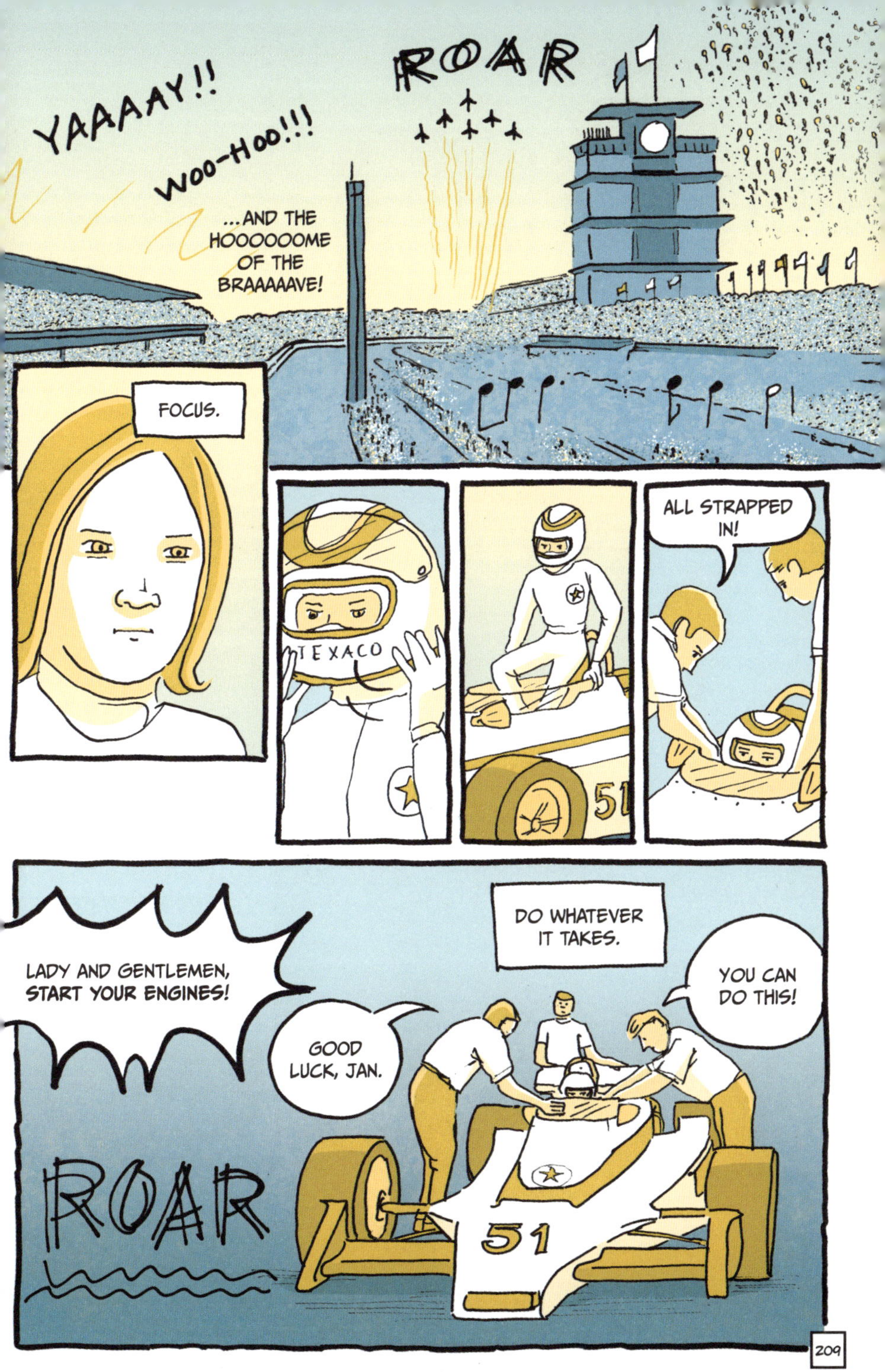
YAAAAY!!
WOO-HOO!!!
ROAR
...AND THE HOOOOOOME OF THE BRAAAAAVE!
FOCUS.
TEXACO
ALL STRAPPED IN!
51
LADY AND GENTLEMEN, START YOUR ENGINES!
DO WHATEVER IT TAKES.
YOU CAN DO THIS!
GOOD LUCK, JAN.
ROAR
51

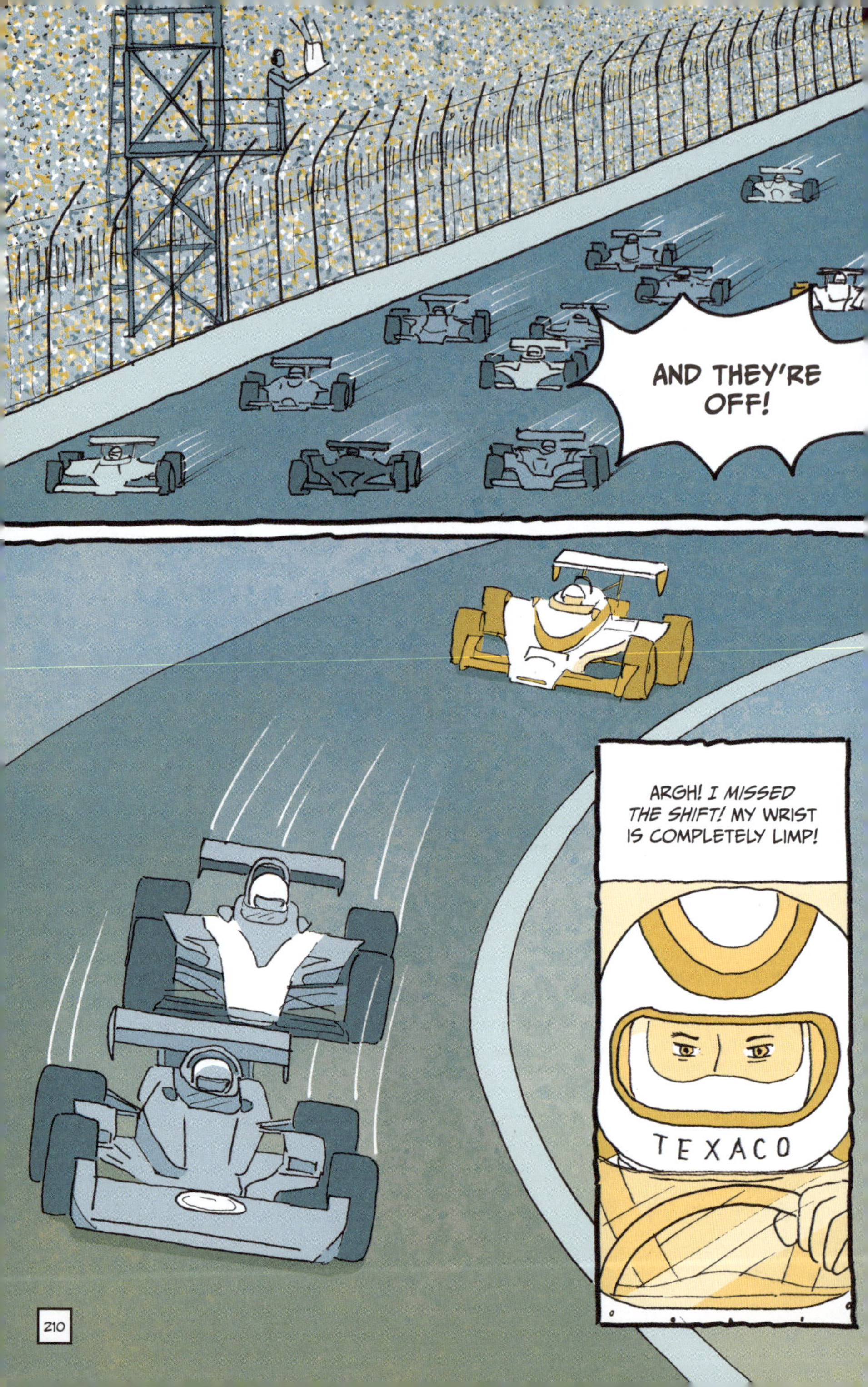
AND THEY'RE OFF!
ARGH! I MISSED THE SHIFT! MY WRIST IS COMPLETELY LIMP!
TEXACO

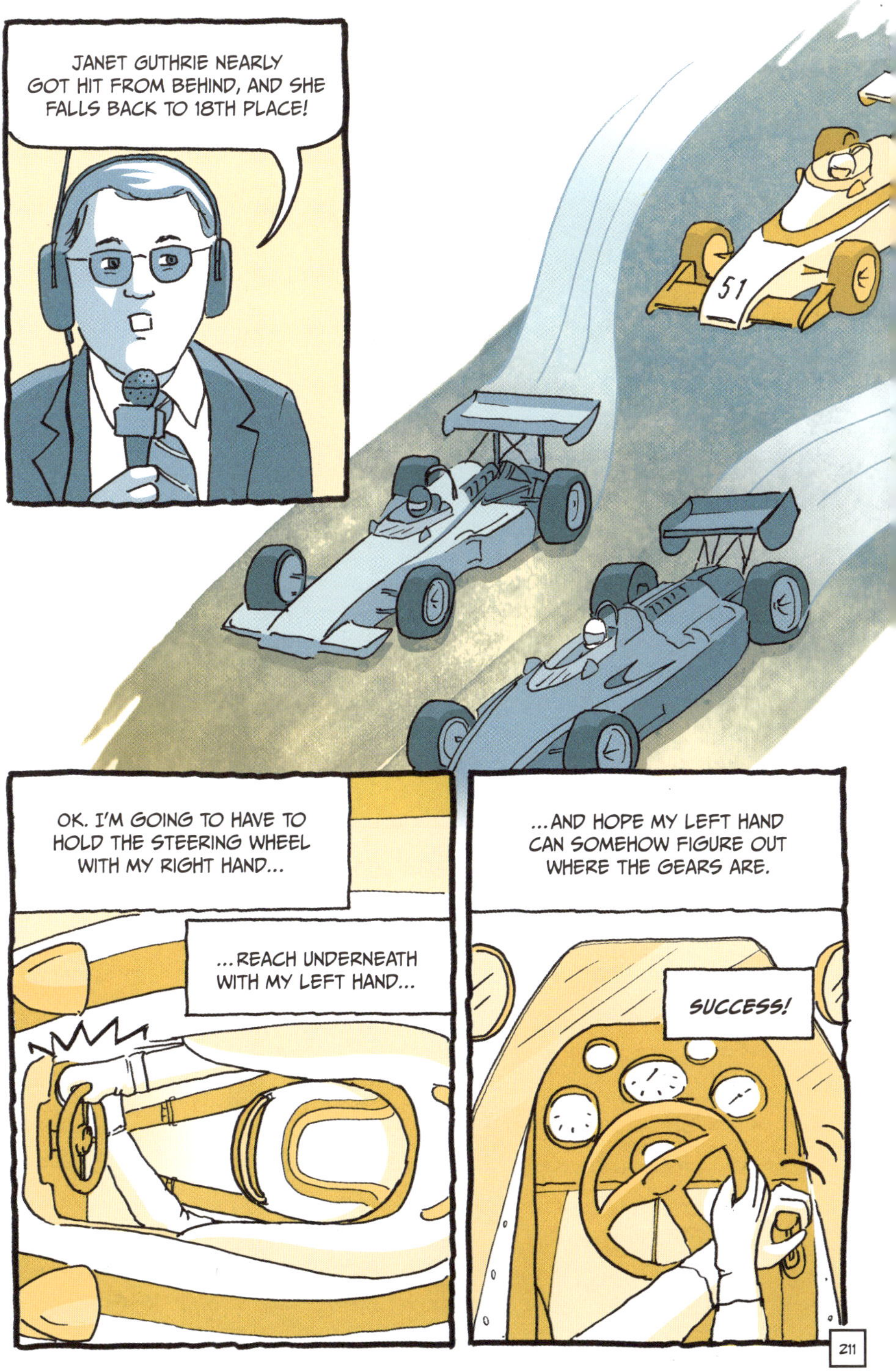
JANET GUTHRIE NEARLY GOT HIT FROM BEHIND, AND SHE FALLS BACK TO 18TH PLACE!
51
OK. I'M GOING TO HAVE TO HOLD THE STEERING WHEEL WITH MY RIGHT HAND...
...REACH UNDERNEATH WITH MY LEFT HAND...
...AND HOPE MY LEFT HAND CAN SOMEHOW FIGURE OUT WHERE THE GEARS ARE.
SUCCESS!

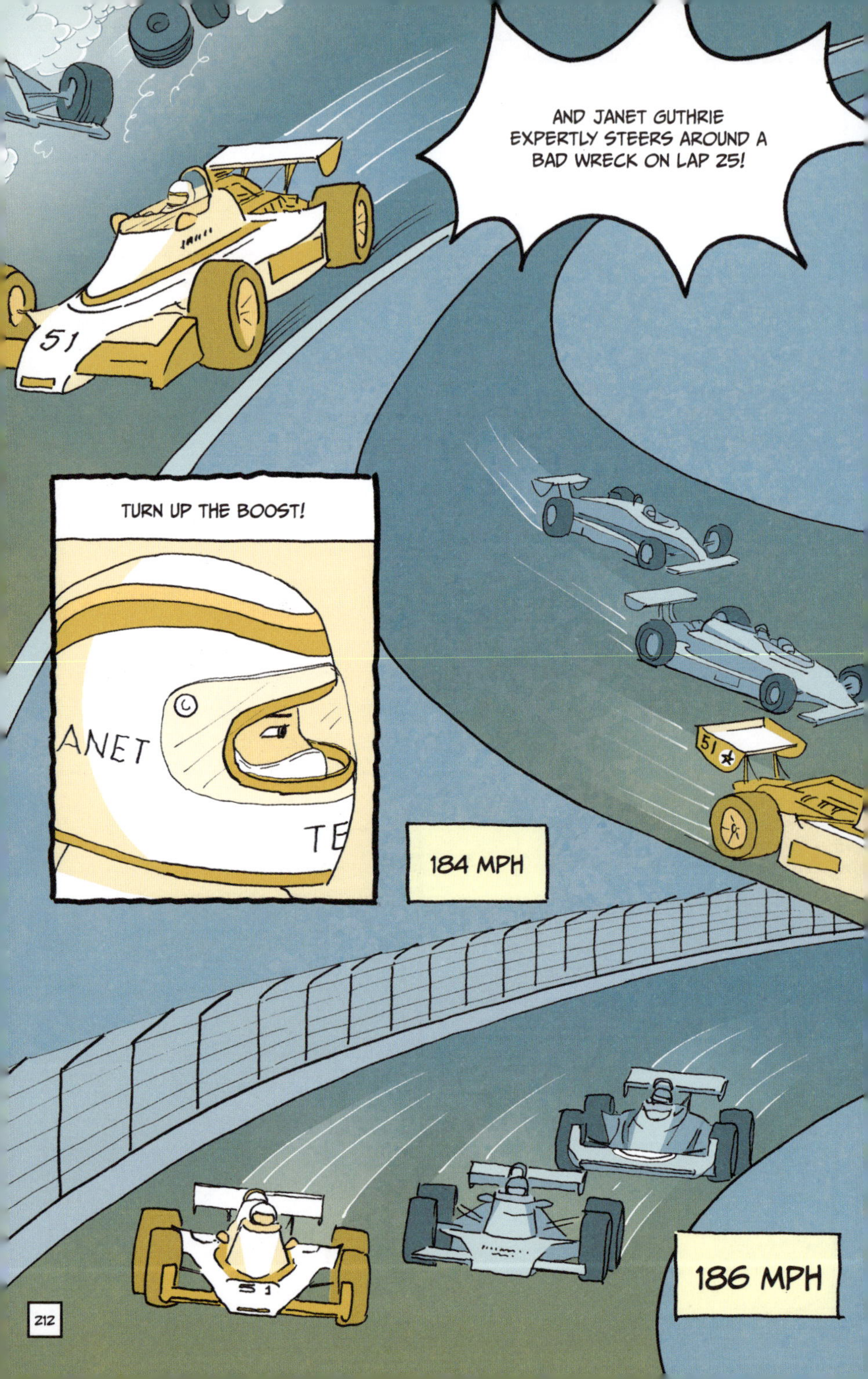
AND JANET GUTHRIE EXPERTLY STEERS AROUND A BAD WRECK ON LAP 25!
TURN UP THE BOOST!
ANET
TE
184 MPH
186 MPH

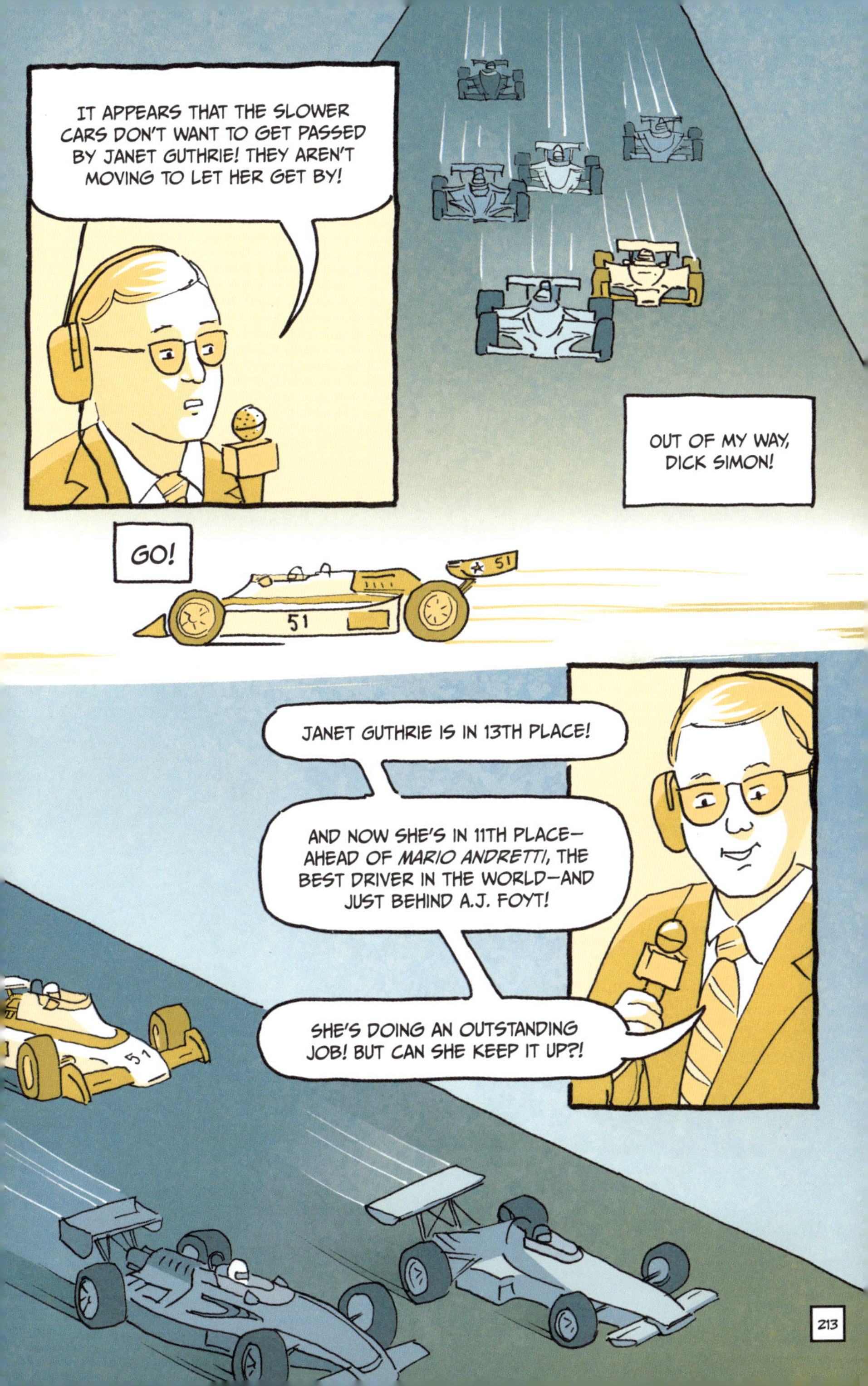
IT APPEARS THAT THE SLOWER CARS DON'T WANT TO GET PASSED BY JANET GUTHRIE! THEY AREN'T MOVING TO LET HER GET BY!
OUT OF MY WAY, DICK SIMON!
GO!
51
JANET GUTHRIE IS IN 13TH PLACE!
AND NOW SHE'S IN 11TH PLACE—AHEAD OF *MARIO ANDRETTI*, THE BEST DRIVER IN THE WORLD—AND JUST BEHIND A.J. FOYT!
SHE'S DOING AN OUTSTANDING JOB! BUT CAN SHE KEEP IT UP?!

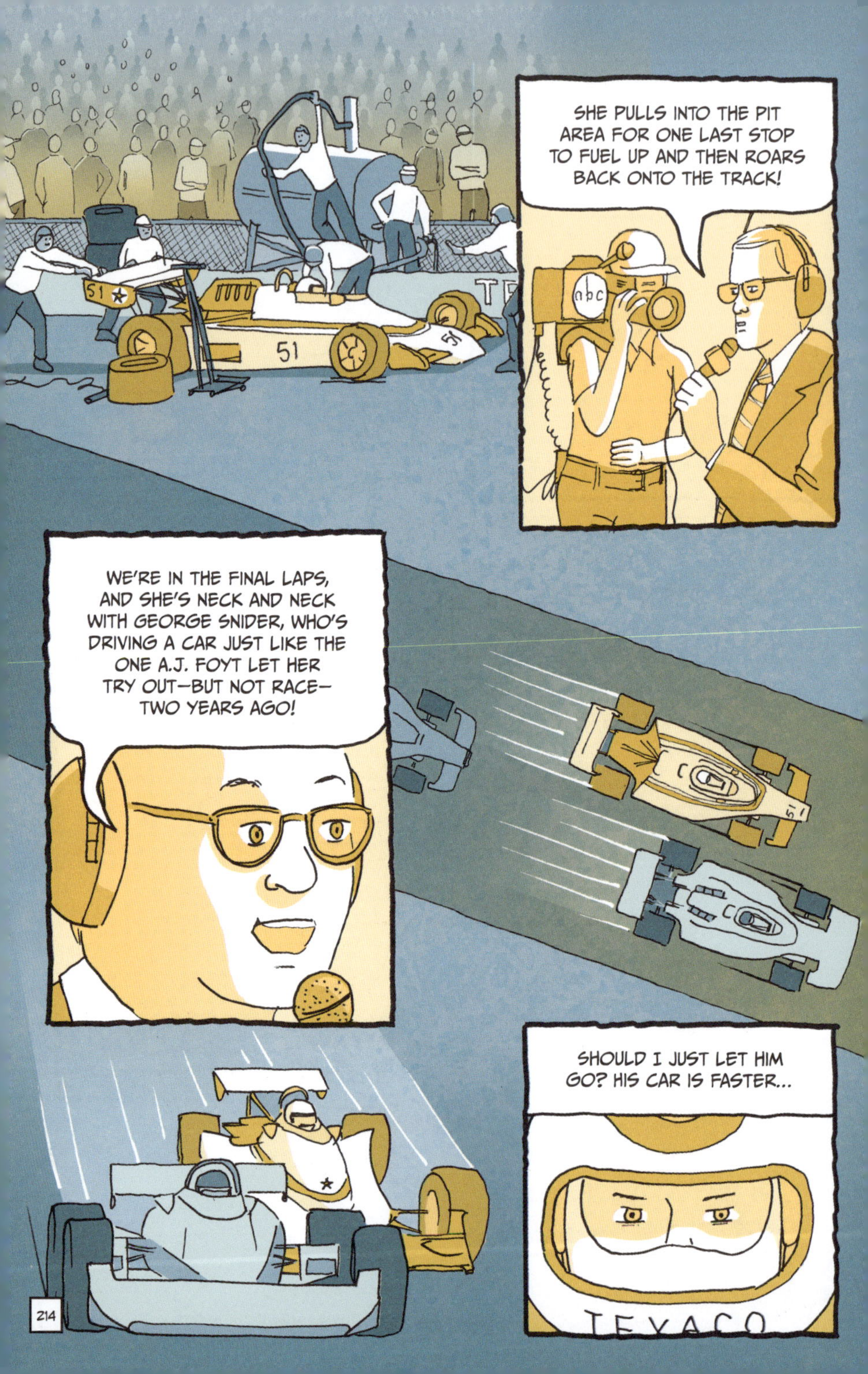
SHE PULLS INTO THE PIT AREA FOR ONE LAST STOP TO FUEL UP AND THEN ROARS BACK ONTO THE TRACK!
WE'RE IN THE FINAL LAPS, AND SHE'S NECK AND NECK WITH GEORGE SNIDER, WHO'S DRIVING A CAR JUST LIKE THE ONE A.J. FOYT LET HER TRY OUT—BUT NOT RACE—TWO YEARS AGO!
SHOULD I JUST LET HIM GO? HIS CAR IS FASTER...
TEXACO

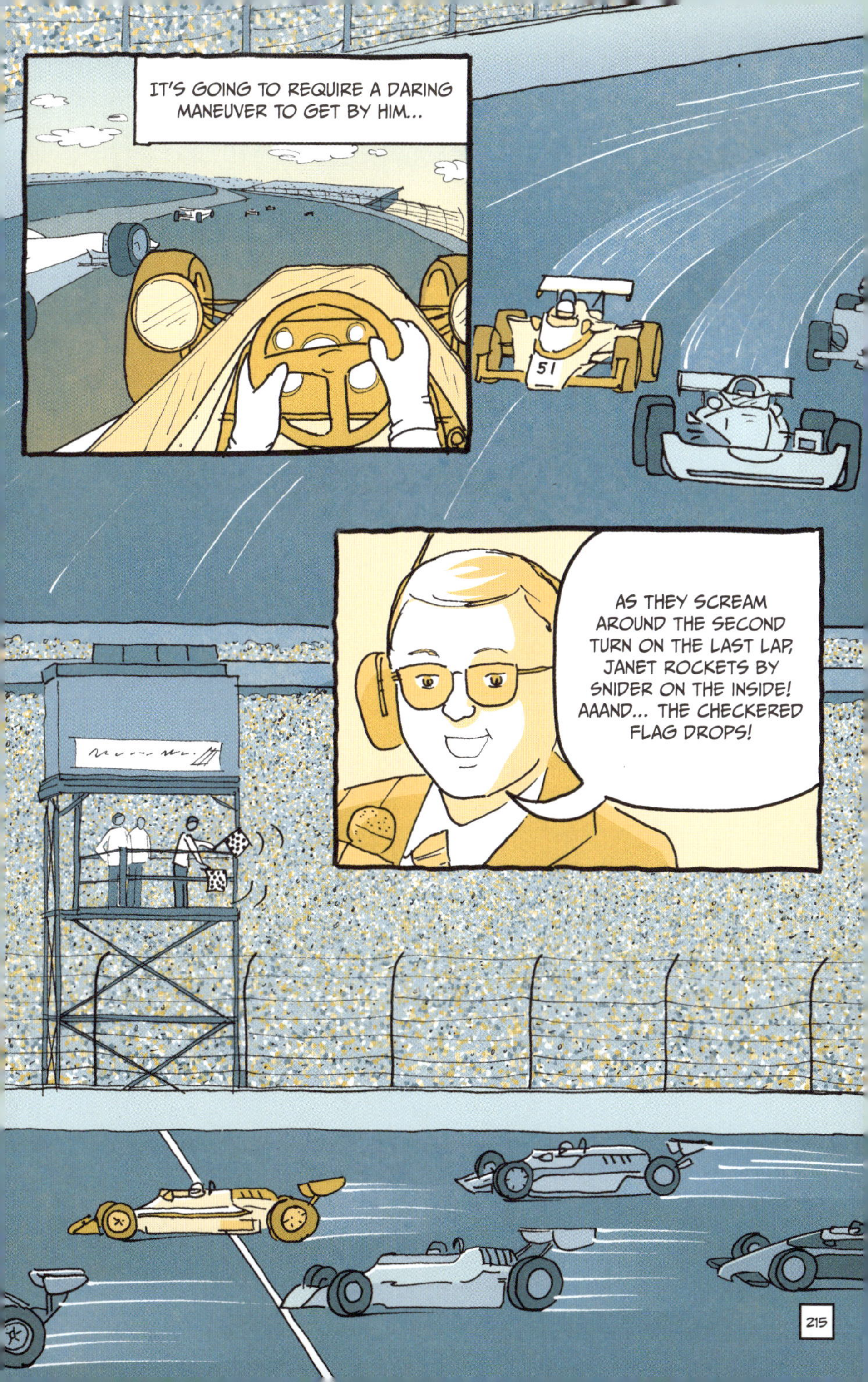
IT'S GOING TO REQUIRE A DARING MANEUVER TO GET BY HIM...
51
AS THEY SCREAM AROUND THE SECOND TURN ON THE LAST LAP, JANET ROCKETS BY SNIDER ON THE INSIDE! AAAND... THE CHECKERED FLAG DROPS!

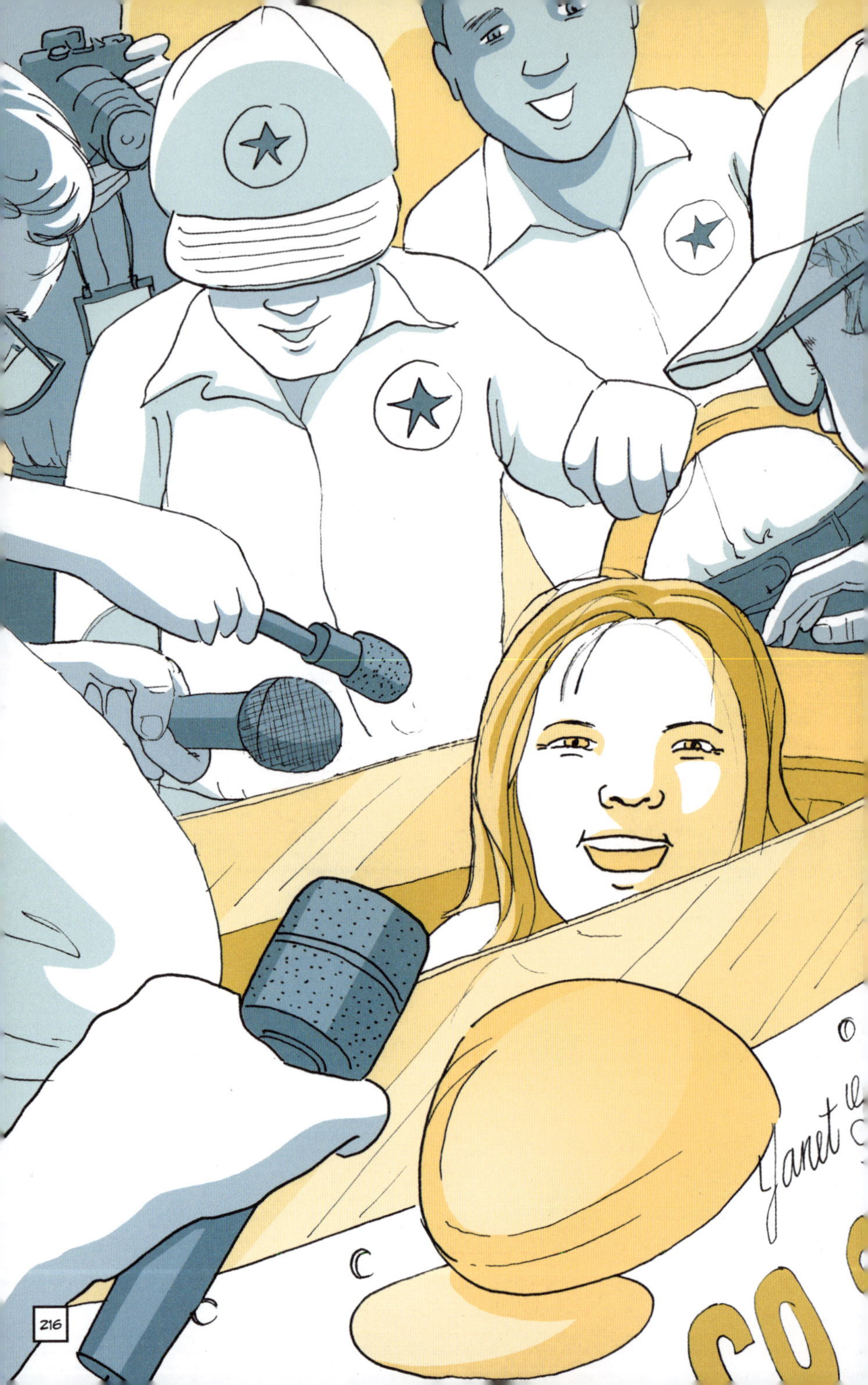
Janet

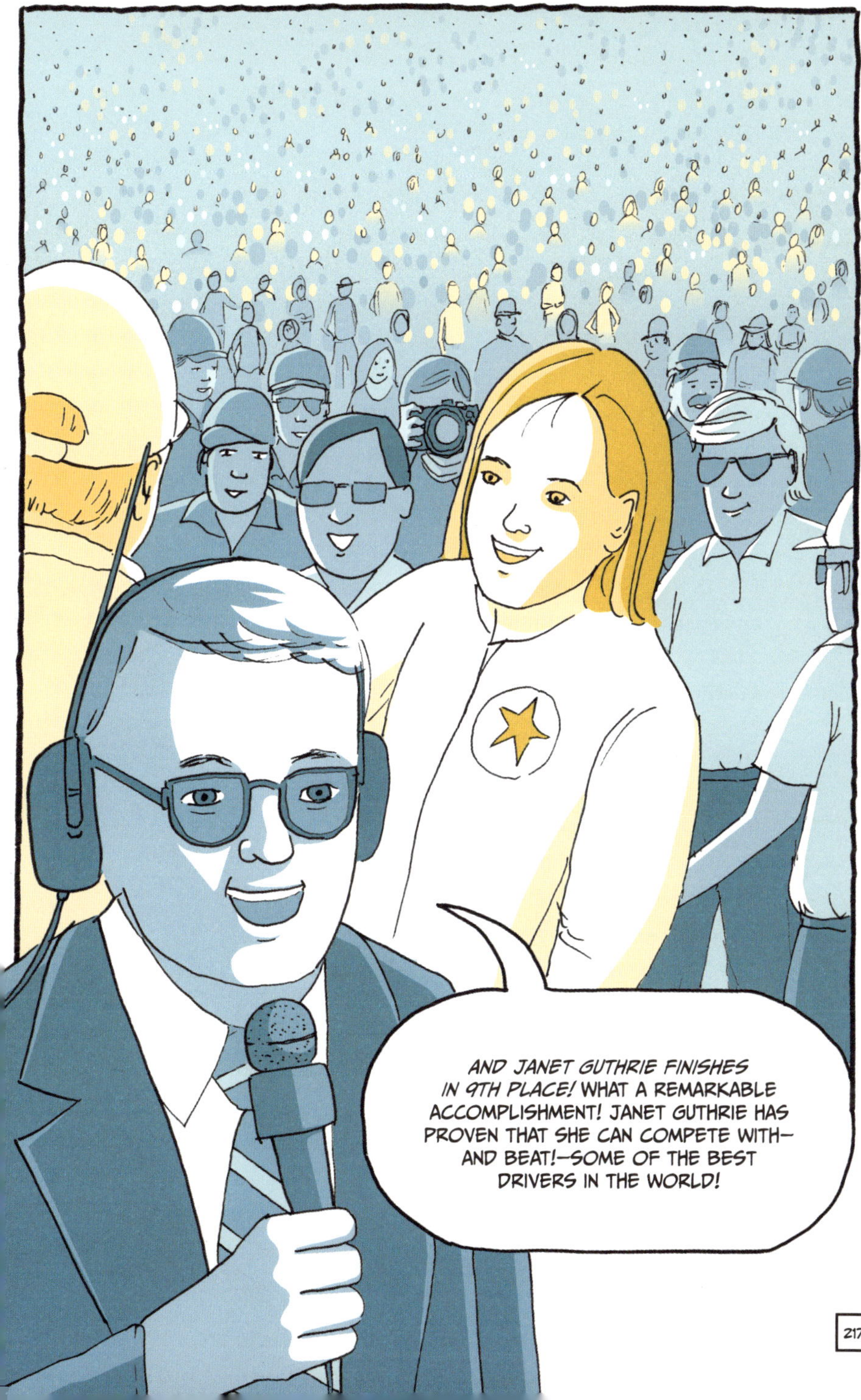
AND JANET GUTHRIE FINISHES IN 9TH PLACE! WHAT A REMARKABLE ACCOMPLISHMENT! JANET GUTHRIE HAS PROVEN THAT SHE CAN COMPETE WITH—AND BEAT!—SOME OF THE BEST DRIVERS IN THE WORLD!

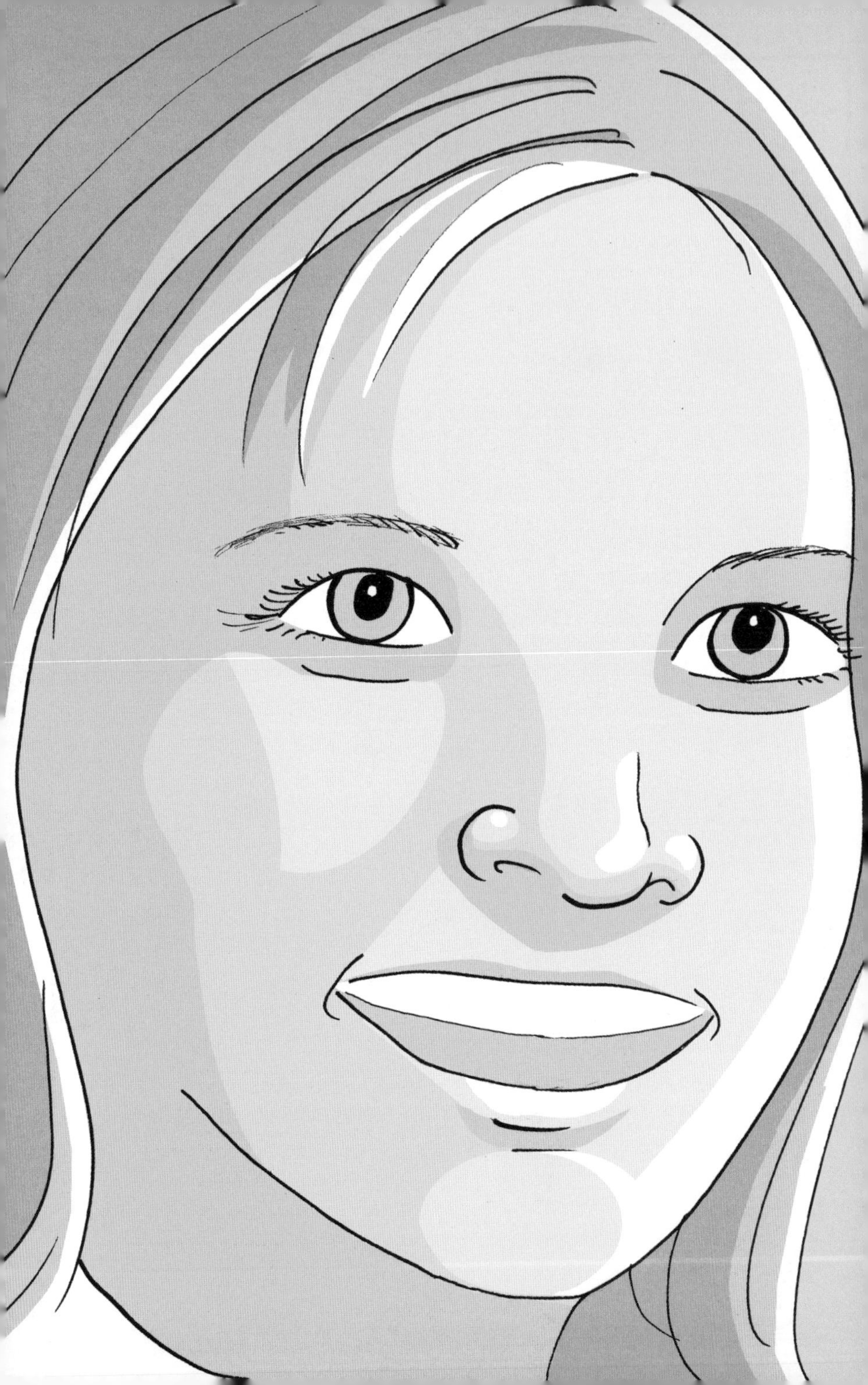

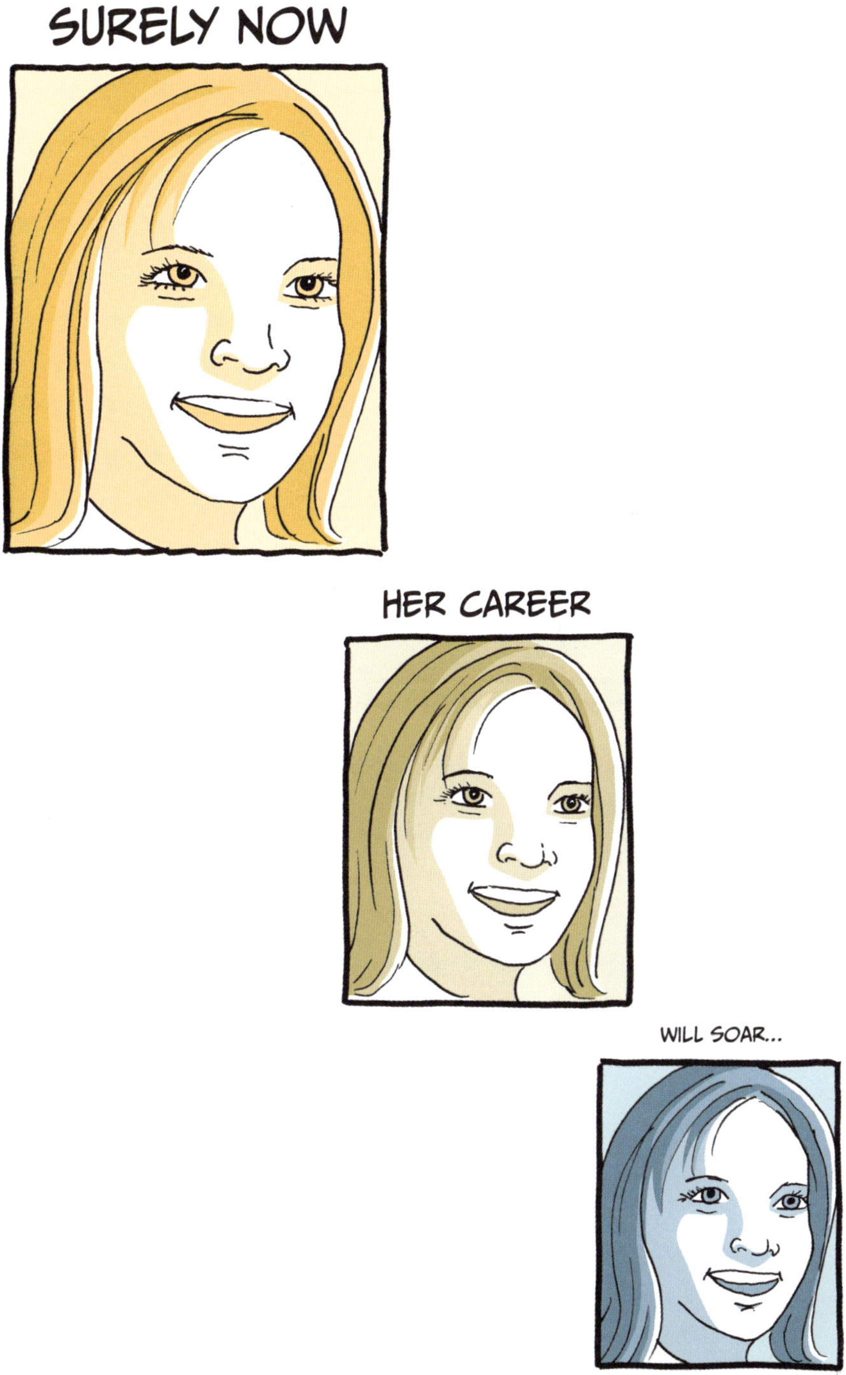
SURELY NOW
HER CAREER
WILL SOAR...

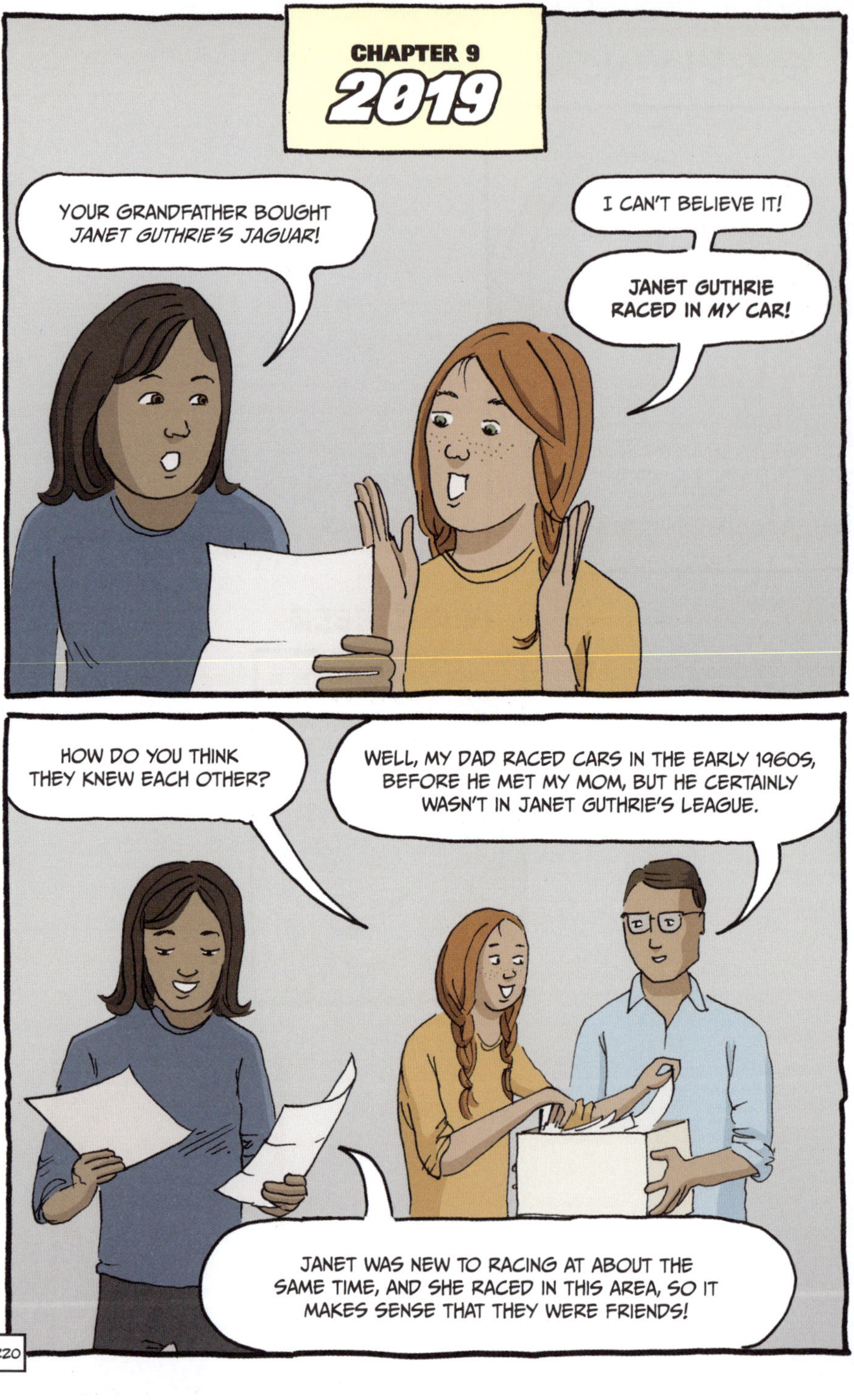
CHAPTER 9
2019
YOUR GRANDFATHER BOUGHT *JANET GUTHRIE'S JAGUAR!*
I CAN'T BELIEVE IT!
JANET GUTHRIE RACED IN *MY* CAR!
HOW DO YOU THINK THEY KNEW EACH OTHER?
WELL, MY DAD RACED CARS IN THE EARLY 1960S, BEFORE HE MET MY MOM, BUT HE CERTAINLY WASN'T IN JANET GUTHRIE'S LEAGUE.
JANET WAS NEW TO RACING AT ABOUT THE SAME TIME, AND SHE RACED IN THIS AREA, SO IT MAKES SENSE THAT THEY WERE FRIENDS!

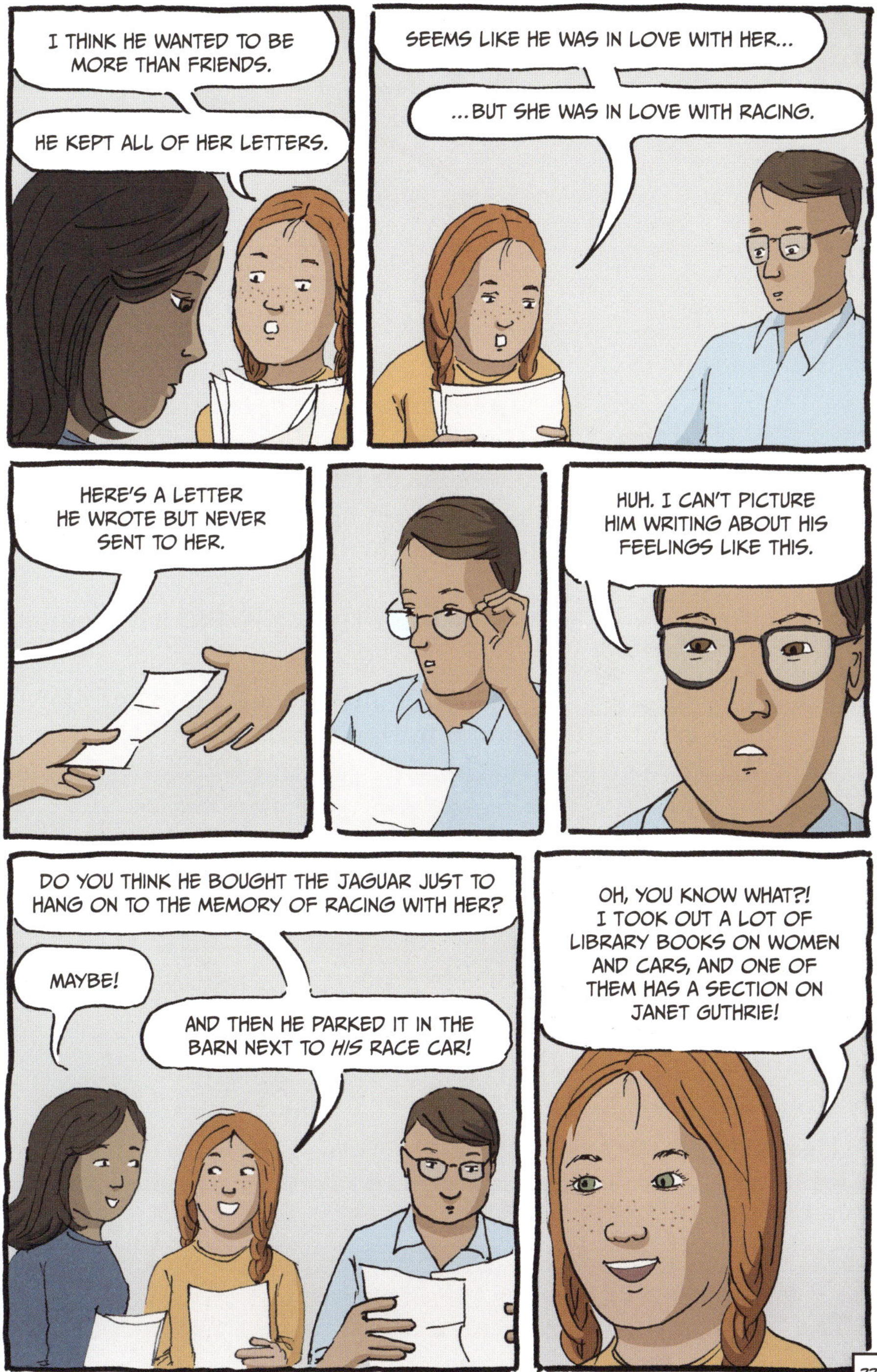
I THINK HE WANTED TO BE MORE THAN FRIENDS.
HE KEPT ALL OF HER LETTERS.
SEEMS LIKE HE WAS IN LOVE WITH HER...
...BUT SHE WAS IN LOVE WITH RACING.
HERE'S A LETTER HE WROTE BUT NEVER SENT TO HER.
HUH. I CAN'T PICTURE HIM WRITING ABOUT HIS FEELINGS LIKE THIS.
DO YOU THINK HE BOUGHT THE JAGUAR JUST TO HANG ON TO THE MEMORY OF RACING WITH HER?
MAYBE!
AND THEN HE PARKED IT IN THE BARN NEXT TO *HIS* RACE CAR!
OH, YOU KNOW WHAT?! I TOOK OUT A LOT OF LIBRARY BOOKS ON WOMEN AND CARS, AND ONE OF THEM HAS A SECTION ON JANET GUTHRIE!

JANET GUTHRIE

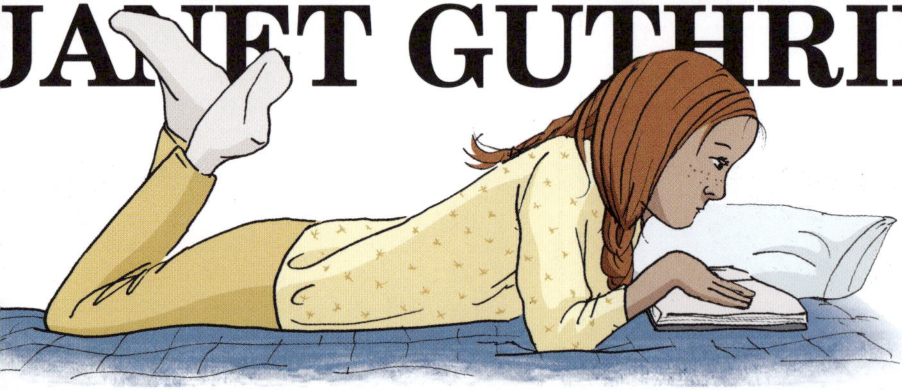

As a teenager, she decided she wanted to jump out of an airplane. There were no lessons or classes available to her, so she practiced her landing by jumping off the roof of the house.

ever felt frightene
uring a race, just
usy. Her level of

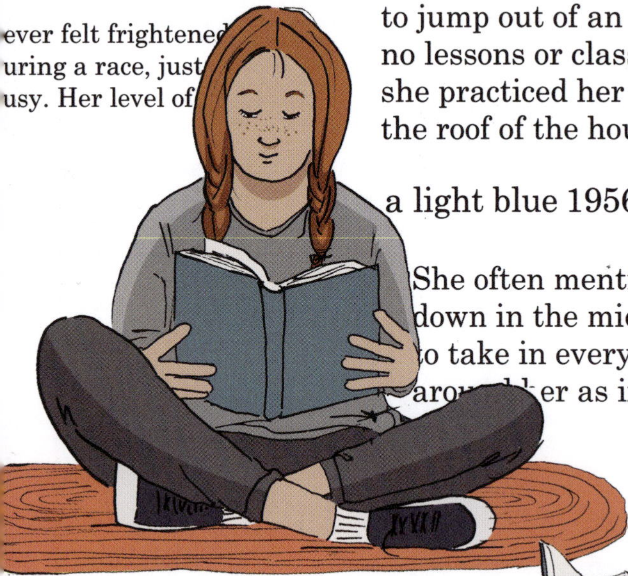

a light blue 1956 XK 140 MC roadste

She often mentioned that time slowed down in the middle of a ... she was ... o take in everythin ... happen aro ... er as if in

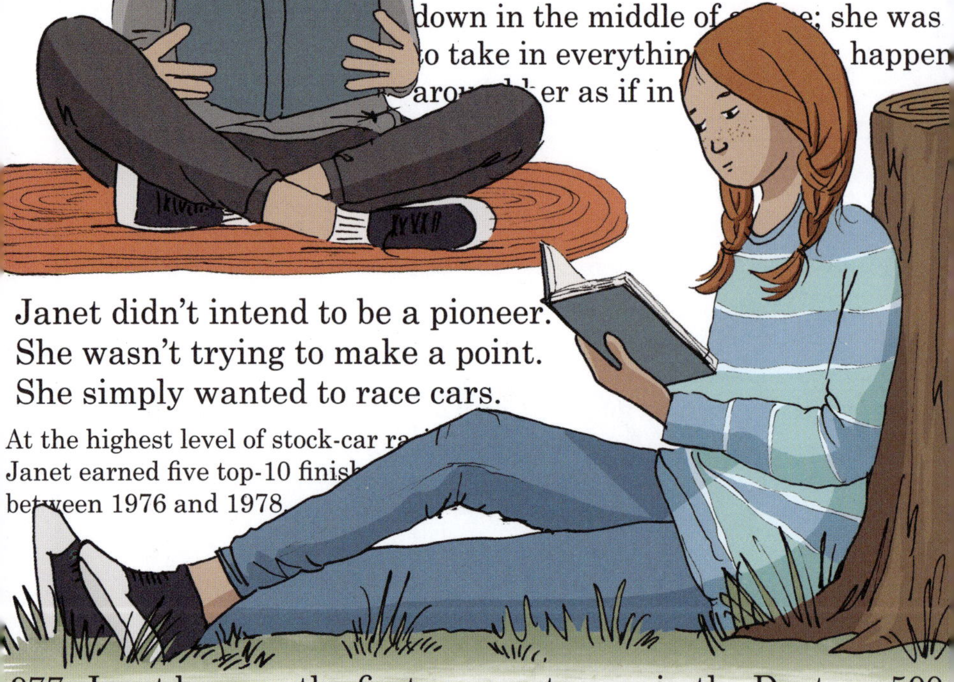

Janet didn't intend to be a pioneer. She wasn't trying to make a point. She simply wanted to race cars.

At the highest level of stock-car ra
Janet earned five top-10 finish
between 1976 and 1978.

977, Janet became the first woman to race in the Daytona 500,
shing in 12th place, beating Richard Petty, who ha long critici

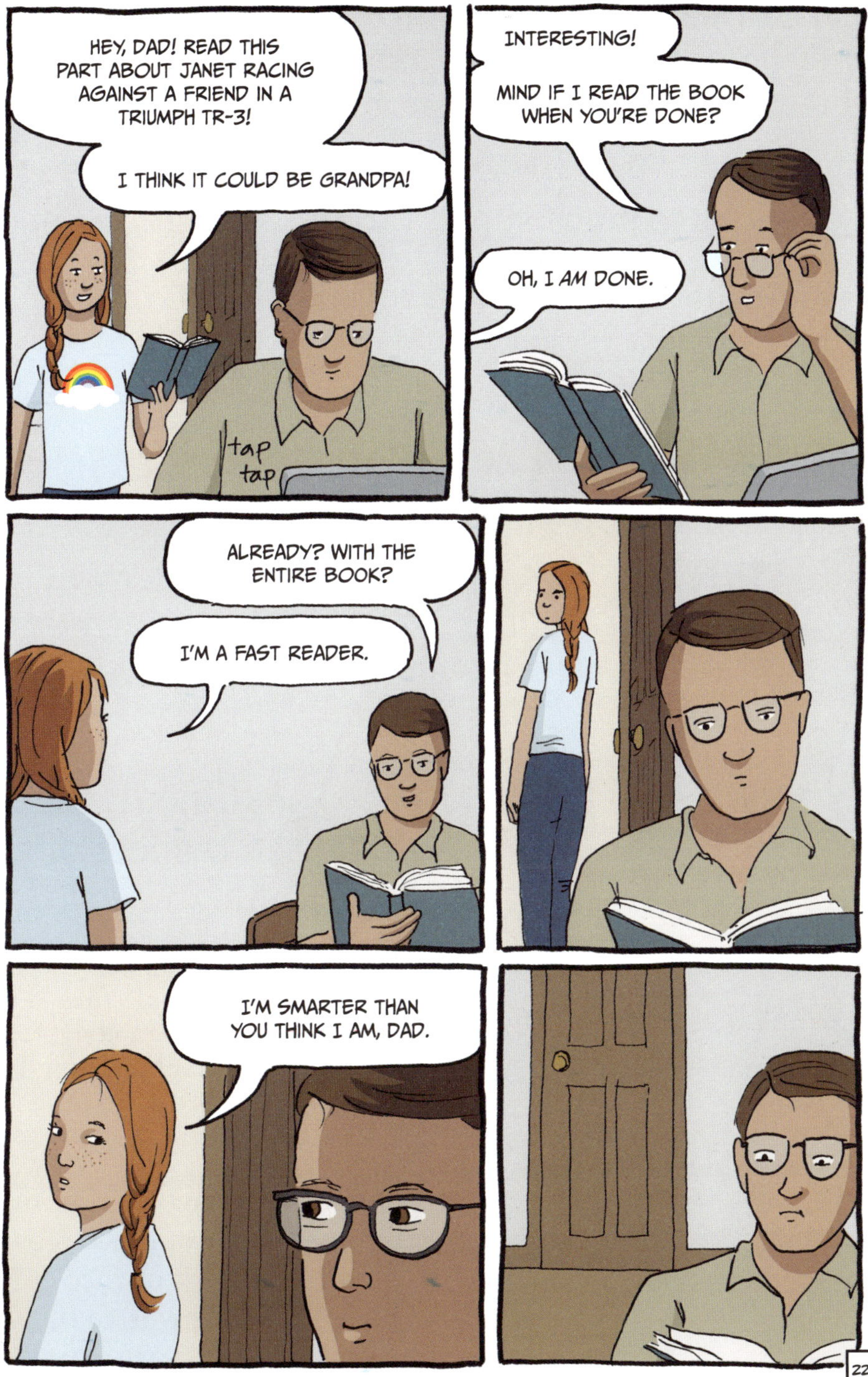
HEY, DAD! READ THIS PART ABOUT JANET RACING AGAINST A FRIEND IN A TRIUMPH TR-3!
I THINK IT COULD BE GRANDPA!
tap tap
INTERESTING!
MIND IF I READ THE BOOK WHEN YOU'RE DONE?
OH, I *AM* DONE.
ALREADY? WITH THE ENTIRE BOOK?
I'M A FAST READER.
I'M SMARTER THAN YOU THINK I AM, DAD.

Her parents prized academic accomplishments, and s
Janet's career as a race car driver didn't please them
Her father, especially, was unhappy about her choice
and felt it was a waste of her mind and talents.

There were times when she felt lonely and discouraged
She didn't have much support from those around her.

Fans felt that the racetrack was no place for a woman
otion that women were too emotional to race and might panic or faint under

The fuss was no necessarily against Janet personally,
but against the entire women's movement.

She didn't want
special treatment,
just an equal chan

so difficult to ear
e respect of th
male drivers des

Drivers who initially were
helpful suddenly turned th
backs; she learned not to
publicly thank another driv
for his support, because of
backlash he inevitably got.

spite her accomplishmer
omen still represent fewe
han 1 percent of race car
drivers and fewer than
3 percent of car mechanics

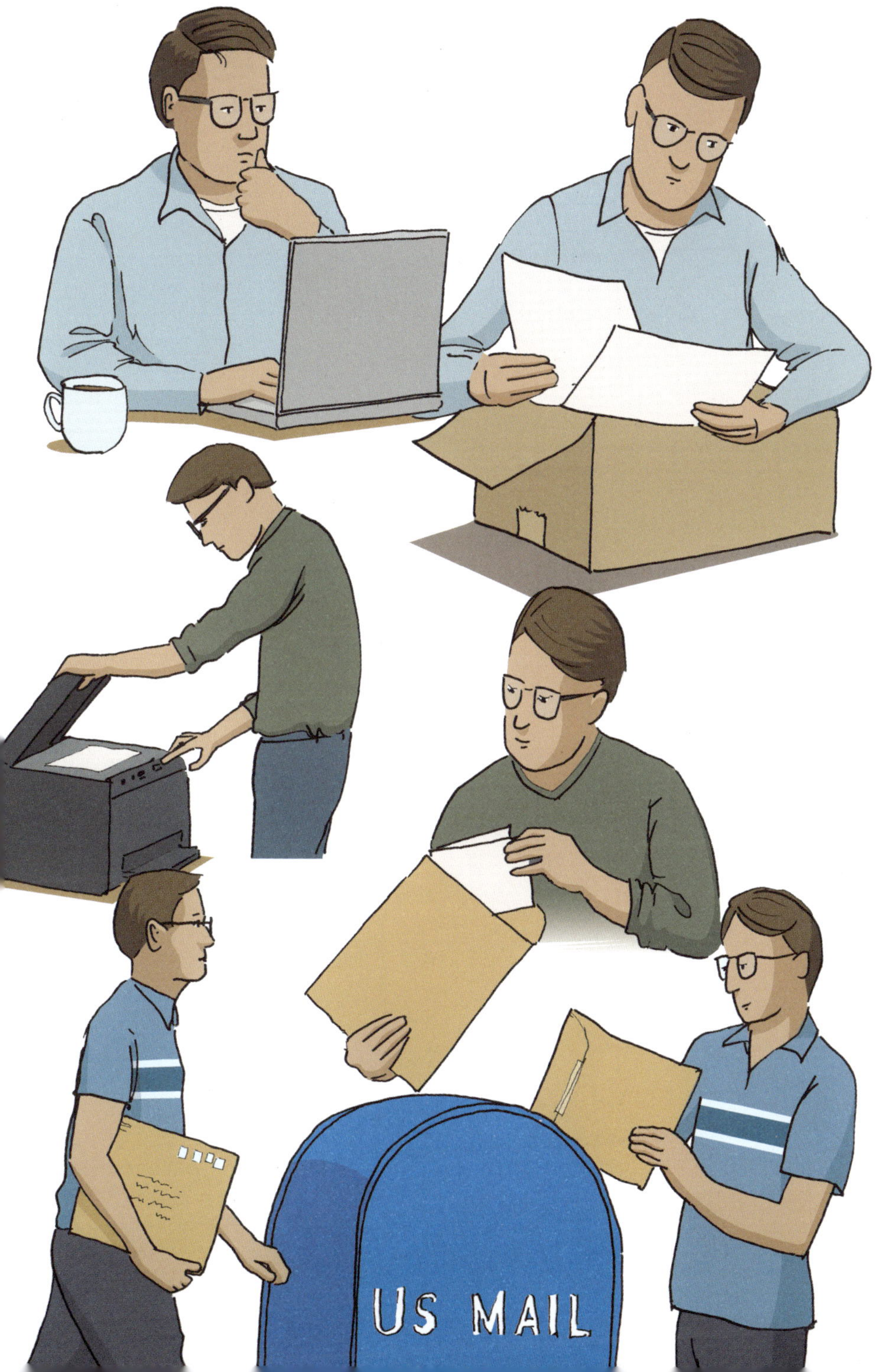
US MAIL

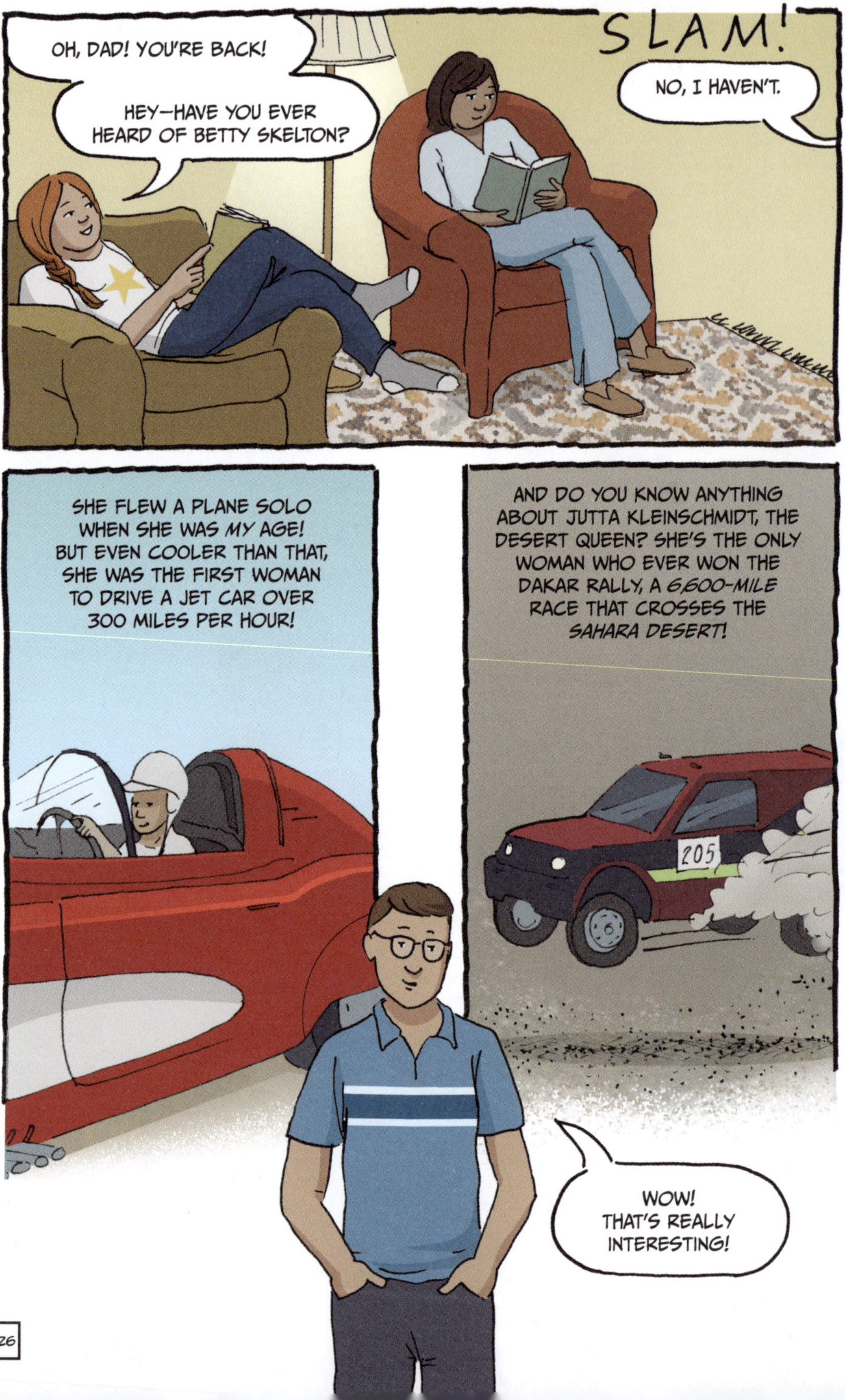
OH, DAD! YOU'RE BACK!
HEY—HAVE YOU EVER HEARD OF BETTY SKELTON?
SLAM!
NO, I HAVEN'T.
SHE FLEW A PLANE SOLO WHEN SHE WAS *MY* AGE! BUT EVEN COOLER THAN THAT, SHE WAS THE FIRST WOMAN TO DRIVE A JET CAR OVER 300 MILES PER HOUR!
AND DO YOU KNOW ANYTHING ABOUT JUTTA KLEINSCHMIDT, THE DESERT QUEEN? SHE'S THE ONLY WOMAN WHO EVER WON THE DAKAR RALLY, A *6,600-MILE* RACE THAT CROSSES THE *SAHARA DESERT*!
205
WOW! THAT'S REALLY INTERESTING!

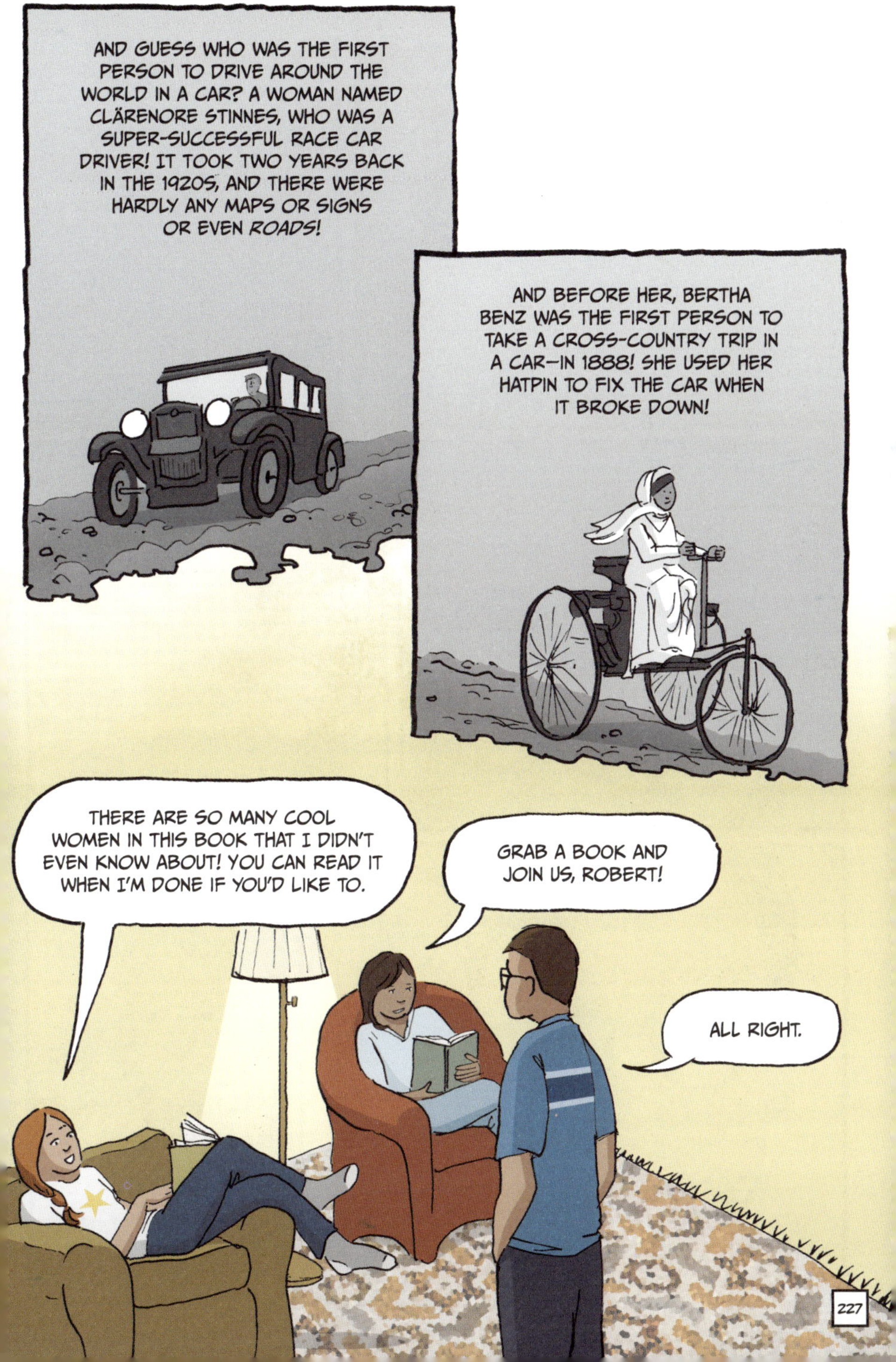
AND GUESS WHO WAS THE FIRST PERSON TO DRIVE AROUND THE WORLD IN A CAR? A WOMAN NAMED CLÄRENORE STINNES, WHO WAS A SUPER-SUCCESSFUL RACE CAR DRIVER! IT TOOK TWO YEARS BACK IN THE 1920S, AND THERE WERE HARDLY ANY MAPS OR SIGNS OR EVEN *ROADS*!
AND BEFORE HER, BERTHA BENZ WAS THE FIRST PERSON TO TAKE A CROSS-COUNTRY TRIP IN A CAR—IN 1888! SHE USED HER HATPIN TO FIX THE CAR WHEN IT BROKE DOWN!
THERE ARE SO MANY COOL WOMEN IN THIS BOOK THAT I DIDN'T EVEN KNOW ABOUT! YOU CAN READ IT WHEN I'M DONE IF YOU'D LIKE TO.
GRAB A BOOK AND JOIN US, ROBERT!
ALL RIGHT.

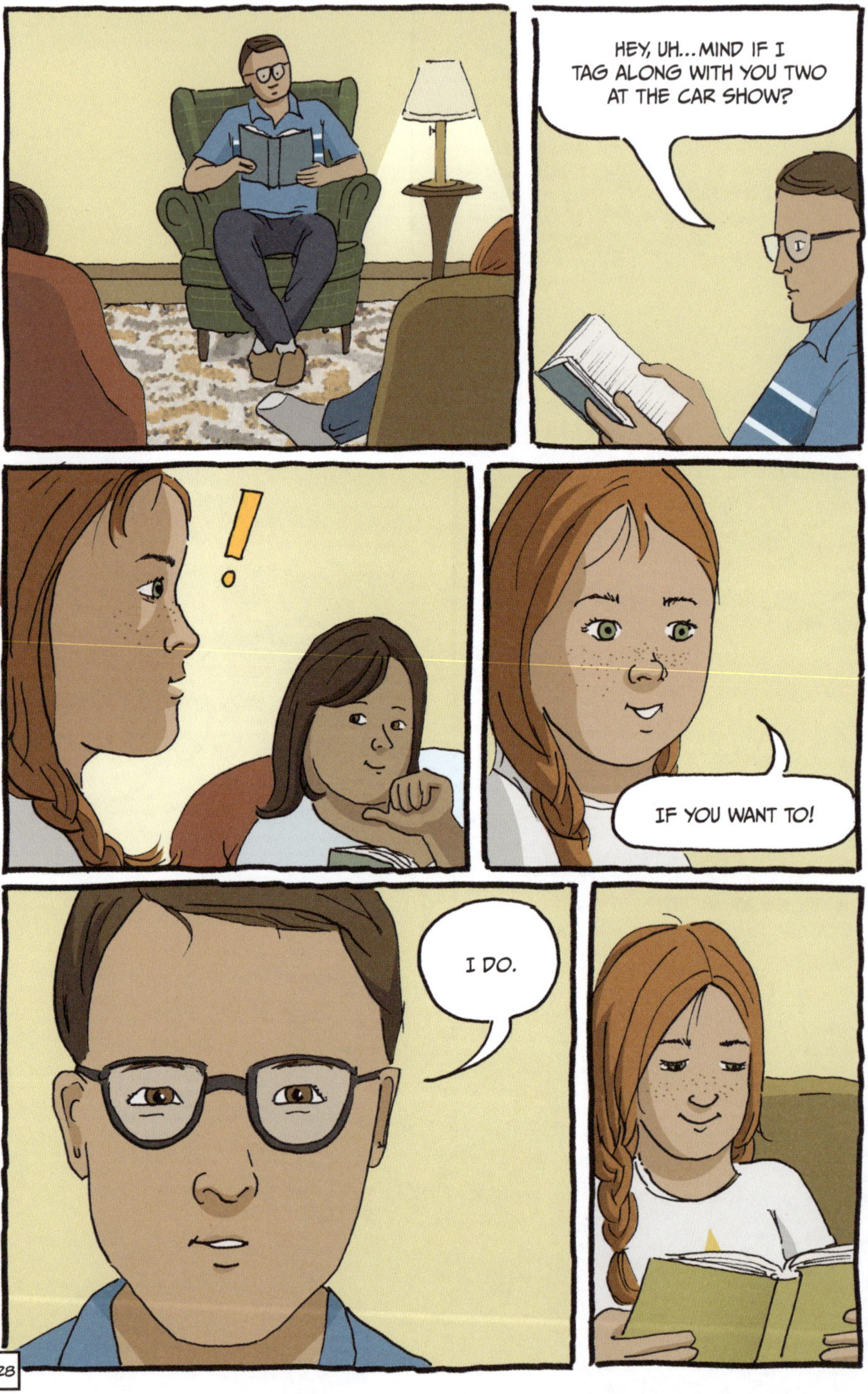
HEY, UH...MIND IF I TAG ALONG WITH YOU TWO AT THE CAR SHOW?
!
IF YOU WANT TO!
I DO.

Lonely Lady:
Whatever Happened to Janet Guthrie?

Janet Guthrie Is Losing Her Sponsors
Pact with Texaco Over, Kelly Girl Running Out

Chapter 10
1982

Janet Guthrie Is Ready to Give Up Racing

The funds aren't there for trailblazing Guthrie

No longer a novelty, Janet Guthrie can't find funding

When All the Hoopla Died Down, Janet Guthrie's Sponsors Exited

Indy 500's first female qualifier Janet Guthrie: "I wish I had some company"

No sponsorship takes Guthrie out of Indy 500 driver's seat

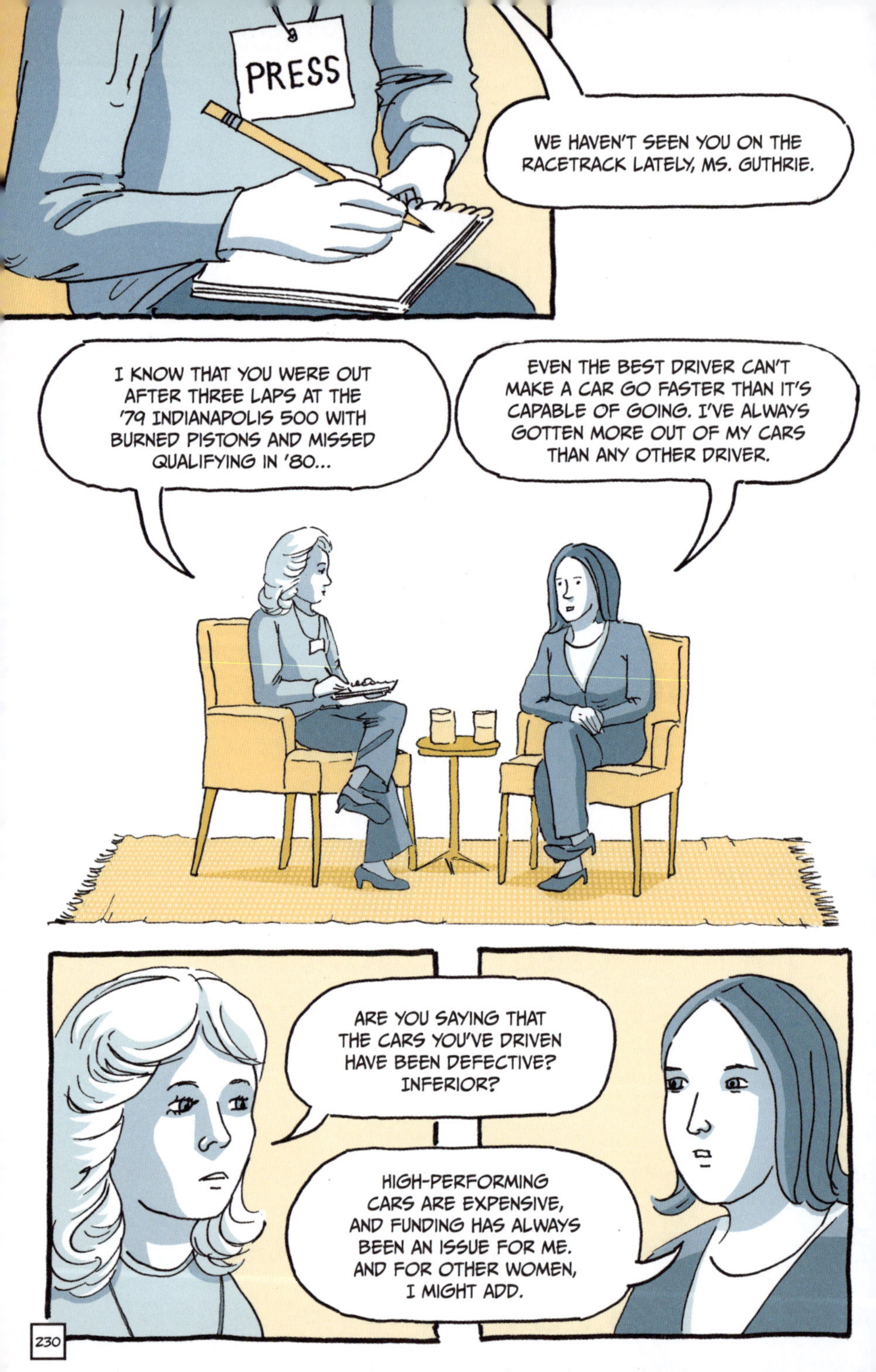
PRESS
WE HAVEN'T SEEN YOU ON THE RACETRACK LATELY, MS. GUTHRIE.
I KNOW THAT YOU WERE OUT AFTER THREE LAPS AT THE '79 INDIANAPOLIS 500 WITH BURNED PISTONS AND MISSED QUALIFYING IN '80...
EVEN THE BEST DRIVER CAN'T MAKE A CAR GO FASTER THAN IT'S CAPABLE OF GOING. I'VE ALWAYS GOTTEN MORE OUT OF MY CARS THAN ANY OTHER DRIVER.
ARE YOU SAYING THAT THE CARS YOU'VE DRIVEN HAVE BEEN DEFECTIVE? INFERIOR?
HIGH-PERFORMING CARS ARE EXPENSIVE, AND FUNDING HAS ALWAYS BEEN AN ISSUE FOR ME. AND FOR OTHER WOMEN, I MIGHT ADD.

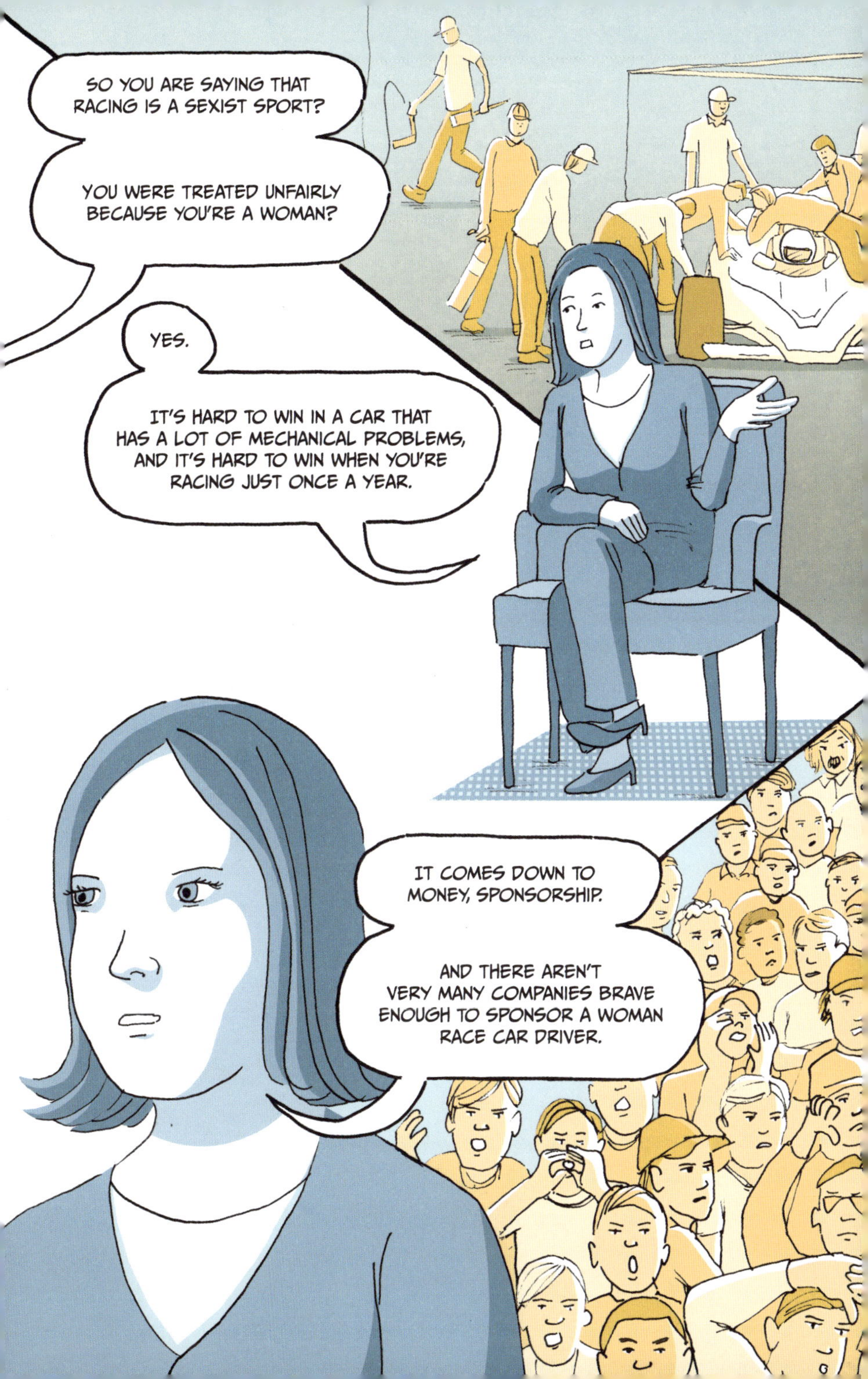
SO YOU ARE SAYING THAT RACING IS A SEXIST SPORT?
YOU WERE TREATED UNFAIRLY BECAUSE YOU'RE A WOMAN?
YES.
IT'S HARD TO WIN IN A CAR THAT HAS A LOT OF MECHANICAL PROBLEMS, AND IT'S HARD TO WIN WHEN YOU'RE RACING JUST ONCE A YEAR.
IT COMES DOWN TO MONEY, SPONSORSHIP.
AND THERE AREN'T VERY MANY COMPANIES BRAVE ENOUGH TO SPONSOR A WOMAN RACE CAR DRIVER.

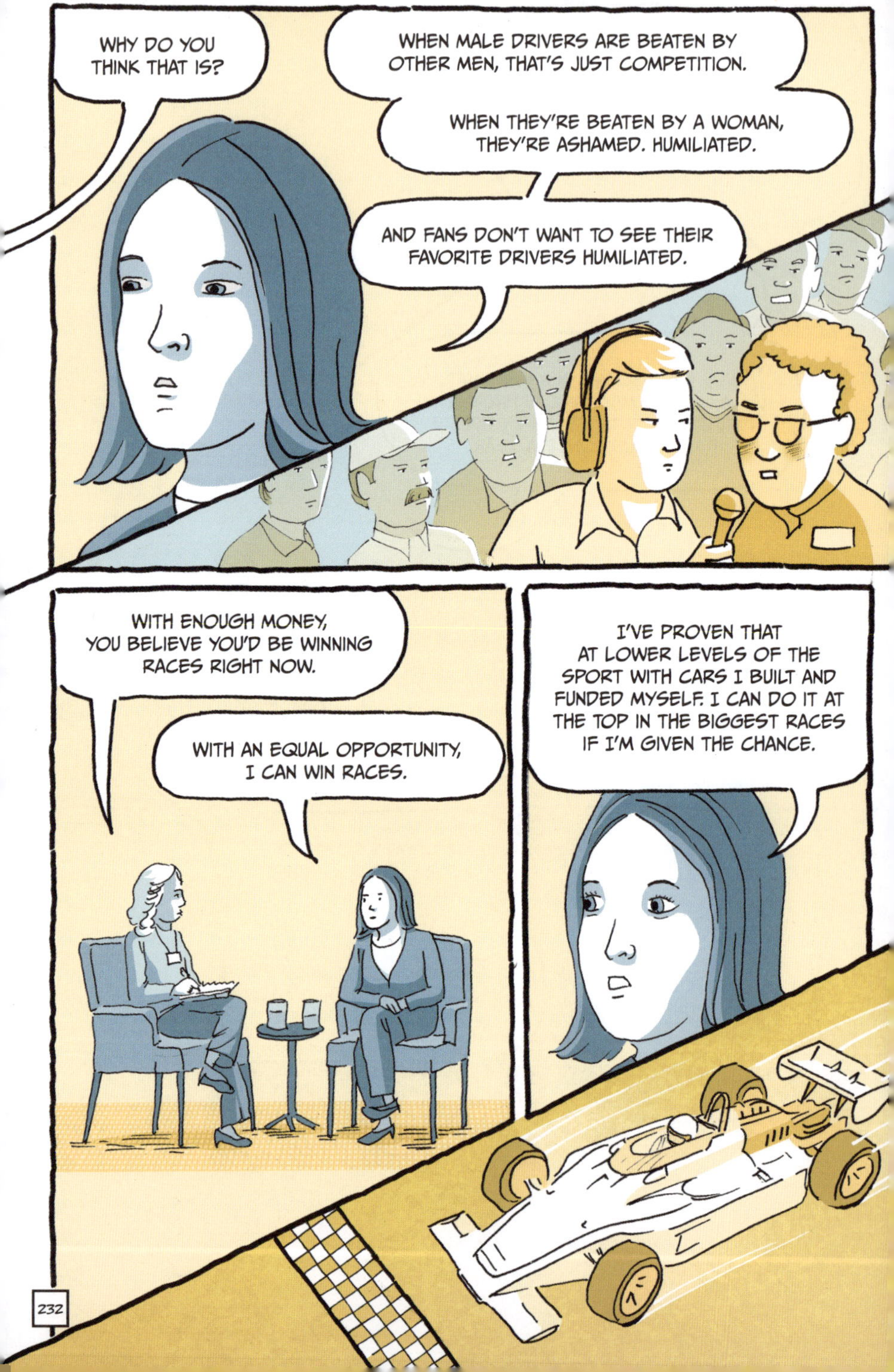
WHY DO YOU THINK THAT IS?
WHEN MALE DRIVERS ARE BEATEN BY OTHER MEN, THAT'S JUST COMPETITION.
WHEN THEY'RE BEATEN BY A WOMAN, THEY'RE ASHAMED. HUMILIATED.
AND FANS DON'T WANT TO SEE THEIR FAVORITE DRIVERS HUMILIATED.
WITH ENOUGH MONEY, YOU BELIEVE YOU'D BE WINNING RACES RIGHT NOW.
WITH AN EQUAL OPPORTUNITY, I CAN WIN RACES.
I'VE PROVEN THAT AT LOWER LEVELS OF THE SPORT WITH CARS I BUILT AND FUNDED MYSELF. I CAN DO IT AT THE TOP IN THE BIGGEST RACES IF I'M GIVEN THE CHANCE.

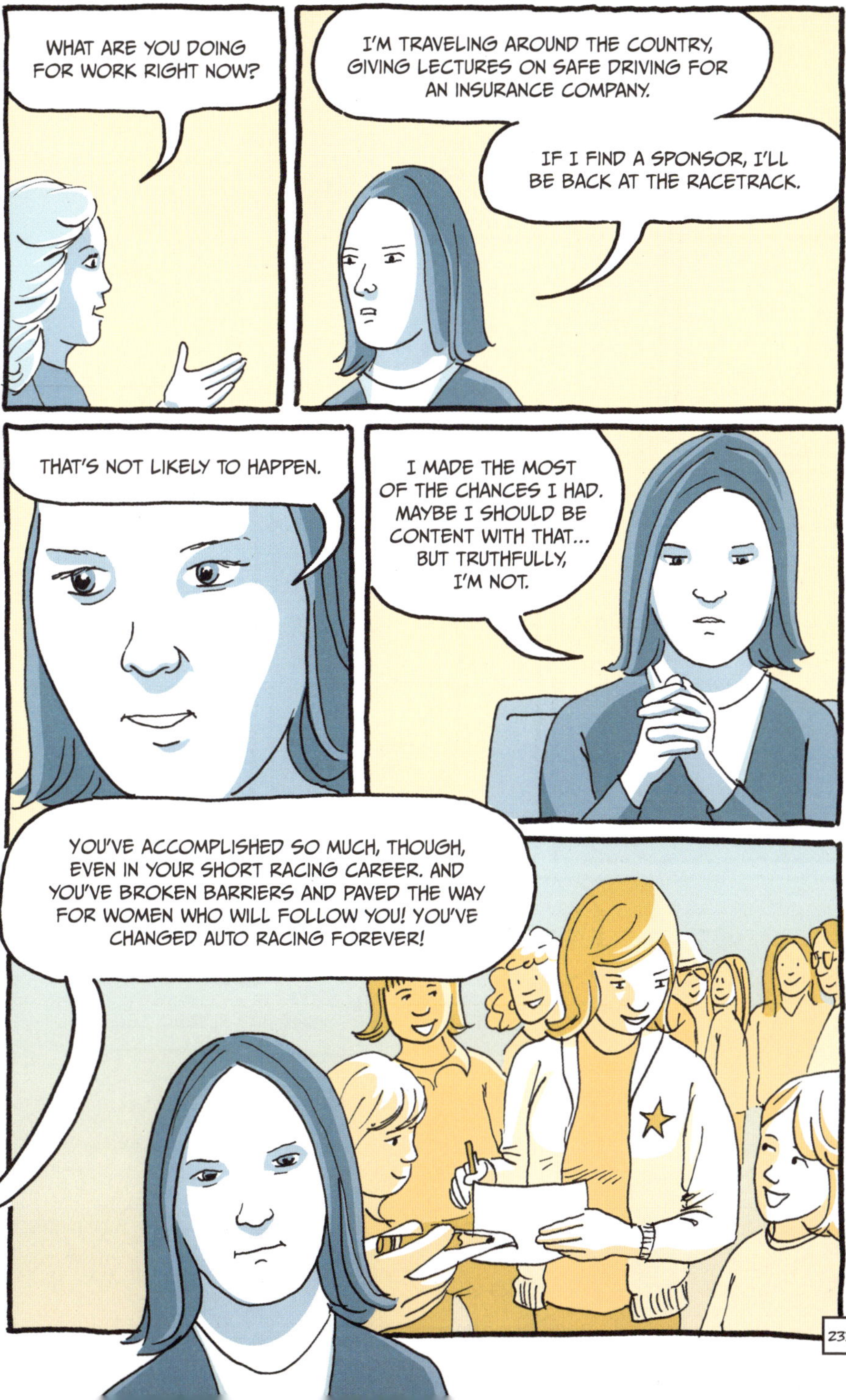
WHAT ARE YOU DOING FOR WORK RIGHT NOW?
I'M TRAVELING AROUND THE COUNTRY, GIVING LECTURES ON SAFE DRIVING FOR AN INSURANCE COMPANY.
IF I FIND A SPONSOR, I'LL BE BACK AT THE RACETRACK.
THAT'S NOT LIKELY TO HAPPEN.
I MADE THE MOST OF THE CHANCES I HAD. MAYBE I SHOULD BE CONTENT WITH THAT... BUT TRUTHFULLY, I'M NOT.
YOU'VE ACCOMPLISHED SO MUCH, THOUGH, EVEN IN YOUR SHORT RACING CAREER. AND YOU'VE BROKEN BARRIERS AND PAVED THE WAY FOR WOMEN WHO WILL FOLLOW YOU! YOU'VE CHANGED AUTO RACING FOREVER!

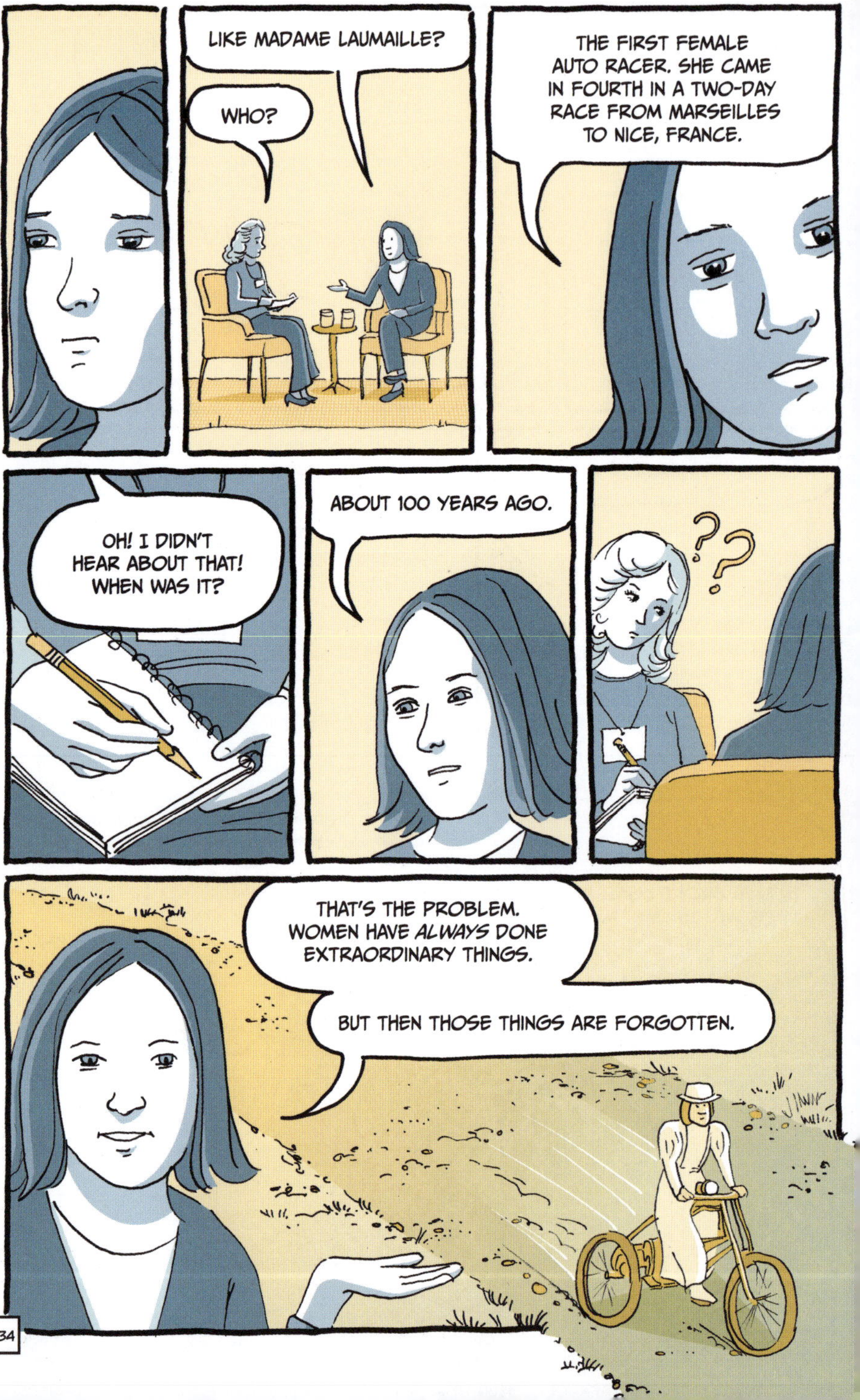

LIKE MADAME LAUMAILLE?
WHO?
THE FIRST FEMALE AUTO RACER. SHE CAME IN FOURTH IN A TWO-DAY RACE FROM MARSEILLES TO NICE, FRANCE.
OH! I DIDN'T HEAR ABOUT THAT! WHEN WAS IT?
ABOUT 100 YEARS AGO.
??
THAT'S THE PROBLEM. WOMEN HAVE *ALWAYS* DONE EXTRAORDINARY THINGS.
BUT THEN THOSE THINGS ARE FORGOTTEN.

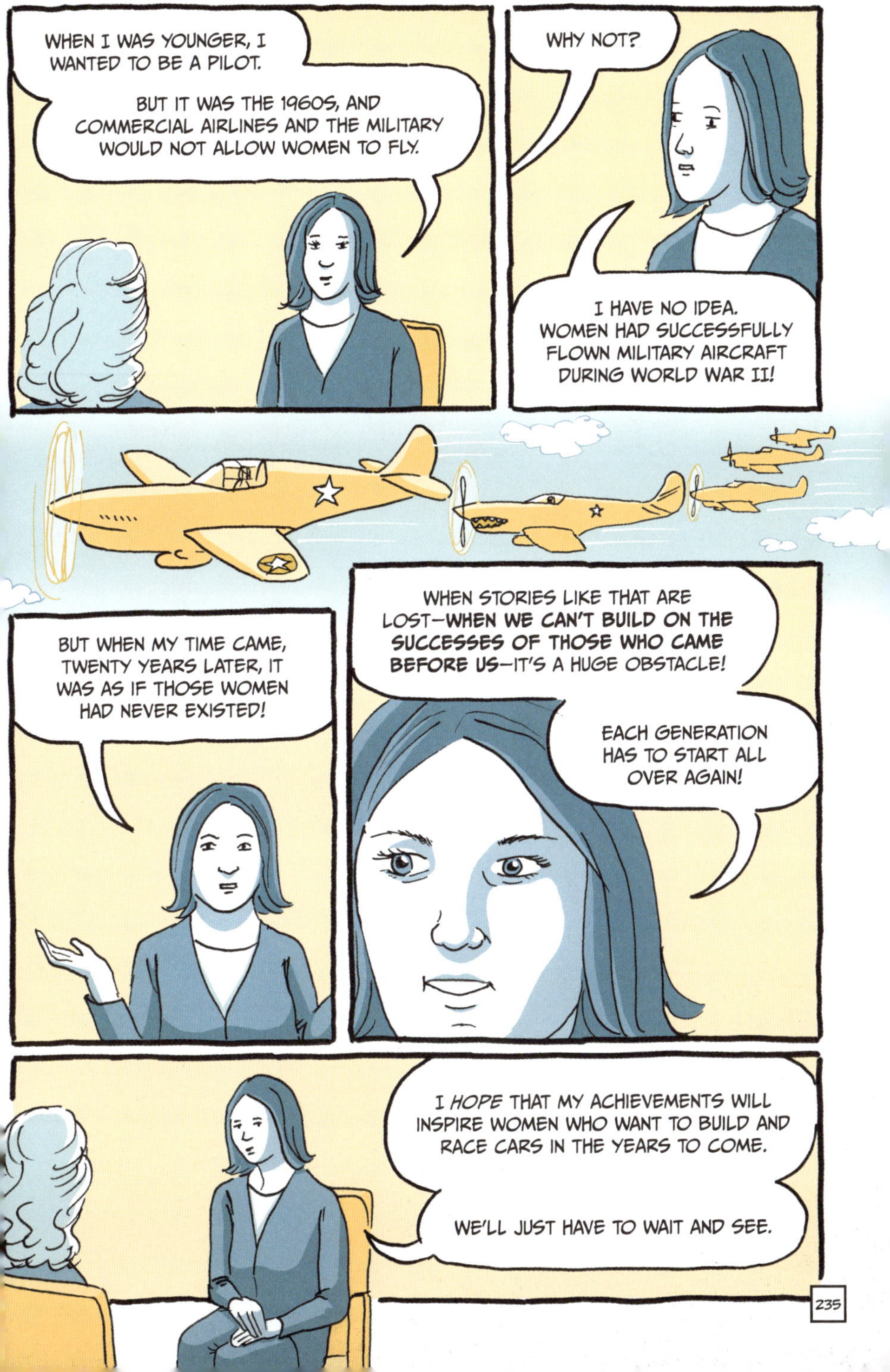
WHEN I WAS YOUNGER, I WANTED TO BE A PILOT.
BUT IT WAS THE 1960S, AND COMMERCIAL AIRLINES AND THE MILITARY WOULD NOT ALLOW WOMEN TO FLY.
WHY NOT?
I HAVE NO IDEA. WOMEN HAD SUCCESSFULLY FLOWN MILITARY AIRCRAFT DURING WORLD WAR II!
BUT WHEN MY TIME CAME, TWENTY YEARS LATER, IT WAS AS IF THOSE WOMEN HAD NEVER EXISTED!
WHEN STORIES LIKE THAT ARE LOST—**WHEN WE CAN'T BUILD ON THE SUCCESSES OF THOSE WHO CAME BEFORE US**—IT'S A HUGE OBSTACLE!
EACH GENERATION HAS TO START ALL OVER AGAIN!
I *HOPE* THAT MY ACHIEVEMENTS WILL INSPIRE WOMEN WHO WANT TO BUILD AND RACE CARS IN THE YEARS TO COME.
WE'LL JUST HAVE TO WAIT AND SEE.

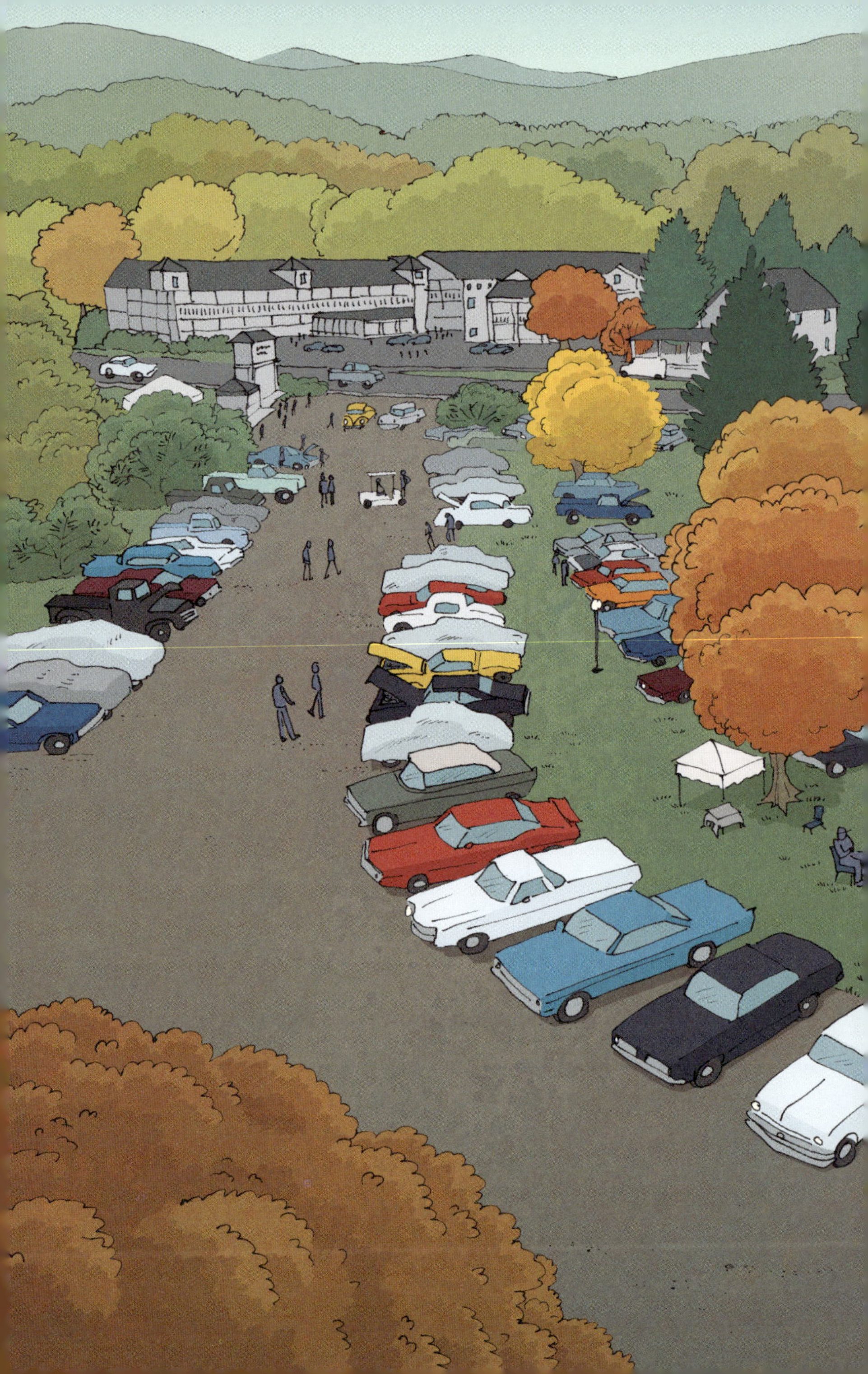

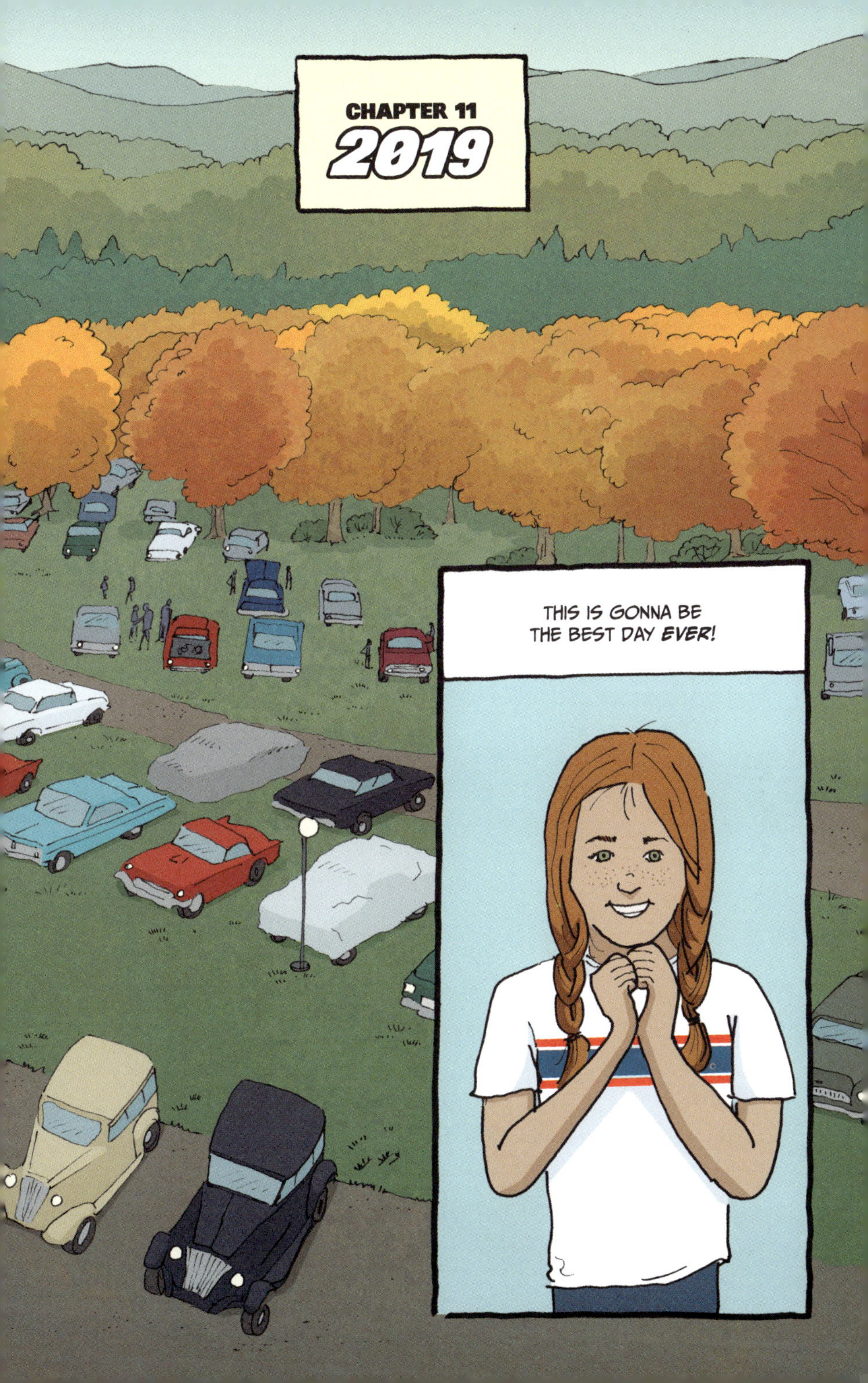
CHAPTER 11
2019
THIS IS GONNA BE THE BEST DAY EVER!

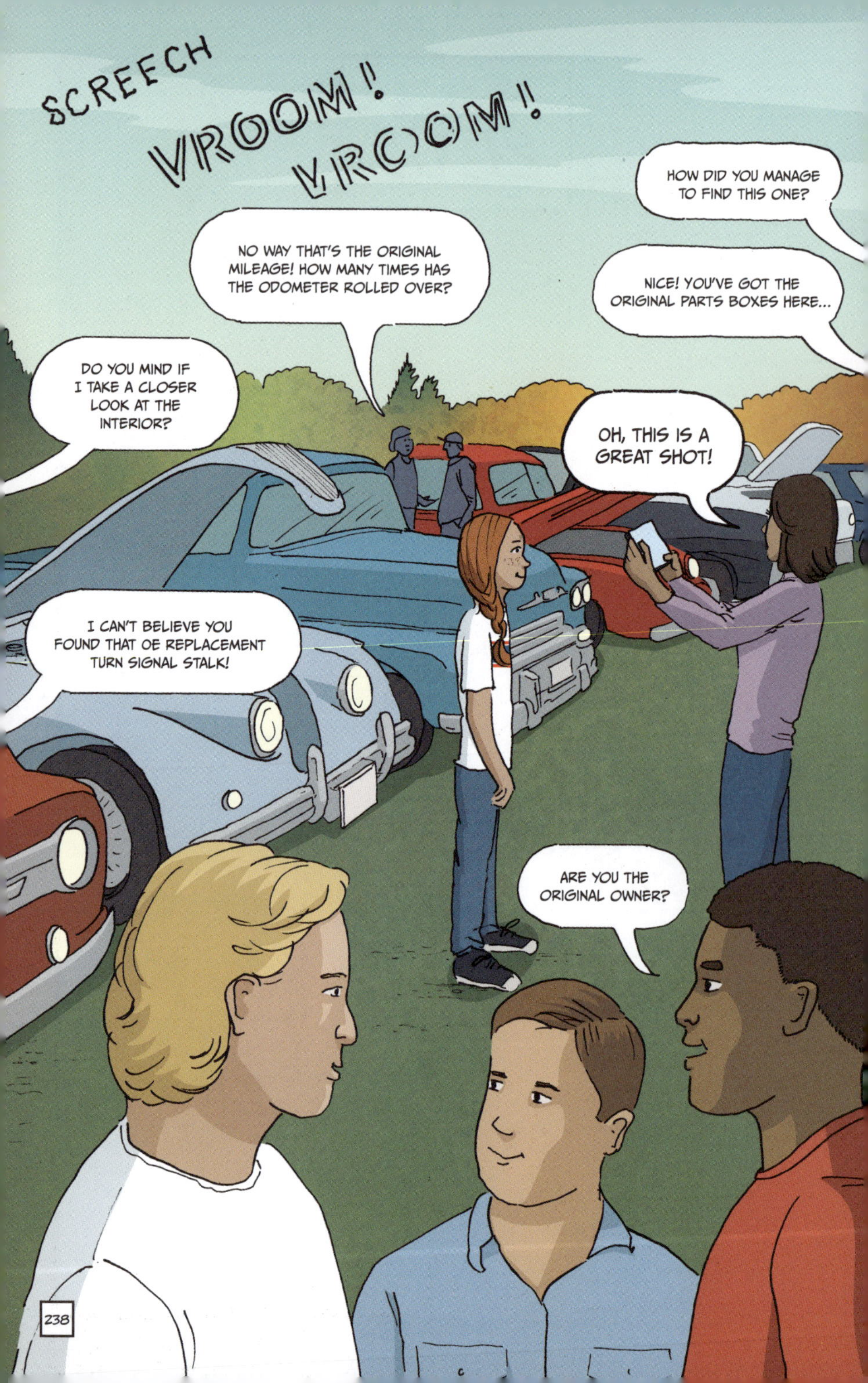
SCREECH
VROOM! VROOM!
NO WAY THAT'S THE ORIGINAL MILEAGE! HOW MANY TIMES HAS THE ODOMETER ROLLED OVER?
HOW DID YOU MANAGE TO FIND THIS ONE?
NICE! YOU'VE GOT THE ORIGINAL PARTS BOXES HERE...
DO YOU MIND IF I TAKE A CLOSER LOOK AT THE INTERIOR?
OH, THIS IS A GREAT SHOT!
I CAN'T BELIEVE YOU FOUND THAT OE REPLACEMENT TURN SIGNAL STALK!
ARE YOU THE ORIGINAL OWNER?

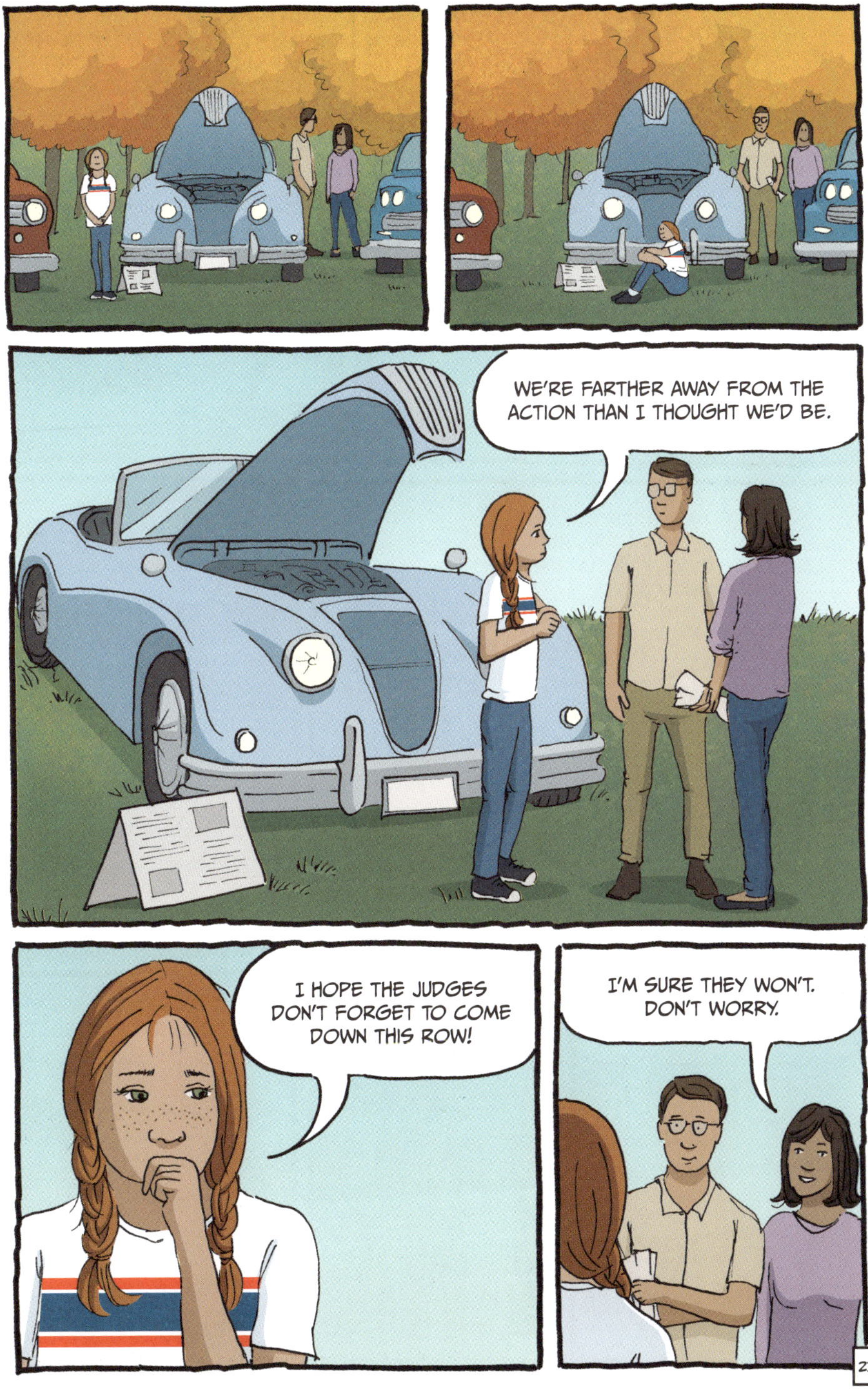
WE'RE FARTHER AWAY FROM THE ACTION THAN I THOUGHT WE'D BE.
I HOPE THE JUDGES DON'T FORGET TO COME DOWN THIS ROW!
I'M SURE THEY WON'T. DON'T WORRY.

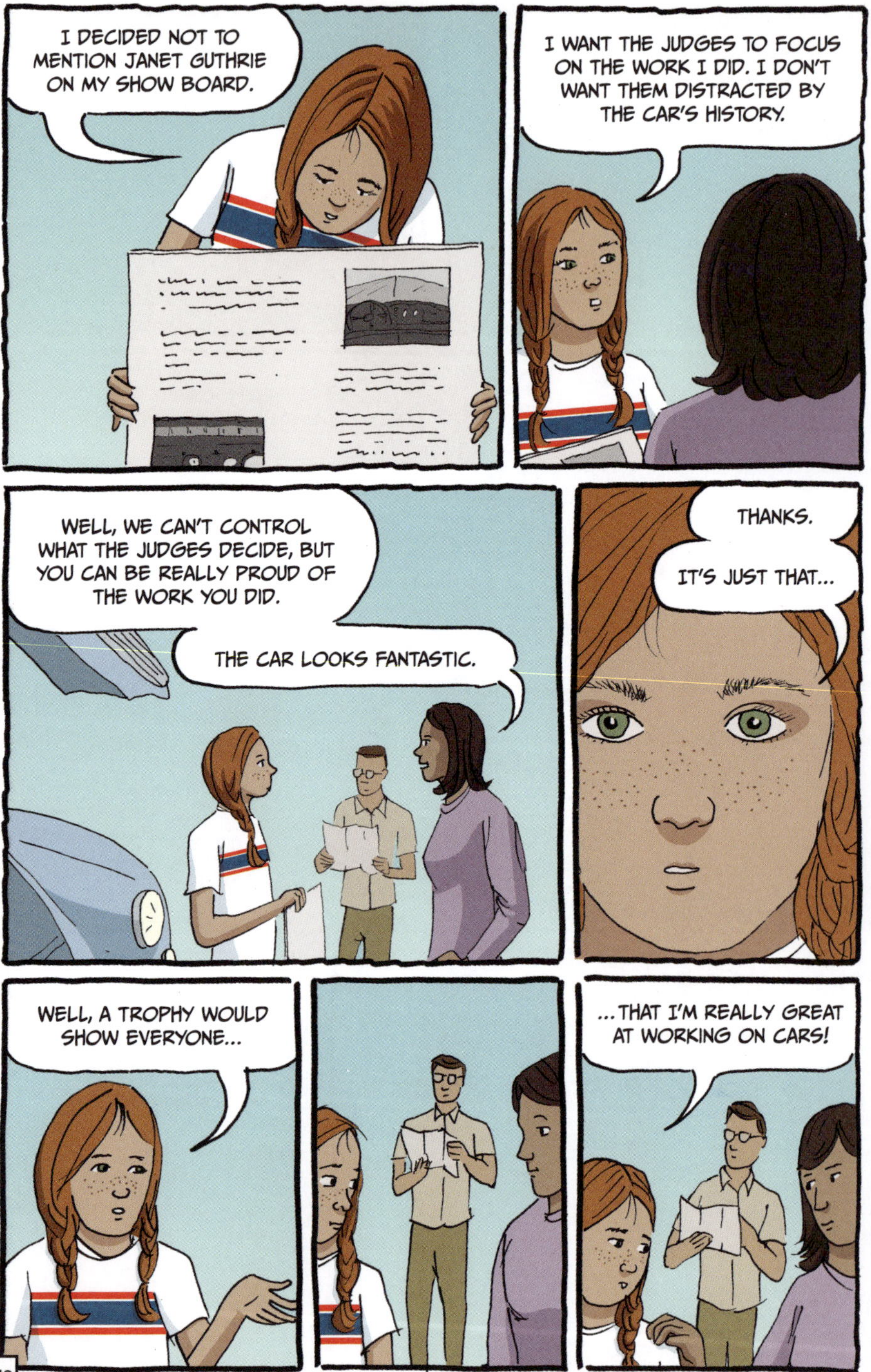
I DECIDED NOT TO MENTION JANET GUTHRIE ON MY SHOW BOARD.
I WANT THE JUDGES TO FOCUS ON THE WORK I DID. I DON'T WANT THEM DISTRACTED BY THE CAR'S HISTORY.
WELL, WE CAN'T CONTROL WHAT THE JUDGES DECIDE, BUT YOU CAN BE REALLY PROUD OF THE WORK YOU DID.
THE CAR LOOKS FANTASTIC.
THANKS.
IT'S JUST THAT...
WELL, A TROPHY WOULD SHOW EVERYONE...
...THAT I'M REALLY GREAT AT WORKING ON CARS!

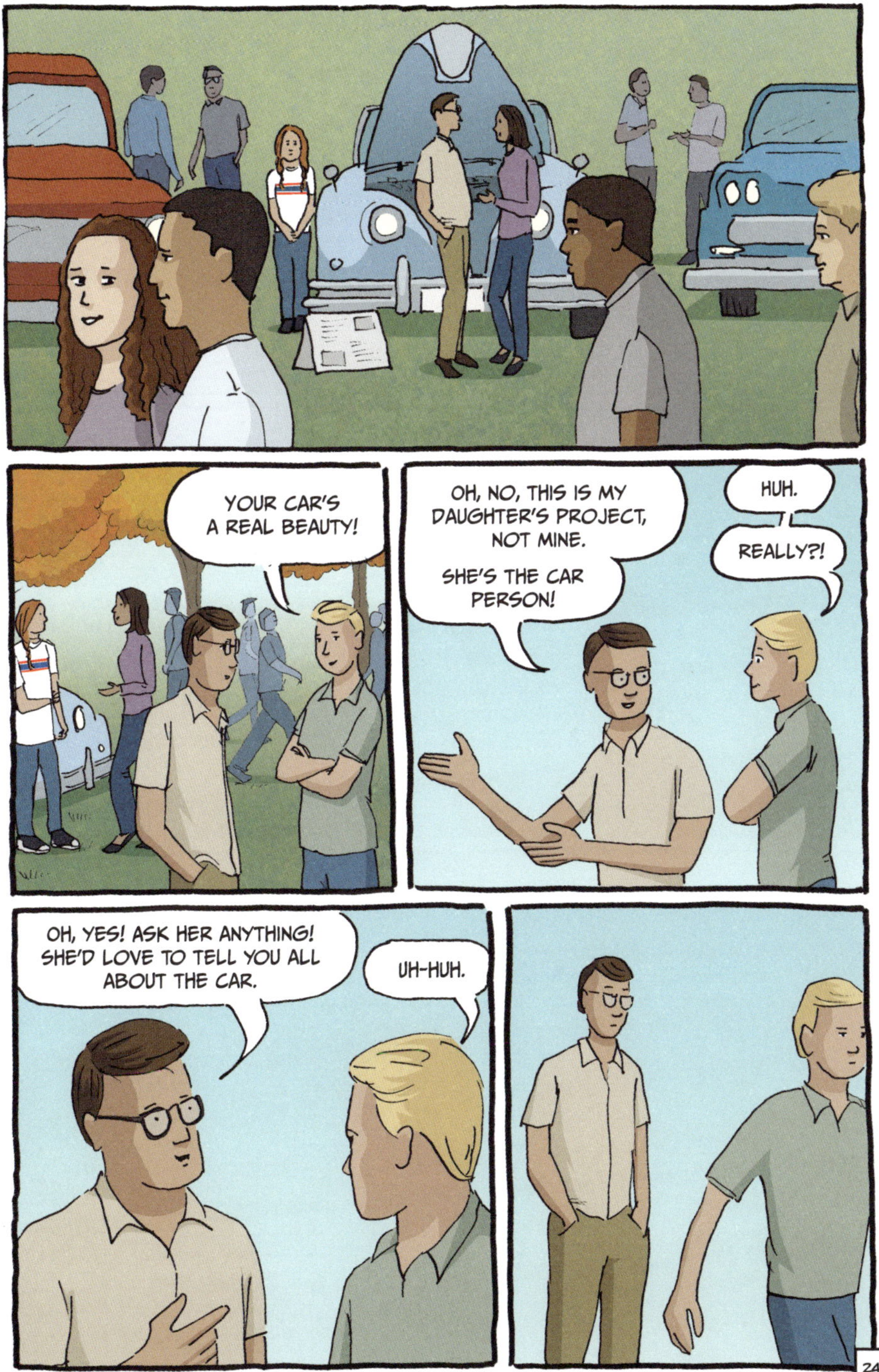
YOUR CAR'S A REAL BEAUTY!
OH, NO, THIS IS MY DAUGHTER'S PROJECT, NOT MINE.
SHE'S THE CAR PERSON!
HUH.
REALLY?!
OH, YES! ASK HER ANYTHING! SHE'D LOVE TO TELL YOU ALL ABOUT THE CAR.
UH-HUH.

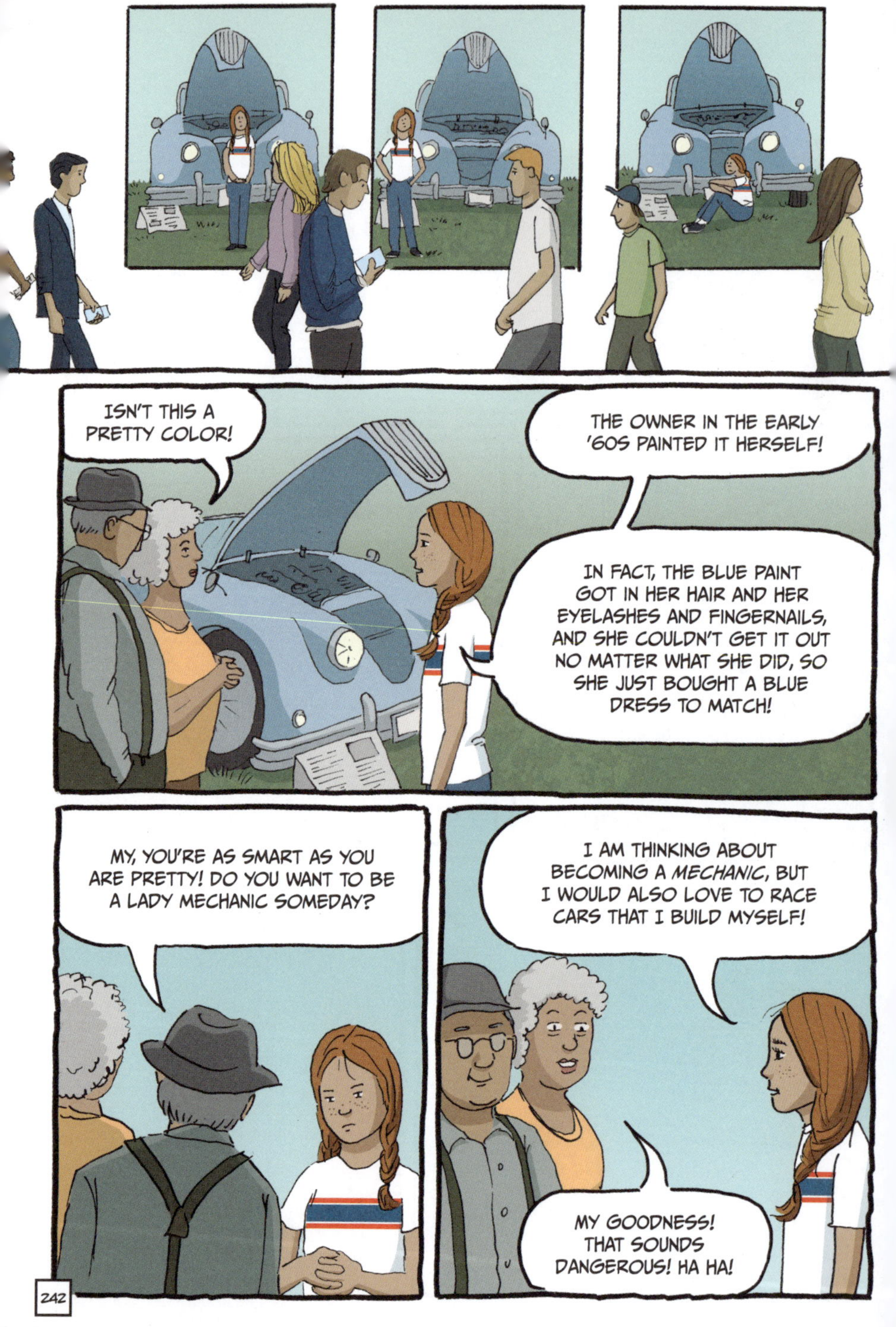
ISN'T THIS A PRETTY COLOR!
THE OWNER IN THE EARLY '60S PAINTED IT HERSELF!
IN FACT, THE BLUE PAINT GOT IN HER HAIR AND HER EYELASHES AND FINGERNAILS, AND SHE COULDN'T GET IT OUT NO MATTER WHAT SHE DID, SO SHE JUST BOUGHT A BLUE DRESS TO MATCH!
MY, YOU'RE AS SMART AS YOU ARE PRETTY! DO YOU WANT TO BE A LADY MECHANIC SOMEDAY?
I AM THINKING ABOUT BECOMING A *MECHANIC*, BUT I WOULD ALSO LOVE TO RACE CARS THAT I BUILD MYSELF!
MY GOODNESS! THAT SOUNDS DANGEROUS! HA HA!

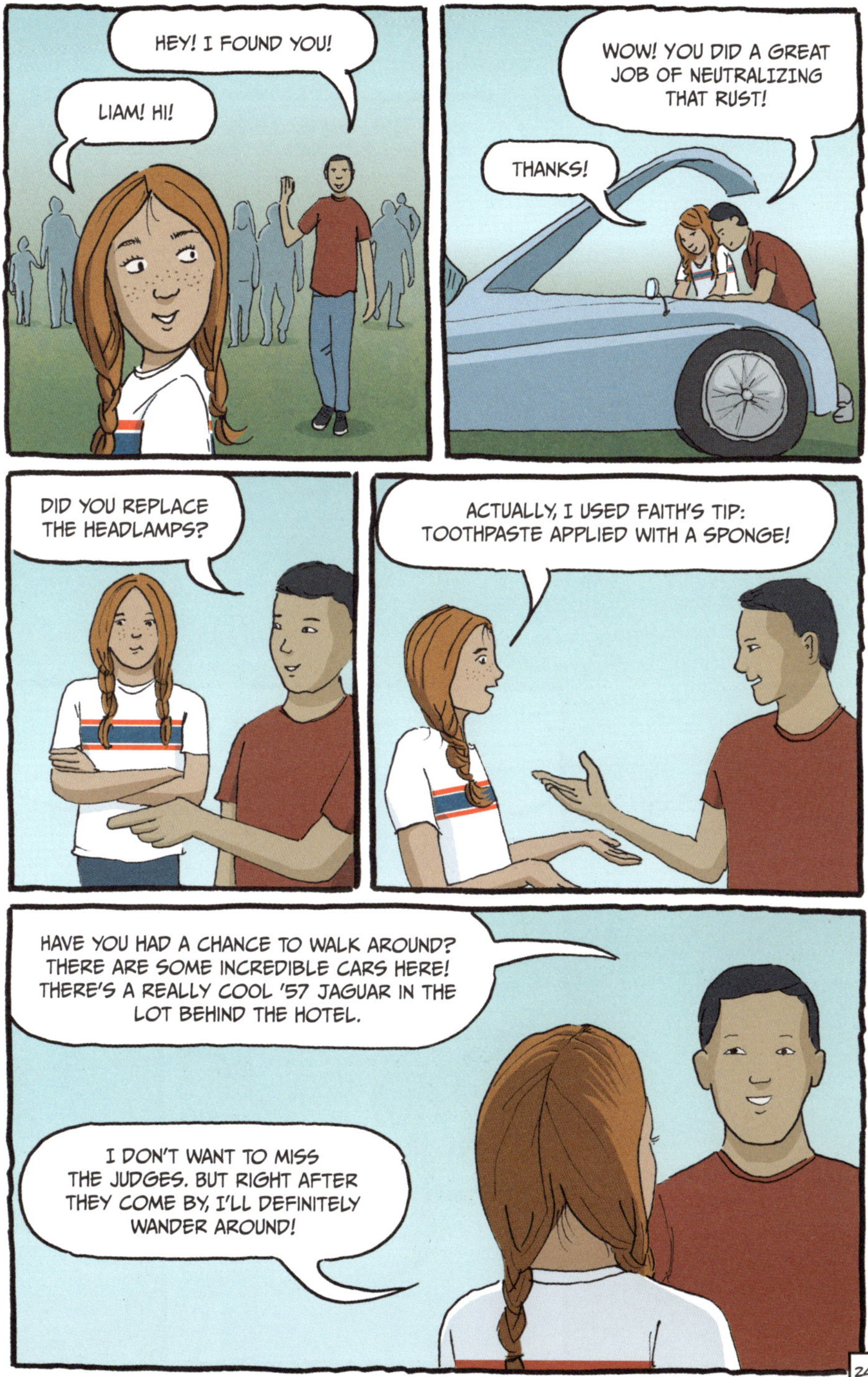
HEY! I FOUND YOU!
LIAM! HI!
WOW! YOU DID A GREAT JOB OF NEUTRALIZING THAT RUST!
THANKS!
DID YOU REPLACE THE HEADLAMPS?
ACTUALLY, I USED FAITH'S TIP: TOOTHPASTE APPLIED WITH A SPONGE!
HAVE YOU HAD A CHANCE TO WALK AROUND? THERE ARE SOME INCREDIBLE CARS HERE! THERE'S A REALLY COOL '57 JAGUAR IN THE LOT BEHIND THE HOTEL.
I DON'T WANT TO MISS THE JUDGES. BUT RIGHT AFTER THEY COME BY, I'LL DEFINITELY WANDER AROUND!

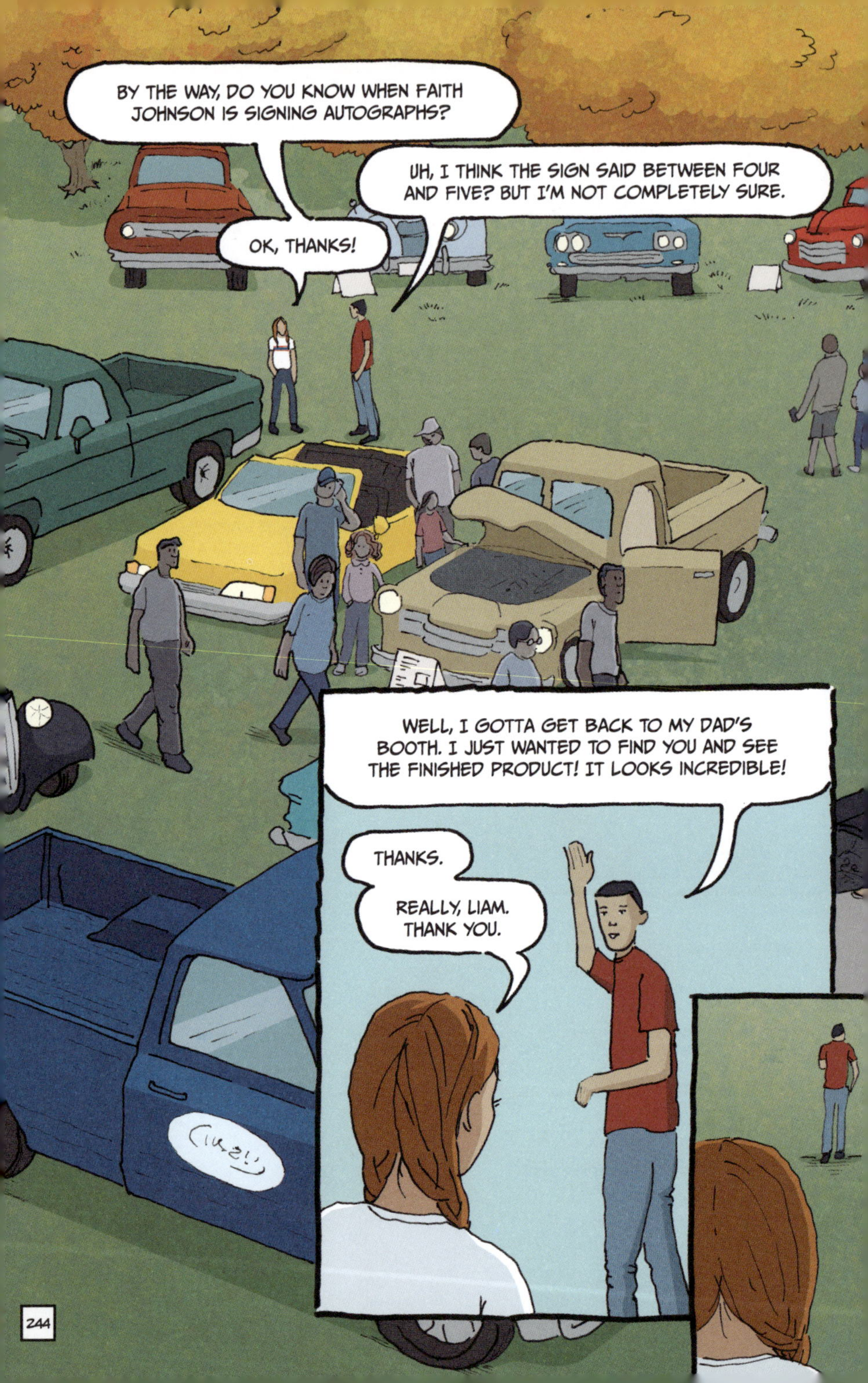
BY THE WAY, DO YOU KNOW WHEN FAITH JOHNSON IS SIGNING AUTOGRAPHS?
UH, I THINK THE SIGN SAID BETWEEN FOUR AND FIVE? BUT I'M NOT COMPLETELY SURE.
OK, THANKS!
WELL, I GOTTA GET BACK TO MY DAD'S BOOTH. I JUST WANTED TO FIND YOU AND SEE THE FINISHED PRODUCT! IT LOOKS INCREDIBLE!
THANKS.
REALLY, LIAM. THANK YOU.

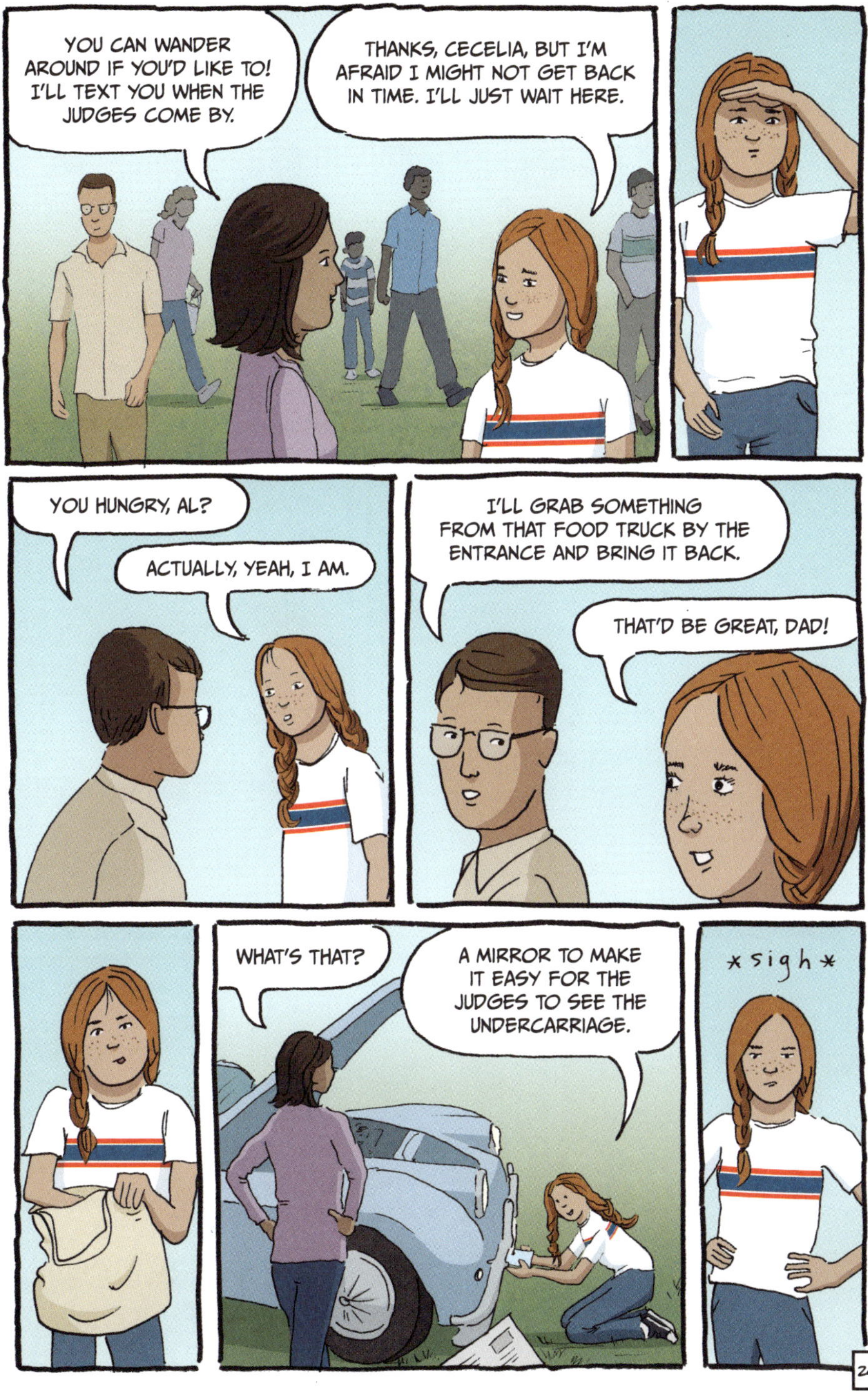
YOU CAN WANDER AROUND IF YOU'D LIKE TO! I'LL TEXT YOU WHEN THE JUDGES COME BY.
THANKS, CECELIA, BUT I'M AFRAID I MIGHT NOT GET BACK IN TIME. I'LL JUST WAIT HERE.
YOU HUNGRY, AL?
ACTUALLY, YEAH, I AM.
I'LL GRAB SOMETHING FROM THAT FOOD TRUCK BY THE ENTRANCE AND BRING IT BACK.
THAT'D BE GREAT, DAD!
WHAT'S THAT?
A MIRROR TO MAKE IT EASY FOR THE JUDGES TO SEE THE UNDERCARRIAGE.
sigh

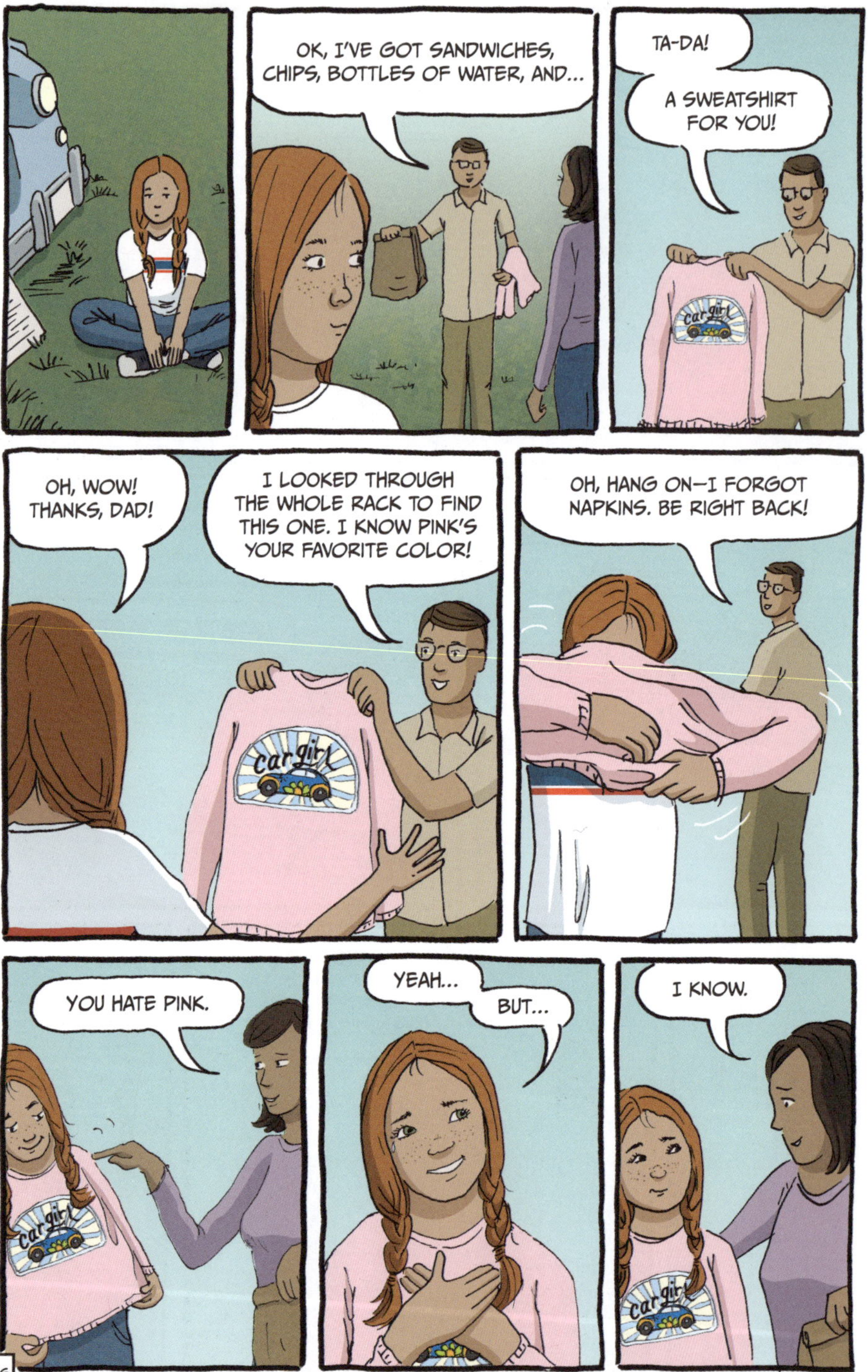
OK, I'VE GOT SANDWICHES, CHIPS, BOTTLES OF WATER, AND...
TA-DA!
A SWEATSHIRT FOR YOU!
OH, WOW! THANKS, DAD!
I LOOKED THROUGH THE WHOLE RACK TO FIND THIS ONE. I KNOW PINK'S YOUR FAVORITE COLOR!
OH, HANG ON—I FORGOT NAPKINS. BE RIGHT BACK!
YOU HATE PINK.
YEAH...
BUT...
I KNOW.

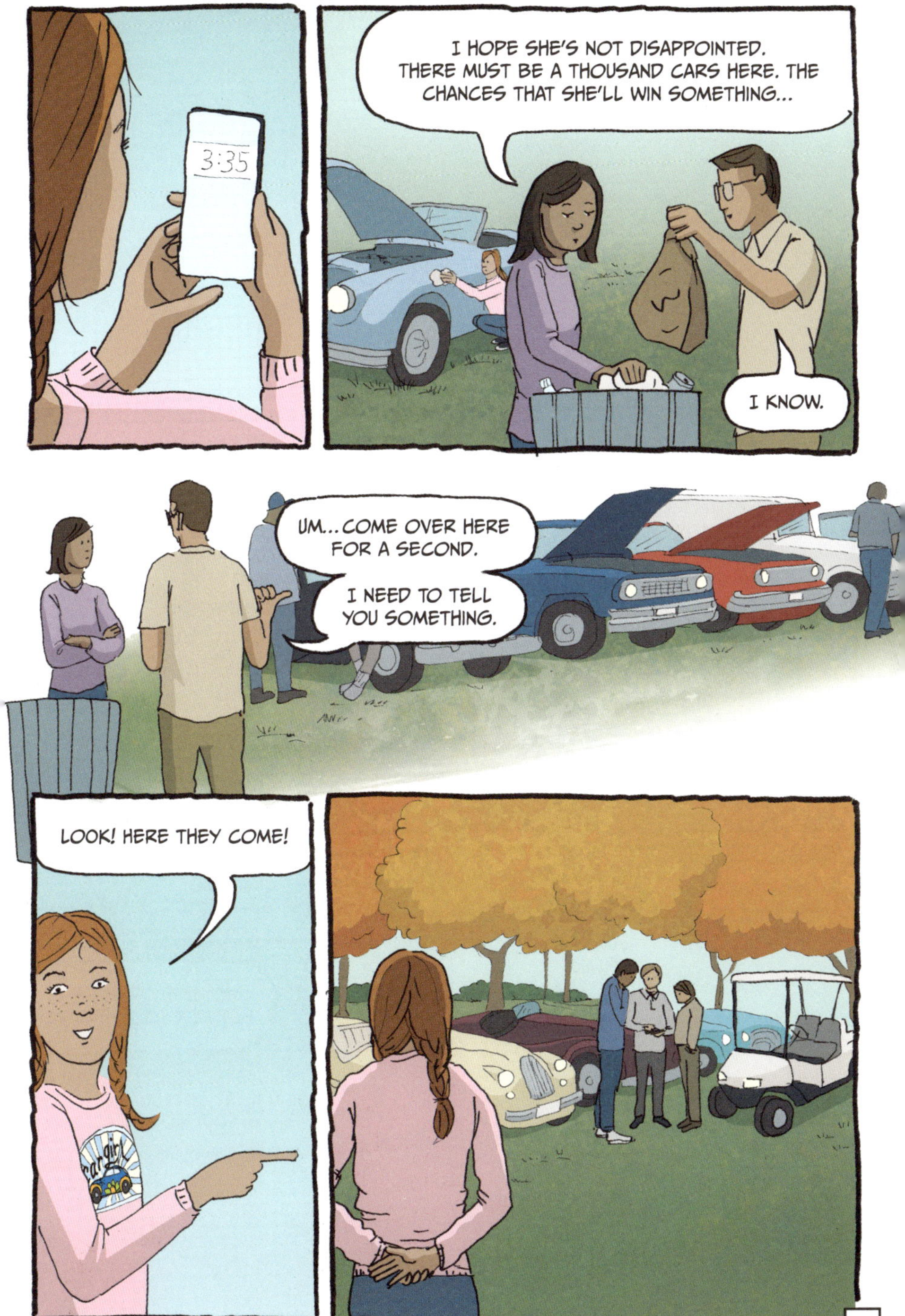
3:35
I HOPE SHE'S NOT DISAPPOINTED. THERE MUST BE A THOUSAND CARS HERE. THE CHANCES THAT SHE'LL WIN SOMETHING...
I KNOW.
UM...COME OVER HERE FOR A SECOND.
I NEED TO TELL YOU SOMETHING.
LOOK! HERE THEY COME!
car girl

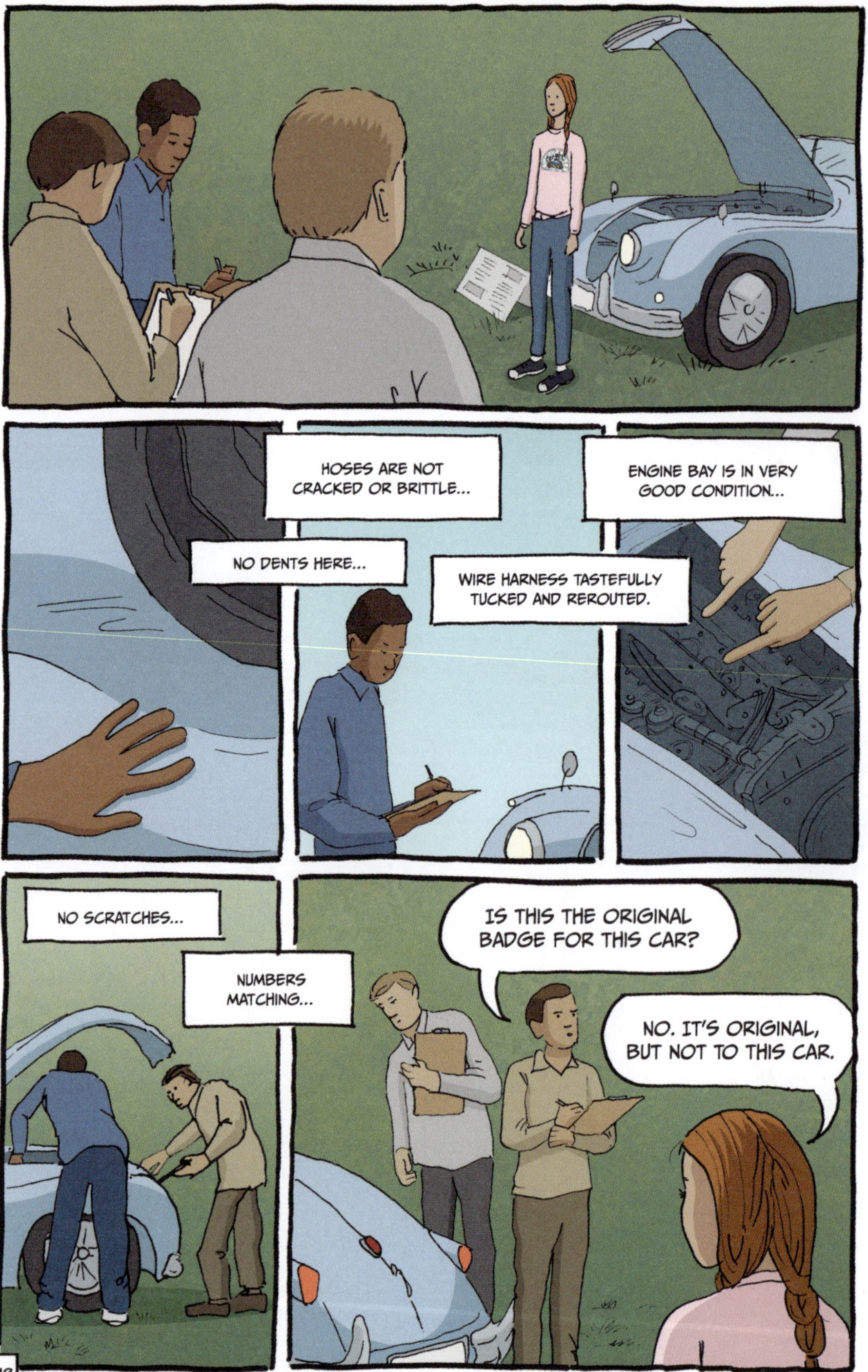
HOSES ARE NOT CRACKED OR BRITTLE...
ENGINE BAY IS IN VERY GOOD CONDITION...
NO DENTS HERE...
WIRE HARNESS TASTEFULLY TUCKED AND REROUTED.
NO SCRATCHES...
NUMBERS MATCHING...
IS THIS THE ORIGINAL BADGE FOR THIS CAR?
NO. IT'S ORIGINAL, BUT NOT TO THIS CAR.

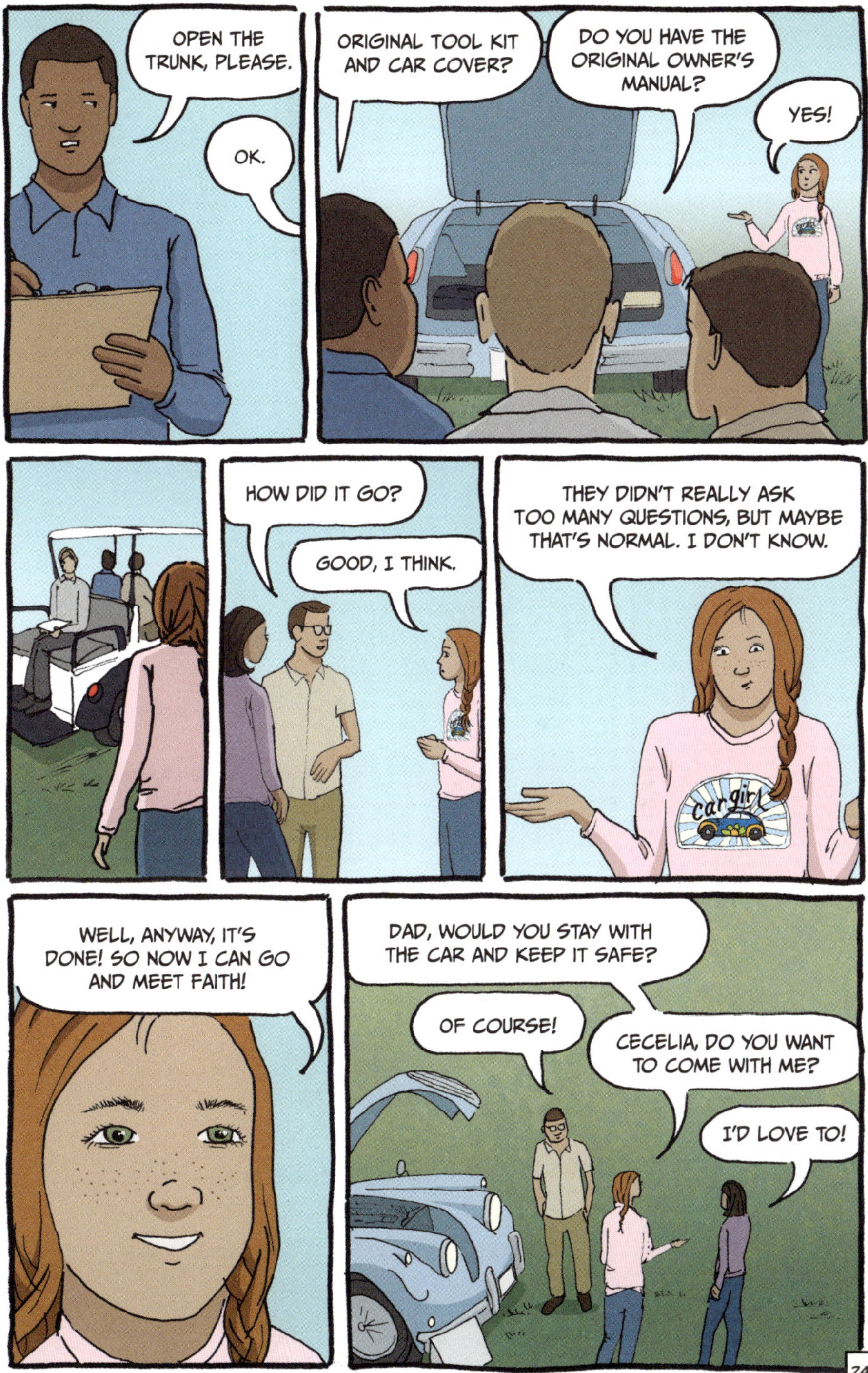
OPEN THE TRUNK, PLEASE.
OK.
ORIGINAL TOOL KIT AND CAR COVER?
DO YOU HAVE THE ORIGINAL OWNER'S MANUAL?
YES!
HOW DID IT GO?
GOOD, I THINK.
THEY DIDN'T REALLY ASK TOO MANY QUESTIONS, BUT MAYBE THAT'S NORMAL. I DON'T KNOW.
car girl
WELL, ANYWAY, IT'S DONE! SO NOW I CAN GO AND MEET FAITH!
DAD, WOULD YOU STAY WITH THE CAR AND KEEP IT SAFE?
OF COURSE!
CECELIA, DO YOU WANT TO COME WITH ME?
I'D LOVE TO!

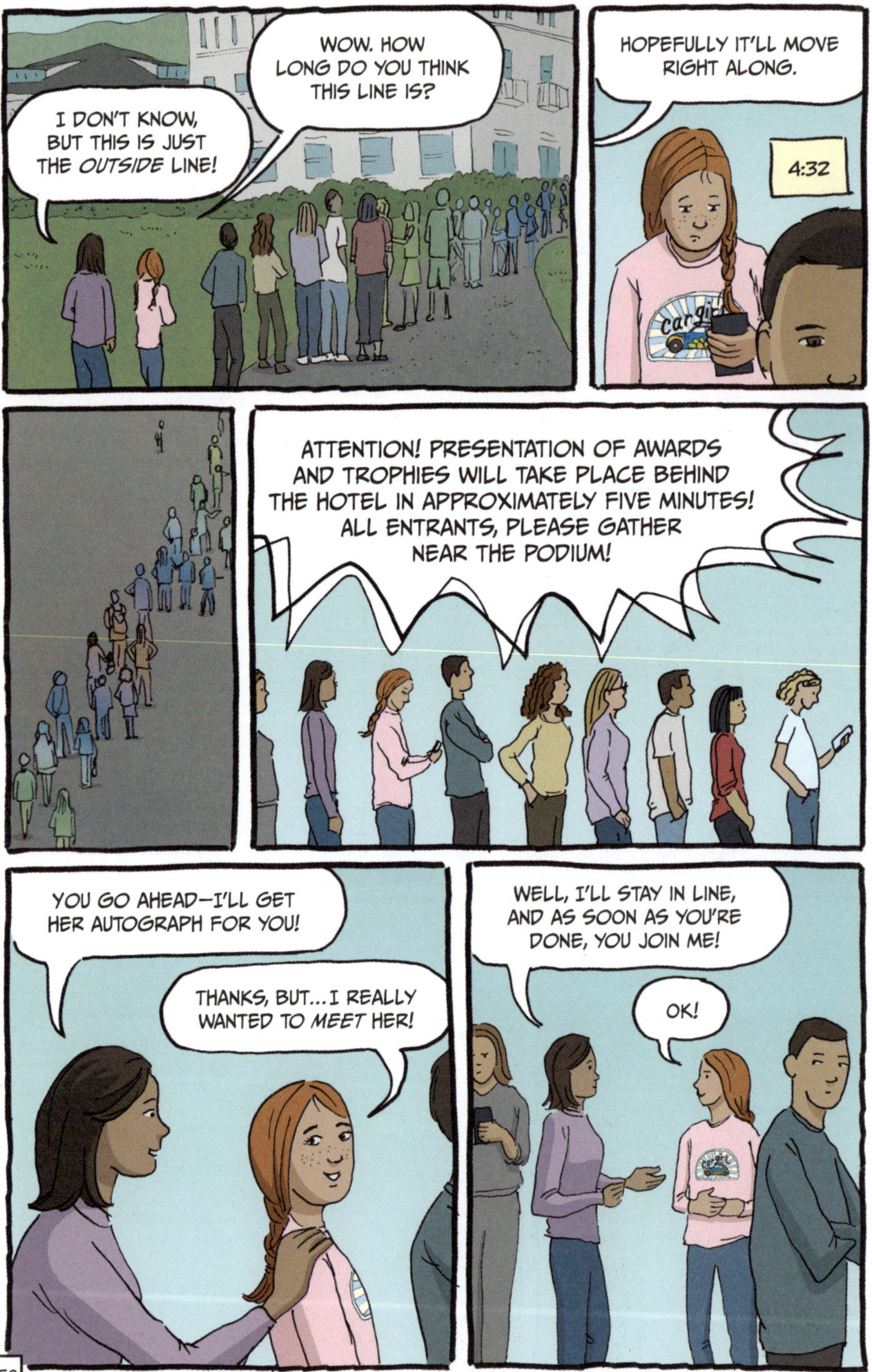
WOW. HOW LONG DO YOU THINK THIS LINE IS?
I DON'T KNOW, BUT THIS IS JUST THE *OUTSIDE* LINE!
HOPEFULLY IT'LL MOVE RIGHT ALONG.
4:32
ATTENTION! PRESENTATION OF AWARDS AND TROPHIES WILL TAKE PLACE BEHIND THE HOTEL IN APPROXIMATELY FIVE MINUTES! ALL ENTRANTS, PLEASE GATHER NEAR THE PODIUM!
YOU GO AHEAD—I'LL GET HER AUTOGRAPH FOR YOU!
THANKS, BUT... I REALLY WANTED TO *MEET* HER!
WELL, I'LL STAY IN LINE, AND AS SOON AS YOU'RE DONE, YOU JOIN ME!
OK!

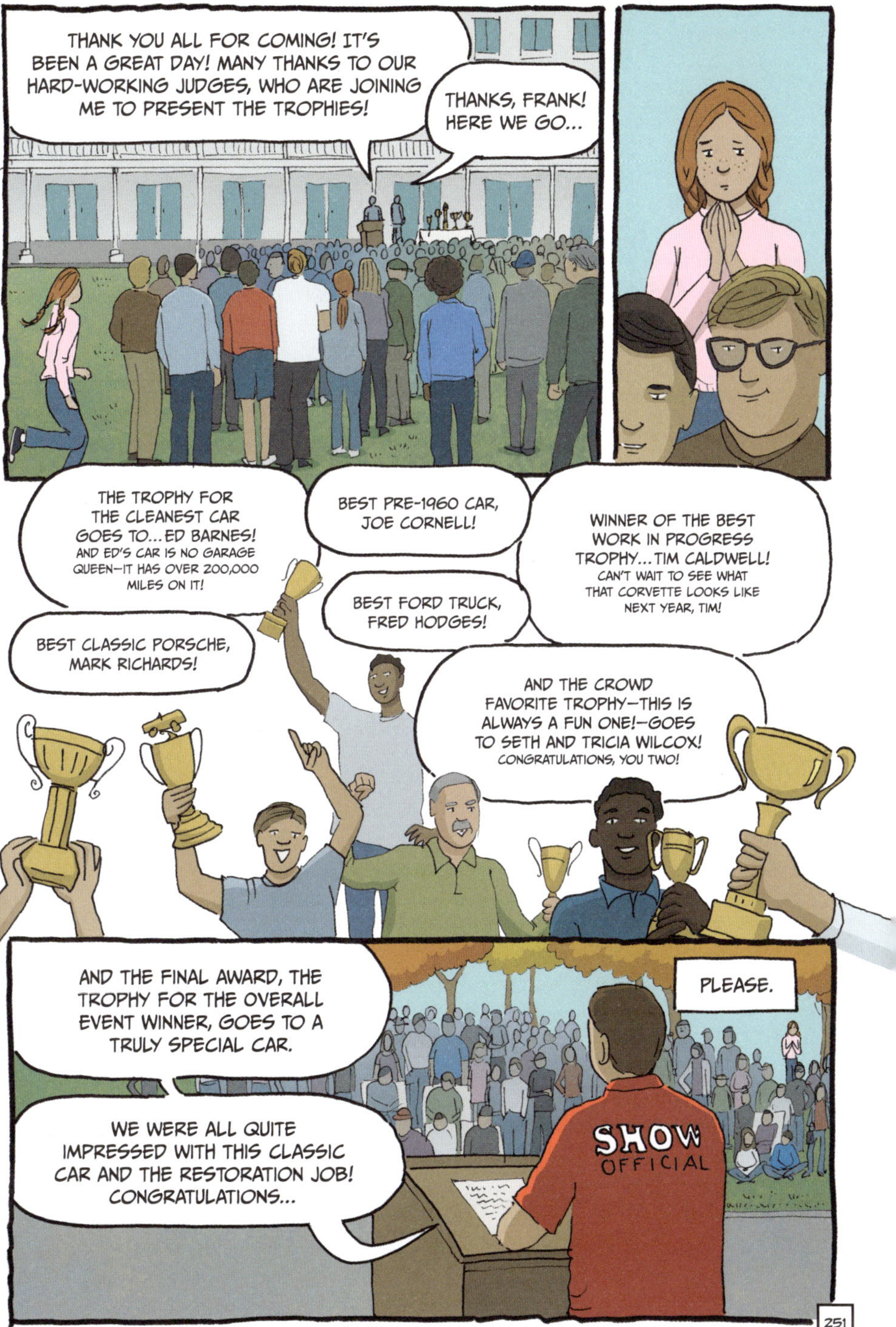
THANK YOU ALL FOR COMING! IT'S BEEN A GREAT DAY! MANY THANKS TO OUR HARD-WORKING JUDGES, WHO ARE JOINING ME TO PRESENT THE TROPHIES!
THANKS, FRANK! HERE WE GO...
THE TROPHY FOR THE CLEANEST CAR GOES TO... ED BARNES! AND ED'S CAR IS NO GARAGE QUEEN—IT HAS OVER 200,000 MILES ON IT!
BEST PRE-1960 CAR, JOE CORNELL!
WINNER OF THE BEST WORK IN PROGRESS TROPHY... TIM CALDWELL! CAN'T WAIT TO SEE WHAT THAT CORVETTE LOOKS LIKE NEXT YEAR, TIM!
BEST FORD TRUCK, FRED HODGES!
BEST CLASSIC PORSCHE, MARK RICHARDS!
AND THE CROWD FAVORITE TROPHY—THIS IS ALWAYS A FUN ONE!—GOES TO SETH AND TRICIA WILCOX! CONGRATULATIONS, YOU TWO!
AND THE FINAL AWARD, THE TROPHY FOR THE OVERALL EVENT WINNER, GOES TO A TRULY SPECIAL CAR.
PLEASE.
WE WERE ALL QUITE IMPRESSED WITH THIS CLASSIC CAR AND THE RESTORATION JOB! CONGRATULATIONS...
SHOW OFFICIAL

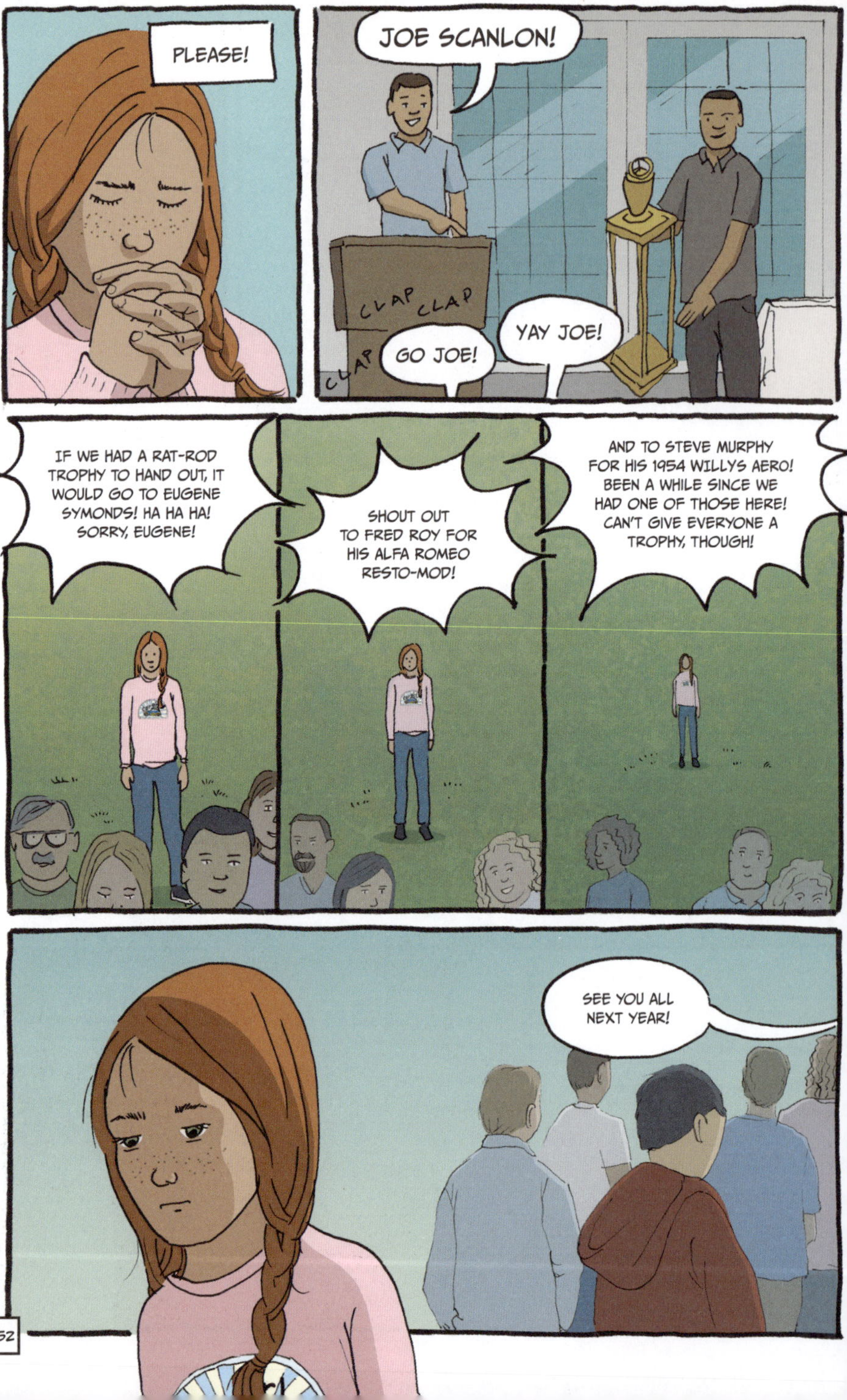
PLEASE!
JOE SCANLON!
CLAP CLAP
CLAP
GO JOE!
YAY JOE!
IF WE HAD A RAT-ROD TROPHY TO HAND OUT, IT WOULD GO TO EUGENE SYMONDS! HA HA HA! SORRY, EUGENE!
SHOUT OUT TO FRED ROY FOR HIS ALFA ROMEO RESTO-MOD!
AND TO STEVE MURPHY FOR HIS 1954 WILLYS AERO! BEEN A WHILE SINCE WE HAD ONE OF THOSE HERE! CAN'T GIVE EVERYONE A TROPHY, THOUGH!
SEE YOU ALL NEXT YEAR!

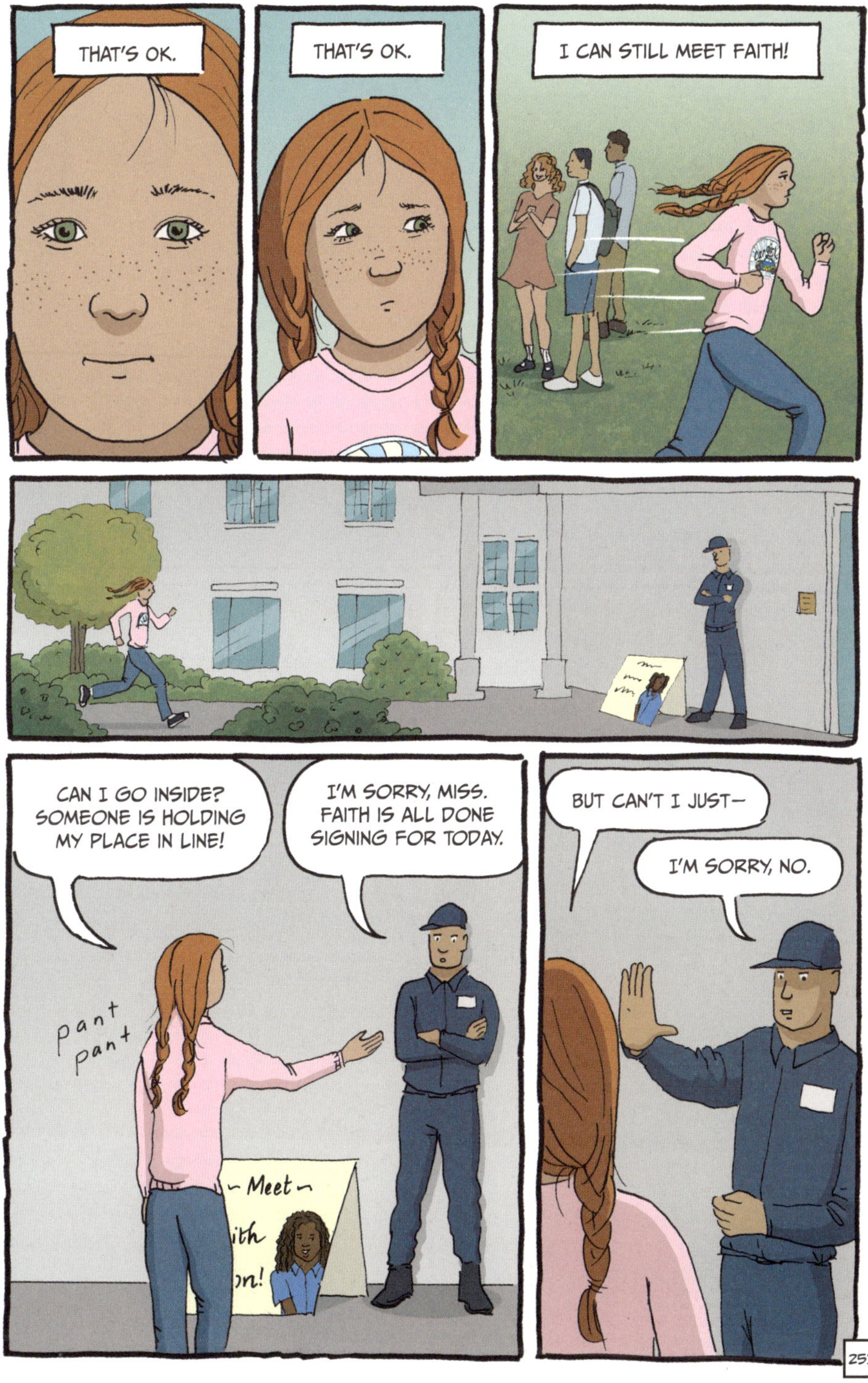
THAT'S OK.
THAT'S OK.
I CAN STILL MEET FAITH!
CAN I GO INSIDE? SOMEONE IS HOLDING MY PLACE IN LINE!
I'M SORRY, MISS. FAITH IS ALL DONE SIGNING FOR TODAY.
pant pant
~Meet~
BUT CAN'T I JUST—
I'M SORRY, NO.

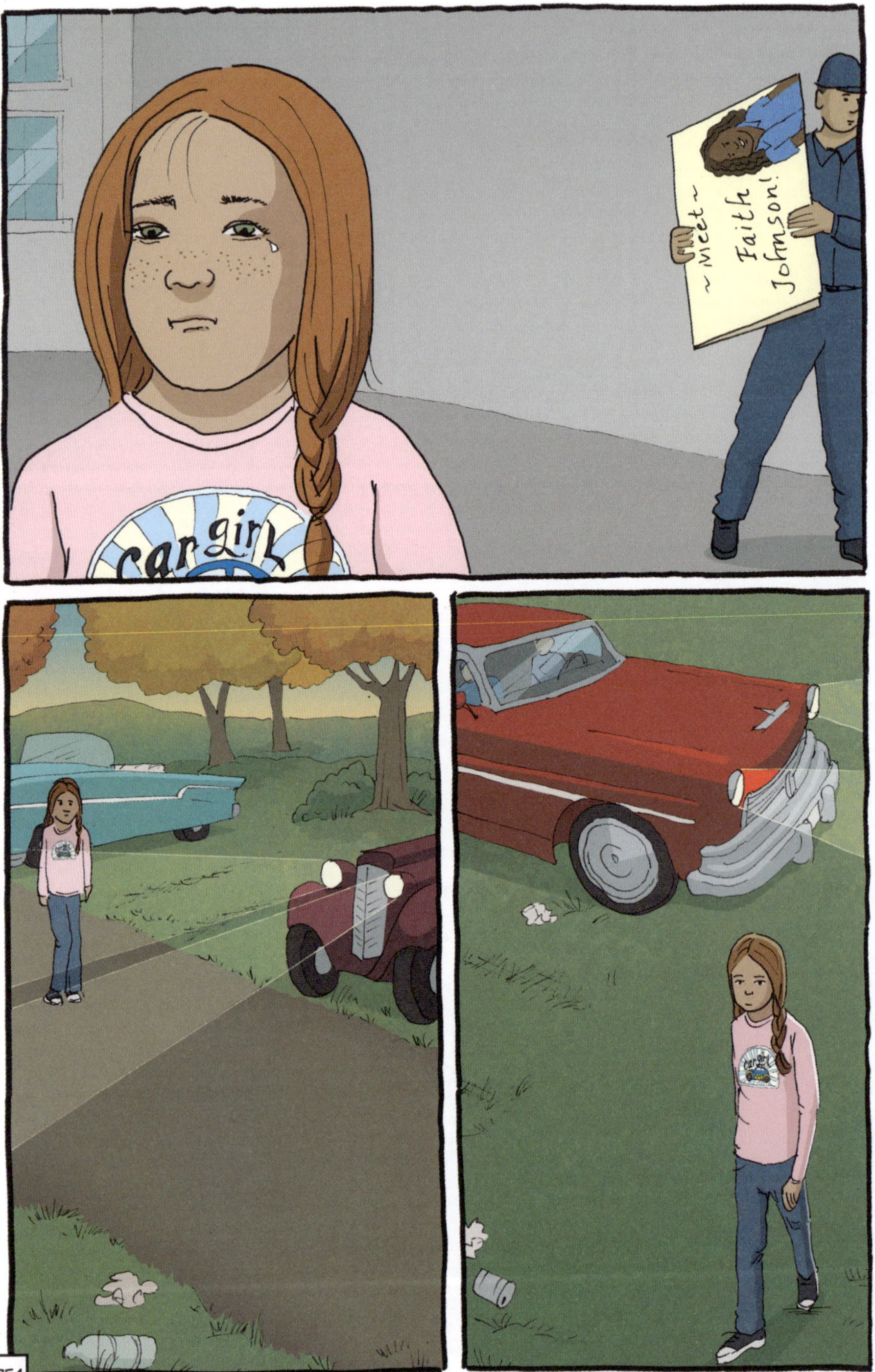

~Meet~
Faith
Johnson!
car girl

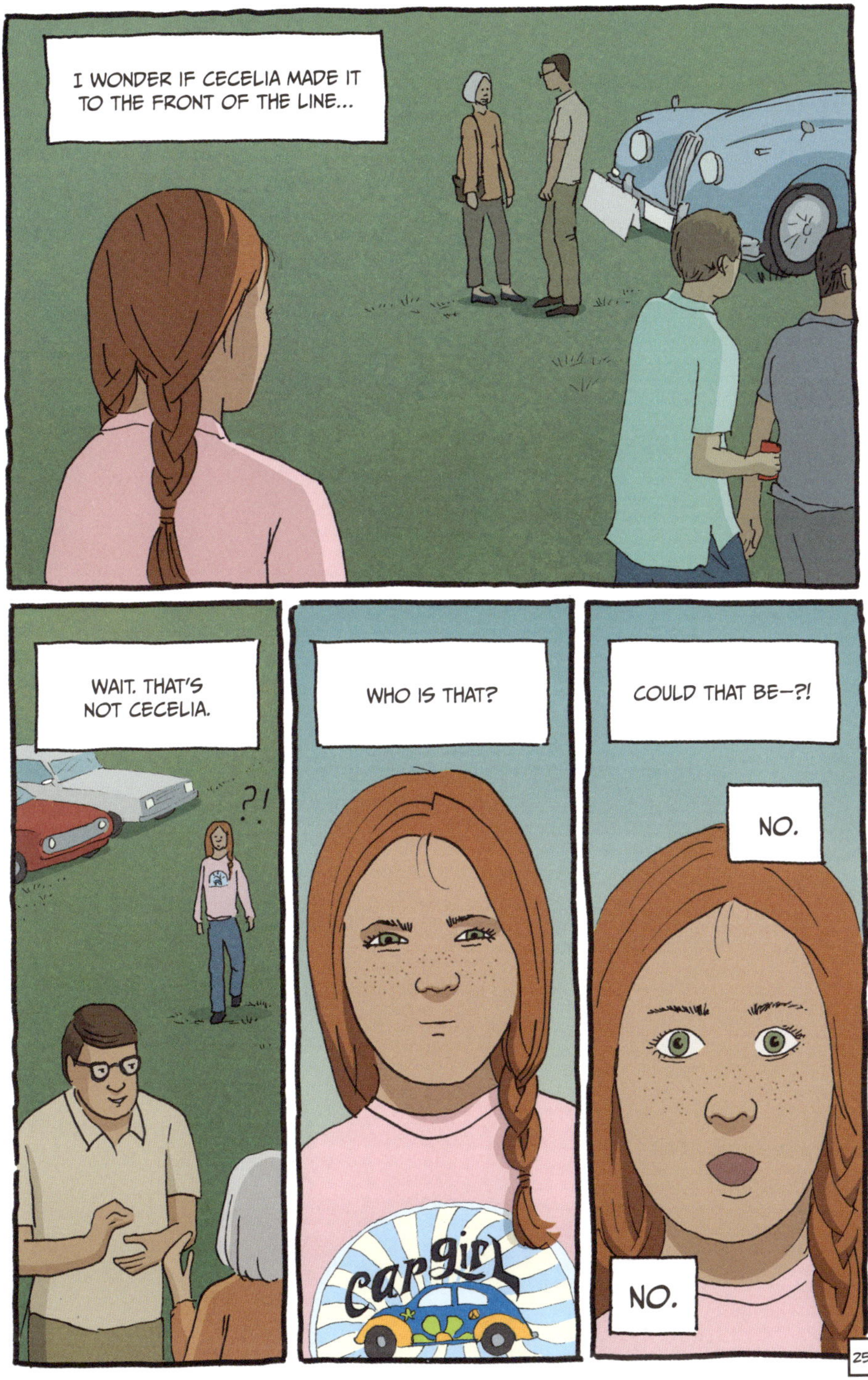
I WONDER IF CECELIA MADE IT TO THE FRONT OF THE LINE...
WAIT. THAT'S NOT CECELIA.
?!
WHO IS THAT?
cargirl
COULD THAT BE—?!
NO.
NO.

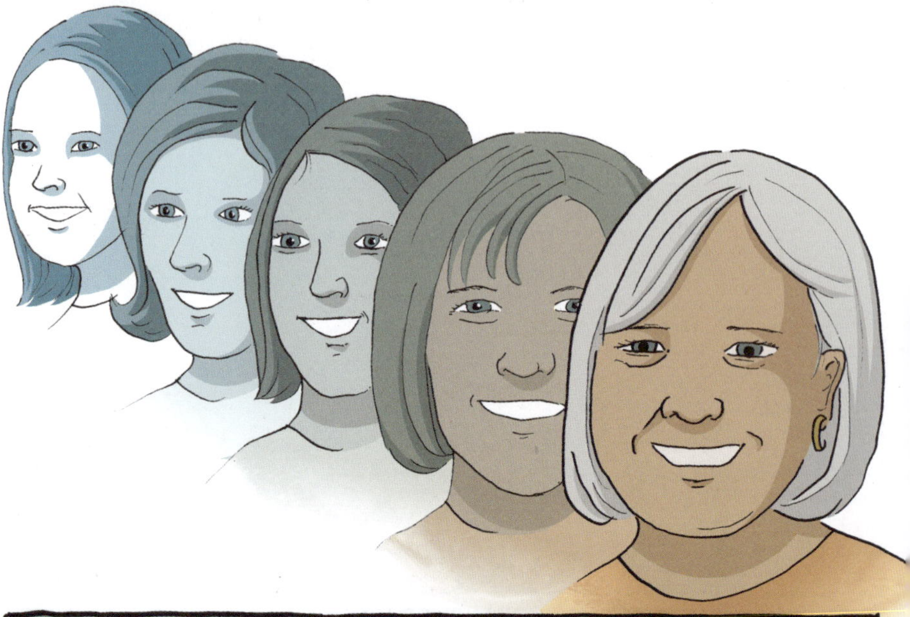

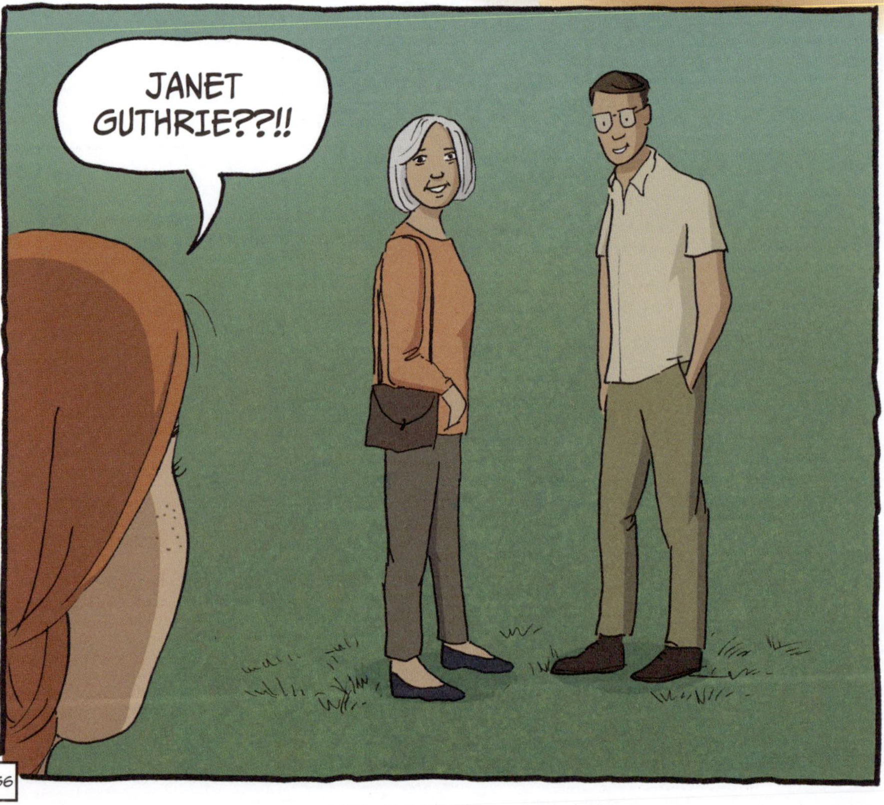
JANET GUTHRIE??!!

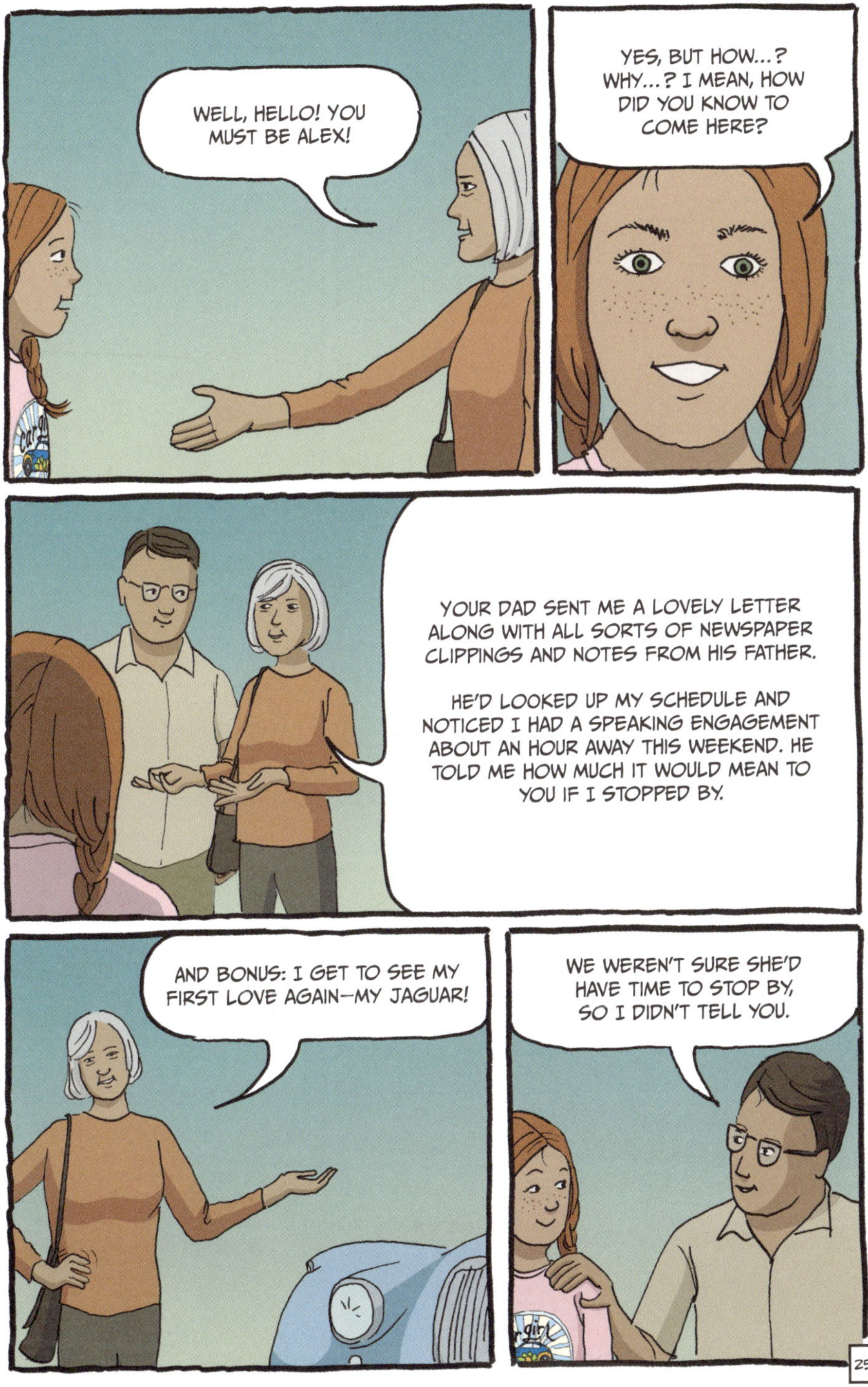
WELL, HELLO! YOU MUST BE ALEX!
YES, BUT HOW...? WHY...? I MEAN, HOW DID YOU KNOW TO COME HERE?
YOUR DAD SENT ME A LOVELY LETTER ALONG WITH ALL SORTS OF NEWSPAPER CLIPPINGS AND NOTES FROM HIS FATHER.
HE'D LOOKED UP MY SCHEDULE AND NOTICED I HAD A SPEAKING ENGAGEMENT ABOUT AN HOUR AWAY THIS WEEKEND. HE TOLD ME HOW MUCH IT WOULD MEAN TO YOU IF I STOPPED BY.
AND BONUS: I GET TO SEE MY FIRST LOVE AGAIN—MY JAGUAR!
WE WEREN'T SURE SHE'D HAVE TIME TO STOP BY, SO I DIDN'T TELL YOU.

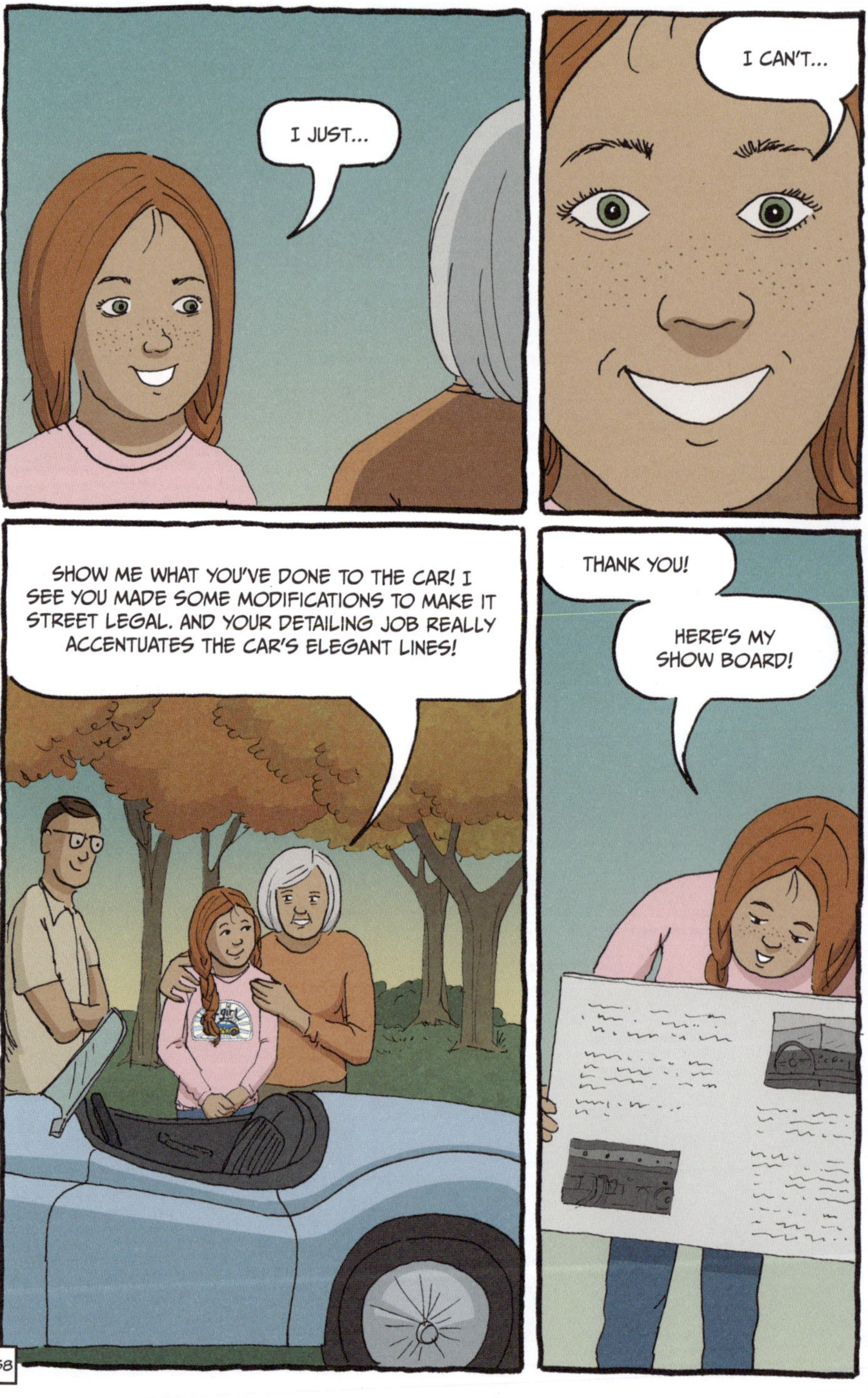
I JUST...
I CAN'T...
SHOW ME WHAT YOU'VE DONE TO THE CAR! I SEE YOU MADE SOME MODIFICATIONS TO MAKE IT STREET LEGAL. AND YOUR DETAILING JOB REALLY ACCENTUATES THE CAR'S ELEGANT LINES!
THANK YOU!
HERE'S MY SHOW BOARD!

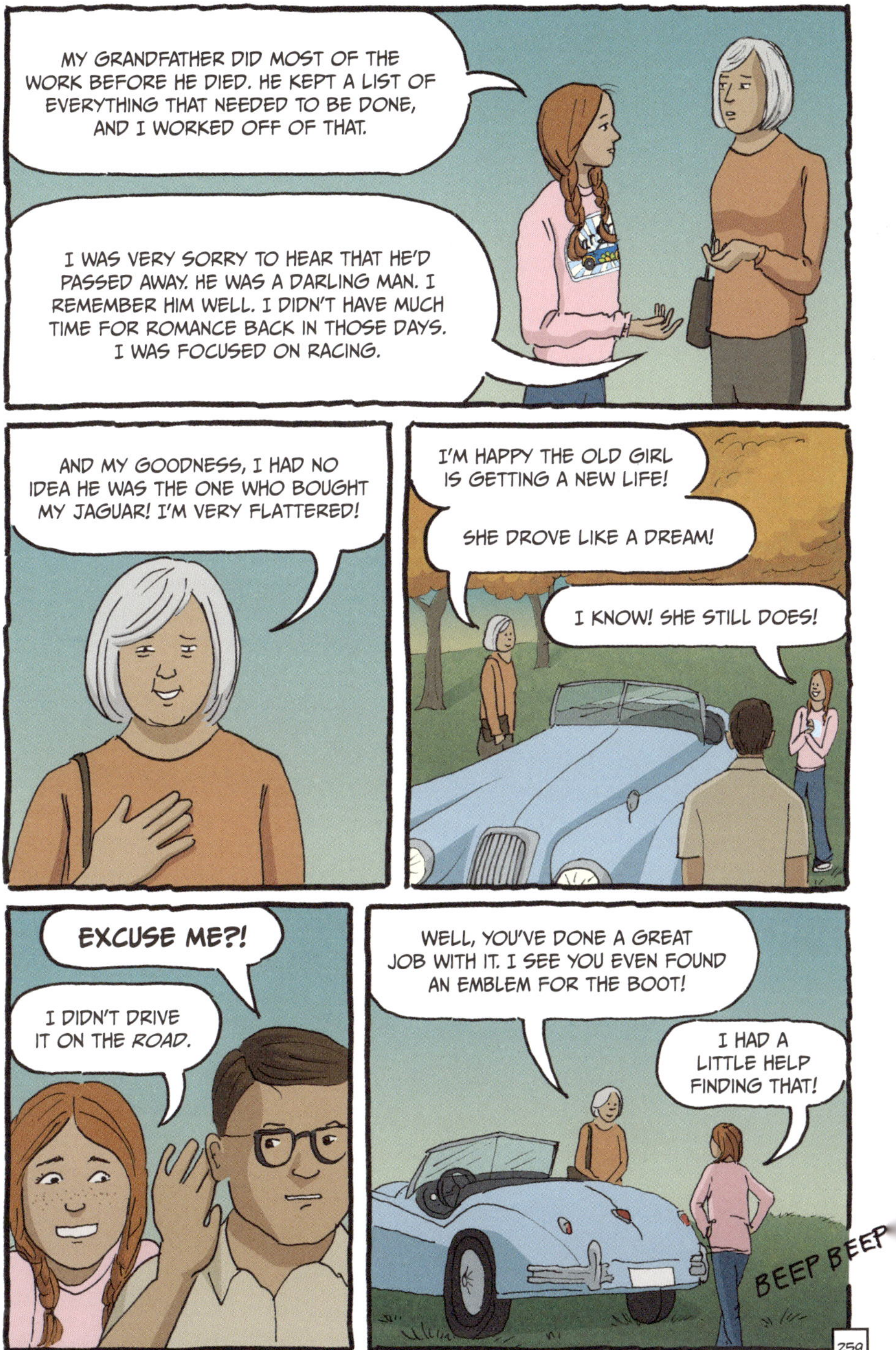
MY GRANDFATHER DID MOST OF THE WORK BEFORE HE DIED. HE KEPT A LIST OF EVERYTHING THAT NEEDED TO BE DONE, AND I WORKED OFF OF THAT.
I WAS VERY SORRY TO HEAR THAT HE'D PASSED AWAY. HE WAS A DARLING MAN. I REMEMBER HIM WELL. I DIDN'T HAVE MUCH TIME FOR ROMANCE BACK IN THOSE DAYS. I WAS FOCUSED ON RACING.
AND MY GOODNESS, I HAD NO IDEA HE WAS THE ONE WHO BOUGHT MY JAGUAR! I'M VERY FLATTERED!
I'M HAPPY THE OLD GIRL IS GETTING A NEW LIFE!
SHE DROVE LIKE A DREAM!
I KNOW! SHE STILL DOES!
EXCUSE ME?!
I DIDN'T DRIVE IT ON THE *ROAD*.
WELL, YOU'VE DONE A GREAT JOB WITH IT. I SEE YOU EVEN FOUND AN EMBLEM FOR THE BOOT!
I HAD A LITTLE HELP FINDING THAT!
BEEP BEEP

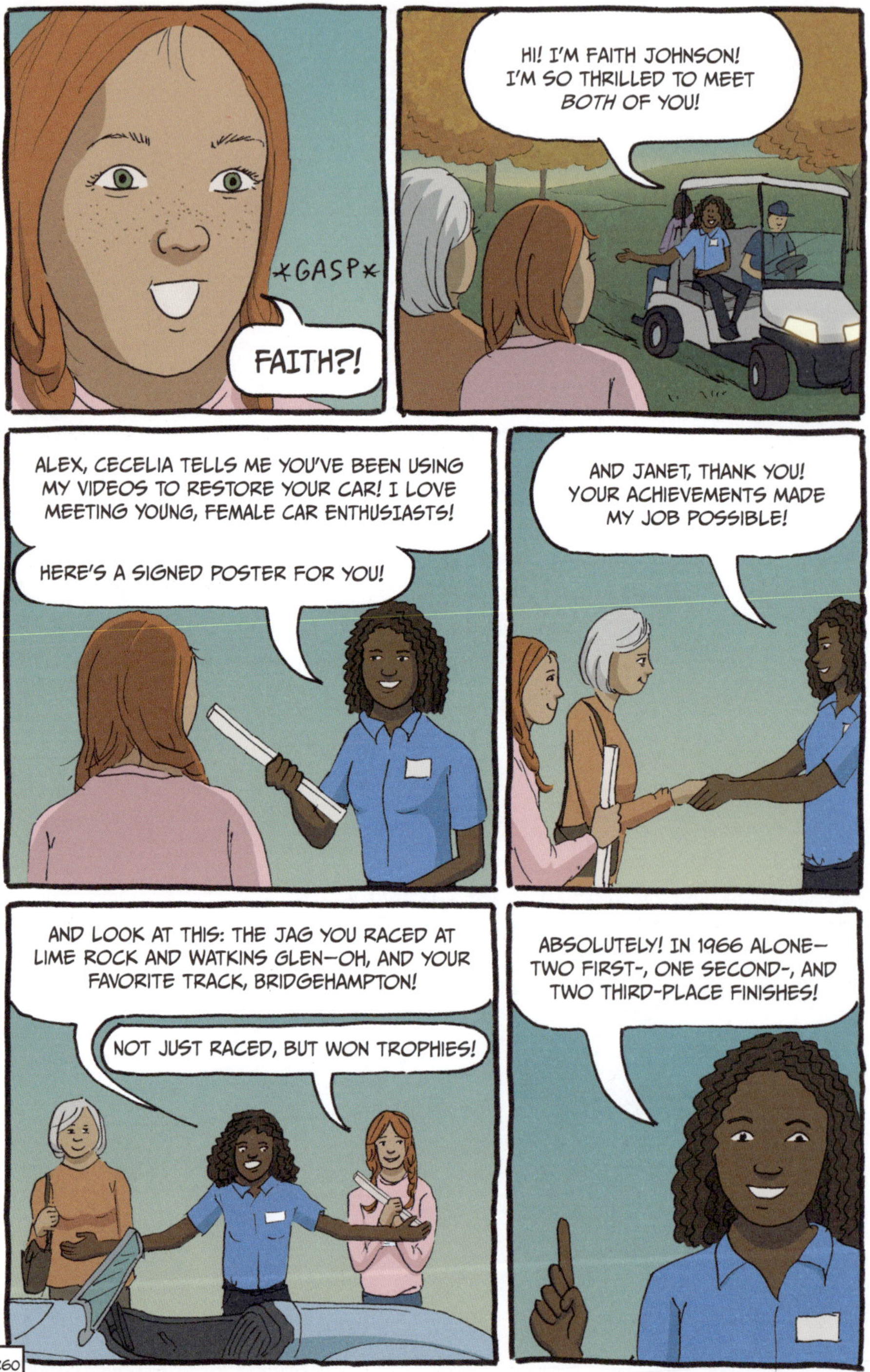
GASP
FAITH?!
HI! I'M FAITH JOHNSON! I'M SO THRILLED TO MEET *BOTH* OF YOU!
ALEX, CECELIA TELLS ME YOU'VE BEEN USING MY VIDEOS TO RESTORE YOUR CAR! I LOVE MEETING YOUNG, FEMALE CAR ENTHUSIASTS!
HERE'S A SIGNED POSTER FOR YOU!
AND JANET, THANK YOU! YOUR ACHIEVEMENTS MADE MY JOB POSSIBLE!
AND LOOK AT THIS: THE JAG YOU RACED AT LIME ROCK AND WATKINS GLEN—OH, AND YOUR FAVORITE TRACK, BRIDGEHAMPTON!
NOT JUST RACED, BUT WON TROPHIES!
ABSOLUTELY! IN 1966 ALONE—TWO FIRST-, ONE SECOND-, AND TWO THIRD-PLACE FINISHES!

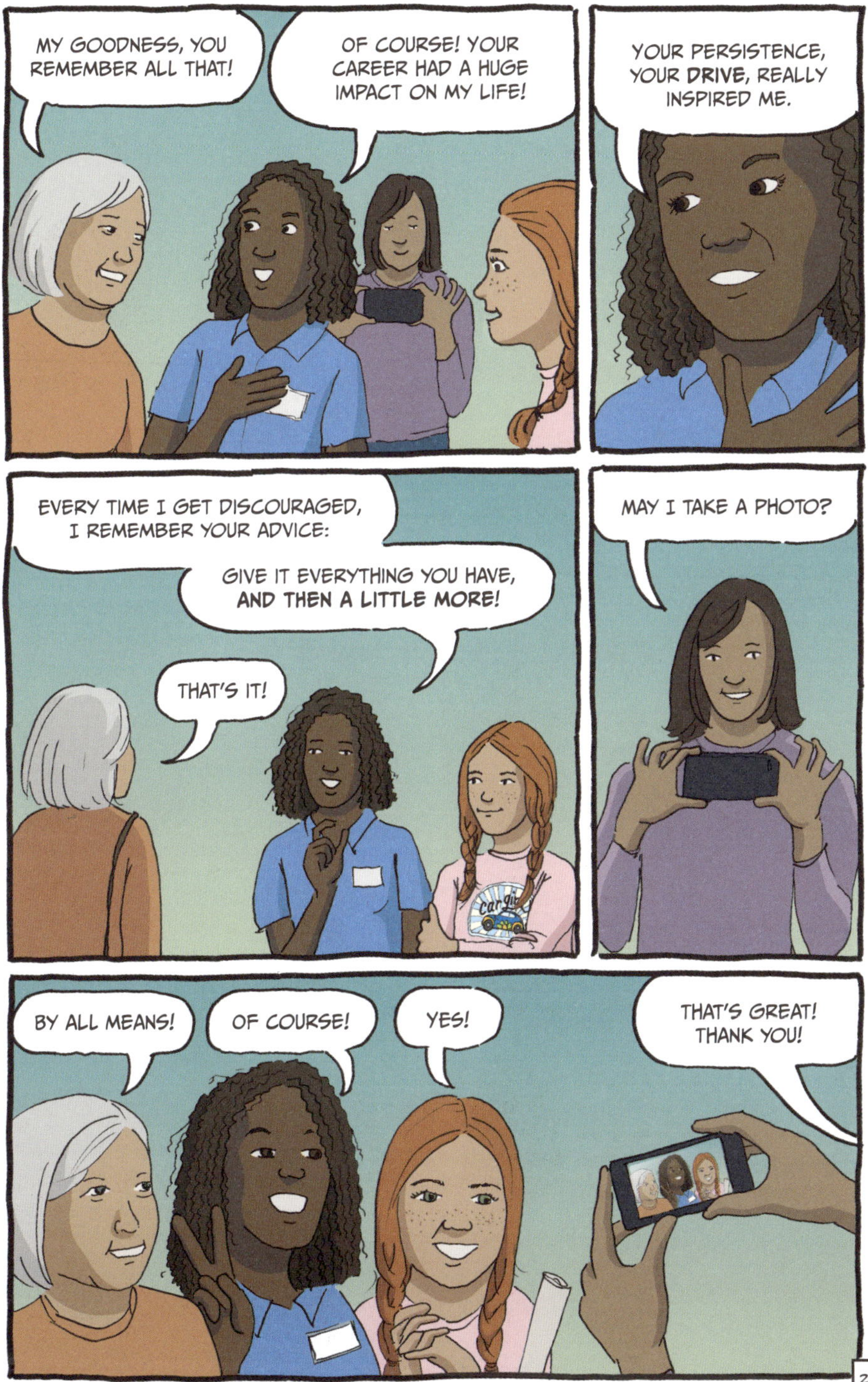
MY GOODNESS, YOU REMEMBER ALL THAT!
OF COURSE! YOUR CAREER HAD A HUGE IMPACT ON MY LIFE!
YOUR PERSISTENCE, YOUR **DRIVE**, REALLY INSPIRED ME.
EVERY TIME I GET DISCOURAGED, I REMEMBER YOUR ADVICE:
GIVE IT EVERYTHING YOU HAVE, **AND THEN A LITTLE MORE!**
THAT'S IT!
MAY I TAKE A PHOTO?
BY ALL MEANS!
OF COURSE!
YES!
THAT'S GREAT! THANK YOU!

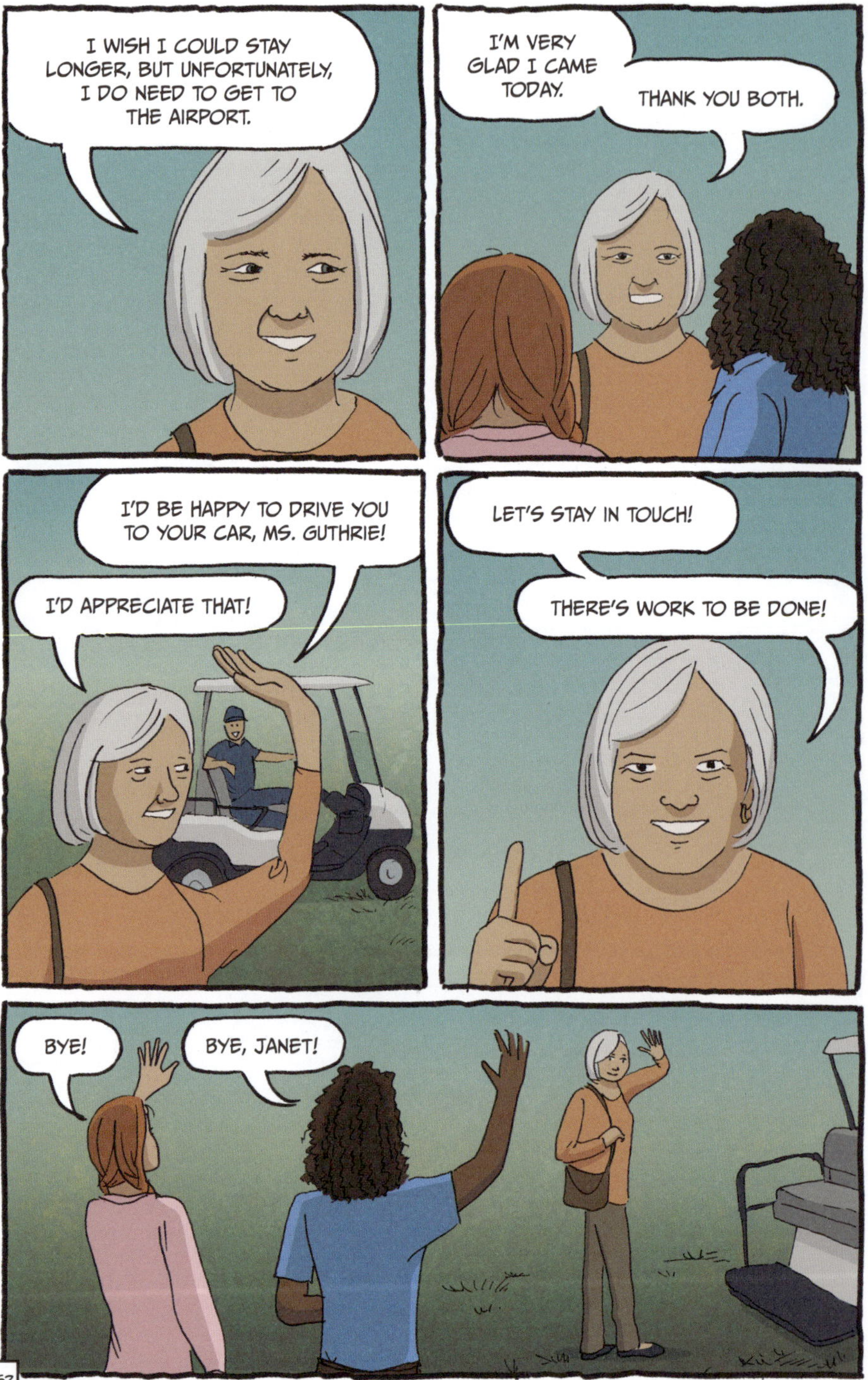
I WISH I COULD STAY LONGER, BUT UNFORTUNATELY, I DO NEED TO GET TO THE AIRPORT.
I'M VERY GLAD I CAME TODAY.
THANK YOU BOTH.
I'D BE HAPPY TO DRIVE YOU TO YOUR CAR, MS. GUTHRIE!
I'D APPRECIATE THAT!
LET'S STAY IN TOUCH!
THERE'S WORK TO BE DONE!
BYE!
BYE, JANET!

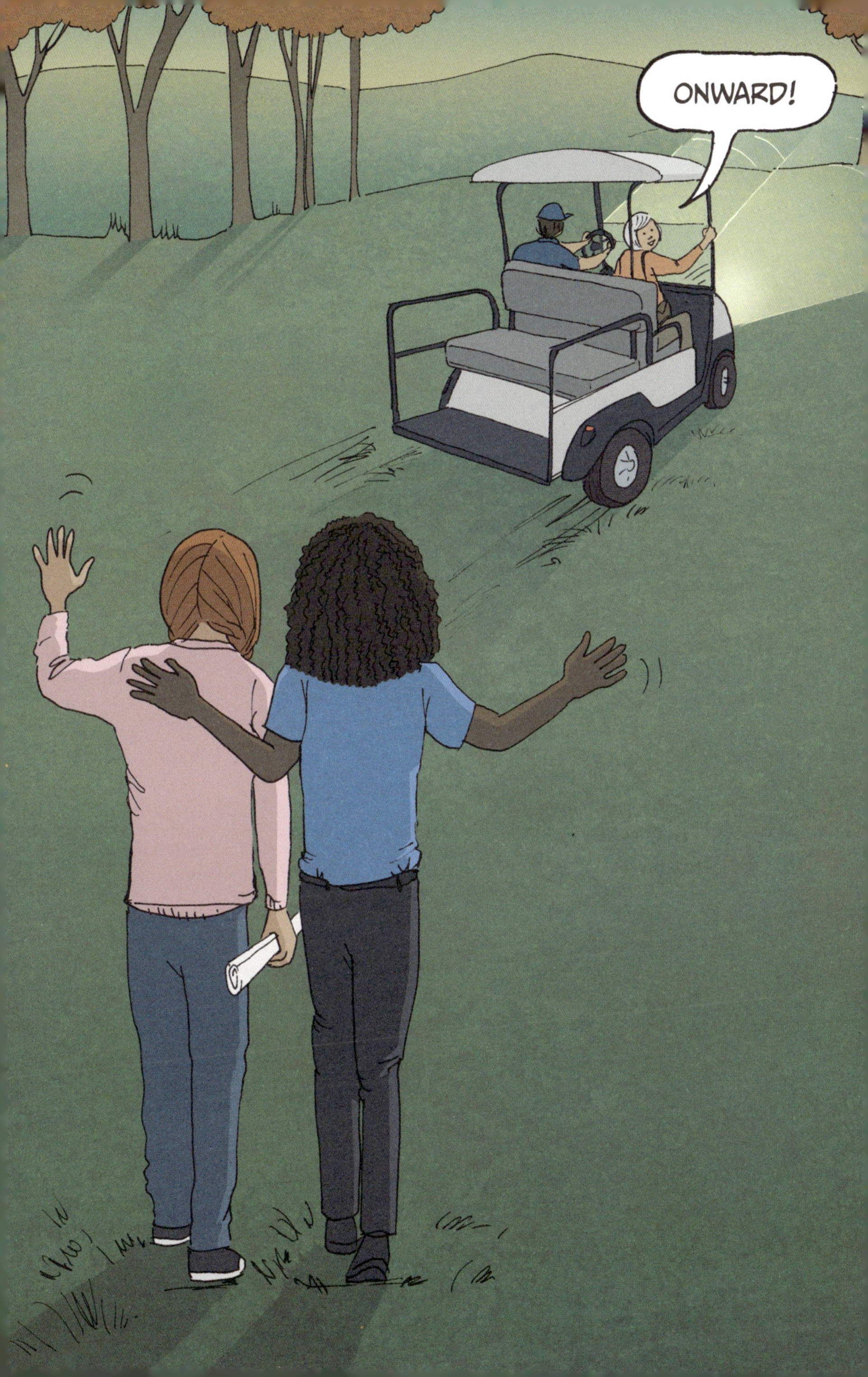
ONWARD!

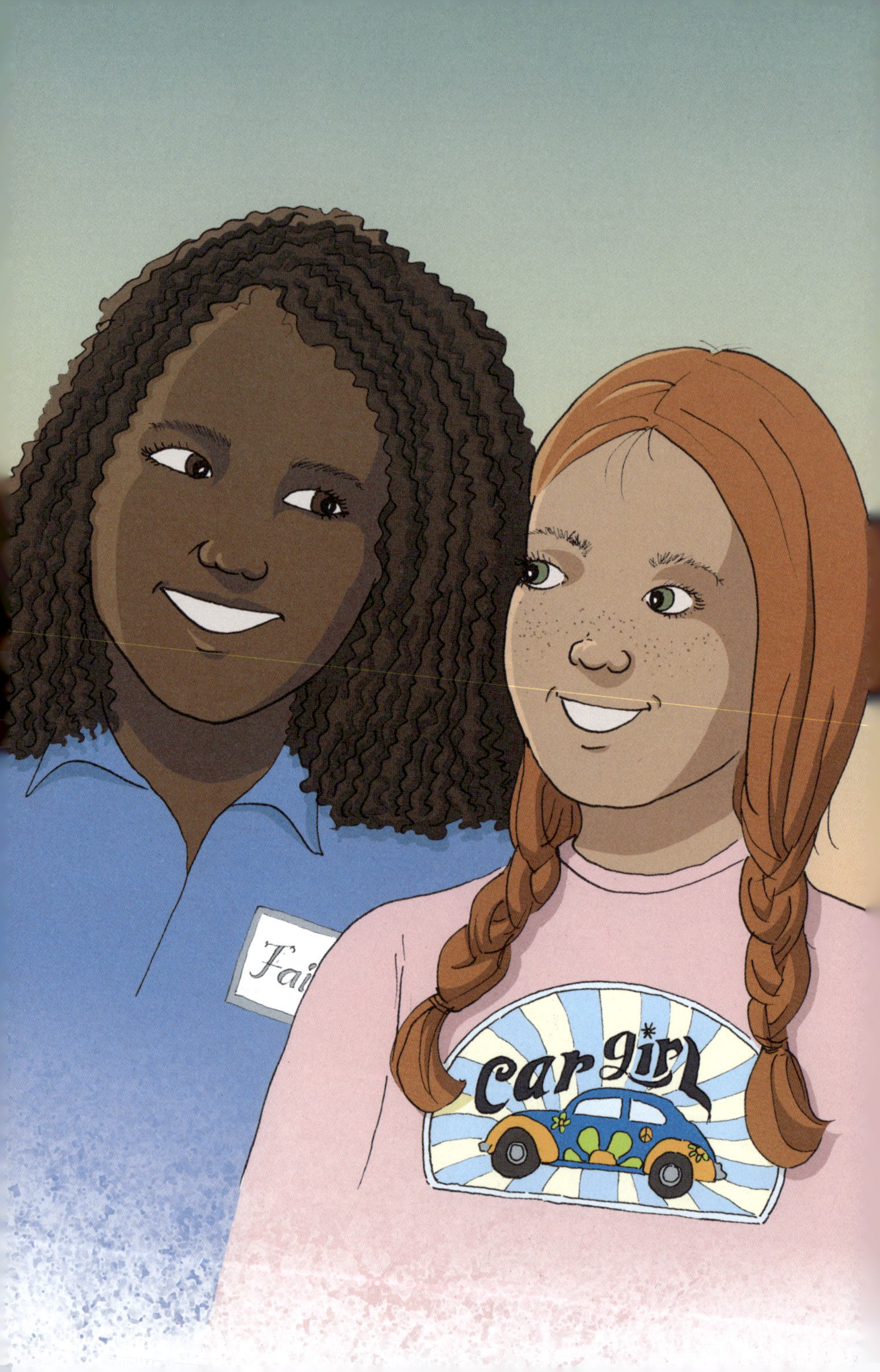
Fai
car girl

AUTHOR'S NOTE

Though in some places this work of historical fiction was simplified to make it more accessible, the important details of Janet Guthrie's racing career are accurate, including competing with broken bones and inferior equipment. In all, Janet competed in 11 INDYCAR events and 33 NASCAR Cup races. Johnny Rutherford, Bobby Unser, Richard Petty, Rolla Vollstedt, Lynda Ferreri, and others are real people whose careers and lives intersected with Janet's as portrayed in the book.

Alex's story is fictional, and so are the characters in those chapters. Alex and her grandfather's interactions with Janet are also imagined. Faith is loosely based on my oldest daughter, Faye Hadley, a top-notch car mechanic and the co-host of MOTOR TREND's *All Girls Garage*. Like Faith, Faye has many supportive fans, but she's also had to contend with backlash and harassment from men who are threatened by women working in the automotive industry. And like Janet, she did not set out to be a trailblazer but has embraced the role and worked hard to broaden opportunities for women.

Janet Guthrie's narrative is important because recognizing the accomplishments of women throughout history creates a foundation for the generations that follow. Girls can stand on the shoulders of those who came before them *only if they know their stories*.

ABOUT THE AUTHOR

CYNTHIA L. COPELAND is the *New York Times* bestselling and award-winning author of more than twenty-five books for adults and children, including her highly praised graphic memoir *Cub*. In the early 1970s she and her family cheered on the race car sponsored by her dad's company, the UOP Shadow, sparking a lifelong interest in auto racing. She lives in New Hampshire with her family. You can find her online at cynthiacopeland.com.